DRAGONLORE

DRAGONLORE

THE COMPLETE TRILOGY

DANIEL ARENSON

ISBN: 978-1-927601-04-4

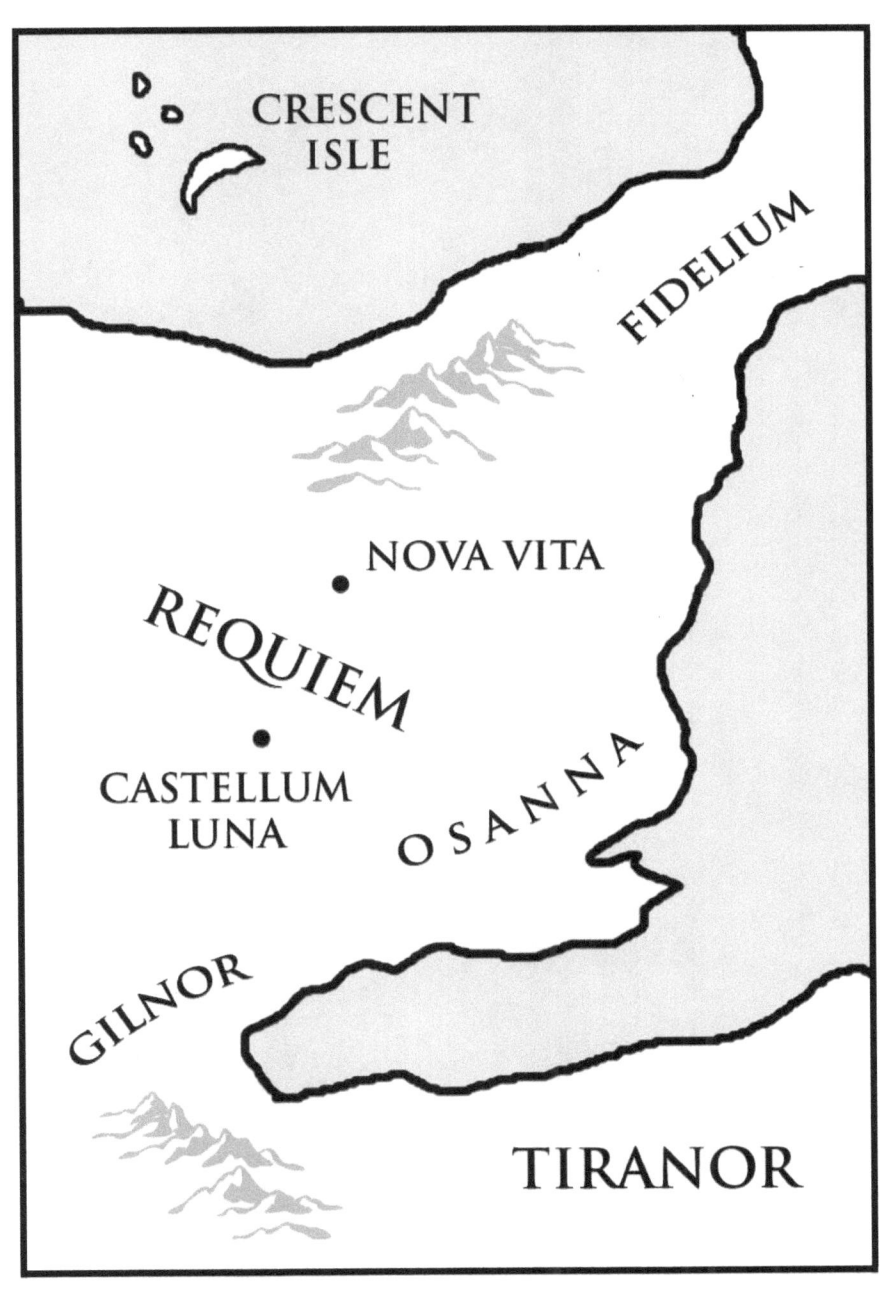

BOOK ONE:

A DAWN OF DRAGONFIRE

MORI

Mori was standing on the fortress walls when she saw the phoenix rise.

A bird of fire, it soared from the snowy horizon, wings outstretched like sunrays. It must have been huge—the size of a dragon or larger. Mori gasped and shivered. The wind whipped her cloak, scented of fire, too hot for winter. She grasped her little finger behind her back, the sixth finger on her left hand, her *luck* finger. Her pet mouse clutched her shoulder; he too had seen the creature of flame.

"Orin!" Mori whispered, lips trembling. She wanted to cry out louder, to sound the alarm, to summon her brother and all his guards... but her fear froze her lips like the frost upon the endless forest before her.

The phoenix coiled in the distance, soaring higher, a creature of grace and beauty. It seemed woven of nothing but fire, and a wake of sparks like stars trailed below it. Mori could hear its distant call, caws like a southern bird of many colors.

Mori wanted to flee. She remembered all those stories her brothers would tell her, terrible stories of griffins attacking Requiem and killing a million of her people. *Even when we took dragon form, we could not stop them,* her brothers would say and squawk like griffins, making Mori run and weep and hide.

"But that was a long time ago," Mori whispered, fingers shaking, even her luck finger. It had been hundreds of years since griffins had attacked, and Requiem was strong now, so powerful no enemy could harm her. Fifty thousand Vir Requis lived in Nova Vita, fair city of the north, and each could grow scales and wings, take flight as a dragon, and defend her.

Still, she reminded herself, Nova Vita lay far north—so many leagues away, she could not count them. Here in the south, in cold and lonely Castellum Luna, only fifty Vir Requis dwelled. Her brother Orin. A few soldiers. And her... the princess Mori, an eighteen-year-old girl with one finger too many, a pet mouse, and enough fear to drown her.

She squinted at the horizon. The phoenix was undulating skyward like a candle's flame torn free from the wick. Its song carried on the wind. Her mouse twitched his whiskers, scurried down Mori's gown, and entered her pocket. Mori envied her pet; she often wished she too could hide so easily.

"Maybe it's good," she whispered. "Maybe it won't hurt us, Pip."

Without Pip, her dear mouse, she would have gone mad down here, she thought. It was just so *lonely* in this southern hinterland. So... so cold and distant and everything frightened her. Mori missed Nova Vita. She missed the city's marble columns that rose between the birches, so beautiful, not like the rough bricks of this outpost. She missed her father the king, her friend the Lady Lyana, and all the minstrels and priests and jugglers and storytellers. Most of all, she missed the library of Nova Vita, a towering chamber with so many books she could read for a lifetime.

Why did Father have to send her here? Why did Requiem even need another settlement? Nova Vita was good enough. Mori had tried to tell Father that, but he only spoke of Requiem recovering from the griffins, and expanding to her old borders, and how the southern air would put some courage into her, and... Mori wanted to weep. None of it made sense to her, and nothing so far had made her any braver. If anything, her fear only grew upon these cold stone walls, staring into this frosted forest, and watching this bird of fire.

As she stood frozen in fear, the horizon kindled. An orange glow rose from distant mist, spreading tendrils across the white sky; it was like sunrise from the south. The snowy forest turned red, and the smell of fire filled Mori's nostrils, spinning her head. Flames crackled and finally she found her voice.

"Orin!" she shouted from the walls. "Fire, Orin! The forest is burning!"

But no, this was no forest fire, she saw. These were no earthly flames. Countless more phoenixes spread wings. Countless wakes of fire rose like comets. The horizon blazed with an army of firebirds, eagles of sound and fury. Their shrieks rose, cries of war. The clouds themselves burned and the forest shook, its frost melting, its trees crackling.

"Orin!" Mori cried. She wanted to use her magic, the magic of Requiem. She wanted to grow scales and wings, breathe fire, and fly as a dragon. But she could only stand upon these walls, a girl with tears in her eyes, a lucky finger, and fear that froze her.

Armor clanked, swords hissed, and boots thumped. Orin ran up the wall, his men behind him. They formed ranks upon the battlements, and their scent filled Mori's nostrils: the smell of oil, leather, sweat, and safety. Her brother clasped her shoulder, staring at the flaming birds that rose in the south. He was a tall man, ten years her senior. His hair was brown like hers and his eyes the same gray, but his face was so much harder, his soul so much stronger. His armor was thick and his sword heavy, and Mori clung to him. He was Orin Aeternum, Son of Olasar, Prince of Requiem, and he was the strongest man she knew.

"What are they, Orin?" she whispered.

His men leaned over the parapets, frowning, each burly and bedecked in steel. Their breath plumed and frost covered their beards. They were the finest warriors of Requiem, sent here to guard this southern fort, this border, and her. Their hands clutched the hilts of their swords. Orin stared with them, frown deepening.

"I don't know," he said softly. "But we're going to find out." His voice rose. "Men of Requiem! We fly!"

He tossed back his head, outstretched his arms, and drew his magic, the magic of Requiem's stars. Silver scales flowed across him. Wings unfurled from his back, claws sprang from his fingers, and fangs grew in his mouth. Soon he roared upon the walls, a silver dragon, fifty feet long and blowing fire. His men shifted around him. They too grew wings and scales, and soon fifty dragons took flight, their fire crackling.

Mori took a deep breath and prepared to shift too. She could not become a burly, powerful dragon like these soldiers, but her scales were still hard, her breath hot, her wings fast. Many called her the fastest dragon in Requiem. Yet Orin, flying from the wall, looked over his shoulder and glared.

"Stay here, sister!" he called, wings churning the falling snow. "Go into the hall, bar the door, and do not emerge until I return."

With that, he roared flame and soared, howls ringing in Mori's ears. His fellow dragons flew at his sides, scales glimmering and breath flaming. Mori watched them, clutching her eleventh finger behind her back.

Help them, luck finger, she prayed. In the distance, the phoenixes screeched, moving closer.

She could see the birds clearly now. Their bodies were woven of molten fire, coiling like storms upon the sun. Their beaks were white and blazing, their eyes swirling stars. With every flap, their wings sprayed fire. Their heat crashed against Mori, even from this distance. The forest wept beneath them, melted snow running in rivulets toward the fort Mori stood upon. Ten thousand firebirds flew there, maybe more. The fifty dragons seemed so small before them—specks of dust flying into a furnace.

"Fly back, beasts of fire!" Orin cried to them, voice thundering. His wings fanned their flame. "Turn from our border."

The phoenixes screeched and swooped toward him.

Mori watched in horror, clutching her finger so tightly she thought she might rip it off. The phoenixes reached out claws of white fire. Flames swirled around their wings and their eyes blazed like stars. The firebirds crashed against the dragons, engulfing them with flame.

"*Orin!*" Mori shouted. She could barely see him, only the fire and smoke... but she heard him. She heard him scream.

What could she do? He'd told her to hide in the fortress, but... they were killing him! She stared, biting her lip so hard she tasted blood. The dragons were howling, kicking, and clawing. She glimpsed their lashing tails, their scales, their maws crying in agony. They tried to fight. Their fangs bit only fire, and their tails only scattered sparks. A few dragons were blowing flames, but that only stoked the phoenix fire.

"Orin, come back!" Mori cried, tears in her eyes. The heat blazed against her, drenching her with sweat. Her gown clung to her body, and her damp hair stuck to her face. She coughed, struggling for breath.

His roars tore at her, cries of pain. Mori wanted to fly to him. She wanted to hide. She could barely breathe, and she knew the phoenixes saw her; their eyes blazed against her. One dragon cried in agony, a sound like tearing flesh. A phoenix claw slashed him, and Requiem's magic left him. Where a dragon had flown, a man now fell, blazing, and thudded dead against the trees. Three more dragons burned, and in the pain of death, their magic vanished. Three more bodies tumbled.

"Mori!" her brother cried from the inferno. Flames engulfed him, white around his silver scales. His wings churned the fire, showering sparks like exploding suns. "Mori, run! Hide!"

"Orin...," she whispered, trembling, clutching her hands behind her back.

"Mori, run!" he cried as the phoenixes tore into him. Their beaks thrust, woven of hardened fire. Their claws dug into him. Their flames surrounded him. Orin Aeternum, Son of Olasar, Prince of Requiem... lost his magic, turned from dragon to burning man, and fell from the sky.

Something tore inside Mori. Her heart shattered. A pain splintered in her chest and shot through her. A cry fled her lips, and before she knew it, she had shifted into a dragon. Golden scales clinked across her, her wings flapped, and she flew into the southern fire.

"Orin, where are you?" she cried, swooping through flame. The fire blazed around her, so hot she could only squint, and her scales felt ready to melt. Three phoenixes dived toward her, each larger than her. Their shrieks tore at her ears. They clawed at her scales, and Mori screamed, tumbled, flapped her wings, and howled. She soared, knocked by them, and rose through an inferno of heat and sound and rage. Everywhere she looked were blazing eyes, beaks of fire, talons that lashed her. She soared higher, burst between them, and swooped again. She had to find her brother. She had to find her Orin, her dear Orin, her hero, her only chance for life. She knocked between phoenixes and falling dragons, crashed toward the earth, and saw him lying in snow.

His clothes smoked. Singed black, they clung to his melted flesh. Half his face was a burnt ruin, red and black and blistering. His skin peeled. He gazed at her with one good eye, and his lips worked, trying to whisper, trying to call to her.

"Oh, Orin," she whispered, horror pounding through her. He was alive. She could still save him. She lifted him with her claws, as gently as she could, but he cried hoarsely and his eyes rolled back.

Was he dead? Had she killed him? She had no time to check. The phoenixes swooped down, an army of wrath, and Mori took flight. Fire bathed her. She shot through flames, wings churning smoke.

I'm the fastest dragon in Requiem, Orin always said so, I can do this. She screamed and emerged from the flames, her brother's limp human form in her claws. The phoenix army on her tail, she flew over the walls of Castellum Luna, down into the courtyard, and landed by the doors of their hall.

They cannot enter, she told herself. *They're too big.* She placed Orin upon the flagstones, shifted back into a human girl, and pushed the doors. They creaked open, revealing a hall full of trestle tables, tapestries, and spears.

The phoenixes shrieked behind her. Their heat blasted her. Mori raced into the hall, dragged her brother inside, and saw countless phoenixes descending into the courtyard. She slammed the doors shut as they landed, sealing their fire outside.

"Mori...," Orin whispered, voice hoarse. "Mori, leave me... fly north. Fly to Nova Vita."

Mori pulled a lever, dropping the doors' bar into the brackets. She stood panting. Could the phoenixes break the doors? They were thick and banded in iron, built to withstand fire and axe. And what of the other dragons? Stars, were any still alive, and had she doomed them to death? She trembled.

The phoenixes screeched outside. Their light glowed under the doors, and tongues of fire reached around the frames. They began slamming at the doors, howling. Mori whimpered with every jolt.

I must go deeper, she thought. *Into the dungeon. The door there is small, too small for them.*

She leaned over Orin, and her breath left her. Tears filled her eyes. Half his face was gone, melted away. Half his body was a wound of welts, smoke, and seared cloth clinging to flesh. Mori gagged, for a moment able to do nothing else. Then she steeled herself. The phoenixes were lashing at the doors. She had to save her brother.

She looked at the eastern wall. A small door stood open there, revealing a staircase that plunged into shadow. Mori tightened her lips. The dungeon of Castellum Luna lay down those stairs. The place had always frightened her—she would imagine ghosts lurking in its shadows—but today she would seek safety there.

"Come on, Orin!" she said, placed her arms around him, and tugged. She grunted, grinding her heels against the floor. "Come on, Orin, get up! On your feet!"

He managed to rise to his knees, coughing, breath like a saw. With strength she had not known was in her, Mori pulled him to his feet. He leaned against her, twice her weight. She thought she would collapse, but she walked, step by step, and helped Orin onto the staircase. She pulled the door shut and began walking downstairs, Orin leaning against her. As the phoenixes howled, and the fortress doors creaked, they descended with blood and tears.

Finally Mori found herself in the dungeon of Castellum Luna, a cold place of shadows, sacks of wheat, barrels of wine, and now the stench of burnt flesh. An oil lamp glowed upon a table, painting the room red. Panting, Mori lay her brother on the floor and touched his hair. His breath wheezed and his flesh still smoked.

Upstairs, she heard the fortress doors shatter. She started. Great eagle cries echoed. Even here in the dungeon, Mori felt the phoenix heat as they stormed into the hall.

"We'll be all right, Orin," she whispered and held his hot, sticky body. "They can't fit down here. The staircase is too small for them. We're safe here. We're safe. I'm going to take care of you."

He only groaned, and she felt his blood upon her, staining her gown, and she held him tight. They trembled together. Above in the hall, she heard the phoenix cries; they seemed to shake the fort, cries of hatred, rage, and bloodlust. *This must be how the griffins sounded when they toppled our halls of old.*

"Mori..." Orin spoke hoarsely, barely able to speak at all. "Mori, you must fly north. You are fast. You..."

He could say no more. Mori held him tight. How could she fly north? How could she escape so many phoenixes, an army of flame? Her head spun. Perhaps she should not have entered this fort, but... Orin had told her to hide here! And now he wanted her to flee? What was she to do? Her head spun, and she shook it violently.

"Rest, Orin," she whispered. "Please. Rest."

She would have to take care of things now. She would have to make the decisions. His life depended on her. *Be calm, Mori,* she told herself. She forced herself to take slow, deep breaths, to steady her trembling limbs.

"We'll wait here until the phoenixes leave," she whispered. "They have to leave sometime. They *have* to. They can't fit down here. When they go away, we'll fly north. I'll take you to the temples, to healers, Orin. They can heal you. They can... they can fix your..."

Your ravaged face, she wanted to say. *Your flesh that melted off. The ruin of your left side, a wound of blood and bone.* Yet could anyone save him now? And could anyone save her?

Gently she pulled back from him; their bodies parted with a sickly, sticky sound like a bandage pulled off a wet wound. In the darkness, Mori crept upstairs toward the dungeon door. Firelight burned behind it. The phoenixes stood in the main hall. She heard their cawing, the crackle of their fire. Squinting against the heat and light, Mori knelt and peeked through the keyhole.

Two phoenixes moved through the hall. Their flames torched the tapestries and trestle tables. One tossed back its head and screeched, and Mori covered her ears. She thought that screech could tear her eardrums and shatter her ribs.

Please go away, she prayed. *Please please leave this place, fly away from here, and let this only be a nightmare.* She clutched her luck finger behind her back, praying to it. *Please send them away. Please let me just wake up and be in Nova Vita again, with Lady Lyana and Father and everyone else.*

Yet the phoenixes in the hall remained. They sniffed, stirring wisps of fire upon their beaks. *Stars, can they smell me?* The firebirds turned toward the door where Mori hid, cawed, and stepped toward it. Their claws rained sparks. Mori caught her breath, too frightened to even flee.

They can't hurt me, she told herself. *They're too big to enter the doorway. Even if they burn the door, they can't enter. And they can't burn the stone walls of the dungeon.* She forced herself to breathe. *We're safe here.*

As she watched through the keyhole, her breath died.

The phoenixes tossed back their heads, cried so loudly that they shook the hall, and outstretched their wings. Their flames rose in fury. They seemed to... not to shrink, Mori thought, but to... fold in upon themselves. Their fire twisted, darkened, shaped new forms. Suddenly the creatures appeared almost human to her, their limbs long and fiery, their heads burning. The flames coalesced, forming a man and woman of liquid fire. The lava hardened. Last wisps of flame clung to the figures, then pulled into crystals they wore around their necks. Finally all the phoenix fire glowed inside the amulets—two small, blazing lights.

Mori gasped and whimpered. She reached into her pocket and clutched Pip so tightly the mouse bit her.

The two figures stood in the hall, smoke still rising from them. Both wore armor of pale steel, gilded helmets, and curved swords upon their waists. Their hair was platinum blond, so pale it was almost white. *They have ghost hair.* Mori trembled to see it.

The man stood facing her, staring at the dungeon door. He was tall and broad, with a face like beaten leather. His eyes were small, blue, and mean. A golden sun was embedded into his breastplate. Mori recognized the emblem—the Golden Sun of Tiranor.

Tirans! she thought. She had heard many tales of them; they were a cruel, warlike people from southern deserts beyond mountain, lake, and swamp.

The woman stood with her back toward the door. She was tall and slender, and her hair was long and smooth. Two sabres hung from her belt, shaped like the beaks of cranes, their pommels golden. Slowly, the woman turned toward the door. Her eyes were blue, her face golden and strewn with bright freckles like stars in sunset. A scar, as from an old fire, ran across her face from head to chin, then snaked down her neck into her breastplate.

Mori gasped.

She knew this woman.

"Solina," she whispered.

Some of her fear left her. Solina was her friend! A princess of Tiranor, her parents slain, she had grown up in Requiem. Mori remembered many nights of sitting in Solina's lap, listening to her tell stories of Tiranor—its white towers rising from the desert, capped with gold; its oases of lush palms, warm pools, and birds of paradise;

its proud people of golden skin, bright hair that shone, and blue eyes that saw far.

Solina won't hurt me, Mori thought, breathing shakily. *Solina will realize this was a mistake, once she sees me, once she realizes it's me, Mori. I was like a sister to her.*

And yet... Mori hesitated. She stayed frozen. That scar that ran down Solina's face... could it be from that night? The night Solina had attacked Father with a blade, and Orin burned her? Mori shuddered. *No, it can't be!* But she knew it was true; that was the scar of dragonfire.

She remembered, Mori realized, and tears filled her eyes. *And now she's here to burn us too.*

The tall, stately woman took a step toward the door, and those blue eyes stared right at the keyhole, right at Mori. Solina's lips curled into a smile.

She saw me! Mori leaped back from the door, heart pounding. She heard footfalls move toward her, and Mori scrambled downstairs. She knelt in the shadows by Orin. He was moaning, body hot, burnt, stinking with death. She clutched his hand.

"Don't be scared, Orin," she whispered as the door above shook. "I'll protect you."

Splinters flew. The door shattered, and firelight bathed the dungeon.

Mori wanted to shift into a dragon. She wanted to let scales cover her, let flame blow from her maw. Yet she dared not. The dungeon was so small, a mere ten feet wide. If she shifted, her girth would fill the chamber, would crush Orin dead. Instead she clutched the hilt of her brother's sword, steeled herself, and drew the blade. It hissed and caught the light.

Solina walked downstairs, hands on her own swords' hilts. Her breastplate sported a golden sun. Around her neck, her crystal of fire crackled, painting her face orange and red. The burly man walked behind her, eyes blazing and teeth bared.

"Stand back!" Mori said, holding her brother's sword before her. Her voice trembled, and the sword wavered. She added her left hand to the hilt, the hand with six fingers, her *luck* hand. *Bring me luck today,* she prayed to it.

Solina approached her. The scar that halved her face tweaked her lips; she was either smirking, or her scar locked her lips in eternal mockery. She seemed inhuman to Mori—her skin made of gold, her hair of platinum, her eyes of sapphire. She was more statue than flesh and blood.

"Why, if it isn't little Mori!" she said, and this time Mori knew that she was smiling. Those scarred lips parted, revealing dazzling white teeth. "Last time I saw you, you were but a girl, a slight thing with no breasts and skinned knees. You've become a woman!"

Mori stood, holding her sword in trembling hands, her brother groaning behind her.

"Stand back, devil!" Tears rolled down her cheeks. "Stand back, or my father the king will hear of this, and he will kill you!"

Solina's face softened—the face of a woman who saw a cute, angry puppy that melted her heart. The man at her side, however, seemed not to share her amusement. He stared at Mori hungrily; she felt his small, mean eyes undress her.

"Oh, dear dear, frightened sweetling," Solina said and clucked her tongue. "But we were such good friends once, were we not? We were as sisters. I remember holding you on my lap, mussing your hair, and reading to you stories of romance and adventure. I promise not to hurt you, my little sparrow... but please, do not stand between me and your brother, or Lord Acribus here will hurt you. And he will hurt you greatly, little sparrow. More than anyone ever has."

The tall man with the golden, leathery face licked his lips. His tongue was freakishly long—it nearly reached his eyes—and white as bone. It looked like a snake emerging from his mouth. His eyes dripped lust, both for flesh and blood.

An hour ago, if somebody had told Mori this would happen, she would have expected to faint, weep, even die of fright. Now she found herself snarling. Her love for Orin, and her fear for him, swelled over fear for herself. Teeth bared, she swung her sword before her, slicing the air.

"Stand back!" she said. "You will not touch him."

Solina sighed. "My sweetling." She ran a finger down her scar, from forehead, to chin, and down her neck. She kept tracing her fingers along her breastplate and finally down her thigh. "Do you see this scar, Mori? I call it my line of fire. It runs from my head to my toe. Your brother gave me this scar. He deformed me. Surely you of all people, with your freakish left hand, know about being deformed." She looked at the burnt, groaning Orin. "So I burned him too. But I am not done with him. He will feel so *much* more pain before I let him die. But you, Mori, need not feel the same pain. You were as a sister to me; I want to spare you this agony. Step aside... or I will give you to my pet. You will scream and beg me for death before he's done with you."

Mori was scared, so scared that she couldn't breathe, and cold sweat drenched her, and her heart seemed ready to crack. She thought of her brother Orin, so handsome and strong, now this ruin of a man. She thought of her other brother, the wise Elethor, who lived up north among the birches.

It's up to me now, Mori knew. *Me, the younger sister, the slim girl who is always so fast to cry, so fast to hide.* She took a shuddering breath. *For years my older brothers protected me; now it's my turn to fight for them.*

With a wordless cry, she swung her blade at Solina.

So fast Mori barely saw her move, Solina drew her left sword. The blade was curved, glimmering with white steel and gold. The two blades clashed, one a northern blade kissed with starlight, the other a desert shard of fire. Sparks flew, and before Mori realized what had happened, Solina's blade flew again, nicked her hand, and blood splashed.

Mori's sword fell and clanged against the floor.

Nearly as fast as Solina's blade, her companion, the snarling Lord Acribus, moved forward. He looked to Mori more beast than man, a wild dog of rabid fangs, cruel eyes, and an appetite for flesh. She screamed when he caught her arms, digging his fingers into her; she thought those fingers could break her bones.

"Solina!" she cried. "Solina, please! How could you do this? We... we raised you as family. You... my brother Elethor loved you, I..."

But her words failed her. Solina stared at her with those cold blue eyes. They were as chips of ice in a golden mask. There was no humanity to them, no compassion, nothing but cruelty.

"Lord Acribus," the woman said, "make her watch."

The lord's fingers dug so deep into Mori's arms, blood trickled to her elbows. "She will watch, my queen, if I must cut off her eyelids."

She shook in his grasp, a tiny mouse caught in a vulture's talons; she was shorter than his shoulders. She watched, trembling, as Solina approached the wounded prince of Requiem.

"Please," Mori whispered, but Solina ignored her.

Orin groaned upon the floor, scorched and convulsing. Somehow he managed to rise to his elbows. Sweat and blood drenched him.

"Sol... Solina," he managed, so hoarse Mori could barely make out the word.

Solina stood above him, sabre drawn, eyes cold. If Orin was a wounded beast, a twisted creature, Solina was a queen of beauty, a statue of gold and steel and ice.

"Hello, Orin," she said softly. "So you remember me too. Perhaps you know me by the scar you gave me." She caressed it. "My line of fire. It is a strange thing, is it not? I used to fear fire. When I lived in Requiem, among you beasts of scales and wings, I feared it." She laughed mirthlessly. "Imagine it! A young, frightened girl from Tiranor, snatched from her home. You could all turn into dragons—noble, ancient children of Requiem, flaunting your magic of starlight. Yes, I feared this fire I could never wield. And I screamed, Orin. I screamed when you burned me."

"You..." He moaned and shivered. His peeling skin hung from him. "You attacked my father, you..."

Again her bitter laugh pierced the air. "I attacked King Olasar, yes. I attacked the man who murdered my parents. Who enslaved me. Who would banish me only because I dared to love Elethor, your brother, the dearest man I've known. Did I ever stand a chance, Orin? Could I ever dream of reaching him with my dagger, when you were there to burn me? The pain of your fire nearly drove me mad; you feel this pain now. So I left, Orin. And I tamed fire." She snarled like a wild beast, and her voice rose. "I wrestled it, and made it my own, until I could become a thing of flame itself. And I burned you. And I will watch you die in agony."

Her sword lashed.

Mori screamed.

Acribus laughed.

With a whistle, Solina's curved, glittering blade sliced Orin's belly and splattered blood across the wall. Mori shut her eyes, whimpering, but Acribus pulled her eyelids open with rough fingers. She tried to turn her head away, but he held it, forcing her to look, forcing her to see it. *Stars, no... no, please, stars, no....* Her tears fell.

Orin screamed. He clutched his wound, trying to stop it, to stop the spilling of it, the glistening, bloody, pink horror of it. Half-burnt and cut open, he cried for Requiem. He cried for their mother. Mori wept.

"Please, Solina, please, please, please...," she whispered.

But Solina only stood frozen, staring down at the dying man, and still no emotion filled her eyes, not a glimmer of pity nor disgust nor even delight.

"You can make it end, Orin," she said softly. Blood sluiced around her boots. "Tell me of Olasar's forces. Tell me how many dragons in his brigades, where they are stationed, who leads them. Tell me everything... and I will plunge my sword into your heart, and I will end your pain. If you do not speak, well... I can stand here for hours. It will take you hours to die without my mercy, do not doubt it. Maybe even days." She smiled softly. "As long as it takes."

He screamed. And he spoke. And he told her everything as he writhed and begged for the pain to end.

Mori trembled, kicked, tried to look away, tried to break free, tried to do anything but see this ruin of her brother, hear his screams, see his blood and entrails spill upon the floor until finally, finally after ages and ages of it, Solina drove her blade into his chest. Finally some emotion filled the queen's eyes. Pleasure. Deep, horrible, hot pleasure. She twisted the blade, and Orin's breath caught, and his scream died... and his pain ended. It was over.

Thank the stars, it's over, Mori thought as she sobbed and shook.

But it was not over. Not for her.

"My queen?" Acribus asked, voice like gravel, breath hot and stinking against Mori.

She looked at him, eyebrow raised, and nodded. "Have your treat, dog."

Now Mori did try to shift into a dragon, even if her girth would slam against the walls, and the dungeon would crush her. She tried to clutch her magic, to grow scales, grow fangs, grow talons that could slash Acribus. But her pain was too great. When she thought she could grasp her magic, his fingers clutched her neck, and it was all she could do to even breathe.

He tore her gown. He shoved her across the table. She felt her mouse flutter against her breast, trapped in her pocket, throbbing like a heart. Shadow covered her world and her eyes rolled back. Pain and blood filled the dungeon, and Solina smiled.

Fire.

Floating stars.

Darkness underground.

Outside, the phoenixes shrieked. Myriads of flaming wings rose, showering heat and light and fire. The forests of Requiem burned, and smoke veiled the sky, red and black. A single fortress rose from the inferno, hiding its shame underground. Deer fled burning, trees toppled, and ash fell like burning tears. The land wept. Her soul tore.

When he was done with her, he shoved her aside. Mori slammed against the dungeon floor, bloodying her elbow. She wept and shook, stars before her eyes. Her mouse lay still in her pocket, a dead heart, crushed under her weight.

"Get up," Acribus told her in disgust. He spat onto her. "You're coming with us. You will be mine every night until we find and kill your father."

She lay on the bloodied floor, her face an inch from Orin's. His right eye stared at her, huge and pained in the dripping, red wound of his face. Mori gasped for breath. She could not rise. She could barely see. Pain dug through her like a cold iron bar. She closed her eyes, so ashamed, praying for death. *Please, Solina, please kill me too, stab your sword into my heart and end this.*

"Stand up, sweet little mouse," Solina spoke above, voice distant as from miles away. "Stand up now, or he will hurt you again."

Mori looked at her brother's body. She forced herself to look. He was no longer Orin, she realized, the hero she had loved, the prince of Requiem. He was nothing but flesh now, a charred and emptied shell. *Your soul now dines in the starlit halls of our fathers,* she thought. *You rest now among the Draco stars, and I know you watch over me.*

The dragonclaw pommel of a dagger rose from Orin's boot. Mori had always feared this dagger, thinking its pommel a true dragon's claw, but today was all about shattering fears. Acribus grabbed her hair, twisted, and pulled. Mori had always been the fastest dragon in Requiem. Fast as she could, she drew her brother's dagger, leaped up, and thrust the blade.

The dagger gleamed in her hand, her *luck* hand. Mori screamed. The dagger scraped against Acribus's breastplate and drove under his arm. He wore only chainmail there, thinner than his breastplate of steel; it was no match to the starlit dagger of a Requiem prince. The blade tore through the mail, blood showered Mori, and Acribus howled.

I'm sorry, Orin, she thought as she ran, tears on her cheeks, blood on her thighs. *I'm so sorry.*

She left him there, racing upstairs. Solina shouted and tried to grab her, but Mori was too fast. Blood pounded in her ears. Every step shot pain through her; it felt like demon spawn had invaded her womb and clawed inside her. And yet she ran, burst out of the dungeon, and raced across the hall. She had always been so fast. *You always said how fast I was, Orin, whenever we'd race through the pure, blue skies over King's Forest.*

Now the sky was red, full of smoke and fire. Mori burst into the courtyard, shifted into a dragon, and soared into the flame. Ten thousand phoenixes roared above her, an inferno; it looked like the sun had engulfed the world. Mori screamed, a hoarse cry that consumed her—for her pain, her rage, the death of her brother. She sounded her howl, a dragon's howl, the howl of a frightened girl who will never more feel joy under this sky. She soared through fire, wings roiling smoke and heat, and shot into the north.

She flew, a thin golden dragon, wings beating, eyes narrowed and wet. The wind roared around her. Behind her, ten thousand phoenixes screeched.

When Mori looked over her shoulder, she saw them following, an army of sunfire. Did Solina fly among them, the woman who had killed her brother? Did Acribus fly there, the man who had... Mori gritted her teeth, shame burning across her. He had done something to her, broken something inside her, taken something she could never retrieve. She ached for it. She wanted to die, to never more feel this impurity, but still she flew.

She still had a second brother in Requiem. She still had a father. *I have to warn them. I have to survive. Whatever more happens, however more they hurt me, I must live.*

She flew north with tears and ice, the fury and heat of Tiranor on her tail.

ELETHOR

He stood in his workshop, white columns rising around him, and stared at the statue. The woman was carved of marble, skin smoothed, body nude and flowing. Elethor had spent hours gently chiseling her full lips, her straight nose, her hair that cascaded like silk. And yet, for all his effort, he thought the statue fell from the true grace of Solina.

If only you were still here, Elethor thought, hammer and chisel in his hands. *If only I could see your true beauty again, not content myself with this cold marble. If only I could caress your soft skin, and kiss your lips, and hold you one last time.*

He sighed, laid his tools on the table, and sat on a bench. Around his workshop, six more statues of Solina stood, some nude, others clad in flowing gowns of stone, all beautiful and all painful for him to see. And yet he kept carving her, laboring for months on each effigy.

I will create one every year until I see you again, he thought. Seven statues. Seven years. Seven lost hopes of seeing his love again.

The sun was setting, he noticed; he had been working all day without sensing the time pass. He rose, lit an oil lamp, then stood between the columns of his workshop. The house rose upon a hill, commanding a view of Nova Vita. Elethor often stood here, between these columns, gazing upon the leagues of birches, the houses of white marble, and the herds of dragons that flew above. The city was still beautiful to him, even if sadness had dwelled here since Solina departed.

Soon the sun dipped below the horizon, and the stars emerged. The Draco constellation glittered before him, the stars of his forefathers, the light of his people. He was a prince of Requiem. Those stars blessed him, and the people of this city served him, yet Elethor would forfeit both for the touch of a hand, a breath on his neck, a whisper of her voice.

"Solina," he whispered. A woman of sunlight and a prince of stars. *Solina.* The fire of his night. The pain that coiled forever in his soul.

As he watched the night, he saw a slim, sapphire dragon flying toward the hill. The starlight glimmered on the dragon's scales. Elethor heaved a sigh.

"Perfect," he muttered. "A visit from Lyana. Just what I need."

The blue dragon glided through the night, fire flickering in her maw. Soon Lyana landed upon the hill beyond the columns, her claws kicking up grass and dirt. She gave her wings a last flap, tilted her head, and regarded Elethor.

"You were missed at dinner," she told him, baring her fangs. "Your father is upset."

"I wasn't hungry," he said flatly.

Lyana spat a flicker of disdainful fire. With a growl, she shifted. Her wings pulled into her back. Her fangs and claws retracted. Her scales faded. Soon she stood before him as a young woman. She wore silvery armor engraved with dragons—the armor of the bellators, Requiem's ancient order of knighthood. A sword and a dagger, their pommels shaped as dragonclaws, hung from her belt.

Elethor hated the sight of her. He hated that upturned nose. He hated those green eyes that always seemed so haughty. He even hated her curly red hair, if only because he knew she was so vain about it.

"Not bloody hungry?" the young knight demanded, chin raised. She was a slight girl, a good foot shorter than him, but always strutted around like a giant. "Elethor, I don't give a damn if you just ate a walrus. You are Prince of Requiem. With your older brother in the south, it's your duty to sit at court. Lord Deramon asked for you, and—"

Elethor groaned. "Lyana! I don't want to hear any more of your lectures."

The girl was insufferable; she had been especially bad since betrothing Orin last summer. If before she had boasted of her knighthood—which was bad enough—Lyana was now set to be a princess, then a queen someday. It had inflated her pride to intolerable levels. She was perhaps shorter than Elethor, and five years younger, but she still acted like she was his mother and he was an errant boy.

She marched up toward him, tightened her lips, and raised her chin so high, Elethor thought her head might fall off. She snorted—a loud sound of pure disdain.

"Oh, I see," she said, hands on her hips. "Maybe you think that because I'm a girl, and because I'm young, that I should just be quiet and pretty. Is that it?"

Elethor sighed. "Here we go again."

He turned and headed back into his workshop, but Lyana followed him, ran around him, and faced him again. She glared.

"Well, I have news for you, Prince Elethor Aeternum. I *will* lecture you, as often as I like. And you will listen to me. I am engaged to your older brother, remember that. I'll be his wife this summer and queen consort when he's crowned, and if you think I will be quiet and subservient to you, well... you better think again. Do you understand me?"

"I understand perfectly," he said.

Her eyes narrowed, shards of green fire. "Do you?"

He nodded. "I understand that you are an intolerable, overbearing, supercilious—"

"Watch it, Elethor!" She raised her hand, prepared to strike him. "You forget that in addition to being intolerable, overbearing, and supercilious, I am also a knight in Requiem's army. And I can kick your backside across this forest if I must."

He snorted. "Yes, you are a soldier. A soldier like my brother Orin. You two are brave, strong heroes of Requiem. And I suppose you think I'm but a lowly sculptor, so weak to your noble eyes."

Her face flushed. "Don't put words in my mouth, Elethor. I don't think you must be a soldier like your brother, but damn it, do *something* with your life. Do something more than stargaze, chisel, and bloody mope all day."

He roared with rage, fingers trembling. "My life is my own to live! Not yours. Not my father's." He raised his fist; it shook with anger. "I'm so sorry, Lyana. I'm so sorry I can't live a life you approve of, that I'm such a failure to everyone. Maybe I should go to court and talk of battles and politics and ancient histories; you and Orin would love that, wouldn't you? Maybe I can grow a couple inches taller, until I *look* more like Orin too. Is that what you want to hear?" He glared at her. "But I'm not him, Lyana. I'm very sorry that I can't be tall like Orin, handsome like Orin, brave or strong like Orin. Maybe *I* should have gone south to Castellum Luna, and Requiem's favorite son could have stayed among you instead of poor, weak Elethor."

He was speaking from anger. He knew that. He knew he'd regret those words later. And yet he could not stop it; Lyana always brought this out from him. He turned his back to her, fuming. He liked to think of himself as a calm man. He was an artist. A scholar. A poet. He was not some hot-headed brute. And yet whenever Lyana was around, he wanted to beat his fists against the walls... or strangle her. Whenever she scolded him, he felt like an angry, hysterical child. He forced himself to take slow, deep breaths and count silently to ten. He stared at his new statue, letting Solina's marble beauty soothe him.

I miss you, Solina, he thought, remembering how they would run through the forest, hide in caves, whisper and laugh about Lyana and Lord Deramon and all the others. *I am a ruined man without you.*

Behind him, he heard Lyana sigh.

"You've carved another one," she said softly.

The sadness in her voice stoked Elethor's anger. He spun toward her, fists clenching.

"That is none of your business. This is my workshop and I will sculpt what I please."

He expected her to shout, to rail, maybe even to strike him. But Lyana only seemed so sad, and somehow that was a thousand times worse. She touched his cheek.

"El, I worry about you," she said, eyes soft. "We all do. Since she left, you... spend all your time here in your workshop. Sculpting her. Whispering her name as you sleep. Gazing at the stars all night as if she glowed among them. When will you let her go?"

Elethor shut his eyes. They stung, but he would shed no tears around Lyana.

"I love her," he whispered.

"And your family loves you!" Lyana said, voice more emphatic. "*I* love you. I know you don't believe me, but it's true. Look at me, Elethor. Open your eyes and look at me, and look at the world you live in. Those days are gone."

He did open his eyes. He looked at his brother's betrothed, this young woman of green eyes and red hair and words that cut him.

"You cannot know what it's like," he said, voice choking. "You did not lose somebody you love."

She sighed, and before he could stop her, Lyana embraced him. She laid her head against his shoulder, arms around him.

"No," she said softly. "But... if I were to lose Orin, I don't know how I would live. I love your brother. I love him like the stars, like the sun after night, like spring after frost. If he were to leave, I would be as a shattered jug." She looked into his eyes, hand against his cheek. "But it's been seven years, El. It's time to return to your family. You must let the past remain what it is—the past. Your future lies ahead, Elethor, if you dare walk down its path."

He turned away from her, almost violently, freeing himself from her embrace. She stared at him with huge, damp eyes, mouth open. Elethor stormed away, leaving her among the statues, until he stood outside in the night. Under the stars he shifted, took flight, and soared as a brass dragon. He roared and blew fire in the darkness, fueling it with his rage.

Once you and I would have laughed at Lyana, he thought. *Do you remember, Solina? You used to imitate her, walking around with nose upturned, scolding the plants for growing, berating the sun for turning, and calling yourself the Lady Know-It-All.*

Now such jokes had lost their humor. Now it seemed life itself had lost its light. Orin had burned Solina and betrothed Lyana, and now Elethor remained here, trapped and lost, his love gone into deserts beyond immeasurable wastelands.

Cold air streamed around him, scented of snow. He circled over Nova Vita, so high that the air thinned, making him heady. Whenever he could, he flew this high, far above the herds, higher than his father flew, or Lyana, or anyone else. He used to tell Solina, *Come, ride on my back and we'll explore the skies.*

But she would never ride him or anyone. *I am a proud child of Tiranor,* she would say. *We do not become dragons, and we are no poorer for it; I walk where I must go.*

Elethor looked over Nova Vita, the heart of Requiem, the only home he'd ever known. The palace stood ahead, white columns rising like pillars of moonlight, and near it rose the Temple of Stars, its dome carved from polished silver. Around these great halls rolled hills covered with birches, the trees rustling and sweetly scented in the night. From the foliage peeked homes of white stone, workshops, and squares full of statues and fountains. Three white archways led to underground tunnels where Requiem stored its treasures: ancient books, magical artifacts, and sacks of golden grain for winter. Finally, two great forts bookended the city, their bricks craggy and their banners thudding: Castra Murus, a squat garrison housing the City Guard; and Castra Draco, its four towers housing the Royal Army.

The structures—even the two forts—seemed part of the landscape to Elethor, blending with the forest as naturally as boulders or rivers. It was a beautiful home—he had always thought so—but for Solina it had been a prison. A place of exile. Of pain.

Once, he knew, a million dragons had flown here, and Requiem had been a wonder for the world. It had been three hundred years since the griffins burned this place, killing all but seven dragons. Today fifty thousand Vir Requis lived here, descendants of the Living

Seven—a small light, a whisper after the great song of the glory days. *Yet we are rebuilding,* Elethor thought. *We are making a new age of glory.* His father carried the torch of Requiem now; Orin and Lyana would follow. Elethor was second in line, and he would not sit upon the throne, for which he was grateful. He wanted nothing more than a life of reflection, sculpture, and stargazing.

"And a life with you, Solina," he whispered. "I pray every night that you return to us someday... that you return to me."

A cry pierced the night.

Elethor frowned and stared south. A lone dragon flew there, wobbling, wings shaking. She was a slim dragon, female, with golden scales. She cried again, a cry of anguish and fear.

Elethor's breath caught.

"Mori," he whispered.

He flapped his wings, narrowed his eyes, and dived toward her. His sister blew weak flame, cried again, and began tumbling toward the forest. Elethor swooped, fear twisting his gut. Air whistled around him. Mori spun toward the distant trees, wings limp, sparks flying from her maw. Elethor caught her ten feet above the ground, wrapping his claws under her. She was so thin, so light in his grip. He lowered her gently onto the snow.

"Mori!" he said. "Mori, can you hear me?"

Birches rose around them, naked and icy. His younger sister blinked at him, thinner than he'd ever seen her. Her wings splayed out around her, and her tail flapped weakly.

"Elethor," she whispered.

His breath caught. Mori had always been a timid thing, but there was new fear in her eyes, a haunting pain that tore through him.

They shifted into human forms. Mori lay in his arms, gazing up with huge gray eyes. Her gown was torn and bloody, her face pale, her lips trembling. Dried blood filled her brown hair.

"What happened, Mori?" Elethor whispered, feeling as if snow filled his belly.

She held him, staring up into his eyes. Her shaky breath frosted.

"They killed him, Elethor," she whispered. Her fingers dug into his back. "They killed him. And they're coming here."

ADIA

Mother Adia, High Priestess of Requiem, stood above the grave of her daughter.

It had been thirteen years since Noela had died—a cherubic child of dark eyes and darker hair. In those thirteen years, Adia had watched her other children grow into adulthood, watched white invade her hair, watched her husband turn from loving man to cold warrior... and yet the pain still lingered.

"I still feel like you only just left me," she whispered to the grave.

She smiled to remember the softness of Noela's hair, the sweetness of her smile, the warmth of her little fingers. Adia's two other children looked like their father. Bayrin and Lyana had the red hair, the green eyes, the fiery temper. But Noela...

"You were like me," Adia whispered. "You had black hair like mine. Soft brown eyes like mine. A sweet sadness like the one that lingers inside me. You wouldn't have been a warrior... you would have been a priestess like me."

A cold wind blew through the night, scented of fire. The wick of her lamp danced. Adia wrapped her white robes around her. *The people are lighting bonfires,* she thought. It was the Night of Seven, a night to remember the seven Vir Requis who had survived the Destruction three hundred years ago, the seven who gave birth to this nation of fifty thousand. Across the hills of Requiem, people would be lighting bonfires of memory, and this midnight Adia would walk through the temples, light incense, and praise the stars for their blessings.

But I'll be thinking of you, Noela. Today we remember the Seven... and today is the day you left me.

Thirteen years. A lifetime of memory and grief.

"Adia."

The voice spoke behind her, deep but soft. Adia turned to see Deramon, her husband, walk between the snowy graves. Frost covered his plate armor, sheathed sword, and red beard. His eyes, deep green, stared at her from under bushy brows. In his left hand he held a lamp; in his right, an axe.

"Why do you bring steel to this place?" Adia whispered. "This is a place of rest. Of beauty. A place for Noela to forever sleep under starlight. Why do you bring axe and sword to the grave of our daughter?"

She saw the pain that caused him. His eyes darkened, his mouth twisted, his knuckles whitened. She had loved him once, Adia thought. Thirteen years ago. Before her world had crumbled. Did she love him still?

Maybe, she thought. *But how can I love another? How can I love anyone when my Noela awaits me in the starlit halls of our ancestors?*

"I am Captain of the City Guard," Deramon said. His voice was gruff, but she heard its pain. "I am sworn to defend this city, my king, and my people. My weapons stay with me... at my post, in my bed, even at the grave of our child. You know this, Adia. You are a priestess; forever the light of stars glows around you. I am a warrior. Forever steel shines with me."

Adia looked away. She looked at the grave, her throat tightened, and her eyes stung with tears. She felt one roll down her cheek.

"She would have been a priestess too," she whispered. "I gave birth to three of your children, Deramon. Two look like you, with red hair and green eyes and steel in their hands. They are warriors. They are proud. And I love them. But Noela..." She trembled. "She was like a young me. A sad, reflective child. Why did she leave me?"

Deramon growled, a low sound like a bear in his cave. He placed his lamp down by the grave. "Noela died in her cradle, Adia. She was not yet two years old. We do not know the woman she might have become."

She spun toward him, glaring. "I knew!" she hissed. Her eyes blurred with tears. "I knew her soul, and her heart, and—"

Deramon grabbed her arm. "Adia," he whispered. His eyes narrowed, drowning in pain. "Adia, I loved her too. More than you can imagine. But I also love Bayrin and Lyana—who still live, who still need us. And I love *you*. We still have a family to protect."

She closed her eyes. "A family to protect. A king to protect. A city to protect. You protect everyone, Deramon, but who protected her?" She opened her eyes. "We were not there for her, Deramon. We didn't even *know* until the morning!" Her voice rose, torn in pain. "She lay dead in the cradle all night, as we slept, and it was dawn before we—"

Deramon howled. "Enough!"

He tossed his axe aside; it thumped into the snow. He held her with both hands. She struggled, but he pulled her into his embrace, and Adia found herself weeping against his shoulder. She shivered against him, and he held her tight and smoothed her hair. She stood with arms at her sides, but then slowly reached around him and embraced him.

Yes, she thought. *I love him. I love Deramon, though he has changed, and I have changed, and joy has left our lives. But I still love him.*

She looked aside at the grave, at the marble tombstone, at the place of all her sorrow and memory.

And I love you, Noela. Always. I will see you again in our starlit halls.

Wings thudded behind her. A dragon's roar pierced the air. Adia spun around to see a blue dragon spiraling down toward the graveyard.

Lyana. My daughter.

The young dragon's wings roiled the falling snow. Smoke plumed from between her teeth, and the moon glimmered against her blue scales. She landed, claws digging into mounds of snow, and shifted into human form. Lyana stood before her parents, her cheeks flushed, her eyes wide and frightened. Frost whitened her armor.

She is like a young Deramon, Adia thought again. *A warrior like him, angry and proud like him, clad in steel and honor.* Mother and daughter—fire and water.

"Mother!" the young woman said, panting. "Quick, to the temple. Princess Mori is hurt."

Adia frowned. "Mori is far south in Castellum Luna. The king sent her to—"

"She's back," said Lyana. She shifted back into a dragon and took flight. Her voice roared. "Follow me! She needs your healing."

Adia's head spun. She took a deep breath and summoned her magic. White scales flowed across her, clinking and glimmering. Leathern wings sprouted from her back, and fire tickled her mouth. She took flight as a long dragon, white as snow. Her husband shifted too, and soon Deramon flew at her side, a burly dragon with clanking, coppery scales.

Parents followed daughter. The three dragons flew over the graveyard, over city streets, and toward Requiem's palace of white marble.

Again the Night of Seven comes to Requiem, Adia thought, *and again sorrow falls.* It had always been a night of destruction.

As she flew over the city, she looked south; the horizon glowed red. Distant fires blazed.

LYANA

Lyana Eleison, a knight of Requiem, stood in the hall of her king. She wore chain mail, a breastplate, and a helmet of steel. She clutched her sword so tightly her knuckles were white.

I will be strong, she told herself, struggling to calm her racing heart. *I am a bellator of Requiem. Whatever evil befell my princess, I will fight it.*

The palace's columns rose around her, pale as moonlight, their capitals shaped as dragons. Braziers stood among them, crackling with embers, filling the hall with warmth and light. Yet no fire could warm Lyana today; her chill gripped her from her belly, sending icy fingers through her.

People filled the hall around her: Lyana's father, the burly Lord Deramon; Lyana's mother, the willowy priestess Adia; King Olasar upon his throne, a crown of gilded oak roots upon his head; Prince Elethor, his eyes dark; a dozen guards with spears and shields. All eyes stared at the young Princess Mori who stood trembling upon the palace's marble tiles.

"Hush, child, you're safe now," whispered Adia. The priestess stepped forward, white robes fluttering, and embraced Mori. "Nobody will hurt you here."

Lyana looked at the two—her mother and her princess—and her throat tightened. *I am a knight of Requiem,* she thought. *I am betrothed to a prince. Yet now I too want to weep into a warm embrace. Now I wish my mother held me, her daughter, the way she holds our princess.*

"You're safe now, Mori," whispered Adia. "You're safe."

The princess wept, a blanket wrapped around her shoulders. Blood caked her hair and tears etched lines down her ashy face. She whimpered and clung to Adia, digging her fingers into the priestess's robes.

"I'm scared," she whispered.

Adia raised her eyes and looked over the weeping girl's head. She stared at the Oak Throne of Requiem, which stood upon a marble dais engraved with gilded leaves.

"Please, Your Highness," the priestess said, "let me take her to the temple. I will tend to her there."

King Olasar sat upon his throne of twisting oak roots. His brows were heavy and black, his beard snowy white. A tall man clad in dark green and steel, he held a sword on his lap—Stella Lumen, ancient blade of the legendary Lacrimosa, the queen who had fought the tyrant Dies Irae and reigned over ruins. He was a wise king, Lyana thought, and a brave warrior. She loved him like a second father.

"Not yet, Adia," the king said, eyes dark. "Let my daughter speak. Mori, look at me. Tell me what happened. Tell me everything."

Still clinging to Adia, the princess looked up at her father. Tears spiked her lashes and her lips trembled.

"They killed him," she whispered. "They killed Orin, Father! They killed him."

Lyana stared.

Her heart shattered inside her.

Orin. My betrothed. No. No...

Tears filled her eyes. Pain gripped her heart and squeezed. She looked up at her mother with burning eyes, at her father who stood by the throne, at Prince Elethor who gasped. Tears blurred her vision and the world spun around her.

Orin. Dead.

The grief swelled through the hall. Lyana found herself clinging to Elethor, digging her fingers into his back. He held her, tears in his eyes, his breath heavy. King Olasar rose to his feet, his chest heaved, and even this great ruler's eyes filled with tears. Lord Deramon gritted his teeth and clutched his axe, and the warriors who served him, guards of the throne, cried in grief.

He's gone. Stars, he's gone. My betrothed. My love. My Orin.

Lyana trembled as the world crashed around her. If the columns of this palace fell and King's Forest burned, she'd have felt no less grief and shock.

Her father spoke first. Captain of the City Guard, Deramon raised his voice above the cries of grief; it boomed across the hall.

"Who killed the prince?" he demanded. He was perhaps the greatest warrior in Requiem, a gruff man of muscle and grit, but even his eyes shone with tears. "Who killed Prince Orin?"

Mori dared not look at Deramon; she had always feared the lord's fiery beard, booming voice, and blazing eyes. Face pale, the princess ran to her father. She clung to the king. For the first time, Lyana noticed that blood slicked the princess's thighs, and an iciness seized her. She shivered. *They killed Orin, and stars, what did they do to Mori?*

"Tirans," Mori whispered, voice so soft, Lyana barely heard. "They bore the sun of Tiranor on their armor. Their swords were curved and gilded; they looked like beaks. They had golden skin, and blue eyes, and hair like platinum. I... they could fly, Father! They flew as firebirds, great beasts of flame. They are coming. They will be here soon. They burned him! And they will burn us. Father... they are coming, they..."

Mori's eyes rolled back, and she fell limp in the king's arms.

Lyana wanted to faint too. She forced herself to breathe, to focus her eyes, to clutch her sword. Tiranor attacking Requiem? She clenched her jaw. Tiranor had not attacked Requiem since the war nearly thirty years ago, a decade before Lyana's birth. She knew little of Tirans, only that they were proud, tall, and fair—a beautiful and cruel desert people with sapphire eyes and blades that thirsted for blood. Why would they attack Requiem?

But of course Lyana knew. She whispered the answer through cold lips.

"It's Solina."

Solina. The orphaned princess of Tiranor, taken captive to Requiem after the devastating war. Solina, who loved Elethor, who had attacked the king, who had fled burnt to her desert home.

Lyana snarled, pulled back from Elethor's embrace, and drew her sword.

"It's Solina!" she repeated, louder this time, loud enough for the hall to hear. "She killed Orin. And I will kill her."

The hall erupted in cries. Father and his men, warriors clad in steel, called for vengeance. Mother called for calm. Only Elethor stood silent, face pale and mouth open.

King Olasar stood, his unconscious daughter in his arms, and raised his voice.

"Silence!" he thundered. Pain filled his eyes, but he narrowed them and stared upon the hall. Mori hung in his arms, head tilted back, blood trickling. The hall fell silent; all eyes stared at the king. Lyana stood panting, sword drawn, grief like a talon clutching her.

The king turned his dark eyes toward Lyana's mother. The priestess stared back, blood smearing her white robes, her eyes huge and haunted.

"Adia," said King Olasar, "take my daughter to the temple. Heal her. Let her sleep. And Adia... prepare the temple for wounded. Many wounded." His jaw was tight. "And for the dead."

Adia nodded, face pale but strong. She walked forward and took Mori from the king's arms. Carrying the girl, she left the hall, robes sweeping behind her. Lyana watched the two leave, throat tight. She knew what this blood meant, this tremble in Mori's voice, the shame in her eyes.

They raped her. They will do the same to me if they can. Her eyes stung and her throat felt so tight she could barely breathe.

Next King Olasar turned to Lyana's father. Deramon stared back, eyes dark under his bushy red brows, his heavy hands upon his weapons. He stood clad in steel and leather, every inch a warrior, but Lyana saw the fear and pain that lurked behind his scowl. *Father is as scared as I am,* she knew.

"Lord Deramon," said the king, "prepare the City Guard. Summon every last man from your barracks, all one thousand. Man the walls and patrol the skies. Protect Nova Vita."

Deramon bowed, one hand on his sword's hilt, the other on his axe. His armor creaked.

"My king," he said gruffly. "It will be done."

With that, Deramon turned and marched out of the hall. His soldiers followed, armor clanking. Soon Lyana heard them shift outside—their wings thudded, and their howls shook the palace. She saw them take flight outside the windows, great dragons blowing fire.

Only Lyana and Elethor now remained before the king. The young prince had not spoken yet. He was pale and his fists shook at his sides. Lyana knew what he was thinking. He was thinking of *her.* The woman he loved. The woman whose parents King Olasar had slain. The woman who, Lyana knew, now marched against them. *Solina, bane of Requiem, forever a curse upon this place.*

She knew Olasar was thinking the same thing. The king was staring at his son, the younger prince, now heir to his throne.

"Elethor," the king said, and for the first time his voice was strangely soft. "Sit upon this throne until I return. You rule in Nova Vita in my absence."

Still pale and silent, Elethor nodded. As the king walked across the hall, Elethor approached the throne and sat, eyes staring at nothing, fists still clenched at his sides. A tear streamed down his cheek.

"My king!" Lyana said as Olasar walked by her. "How shall I serve you?"

Olasar paused and stared at her, and Lyana lost her breath. She saw such pain in Olasar's eyes, such grief and rage and terror, reflections of her own turmoil. Olasar's lips trembled only slightly, and his brow remained strong, his jaw squared.

"You will fly at my side, Lady Lyana," he said, voice soft. "We call the banners. We summon the Royal Army. And we fly south. We fly to war."

Lyana sucked in her breath. Not since the war thirty years ago had the Royal Army—five thousand warriors led by the king and his knights—flown to war.

Orin. My love. My eternal prince. Tears stung her eyes, but she bowed her head. She gritted her teeth, grief and rage like ice and fire crashing inside her.

"To war," she whispered.

They marched across the hall, boots echoing against the tiles. Around them between the columns, Lyana saw thousands of dragon wings and blasts of flame. When they reached the hall's end, the gatekeepers bowed and opened the doors, revealing Nova Vita. Deramon's guardsmen ran between the birches, shifted into dragons, and took flight.

King Olasar marched into the courtyard and shifted. His wings thudded, and he flew as a great black dragon, flames seeking the sky. Lyana was prepared to shift too, but paused and looked back over her shoulder.

Elethor sat upon the throne across the hall, staring at her. He looked so small in the empty palace, nearly lost in the grip of the twisting Oak Throne.

"Lyana," he said and stood up. In the empty hall, his voice echoed and flowed to her. "Lyana, I'm sorry. Be careful tonight."

For the first time, Lyana realized that by the law of Requiem, she was now betrothed to Elethor. *His older brother is dead; he inherited the right of succession, and he inherited me.*

Lyana nodded, silent, jaw clenched. She turned and left the palace, leaving him among the marble columns. The dragons of Olasar's army, five thousand warriors, were taking flight, following their king to the south. Already Lyana saw a fiery glow upon that horizon, sending red claws toward their home. She shifted, flew to join her king, and roared her flame.

A wall of fire rose ahead, shimmering with sound and heat.

OLASAR

A fire rose in the south. From the inferno flew the phoenixes, beasts woven of flame, large as dragons and cruel as wildfire. Thousands shrieked and beat blazing wings, showering sparks. Their cries seemed to shake the world.

"The sun herself has hatched," King Olasar whispered, "and given birth to countless birds of prey."

The enemy soared, lighting the night with fury. The clouds themselves seemed to burn, roiling and raining ash. The phoenix army swallowed the sky and stormed forward; they would reach him soon.

Olasar flapped his wings and blew fire. He roared, a dragon roar that could shatter men's ears. Behind him, his army answered his call. Five thousand dragons howled, a song of rage and fire.

He turned to face them, his wings churning the falling snow. They flew in phalanxes, each lead by a bellator with gilded horns, each a terror of a hundred dragons. Fifty knights and thousands of hardened warriors; they all roared in the night. Their jets of flame rose like pillars of a burning cathedral, blazing against their scales. Their fangs shone like whetted daggers.

"Dragons of Requiem!" King Olasar called to them. "Show the enemy no quarter. Defend our land. Destroy these beasts of unholy fire!"

Their cries shattered the night. The falling snow flurried and steamed around them. Olasar turned back toward the enemy, the countless phoenixes that had swallowed their southern lands, slain his son, and now flew toward Nova Vita itself. The firebirds screeched and burned with the fury of the sun.

"To war!" Olasar shouted and flew toward them.

"To war!" cried five thousand voices behind him.

Their wings thudded. Their flames roared. Thousands of dragons, warriors of Requiem, soared through wind and darkness. Their cries rose in the night—for war, for fire, and for glory. The smell of smoke and fear filled Olasar's nostrils, and he bared his fangs.

As my forefathers fought for Requiem, I will fight too. For the memory of my son. For the eternal light of our people. I will not let Requiem fall again.

The phoenixes flew toward them, a mile away, then a hundred yards. Their heat blazed. Olasar had never felt such heat; it stung his eyes and throat. The firebirds soared and swooped, their cries thudded in his ears... and then they were upon him.

Roaring, Olasar blew a jet of fire. It crackled, spun, and slammed into a phoenix. The great bird tossed back its head and screeched. The dragonfire only seemed to fuel the creature; it grew larger, and its talons lashed.

The claws slammed into Olasar, and he howled. The fire roared across his chest, raising welts. The heat consumed him, and all around, countless other phoenixes flew. He swung his claws, tearing into one. It was like clawing a campfire; there was no flesh to cut. The phoenix roared, a sound like an erupting volcano, and thrust its beak.

Fire blasted Olasar and raced across his scales. He reared and beat his wings, trying to scatter the phoenix flames; it only fanned the fire, making the bird larger, hotter, crueler. Its eyes crackled, white pools like smelters.

Olasar bared his teeth and soared higher. The phoenix chased him through the clouds. All around, he saw dragons battling more phoenixes. The flames and clouds roiled, and cries shook the sky.

"We cannot kill them, my lord!" cried a dragon to his left.

"The demons cannot be burned or cut!" shouted another dragon.

Everywhere he looked, Olasar saw dragons burning. Their wings flamed and they howled in the night. They fell around him. In death, Requiem's magic left them, and they took human forms. The bodies of men and women fell like comets.

"They must not reach Nova Vita!" Olasar shouted. Thousands of his people dwelled there—women, children, the elderly. He howled. "Dragons, hold them back!"

Five phoenixes soared toward him, a shower of flame. Their wings battered him. Their claws burned him. Their beaks of fire dug into his flesh. He roared, flapping his wings, beating them back. When he scattered their fire, they reformed. When he cut their bodies, the flames only burned his claws.

"We must retreat!" cried a slim blue dragon beside him. Her gilded horns shone in the firelight—a bellator's horns.

"Lyana!" Olasar cried to her. "Lyana, fly to Nova Vita! Get everyone into the tunnels and seal them! We will hold them back. Go underground!"

The young blue dragon howled. She blew flame at a swooping phoenix but could not stop its dive. It slammed into her, knocking her into a spin.

"I will not leave you, my king!" she cried, dodging the phoenix claws. "I will not leave my men!"

"Fly!" he cried to her. "Save those that you still can. Lead the city into the tunnels, Lyana! That is my command."

Three phoenixes crashed into him, and Olasar howled in pain. Welts rose across his belly. The scales covering his back blazed; he felt that they would soon melt. He could barely see; smoke and flame filled the night.

"Fly, Lyana!" he shouted.

He thought he glimpsed a flash of blue scales shooting into the distance. *I must only hold the phoenixes back long enough,* he thought. *Long enough for Lyana to evacuate the city underground, to save herself and my living son.* He gritted his teeth. *I will hold them back.*

"Dragons of Requiem!" he shouted into the inferno. "Cut them with claws, scatter their flames, do not let them fly forward! Hold them back!"

The phoenix beaks bit. Their wings slammed into him like fountains of lava. All around he saw dragons blazing, shouting, and turning into men who burned and fell. The smoke filled Olasar's lungs. He could not breathe. Soon he could no longer see; he seemed to fly inside the sun.

Will Requiem fall again? Will it fall like in the days of King Benedictus, when the griffins toppled our halls?

A great howl rose before him, a sound of collapsing mountains, of primal rage, of shattering kingdoms.

The smoke parted. The flames rose in a wall. From the holocaust soared a phoenix, brighter than the others, slender and graceful. Its eyes were molten stars, blazing white. Its wings stretched out, red and orange, tapestries of inferno. It was the most beautiful creature Olasar had ever seen, a deity of punishment and brimstone.

The great firebird soared toward him. Its claws were shards of purest white, hotter than forge fire. They slammed into him, and the world burned, and white light flooded him.

Olasar the First, King of Requiem, fell from the sky.

He crashed through the clouds, tore through burning trees, and slammed into the snow. The shock and pain tore his magic from him. His wings pulled into his body, his claws and fangs retracted, and his scales vanished. He lay as a man, burnt and cut, dying. When he looked around him, he saw the bodies of slain soldiers; they too were only men now, their magic extinguished, their bodies seared red and black.

Olasar looked above him. The phoenix army covered the sky; he could see no end to them. They were flying north, heading to Nova Vita, the capital where forty-five thousand of his people still dwelled.

"Save them, Lyana," he whispered, feverish and trembling. Smoke rose from him. "Save our people."

The great, beautiful phoenix descended toward him, burning with the fire of the sun. *So graceful,* Olasar thought in a haze. *So beautiful. How could something so beautiful be so cruel?*

The phoenix landed in the snow before him. It regarded him for a moment, and then its fires flared, twisted, pulled inward. It shrank and reformed, taking the shape of a human. It was a woman, he realized—a woman with platinum hair, a golden mask, and sabres at her hips. She walked toward him as the sky burned. A crystal hung around her neck, a flame dancing inside it.

"Who are you?" Olasar whispered, staring up at her.

She came to stand above him, staring down through her golden mask. In one hand, she held a sack. Her other hand rested on the pommel of her sword.

"Olasar," she said to him, her voice itself like caressing flame. "Hello again."

He squinted, staring up at her; she stood dark before the wall of fire. Her golden mask glimmered. He tried to rise but could not. Welts rose across him, seeping. The pain spun his head and sweat drenched him.

"Show yourself," he managed to say, reaching for his sword with charred fingers.

Slowly, the woman removed her golden mask... and Olasar snarled.

You were right, Lyana. Stars bless us.

"Solina," he whispered hoarsely.

Her face was golden, her eyes blue, her lips cruel. A burn mark ran across her face, from forehead to chin and down her neck. She traced the scar with her fingers.

"My line of fire," Solina said softly. "You remember how your son, the great Prince Orin, burned me." She opened her sack and held it upside down. A severed head rolled out. Half the head was burned into pulpy, red flesh. The other half was locked in a cry of anguish.

"No," Olasar whispered, then howled in the night. "My son! My son." Tears filled her eyes.

Solina nodded, smiling softly. "He burned me... and so I burned him. And so I will burn all of you."

Olasar shook his head. Though the pain suffused him, he managed to rise to his feet. He drew Stella Lumen, his ancient sword. The fire of the phoenix army blazed against the blade.

"I took you into my court," he said, voice trembling but still strong. "I raised you as a daughter. I—"

"You lie!" Solina screamed. Suddenly her eyes blazed, and her fury twisted her face. "I was no daughter to you. I know, Olasar. I know what happened to my true parents. I know that you killed them." She laughed and touched the crystal at her neck; the flame inside it danced. "But I am strong now; I have the strength of the Sun God. As you killed my parents with steel, so will I kill you. Goodbye, tyrant. May your soul forever burn in the court of my lord."

She drew her sword. It crackled with fire and she drove it forward. Olasar parried, sparks showered, and his blade shattered. Shards of steel flew.

Solina snarled and her blade thrust. It drove into Olasar's chest, burning, blazing, twisting inside him.

He fell. Solina laughed above him, and all Olasar saw was the thousands of firebirds flowing north, burning all in their path, heading to the heart of his realm... and then the flames flooded his world, and he saw nothing else.

LYANA

"No," she whispered, eyes stinging. Her breath died within her. "Stars, please, no... Stars, no."

The image seared her. Orin's head, severed and charred, rolling from a sack. It stared up at her from below, hundreds of yards away, but dragon eyes were sharp, and she knew it was him. Tears blurred Lyana's vision.

"Orin, stars... my Orin."

My love. My betrothed. My prince.

She watched as Solina pulled her sword free from the king's body, this woman who had once been like an older sister to her. Smirking, Solina sheathed her blade, leaped into the air, and flames engulfed her. She spread fiery wings and took flight as a phoenix, a flaming beast the size of a dragon. Her shrieks tore the air.

"Kill every last dragon!" Her voice stormed through her beak of fire. "Soon we fly to Nova Vita."

Lyana had heard enough. She had to warn them. The king had commanded her. Growling, she spun around and began flying north. *I will warn them. I will save our city.*

She shot through the battle, eyes narrowed. Around her, dragons were still dying, burned in the grip of phoenix talons. Three of the firebirds dived toward her, leaving trails of flame. Lyana flew sideways, dodging them, and flashed around them. She soared, jaw clenched.

You will not have died in vain, Orin, she vowed. *I will save our people.*

She had always been fast—not as fast as Mori, perhaps, but faster than anyone else she knew. Her body was slim, her scales smooth, her wings strong. She burst through walls of fire, howling, and shot into the clouds.

Snow flurried and filled her maw. Its ice stung the welts that covered her wings. She flew higher and higher until her eyes burned, her lungs ached, and she could barely see or breathe. She straightened, glided forward, and looked down.

The battle raged below, hidden under the clouds. She saw bursts of light where phoenixes flared. She heard their shrieks and the death cries of dragons. When she looked north, she saw only darkness, but she knew Nova Vita lay ahead across lake and mountain.

Capital of Requiem. Home to thousands of Vir Requis she had to save.

The shame of leaving her phalanx—a hundred soldiers sworn to serve her in battle—dug through her chest. She was a knight, a leader of warriors... and she was leaving them to die. She gritted her teeth and fire flared inside her.

Yet I will obey my king. I will save the people of Nova Vita. I will do what I must.

She flew toward the city. She cut through the night, the cold air stinging.

Shrieks sounded behind her, moving closer. When she looked over her shoulder, she cursed. Three phoenixes emerged from the clouds, flames blazing, and flew toward her.

"Damn it!" Lyana gritted her teeth and flew faster. She could not let these beasts follow her home. She dived, plunging into the cloud cover. The snow slammed against her and the wind screamed.

The phoenix cries rose behind her. She turned her head and saw blazes of light through the clouds, like three suns chasing her. She flapped her wings mightily.

Even three could destroy our city, she thought. *I can't let these ones reach Nova Vita before I evacuate everyone into the tunnels.*

She kept flying. They kept chasing, orbs of light inside the clouds. *They will not leave me.* Lyana swerved sideways and flew east, cursing the delay; every moment she lingered could mean another life lost. When she looked back, she saw the flames follow, blazing among the clouds.

Stars! How could they keep following her? The clouds were surely too thick to see a slim, blue dragon who blew no fire. *I must be leaving a wake through the clouds... that, or they can smell dragons.*

She flew up and down, left and right, but the phoenixes followed. Their shrieks grew closer. The clouds began to thin, and Lyana cursed under her breath. Soon the flurries of snow died, and only wisps of clouds raced across her scales. Sky burst open before her, black and tainted with the orange glow of distant fire. Smoke billowed above, umber and gray. Behind her, a wall of fire rose from the battle, casting red light like blood across the land.

The phoenixes cried behind her. Lyana glanced back and cursed. They tore through the last clouds, comets of fury, blazing toward her. Their wings burned red and yellow. Their beaks opened, revealing gullets like flowing lava. Their eyes flared, collapsing stars. They left wakes of flame as they soared toward her. Though the night

was black, their light filled it; they saw her, and they cried with
bloodlust.

What unholy magic had created these beings? Lyana growled
and swooped. She had seen one turn into Solina, adopted sister to her
fallen betrothed. *These are no demons,* she thought. *They are men and
women with magic similar to ours. We can turn into dragons; they turn into these
creatures.*

She could not fight fire. If she could face them in their humans
forms, she could kill them.

She dived toward Aranath Mountains below, chunks of black
rock in the night. The phoenix light blazed against them, racing across
the black stone and patches of snow. Lyana would come to these
mountains with Orin—sweet, handsome Prince Orin—and they
would walk through caves, whispering, holding hands, stealing kisses.
If I must die today, let these caves be my place of eternal rest.

"Come on, you bastards!" she shouted over her shoulder. She
blew a jet of fire back toward the three chasing phoenixes. "You killed
him. You killed my love. Now come face me."

She swooped, claws extended. She knew these mountains better
than anyone in Requiem. Wind whistled around her, and the
phoenixes cried so loudly, snow cascaded and melted below. She saw
the cave there, *her* cave, hers and Orin's, its mouth round and five feet
tall, short enough that she'd always had to stoop to enter.

She landed outside the cave. As soon as her claws hit the
ground, she shifted into human form. Her wings pulled into her back.
Her fangs and claws retracted. Instead of scales, steel armor covered
her body. Her sword—as much a part of her as her arm—still hung
on her belt. She ran into the cave, hand on its hilt.

She spun around, the cave walls close around her, and saw an
inferno.

Damn them. This delay shot fear through her. She needed to
reach Nova Vita quickly. Mori had fainted after only a vague warning
and might still be sleeping. Did the city know of this phoenix fire?
Did they know they could not fight, only hide? Lyana had to warn
them. She had to fly now. She had to kill these beasts quickly, or it
would be too late.

The phoenixes landed outside the cave. Snow melted and fell
like rain around them. Wings thrashing, they reached into the tunnel
with claws of fire. The flames blazed. Lyana leaped back; the heat
blasted her armor, and she felt like her eyeballs could melt. She
retreated into the darkness.

The first time we made love was here, sweet Orin, she thought, eyes stinging and throat burning. The image kept playing before her eyes—his head rolling from the sack, burnt and grimacing—even now as these beasts of sunfire clawed outside.

"Come in and face me!" she cried. "You are like us children of Requiem. You have human forms; I have seen it. Come face me, or are you such cowards that you dare not face one woman?"

They howled and flared. Their heat drenched Lyana with sweat; locks of her damp, red hair stuck to her face. She snarled, holding her sword before her. With her left hand, she drew her dagger, its blade shaped as a dragonclaw. The heat of battle raged over her loss of Orin, simmering over her grief.

"Be with me, stars of Requiem," she prayed. "May your light shine upon my blades."

With cries of fury, the phoenixes outside shifted.

Their fire pulled into them, twisting and coiling into human shapes. The flames darkened and hardened, like lava cooling into stone, until they became flesh. They stared at her, eyes still burning like coals. They wore breastplates of steel emblazoned with the golden Sun of Tiranor, and swords hung at their sides. Their hair was a blond so pale, it was almost white. Their skin was golden, their eyes blue and cold. Each wore a chain holding a crystal glimmering with fire. Two were men, their faces bearded and cruel. The third was a woman holding a sabre and a spear. The sides of her head were shaven, revealing sun tattoos, and her lips were pierced with rings.

"See how she cowers in darkness," said the woman to her companions. Her voice was cold, her eyes ruthless. "When the dragons burned our homeland, they howled with their pride, their bloodlust, their cruelty. See what pathetic creatures they've become." She snarled and her voice rose to a shout. "Hail the Sun God, destroyer of Requiem!"

"Tirans," Lyana said, eyes narrowing. "Return to your homeland that we burned. Leave Requiem, or we will kill you on our mountains, like we killed you in your deserts."

The female Tiran smirked. Her armor was bright, and her blades glimmered like shards of light, flames racing across them.

"You may call me Phira of the Two Blades," she said, raising her sword and spear. "Do you see them? They will cut your tongue from your mouth, weredragon." She spat out the last word in disgust.

Lyana snarled. *Weredragon.* It was a dirty word, an ugly curse. She was Vir Requis, a proud daughter of Requiem, descended from the hero Terra Eleison himself. Hers was old blood, proud and pure.

Like every child of Requiem, she could grow wings and scales, breathe
fire, and take flight as a dragon. It was a magic old and noble, kissed
with starlight. *Weredragon* meant a reptile, a filthy beast.

"And you may call me Lady Lyana Eleison, a knight of
Requiem, daughter of Lord Deramon and Mother Adia," she said.
"May the stars burn your souls."

She ran toward them.

The two men ran to meet her. Lyana lashed her sword and
dagger. The soldiers parried. Flames leaped from their swords and
burned her sleeve. She screamed, swung her sword, and blades
clashed again. She raised her dagger, parrying a thrust. Flames hit the
cave walls and steel rang.

"Requiem!" she cried. "May our wings forever find your sky."

The words of her fathers. The words of battle, of death, of
blood and hope.

Her blades swung and thrust, glowing bright. She knocked
one sword against the wall, thrust her blade, and pierced the man's
neck. The second Tiran swung down his sword, and she raised her
dagger. The blades sparked. The blow nearly dislocated her arm, and
she screamed, but pulled her sword free and swung low.

Her blade slashed the leg before her, and the second man fell.
She leaped back, dodging his sabre, and thrust. Her sword slammed
into his mouth, muffling his scream. Blood spurted and he fell. More
blood painted the cave walls and floor, congealing in the heat of fire.

Two men lay dead, sabres still crackling.

Phira, the Tiran woman, snarled. She stepped over the bodies
and raised her blades. Fire wreathed her, glittering upon the rings
piercing her lips. The suns tattooed onto her head seemed to burn
with real fire, but her eyes were cold, chips of ice. There was no
humanity in them, only hunger and cruel amusement.

"Very good, girl," she said and licked those pierced lips. "Not
bad for a weredragon. But now you will taste true steel."

Phira thrust her spear.

Her arms ached, but Lyana parried. The blades clanged.
Phira's sabre swung next, and Lyana barely checked the blow.

Phira was strong, stronger than Lyana had expected. She cried
in pain. Her sword nearly flew from her arm, and her bone felt like it
could snap. The sabre swung. Lyana parried with her dagger. Phira's
spear sliced her hip, and she cried.

"Do you like the taste of my steel?" Phira asked, smirking.
She thrust her blades again. Lyana parried, grunting in pain. Sweat

dripped into her eyes. The spear sliced a lock of her hair, and the Tiran laughed.

"Yes, groan for me, weredragon," she said and spat. "That's how I like to hear reptiles die."

Lyana screamed and thrust her sword. Phira parried, caught her wrist, and bent her hand back. *Fight her!* Lyana cried to herself. *You are a knight of Requiem!*

Phira clutched her right wrist, twisting, her strength almost unreal. Lyana felt like her bones could shatter. As her fingers uncurled and her sword fell, she thrust her dagger. She aimed for Phira's neck, but the Tiran moved aside, and Lyana's dagger scraped across her pauldron. Sparks flew. Phira laughed and punched, slamming her fist into Lyana's face.

Light blazed. Blood filled her mouth. Lyana fell, hit the ground, and tried to rise. Phira kicked her chest, knocking her onto her back. Her boot stepped onto Lyana's left wrist, and she yanked her dagger free. Stars floated before Lyana's eyes.

Up! Up, daughter of Requiem! She growled and tried to rise, but the boot crushed her hand. Phira's second boot pressed down on her neck. Lyana couldn't breathe, couldn't even scream. She groped for her weapons, but couldn't reach them.

Phira smirked above her. "You must be that Lyana the Weredragon Prince spoke of," she said. "The troops speak of this Prince Orin. When my queen tortured him, he cried your name. *Lyana, Lyana!* All the while as Queen Solina's blade cut him, he shouted for you." Phira laughed. "He cried like a girl, they say, and squealed like a pig when my queen finally ran him through."

No. No, stars, it can't be. Tears blurred Lyana's eyes. She wanted to see him again, to hold her Orin, kiss him, heal him. *But he's dead now, dead like the king, like so many upon the battlefield.*

The smirk never leaving her face, Phira knelt. Her knee drove into Lyana. She gasped in pain, and Phira's hand clutched her throat. Lyana struggled, and Phira backhanded her, rattling her jaw. She spat blood and coughed, gasping for breath.

"We shall see," the Tiran said, "if I can make you squeal and beg for death too."

She kept one hand on Lyana's throat. Her second hand drew a serrated knife from her belt. Despite the heat that still lingered, her hand was icy. Lyana kicked the air, trying to hurt her, trying to break free. She could not. She could see only stars, the Tiran's snarl, her cold eyes. Her knife ran down Lyana's cheek, drawing blood.

"Filthy weredragon," Phira said in disgust. "Will you beg for death too before I pull you entrails from your body?"

Lyana clenched her fists. She was a bellator, a knight of Requiem. *I will not die today.*

With a howl, she grabbed Phira's wrist, twisted, and shoved the knife up.

The blade slammed into the Tiran's neck. Blood gushed, showering onto Lyana's face. Screaming, she twisted the blade.

For an instant, Phira stared in shock, eyes wide, spittle on her lips. Then she screamed, a gurgling sound. Lyana shoved the woman off, rose to her feet, and lifted her fallen sword.

Phira convulsed on the ground, knife still buried in her neck. Fear flooded her eyes. Lyana looked down at her, dripping sword in hand. With her other hand, she wiped the blood off her face.

"Will you beg for death?" she whispered.

Phira stared up at her, eyes blazing.

I didn't think so.

Lyana drove her sword down, blood splashed, and it was over.

She turned, ran out the cave, and stood upon the snowy mountainside. Screeches and howls rose in the night. Lyana was slick with blood, her eyes stung, and her knees shook. She had never killed before; tonight she had taken three lives.

No, she told herself and forced a deep, shuddering breath. *There's no time for horror now.* She allowed herself to count to five. That was all. *One. Two. Three.* She trembled, forced another breath, and clenched her jaw. *Four. Five.*

She leaped and shifted into a dragon.

I must save Requiem. I can feel no fear. No pain. Not now. Not yet. There will be time for pain later. A blue dragon, she flew north, heading toward the city of Nova Vita. *I will warn them. I will save them, even if I can no longer save those left behind.*

She shot through the night. Behind her, flames rose and all the horrors of the world seemed to cry for her blood.

ELETHOR

My brother is dead.

    The thought clutched him like claws of ice. Fear for his father, his sister, and his friends filled him too, but all drowned under the flood of grief. *Orin. My brother. My pillar of strength. Gone.*

    He stood in Gloriae's Tomb, a towering hall of marble, its ceiling domed, columns lining its walls. There were many places Elethor could have gone this night. He could have gone to the temples and sat by Mori's side. He could have stayed on the Oak Throne, gazing upon an empty hall. He could have flown over the city with Lord Deramon, waiting for danger in the dark. But he had come here, to this place of shadows and solitude, to think and to pray.

    The statue of Gloriae towered above him. Carved of marble, the legendary Queen of Requiem rose fifty feet tall. She held a sword of stone, and her hair was gilded. Her stone eyes stared forward, brave and determined. Elethor stood before the monolith, gazing upon the queen who had defeated Dies Irae, rebuilt Requiem from ruin, and founded this city of Nova Vita.

    "I am descended from you, my queen," Elethor said softly to the statue. "But I lack your strength." He lowered his head. "In the stories you are always strong, brave, and noble. Even when Dies Irae murdered your parents, you fought with fire and defeated your enemies. Lend me strength now."

    The statue was silent, staring into the shadows of the hall, eyes forever strong, sword forever drawn. The true Gloriae was entombed beneath the statue, Elethor knew, her bones resting eternally in the earth of the city she'd built. Would her city now fall?

    He clutched the hilt of his sword, seeking strength from the leather grip. Ferus was an old longsword, forged in dragonfire a century ago. Its blade was three feet long, pale and grooved. Its crossguard and pommel were dark, unadorned steel. Many lords of the court wore decorative blades, pieces of art that glittered with gold and jewels. Today Elethor had chosen a simple sword; a weapon meant for battle, not ceremony. He had trained with Ferus for years—every prince of Requiem learned swordplay from childhood—but had never swung it in battle.

Orin was the warrior. He should be the one standing here, preparing for war.

Elethor clenched his fists and lowered his head. The pain constricted his throat, and his eyes stung.

"My brother is dead. My father flew to war. Tiranor attacks, and... what if Solina is among them? What if the woman I love returns with fire and death?" His chest felt tight, and he could barely see the floor's tiles. "What do I do now, Gloriae? Give me advice, my queen."

A voice rose in the temple, speaking in exaggerated falsetto.

"Well, first thing, my lad, I advise getting a haircut and a shave. You look like a bloody sheepdog. I don't know whether to help you or pat you."

Elethor raised his head and frowned. From between the columns stepped Bayrin Eleison, a gangly young guard with large ears, a head of orange hair, and mocking green eyes. An impish smile split his wide, freckled face. He wore a steel breastplate engraved with the Draco constellation. A sword, its pommel shaped as a dragonclaw, hung at his side.

"Bayrin!" Elethor said and grimaced. "How could you joke in a place like this, in a time like this?"

The young man shrugged. "The world is burning, my friend. What better time to joke?"

Eldest of Lord Deramon's children, Bayrin was nothing like his fiery sister Lyana. When Lyana would lecture, Bayrin would joke. When Lyana would drill with sword and dagger, Bayrin would sneak into the armory and draw rude pictures on shields. Lyana was a warrior, Bayrin a prankster. Ostensibly a city guardsman in his father's force, Bayrin spent less time patrolling the streets, and more time singing hoarsely in alehouses.

He's just as insufferable as his sister, Elethor reflected with a sigh. *But he's also my best friend.*

"Bayrin, you think every time is best for joking."

The young man gasped. "Me? Never in the bedroom. No, Elethor. That is all serious business in there." He looked around him. "But unless you plan on bedding a fifty-foot statue of a dead queen, I think we're safe." He stepped forward, and now his smile did vanish, and his eyes turned somber. He clasped Elethor's shoulder. "But I'm also sorry, my friend. Deeply and truly. I heard about your brother."

Elethor nodded and looked away, blinking. He did not want to cry in front of Bayrin, his friend who seemed to live for laughter, but couldn't help a tear from falling.

"I can't stop thinking that... that *she* did it. Solina." He looked back at his friend. "When Orin burned her, she swore that she'd kill him someday."

Solina. Queen of Tiranor. My love and fire.

"We don't know that yet," Bayrin said softly. "Mori is still sleeping; she's hurt and in shock, and might not wake for a while. We'll have answers in time. But come now, El. A fire burns in the south and the sky turns red. The city needs you."

Elethor nodded, eyes lowered, and they walked across the tomb to its towering doors. The weight of the sky seemed to hang on Elethor's shoulders. He forced himself to walk straight, to hold his head high, to square his shoulders, to be a prince of Requiem. Inside, however, he felt ready to collapse.

My sister is hurt. My brother is dead. My father flew to war. He clenched his jaw, eyes stinging and throat burning. *Be strong, Elethor. Keep walking. The city needs you. There will be time for grief later.*

They stepped under a towering archway, its keystone embossed with golden dragons, and exited Gloriae's Tomb. From atop the marble staircase, Elethor saw the city roll across hills below. Domes and towers rose from the birch forest, glittering with icicles. Towering walls circled the city, rising from among the snowy trees like a crown of stone resting in white hair. Lord Deramon's dragons perched upon the towers and walls, watching the south where red light glowed.

The fire of Tiranor flies there, Elethor knew. *Stars protect you, Father.*

Elethor had been born after the war with Tiranor. Orin had been only a babe. But he had heard the tales countless times. In his mind, he could see that old war as if he himself had fought it. Father, then a young brash king, had flown against the deserts of Tiranor, howling with rage and vowing to avenge the death of his brother, whom Tiran soldiers had slain with arrows. The Tirans had no dragon forms; theirs was a doomed battle. They fought in caves, in forts, in mountains, firing arrows and spears against the wrath of Requiem's dragons. They died. Their palace fell. Father himself slew the king and queen of Tiranor.

But he spared the young princess, Elethor thought, heart wrenching. Father had spared Solina. He returned to Requiem with scars, dark eyes, and a girl who grew to bring fire, passion, and unending sweet pain to Elethor's life.

Standing upon the stairs of Gloriae's Tomb, Elethor shifted, growing and hardening into a brass dragon. Bayrin shifted at his side, becoming a green dragon with white horns. The two took flight, fire flickering between their teeth, and dived over temples, cobblestone squares, copses of birches, and marble homes. Soon they reached the southern wall, a curving battlement fifty feet tall. They landed upon its crenulations between dragons of Deramon's City Guard. Before them in the south, firelight rose over King's Forest, and smoke billowed to paint the sky dark red.

"A forest fire?" Bayrin asked, frowning. His own fire danced in his maw. Scales clinking, he clutched the battlements so tight his claws dug grooves into the stone.

Elethor shook his head, scattering the smoke that rose from his nostrils. "It is the fire of Tiranor herself." He clenched his jaw, remembering the fire that had burned Solina, and how she trembled and cried in his arms.

A distant blue glimmer caught his eye. He stared. A dragon was flying from the south, a speck fleeing a wall of fire.

"Blue dragon," Elethor whispered. "Lyana?"

Bayrin stared, squinting. With a grunt, the young guard took flight from the wall, wings thudding. His tail snaked behind him, and his green scales turned red in the firelight. With a curse and icy fear twisting his gut, Elethor flew too. The wind tasted like smoke, too hot for winter. The two dragons, brass and green, flew toward their distant comrade. The farms of Requiem rolled beneath them: fields of wheat and barley, rows of apple trees, pastures of sheep and cattle. Fifty thousand Vir Requis lived off this land; in his mind, Elethor already saw it burning.

They reached the blue dragon two leagues from the walls of Nova Vita. It was Lyana, and she was hurt.

"Sister!" Bayrin cried and circled around her.

Blood splashed Lyana's scales. A burn mark ran across her belly and leg. Her eyes, large emerald orbs, were haunted.

"Bayrin," she whispered, voice trembling. Her wings shook. "Elethor. Help me to the city. Quick! The phoenixes. They're coming. Faster!"

Elethor stared into the southern horizon. From here, he could see the flames rising, thrashing the sky and racing across the land. When he squinted, he thought that the fire took the form of great eagles, dragon-sized, their wings like fountains of sunfire. The fire crackled and he could hear their shrieks.

"Where are the others?" Elethor demanded. "Where is my father, his five thousand dragons?" Horror pounded through him, shaking his limbs. Were they all gone like his brother?

But Lyana was already flying back to the city.

"To Nova Vita!" she called. "Hurry!"

Elethor cursed and followed. Bayrin flew at his side.

As they flew, Elethor watched the city grow closer. Its walls rose, white and craggy, defending temples, homes, and workshops. Three hundred years since the Destruction when the tyrant Dies Irae had razed this land, Requiem's dragons were recovering. Trees grew where once fire and war had raged. Vir Requis sang and prayed where once skeletons had lain burnt. A million dragons had once flown here; Dies Irae had killed all but seven, but now myriads lived behind these walls, a renaissance for their race.

I will not let Requiem fall again, Elethor vowed.

When they landed on the walls, they shifted back into human forms. When their wings and scales vanished, they stood panting on the parapets. Lyana faltered, and Elethor caught her.

"Lyana!" he said. "What happened?"

Ash covered her face and darkened her hair. Her armor was singed and bloody. Pain filled her eyes, and something else... a haunting fear.

"They're coming," she whispered through pale lips. "The phoenixes. Great birds of flame." She clutched his shoulders. "We must get everyone into the tunnels. Everyone! And barricade the entrances. They will be here soon."

Bayrin stared at her, slack-jawed. The gangly young man rubbed his eyes.

"Sister, who is coming? What are these phoenixes?"

She glared at him, five years his junior and nearly a foot shorter, but twice as commanding. "I'll explain later. Now fly over the city, both of you! Sound the alarm. Roar the call. I'll run between the houses. Go, you blockheads!"

With that, she ran down the wall's stairs, dashed across a street, and began pounding on house doors.

Elethor looked back south. He could see them clearly now—countless firebirds, huge eagles blazing with fury, flying their way. With a growl, he shifted back into a dragon and began circling over the city.

"People of Requiem!" he roared. The city streets and houses spun beneath him. "This is Elethor, son of King Olasar. On my command, leave your homes and head to the tunnels. Now! Everyone must enter the tunnels at once!"

Bayrin was flying too, wings churning the hot air, roars shattering the night. "Enemies at the gates! Into the tunnels! Into the tunnels!"

Below them, Lyana was banging on doors and helping people outside. Soon thousands crowded the streets, shouting and weeping.

Three entrances led to Nova Vita's tunnels. Originally a network of natural caves, the tunnels now held stairways, cobbled floors, archways, and bridges—masonry added over centuries. In those underground chambers, Requiem stored its winter food, its ancient books, its magical artifacts. They were secret places for kings, priests, and scholars. Today thousands raced toward them.

As Elethor flew, sounding the alarm, fear pounded through him. Nobody else was flying back from the inferno. Was Lyana the only survivor? Was his father... *No.* Elethor swallowed the thought. *Do not panic,* he told himself. *Not now. Not until everyone is safe.*

When he looked back south, he saw them closer. The phoenixes were only a league away. The farms outside the city kindled, and their fire raced toward the walls. Smoke unfurled like demons. The farmers were shifting into dragons, taking flight, and heading toward the city.

"Everyone move calmly!" Lyana shouted below, still in human form, herding the people into lines. "That's right, form lines, head into the tunnels one by one. Stay calm and move quickly."

Father, Elethor thought. *Where are you? Why don't you fly here too?*

Shrieks sounded behind him, and Elethor turned to see the phoenix army fly over the walls.

The inferno stormed with heat, sound, and fury. It felt like a sun exploding over Nova Vita. Fire howled around Elethor. He reared and flapped his wings to blow back the flames. He only fanned them. The phoenixes swooped, larger than him, wings crackling and beaks flowing with fire. Their claws reached toward him, shards of lightning.

Below him, the people screamed. They ran through the streets, blazing. Cries of pain and fear rose across the city, muffled under the crackle and shrieks of the firebirds.

Elethor blew fire. The jet spun and slammed into a phoenix. The great firebird screeched, unharmed; the dragonfire only seemed to enlarge it, as if it sucked up the fire's strength. It dived and slammed its claws into Elethor.

He screamed. It felt like hot irons pressed against him. He soared, spun, and swooped. His claws tore into the phoenix's head, and he cried in pain. Its fire blazed across his legs; he thought his scales might crack from heat.

"Elethor!" rose Bayrin's voice somewhere in the distance. "Elethor, come, into the tunnels!"

The phoenixes swarmed everywhere. Houses cracked in the heat. People fell burning. Some Vir Requis became dragons and tried to fly, only to crash into the phoenixes. A young girl ran from her house, shifted into a lavender dragon, and took flight. Before she could fly ten feet, phoenix claws tore her apart. She crashed back onto the cobblestones as a girl, her neck and chest slashed open.

Smoke unfurled and flames filled the night. Elethor flew, dodging phoenix claws and beaks. He crashed through one's flaming wings, and the heat seared him. His eyes and throat burned with smoke.

"Bayrin, where are you?" he shouted. He could see nothing but fire. "Lyana! Mori!"

He heard Bayrin's voice again; it rose from the flames below. "Elethor, down here, into the tunnels!"

Elethor dived through flames and flew down the streets, wings beating back fire. People were still running toward the tunnels, some of them burning. Many lay dead; Elethor could see their seared bodies through the fire. The phoenixes were swooping, burning the fleeing people. Some Vir Requis were shifting, taking flight, and fleeing into the night. The phoenixes flew at them, caught them in their talons, and bit with fiery beaks.

One phoenix surged between buildings toward Elethor and slammed into him. It felt like a furnace door opened and the flames knocked him back. He hit a building, cracked the stone wall, and howled. He clawed and blew fire, but could not hold back the phoenix. Could nothing kill these beasts? Around him, dragons soared, only to be slammed down and burned. Bodies littered the streets.

"Into the tunnels, go!" Elethor shouted to the people. "Don't try to fight, just run!"

A long, green dragon soared from the inferno, howling. Leathern wings beat back the flames. Bayrin roared and grabbed Elethor's shoulders.

"El, we must go!" he shouted. "Now!"

Elethor shook himself free. "There are still people in the houses! We must get them into the tunnels. We must find Mori!"

"We can't help anyone if we're dead!" The flames burned around Bayrin; his scales blazed red. "The phoenixes are—"

Three firebirds dived and slammed into them. Elethor shut his eyes under the flame. He felt weight and heat pushing him down. He crashed against a road, cracking the cobblestones. When he opened his eyes, he saw bodies everywhere. No more people ran through the smoke. Bayrin was gone. The phoenixes screeched above him, beaks and claws lashing him. Elethor leaped aside, dodging the flames, and soared.

"Mori!" he called. "Mori, do you hear me?"

Was his sister still alive? Had she managed to flee the temple where Mother Adia had taken her? He'd already lost a brother; if he lost his sister too, there would be no meaning to his life.

Elethor looked around, but saw only phoenixes, an endless swarm of them, and smoke, and fire, and bodies burning into bones. Nova Vita flamed. The smoke was so thick, and the light was so bright, he could barely see.

"Elethor!" rose a voice from the distance.

"Lyana!" he cried.

"Elethor, we're sealing the tunnels! Come on!"

Ten phoenixes soared toward him. Elethor cursed, snarled, and swooped. He shot through walls of fire. He crashed against a temple's column, cracking it. Bricks rained. The body of a child burned below.

"Lyana, where are you!"

"Elethor, here! In Benedictus Square!"

He could just make out the columns surrounding the cobbled square. Only yesterday, philosophers, priests, and scribes would wander this square between the birches, praying and singing and studying the stars. Today bodies and smoke filled it. Elethor dived toward it, the forge of phoenixes in pursuit. He barely discerned Lyana standing at an archway; beyond it, stairs led underground. Elethor hit the cobblestones and shifted into a human. He leaped into the stairwell with Lyana, then spun to face the archway.

Phoenixes landed outside, screeching. Their flames shot into the tunnel, forcing Elethor and Lyana to leap back several steps. The craggy staircase led into darkness below. Hundreds of people crowded the stairs, weeping and moaning and screaming.

"Quick, seal the doors!" cried a burly man in armor, his red beard singed.

Elethor recognized Lord Deramon, father to Lyana and Bayrin. He had never liked the man. A harsh soldier with a face like a craggy cliff, Deramon seemed to always scowl and mutter around him. Elethor's hatred had only grown seven years ago, after Deramon

caught him kissing Solina in the forest. The lord had marched to the
king, revealed the secret love, and doomed Solina to exile.

"There are still people out there, Deramon!" he shouted.
"They're dying!"

The phoenixes scratched at the archway but were too large to
enter.

"They're dead already!" Deramon shouted back. His face
flushed as red as his beard.

Elethor wanted to run outside, to find and save whoever he
could. Had Bayrin made it into the tunnels? What of his father and
sister; where were they?

"You don't know that, Deramon!" he shouted and drew his
sword.

He watched the tunnel entrance and grimaced. Before his
eyes, the phoenixes shrank, twisted, and took human forms. Soon
they stood as warriors in bright armor, golden suns upon their
breastplates. *The sun of Tiranor,* Elethor knew. The Tirans drew sabres.
The Vir Requis in the tunnel shrieked in fear.

Lord Deramon drew his own sword—a thick, heavy blade of
northern steel. Lyana already held her blade before her; it was
bloodied and darkened with ash. Flickers of fire still clinging to them,
the Tirans ran onto the staircase and blades clashed.

Elethor parried a thrust, grunted, and riposted. He was no great
warrior; his father and Orin were the fighters. Today everything his
swordmasters had taught him vanished, and he swung his blade with
blind fear and fury.

"You will die, weredragons," said a Tiran, a tall man with blazing
blue eyes. A crystal hung around his neck, a flame trapped inside it.
His sword swung, and Elethor parried, raising sparks. Deramon
fought at his side, his thick sword slamming at the enemy's thin,
curved sabres. The tunnel was only wide enough for two men to fight
side by side.

A dagger flew over Elethor's head and slammed into a Tiran's
neck. Blood spurted and the man pitched forward, hit the stairs, and
crashed down between Elethor and Deramon. Standing behind them,
Lyana slammed down her sword, finishing the job. Vir Requis guards
were racing up from the shadows below, drawing their own swords.

"Get down into the tunnels, boy!" Deramon howled at Elethor,
swinging his sword. "We'll hold them back."

Elethor cursed and grumbled. "You will not call me 'boy'. I am
still your prince, Deramon."

The man growled. "You are a boy, and you will enter the tunnels. Make room for men to fight by my side."

As he parried blows from Tiran sabres, Elethor fumed. He was no warrior, but he was still these people's prince; how could he run and cower among the women and children?

"I'm staying here to fight and die, old man!" he shouted, parried a blow, and thrust his blade.

Deramon slew a man. The body crashed down the stairs into darkness. "I'm not risking your life, not until I know if your father is alive. We're not losing another prince. Down, into the tunnels! Take my daughter with you."

A blade flashed. Elethor parried. Blood spurted and the enemies crowded at the doorway; there seemed no end to them. Nova Vita's survivors wept and shouted behind in the darkness.

"You think I'll run and hide instead of fight?"

"You will do what I tell you!" Deramon shouted, still swinging his blade. "As you like to remind me, you're our prince... not our champion."

Lyana rushed up behind him and grabbed Elethor's shoulder. "Come on, El. He's right. With me, down into the darkness. We have to protect you."

A Tiran broke past Deramon, leaped three steps, and lunged at Elethor. Blades clashed. Elethor grunted in pain. The Tiran's sword sliced his shoulder. Lyana's blade thrust, the Tiran leaped back, and Elethor drove his sword into the man's neck. He stared, gritting his teeth, at the blood dripping down his blade. It was the first man he'd killed.

More Vir Requis warriors, clad in the armor of the City Guard, raced upstairs from the shadows. Their heavy longswords clashed with the Tirans' sabres. Blood flowed down the stairs.

"Come with me, El," Lyana said, voice soft. "You're hurt."

He stared at the tunnel entrance. Deramon and three of his men now fought there. Thousands of Tirans seemed to fill the night outside. With a curse, Elethor tore his gaze away and took several steps down into the shadows. Survivors crowded around him, reaching out to touch him.

"Our prince," whispered an old woman, hands patting his shoulder.

"My lord," said a child, bowing his head.

They filled the darkness around him, burnt, bloodied, and weeping. Their arms reached to him and their eyes shone. The stench of burning flesh and blood and fear filled the tunnels.

Lyana held Elethor's arm and led him deeper into the darkness. "This is where the people need you, Elethor. They need to see you, to know that you lead them. You need to be their leader, not their soldier. You will be our king."

He froze, grabbed her arms, and stared at her. "What do you mean, Lyana?" he said through clenched teeth. "My father is king." His voice shook. "King Olasar, son of Amarin, descended from Queen Gloriae herself." His fingers shook around her arms.

Lyana lowered her head. "Elethor," she said softly. "Oh, Elethor."

She embraced him, this girl who would steal his toy swords when they were little, who once peeked into the bathing chambers as he undressed, who always looked down her nose at him and Bayrin and scolded them for being immature, good-for-nothing layabouts. Today this girl, now a woman stained with the blood and fire of war, placed her head against his shoulder, shed tears, and whispered into his ear.

"I'm sorry, Elethor. I'm so sorry. He fell." She touched his cheek. "Your father is dead."

The flames roared outside. Steel rang and the screams of dying echoed. Elethor closed his eyes. A tremble took him and he could not breathe. It felt like a vise clutched his head, twisting and cracking his skull. He forced himself to breathe. His head spun and he had to hold the tunnel wall for support.

Calm down, he told himself. *Don't panic yet. Not when these people need you... when Lyana needs you.*

Breathing through clenched teeth, he opened his eyes, still holding Lyana. She looked at him with huge, damp eyes.

"I'm sorry too, Lyana," he said. He tried to sound strong, comforting, a powerful man who could protect her—but his voice cracked. It sounded to him like the voice of a frightened child. He took another deep breath.

The survivors in the tunnel jostled and moved aside. Bayrin walked through the crowd, heading upstairs toward Elethor and Lyana. Burn marks covered his arms, and his face was damp and red. He stared with cold eyes.

"I found Mori," he said. "She's in the wine cellars. She's banged up and a little singed, but she's alive."

Elethor inhaled shakily—a breath of such relief that his knees shook and he nearly collapsed. *Thank the stars.* His eyes stung. *My sister is alive. Not all our family is dead.*

"Thank you, Bay," he said, voice choked.

Bayrin stared back solemnly. "And El... my mother is waiting for you. Come with me. She's going to crown you."

Elethor couldn't help it; he made a sound halfway between gasp and guffaw. He stared over Lyana's head at her brother, his best friend since childhood.

"You've gone mad, Bay," he said. "Adia wants to crown me? Now, here?" He shook his head wildly.

Lyana held him and stared at him. A fire blazed in her eyes.

"Yes, now and here," she said, voice stern. Curls of her red hair clung to her face with sweat and blood. "The people need a king, Elethor. They need a leader." She sighed. "You might be a blockhead, but you're all we've got now."

He laughed mirthlessly. "You've both gone mad! Both of you. My father... my brother..." His voice cracked. "Oh stars, we haven't even buried them. I don't want a crown. I never wanted to be king. Find somebody else." He looked back over his shoulder at the fighting. "Get your father down here! Crown him; the people love Deramon."

He sounded like a child, he realized and cursed himself. But what else could he say? He had never served in the army like Orin. He had never dreamed of the throne like Orin. He had never gone to countless ceremonies and feasts and met with foreign kings. He was just Elethor, the younger brother who'd count the stars, or sculpt, or walk for hours through the forest with Solina, or...

But those days are gone now, Elethor, he told himself. He clenched his fists. *You must do this. They're right. You can't abandon your people. They need you.*

As soldiers raced up the stairs and blood spilled down, his friends pulled him deeper into the tunnels. The shadows spun around him. Everywhere hands reached to him, the wounded lay moaning, and the stench of death spun his head. He moved in a daze, eyes burning.

My father. My brother. Gone.

Mother Adia, Priestess of Requiem, rose from the darkness toward him. A tall woman, she looked nothing like her red-headed, light-eyed children. Adia's hair was black and smooth as the night sky. Her eyes were pools of darkness. She could have been one of Elethor's statues—pale, beautiful, her skin like marble. Ash and blood stained her white robes.

"Elethor," she said, voice as deep and solemn as her eyes, and took his hands.

She whispered prayers to the stars in a shaky voice. Around them the people answered her prayers, reaching to the ceiling. Elethor did not know if starlight could ever glow here—or in the world again—but he answered the prayers in a hoarse, low voice.

They had no crown to place upon his head, no holy oil to anoint him with. There were no lords and ladies, no songs, only this stench of burnt flesh and sweat and nightsoil and death.

"Requiem!" Adia called, voice rising and shaking. "May our wings forever find your sky."

The words of their fathers, their people, their life. Those were the words the first kings had spoken when building temples in King's Forest. Those were the words the legendary Queen Gloriae had shouted in battle against Dies Irae the Destructor. The survivors in the tunnels repeated the prayer. Elethor spoke with them, his voice finally finding some strength.

"Requiem! May our wings forever find your sky."

Mother Adia turned to the crowd in the tunnels. Voice trembling, she said, "Kneel before King Elethor Aeternum, Son of Olasar."

Those who could, knelt, and Elethor looked over the survivors, his eyes dry. They filled the narrow tunnels, disappearing far into the darkness. Lyana knelt before him, holding her sword drawn, her eyes lowered. As Elethor looked at her mane of curls, he realized that by the law of the land, he had inherited not only his father's throne, but his brother's betrothed. If they survived this war, Lyana and he would be wed.

"Rise," he said to the people. They rose and wept, blessing his name.

Lyana looked at him, eyes huge and haunted. "My lord," she whispered, the first time she had ever called him that. "There is something more you must know."

Elethor stared at her, silent. His father and brother were dead. He had inherited the throne, and he was now betrothed to the girl who would torment him throughout his childhood. His city burned above him, and hundreds—likely thousands—were dead. What more news could she give him?

"Speak," he said.

She stared at him steadily, holding his arm. "Elethor... the leader of the phoenixes, and the one who killed your father and brother, is Solina."

He stared at her. The memories of Solina pounded through him: her kisses, her naked body against his, their forbidden love in secret forests and chambers. His world burned. He saw nothing but fire.

He spun around and began marching upstairs to the tunnels' exit.

"I will speak to her," he said, voice strained, fists clenched to stop them from trembling.

For the first time in seven long, aching, lonely years, he would see her again. He had dreamed of this moment. Today it chilled his belly and filled his throat with bile.

SOLINA

The city of Nova Vita, fair capital of Requiem, burned below her.

Solina flew above the carnage, woven of fire. The marble columns and towers undulated in the heat waves. With every thud of her wings, sparks flew and light flared like the beat of her flaming heart. The sound and fury pounded through her, crackling, buzzing, roaring for eternal pain and glory. She had been burned. She had lain for days in a temple, bandaged and crying for vengeance. She had tamed her fire, and now she soared through it, a goddess of inferno.

Bodies littered the streets below, the fire stripping flesh from bones, leaving blackened skulls that gaped. A scattering of dragons still flew, only for her phoenixes to hunt them, tear them down, and feast upon them. The rest huddled in the tunnels below, but Solina knew she would burn them too. She knew every twist and cavern in those tunnels. She had spent so many hours in their darkness, stoking her fire with Elethor.

Do you hide there now, my prince of tears? she wondered. *Will we meet again this night, after all these years?*

Elethor. The very name sent pulsing memory through her. She still remembered his birth. She had been only five, an orphan raised in the king's court, a timid girl still so scared of the world. When King Olasar let her hold the babe, she vowed to forever love him.

And I love you, Elethor, she thought. *I loved you when I held you as a babe. I loved you in our youth, when our lips touched, and our hands felt, and our naked bodies pressed together. And I still love you now, even as I burn your home.*

She dived toward the palace. It shimmered between the flames, its columns like bones. Her claws hit the cobblestones, splashing fire. She shifted, sucking the flames into her. Her wings drew in, forming arms. Her fire twisted, formed flesh and bones, and soon she stood upon human feet. The last tongues of fire pulled into the firegem around her neck, where they danced. She clutched the amulet and smiled, looking around at her old prison.

Requiem's palace. The place where they raised me... and where they burned me. She ran her finger across her line of fire, the scar that snaked down her face, between her breasts, and along her thigh. *But their fire can no longer hurt me.*

The columns rose around her, two hundred feet tall, carved of white marble. Between them, the birches blazed and crackled. When Solina was young, these columns had seemed so large to her, colossal monuments kissed with starlight that would never bless her. Orin and Elethor, like brothers to her, could become dragons, fly above them, soar so high the columns were as mere twigs to them. They had offered to carry her upon their backs, but Solina had always refused.

To ride you would mean I'm a cripple, she would think, fists clenched. *I am a proud Tiran, a desert daughter, a princess of the ancient Phoebus Dynasty. We do not ride dragons.*

"We kill them," she whispered.

Several phoenixes landed beside her, flaming and shrieking, their fire pounding the cobblestones. They shifted, flames pulling into their firegems, and soon stood before her as men clad in pale armor. They saluted, slamming their fists against their breastplates. Acribus stood among them, chief of her warriors, his armor bloody and his arm bandaged.

"My lady Solina," he said and bowed his head.

She stared at his blood. "The wound Princess Mori gave you is still bleeding. You need it stitched."

He bared his chipped, yellow teeth. "Princess? You mean a lizard whore. She will bleed worse when I catch her."

Solina shrugged. "Call her what you like. Hurt her how you like. You can cut off her freak finger, if it pleases you. Just don't bleed to death first."

Seven years had passed since she'd set foot in Requiem, but Solina had never forgotten Princess Mori, or the Lady Lyana, or any of the other girls who would torment her.

Mori was only a child then, Solina thought, *but I remember how she'd pity me, a mere Tiran who could not become a dragon.*

Lyana, meanwhile, had been only a snotty youth, a bookish girl whose nose was always upturned and whose father—Captain of the City Guard—would pamper her. *Lyana too always looked down upon me*, Solina thought. *She saw only an orphan, an outcast, a cripple.*

She clenched her jaw. *Acribus will hurt them well. They will hurt like I hurt. We'll see how they pity me when Acribus thrusts inside them, when he cuts them, when he feeds their fingers to the dogs.*

As if he could read her thoughts, Acribus licked his lips with that ridiculous white tongue of his. It always looked to Solina like a snake nested in his mouth.

"My lady," he said, "the weredragons have crowned a new king. He fights at the entrance of a nearby tunnel, and he wishes to treat with you." He laughed, a sound like snapping bones. "Would you like to hear this boy king beg for life before we kill him, or shall I gut him now?"

Solina felt like a bellows blasted hot air against her. She froze, fingers tingling, sweat dripping down her forehead.

"Elethor," she whispered.

Acribus barked a laugh. "Yes, that was his name. A soft boy; looks like he never swung a sword in battle until today. I will break him. I will shatter his spine. I will crush his limbs with a hammer, sling them through the spokes of a wheel, and hang him to die upon the palace walls."

She glared at him, baring her teeth. "You will not touch him, Acribus. If you do, you will be the one broken. Show me to the weredragons' new king. I will speak to him."

They marched down the streets, leaving the palace behind. Ash swirled around their boots. Trees and bodies burned at their sides, raising black smoke. Phoenixes soared and screeched above; the sky itself seemed to burn. The sounds of battle came from ahead: swords clanging, battle cries, and the shouts of dying men calling for mothers, lovers, or the mercy of death.

Soon Solina saw an entrance to a tunnel. The stone archway rose ten feet tall, its keystone engraved with dragon reliefs. The bodies of Tirans and weredragons littered the cobblestones around it. Living soldiers fought above the bodies, clanging swords. Blood puddled and flowed toward Solina's boots.

A memory thudded through Solina, aching in her chest. *Come on, Elethor!* she had cried, laughing, and pulled him down the streets. She had been twenty, maybe twenty-one, a young woman blooming into her beauty. He had still been a youth, awkward and gangly, but she was determined to make him a man. They explored the tunnels that day, moving between wine cellars, libraries, silos, and finally finding a nook full of rugs where they made love—fiery, passionate love that made her scream and scratch her fingernails down his back. *We returned to these tunnels most nights after that,* she remembered.

"Tirans!" she shouted. "To me. Form rank. Leave the weredragons to cower in their burrow."

With a few last sword swings, the men fell back and formed rank around her. Blood splashed their armor, and they glared at the tunnel archway. Weredragon warriors stood there, panting over the bodies of their fallen. One man clutched a hole where his ear had been, and another sat against a wall, cradling an arm that ended with a stump. The place seemed strangely silent without the clash of steel and cries of battle; Solina heard only the fire of phoenixes above and the moans of the dying.

"Elethor," she said, speaking to the gaping shadow of the tunnel. "Elethor. Come see me."

Flames crackled. Smoke unfurled. From the blood and shadows, the pain and hope of her youth emerged. All that sweet pain—the secret kisses, the forbidden taste of love—flooded her, made her fingers tingle, and she stared in silence.

He had been only eighteen when she last saw him, a tall and gaunt youth; she would poke him and laugh at how thin he was. He had grown into adulthood since then, a man of twenty-five with dark, haunted eyes and brown hair that fell over his brow, caked with blood and ash. And yet those were the same lips she would kiss, the same eyes she would gaze into—hound dog eyes, she would call them.

"Solina," he said softly.

Her eyes stung. She had not expected this to be so difficult. She had not expected to still feel so much, hurt so badly. She remembered him speaking her name so many times—as a child growing up in her arms, a lover in her bed, and that last time he called her name, shouting it from the walls of Nova Vita as she fled into exile, her line of fire burning down her body.

"Elethor," she whispered. She beckoned him closer. "Come. We will speak." She snapped her fingers, and her men formed lines around her. "Follow me; we will find someplace quiet."

He stood still, staring at her between strands of damp hair. "We will speak here."

She couldn't help it; she laughed, tears stinging her eyes. "I won't harm you, Elethor. And my men will not hurt yours until we've spoken. You have my word." She stepped toward him and took his hands. They were bloody and hot. "Come with me, Elethor. Let's work out this mess."

He stared into her eyes, scrutinizing her, and she saw the same memories and pain pound through him. He still loved her, she knew then. That soothed her. *This will make things easier.* She did not want to hurt him. Finally he nodded and took a step forward.

At once, two more wereragons emerged from the tunnels, making to follow him. Both held drawn, bloodied swords. Solina recognized them. One was Lord Deramon, Captain of the Guard, a burly man with a red beard now grizzled. *He is the man who caught me with Elethor,* she remembered, a deep rage simmering inside her. *The man who doomed me to exile.* The second weredragon was his daughter, the Lady Lyana. The girl Solina knew had been overbearing, an imperious brat. Today Solina saw a woman with fear and grief in her eyes. *We hurt her. Good.*

Solina held up her hand. "No. You two stay here. Elethor and I speak alone. Just me and him."

They began to object.

"She'll kill you, Elethor," Deramon said, eyes dark.

"We go with you," said Lyana and bared her teeth at Solina.

Elethor's eyes never left Solina; they were narrowed, seeking answers, reliving old years. He hushed his companions with a raised hand.

"Just me and her," he repeated softly. "They won't touch me. Deramon. Lyana. Stay and tend to the wounded. I'll be back soon."

They walked through the streets, she and Elethor. Her men snaked around them, forming a hallway of steel. Phoenixes circled above, bodies lay scorched, trees burned, and columns lay smashed. The battle had surged; for now it simmered.

The smell of burnt flesh filled Solina's nostrils. She remembered that smell from seven years ago; she had smelled it on herself. She felt her line of fire tingle across her body. She clenched her teeth and smiled.

"Here," she said to Elethor, gesturing at a gazebo rising from a stone square. "We will talk here."

He stared at the gazebo, eyes dark. *He knows why I chose this place.* The gazebo rose upon a dais, fifty steps leading toward it. Its columns were white marble engraved with dragon reliefs. The roof was domed and set with frosted glass panes. Solina remembered sitting here with Elethor at night, watching the stars and moon glimmer through that glass, a shower of fireflies. It was the first place she had kissed him.

He nodded. "We will talk."

She left her men below in the square. They stood at attention upon the flagstones, fists against their breastplates. She climbed the stairs toward the gazebo, Elethor at her side. When they stepped inside, she could see firelight through the frosted glass roof—countless phoenixes diving through the night, casting orange dapples upon her and Elethor.

She turned toward him, placed her hands in his hair, and pressed her body against his. She kissed his lips, and for a moment, their heat mingled like in the old days.

"Elethor," she whispered, eyes stinging. "I missed you. I love you."

He turned his head away, breaking their kiss, and pushed her back. His bloodied hands stained her breastplate.

"Solina, did you bring me here for that? You killed my father. You killed my brother." His voice shook. "How dare you kiss me now?"

She glared at him, teeth bared. Her line of fire blazed. "Your father?" She snorted. "He banished me, El. You remember. He banished me because of our love, cast me out into the desert." She clenched her fists. "Your brother? Orin burned me. He blew his fire upon me and left me scarred, deformed." She ran her finger along her scar, from her forehead, across her face, and down her neck. "But I tamed fire, El. I told you I would." She clutched his arms. "They can no longer banish me, no longer burn me. I did this for you. So we can be together, with no fear, no pain. No more hiding." She tried to kiss him again. "I've returned to kill those who hurt us and to be with you again. I love you."

He stared at her, and something filled his eyes... something dark, shocked, frightened. He shook his head. "Solina... what have you done?" He clenched his fists and looked aside. "Stars, Solina, how could you do this?"

She snarled and slapped his face, hard, driving all her strength into the blow. "How dare you speak of your stars here? Your stars are worthless." She laughed bitterly. "Starlight never blessed us, Elethor. It never protected Requiem. But fire..." She breathed heavily. "Fire is strong. Fire burned me. Fire is now my ally." She felt it burn inside her, and she dug her fingers into his shoulders. "You do not know the power of the Sun God, Elethor. He cured me from Orin's flames." She grabbed her firegem. "He gave me his power, so that I could become a phoenix, a deity woven of his flame. He has given me so much. He can give this fire to you too."

He shoved her back again, more roughly this time. "Do not speak to me of this Sun God. I know of him. I know that he destroyed Requiem once, driving the evil of Dies Irae the Tyrant. I know that his flame will burn everything it can consume."

"It will not consume those who serve it." She was panting now, and she touched his cheek. "Elethor. Oh, my Elethor; you were the fire of my youth. Now join your flames to mine. I will grant you a firegem; you will become a phoenix, a great firebird, no longer a lizard of scales. Join me in Tiranor and worship my lord at my side. We will rule together. We will cast our flames across the world and watch it burn." She held him, pressed her lips against his ear, and whispered.

"Elethor, don't you love me? Don't you remember all those nights we spent here?"

He let out his breath slowly, and his head lowered; suddenly he felt so sad to her, the weight of the world upon his shoulders.

"I remember," he said softly. "Solina, I loved you more than anything—so much that it ached. For seven years since you left, I thought of you every day." He laughed bitterly. "Every minute of every day. I never loved another woman since you. I don't know if I ever will."

She held him tight, eyes stinging. "So come with me, El. Come south with me. They can no longer hurt us, no longer drive us apart. I will kill anyone who comes between us again."

She trembled, remembering those years so long ago, her life in the courts of Requiem. The pain flooded her, memories like rivers, streams of faces and words and feelings.

She had been only three years old when the dragons of Requiem burned her home. Their claws toppled the white towers of Tiranor, and their flames burned their oases in the desert. Solina had been too small to understand why the war raged. She did not understand why her parents would not wake, why their blood covered her. The dragon who slew them, the vile King Olasar, pitied her that day. He kidnapped her from her home, brought her to his cold realm of snow and birches, far from the warmth and light of Tiranor.

She grew in his court. A freak. An outsider. A Tiran girl not blessed by Requiem's stars. She could not shift into a dragon like Prince Orin, like King Olasar, like all the Vir Requis she grew up among.

Deformed, the children of the court would call her. *Freak. Cripple.* They would shift into dragons, slap her with their tails, and blast fire at her feet and make her dance. How she tried to shift too! How she dreamed of becoming a dragon! Yet she was a southerner, a desert child, doomed to be weak, scared, tormented.

And then... then her life changed. Then Elethor was born. A pure baby, younger brother to Orin and like a brother to her. Solina vowed to protect this soft, beautiful child, to make sure he never felt loneliness or pain like she did. She watched Elethor grow. He was her treasure, her foster brother, her reason to live. Even when he grew old enough to become a dragon, she still loved him. She would run her fingers over his brass scales and kiss him, and he was *her* dragon, her protector.

He was only fifteen when she kissed him in this gazebo. She was twenty, but still clinging to all the fear and rage of youth; in her mind, she felt no older than him. They conquered their fear together. For three years, they would hide in this gazebo, or in the forests, or in the tunnels beneath Nova Vita, and they would love each other. A forbidden, secret, wonderful, horrible love. For three years Solina felt pure joy... until Lord Deramon caught them in the forest, and told his king, and Requiem's rage rained down upon them.

"Solina of Tiranor!" King Olasar shouted in his court. She stood before him, head lowered, tears on her cheeks. "Despite the crime of your parents, who attacked our borders and sacked our temples, I raised you as a daughter. I sheltered you, taught you, protected you. And yet you cast your sin upon my son." His fists trembled at his sides. "Elethor is like a brother to you. How dared you seduce him? He is only a youth, five years younger than you. How dared you bring such perversion into my hall?" He pointed a shaky finger at her. "You are banished from Requiem! Leave this place now, and wander whatever lands you may please; if you are caught within our borders, your life is forfeit."

Rage bloomed within her. She drew her dagger and screamed.

"You will not speak of my parents!" Her voice was hoarse, torn with years of pain. "I know what you did to them. I know that you killed them, framed them for stealing jewels from your temples. Liar!" She ran toward him, knife raised. "You cannot know how Elethor and I love each other. You will not tear us apart!"

She almost killed him that night. A few steps more, and she could have plunged her blade into his heart. Yet Orin—brutish, cruel Prince Orin—stood as a dragon by the throne. Like a coward, he did not face her as a man, but blew fire upon her. The flames shot toward her, a screaming inferno.

Elethor shouted and pulled her aside. He saved her life, she knew... but dragonfire burned bright, and tongues of its flames still seared her. She screamed, ablaze, and fell. Welts and smoke rose across her. Never had such pain filled her. It made her weep, roll on the ground, and claw the air.

For days she lay abed in a temple, bandaged and feverish. The priestesses tended to her in darkness. She cried for Elethor, but they would not let her see him. When finally she rose from her bed, and her bandages were removed, she bore her line of fire. The scar split her face, snaked down her torso, and crawled down her leg. *A reminder,* she knew. *A pledge. A battle scar.*

"Solina!" he shouted from the walls as they cast her out, goading her with spears, sending her into the wilderness with nothing but a waterskin and loaf of bread.

She dared not look back at him. She walked, barefoot, leaving the city behind. She heard his dragon roars calling her name, but she did not want to remember him this way. She would remember the Elethor who held her in the tunnels, laughed with her, whispered with her. She walked south for days, leaving Requiem, heading into the swamps of Gilnor. All of autumn she walked, until in winter she reached a land where no snow fell, and heat rose from sand.

Tiranor. Land of her parents. Land of the Sun God, of flame, of power. Her people welcomed her with joy—the last, lost daughter of the great Phoebus Dynasty. They crowned her with ivory and raised her to be their queen. In desert temples of stone, she worshipped her new lord the Sun God. She swore that if he gave her the strength, she would kill his enemies in Requiem.

"He gave me so much."

A chest of firegems, crystals that held flames from the sun itself. With them, she could become the phoenix. With them, her followers could soar as beasts woven of sunfire. Soon all the temples of Tiranor praised her name, flew with her to battle, and vowed to destroy the weredragons who worshipped night and stars.

"But you, Elethor," she whispered in the gazebo as Requiem burned, "you don't need to die. Come south and rule with me. We will be together again... like we were born to be."

She saw in his eyes that he had relived their lost years too. He removed her hands from his shoulders, took a step back, and stared at her.

"You come with fire," he said. "You come with death. You murdered my family and you burned my home. How can you now ask me for love? Did you do all this from some... some mad notion that if you destroyed everything I have, I would be with you?" Pain cracked his voice. "I loved you so much, but I don't understand this."

She shook her head sadly. "Elethor, oh Elethor, how to make you understand? I did not kill and burn for you alone." She touched her scar. "I killed for this. For how they hurt me, and how they hurt you. I killed for my lord, the Sun God, and all that he's given me. But I do not wish to kill you." She took a step toward him, breathing heavily. "But if you refuse me, Elethor... if you fight me, I will hurt you. Turn me down and I will kill you. I will kill everyone who huddles in your tunnels."

He stared away from her, watching Requiem burn between the gazebo columns. "I am king of this land now. I never wanted the crown. I never imagined that I'd wear it. But I am King of Requiem, and I cannot abandon her. I cannot abandon all those who still live here."

"You will abandon them." She grabbed his shoulder, digging her fingernails into it, and spun him around. She snarled. "You will surrender this land to me, Elethor. You will return with me to Tiranor. Do this, and I will spare your life, and I will spare those of your people who still live. Refuse me, Elethor... and you will all die. You will die in fire."

He stared aside, jaw tight, fists clenched at his sides. She saw the turmoil on his face.

"You know my answer," he said.

She pulled his face to her and stared into his eyes. "You are loyal to your friends. That is admirable. How would you serve them by refusing me? Would you watch me burn them? Because I would make you watch, Elethor. You would watch them die in agony before I killed you." She turned her back to him and spoke through clenched teeth. "Go to your tunnel, weredragon, and think. Think of those you love. Return here at sunrise to surrender to me. If you still choose to fight me, my fire will consume the world."

With that, she left him and walked downstairs to the courtyard. Her fingers tingled and a trembling smile found her lips.

I love you, Elethor, she thought, breathing hard. *But if I cannot have you, I will destroy you.*

MORI

She stood in the corner, hugging herself, and listened to the adults argue. Elethor had returned with the news: They had until dawn to surrender. Everyone seemed to have an opinion, which they were shouting. Bayrin Eleison, who would tug her pigtails in childhood, shouted that he'd charge through the Tirans and kill Solina himself. Lord Deramon grumbled that surrender might be the only option they had. Others stood around them—the Lady Lyana, a priest, two wounded lords, a group of guards—calling for war, for prayer, or for surrender.

Only Mori was silent. She stood in the back, cloaked in shadows, and dared not speak. She worried that if she opened her mouth, her voice would tremble, and tears would fill her eyes. An iciness lived in her belly, twisting and growing. Her shame still ached, a deep pain she worried would never leave her.

She remembered his tongue, a wet serpent, licking her cheek. She remembered his stale breath, his hands crushing her, his body above her, her mouse dying under her chest. She remembered the pain, and she closed her eyes and forced herself to take deep breaths. Before, in the battle, she had found no time for shame. Now it flooded her.

"Stars, I've heard enough!" Bayrin shouted, so loud that Mori's ears ached. "You can't be serious, Father. To let Elethor go with this... this creature of fire back to her lair?"

Lord Deramon was glaring at everyone and everything. "How do you suggest we fight the phoenixes? Dragonfire only feeds them. Claws cannot cut them. Even if we could stop them from entering the tunnels, we'd eventually die of starvation and thirst."

Bayrin crossed his arms. "Our water reservoirs and our silos are here underground. We have enough to last all winter."

"And what then?" Lady Lyana interjected, clutching her sword so tightly her knuckles were white. "Will you have us linger underground all winter, only to starve in spring? That's assuming we can even hold back the Tirans that long."

For a moment everyone shouted together, and Mori felt like a mouse herself, a small thing that made its home in shadows, unseen and frightened. She looked at her brother Elethor. He stood between her and the others, eyes dark. Only he seemed to notice Mori; he looked toward her, and his eyes softened. His chest rose and fell, and such sadness seemed to fill him that Mori wanted to embrace him.

Our father is dead. Our older brother is dead. Elethor and I are all that's left of our family. We're all we have. Tears filled her eyes and her lip trembled.

"What do you think, Mori?" he asked softly, his voice barely heard over the shouts of the others. It was not a plea for advice, she knew. Elethor was not asking for help. What he was really asking was: *How are you holding on?*

She looked away. His eyes were too much like Orin's. Gazing into them hurt too much.

"I don't know," she whispered, and that pain between her legs flared, and the shame inside her cried to her, calling her a harlot, a disgrace, a soiled thing.

Bayrin, her brother's gangly oaf of a friend, laughed mirthlessly. "Finally, an honest one among us. The Princess Mori doesn't know what to do. Neither do I. Neither do any of us. At least the girl is honest." He guffawed; it sounded close to tears, close to panic, a last attempt at humor to hold back the horror. "So tell me, Mori, maybe you know this: Will we die from starvation, fire, or the thrusts of Tiran swords?"

Bayrin would always tug her braids in childhood, stuff frogs down her dress, and mock her mercilessly for having one finger too many. Today Mori missed the trickster Bayrin; the frightened and bitter Bayrin seemed infinitely worse. She clutched her hands behind her back, twisting her fingers. She felt her eleventh finger there, her luck finger, the plucky pinky itself as she sometimes called it. *Bring me luck today,* she thought.

"I need to learn more," she said softly. "About the Sun God. About this magic of phoenixes." She turned and began walking away. "I'll visit the library; it's not far from here. I'll learn what I can and return."

She felt their eyes on her back. Their argument died, and an odd silence filled the tunnels. The wounded lay around her feet, moaning and clutching wounds. Other survivors stood along the walls, rows of them leading into the darkness below. These tunnels delved deep, Mori knew, eventually leading to the Abyss itself, a realm of hidden horrors.

She heard her brother speak softly behind her. "Mori. Mori, are you all right?"

What could she tell him? *A man with yellow teeth and a white tongue broke me, Elethor. He shoved my legs open and thrust himself inside me, and I'm a princess of Requiem, a daughter of starlight, but I cried like a child and could not fight him. I could not even kill him. I watched my brother tortured to death, and my father is gone, and I'm so scared, and I'm so hurt, and I can't get rid of this iceberg inside my belly.* She smiled bitterly and said nothing. She kept walking, leaving them all behind, and plunged deep into the tunnels of Requiem.

The craggy stairs led to a rough, sloping tunnel. Candles filled alcoves in the walls, their wax dripping like the faces of burnt men. These tunnels wound for miles under Requiem, Mori knew; she would often explore them as a child. The great elders of Requiem had placed their scrolls here underground. The legendary King Benedictus had fought the Destroyer, Dies Irae, in these tunnels. *And today once more Requiem's fate will be written here,* she thought.

As she kept walking, she saw no end to the survivors. Hands reached out to her in the darkness. Mothers held crying children to their breasts. The elderly stared with teary eyes. Most people were burnt. Most whispered prayers to the Draco Constellation, the stars of Requiem.

"Our princess," they whispered, kneeling, tears in their eyes.
"Princess Mori, thank the stars."
"The stars bless you, our princess."

Their hands reached out, touching her, and she shivered. *His hands touched me too, and his tongue, and...* She closed her eyes, trembling.

One old woman began to chant the Old Words, the whispers of Requiem since time immemorial. The others whispered with her, their voices chanting together, and Mori added her voice to the song.

"As the leaves fall upon our marble tiles, as the breeze rustles the birches beyond our columns, as the sun gilds the mountains above our halls—know, young child of the woods, you are home, you are home." Tears filled Mori's eyes, the holy words soothing her. "Requiem! May our wings forever find your sky."

She looked above her and saw only cold stone. She had never understood the meaning of those words until now, trapped under rock and grief. *Requiem. May I find your sky again.*

She walked for a long time, hugging herself, passing by silos, pantries, wine cellars, and reservoirs. Sunrise couldn't be more than two hours away. *I must find a way to defeat the phoenixes before then... or we'll have to surrender and live forever under the bane of Solina.*

"And under his bane," she whispered, remembering his fingers gripping her. How many more times would he hurt her, if they could not defeat the Tirans? Would he claim her as his own, take her to his chambers, chain her and invade her every night?

"We must defeat them." Mori's lips trembled. "We must."

Soon she reached the Library of Requiem. Its doors rose tall above her, set into the stone walls of the tunnel. Mori carried the old, filigreed key around her neck on a chain. This library was ancient, and its books were priceless; each codex of parchment and leather was worth more than a chest of gold. Only the royal family bore the keys to this chamber of secrets. With trembling fingers, Mori unlocked the doors, stepped inside, and found herself in a world of books.

Thousands of years ago, before the Vir Requis had built columns of marble, they lived in these tunnels. Before they wrote books, they wrote upon scrolls of parchment and kept them here in alcoves, safe from the dangers of rain and snow and war. None of those original scrolls remained; they had all burned in the Great War three hundred years ago, when King Benedictus fought Dies Irae underground. But today the library was rebuilt, and new knowledge filled the alcoves and shelves that lined the walls. A hundred thousand books, leather-bound and beautiful, rose all around Mori.

It was a lot to read within two hours.

For the first time since the phoenixes had invaded Castellum Luna, Mori felt peace flow over her. There was some solace here, some goodness hidden from fire. So many hours of her childhood had been spent here. While Orin would go hunting with Father, and while Bayrin and Elethor were drinking in alehouses, Mori would come to this place. She had read her first book here at age five, and she kept returning every day for more. She would devour poems of epic adventure; codices full of delicate illustrations of birds; tomes of herbalism, astrology, history; and more. More than anything—the softness of her gowns, the beauty of Nova Vita's gardens, or the warmth of her quilt—Mori drew comfort from books. As she stood here today, a hurt and damaged woman, she could still feel that comfort, that wonder of childhood. Centuries of knowledge surrounded her. The wisdom of thousands of poets and philosophers filled this one place.

"It's the best place in the world," she whispered. "May today it bring us salvation."

She walked across the tiled floor, approached a ladder, and climbed to a high shelf. She ran her hand across the books, caressing their smoothed leather spines, and smiled softly. *There is still some goodness in the world.* She knew the library well; this shelf held her favorite books, ancient tomes about creatures and monsters of legend.

She remembered one book, a heavy codex her father had claimed was a thousand years old, and between its pages dwelled a hundred monsters. The book was so old, Father claimed that even the legendary Queen Gloriae had read it, and the book had been ancient then too. Mori had always feared that codex and never dared read it; when Father would try to read it to her, she would run and he would laugh softly.

He thought me scared of the monsters inside, Mori remembered. But it was not the monsters that would scare her; it was the book's age. So many generations had passed since its author scribed its words and pictures, so many ages of men who lived and fought and died. So many generations read the book, laughed, whispered, loved and hated. It was a thing of ghosts, of ancient life that spun Mori's head. But how could she have told Father that? So she had pretended to fear its pictures of griffins and serpents, and she would instead read poems of love and heroes.

Today she sought this old tome. Today was all about conquering fears. Would the book tell her of birds woven from fire? She let her fingers dance across the spines, and soon her fingertips rested upon a large codex wrapped in leather so old, the binding formed a landscape of crevices, canyons, and valleys. Words of gold crawled along the spine, written in the tongue of Osanna, the realm of men to the east. Mori did not read that ancient language well, but she knew enough to read these words. It was the book she sought: *Mythical Creatures of the Gray Age.*

Perhaps it was the fear inside her, or perhaps the solace of this place after the storm of battle, but Mori felt like the book's wisdom crept into her fingers, pulsed through her, whispered comfort into her soul. Smiling softly, she pulled the book off the shelf, and dust rained.

She blinked, coughed, and clung to the ladder. She struggled for long moments to pull the book free, stuff it under her arm, and hold it tight. The tome was large, over a foot long, and its spine was wider than her palm. Clinging to the ladder with one hand, Mori descended to the floor, placed the book down, and sat crossed-legged before it.

A digging pain thrust through her, and she closed her eyes. Her pulse quickened. His eyes blazed, and his lip curled, baring yellow teeth. His breath blasted her, scented of rot, and she screamed as he invaded her, hand around her throat, and she shook and wept and—

No. She forced her eyes open, forced herself to take slow breaths. Cold sweat drenched her, and slowly as she breathed, the flaring pain faded to a dull throb. She wiped tears from her eyes. *Don't think of him, Mori,* she told herself. *Think of saving Elethor. He is the only family you have left. You must save him from Solina... and you must save yourself.*

She leaned forward and blew dust off the book. It flew in a cloud, covering the tiles, and Mori sneezed. She opened the book, revealing crinkly pages of parchment. The first page sported an illustration of a griffin, and Mori shuddered, remembering the stories she'd heard of griffins attacking Requiem long ago. Small letters covered the page, written in the tongue of Osanna, speaking of the beasts. Mori began to leaf through the pages. The parchment was so old, she worried it would crumble in her hands. As the pages flipped, they revealed and hid creatures great and small: the mythical salvanae, true dragons of the west, who had no human forms; the nightshades, demons of smoke and shadow; the cruel mimics, undead warriors sewn from dismembered corpses; and even a page about the Vir Requis themselves, warriors of Requiem who could become dragons.

Mori laughed, eyes still stinging with tears. She didn't feel like a mythical creature, only a girl—scared, alone in darkness, seeking answers. She sniffed, knuckled her eyes, and flipped the page. Her eyes widened and her breath died.

"The phoenixes."

The page seemed to stare back at her, screaming from years beyond counting, and Mori hugged herself. The scribe had drawn an eagle woven of fire in red and orange, its claws outstretched, its beak wide, its eyes of fire incensed. Mori could imagine that she heard its shriek, and she shivered. The phoenix seemed to move upon the page; Mori almost saw its flames crackle, almost felt its heat. Suddenly she feared that the drawing could burn the book, that the phoenix could rise from the page and turn into Acribus, grab her and toss her over a table, and she would scream and her pain would never leave her. The fire and the screams engulfed her, and her head spun.

She gritted her teeth, clenched her fists, and closed her eyes. She forced herself to breathe deeply, like Mother Adia had taught her. She inhaled through her nose, slowly, counting to five, until she filled her lungs from top to bottom. She held her breath, counted to five again, and exhaled slowly. Hugging herself, Mori forced herself to keep breathing, again and again—into her lungs, into her limbs, into every part of her that trembled, until the fear passed. When she was ready, she opened her eyes again, and found that the book was silent and cold, the library only a place of shadows and solitude.

It's only a book, Mori, she told herself. *It's only a drawing. It can't hurt you.*

She leaned down so that her nose almost touched the parchment and squinted. The letters were old and small, faded in places, and Mori had never found it easy to read the tongue of Osanna. She mumbled to herself, reading aloud:

"In the days of Chaos, the lights of the heavens fought a great war, casting light and fire upon the earth. The Sun God, lord of heat and flame, birthed the phoenixes to champion his cause. Great birds of sunfire, they flew upon the earth, burning forests and boiling lakes, and men died between their talons. The stars, guardians of Requiem, and the moon, goddess of the northern children, held council and forged weapons to fight the Sun God. The stars granted their children a Starlit Demon, a creature of rock and light, a devourer of fire. The moon crafted a Moondisk of stone and light, and its beams could douse all sunfire. The Starlit Demon consumed the phoenixes, and the Moondisk stripped them of their fire, until the Sun God returned to the heavens, and peace reigned upon the earth."

Her fingers tingled, and Mori rose to her feet so fast, her head spun. Was this the answer? A Moondisk? A Starlit Demon? Those sounded like fairytales to her, no different from the stories of knights, princesses, and unicorns she'd read as a child. But Mori was a woman now, eighteen years old; she had watched fire rain upon the world, and she had watched her brother die, and she had lain with a man, and...

Tears stung her eyes, and she wrapped her arms around her stomach, and suddenly she was trembling so violently that the library spun around her. That is what had happened, she realized; for the first time, she fully understood what he had done. She had lain with a man, with the cruel lord with the white tongue, like the princesses with the knights in her stories. Did his child grow within her now, a demon babe with a white tongue, and yellow teeth, and fingernails that could cut her? She felt evil inside her, shame and filth, and she fell. She curled up, hugged her knees, and lowered her head. Her tears claimed her, and she could not stop seeing it—Orin burnt, his entrails spilling, and how he gazed at her as Acribus stifled her screams, thrusting inside her, grunting, and she had let him do it, she *let* him. She could not shift into a dragon, not in a chamber so small, not with him choking her... but she could have fought him somehow, and she hadn't. *I let him do it. It's my fault. What kind of creature am I now?*

"Mori," whispered a voice, and a hand touched her hair.

She screamed and cowered.

"No! Don't touch me, please, don't. Please..."

Through her tears, she saw a figure lean above her, and Mori was sure it was him again, come to hurt her, come to place a demon child inside her, but the voice that spoke again was soft, soothing.

"Mori, it's all right. It's me, Lyana. You're safe."

Mori blinked, still cowering on the ground, and saw a head of red curls, a freckled face, and soft green eyes. *Lyana. My friend.* Mori sniffed, rose to her knees, and found herself caught in Lyana's embrace. She held her friend close, her tears wetting Lyana's shoulder. She could not stop trembling.

"Hold me," she whispered. "Don't let me go."

Lyana held her tight and stroked her hair. Her friend's armor was cold against Mori's cheek, but she didn't care. Lyana was a great warrior—a real bellator, a member of Requiem's ancient order of knighthood. There were only a few bellators in the whole kingdom, Mori knew. More than anyone, Lyana could protect her, hold the horror at bay.

Growing up, Mori had always wanted to be like Lady Lyana. *I've always been too thin, too frightened,* Mori thought, *a meek child running from shadows.* Lyana was two years older, a heroine to Mori. While Mori was afraid of swords, Lyana was a deadly fencer. While Mori cowered from spiders, Lyana dreamed of slaying griffins and nightshades. While Mori could charm the lords of the court with her needlework and poetry, Lyana could discuss warfare, politics, and governing.

I've always wanted to be brave like you, Lyana, she thought, holding her friend tight. *Especially now, give me some of your strength, some of your courage.*

"I'm with you, Mori," Lyana whispered and kissed her forehead. "We're safe here underground, and I'll watch over you."

Mori looked up at her, eyes blurred with tears. "Do you promise?"

Lyana nodded. "I promise. No one will hurt you while I'm with you."

Unless they kill you, Mori thought. *Unless they burn you, and gut you like a fish, and rape me as you lie dying.*

She shivered, her insides throbbing, and pressed her cheek against Lyana's breastplate. She closed her eyes but only saw yellow teeth, a white tongue, and never-ending fire.

LYANA

As Lyana held her princess, a chill ran through her, trickling down her spine and along her limbs. She did not know what Mori had seen at Castellum Luna. She did not know how Solina and her men had hurt her. But she saw Mori hug her belly and shiver, and Lyana knew enough of men at war to know what that meant.

They raped her, Lyana thought, *to fulfill their desire and to send us a message. They come to hurt us. They come to conquer us. If they break into these tunnels, they will rape Mori again, and me, and all the women they can capture. They will slay the men and children.*

Gently, Lyana kissed Mori's forehead, smoothed her hair, and whispered soft comforts. It had been thirteen years since little Noela had died in her cradle, leaving Lyana without a sister; since then Mori had become like a sister to her.

I won't let Mori die too, she thought. *I won't let her leave me like Noela did. We will stop the Tirans. We will fight.*

Huddled in her arms, Mori sniffed and pointed at the book. It lay open on the floor, showing a drawing of a phoenix.

"I found this about the phoenixes," the princess said, her voice small. "It talks about a Moondisk and a Starlit Demon. Do you know of these things?"

Lyana sat by her, arm around her waist, and the two young women leaned forward to read the book. Lyana scrunched her lips and tapped her chin.

"I remember hearing stories of the Starlit Demon," she said. "My mother would tell me of it. I don't remember much, only tales of Requiem's old kings trapping the beast, burying it deep underground in the Abyss itself, and placing many guardians around it. Does the book have an entry about it? Let's look."

They began flipping the pages, skipping entries about various beasts: undead skeletons from Fidelium, a northern land of ruins; the snowbeasts, gangly creatures of many limbs; the Poisoned, deformed men and women with webbed hands and eyeballs on stalks; the Dividers, hairy beasts who guarded the western borders; and many other creatures, each more hideous than the last.

Finally they found a page titled "The Starlit Demon" and Mori shuddered. An illustration appeared of a creature that seemed hewn from craggy stone. Its claws, spiky tail, and teeth glimmered like obsidian, and its eyes shone like stars.

"It eats fire," Mori whispered, pointing at words on the next page. "Look, Lyana."

The book spoke of the Draco Constellation, holy stars of Requiem, weaving the creature of stone and starlight to fight the phoenixes.

Lyana nodded and read aloud: "The Starlit Demon, ancient and powerful deity of wrath, feasted upon the sunfire of the phoenix and drank from the lava of the Sun God's fury."

Mori gasped and clutched Lyana's arm. Her damp eyes shone. "That's it! The Starlit Demon can defeat them. But where is it? Does the book say?"

She's still a child, Lyana thought, *and she's hopeful, and she's afraid, and she will believe anything that can hold her terror at bay.* Sadness ran through Lyana, like water dripping through her bones. There was pain in Mori, pain that would perhaps always fill her... but life and hope still flickered in those teary gray eyes. *Will I live to see joy return to her or those last flickers extinguished?*

She shook her head and sighed. "This book is ancient, Mori, written in the early days when many beasts roamed the earth. Who knows if any still live?"

"The phoenixes still live," Mori whispered and clung to her, pressing her face against Lyana's armor.

"Yes," Lyana whispered. "They do." She stroked the girl's hair and tried to remember the stories her mother would tell her. "In my bedtime stories, the Starlit Demon was wild, dangerous, a creature too powerful to tame. It would topple columns and eat dragons when it found no phoenixes; it was a menace as often as an ally. An old queen—Queen Luna the Traveler, I think, daughter of Gloriae—buried the Starlit Demon leagues under Requiem. It's said only Requiem's monarch can free the Starlit Demon and tame him; all others would die in his starlight."

Mori shivered and clutched Lyana's arms. "Is the demon buried here in these tunnels?" She looked around, as if seeking the demon between the book shelves.

"Deeper," Lyana said. "Many leagues underground, down in the Abyss itself." She shuddered to remember stories of that nightmarish realm. "Around its lair, Queen Luna placed many riddles and ancient guardians that would not die. Mother would tell me that it still lives underground, locked behind a Crimson Archway. When I'd misbehave, she'd tell me that the Starlit Demon ate bad children."

"But that's not true, is it?" Mori asked, eyes pleading. "It eats phoenixes. It *has* to. The book says so. Right, Lyana?"

Lyana sighed. She had never believed in Starlit Demons, or Moondisks, or old stories of legendary magic. But then again, until today she had not believed in phoenixes either. If stories of an old demon gave Mori hope, well, they were real enough. She stroked the girl's chestnut hair, again and again, until her shivering stopped.

"That's right, my princess," she said and kissed Mori's head. "If we can find the Starlit Demon, he'll help us. He'll eat all the phoenixes."

Mori nodded, closed her eyes, and mumbled, "Eat all the phoenixes..."

I wish I could turn back time, Lyana thought, a lump in her throat. *I wish I could have kept you here in Nova Vita, my princess, you and Orin my love. I wish I could have saved Orin's life, saved your innocence, saved everyone who died tonight. I will keep fighting for you, Mori, and for the memory of your brother, and for our home.*

Suddenly Mori rose to her feet, freeing herself from Lyana's arms. She bounded across the chamber, scurried up a ladder to a shelf, and pulled out another book. This too was an ancient tome, its leather old and cracked, its pages dusty. Holding it to her breast with both arms—the book was a good foot long—she walked back to Lyana and placed the codex down with a shower of dust. Its cover read: *Artifacts of Wizardry and Power.*

"I used to love this book as a child," Mori said. "It has pictures of magical rings, and amulets, and bracelets, and all sorts of jewels with special powers. When I was little, I liked to pretend that I owned these jewels, that I had magic that could stop Bayrin from tugging my braids, turn my hair red like yours, or save me from the spiders that crawled in my room." She opened the book and began leafing through it. "But the book has pages about other artifacts too, not just jewelery." She gasped and slapped a page. "Here! The Moondisk."

Lyana leaned down and examined the book. The page showed an illustration of a green disk, chipped and dented; it seemed made of bronze. Golden symbols were worked into the bronze: a crescent moon, a full moon, and a cluster of three stars.

Mori tapped the page. "See? The Moondisk that can extinguish phoenix fire!"

Lyana read from the book: "In the Days of Mist, the Children of the Moon sailed upon ships to the Crescent Isle, built rings of stones among the pines, and danced in the moonlight. A Moondisk they forged of bronze inlaid with gold, and upon it the moon turns, and the Three Sisters glow, and its light can extinguish all sunfire, so that the Sun God may never burn them."

Mori nodded emphatically. "See, Lyana? See?" Her eyes lit up. "We can defeat them! We can kill the phoenixes! I'll find the Moondisk so we can put out their fire. You can find the Starlit Demon, who will eat them." She clutched Lyana's shoulders, panting, eyes desperate. "We can do this, Lyana. I know it. I believe."

Lyana sighed. Magical disks of moonlight? Ancient demons of stars? Were these but myths, fairytales for children? Lyana was a warrior. She believed in the heat of her dragonfire, the sharpness of her claws, the steel of her blade. She knew nothing of ancient magic and enchanted beasts.

"Come, Mori," she said. "Let's take these books to my mother. She knows much of old lore and can interpret these words better than we can."

The young princess shivered. "Do we have to? Adia is near the tunnel entrance, where the phoenixes are, and..." She gulped, nodded, and knuckled her eyes. "But we must, yes. I'm not afraid. Not with you by my side. Let's go."

Each holding a book, the two young women left the library. They walked through the tunnels. As the wounded moaned and prayed, and as the shadows swirled, Lyana's throat constricted.

They had until sunrise, Solina had said. *We can surrender and live under their yoke, let them torture us, rule over us with fire and steel...* She clutched the book tight to her chest. *Or we can go chasing a dream from old books.*

She did not know which path led to greater darkness, and the book seemed so heavy in her arms, Lyana wanted to lie down, to place her head against the floor, and to sleep until this nightmare ended. But she kept walking—for Mori's eyes full of grief and hope, for the memory of Orin, for her family, for all those who prayed and wept around her.

I am a soldier, she told herself. *Whatever horror dawn brings, I will face it.* She walked through blood, fear, and pain, head high and heart trembling.

ELETHOR

He stood in the wine cellar, arms crossed and head lowered, staring at the cobbled floor where centuries of boots had trodden. Dozen of oak caskets rose around him, holding wine from Requiem's vineyards. *If we go to siege,* he thought, *at least we can get royally drunk before the Tirans break down our doors.*

He had chosen this cellar as his war room. *My father ruled among columns of marble and gold; I think caskets of wine are a far wiser choice for a king.* He did not know how long he'd live to rule. Perhaps future poets would sing of the Drunk King—Elethor Aeternum who was crowned in darkness, reigned from a wine cellar, and died the next day.

He sighed and turned around. Lyana and Mori stood there, staring at him with solemn eyes. Their ancient codices lay on a scarred table between rolled-up maps, mugs of wine, daggers, and a helmet. Around them stood the rest of his inner council: Lord Deramon, a bloody bandage covering his neck; Mother Adia, her eyes solemn and her white robes splashed with blood; and their son, Bayrin, ash in his red hair and fire in his green eyes.

They want me to fight, Elethor thought. *Even Mori.* He couldn't help it; he laughed bitterly.

"You can't be serious," he said and slapped the old books. "A magical disk that can extinguish sunfire? A Starlit Demon? My nurse told me such stories at bedtime—until I was about nine and stopped believing them."

Bayrin raised an eyebrow and whistled. "Well, there's a trick. I never believed in phoenixes either, until about ten thousand of them nearly burned my backside to a crisp." He clutched the hilt of his sword. "I don't know if this Stardisk or Moonlight Demon are real, but I'd rather go find a fairytale than surrender to your old flame, El—literally an old flame, in this case."

Face still ashy from the battle, Lyana glared at her brother. "It's the *Moon*disk and the *Starlit* Demon, you dolt. And it's not about what you'd rather do. It's about our best chance of saving lives. You might want to go on some adventure in the great outdoors, not caring if the Tirans kill us all in the meanwhile, but I'm sure Elethor cares." She looked at him and sighed. "At least I hope you do, El."

He looked into her green eyes and saw the fear in them. They were all afraid, he knew, even grizzled Lord Deramon.

What would my father do? Elethor thought. *What would Orin do? They would rally the troops. They would never surrender. They would fight at all costs.* He closed his eyes. *And they are dead, while I survived.*

He dug his fingernails into his palms. It wasn't fair. He didn't want to be king. He didn't want to make these decisions. He had never asked for this, for any of this! He was only Elethor, the young prince, the sculptor. How did he end up here, bearing the yoke of monarchy, his people depending on him, waiting for his decree? He opened his eyes and looked at them, one by one. A gruff warrior. A priestess. A friend. A betrothed. A sister.

He let his eyes linger on Mori, his dearest love, the last living member of his family. She stared back at him, eyes soft and damp, face so pale. She was a frail, pretty thing, and more than anything Elethor wanted to protect her. *If I surrender to Solina, what would become of my sister? Of Lyana and Adia? Of the other women who hide in these tunnels?* Elethor was no soldier, but he knew enough of war and conquest. *Solina's men would plunder our halls, eat our food, ravage our women. They would spare our lives, but they would make those lives miserable.*

And what of him? If he accepted Solina's offer, he would need travel south with her, rule by her side in Tiranor. She still loved him; he'd seen that in her eyes, felt it in her kiss. He could rule there with her, feel those kisses a million times, make love to her like in the old days, forever be with the woman he'd spent seven years sculpting and missing and craving.

And meanwhile, my people would suffer in chains. He shook his head. No. He could not allow it. Even if it tore his soul, even if meant giving up Solina forever, he would fight for Mori. For Lyana. For his people.

"What do you choose, my king?" Mother Adia asked. She stared at him, her eyes deep and penetrating. "Sunrise looms and you must decree."

Elethor stared back at her, though her eyes felt deep as midnight sky, stronger than steel, as wise as the true dragons of old. More than ever, he was struck by how different Adia was from her daughter. Lyana was free and fast as fire, while Adia was like an ancient forest, wise and full of secrets.

He spoke softly. "Solina and her men wore crystals around their necks. When they shifted into humans, their phoenix fire seemed to flow into those amulets. I've heard stories of the Griffin Heart, the magical amulet that once tamed the griffins. I've heard stories of the

Animating Stones, glowing gems that let the tyrant Dies Irae animate corpses and send them to war. I thought those only stories, legends, but... if Solina found amulets of fire, perhaps all those legends are true. Magic is real. Who's to say the Moondisk or the Starlit Demon are not?" He took a deep breath, struggling to calm the turmoil inside him. *For the memory of the dead. For the living. For Requiem.* "Let us find these weapons... and let us fight."

Bayrin slammed his fist into his palm. "Stars yeah! We fight."

Lyana stared at him solemnly, hand on her sword. "We fight," she whispered.

"We fight," whispered Mori, face pale but eyes staring steadily.

Lord Deramon nodded and clenched his fists around his weapons. "For blood and war."

"For peace and starlight," said Mother Adia and raised her eyes to the ceiling, as if gazing upon the stars. "Requiem! May our wings forever find your sky."

They all repeated the prayer, and a tremble ran through Elethor. *Be strong,* he told himself. *Be strong like your father, like your brother, like the great kings and queens of old.*

In the silence that followed, Bayrin cleared his throat.

"There is, ahem... one small problem." He sucked his teeth. "How the stars do we find this Moondisk and Starlit Demon? I can't find my socks most days, and Lyana once couldn't find a dagger she'd already strapped to her belt. And as for you, Elethor, I saw you get lost in the palace once, and you're our bloody prince. Well... king now, but the point stands. Finding these things won't be easy."

"Nothing's ever easy," Elethor said. He unrolled a parchment map across the table, then pinned it open with mugs. "Mori's book says the Moondisk belongs to the Children of the Moon on the Crescent Isle. Well, I only see two groups of islands on this map. One is far in the east, where the griffins live, and I've never heard them called Children of the Moon. And then there's this place." He tapped a cluster of islands in a northern sea, many leagues away, northwest of Requiem above distant realms of myth. "I don't know much about this place. I don't know if anyone alive today does; these maps predate Requiem's fall three hundred years ago, when most other maps were burned."

Bayrin frowned at the map. "Crescent Isle? Never heard of it. You reckon our Moondisk is there?"

"I don't know," Elethor said. "But look here. One island is shaped like a crescent moon. Three smaller islands surround it. Does this remind of you of anything?"

For a moment everyone stared at the map, silent. Mori understood first and gasped.

"They're shaped like the moon and stars on the Moondisk!" She tapped the page in *Ancient Artifacts* where the Moondisk was drawn in delicate ink. Indeed, it seemed like the golden stars adorning the bronze disk formed the shape of the smaller islands, rising above the larger Crescent Isle. Tears filled Mori's eyes. "It's true. I knew it."

Bayrin raised his eyebrows and bit his lip. "Well, seems like a long chance—literally, since these islands are a long, very long flight away. But... I'm up for a flight. In fact, flying hundreds of leagues away from Solina sounds just about perfect now. Who's going with me?"

"Mori is," Elethor said.

As he expected, the room erupted with raised voices. Mother Adia glared and spoke of Mori needing time to recover from her flight and wounds. Lyana cried that she was a warrior of Requiem, and sworn to defend her princess, and would keep her here under guard. Even Bayrin objected, shouting that Mori would only slow him down, and that he couldn't drag along the princess if he were to find the Moondisk and bring it back for war. Even Lord Deramon spoke up, claiming that he'd send a squad of tough, battle-hardened warriors to find the Moondisk, letting the princess remain in shadow.

Elethor waited for the voices to die down. When they were all silent and staring at him, he said, "Mori needs time to heal. That will not be in underground tunnels, under siege, under constant threat of violence. If I fall, she is the last member of House Aeternum. I will not have her here, in a burrow, with the wrath of Tiranor outside our doors. Let her fly north! She will be safer in the wilderness, a single dragon in a wide world, while we fight here in a few chambers and halls. You say she would slow you down, Bayrin? Mori is the fastest dragon in Requiem. She's won every flying race she's ever flown. She flew from Castellum Luna to Nova Vita in only two days. As for sending strong warriors north, Deramon? We need them here, every last man, to protect our people. We don't know if anyone survived the battle over King's Forest other than Lyana. All those soldiers might be dead now, five thousand of them; those we have left cannot be spared." He stared into Bayrin's eyes. "Bay. You are my oldest, dearest friend. Fly north to the Crescent Isle with Mori. Protect her."

Bayrin stared back in silence for long moments, lips tight and eyes fiery. Elethor stared back at his friend, refusing to look away. He knew Bayrin; the man would grumble and quip as easily as he breathed, but he was also an honest man and a good friend, and

Elethor trusted him. He could think of no one better to protect his sister.

Finally Bayrin's eyes softened and he heaved a sigh. "Oh bloody stars," he said, "I'm going to regret this, but all right." He walked toward Mori, slung his arm around her waist, and pulled her close. "Looks like it's me and you, Mors. I am sworn to protect you, my princess, and all of that."

Mori looked so slim and frail, pulled against Bayrin's gangly frame.

"Just try to keep up, Bayrin," she said in a small voice.

He snorted. "Just try not to fly into any cobwebs, little one." He turned to Elethor. "Of course, there is one small, tiny flaw in the plan—more a quibble than a flaw, really, but hear me out. How are we to, well..." He cleared his throat and raised his voice. "...leave these tunnels with about a million phoenixes and their mothers outside? I mean, I reckon Mors and I could just walk outside, wave, and say, 'Sorry, old friends, but we'd really like to fly off and fetch a weapon that could kill you all, how about you be good phoenixes and let us pass?' Yes, I think that'll work well."

Lyana groaned, rolled her eyes, and punched her brother. "Bayrin, you go do that, and spare the world your stupidity. Mori will escape the sensible way—using the Portal Scrolls."

Bayrin scratched his head of red curls. "The porta-what-now?"

Lyana groaned even louder. "You really are an idiot, aren't you? Are you sure we're related?" She slapped his head. "The Portal Scrolls! You should have spent less time chasing girls with Elethor, and more time listening to your teachers' lectures."

"I sense another lecture coming on," Bayrin muttered.

Lyana seemed not to hear him; she kept speaking, nose raised. "King Elaras, son of Queen Luna the Traveler, crafted the Portal Scrolls in the year 3318. That's 232 years ago; don't break anything trying to do the numbers in your head. Each Portal Scroll has a map with a star on it. When you read a scroll, it will magically whisk you away to that place on the map."

Bayrin whistled. "Some magic! So, you don't happen to have any Portal Scrolls leading to the Crescent Isle, do you?"

Lyana glared at him. "Bayrin! If you had ever listened to anything your teachers told you, or even bothered to visit the Chamber of Artifacts, you would know. But of course, the Chamber of Artifacts is next to the library, and I forgot that you avoid being within a league of any book." She sighed. "King Elaras and his descendents used most of the Portal Scrolls, visiting many distant realms. Only two scrolls remain in the chamber, both pointing to Lacrimosa Hill."

"But...." Bayrin rubbed his eyes. "Lyana! Lacrimosa Hill is only about a league from here. You can bloody walk that far in an hour, or fly in a second. Why would Elaras even bother crafting a magical scroll leading to a hill just outside the city?"

The groan that escaped Lyana's mouth was so loud, it echoed in the chamber. "My stars, you really are the dumbest man in Requiem, aren't you? He crafted those scrolls to get *back* home. A scroll leading to Salvandos isn't very useful unless you can get home, right?"

"Me, I'd stay in Salvandos if it meant escaping a know-it-all sister," he muttered.

Lyana placed her hands on her hips. "That's as may be. In any case, the Chamber of Artifacts has two scrolls; they will take you and Mori into the forest." She glared at her brother. "Do you understand now, Bayrin, or do I need to get some puppets?"

"All right, all right, I get it!" Bayrin said. He rolled his eyes. "Do you see what I have to put up with, El? The real reason I volunteered to grab the Moondisk is to get away from the constant history lessons. So, Mors and I visit the Chamber of Artifacts, find those Portal Scrolls, and zoom into the forest, nice and far from all those phoenixes. Then it's off to the magical lands of moonlight."

Elethor stared down at *Mythical Creatures of the Gray Age*. The illustrated Starlit Demon stared back up at him, carved of stone, its eyes two stars. Did this ancient being still live below Requiem, entombed in the Abyss, the mythical caverns far below these tunnels? Like everyone, Elethor had heard stories of the Abyss. As youths, he and Solina would even creep down to the Abyss Gates—a towering archway of stone and iron. Solina had once wanted to enter them, to make love in the Abyss itself, but Elethor had become frightened and hurried back to the surface. *Do I dare approach these doors again... and this time step through them?*

He spoke softly, still staring at the book. "Only the King of Requiem can wake the Starlit Demon, if the stories are true." He took a deep breath. "It seems I am the king now, so this task falls to me. I've been to the Gates of the Abyss, though I don't know what lies beyond them. They say that beyond those doors, evil dwells, and tunnels plunge for leagues into shadow and fire." He looked up from the book and found Lyana staring at him. He stared into her eyes. "I don't know if this demon is real. I don't know what awaits in the Abyss; none have entered that evil place for centuries. But if more hope lies there, I will go on this journey. If the Starlit Demon truly lives and truly sleeps in the dark deep, I will tame him and bring him to Nova Vita to slay whatever enemies the Moondisk cannot."

Lyana stared at him steadily, cheeks flushed, and nodded. "And I will go with you."

Her parents began to protest at once. Deramon spoke of needing her here, by his side, to help him defend the tunnels. Mother Adia spoke of Lyana being only a child, of the dark depths being too dangerous for her. Lyana shook her head.

"Elethor needs my sword," she said. "And he needs my knowledge. According to this book, many traps and riddles guard the way to the demon's lair." She smiled crookedly. "I've always been good at riddles. Mori might be the fastest dragon, my father the strongest, my brother, well... I'm sure he has *some* talents somebody will discover someday. As for me, I like to think I'm the smartest of the group. Elethor will need my knowledge."

Elethor was about to say more when the room shook. The mugs rattled on the table, and shrieks echoed outside in the tunnels. The cries of men and ringing blades filled the cellar. Deramon and Lyana drew their swords.

"It's sunrise," Elethor said softly, his insides chilling. "And Solina's wrath is upon us again." He looked at them all, one by one. "We know our tasks. Deramon, lead the men. Defend these tunnels. Adia—heal the wounded, and pray for us."

Deramon approached him, axe in hand, and gave him a hard look.

"You better not let any harm befall my daughter," Deramon said, eyes narrowed. "If you do anything stupid down there, Elethor... if you let any harm come to Lyana... I will hunt you down with more wrath than ten thousand phoenixes." He growled. "It's your lover who burns our city. I don't forget that. You find a way to extinguish her flames, or by the stars, it won't be a phoenix who kills you. It will be my axe."

Elethor stared back at the gruff, grizzled face. "You keep these tunnels safe until I return, old man. Swing your axe at the Tirans, not at me. I will extinguish Solina's fire."

Deramon spat onto the floor, gave Elethor a last glower, then turned toward his daughter. When his eyes fell upon her, they softened. The gruff warrior suddenly looked like a mother bear. He pulled Lyana into his embrace and held her tight. She clung to him.

"Take care, daughter," Deramon said. "Come back to me. Don't let the boy do anything stupid."

She nodded, tears in her eyes, and kissed his cheek.

"Goodbye, Father," she whispered.

Lyana turned to her mother next. The stately priestess stared at the young knight, tall and proud as ever, but then her eyes filled with tears, and she seemed no longer a great figure of starlight, but a mother overwhelmed with grief and worry. She hugged her daughter close, and their tears fell.

"I love you, child," Adia whispered. "I will pray for you."

Elethor turned away from them, his own eyes stinging, and found Mori and Bayrin staring at him, silent. *My best friend. And my sister. I'm sending them both into danger, and I don't know if they'll return.* A lump filled his throat, and he could not curb his tears. He approached them hurriedly, so they would not see his turmoil, and pulled them into an embrace.

"Goodbye, Bay," he whispered to his friend. The young man's shaggy head pressed against his cheek. Mori clung to his other side, her face pressed against his chest. He kissed her head, and she looked up at him with huge, damp eyes. "Goodbye, Mori. I love you, sister. Be careful out there. Fly fast and return to me."

She nodded, lips trembling, and held him tight. "Goodbye, El. Please be safe. *Please.* Listen to Lyana and don't do anything stupid, okay? And if you see anything dangerous, don't be brave, just run. *Promise* me."

He laughed softly through his tears and mussed her hair. "Okay, Mori, I promise."

He wiped his eyes and pulled away from the embrace. The sounds of battle echoed through the chambers. Deramon and Adia were gone already, off to fight and heal. Swallowing a lump in his throat, Elethor approached Lyana and smiled thinly.

"Are you ready?" he asked quietly.

"No," she said. "I was never ready for this. Nobody was. But let's go." She tightened her lips, nodded, and her eyes flared with rage. "Let's find this Starlit Demon and kill Solina."

SOLINA

The statue of King Benedictus—the vile weredragon who had fought the griffins three hundred years ago—lay fallen and cracked in the square. Solina stood upon it, her boots smearing mud across its marble face. Hands on her hips, she stared at the archway before her, which led into the tunnels. Her men fought there, slamming sword and spear against defenders who lurked in shadow. The sun rose around them, painting the ruins red, and smoke unfurled like dark phoenixes. It stung Solina's eyes.

He did not return to me, she thought, pain pounding through her. *He did not surrender. He wants to kill me.*

Watching the fight, she clenched her fists and snarled. Her rage bloomed inside her like the fire of her amulet. She had given everything for him! She had raised an army for him. She had killed a cruel king and a vain prince for him. In her palace in Tiranor, she had built chambers for his sculptures, dreaming of the day he ruled by her side.

"You could have ruled in luxury," she whispered through clenched teeth. "You could have ruled me, my body, my soul. I would have given myself to you. I would have made love to you every night, kissed you until you cried with the sweet pain of it." She pounded her fist into her palm, growling. "But you choose to fight for the reptiles. You choose their love over mine. You will die for this, Elethor. You will die in more agony than any weredragon ever knew."

As she watched the blood sluice the street, she imagined Elethor's blood washing her. She swore that she would break him. She would shatter him with hammers. She would gut him alive. She would let him linger in life, deformed and begging for death. And finally, when he could bear it no more, she would burn him with her phoenix fire, then watch his ashes rise into the wind and scatter over the desert she ruled.

"That will be your fate, Elethor," she whispered. She shook her head, eyes burning and throat tight. "You will regret this. You will beg me to love you again, and I will laugh."

She drew her twin sabres with a hiss, leaped off the fallen statue, and marched toward the tunnel entrance. Her men fought around her, stabbing spears and sabres at the shadows. Solina saw weredragons fighting inside in their human forms, eyes dark and blades bloodied.

"Move aside!" Solina said to her men, snarling. "My blades thirst for blood."

Her men stepped aside, and Solina stepped toward the archway. Its stones, once white and carved with golden reliefs, were now slick with blood. Three weredragons stood at the entrance, hiding their lizard forms in facades of gruff men in armor. They raised the thick, double-edged longswords of the north—hacking weapons so crude compared to Tiranor's curved steel. More weredragons spread behind them into the shadows.

"Where is Elethor Aeternum?" Solina demanded, rushing toward the weredragons. "I will kill you instead, if he is too cowardly to die at my blades."

They thrust their swords at her, graceless hunks of metal. Grinning savagely, Solina swung both her blades. She parried two blows and swung again, slicing a man's face. Blood showered. Solina snarled, sabres whirring, shards of sunlight. Steel clanged and blood splashed. She parried more blows, sliced into a man's mail, and opened another's neck. He fell, blood spurting, and another replaced him only for Solina to slash his face.

She smirked. These were no warriors. They were brutes, their armor heavy, their legs stiff and their muscles slow. She was a dancer. She was wildfire. Her feet were quick, her sabres like striking asps, her teeth bared in a grin.

"We killed you in the sky," she said and growled. "We will kill you underground."

She swung her blades, reveling at the taste of splashing blood. She severed a man's leg, snarled, and swung her sword down so hard, she cut through another man's helmet. A sword hit her breastplate, knocking the breath out of her, but she only growled and kept fighting.

"Come face me, Elethor!" she shouted into the darkness. "Come taste my steel."

She kicked a soldier, cut down another, and forced her way into the archway. She found herself on a staircase that plunged into darkness. Her men cried for the Sun God and ran to fight with her; one stood at each side, and a hundred shouted for blood behind her. She swung her blades, kicked, sliced, and pushed her way down a step. Bodies fell before her. A hundred weredragons cried below upon the stairs, awaiting her steel. She slew three, suffered a cut on her arm, but pushed forward and descended another step.

"I will find you, Elethor. Step by step, I will descend into your lair."

Cries of war filled the darkness. Solina smiled and licked blood off her lips.

Time vanished. She fought for hours—maybe for days. Her sabres were parts of her, extensions of her arms, demons of her wrath. Soon her face, armor, and helmet were covered with blood; she was a red devil of death, blades always whirring, throat always growling. Her men shouted at her sides, dying, killing. A blade cut Solina's leg. She fell, pushed herself up, and drove her sword into a man's throat. Snarling, she pulled her sword back with a red shower, swung it again, and cut down another man.

She fought in darkness. The archway was far above her now, and she had descended many steps into this den of evil.

"You pitied me, weredragons!" she called, the blood of her enemies in her mouth. "You saw me as an orphan, a cripple, a sinner to burn and banish. Now you die at my feet, reptiles."

She swung her blades, cutting down more weredragons, and took another step into the darkness. Soon she saw the end of the staircase where a tunnel sloped into shadow. Corpses piled up there, a hill of her victory. A burly man emerged from the shadows and stood above the bodies, a sword in one hand, an axe in the other.

Solina grinned. "Deramon!" she cried to him and bared her bloody teeth. "Do you remember me, weredragon? Will you come die at my feet too?"

The memories filled her like fire in an oven. Deramon, cruel Captain of the City Guard, had always loathed her. He had once accused her of stealing from a temple—she had only taken one gem!—and twisted her arm, and would have beaten her had she not kicked him and escaped. Today she would do more than kick him. Today she would twist his arm too, until flesh ripped and bone snapped, and she would laugh as he screamed.

"Come to me, weredragon! You would torment me as a child, but I've grown. Come die."

He stood below, bodies around him, and stared at her. His eyes were narrowed and cruel. A cut ran down his face, dripping blood. For a moment the battle died, and the only movement was the thrashing of the wounded, the only sound their moans. Solina and Deramon stared at each other, and she grinned, prepared to dance.

Deramon nodded and stepped back.

Solina snarled and ran down toward him.

A dozen weredragons emerged from the shadows, shoving boulders.

Solina screamed. "Cowards! Fight me!"

They shoved the boulders and cried, and Solina slammed into the stone. She tried to climb above a boulder, but more piled up. She growled and punched the stone, bloodying her knuckles. Her men ran down to join her and pushed against the boulders, shoving them back.

"Break down their barricade!" Solina cried. "Kill them all."

But the weredragons were cowards. They piled up more stones, and she could not break through. She shouted to them.

"Deramon! Deramon, you coward! Fight me like a man. Or will you hide like a rat? Do you think your stones can hold me back for long?"

Soon she was forced to stop. She stood panting before the pile of boulders. Sweat and blood covered her. She spat, licked blood off her blade, and screamed. Her voice echoed like a hundred demons. Her men crowded around her, breathing heavily, swords drawn.

"Get hammers," she told them when she'd caught her breath. "We're breaking through."

Not waiting for a reply, she shoved her way through them so roughly she knocked one man down. She stormed upstairs, teeth gritting, until she emerged back onto the surface. She stood in the courtyard, dizzy with the heady smell of death.

Lord Acribus came marching across the courtyard, armor and sword bloody. He nodded his head at her.

"My queen." His voice was like crackling gravel.

"How are the other tunnel entrances?" she asked him, holding her blades crossed.

Acribus spat out a tooth. "They blocked them," he said. He uncorked his flask, took a draft of spirits, and swished it. When he spat it out, it was bloody. "Bastards put up walls of rock. My men are hammering at them. We will break them down soon."

Solina shook her head. None of this made sense. Did Elethor truly think he could win this way? Did he expect to survive, locked in darkness behind rock, forever buried underground?

"He'll die down there," she said. "He has enough food for winter, maybe. When spring comes, they will all starve. Unless..."

She thought back to the days she'd enter those tunnels with Elethor. Years ago, they would sneak underground most nights, undress in darkness, kiss each other across their bodies, make love in shadow where none could find them. She would scream in the darkness with nobody to hear, nobody to hurt her, pity her, judge her.

One midnight, they had made love in the Chamber of Artifacts, their bodies pressed together as the wonder and secrets of the world covered shelves around them. Elethor had pressed her against a cold stone wall. She dug her fingers into his shoulders, head tossed back, and gasped at amulets, crystals, and...

She snarled.

"The Portal Scrolls," she said.

Acribus grumbled and scrunched his face, as if seeking more loose teeth with his tongue. "My queen?"

She growled and clenched her fists. "They have two Portal Scrolls down there, magical artifacts that can send two weredragons into the forest." She nodded. "Elethor will try to flee that way, or send his sister to safety. Come, Acribus." She started walking across the square. "We head into King's Forest."

Acribus snarled and followed. "If Mori the weredragon whore tries to escape, I will catch her." He clutched his wounded arm where the princess had stabbed him. "I will make her envy her dead brother. I will make her beg for death."

As they walked through the streets, Solina remembered the sight of Acribus thrusting into the princess as Orin lay dead, and she smiled.

BAYRIN

Soldiers rushed around them, shouting and drawing weapons. Survivors huddled in shadows, some weeping, others nursing wounds, all pale and trembling. Priests ran from wounded to wounded, praying, healing, comforting the dying. As Bayrin walked down the tunnel, stepping over and around survivors, he kept looking at Mori. The princess, he thought, looked just as hurt, pale, and haunted as any one of the dying souls on the floor. Her eyes were rimmed with red. She kept sniffing and looked close to bursting into tears.

"Hey, Mors," he said hesitantly and tapped her arm. "Chin up, huh? We're going to find those scrolls, find the Moondisk, and kick Solina's backside."

She only sniffed, twisted her fingers, and a tear rolled down her cheek. Bayrin touched her shoulder awkwardly, not knowing what to do. She flinched and shied away. How could he comfort her? Would she be like this the entire journey, trembling and weeping? He would go mad within a day!

"I know," she whispered, and her lips wobbled. She dared not meet his eyes, only twisted her fingers behind her back and stared at the floor.

Bayrin looked away from her and stared forward into the darkness. He held a tin lamp, but its wick cast only soft light; he could barely see three feet ahead. He kept walking, stepping between the crowds of survivors.

Why couldn't somebody else have gone on this quest with him—if not Elethor, then maybe Janith the blacksmith, or one of Father's men... or really anyone other than the weepy, frightened princess. Even his sister Lyana, for all her lectures and scoldings, would have made a better companion; though Bayrin hated to admit it, at least Lyana was brave and strong. But Mori? All his life, Bayrin knew Mori as the girl who screamed when spiders crept into her room, who cowered when dogs barked, who always stared at her toes shyly whenever he tried talking to her. The king had thought sending her south to Castellum Luna would toughen her up, but now Mori seemed even *more* timid and weepy. Bayrin sighed.

"Here we are, Mors," he said and pointed at a doorway in the tunnel ahead. "The Chamber of Artifacts."

The archway loomed above them, its keystone engraved with the Draco constellation. Its doors were thick oak clasped with a heavy lock. The archway only seemed to scare Mori further, and she hugged herself. She glanced longingly at the entrance to the library, which lay across the tunnel, then gulped and looked back the Chamber of Artifacts.

"I have the key," she whispered.

The Chamber of Artifacts, like the library, was locked to most people; the treasures within were too valuable. Only the royal family carried the old, filigreed keys to these tombs of secrets. Mori produced hers—she wore it around her neck on a chain—and unlocked the door with trembling fingers. She closed her eyes, whispered a prayer, and tugged the doors. They creaked open, revealing a room of shadows.

"After you," Bayrin said, but Mori only trembled.

Bayrin sighed. He considered holding her arm to guide her into the chamber, but knew she'd only cringe at his touch. Instead he stepped into the chamber alone and beckoned her to follow. With a shiver, she took small steps into the darkness.

Bayrin raised his lantern... and his breath died.

He was no prince; he had never been in this chamber, one of the holiest places in Requiem. All the magic, power, and history of the realm filled this place. On one shelf, he saw three golden skulls, twice the size of human skulls. *The Beams*, he knew; in countless bedtime stories, he'd heard how the old heroes of Requiem shone their light against the nightshades. In a chest on the floor, a thousand red gemstones glowed. *Animating Stones*, Bayrin thought—the magical gems that had given life to Dies Irae's monsters of rotting bodies. On other shelves he saw the Summoning Stick, an enchanted candlestick that could call griffins for aid; a jar of shards labeled "The Griffin Heart"; and dozens of jewels, statuettes, quills, and... two parchment scrolls.

"Look, Mors, some scrolls," he said, hoping that at least would cheer her up. "You reckon those are the Portal Scrolls, or some naughty drawings your brother hid here? Either way, we're winners!"

She only sniffed, and Bayrin groaned inwardly. *This is going to be a long quest.* He stepped around a few golden vases, reached up, and grabbed the two scrolls. Tied with blue ribbons, they felt unnaturally cold. He tossed one to Mori, untied the ribbon on his scroll, and began unrolling it.

"Wait," Mori whispered.

Bayrin paused, the scroll half-unrolled in his hands. "What is it?"

She shivered, the scroll rolled up in her hand. "What if... what if there are phoenixes out there? In the forest." She sniffed. "Lacrimosa Hill is only a league away. What if he sees us?"

Bayrin frowned. The princess was trembling and pale; Bayrin had never seen anyone look so frightened.

"Who is *he*, Mori?" he said, scrutinizing her.

She knuckled tears from her eyes, bit her lip, and clutched the sixth finger on her left hand.

"I mean... the phoenixes." Her voice was so quiet he barely heard.

Bayrin patted her shoulder, but she flinched and lowered her eyes. He sighed and said, "Mori, the phoenixes want to kill us. And they think we're all in these tunnels. They won't waste time searching a bleak forest a league away. Once we magically appear there, we'll find a nice, empty hill far from any phoenixes. And if they *are* there? Well, you're the fastest dragon in Requiem, right? You escaped thousands of those phoenixes before. If any lurk in the forest, just fly away, fast as you can. I'll be right behind you."

That seemed only to terrify her further. For the first time, she met his eyes. Tears rolled down her cheeks. "But I don't want to flee them! I want to hide here." She clutched his sleeve. "Please, Bayrin, please let's not go. *Please!* Let's just find a place to hide here underground, or... or look for a different, better magical artifact."

"Mori!" Bayrin groaned inwardly, and he felt his anger rise. "You're the one who wanted to find the Moondisk in the first place, remember? You can't back out now! I know you're scared, but... stars, Mori. Crying and trembling won't help us defeat the phoenixes, will it?" She began to sob, and Bayrin rolled his eyes and softened his voice. "Look, Mors, I know you can do this. I believe in you. So chin up. Stand straight. Be brave. I'm with you, remember?"

She nodded, sniffing and rubbing her eyes. "All right." Her voice was so soft, he barely heard.

He helped her untie the ribbon binding her map. "On the count of three, all right?"

She nodded, face white and lips trembling, but she met his gaze. Her voice was but a whisper. "All right."

Just to be safe, Bayrin clutched the hilt of his sword. "One... two... three..."

They unrolled their Portal Scrolls, and Bayrin looked at his. It showed an ancient map, torn in one place, its ink faded. He recognized Nova Vita in the north and the ruins of Draco Murus in the east. And in the center, between small ink trees, a red star was drawn above Lacrimosa Hill.

The star began to spin and glow.

Bayrin looked over the map at Mori. She stood before him in the Chamber of Artifacts, staring at her map. She looked up to meet his gaze...

...and the world swirled.

The chamber twisted like a whirlpool. Mori's face stretched, ten feet long and curving. Light pulsed. Bayrin felt nausea rise in him. He winced and raised his hands, but his fingers extended across the room, and the shelves coiled, and shadows leaped. Then the room bulged and rippled, like a reflection in a pond under rain, and sparks rained. With a pulse of light, branches rustled, smoke filled his nostrils, and black streaks settled into the forms of burnt birches. The shadows faded, and Bayrin found himself standing in puddles of melted snow in a smoldering forest.

Mori was nowhere to be seen.

Frowning, Bayrin drew his sword and looked around. Something had gone wrong. The smell of smoke filled his nostrils. He was in the right place—this was the hill where, according to legend, the tyrant Dies Irae slew Lacrimosa, Queen of Requiem. But shouldn't Mori's scroll have pointed here too?

"Mori!" he whispered, belly churning.

Figures stepped out from behind the trees.

Bayrin cursed.

There were six of them. They wore breastplates over chain mail, the steel so bright it was almost white. Their hair was platinum, their skin golden, their eyes blue. Their sabres bore pommels shaped as rising suns.

Tirans, Bayrin knew. *These are their human forms.*

One of them—a tall and slim woman, her breastplate snug against her body—wore a golden mask. She removed it slowly and smiled at him.

"Hello again, Bayrin."

It was Solina.

Still clutching his sword, Bayrin raised his eyebrows and clucked his tongue. "Well hullo, Soli old friend. Been what, seven years? Time does fly. You must be looking for your old lover, El. Sorry to say he's not here at the moment, but if you'd like a roll in the hay—you know, for old time's sake—I'm more than happy to fill in."

She sighed. "Time has not made you any wiser." She turned to one of her men, a beefy warrior who looked like a rabid bear with yellow teeth. "Acribus, kill him."

The man snarled, drooled, and burst into flames.

Bayrin caught his breath.

The fire raced across Acribus. The man's flaming arms outstretched, and he rose into the air, ballooning and crackling, until he soared as a phoenix.

With a growl, Bayrin shifted into a dragon, flapped leathern wings, and shot into the sky.

He crashed between burnt branches, scattering chips of wood. Flames crackled and phoenix screeches rose. Bayrin growled and flew higher, as high and fast as he could. Below him, the other Tirans combusted into phoenixes. Their inferno rose, and heat blasted Bayrin.

"Stars damn it!" he shouted and flew forward, circling the hill. Phoenixes rose around him, their flames reaching toward him. One firebird shrieked behind him, and talons blazed against Bayrin's tail. He howled, spun around, and blew his own fire. The jet slammed into the phoenix, its beak lashed, and Bayrin screamed.

I can't fight it, he knew. *Fang or fire can't kill it.* He cursed and swooped, crashed between branches, and soared again.

"Mori!" he shouted. "Mori, where the stars are you?"

A phoenix swooped from above. Two more took flight from each side. Bayrin cursed, dived, and flew between trees. Smashed branches flew around him. He soared again, covered with ash, his scales blazing.

"Mori!" he shouted. "Stars damn it, Mori!"

He saw a flash of blue below. He dodged a phoenix, suffered a blast of fire, and dived. He saw the color again—a girl in a blue cloak, huddling between the trees.

"Mori! Mori, fly!"

She looked up at him, shivered, and seemed ready to faint. The phoenixes swooped toward Bayrin, and the trees below crackled. The snow melted.

"Mori, shift into a dragon! We're getting out of here!"

With a cry of fear, Mori became a slim golden dragon and took flight. A phoenix dived toward her, lashing fire. So fast Bayrin gasped, Mori skirted around the phoenix and soared higher. She flew toward him.

"Bayrin, behind you! Fly!"

He spun in time to see the phoenix shoot toward him, a blazing comet. The firebird crashed into him, and flames engulfed Bayrin. He howled in pain. Golden scales flashed, and Mori flew toward them. Her wings beat and her claws slammed into the phoenix, kicking it off. She cried in pain.

"Come on, Mori, we're out of here!" Bayrin shouted.

He began flying west. She flew at his side. When Bayrin looked over his shoulder, he saw five phoenixes following.

"Catch them!" Solina cried below, the only Tiran still in human form. "Bring me their heads, Acribus, or I will content myself with yours!"

Bayrin flew as fast as he could. Mori flew at his side, panting. The flames howled behind them, the heat bathed them, and ten thousand more phoenixes flamed a league north above the city. Bayrin cursed, narrowed his eyes, and flew.

LYANA

"Well, here it is," she said quietly and couldn't suppress a shudder. "The Gates of the Abyss."

Lyana raised her tin lamp, shining its light against the archway. It rose fifty feet tall, dwarfing her; she could have walked through this archway even in dragon form. Its keystone was shaped as a dragon's skull, horns blood red. Its remaining stones bore engravings of screaming mouths full of shattered teeth. Heavy doors filled the archway, wrought of iron that had not rusted in two thousand years. Cold air blew from beneath those doors, sneaking under Lyana's armor to chill her flesh. She clutched her sword's hilt like she would clutch Mother's hand as a child.

Standing at her side, Elethor drew a silver key from his tunic; it hung around his neck on a chain. All members of royal House Aeternum owned these keys, Lyana knew, even the young Princess Mori. They unlocked all forbidden places here in the underground: the library of ancient codices, the Chamber of Artifacts... and these dark doors to the Abyss.

"Are you ready, Lyana?" he said. "Are you afraid?"

Lyana shuddered to remember the stories her nurse would tell her of this place. The old woman whispered of horrors that dwelled below—rotting bodies that walked, naked moles the size of horses, ancient demons that could shrivel your body with a glance. Lyana had never believed those stories, not even as a child, but then again, she had never believed in phoenixes either. She had never believed she would lose her beloved. She had never believed she would see her friend and princess, the dear Mori, broken and ravaged and left a trembling shell of a girl. Who was to say what horrors truly existed in the world, and what were the whispers of old wives?

Yet she only glared at Elethor. She would show him no fear.

"I'm not afraid," she said. "I am a knight of Requiem. We will find this Starlit Demon, and we will tame him."

Elethor looked at her strangely, as if trying to read her mind.

"But I am afraid." His voice was soft. "This is a dark place, and I wonder if, on our quest to defeat the phoenixes, we unleash more beasts whose evil we cannot expect." He lowered his head, took a deep breath, and looked back up at her. Compassion softened the fear in his eyes. "It's okay to fear this darkness. Even great warriors feel fear; Orin would too."

Her insides trembled, cold sweat trickled down her back, and her head spun. But Lyana only raised her chin, tightened her jaw, and whispered, "I don't."

Slowly, Elethor placed his key in the heavy lock. It scraped against the metal, a sound like a banshee. Suddenly Lyana wanted to stop him. *Don't!* she wanted to cry. *Don't unleash what horror dwells there! There must be another way!* Yet she only tightened her lips, clutched her sword, and took a deep breath. *Be brave, Lyana,* she told herself. *You are a bellator. You are a warrior. Whatever waits behind these doors, you can slay it.*

Elethor paused, key in lock, and looked at her. She stared back, silent. He took a deep breath and shut his mouth. He seemed to be considering his words, then spoke again in a low voice.

"Lyana, I don't know what lurks beyond these doors. I don't know how long we will live once we walk past them, or if we'll even live long enough to enter. Before I unlock these doors, I want to tell you how sorry I am for your loss."

A deep sadness seeped into Lyana, like an underground river of ice. She sighed and lowered her eyes. Suddenly thoughts of demons and skeletons paled in her mind, overcome with this sadness, the tragedy of all this death.

"I know," she said softly. "I'm sorry too, Elethor."

Pain filled his eyes like ghosts in old castles. He placed a hand on her shoulder. His voice was hoarse.

"Lyana, I know this might not mean much now, in these tunnels, in the cold dark. And I know that you're a strong, capable woman, and I know you're not afraid. But however I can, I swear to you: I will look after you. I..." He swallowed. "I'm not a warrior like Orin was. I'm not strong as he was, nor as wise. But I promise you, Lyana. I will protect you however I can—in the Abyss, and if we return from it. For whatever it's worth, you have my sword, and you have my loyalty."

She couldn't stop a sad smile from touching her lips. She stood on tiptoes and kissed his cheek.

"Thank you, Elethor," she said. "But for now, focus less on protecting me and more on finding this Starlit Demon. All right?"

His eyelids flinched, as if her words stabbed him, and Lyana sighed inwardly. What did he want her to do? To throw her arms around him, weep and kiss him, and vow her eternal love? He was her betrothed now; his older brother had died, so he had inherited all of

Orin's claims, his titles, and his woman. Lyana was a daughter of Requiem, and she accepted her laws. That did not mean her grief left her. That did not mean she could forget how Elethor had spent years shunning the court, yearning for the woman who now burned it. He confessed that he lacked Orin's strength and wisdom. Did he want her to deny it? She could not. He was her king now. She would respect that. But love him... love him like she loved Orin? Accept him as a hero, a protector? She could not.

"All right, Lyana," he said softly, and pain lived in his voice. "We enter the darkness."

He turned back to the lock, took a deep breath... and twisted the key.

The lock clanked.

The doors to the Abyss, this dark lair of secrets deep below Requiem, began to creak open.

Lyana shuddered and gritted her teeth. Iciness stung her fingertips and roiled her belly. She would never admit it, of course. She was a soldier. A heroine of Requiem. She must show strength, especially now, especially to Elethor. And yet as the doors creaked open, revealing mist and shadow, cold sweat washed her.

She did not know what she was expecting. Demons to attack? Rotting bodies to lunge at all? Soon the doors were opened wide, and she saw nothing but shadow, smoke, the glimmer of smooth stone walls. That was all. Just a tunnel. And yet this darkness filled her with more fear than skeletons or demons would. She could kill skeletons or demons, smash them with her sword, beat them down, defeat them with all her skills of war. It was the darkness she feared. The secrets. The unknown.

"Are you sure you're all right, Lyana?" Elethor asked, standing at the doorway. "You're pale, and your fingers are trembling."

She snorted and shoved by him.

"Out of my way, Elethor." She drew her sword. "I'm going in."

She walked through the archway, sword drawn in one hand, tin lamp in the other. She delved into the darkness.

The chill filled her bones. Mist swirled around her legs. As she walked, her boots clanked, echoing like the laughter of demons. Her lamplight flickered against smooth walls carved by old streams. The floor curved steeply, forcing her to move slowly. The tunnel plunged into darkness like a giant's gullet. She kept listening for enemies, but heard nothing—no grunts of beasts, no scuttling feet, no screeches of ghosts.

There is nothing here, she told herself. *No demons. No skeletons.* She clenched her jaw and held her sword high.

Bring me strength, Levitas, she prayed to her sword as she walked. It was an ancient weapon, its blade engraved with coiling dragons, its pommel shaped as a claw. Her father traced its lineage back to Terra Eleison, a knight of Requiem who'd survived the griffin war, helped found Nova Vita, and restored their house to glory. Many Vir Requis today carried longswords, heavy weapons for both hands; Elethor carried one at her side, the old blade Ferus. Lyana's sword was shorter, faster, easy to wield in one hand; the weapon of a knight.

Your sword was ancient even then, Father had said when giving her the blade five years ago. It had defended Requiem for centuries and slain many of her foes. Lyana tightened her fingers around the leather grip. Under the sky, she fought with claw and fire, a dragon roaring her fury. Here she would wield this ancient shard of steel.

May Levitas defend me underground, she thought, *in darkness, far from the sky of Requiem. Shine bright, Levitas. Shine bright, for the world is full of more darkness than I can bear.*

They kept walking down the tunnel. Lumps rose upon the walls like warts. When Lyana touched one, she found it clammy. She imagined herself walking through the veins of some great beast of stone, and she shuddered. She held her lamp out at arm's length, but could see only several feet ahead.

A screech filled the darkness.

Lyana froze, panting. She raised her sword.

"What was it?" she whispered. A shiver ran through her.

Elethor stood frozen by her side, his own sword raised. He stared ahead, but the darkness nearly swallowed their lamplight. They saw nothing. Silence filled the tunnels.

"I don't know," he whispered. "Was it the Starlit Demon?"

Lyana squared her jaw. "If it is, we will tame the beast. Come, we go farther."

They walked five more steps before the screech sounded again.

It was so loud, Lyana grimaced. She nearly dropped her sword and lamp to cover her ears. The tunnels shook and a crack ran along a wall. Many feet pattered in the distance, clanking, scratching. The screech went on and on, rising and falling, a banshee cry. Lyana's insides trembled and she could barely breathe. A ghostly light glowed ahead and shadows scurried.

"Stay by me, Lyana," Elethor said, hand clutching his sword. Sweat beaded on his brow.

Keeping her eyes on the tunnel ahead, Lyana laid down her lamp and drew her dagger. She held both blades before her, ready to fight whatever enemy approached.

A shadow lurched.

A creature emerged from the darkness.

Lyana grimaced. Her heart burst into a gallop, and cold sweat flooded her.

With a screech, the creature scuttled forward on many legs. It looked like a great centipede, many feet long and wide as a tree trunk. Its body was made of segments, each bloated and furry like the body of a spider. Its curved legs looked sharp as blades. Worst of all, however, was not the body that snaked behind, but the front of the creature.

It had the head, torso, and arms of a human girl, no older than ten. Her flesh was pale, her red eyes rimmed in black, her hair scraggly. Her bloated belly was slashed open, revealing cockroaches that nested and bred inside her. The girl grinned, showing rotting teeth, and raised her arms. Her hands ended with curving, yellow claws that dripped sizzling liquid. Below her belly, her centipede body pulsed black and hairy, coiling into the shadows behind her.

"Stars," Elethor whispered.

"What are you?" Lyana shouted at the beast, baring her teeth. "Why do you dwell in Requiem?"

The creature stared at her, eyes dripping pus, and tilted her head. She opened her mouth wide, and her tongue rolled out, a foot long and covered in ants. She screeched, a deafening sound that made Lyana grimace and scream.

"This is... not... Requiem!" the creature said, voice like shattering glass. Blood dripped from her eyes down her cheeks. "This is the Abyss. I am Nedath, guardian of this realm. Turn back, creatures of sunlight! Leave our... world..."

Her voice turned to wind that howled, blowing back Lyana's hair. The creature thrust herself up, rising ten feet tall upon her bloated segments. Her spider legs stretched out like black blades. Blood spurted between the demon's sharpened teeth, spraying Lyana's face. The droplets stung like acid.

"Turn back, Nedath, guard of the Abyss!" Elethor cried. He waved his lamp, as if light could cow this creature of darkness. "I am King Elethor Aeternum. My forefathers sealed you here. Now obey me."

The creature cackled, hair rustling with maggots. With a screech, she spat a glob of blood and mucus at Elethor. He swung his blade, blocking the discharge. What droplets sprayed him sizzled, and he cried in pain.

"Turn back, creature!" Lyana cried, waving her sword. "I am Lyana Eleison, daughter of Lord Deramon, knight of Requiem! You will kneel before me."

She swung her sword, but Nedath pulled her body back, and the blade whistled through air. The creature cackled and spat a glob of bloody mucus. Lyana had no time to parry, and the glob hit her face.

Her eyes blazed with pain. She could not breathe or see. She screamed; it felt like her face was being ripped off.

"Elethor!" she tried to shout, but the mucus entered her mouth, choking her, running down her throat like a living thing.

"Back, creature!" Elethor cried, voice muffled, a million leagues away. "Turn back into the darkness."

Lyana could not see him. She swung her sword blindly, not knowing if she hit anything. The creature screeched again, but she could barely hear.

She fell. She hit the ground. She dropped her weapons, clawed at her face, tried to tear the slime off her eyes, her nose, her mouth. Her head hit the ground, and she heard only a distant screech, a cry of horror, and then nothing but cruel cackling.

ADIA

She moved between the wounded, her robes soaked with blood. Her fingers stitched wounds, her eyes shed no more tears, and her heart felt no more pain. Around her the wounded shivered, wept, and screamed; she healed them. The dying lay feverish; she comforted them. The dead lay stinking; she prayed for them. She was a healer, a priestess, and a mother grieving.

Come back to me from your wilderness, Bayrin, she prayed silently as she bandaged a burnt, trembling man. *Come back from the darkness, Lyana. I love you, my children.*

The man groaned, his face melted away, his hands burned to stumps. If he died, Adia thought, it would be a blessing for him, and yet she fought for him, gave him the nectar of silverweed to dull his pain, and she refused to surrender his life. He was somebody's son, and Adia too had a son. What if Bayrin returned to her like this, burned into red, twisted flesh and pain? She moved to a young girl, her legs shattered, her hand severed, and she prayed for her, bandaged her, set her bones as best she could. What if Lyana returned to her broken and bleeding too?

Stars, please. I already lost one of my children. I already lost my sweet Noela. Don't let me lose Bayrin and Lyana too.

Her worry seemed too great for Adia to bear, and yet she bore it. She was High Priestess of Requiem. All these bleeding, broken, burnt souls were her children too. They lay in rows upon the floor, dozens of them filling the armory. The swords and shields were gone from this place, taken to battle; the wounded were returned. Every few moments they were carried in: men whose legs ended with stumps, men with entrails spilling from sliced bellies, men burnt and cut, men crying for wives and mothers. In battle they were brave warriors, heroes of Requiem. Here in her chamber, they were sons and husbands, afraid, the terror of battle too real.

"Mother Adia... Mo..." A wounded man reached out to her. Skin hung from his hands, the flesh of his fingers blackened, falling to show the bone. "Mother, a prayer, please..."

She turned to him, placed her hand on his forehead, and prayed for him. She prayed to the stars to comfort him, to heal him or lead him peacefully to the halls of afterlife. And yet Adia did not know if starlight could reach these tunnels. All her life, she had prayed in temples between columns and birches, watching the sky. Now that sky burned, and here they hid, in darkness and pain. *The world has become fire and shadow, and all starlight is washed away.*

But still she prayed. Still she believed, forced herself to. If her stars had abandoned her, what purpose did her life hold? So she prayed for this burnt man, kissed his bloodied forehead, and bandaged his wounds. She gave him the nectar of silverweed, until he slept, feverish and dying.

"As the leaves fall upon our marble tiles," she whispered, lips sticky with blood, "as the breeze rustles the birches beyond our columns, as the sun gilds the mountains above our halls—know, young child of the woods, you are home, you are home." She held him as his breath stilled and his face smoothed. "Requiem! May our wings forever find your sky."

She closed his eyes, covered him with his cloak, and stood up. She pulled him to the corner and placed him among the piles of bodies. There he would stink, decay, lie as rotting flesh until they found room to bury the dead. Adia needed men to dig graves underground, or soon the disease of bodies would claim them all. She needed healers to help her. She needed her husband by her side, and she needed her children back, and she needed this war and death to end. But all she had were her hands that could stitch a wound and hold a dying man, her bandages and nectar, and whatever faith still remained in her heart. And she used them all as the blood flowed, the stench of bodies wafted, and soldiers kept dragging new death into her chamber.

Stay safe, Bayrin and Lyana. Stay alive. Return to me.

She did not know how many hours or days passed as she worked, healing and praying. She did not know night from day. When her husband appeared at the doorway, armor splashed in blood and eyes dark, her fingers were sore, her eyes stinging, her head light. She walked to him, embraced him, and kissed his bristly cheek.

"Adia," Deramon said to her, voice deep as these tunnels, rough as his hands and hair and body. "You need sleep. You need food and drink. Come, we will rest. Sister Caela will take over."

The young healer stood by his side, a girl no older than Lyana, her hair braided tight behind her head, her eyes haunted but strong. She held bandages, towels, and vials of herbs and silverweed.

Adia shook her head. "Sister Caela is too young. She is only a healer in training. She... come, sister. Work with me. Help me."

A man wept at her left, crying for his mother. His hands clutched a wound on his stomach; it gaped open, glistening and red, gutting him.

"I want to go home," he whispered, lips pale, eyes deathly. "Please. Please, I want to go home."

Adia realized that he was just a boy, younger than her own children, and she turned to him, to heal him, to pray for him, but Deramon held her fast.

"Let Sister Caela tend to him," he said, voice low, touched by a softness Adia rarely heard in him.

He held Adia's arm, gently but firmly. His hands were bloody and rough, and Adia wanted to break free, but she was so tired. Her head felt so light. His second hand held the small of her back, keeping her standing.

Sister Caela moved forward, lips tight, and knelt by the dying man. With sure fingers, she uncorked her vials, then poured silverweed nectar into the man's mouth.

"Sister," he whispered, shaking now. "Hold me. Hold me as I leave."

The young woman held the dying man, praying for him, until he lay still in her arms. Adia watched, eyes moist, and she shed tears, all those tears she had not cried for hours, maybe days. Her body shook with them.

"Come, my love," Deramon said softly. "You've not slept in three days. Sister Caela will tend to these men for a few hours."

They left the armory, this place of death and blood and screams. They walked down a tunnel, moving between soldiers who ran and survivors who huddled and prayed. Darkness, stench, and whispers of fear swirled around them. Adia's head spun. Three days. Had it truly been that long? Only several lamps lined the tunnels, casting shadows like dark phoenixes. From above came hammering and cries of battle.

"How are the defenses?" she asked.

Deramon clenched his jaw. "Holding. Barely. The Tirans broke through one blockade—the entrance at the temple. Many died. We raised more boulders and are holding them back. For now." He looked at her. "We will not hold out for long, Adia. But we will hold out for the night."

She realized that Deramon too had not slept for three days. His face was haggard. New lines creased his face, and more white streaked his red beard. His clothes and armor were covered in dust and blood.

"You look like you've been to the Abyss and back," Adia said. She shivered, realizing the grimness of the phrase she'd chosen. *No, he had not been to the Abyss, but Lyana now delves into that place. Our daughter. Our sweet, brave light.*

Deramon seemed to read her thoughts. He held her hand tight.

"I trust Lyana," he said, voice a low growl. "She is the finest swordswoman I know. She is wise and strong and fast. If anyone can survive down there, it's our girl. She'll return to us with the Starlit Demon. I promise you."

Adia looked at him, and she wanted to believe, but she saw the fear in his eyes. She knew that he himself did not believe those words.

Lyana will die, she thought. *We will die. Requiem will fall. But if we are doomed, we will go down fighting, and we will not give up until death's grasp pulls us to the stars. Does my Noela wait for me there?*

Survivors covered every corner of these tunnels, sleeping on the floors, standing against the walls, huddling into nooks. Adia made her way between them, until she entered the wine cellar which had become their war room. She and Deramon stepped in, and the chamber seemed so bare to her. This was Requiem's new center of power, but where was their king? He was gone into darkness. Where was their princess? She had flown into the night. Where were Olasar and Orin? Their bodies lay burnt in the inferno of the world.

Who will lead us now? Adia thought. How could this lost, hunted people survive underground with no father or mother? She would be that mother, she knew. She was a priestess, a leader, a healer. *Let me lead and heal as best I can until my king returns.*

Deramon moved about the room and found them mugs of wine, old cheese, and bread, but Adia could not eat nor drink. She huddled on the floor by a casket, pulled her knees to her chest, and wept.

"My love," Deramon whispered. He sat by her, wrapped his arms around her, and held her. She trembled against him. He was all cold steel and rough flesh; he seemed so strong to her, forever her lord and soldier.

"I'm so scared," she whispered to him. "I'm so scared, Deramon. I'm so scared for Bayrin, for Lyana, for everyone." Her tears claimed her.

He kissed her head and held her close, his arms so wide and strong; when she was younger, Adia used to think he could lift the world with those arms.

Finally she slept, held in his embrace, her cheek against his shoulder. She dreamed of gaping wounds and burning flesh and haunted, bloody eyes.

MORI

She could not breathe. She could see nothing but clouds and stinging snow. Her fear gushed through her, she blew fire, her wings beat madly, and it was all she could do to keep flying.

I'm suffocating, she thought. Her head spun and her lungs ached. *I can't breathe. Help, stars, help.*

The shrieks rose behind them, cries like great eagles, like crashing flame, like the pain that still dug through her. The phoenixes soared, chasing suns of fury, crackling and howling.

It's him, Mori thought, eyes burning and wings trembling. The clouds streamed around her. *He flies there as a firebird. The man who... who...*

Once more she lay upon that oak table, staring into Orin's dead eyes. Once more his hand clutched her throat, and his pain drove into her, and her mouse fluttered in her pocket like a heart, until her weight crushed him. Once more Solina stood above her, watching, laughing.

"Mori!" rose a shout, distant and muffled, as from leagues away. "Mori, *fly!*"

She blew fire, clearing the haze, and saw Bayrin flying at her side. His green scales flashed between the clouds, and his tail nudged her, steadying her flight. The fire of the pursuing phoenixes gilded the clouds.

"Mori, fly!" Bayrin shouted. "Faster!"

She flew, neck outstretched, tail straight, wings churning the clouds. She sliced the sky, wind blowing around her.

Orin always said I was the fastest dragon in Requiem.

Bayrin flew at her side, flames seeping between his teeth. Soon he was falling behind, and Mori forced herself to slow down, though all her horrors blazed behind. She could not see them clearly—the clouds still hid them—but their shrieks tore the sky, and their fire blazed like sunset.

If he catches us, he will kill Bayrin, she thought. *But he will not show me that mercy. He will chain me, and rape me again and again, and force me to watch Solina kill Elethor.*

A growl found her throat, surprising her. She had not thought any anger remained in her, only fear, and yet her rage now blazed.

So I will not let him catch me.

"Bayrin!" she cried, flying at this side. "Keep your neck and tail straight! Keep your body smooth! Cut through the wind, like this."

She was slim and small; he was long and gangly. She shot forward, as straight and flat as she could, until she flew before him. The wind flowed around her.

"Fly in my slipstream, Bay!" she shouted. "I'll shield you from the wind."

They drove forward, the shrieks rising behind them, the wind howling. The clouds parted, and Mori found herself under blue sky. Mountains rolled below, their slopes golden, the peaks white with snow. Between them, silver strings of frozen rivers snaked through forests of evergreens. Red light blazed against the landscape, and when Mori turned her head, she saw the phoenixes emerge from the clouds.

There were five. Their flames twisted and rained sparks. Their beaks like molten steel cried in fury. One phoenix led the pack, larger than his brethren, his wings a hundred feet wide. He was Lord Acribus. Mori knew it was him; she knew the cruelty in those white eyes.

"Bayrin, fly!" she shouted.

He was lagging behind, tongue lolling, chest rising and falling. He stared at her, eyes glazed; he had reached the end of his strength.

Again she saw Solina in her mind, scarred face cold, blue eyes staring. Again she heard that voice.

Have your treat, dog.

The fingers dug into her, and she could not breathe, not even scream.

"No," she told herself, wings flapping. *I won't let them catch us.* Her breath ached in her lungs. *Never. Never again.*

She looked around madly, over mountain and river and forest, seeking a place to hide. When she saw the fallen tower, she gasped. It lay upon a mountaintop, jagged and crumbling. These were the ruins of Draco Vallum, she knew. She had always loved books of maps and histories; she had spent so many hours poring over them in the library. She remembered reading about these ruins—the crumbling remains of proud, ancient forts from Requiem's Golden Age before the griffins destroyed the land.

"Bay, fly to the ruins!" Mori shouted into the wind. "Do you see them?"

She slapped him with her tail, nudging him in the right direction. He panted and his eyes rolled, but he managed to nod. The two dragons, gold and green, began diving down toward the mountains. Wind howled and Mori's belly twisted. She swooped so fast that she nearly fainted, and the tug of the world pulled her stomach and skull. She gritted her teeth and kept diving.

"We'll have to fight them in the ruins!" she said.

Memories pounded through her, and she saw herself again in Castellum Luna, slamming the doors shut, racing into darkness.

That is where he killed Orin, hurt me, and spat on my bleeding body. Suddenly Mori wanted to turn away from these ruins. She wanted to fly to the phoenixes, to die in their fire, to fall burnt upon the forests of her homeland. Anything seemed better than hiding underground, waiting for him to shove her down, clutch her throat, grunt above her as she wept.

But she growled and kept swooping.

I'm stronger now. Bayrin is with me, and we both bear swords. This time I will fight him... and I will kill him.

She looked over her shoulder. The phoenixes swooped behind her, talons outstretched. Fire rained from them, and their wings crackled like crashing pyres. Mori stared into his eyes—white orbs of swirling flame. There was so much hatred there. Mori had never known such hatred and madness could exist. Though the phoenixes drenched the world with searing heat, she felt cold.

"Mori, come on!" Bayrin shouted.

The dragons were near the ruins now. Little remained of Draco Vallum, this old fortress of fallen heroes. Only one wall still stood, craggy like the gums of an old stone giant. The rest of the fortress lay as fallen bricks. Mori discerned half of an archway leading into a cellar, and she dived toward it.

"We'll kill them in shadow," she shouted and swooped.

The ruins rushed up to meet her. She landed, claws digging into snow. At once she shifted, becoming a girl again, and drew her sword. She ran, blade in hand, and leaped through the archway. She found herself upon a staircase plunging underground.

"Bayrin, in here!"

She turned to see him land in the snow outside. The lanky green dragon shifted, and Bayrin ran forward in human form, drawing his sword. He leaped onto the staircase to join her.

Mori had time to see the phoenixes land too, melting the snow, before she turned and ran downstairs into darkness.

The steps were narrow and craggy. She tripped, pitched forward, and just barely righted herself and kept running. Bayrin ran behind her, boots thudding and scabbard banging against the walls. He cursed as he ran, such foul words that Mori had never heard. She cursed too, repeating words she had never dreamed a princess would utter.

Soon she heard other voices—calling for her blood, calling for her flesh. When she glanced over her shoulder, she saw the Tirans, and she saw *him*.

In human forms they were no less frightening than phoenixes. The Tiran soldiers wore armor darkened with soot, and their sabres were bloody. Her tormentor walked at their lead, the Lord Acribus, his face like beaten leather and his eyes cruel, blue chips. He opened his mouth, revealing his yellow teeth, and his tongue licked his lips, serpentine.

"Mori!" he called to her. He grinned like a rabid animal, drooling. "Are you ready for more, weredragon? Are you ready to scream?"

Fear pounded through Mori, nearly freezing her. Her heart thudded, tears leaped into her eyes, and she whimpered. But then she saw that his arm was bandaged. She had cut him there with Orin's dagger. *He can be hurt. He's just a man now, not a phoenix, not a demon, and I can kill him.*

She and Bayrin reached the end of the staircase. They found themselves in a dusty, ancient cellar, too narrow for shifting into a dragon or phoenix. Rusted blades lay upon the floor between fallen bricks, the wood and leather of their hilts rotted away. The back of the chamber lay in shadow. Mori raced into the darkness, seeking a tunnel, a doorway, somewhere to flee, but found herself facing a brick wall.

She spun toward the Tirans, her back to the wall. Bayrin stood by her, panting and holding his sword before him.

"Bayrin," Mori whispered. She reached out and clutched his hand. "Bayrin, we will fight them."

He nodded and spoke with a choked voice. "Be brave, Mori. I won't let them hurt you."

At that moment, she loved him—loved him like she loved Orin, her fallen hero, like she loved Elethor, her new king. Bayrin was no warrior, she knew. To her he'd always been a fool, a jokester, Elethor's gangly friend whom she always thought looked like a grasshopper. Yet now he stood by her, sword raised, sworn to defend her... and in the darkness of this chamber and her fears, she loved him.

Acribus came walking toward them, a half snarl, half smile on his lips. His firegem blazed around his neck, painting his face red. Drool dripped down his chin. He was tall, even taller than Bayrin, and twice as wide. He cracked his knuckles and stripped Mori naked with

119

his eyes. His tongue licked his chops, dropping as far as his chin. Lust for her body and blood filled his eyes.

"Men," he said to his four companions. "Kill the boy. Keep the girl alive. We'll have our fun with her."

The four soldiers eyed her, no less hunger in their eyes, and raised their swords. They approached Bayrin, their firegems crackling; in the flickering light, they looked like demons of shadow and fire.

Mori raised her sword and prayed.

BAYRIN

Cold sweat washed him, and his fingers shook, but he forced himself to grin—a terrified, trembling grin.

"So, dear friends." He forced the words through stiff lips. "Thank you so much for visiting Requiem. We do love visitors up here in the north. I hope you enjoyed our tour, but now we really must be on our way."

The Tirans kept advancing toward him, sabres raised. They bared their teeth. Their faces became demonic masks in the light of the firegems.

Bayrin gulped, his own sword raised. His limbs throbbed. His every instinct called for him to retreat into the corner, to press his back against the wall, to move as far as he could from these men—even if that meant retreating only a foot. He forced himself to step forward instead, feet numb. With his left hand, he pushed Mori behind him, shielding her with his body.

Stars, he thought. What had that rabid, leathery-faced Acribus meant? *Are you ready for more, weredragon?* he had asked. Nausea filled Bayrin. Had he meant that... had this man met Mori before... and hurt her? Even now the Tiran eyed her with lust, that white tongue of his licking his lips and dripping drool.

"Well," he said to the five Tiran soldiers. He forced a laugh, sweat dripping down his forehead. "I suppose now is the time that you try to stab me, and I try to stab you, and swords clang and blood pours. I do love swordplay—I'm quite good at it too—but I suppose I'll show some mercy, and I'll offer you a chance to settle this over a nice game of dice. What do you say?"

The Tirans laughed.

One lashed his sword at him.

Bayrin parried, and steel clanged, and he couldn't help but yelp. That drew more laughter from the Tirans. They formed a semicircle around him, like vultures over prey.

His heart hammered so powerfully, Bayrin thought it would burst from his mouth. His belly roiled. How had he come to this? He was no warrior like his father. He knew no swordplay like his sister. He... he was only Bayrin the prankster, the fool, the young man nobody expected anything of. And yet here he was, in a dark dungeon, defending his princess against five soldiers.

A Tiran swiped his sabre, and Bayrin parried madly, holding his sword with two hands. The Tirans laughed again, and Bayrin realized they were toying with him. They knew he was no fighter.

"The boy wants to play dice!" one said and laughed, a hoarse sound, almost inhuman. "Maybe we'll carve dice from his bones."

His comrades laughed, and one swung his sabre so fast, Bayrin could not parry. The blade sliced his shoulder, blood sprayed, and Mori screamed.

"We'll play with his bones after we play with the girl," said another Tiran, voice a deep growl. "I haven't had a girl since we left home."

Two more swords flew. Bayrin parried left and right. He thrust his weapon, trying to kill a man, but the Tiran parried and nearly yanked the sword from Bayrin's hand.

None of this should have happened, he thought. The scrolls should have taken them to safety. They should have been on their way to find the Moondisk now. It should have been King Olasar fighting, or Prince Orin, or...

He gritted his teeth. *But they're dead, Bay. They're dead, and you're alive, so man up and defend your princess.*

With a wordless cry, he thrust his blade at Lord Acribus.

The Tiran swung his sword, blocking the blow. His left hand drove forward, and his fist slammed into Bayrin's face.

"Bayrin!" Mori screamed behind him.

White light flooded him. He fell back, hit Mori, and she screamed. He swung his sword blindly, pain suffusing him. A blade bit his left arm, and a chill washed him. Another blade flashed, and Bayrin raised his sword, blocking most of the blow. But the sabre still sliced along his arm, cutting his sleeve and skin. Another sword slashed. Bayrin parried and tripped on a fallen brick. He fell down hard, knocking the breath out of him.

He spat out a glob of blood, coughed, and said, "Do you..." He coughed again. "Do you give up yet?"

The Tirans stared silently for a moment, then laughed—cruel laughter like crashing stones. Bayrin chuckled through the blood in his mouth. He nodded, raised his eyebrows, and laughed harder until the Tirans' laughter grew too. *This is what I've always known how to do... make people laugh.* As his bloody laughter roared, he grabbed the fallen brick and hurled it.

It smashed into Acribus's firegem.

The laughter died when the gem shattered. Acribus howled. Fire burst from the shattered gem like demons escaping a tomb. It raced across him, until Acribus blazed, a creature of fire.

He's turning into a phoenix, here, underground, Bayrin thought. He leaped to his feet and grabbed Mori's hand.

"Come on, Mori!" he screamed. "Run!"

He pulled her forward, sword swinging. Fire blazed. He could barely see. He knocked aside a Tiran's sword, plowed forward, and drove his shoulder into the man. The soldier crashed down, flames roared, and Bayrin and Mori whipped around him.

Firelight filled the chamber. Behind Bayrin, a phoenix shriek rose, deafening. It was a small chamber; the phoenix would be crushed, he knew. It would burn everything alive inside. He leaped onto the staircase. He ran, pulling Mori behind him.

"Mori, run, faster!" he shouted.

Smoke and flames blasted their backs. They raced upstairs into the fort's courtyard. Tirans shouted and cursed behind them, running upstairs too.

Bayrin spun around and shoved Mori aside. He shifted into a dragon, so fast that his head spun, and blew a jet of fire into the dungeon.

His flames roared, spinning and blazing down the stairway. Tiran soldiers burned and fell back, dragonfire before them, phoenix fire in the dungeon behind. They screamed. Their screams filled Bayrin's ears, cries of such agony, that he knew he would forever hear them. He kept blowing fire. He could make out one Tiran, his skin bubbling, his flesh burning away, until the blackened thing fell back into the inferno and vanished in fire.

"Bayrin, fly!" Mori cried. She shifted into a dragon and panted. Firelight blazed against her golden scales. "Acribus is a phoenix down there, he's still alive!"

Bayrin let his flames die. He growled, spun, and slammed his tail against the entrance to the dungeon. The crumbly archway collapsed, raining stones. He slammed his tail again, shoving down more bricks and dirt.

"So we'll bury the bastard," he said. "Help me."

The slim golden dragon trembled but began lashing her own tail and claws, shoving dirt and stones into the dungeon. Soon the fire was contained. Smoke rose between cracks and fissures. Inside the tomb, the phoenix was screeching.

Bayrin surveyed the ruins, seeking more bricks. He found only a few pieces of shattered columns. He began shoving them. With

Mori's help, he placed them over the dungeon. The phoenix inside was slamming against the blocked entrance, and the bricks and stones jostled. Searing heat rose from below, almost intolerable against his claws.

"This won't hold him for long," he said and heard the grimness in his voice. "Let's get out of here."

The two dragons took flight. They soared over the ruins, smoke and heat rising around them. They righted themselves and began flying north, the scent of fire in their nostrils. The frozen valleys of pines blurred beneath them. The shrieks of the phoenix, and the screams of the burning men, still echoed in Bayrin's ears. Most of all, he kept seeing Acribus lick his chops and heard the man's voice again: *Are you ready for more, weredragon?*

Bayrin growled, belly cold. He began to descend toward the evergreens.

"Bayrin, fly, come on!" Mori cried above him. "We have to fly fast before he escapes."

Bayrin shook his head. Fire caressed the inside of his mouth.

"We're not flying anymore," he said. He spiraled down toward a valley. "We're too easy to spot in the air. We're a beacon up there. Tirans might still crawl this land. We go on foot from here."

He crashed between branches and landed by a frozen stream. His claws dug into snow, and when he shifted into human form, he shivered. The pines creaked in the wind and sap covered him. Blood dampened his clothes and his wounds blazed. He sniffed the air and could still smell the phoenix fire, and when he looked south, he saw a plume of smoke rising between the trees.

Golden scales glimmered and Mori landed by him. She shifted into human form and stood trembling, hugging herself. She stared at him, her eyes huge and haunted, and for a moment, Bayrin could only stare at her. So much pain lived in those gray eyes that his chest ached.

At home, he always knew what to say—he could spout countless jokes, bawdy lyrics, taunting puns. Now he was speechless. He took three steps toward her, reached out his arms, and embraced her. She flinched and trembled like a bird caught in his palm, but soon her trembling eased and she laid her head against his chest.

"Oh Mori," he said softly, remembering those rabid teeth, that lolling tongue, those lustful eyes. "Did..."

Did he hurt you? he wanted to ask. *What did he do to you?* But the words caught in his throat. He feared that if he spoke them, her heart would shatter. So he only held her, kissed her forehead, and smoothed her hair.

"You did well," he said instead. "But damn it, Mors, you make me look bad! Flying fast like that... I'm going to tie some weights onto you next time so I can keep up."

A soft smile touched her lips, and Bayrin couldn't help it. He grinned, a huge grin that made his cheeks hurt. It was the first time he'd seen her smile since the Tiran invasion.

Her eyes were lowered. She spoke, her voice so soft, he could barely hear.

"I bet I walk faster than you too."

He snorted. "No way. You walk like a turtle, I've seen it."

Still staring at her feet, she whispered, "You walk like a snail."

"Oh that does it!" he said, still holding her. Mockingly, he pushed her back and started stomping through the snow. "It's a race, turtle girl. See if you can catch up."

The Crescent Isle lay countless leagues away. They walked between the trees, smoke and phoenix screeches rising behind them.

ELETHOR

He ran down the tunnel, eyes stinging, heart pounding, searching for
Lyana in the darkness. He saw nothing but black mist, craggy walls,
and shadows. His boots thudded against soft ground, as if running
over moss. *Or over corpses*, he thought.

"Lyana!" he cried, and his voice echoed, taunting him, twisting
through endless caverns. His heartbeat pounded in his ears, and his
clothes clung to him, damp with sweat.

The image still burned against his eyes—Nedath the Guardian, a
rotting girl with the body of a centipede, lifting Lyana in her arms.
Licking her. Biting her. Elethor had tried to stop the demon, but
Nedath moved too quickly. She had vanished into the bowels of the
Abyss with her meal—with Lyana.

"Lyana!" he called again, and again his voice echoed like a
hundred ghosts. Was she still alive?

As he ran, shadows swirled. Feet clattered all around. He could
not tell if they moved near him or echoed from a distance. Cobwebs
hung from the ceiling, slapping against him.

"Elllethorrrrr..."

The voice rose ahead, high-pitched as wind between canyons,
mocking him. Laughter rolled.

"Nedath, come and face your king!" he cried again. "Bring back
Lyana or I will kill you."

Somewhere ahead, Nedath laughed and sang. Her voice echoed
from countless tunnels, a symphony of chaos. "Again the humans
run... again their sweet stench rises... again Nedath shall feed!"

Elethor ran, slapping cobwebs aside, trying to find the demon.
The tunnels branched, a labyrinth of them. Whenever he thought he
heard footsteps or laughter, he headed that way, but then heard the
sounds from behind him.

The cobwebs flapped against him, heavy and thick. Moans
and pleading whispers rose from them. Elethor raised his lamp... and
felt nausea swell.

Some cobwebs held severed arms with fingers that still moved.
Others held ruined bodies stripped down to bones; the spines ended
with withered heads whose mouths gasped, whose eyes spun, whose
voices begged for death.

"Boy... boy, are you a skeley, are you skeley yet?" whispered one creature, an upside down, mummified thing, no thicker than Elethor's arm, its head shrunken and its lips smacking, its gums toothless. "Boy, it's skeley good, do you think?"

Elethor screamed and shoved past the hanging, mummified creatures. They gasped around him, eyes spinning and fingers twitching, swinging wildly on the cobwebs that bound them. *Stars, what are these things?* Elethor's head spun and he tasted bile. *Were they humans once? Will Nedath turn Lyana into one of them?*

In the shadows, the demon's laughter rolled.

"Poor poor humans, yes, Nedath. See how they cower! See how their fear fills the air, so sweet. Soon they will rot, and shrink, and hang, and lick, and smack, and whisper, and weep, and beg, and we will eat them slowly, yes Nedath, we will suck their juices dry, and the marrow from their bones, and their eyeballs, and their sweet innards, as they rot, and shrink, and hang, and..."

"Silence!" Elethor shouted, spinning around, seeking her, seeing only mist and cobwebs. He wanted to rage, to find this creature and fight, to be strong and proud and a warrior like Orin. But he felt close to tears. His legs shook. He gritted his teeth, and would have crumbled and wept had Lyana not needed him. Around him the withered, hanging creatures swung on their cobwebs, sucking the air and whispering madness.

Be strong, Elethor told himself. *For Lyana. You must find her. You can't let her turn into one of these hanging things.*

"Nedath!" he shouted, hoarse, close to panic. He swung his sword, cutting cobwebs. "Nedath, come and face me!"

Mist rose, cobwebs parted, and the demon emerged.

She was more hideous than Elethor remembered. Her centipede body rose, each segment bristling with black fur. Mounted atop the last segment, the torso, arms, and head of the rotting girl were slick with drool and blood. The girl's mouth opened, revealing chewed flesh. With a screech, she vomited, spraying meat and broken bones and fingers.

"Elethor!" she screamed, a sound that shook the tunnels. "King Elethor of Requiem, fell lord of lizards!"

With a shout, Elethor swung his sword.

The blade sliced Nedath's top half, cutting into the rotten girl's belly. Snakes spilled like entrails, bloody and hissing.

Nedath screeched, a sound like shattering bones. Cobwebs tore and the bodies within them burst, spraying white ooze.

Elethor swung his sword again, aiming for Nedath's head, the head of a rotting girl. The demon raised her arm, and the blade halved her hand, cutting down to the wrist. Her spider legs lashed. Two slammed into Elethor, cutting him, shoving him down. He struggled to rise, but more legs hit him.

Nedath leaned over him, snarling. Drool dripped down her chin. Her eyes shed blood. Three tongues slipped from her mouth, fell onto Elethor, and squirmed across him like snakes. Around them, the hanging creatures twisted and smacked their withered, pursed lips, gasping for air and mumbling.

"The numbers don't line, the numbers don't line, they say, I heard them line it!" said one creature, a spine with clinging skin, its head a mere mouth with two eyeballs on stalks.

"Into my lair, boy, into my lair, we will drink somebody, boy, in here I say, listen, yes," said another, a twisting stem of a thing, its head a wilting cloth bound in iron wire.

They spun around him and Elethor screamed. He swung his blade, cutting at Nedath, but she pinned him down with her legs. She laughed, blood bubbling in her mouth.

"The new Boy King of Requiem," said the demon, voice twisting and rising. "You will be king of my withered things, and you will hurt more than them all."

He drove his fist up and shattered her face. Her skull cracked and cockroaches fled from it, the insects' faces almost human. Nedath laughed. She leaned down and bit Elethor's shoulder, and pain blazed—more pain than he'd ever felt. He writhed and screamed.

Darkness spread across his eyes, closing in until the world was black, and all pain dulled to throbbing cold. In the shadows he saw blue eyes, cruel and mocking, lips that kissed him, a golden face.

"Solina," he whispered hoarsely.

She leaned over him, her naked body pressed against him, and kissed him with the kisses of her mouth, and he ran his fingers through her hair of molten gold. She whispered into his ear, laughing softly, and he held her close.

"I love you, El," she whispered and laughed. "My secret prince."

He wept, clinging to her. "Don't leave, Solina, don't leave, stay here, don't go into fire, don't go into fire..."

But she burned. She burned atop him, screaming, her flesh peeling and melting, until he saw her skull, and still she screamed and clung to him.

No, he thought, shaking. *No, I can't let her burn. I can't let this happen. I can't turn into one of these things, these hanging twisting things of memory and pain and madness.*

He shouted Solina's name as he drove his blade upward.

Ferus, his sword forged in dragonfire, shone with starlight. It pierced through the burning apparition of his love. Blazing, it drove into the rotting, mad Guardian of the Abyss. With the howl of collapsing stars, the steel blazed into darkness, and Nedath howled too, and the world seemed to explode.

The demon's head shattered. Fragments of bone and gore flew. Behind her, her snaking body of black, furry segments burst, showering the tunnel with blood. Her scream echoed and the hanging things swung, eyes spinning and mouths gasping.

Elethor rose to his feet, breathing raggedly. He looked around him. It looked like the innards of a dead whale. Blood and entrails covered the tunnel. His lamp had fallen and set fire to cobwebs. He stamped out the flames, lifted the lamp, and surveyed the darkness.

"Lyana!" he shouted.

The withered bodies cackled around him, swinging on the cobwebs. They cried out in a mocking cacophony. "Lyana! Lyana! Lyana!"

Elethor began shoving his way between them, knocking them aside. They careened around him, some only spines and skin, others pale creatures whose hearts beat red behind transparent skin. Was Lyana hanging here too? Had she become one of them?

"Lyana, answer me!" he cried. His eyes stung. Stars, he couldn't leave her here. He couldn't let her become a creature. "Lyana!"

Coughing sounded in the distance. A muffled voice cried out. "Elethor!"

His heart leaped. He ran, boots sucking at blood, sword swinging at hanging creatures. His lamp swung and shadows swirled. Down a tunnel and around a bend, he saw a figure cloaked in webs, hanging from the ceiling.

"Lyana!"

Tears stung his eyes. He ran to her and began tearing the cobwebs off. She hung upside down, coughing and blinking. He kept ripping off webs, not knowing what he'd find. Would her body be withered, her skin clinging to bones, her heart beating behind clear skin? When the cobwebs were torn and he pulled her free, he breathed in relief. Blood covered her armor, and black ooze covered her face, but she was whole. Her drawn sword clattered to the floor.

"Lyana, talk to me, are you all right?" He wiped her face, revealing her pale skin.

She coughed, gasped for breath, looked at him silently... then crashed into his embrace. She clung to him.

"I... saw him," she whispered. "I saw Orin. He was here, Elethor!" She looked at him pleadingly. "He was hanging here from the webs, and I could see his spine, and his head looked like, like... it was just a flat piece of leather, but his eyes moved."

"It was a dream, Lyana," he said softly. He picked webs from her hair. "I saw Solina too. We see the ones we love here, I think."

She gulped and lifted her sword. Blade raised, she looked around her: at the blood on the walls, at the creatures who still hung and stared at them, at the torn segments of Nedath's body. With a sigh, she closed her eyes and leaned her head against Elethor's chest.

"Thank you," she whispered. "You killed the guardian. You did what I could not."

They stood silently for long moments, holding each other in the darkness. Lyana's mane of curls tickled Elethor's nose, and as he held her, he too thought of Orin. In the old days, some claimed that the souls of dead sinners landed in this place, while the pious glowed among the stars.

Elethor clenched his jaw. *No. Orin was a hero. A noble son of Requiem. He dines now in our starlit halls, and his soul will never see this cursed place.*

"Elethor, look!" Lyana said. She gasped and fear filled her eyes. Slowly, she stepped away from him and raised her left hand. Her fingertips were gray and withered, thinned to sticks.

Elethor's stomach churned. Cold sweat dripped down his back. He forced his fear down and spoke through a tight throat. "Adia can heal them, Lyana. She is a great healer."

Her chest rose and fell as she panted. "Stars, Elethor, stars, am... am I turning into one of them?" She gestured around her at the chamber. The shrunken, withered creatures snorted and cackled and licked their toothless gums.

"No," Elethor said and clenched his fists. "Nedath is dead now. She can no longer harm you. And your mother will heal your fingertips, I promise you." He reached out, held her good hand, and squeezed it. "Now come, Lyana. We go find the Starlit Demon. The faster we leave the Abyss, the better."

She nodded and wiped a tear off her cheek.

"Let's go," she said and raised her sword. "We delve deeper... and I pray that the worst is behind us."

As they walked deeper into the darkness, Elethor prayed too. But he knew in the pit of his stomach: The worst still lay ahead.

SOLINA

With a trembling heart and the whispers of old pain, she walked toward his home.

Solina had told herself she would be strong this day. She was a queen of Tiranor, a great warrior clad in steel and gold. Her twin blades were sharp, her army was vast, her power endless. She was hardened by fire, then by sand, finally by blood. She had not thought this place could hurt her.

Yet some pain drove past armor, and some memories haunted even great queens of cruel desert lands. As Solina walked toward Elethor's old home upon the hill, that pain clutched her heart and twisted.

It was a small home for a prince—a narrow hall, its walls lined with columns, their capitals shaped as dragons. It rose upon a hill where grass had once rustled, pines rose like sentinels, and birds always sang. Solina remembered the old smell of the place, the sweetness of lilac in the gardens, the wine that forever poured here, the musk of him as they made love between these walls. Now the grass was burnt, the pines fallen, and she only smelled smoke and blood. The columns still stood, but while they were once snowy white, soot now stained them.

"This was a good place," Solina whispered as she walked uphill. "This was the only place we found peace, away from the court of the cruel king."

She stepped between columns toward the hall's doors. Once carved with dragons and stars, they were now charred and cracked; the phoenix fire had reached even this place, the doors to her chamber of old secrets. When she shoved them, the doors opened, showering ash. Solina stepped inside, heart like a bird caught in her ribcage.

She saw the chambers as they had been, lush with flowers from the gardens, warm with pillows and divans, sweet with the secrets of forbidden love. She would lie naked here by his side, holding him, and they would talk and kiss and laugh until dawn rose. She remembered the wooden turtle with emerald eyes he had carved her, and his songbirds in their golden cage, and the tears she cried here when the pain of exile was too strong.

The room now lay in ruin. The fire had burned those pillows, divans, and flowers. All that remained were seven marble statues, life-sized, and Solina's breath caught.

They were her.

She stepped toward one, tears stinging her eyes, and touched its cheek. The statue stared back, a girl blossoming into womanhood, pure and beautiful, her eyes soft and her lips smiling. She was draped in cascading robes that revealed her left breast, and her hands were held out as in offering.

"Oh, Elethor," she whispered.

He had not forgotten. He still loved her, had missed her like she missed him, and suddenly Solina was trembling. She wanted those days back, if only for a respite from this pain and fire. She wanted to see the wooden turtle again, and hear the birds sing, and lie with him and kiss him with all those forbidden kisses.

She looked away.

"But those days are gone," she said and clenched her fists. "I was an exile then. I was afraid. I was weak. I was burned. I returned to my southern land, and now I come here as a queen."

Sudden rage exploded in her. Who was that smiling, beautiful woman carved of marble? That was not her. Not anymore. The dragons had burned her, ruined her beauty, scarred her face and soul. With a snarl, Solina drew her dagger and pulled it down the statue's face. The marble chipped, and she kept hacking at it, until a rut halved the statue's face.

"There," Solina said and touched the scar that rent her own face. "Now you are Solina of Tiranor, burned with fire, seeking revenge."

She moved between the other statues, hacking at them, until scars snaked down their faces, torsos, and legs. She would allow no more memories of pureness to fill this chamber. Those memories were lies.

"My power is truth," she whispered.

She opened her leather pack and looked inside. Nestled between rations, sharpening stones, and bandages lay a box carved of olive wood, a foot long and half as wide. Golden runes of suns and flames lined the wood, twisting and glowing. When Solina touched the box, it nearly seared her hand. The weapons within buzzed as if begging for release.

"Soon your fire will be unleashed," Solina whispered. With an angry jerk, she sealed her pack, spun around, and marched out of

Elethor's house. She walked downhill between charred pines and birches, jaw clenched, refusing to look back. She would never return.

"I will scar you too, Elethor," she whispered as ash blew around her boots and phoenixes shrieked in the sky. "I will destroy all memories of this place. I will fill it with only my strength and majesty."

She made her way through the ruined city of Nova Vita. The birches still smoldered, charred sticks rising from mounds of ash. The palace rose ahead, its proud columns blackened, its lush gardens now crackling with scattered flames. The city amphitheater dipped into a hillside, a bowl cut into the earth, its tiers of seats holding charred bones, its stage splashed with blood. A hill of bodies burned between the columns of a temple, an offering of death for the cruel stars of Requiem.

No more weredragons filled this place—their vile, shapeshifting bodies now cowered underground. Her troops of Tiranor lined the roads, tall and proud men and women, their skin golden and pure, their hair shimmering platinum, their eyes sapphire jewels. They were as noble a race as weredragons were foul. Even as smoke rose across the city, their armor glimmered, and the firegems around their necks cast ten thousand lights. They stood with swords drawn, the blades curved like the beaks of sacred ibises, their pommels carved as sunbursts. Above them a hundred phoenixes circled in patrol of the skies. Ash rained and smoke rose in pillars.

Solina called out as she walked. "Sandfire Phalanx, fall in behind me! Jade Phalanx, follow! Deserthawk, follow!"

Her troops slammed blades against shields and cried for blood. They marched down the road behind her, boots thudding as one. As they moved between the ruins, Solina summoned more troops, and soon a thousand marched behind her. A snarling grin twisted her lips.

"It is time," she said, "for a fire in the deep."

This would be no long siege. She would not wait here for moons, even years, until the weredragons' food and water dwindled. She would break through their defenses. She would burn them all, and her men would take their women, and her blades would cut her old love.

"For your glory, Sun God," she whispered and looked to the heavens. The sun burned there behind smoke and cloud; it was smaller here in the north, and colder, but Solina would bring all its wrath to this place. She would serve her lord with the flames he'd given her. Her hand clutched the firegem around her neck and its heat shot through her, rivers of flame in her veins.

Soon they reached the tunnel entrance, where a hundred Tirans stood with drawn steel. The archway rose around the darkness, stained with fire and blood. The stairs plunged into shadow.

Elethor waits down there.

Lord Deramon had raised barricades of stone, sealing her outside. He would find that no rock could face the flame of Tiranor.

As her troops stood behind her, swords raised, Solina opened her pack. Delicately, as if handling a holy artifact, Solina withdrew the long box of olive wood. It thrummed and its runes blazed, nearly blinding her.

She whispered a prayer to the Sun God. "May your light forever cast out the darkness. May your fire forever burn out the cold."

She caught her breath and opened the box.

Six clay balls lay there, placed into holes lined with cloth. They nearly burned her hand when she touched them. Decorative red lines, shaped as flames, ran across them.

"Tiran Fire," she whispered. A hungry smile touched her lips.

Her priests had labored for moons to produce these weapons. Each clay container had taken many nights of work and prayer. One alone could destroy a phalanx of troops. Six would destroy Requiem.

She raised the box over her head, ignoring the heat that ran down her arms, and faced her troops. Firelight blazed in their eyes.

"For the glory of the Sun God!" she called. "We cast out the darkness!"

Her troops howled and waved their weapons. Their roar shook the ground. Snarling, Solina turned back toward the tunnel, thrust the box forward, and sent the six balls of Tiran Fire tumbling into darkness.

She stood facing the stairway, panting, teeth bared. She let the empty wooden box thud to the ground. The clay balls clanked down the stairs, and Solina snarled and waited... one breath, two, three...

An explosion rocked the city.

Fire and wind blasted from the darkness, and Solina turned aside, gritting her teeth. Dust flew and coated her. Rocks fell. The ground shook beneath her boots. The flames roared so loudly she could hear nothing else.

Soon she heard more sounds—screams from below.

A smile spread across her face, becoming a grin.

When the dust settled, she found the staircase coated with debris, some stained with blood. Black lines stretched along the walls.

Solina drew her twin blades, Aknur and Raem, and the golden runes upon them blazed. She would lead the charge.

"For the Sun God!" she shouted. "And for Tiranor!"

Her army answered the call behind her, shouting so loudly, the ruins shook. "For the Sun God! For Tiranor! For Queen Solina!"

Solina charged into the darkness with her light and heat. She raced down stairs covered with dust and rock. Her men charged behind her, shouting for sun and glory. The walls rushed at her sides, stained with blood and ash and weredragon stench. Her blades blazed like the sun, casting out the shadows.

This is my purpose, Solina thought with a snarl. *This is my glory. I will banish the darkness of reptiles with my lord's light.*

At the bottom of the staircase, the barricade Deramon had raised was gone. The boulders were smashed to shards. Grooves dug into the walls. Blood, dust, and chunks of flesh covered everything. Blades raised, Solina stepped over the debris... and crashed against an army of weredragons.

Dozens of them filled the darkness, thrusting their straight, heavy blades of the north. The stains of fire and blood coated them. Stubble covered their faces and pain filled their eyes. They were desperate men, pushed into a corner, and wild; but Solina was glorious and strong and she would defeat them.

Her twin sabres lashed. Aknur, her left blade of nightfire, parried a blow from a weredragon's sword. Raem, her right blade of dawn, sliced into a man's neck. Blood sprayed like sunrise. Her troops roared behind her and burst into the chamber, sabres clashed against longswords, blood spilled, men fell. They fought over the bodies of the fallen, boots snapping bones and crushing faces.

She fought for hours. Aknur and Raem spun like disks of light. Blood coated her armor when she finally drove into the deeper chambers, where tunnels snaked wide and tall, lined with doors. The women and children of Requiem cowered here, wailing. They began to flee, a mad rout into darkness.

"Kill the reptiles!" Solina cried hoarsely. "Kill them all."

She marched through the tunnels, swinging her blades. Soldiers still hacked at her. A child ran to her left, wailing. Solina swung Aknur and cut him down. More soldiers raced up from the darkness, blades lashing. She parried and thrust, shedding their blood upon the fleeing survivors.

"Solina of Tiranor!" howled a deep voice, and Lord Deramon himself marched toward her. He bore a sword in one hand, an axe in the other. His armor was thick, his arms wide, his face cold.

She smiled at him and raised her sabres in salute. "Come die at my feet."

They circled each other, blades raised, and blood pounded in Solina's ears. It was Deramon who had caught her making love to Elethor. It was Deramon who had told her secrets to the king—who had her burned, exiled, torn apart from her lover. It was Deramon who would now die in pain and fear.

Her sabres lashed. He parried. His axe flew and she blocked, riposted, shouted in rage. Steel rang and pain thrust up her arms. Men fought around them, but Solina would not remove her eyes from her foe. He was a tall, broad man—almost twice her size—and his blades were heavier than hers. But she was younger and faster. Aknur blocked a thrust of his sword, and Raem, her blade of dawn, slammed against his breastplate.

Steel dented and Deramon grunted. His axe thrust, and Solina fell to one knee as she parried. Aknur, blade of nightfire, clanged against his axe. Raem swung against his leg, steel sparked against steel, and Deramon grunted. She leaped up and swung both blades down.

He blocked one. The other hit his shoulder, cleaving his pauldron, and blood seeped.

She lashed again at once. This was her chance to slay him. But despite his wound, he did not miss a step of the dance. His sword rose, blocked her blow, and his axe slammed against her breastplate.

Steel bent. Pain blazed. She gasped for breath and found none. His sword clanged against her pauldron, and she thought her arm would dislocate. She fell, armor dented, by the body of the child she'd slain.

Deramon stood above her and stared down, eyes cold, blood seeping. A lesser warrior might have given her some last words, spoken some poetry of farewell or justice. Deramon wasted no time on dramatic partings; he lusted for nothing more than the kill itself. His axe swung down.

On her knees, Solina raised her blades and crossed them. The axe slammed down, chipping Aknur and shooting pain down her arms. Keeping Raem raised, Solina dropped Aknur, snarled, and grabbed the dead child's hair. She tugged the head up and tossed the small, lacerated body at Deramon.

The child slammed against him, and Deramon fell back a step. Solina leaped up, swung her blade, and hit Deramon's helmet. He staggered.

She would have killed him then. She would have ended this. Yet Deramon had no honor; he would not even duel her to the death.

Five of his men rushed forward from the shadows, blades lashing. With a snarl, Solina grabbed the fallen Aknur, parried a blow, and stepped under an archway. Here she could slay them one by one.

Men lashed at her. Moans and wails rose behind her. Solina glanced at the reflection in her blades. A wild smile tingled across her face. *Perfect.*

As men thrust blades at her, Solina retreated through the archway and into the chamber of wails. She found herself fighting in Requiem's old armory, now a hospital crowded with dying weredragons. They lay around her on the floor, bandaged, burnt, some with severed limbs, others with gaping wounds. A hundred filled this place. A single healer, a young woman with a stern braid of dark hair, huddled over the wounded.

Soldiers of Requiem came spilling into the chamber, and Solina fought alone. The hospital was wide, fifty feet deep, its ceiling twenty feet tall. She licked her lips. *It is large enough. It is time for fire.*

She parried a blow, clutched the firegem around her neck, and smiled.

She summoned her lord's gift.

At once, she burst into flames. They raced across her, scorching, intoxicating. She reached out her arms, and flaming feathers grew from them. She howled, and her voice became the shriek of an eagle. Men cowered before her. The wounded burst into flame. The young healer screamed and ran, a living torch. Solina grew in size until she was a great phoenix, dragon-sized, an inferno of flame and smoke and wind.

The hundred wounded weredragons blazed. A few were well enough to run, but none made it to the doors. They fell, burning into charred bones. The fire filled the chamber until it was a furnace, a pyre for her glory. The weredragons at the door howled. Some brought crossbows but their darts only passed through her flames, and Solina screeched, a great bird of sunfire.

She was a queen. She was a goddess. Soon she would destroy these tunnels, find her cowering Elethor, and she would burn him too until he screamed and begged and knew her glory.

MORI

She huddled under the trees, cloak pulled over her, and prayed.

"Please, stars, please *please* don't let him see us, please stars, send him away."

Above in the clouds, the phoenix dived and shrieked. Its wake of fire spread behind it like a comet's tail. Mori pushed herself against the tree, as close as she could. Bayrin huddled at her side, also covered in cloak and hood. They had strung branches and leaves over their cloaks, but would that fool the phoenix? It circled the veiled sun, crackling.

Mori did not know if Acribus could still take human form. Bayrin had smashed that crystal he wore around his neck, the one with the fire inside. She knew little of southern magic, but thought that the firegem let the Tirans turn into phoenixes. Solina had worn one too, which she never had back in those days in Requiem. With his firegem smashed, could he still turn into a man? A man who could choke her with cracked hands, tear off her clothes, thrust into her with such blazing pain that she wanted to die? Or would he remain forever a phoenix, a questing demon of fire that would forever hunt her?

"Bayrin," she whispered. She wanted to ask him about the firegem, but he hushed her.

They huddled together, frozen in the cold. The wind cut through their cloaks, icy but scented of fire. It seemed ages before the phoenix turned east and flew away, and its shrieks faded in the distance. Mori shivered and rose to her feet. She clasped the hilt of her sword, that sword she had never wielded in battle, and watched the wake of fire disperse above.

Bayrin too stood up. He spat. "Good riddance. I thought the damn bird would never fly away. Peskier than bees in your underpants, these phoenixes are." He squinted and watched the skies for a while. "We might be fine for flying soon. The phoenix is heading east, and we're going north."

"No!" Mori clutched his sleeve. "Please, Bayrin, please don't make me fly. He'll see us. I know he will. Phoenix eyes are sharp, and if we fly, he'll see us, and he'll burn us." She trembled and tugged on his cloak, as if that could convince him. "Please, Bayrin, I don't want to fly. Not yet."

He sighed. Circles hung under his eyes. "All right, Mors. We'll walk for a while under the trees. But sooner or later we'll have to fly again. Walking all the way to the sea can take moons; flying would take days. And once we reach the sea, we'd *have* to fly, unless you know how to build a boat with your bare hands."

"We'll walk for today," she said and drew her sword, wondering if she'd ever dare swing it at an enemy. She lowered her head, remembering how even in the dungeon of Draco Vallum, she had only cowered, and dared not fight like Bayrin did. She took a shaky breath. "We'll fly tomorrow."

They walked through the forest in silence. The pines rose around them, frosted with snow, their branches snagging at their cloaks and smearing them with sap. Soon snow began to fall. The cold air drove into her bones. Mori pulled her cloak tight, but the wind kept creeping under her clothes to caress her skin. She missed home. She missed sitting by the fireplace with a good book, maybe one with maps, or one about adventure. She missed drinking mulled wine and talking to Lyana about what gowns the ladies of the court wore, or talking to Elethor about the stars, or even just cuddling with her pet mouse and whispering her secrets to him. Would that world ever return? So many had died. So much of the city had fallen.

Mori lowered her head. For the first time, she realized that she was an orphan now. True, she had not stopped thinking about her dead father, not for an instant. And even now, years after her mother's death, she still thought about the queen every day. But that word—*orphan*—only now filled her mind. To Mori, orphans had always been poor children with shabby clothes and hungry bellies, figures from books and stories. She had never thought she would one day tread in the wilderness, her own clothes torn, her own belly twisting with hunger, her own two parents gone.

But I have Elethor, she thought. *He's still alive, and he'll protect me. And I have my friend Lyana.* She shivered and wrapped her cloak as tight as she could. *Unless they're dead too. Unless some creature in the Abyss killed them.*

"Mori, you're shivering," Bayrin said. He looked at her, his black cloak now white with snow. Snow even coated his eyebrows. And yet he began to doff his cloak. "Here, wear this too."

She held up her hands. "No, Bay. You're cold too. Keep your cloak, I'm all right."

His words, if not his cloak, warmed her. She wasn't sure why, but since battling Acribus underground, Bayrin had seemed much nicer. He sighed and rolled his eyes less often. He made fewer quips.

He even held her hand when they stepped over ice—the hand with six fingers, which he would mock so much back at home. Had something happened underground to change him? Maybe he was only scared too... scared that the other Vir Requis were all dead, that the city of Nova Vita had fallen, that they would die out here.

Mori did something she never thought she would dare, something that a moon ago would terrify her. She stood on her tiptoes, leaned forward, and kissed Bayrin's cheek. His red stubble tickled her lips.

"But thank you, Bay."

He raised his eyebrows and whistled. "Oh my." He made to remove his boots. "Here, take my boots too! And my pants and shirt. Would you like some nice warm socks?" He wiggled his eyebrows. "Does that get me a kiss on the lips?"

Mori couldn't help but giggle. She shoved him back. "It'll get you frostbite, that's what."

As they kept walking, Mori hugged herself and wondered: What would it be like... to truly kiss Bayrin on the lips? Mori was eighteen already, but she had never kissed a boy. Her mother had been married at her age, and Lyana had kissed her first boy at age fourteen, but Mori had always feared it. Would it be painful and cold like... like when...?

She shook her head wildly, scattering snow. *No. Don't think about that, Mori. Love isn't like that night, and if I ever kiss a boy, it will be for love. He would love me, and I would love him, and it will feel like those old days, when I'd sit by the fireplace and read books with maps.*

She slipped on some ice, and Bayrin caught her hand to steady her, and she let him hold it as they kept walking. The forest spread cold ahead, as far as she could see. In the distance, upon the eastern wind, she thought she could hear a phoenix shriek.

LYANA

They walked down a twisting tunnel. Its floor was rubbery like skin and strewn with eyeballs like pebbles. Shattered spines rose in ridges along the walls, seeping blood. Fingers rose in tufts from nooks and crevices, nails cracked, snagging at them.

Lyana could see only several feet in each direction; shadows pushed deep around her, swirling and cackling, red eyes blazing in their depths. When the tunnels forked, Elethor did not hesitate, but always chose the path that sloped deeper down.

"Do you know where we're going?" she asked him.

He stared ahead, holding his tin lamp high. The flames flickered. They had oil enough for another day, two days at most.

"This tunnel is steeper," he said. "So that's where we go. Deeper into the darkness."

"You don't know that'll take us to the Starlit Demon," Lyana said. "This labyrinth is vast, Elethor. It might be larger than Requiem itself, larger than the world. According to the stories, the Starlit Demon is locked behind the Crimson Archway, and I haven't seen a single archway here. We need to find a map, or a source of knowledge, or—"

He spun toward her and glared. "Lyana, what map? What 'source of knowledge'? The last creatures we met who could talk were dangling on cobwebs, mumbling nonsense about numbers not lining up, and hairs that grew too slowly, or stars know what else."

"So your answer is to just walk blindly?" she demanded, voice rising now. She swept her sword around her. "Elethor, we are getting lost down here. You have no idea where to go. No idea what to do. No idea how to get back home. You—"

"Well, do you?" He raised his eyebrows. "Do you have answers? You're just as much in the dark. So unless you have suggestions, keep walking."

"Well, I..." She searched for words but found none and fumed. All her life, she had always had an answer to any question. She knew everything about geography, heraldry, warfare, swordplay, history, astronomy. She was the smartest person in Requiem, she was sure of it; yet now she felt so lost, so afraid.

She raised her left hand and shivered. Bandages covered her fingers, hiding the gray, withered flesh. A day ago, only her fingertips had been shriveled and pale. Now lines of rot stretched from under the bandage, spreading across her palm to her wrist. The skin looked old, spotted and wrinkled, the bones beneath it brittle.

Elethor looked at her, his eyes softened, and he sighed.

"Does it hurt?" he asked quietly.

She shook her head. "I can't feel my hand anymore. At least there's no pain."

She shivered and lowered her eyes, remembering the withered creatures back at Nedath's lair. She had hung among them for hours. Most were no wider than snakes, nothing but spines with loose skin, their limbs wilted stalks. Their skulls had long crumbled to dust, leaving loose faces like old rags.

"We are the Shrivels," one had told her, swinging on its cobwebs. "We are the lost ones, the cursed, the counters of the numbers... or maybe the numbers themselves." It grinned, showing toothless gums. "Soon you will be one of us, soon you will help us count, we will count all the numbers, we will line them, or she will hurt us, she will eat us, she will feed upon our sweetest meat."

How long will it be? Lyana wondered. She no longer doubted that their curse infected her. How long until her palm withered completely and the disease spread to her arm, then her body, and finally left her a shrunken creature that could not die? Would she remain here in the Abyss, mumbling of shattered teeth that must be found, screws to turn, and more ramblings of the dark? Or would they hang her on a post in Requiem, a thing to pity, and she would linger there as seasons turned, unable to die?

Suddenly she laughed. She couldn't help it.

"Imagine it, Elethor!" she said, tears in her eyes. Laughter shook her. "Me, only a piece of shriveled skin on a hook! Would you hang me by your throne so I could still watch the court?"

She laughed so hard that she didn't realize she was crying, that her laughter was becoming a panicked pant. She jerked when Elethor touched her shoulder, sure for an instant that it was her, Nedath, the demon who had bitten her shoulder and spoken of sucking her bones. She found herself wrapped in Elethor's arms, like the cobwebs had wrapped her, and she wept against him.

"I won't let that happen," he said softly, stroking her hair.

She shivered, unable to stop her tears from falling. "I'm so scared, Elethor. I saw things in there, in the darkness she showed me. I saw... there was a black hill, and a black rose on it, and horror filled the air, as if fear were a physical thing. And... Elethor, I have to stop the bones from lining up! I have to *count* them, Elethor. I have to count the hairs that are growing sideways."

He shook his head, eyes narrowed. "What, Lyana? What do you mean? There are no bones. There's nothing to count."

She sobbed, body shaking. "I don't know! I don't know, Elethor. But..." She sniffed. "If my teeth fall from my gums, I..." She gritted those teeth and rubbed her eyes. "No! No. I can't think like them. I can't talk like them." She clung to his clothes with her good hand, staring into his eyes through her tears. "I won't turn into a Shrivel. Promise me that, Elethor. Promise you won't let me go."

He held her. "I promise you, Lyana. As King of Requiem, I will do whatever I can to cure you; I will summon healers from across the world, from Salvandos in the west to Leonis in the east. I won't let you turn into anything." He touched her hair. "Do you remember how, when we were children, we'd go to Lacrimosa Hill, eat walnuts from a pouch, and look at the stars? You and Mori would whisper, and Bayrin and Orin would laugh, and I'd try to tell you all about the stars, but you'd never listen." He smiled softly. "We'll do that again, Lyana. We'll go stargazing, and eat walnuts, and laugh..."

He fell silent. They stood holding each other, and Lyana tried to remember those days of her youth, the glow of the stars, the warmth of the breeze, the sound of her laughter, and she knew those days could never return. Orin was gone now. Mori was hurt, maybe too much to ever recover. As for herself... could she ever be the woman she had been? When fire rained, and darkness clutched her, was there still a path home?

"Let's keep going," she said and pulled back from his embrace. She raised her lamp, casting its light upon a dead, dark land. "Let's find this Starlit Demon and go home."

They walked across the grass of fingers, crushing them. They moved through darkness, lashing their swords at red eyes that blazed around them. Shadows swirled, taking the shapes of bloated dragons that burst, shedding bodies of smoke from their bellies. Ribs rose around them, framing the tunnels, columns of dead cathedrals. Bodies hung from the walls on meat hooks, their faces burnt. Some bodies looked almost like Orin, others like Lyana's parents, some like herself. Their bellies were split, revealing nests of transparent eggs, snakes moving inside the shells. Hatched snakes squirmed along the tunnel floor, bloated, screeching, laughing, mocking them.

"Walk deeper, weredragons!" spoke the bodies on the hooks. "Enter our darkness. You will hang here too! You will rot and burst and feed our hatchlings."

The bodies' faces twisted, mouths gasping. They screamed, begged for death, and wept tears of blood.

"Don't look at them," Elethor said, jaw clenched. "It's not real, Lyana. It's just a dream. It's just a nightmare they're showing us."

Lyana nodded, desperate to believe him. When bodies rubbed against her, she shoved them aside and stabbed them, shedding blood and pus and maggots. Their stench filled her nostrils. Their flesh against her felt hot, sticky, too real to be a vision. Yet she kept walking, forcing herself to stare forward, to ignore them.

"They're just a dream," she repeated through stiff lips. "Just a dream."

"Are we just a dream?" asked a hanging body, speaking through a gaping wound in its rotted face.

"You have been kissed by Nedath!" said another, the skinned body of a man with a bull's head.

A snake coiled toward her, spine peeking through rents in its skin. It hissed and stared with blazing red eyes. "The Guardian of the Darkness bit her, children! She will soon be a Withered One. Look at her arm!"

The bodies on the hooks stared and hissed. Tongues thrust out from their wounds and licked their blood. Lyana looked at her arm and saw that Nedath's disease had spread to her elbow. Her forearm was now thin as bone, her flesh gone, her skin dangling.

"Can you cure her?" Elethor said, raising his voice over their cries and laughter. "How can we stop the curse?"

The bodies on the walls growled, revealing fangs. "Feed us! Feed us and we will tell you. We know of a cure. Feed us and we will help."

Fingers trembling, Lyana opened her pack. She had brought food from Requiem: sweet apples, grainy rolls of bread, cheese, oranges, and dried fish. Maggots filled the food now, and Lyana grimaced.

"I have food for you!" she shouted. The bodies were twitching around her, legs kicking, as if trying to escape the meat hooks.

"We do not want your food of sunlight and soil!" one said.

"Feed us ourselves!" cried another. "Let us feast upon our comrades, upon our sweet hands and feet!"

They opened their maws wide, drooling, begging for meat. Those with arms reached out and pawed at her. Their bellies bloated, pulsing with eggs.

"Stars, they're cannibals," Elethor whispered. He was pale and his sword wavered in his hand.

Lyana wanted to gag, to weep, to run. How could she do this? To take a squirming body from the wall, hack it apart, feed it to its comrades?

"It would be like cutting meat, just like cutting meat!" they begged. "Feed us, feed us our comrades!"

"Tell me of a cure first!" Lyana shouted. Their voices rose so loudly, her ears hurt. "Tell me how to cure Nedath's curse and I will feed you then!"

A halved body, ribs white and twisting, hissed at her. "You must find the Feasting Table!" it said. "You must eat there from the sweet meats. Then you will be cured. Then you will be a Withered One no more. Then you must feed us!"

Elethor shouted, swinging his sword to hold back the groping arms. "Where is this Feasting Table?"

The bodies pulled aside, like sweeping curtains of flesh, and revealed a gaping doorway. Lyana could see nothing but shadows through it, but scents hit her nose. She could smell... food, *real* food! Fresh bread, and cakes, and fruits. The scents mingled with the stench of the hanging bodies, a sickening mix of the delicious and rotting.

"Enter and feast, child of starlight," said the bodies. "But choose wisely, so we may feast too."

Lyana looked at her arm. The disease was spreading up to her shoulder. Through her hanging skin, she could see the bones of her elbow, pale and full of worms. She no longer cared for danger. She rushed past the bodies into the dark chamber of scents. Behind her, she heard Elethor follow.

They walked for a moment in darkness until they saw candles burn ahead. The craggy walls widened, revealing a chamber with a tiled floor, white walls, and a chandelier.

A table stood in the room, and upon it lay a feast—such a feast as Lyana had never seen, not even in the courts of Requiem. Golden platters, bowls, and plates held roast ducks on beds of mushrooms, glazed hams, grapes and apples and peaches, thick gravy, bread still steaming from the oven, stewed vegetables, and every other delight Lyana could imagine. She realized that she was famished. Her mouth watered.

She would have leaped toward the food, were it not for the figures that sat around the table.

Seven chairs surrounded the feast. In all but one sat a Shrivel. Their limbs had atrophied into mere twigs wrapped in loose skin. Their spines were slung across the chairs, and their heads dangled over the backrests, forever looking at the walls behind them. Their faces gasped and sucked at their toothless gums. Dark liquid dripped from them, forming pools below their heads. The last chair, the one at the head of the table, was empty.

That chair is for me, Lyana knew.

A portrait of King Olasar of Requiem hung upon the wall, framed in giltwood. Somebody had smeared blood across it, giving the king horns and a forked tongue. The eyes had been gouged out. Words were scratched across the canvas, and Lyana read them, a shiver running through her.

> *At the table of lost souls*
> *A feast awaits the withering*
> *Nedath's cursed seek a cure*
> *For skin, flesh, and bones decaying*
> *Feed upon our sweetest meats*
> *Your tainted blood again shall bloom*
> *Crave and eat the lesser treats*
> *And rot forever in our room*

"What does it mean?" Elethor asked, standing beside her. He was pale, and his dark hair clung to his damp forehead.

Lyana looked back at the feast covering the table: roast ducks, fresh fruit, pastries, breads... Would one of these heal her?

"What is the sweetest meat?" she asked. "Feast upon our sweetest meats, and your tainted blood again shall bloom. Does that mean that if I eat the right food, I'll be cured?"

Elethor shivered. "Eat the lesser treats, and rot forever in our room." He gestured at the Shrivels who gasped upon the chairs. "That must be what happened to them. They ate the wrong dish."

Heart hammering, Lyana walked to the table. The scents of the feast filled her nostrils. Her left arm dangled at her side, a flap of useless skin, its bones so brittle now, no wider than a porcupine's quill. When she looked at a golden bowl, she saw her reflection. Already her left cheek sagged, the skin gray.

"What should I eat?" she called, turning to the Shrivels on the seats. She grabbed one and shook it. Its skin was clammy, and its spine rattled. "What did you eat?"

The creature's head flapped from side to side. It gasped and sucked its gums. "Eat, child, eat the treats, join us, count with us..."

Tears stinging her eyes, Lyana tossed the creature aside. It slapped against the floor and squirmed. She grabbed another Shrivel.

She shook it, and its heart pulsed behind its clear skin, shooting black blood down a single vein.

"What do I eat here?" she demanded, tears on her cheeks. "Tell me!"

The Shrivel whispered, and its eyes shed black tears. "Please, light one, please, tell him, tell him to turn, he has to turn it, he has to turn the *screws*, please tell him!"

She tossed this creature aside too and spun toward the table, trembling. Her left leg shook, and when she took a step, her foot pulled out from her boot.

"Lyana!" Elethor cried. He ran toward her and held her, and she gasped, clinging to him. Her sock fell off, revealing a shriveled foot, no larger than the foot of a baby. Her toes curled inward, white and brittle.

"Oh stars, Elethor, stars," she whispered.

"Eat something!" Elethor said. He pulled her toward the table. "Eat... what is the sweetest meat? Duck? Veal? Ham?"

Lyana looked at the feast. For the first time, she saw that drool covered the dishes. The marks of toothless gums filled the geese, the ham, the fruit.

The Shrivels had tried eating these foods, she knew. *They all chose wrong.* She raised her head and looked at the empty seat. She trembled, wept, and held Elethor tight.

"Please, Elethor," she whispered. "Please, don't let him turn the screws, please, tell him, *tell him*."

She tried to say more, but felt a tooth come loose. She spat it out, and she wanted to sink her gums into the meat, to feed, to count, to line things up, to...

No! No, not yet. You are not a Shrivel yet. She fumbled toward the table, tossed her sword down, and lifted an apple with her good hand. Even that hand was shrivelling; it looked like the hand of an old woman. She raised the apple to her lips. Was this the fruit? Was this the sweetest meat?

I will feast upon you... I will feast upon your sweet meat...

The words echoed in her mind, and Lyana gasped. She had heard this before! She had hung in cobwebs in Nedath's lair. The great demon had bitten her shoulder, wrapped her webs around her, and whispered and cackled in her ear. *You will be my sweet meat, child, I will feed upon you....*

"It's the Shrivels!" she shouted. She turned toward them, trembling. "It's not the food. Those are just lesser treats. This is Nedath's Feast, and she eats what lies on the chairs, not the table."

She stepped toward one seat, where lay a Shrivel with hairy tufts on its hanging skin. Her right foot pulled out from her boot, skin and bones twisting and rotting, and Lyana fell to the floor. She reached out her right arm, which was now thin as a twig, and grabbed the Shrivel on the seat. She pulled it down to the floor, like pulling down a wet cloth. Ignoring the nausea that twisted her belly, she bit into the creature.

It was stringy and cold, like biting into raw chicken skin. She forced herself to bite, though her teeth were loose, and she chewed, swallowed, bit some more.

"Lyana, don't!" Elethor cried, and she heard the terror in his voice, but she ignored him. She had to keep eating. She dug her teeth deeper, and liquid exploded in her mouth. The Shrivel flapped, screaming and squirming, and she kept biting and chewing, eating it alive.

It is the sweetest meat, she thought. *I am a huntress, a feeder, a creature of darkness, and—*

Starlight blazed.

Above her shone the Draco Constellation, the stars of Requiem, her homeland. Hot tears flowed down her cheeks, and she gasped, shook, blood on her fingers, blood on her lips.

I am a creature of starlight, she knew. *I am... I am Lyana! I am a knight of Requiem. I am a daughter, a sister, a warrior.*

She rose to her feet, the dead Shrivel hanging from her mouth. She spat it to the floor and cried for her betrothed.

"Elethor! Elethor, where are you?"

He ran toward her. He held her, shook her, touched her cheek. Tears filled his eyes.

"Lyana, I'm here! You're changing. You're healing. Can you see me, Lyana?"

She kept gasping for air, and the chamber swirled around her. She saw the hanging things move and laugh and swing, and Nedath's fangs, and that black hill with the black rose, but... she also saw marble columns rising from a forest of birches, and she heard harpists play, and she saw—

"Dragons!" she said, digging her fingers into Elethor's shoulders. "I see dragons, Elethor, herds of them. They fly over our home." She wept. "We are from Requiem. I am Lyana. You are Elethor. Don't forget that, *never* forget."

She trembled so violently, and he held her so tight, not letting her fall, not letting her forget herself, drown in that dark place.

"You are Lyana Eleison, daughter of Deramon and Adia," he said, stroking her hair. "You will not forget. You will see dragons again. We will return to Requiem." He held her tight. "We will return, and we will save our home, and we will destroy this place with fire." He kissed her forehead and touched her cheek. "You are healed, Lyana."

She turned to face the golden dishes and saw her reflection. Her red curls fell around her shoulders in a mane. Her skin was once more white, young, and strewn with freckles. Her limbs were strong again. She pulled her boots back on, lifted her sword, and marched toward the doorway.

"Let's go, Elethor," she said, her voice cold. "Back to the bodies outside."

She walked through the darkness. Soon she stepped back into the tunnel where bodies hung on meat hooks, snake eggs in their bellies. They howled and smacked their lips, drooling.

"Feed us!" they cried. "Feed us, child of starlight! You promised."

Lyana took several steps to where the tunnel widened, ten feet between the walls. It would be a tight squeeze, but Lyana narrowed her eyes. She would do this.

"Stand behind me, Elethor," she said softly. She pushed him behind her. "Go farther back. Fifty steps. Go."

"Lyana, are you sure?" he said, and from the softness in his voice, she knew that he understood.

She nodded and looked into his eyes. She saw something new there, something she had never seen when he looked upon her: warmth, caring... even love. It made her eyes sting, and she couldn't help it. As the bodies shrieked around them, she touched his cheek and kissed his lips.

"I'm sure, El," she whispered. "I'll do this. Now go."

He nodded and walked down the tunnel into the darkness. The bodies lined the tunnel in front of Lyana, screaming on their hooks, thrashing their limbs.

"Feed us ourselves!" they demanded. Some began to eat their own limbs, coating their teeth with blood. The eggs inside them squirmed. "You promised! You promised!"

Lyana took a deep breath, lay down on her stomach... and shifted into a dragon.

Wings burst from her back and slammed against the tunnel ceiling. She pulled them close to her body. That body grew scales and ballooned until it pushed against the tunnel walls. Her tail flapped behind her. Fangs grew from her mouth, fire filled her maw, and with a howl, she shot a stream of flame.

The jet blasted the bodies. They screeched. The tunnel shook and rocks fell from the ceiling. They screamed and screamed as they burned, and the eggs inside them popped, and small snakes fled only to burn too. Lyana could not believe how long they screamed. They screamed as their flesh charred, until nothing was left but bones, and still they screamed and thrashed. She thought that they would never die, and she blew all the fire inside her, until finally their screams faded to whimpers.

"You promised," the charred remains begged. "You promised to feed us. You are cursed, daughter of Requiem! Your kingdom is cursed! We will seek our vengeance. Your land will turn to our darkness! We will find your kingdom and we will twist it!"

With a last howl, their bones shattered, and they fell to black dust.

Lyana crawled forward, craned her neck around, and blew flames through the doorway. The dragonfire crackled into the white banquet room. Inside, the Shrivels screeched, voices high and twisting.

"She burns us!" they called. "Black! Pain! She turns the screws, skeleys. She counts the pain. Count the hairs that burn sideways, Withered Ones!"

A few Shrivels came crawling from the room. They squirmed until the fire consumed them and they collapsed. They lay as crisp, blackened things, stared up with melting eyes, then crumbled to ash.

Lyana let her fire die, and silence filled the tunnels.

She shifted back into a human. She lay in the ash, shaking, smoke rising around her. Elethor rushed toward her, helped her up, and she embraced him. She stood for long moments, her head against his shoulder, his arms around her.

"Elethor," she said softly.

He pushed back a curl of her hair. "Lyana."

She swallowed and stared at him. "It's time to find that Starlit Demon. I want to leave this place."

He nodded. They walked into the darkness, swords raised, smoke curling around their boots.

ADIA

She tried to run past her husband's soldiers. They held her—broad men in armor, their eyes hard. She tried to push them aside, but they stood firm.

"Let me through!" she demanded, glaring at them. "I am High Priestess of Requiem, and I command you move aside."

Adia was a tall woman, and she knew that men often whispered of her stern eyes, her cold face, her commanding voice that could wither flowers. Yet none of that held sway in these tunnels, as men clashed and cried and died ahead in the darkness. She looked over the men's shoulders and saw their comrades pile rocks and wood, sealing the chambers above—the library, the wine cellar that had become their war room, the armory where Solina had burned all those Adia had labored to heal.

"I'm sorry, Mother Adia," one of the soldiers said, eyes lowered. "Your lord husband commands it. The upper tunnels have fallen, from the library to the armory."

"It is no longer an armory!" Adia said. "It ceased being an armory once you donned your armor, and once we started moving the wounded in. It's a hospital now, and I'm a healer, and you will let me through."

She was about to shove them again when she felt a hand on her shoulder. She spun around, glaring, to see her husband. Dust covered Deramon, painting him gray. Blood trickled from a wound on his shoulder, thick with dirt. Dents and scratches covered his armor, and welts ran down his cheek.

"The upper chambers have fallen," he said, voice low and gruff, but tinged with softness. "They're dead, Adia. They're gone."

She spun back to the soldiers, then back again to Deramon, and felt close to panic. She forced herself to stand still, to take deep breaths, to ease the hammering of her heart. Her eyes stung and her belly felt so cold and heavy, as if ice filled it.

I swore to heal them, she thought. *They depended on me. I shouldn't have left them. I shouldn't have gone to sleep while they burned. Now the hurt are gone, while I, the healer, linger.*

She turned and faced the other direction, staring into the darkness. Survivors huddled before her, lining the walls. There were so few of them. So many had not managed to escape the upper chambers. From behind her, she heard the cries of the Tirans, clashing steel, and a scream. A voice cried out the words of Requiem—"May our wings forever find your sky!"—torn with pain.

"There are still Vir Requis alive up there," she whispered, a tremble running through her.

Deramon nodded, grim. "They're beyond our help now."

The voice behind her rose in a scream—a cry of more anguish than Adia had ever heard, even in her hospital.

"They're torturing our men," she whispered.

Deramon held her shoulder and began leading her away. "We can no longer help them, only pray. Come with me, Adia."

How could she just leave this place? How could she abandon those Vir Requis who still lived beyond the line of battle, cut and broken and tortured by Tiran steel? And yet she walked, head raised, eyes staring ahead. She would pray for those still left behind... pray that death found them quickly.

They walked deeper into darkness and found a corner to huddle in. She sat on the cold ground, Deramon's great arms holding her, and Adia closed her eyes. She could still hear the screams, even down here, and she clenched her jaw so tight, her teeth ached.

Did her children scream like this too? Had the phoenixes caught Bayrin, her firstborn, the son she loved with all her heart? Did the terrors of the Abyss now torture her daughter, the brave and beautiful Lyana, the light of her life? Would her children leave her like Noela?

I should not have let them go! Adia thought, fingernails digging into her palms. *I should never have let them leave me! They need me now. They need me to protect them.*

"Mother Adia," spoke a soft voice. "Mother Adia, I beg you. My wife, she's... she's giving birth, and... the midwife is in the upper chambers. Please, Mother, can you help?"

Still held in Deramon's arms, Adia opened her eyes. She saw a young man with a wide, pale face. Sweat soaked him and his left arm was wrapped in bloody bandages. Adia stared at him in silence, and for a moment she only thought: *What of my children? What of those I gave birth to? Leave me. Your child will die with the rest of them.*

She wanted him to leave, and she hated herself for it, and her thoughts scared her more than anything in this darkness.

She rose to her feet.

"Lead me to her," she said. She was still Mother of Requiem, and all the survivors were her children. She would protect them, heal them, comfort them... until the fire consumed them all.

BAYRIN

Dawn rose cold and bleak. Bayrin lay under his cloak, his head on a rolled-up blanket. Mori lay at his side, her cheek upon her hands. She still slept, face pale in the dawn, her hair spread out like a halo. Even in sleep, she seemed fearful; her lips were scrunched, her eyelids were closed tight, and she occasionally winced. Bayrin lay watching her as the sun rose. Her thigh pressed against him, a hint of warmth in the icy forest.

"No, please," she whispered in her sleep, and her legs kicked. "Please, Solina, please, please don't."

Bayrin sighed. He raised his hand, hesitated for a moment, then stroked her hair. It felt soft and smooth, like running his hand over silk. She calmed, her face smoothed, and her breathing deepened.

A deep anger filled Bayrin as he watched her. She was only a thin, pale thing, the last petal of a flower in snow. Bayrin knew of the shame she carried. She had spoken in her sleep of that night, begging for Acribus to release her, begging for the stars to forgive her for her shame.

She's only a child, he thought. *Eighteen years old, but so much younger in spirit. How could anyone have done this to her?*

With a pain like a dagger in his gut, Bayrin regretted all those years he had taunted Mori, all those times he'd mock her extra finger, tug her hair, and joke of her tears and trembles. It had been easy to roll his eyes at Mori back in Nova Vita, when walls and guards surrounded them, when wars were merely the words of old stories. Here in the wilderness, the phoenix on their trail, he felt ashamed. Careful not to wake her, he kissed her pale cheek. It was cold against his lips.

She mumbled and her brow furrowed.

"Mmmm... Bayrin?" She opened her eyes and blinked. "Did I kick you?"

"You damned near cracked my ribs," he said. "Horse kicks are weaker than yours."

She blinked and kicked his leg. "How's that?"

He feigned a look of pain and let out a long, exaggerated groan. "Oww... my bones are shattered!"

When she smiled sheepishly, eyes lowered, Bayrin couldn't help but feel warmth inside him, like butter melting.

You are my princess, he thought. *I might only be a lowly guard, the lesser son of a great house, but I will serve you as best I can.*

They rose in the cold morning, breath frosting before them, and wrapped themselves in their cloaks. Snow filled Bayrin's hair and his boots were soggy. Clouds glided across the sky and flurries fell. In their packs they found only some bread, cheese, and dried fruit. They shared the breakfast, eating with numb fingers.

"Mori," he said, "we should fly today."

She bit her lip and shook her head silently.

"It's been two days since we saw the phoenix," Bayrin continued. "If he's still hunting us, he's hunting us leagues away. We should shift into dragons and fly to the sea. It still lies hundreds of leagues away; walking is too slow."

She lowered her head, and a tear ran down her cheek. "But Bayrin, if we fly, he'll *see* us. I know it." She raised her eyes; they glimmered with tears. "Can't we walk for just another day, to be sure he's gone?"

Bayrin placed an awkward hand on her shoulder. "Mori, Requiem needs us. My sister needs us. Your brother needs us. Solina is still attacking them, and if we can't bring the Moondisk back soon, more will die. We can't dally any longer."

She hugged herself. "But... but what if he *sees* us, Bayrin? What if he's flying up there? We're little as humans. But dragons are too large, our scales are too bright, and..."

"We'll have to take that risk. For Requiem. We'll have to be brave. We'll be brave together, all right? I know you can do this."

She looked at her feet, trembling, then looked up at him again. Her eyes were so large, so haunted, so full of pain, that Bayrin felt his chest twinge. Without breaking her stare, she shifted.

Wings sprouted from her back, a pale gold like honey. Scales clanked across her, fangs and claws sprouted from her, and soon she stood before him, thirty feet long, a golden dragon with sad eyes. Bayrin shifted too and stood before her, a long green dragon, fifty feet from snout to tail's tip. Snow fell around them, their breath plumed, and their scales frosted.

They leaped, scattering snow, and flapped their wings. With a shower of twigs and snow, they crashed through the treetops into the sky. Snow flurried and wind howled in Bayrin's ears. Their wings thudded, bending the trees, and they soared until they flew among the clouds. Hidden among them, they leveled off and dived north. Wind and snow flowed around them.

As they flew, Bayrin kept looking around him, seeking phoenix fire. Once he thought he saw the beast, and his heart leaped, but it was only the sun glowing dimly through the clouds.

He's leagues away, he told himself. *Stars, I hope we never see that bastard again.*

They flew for several leagues before the clouds parted, revealing a rolling landscape. Cliffs and mountains rose like battlements, their eastern facades gilded with sunlight, their western slopes melting into mist and purple shadow. Evergreens rose tall and frosted, and a frozen lake glimmered like beaten silver. Herds of deer swept across valleys, while eagles soared from mountainous nests. The two dragons' shadows raced across the land. Even this high up, the smells of pine filled Bayrin's nostrils.

He saw no towns, no farms, no sign of civilization. Mori was better at maps, but Bayrin thought they flew beyond the Old Kingdom's borders, heading toward the distant Terius Bay. This was a cold hinterland north of Requiem, west of the fallen kingdom of Fidelium, and east of the mythical land of Salvandos. Few bards ever sang of these lands. Few scrolls told their tales. In most maps, they were empty spaces of canvas. It was a realm untouched by man or dragon, wild and beautiful.

As he flew, Mori at his side, his thoughts kept returning to Requiem, to his family and friends. While he flew here, the cold air in his nostrils, they huddled underground. While he fled one phoenix, they fought an army. Suddenly he wished Elethor had not chosen him for this task. He was no explorer, no hero, no warrior. He should be back home, helping his family and friends. Even if he couldn't fight well, he could still comfort them, make them laugh, bring some light to the darkness. But here... was he truly helping Requiem here? Was there truly a Moondisk beyond mountain and sea, or did Elethor merely send him here to spare his life, to save the princess from death underground? Bayrin didn't know. If all should die and he lived, the shame would be too great to bear, he thought.

They should have sent my sister. Lyana would know where to fly, what to do, how to fight. They should have sent my father; he's a great warrior and would have killed Acribus in the fort. They should have sent my mother; she's a healer, and could have healed the pain inside of Mori. But they sent me... Bayrin. A lowly guard. A jokester. A fool. Why should they fight and die, while I flee over wild country?

He ground his teeth. He had to believe. He had to find this Moondisk, if it truly existed, or die seeking it. He would not be a coward, hiding beyond map and measure as his kingdom fell.

"We will return, Requiem," he whispered into the wind. "Fight. Stay alive. We will bring aid."

Mori looked at him, wings churning the clouds, smoke seeping from her nostrils. He could see the same thought in her eyes.

They glided over mountain and forest. In the afternoon, they spotted goats upon a mountain and swooped to hunt. They flew again with bellies full, soaring over an icy lake, a frozen waterfall, and cliffs bristly with pines. At night they slept as dragons, curled up in the snow, coiled together for warmth. At dawn they flew again, frost on their scales, blowing fire to warm them.

For three days they flew—over ancient forests, plains of snow, and mountains that rose around them as jagged walls. On the fourth morning, the sun cold in an iron sky, they saw Terius Sea ahead.

It stretched beyond Bayrin's sight, curving to span the horizon. Lines of foam ran across it. The water was deep iron, stained cobalt where hidden valleys plunged. Jagged boulders rose from the depths like the hands of drowning gods. Bayrin had once flown east to Altus Mare, a port city in the kingdom of Osanna. There the waters had been green and bright, but here they spread like oil, dark and foreboding. He hovered before the sea, wings flapping.

"I'm scared," Mori said, flying beside him. There was no wind, and he could hear her words clearly, even above the thud of their wings.

He gestured with his head toward the rocky beach, snorted a blast of fire, and spiraled down. Soon he felt the spray of crashing waves. He filled his wings with air, reached out his claws, and landed, smoke rising from between his teeth. Mori landed beside him, claws nearly silent against the rocks, and folded her wings. The sea grumbled before them, spraying them with salt.

"Mori," he said, "you used to love books of maps. How far is the Crescent Isle from this shore?"

She stared into the sea. "Hundreds of leagues," she said. "A distance as wide as Requiem. But... those maps are very old, and the Crescent Isle appears only in ancient myths. I don't know what the true distance is." Her claws dug into pebbles. "Maybe the island doesn't exist at all."

Bayrin shot a jet of flame over the waves. Was this a fool's errand? They could perhaps navigate by the stars—he knew some of the skill—but how far could they possibly fly at once? Fifty leagues? A hundred? Soon or later, they would need rest. What if they found no island; were they doomed to drown?

Despite his earlier vows of heroism, he was tempted to turn around, find a quiet forest, and spend the rest of his days there with Mori. They could live forever here in the hinterlands, far from any phoenix or war. They would hunt goats, and sleep in their cloaks, and Mori would kick him at night, and he would smooth her hair, and kiss her cheek, and never have to feel like a failure again, the lowly son of a great father.

So don't act like a lowly son, whispered a voice in his head. *All your life, you've watched men praise your father, worship your mother, admire your sister for her courage and knighthood. So you would mock them, and run off with Elethor to alehouses, and forget the world. But now Requiem needs you—not the great Lord Deramon, or the beloved priestess Adia, or the brave knight Lyana, but you... Bayrin. Now is your time to be the hero.*

Bayrin didn't know who spoke to him. Was it a part of his own mind? The stars of Requiem? Was it the voice of Elethor, his best friend and now his king?

"Bay, are you all right?" Mori asked. She touched him with her snout, her breath warm against his scales.

He shrugged his wings. "I could use a ship. And a night's rest in a soft bed. And some tavern wenches with big eyes and bigger mugs of ale. But otherwise I'm fine. Are you ready for the longest flight of your life?"

She lowered her head and whispered. "I flew from Castellum Luna in the south to Nova Vita, and it took me two days with no rest." She raised her head and stared at him, her eyes haunted with the death of her brother, the death of her father, and her own tragedy. "I am ready to fly as far as it takes."

Bayrin briefly considered waiting, resting, spending the day here on the beach, then flying tomorrow. But Solina would not wait; she would be slaughtering his people as he stood here on the shore. With a blast of fire, he kicked off the beach, his wings flapped, and he soared into the sky.

Mori flew beside him and they streamed forward, shooting so low the sea sprayed their bellies. Their reflections raced along the water beneath them, and Bayrin saw the shapes of submerged boulders, valleys, and hills. When he looked behind him, he could see distant forests under mist. Soon they too were gone, and they flew over endless water.

The sea stretched into the horizon, cold and cruel as a grave.

ELETHOR

He flew, a brass dragon with white claws, wings roiling ash, flames trickling from his mouth like the tails of comets. Lyana flew at his side, squinting. The sea of lava below painted her blue scales a deep purple. The liquid fire gurgled, whirled, and shot up fountains. The dragons flew side to side, dodging them. A stone ceiling rose above them, embedded with countless skulls of dragons, spiders nesting in the eye sockets.

"We must be close now!" Lyana cried, voice dim under the roar of lava and wind. "In the books of Requiem, the Abyss is said to end where rock turns to fire. We will find the Starlit Demon here."

Elethor was less hopeful. They had been flying for hours—since the tunnels had given way to this sea of fire. He had seen no sign of a demon, no sign of life but for the spiders that crawled in the skulls. This place could be vast, larger than the world aboveground. And yet what other hope did they have? And so he flew, wings aching, the heat baking his belly, the smoke stinging his lungs.

A fountain of lava gushed from the sea. Elethor cursed, banked, and knocked into Lyana. They tumbled aside, nearly hit the burning sea, and soared. The stream of liquid fire crashed into the ceiling and boulders fell. One knocked Elethor's tail, and he shouted a curse but kept flying. Drops of lava fell like rain.

"Are you all right?" he asked Lyana.

She nodded, but weariness filled her eyes, and a burn spread across her wing.

Damn this place, Elethor thought. His tail ached and droplets of lava sizzled on his wings. He was tired, so tired that he could barely flap his wings, barely breathe the smoky air.

"I see a rock ahead!" he shouted to Lyana. "Let's rest for a bit."

The boulder rose from the lava, fifty feet tall, black and craggy. Elethor flew toward it, narrowly dodging another shower of lava. He landed on the rock with a grunt, claws clacking against stone. Lyana landed beside him.

Elethor perched upon the rock, tail curled around it, as fire rained from the stone ceiling like falling fireflies. Lyana lay beside him, her head against his neck, and he folded his wing over her. He dared not return to human form, not as lava still boiled around him, spreading for leagues.

"Are you all right?" he asked Lyana, voice soft.

She nodded, smoke rising from her nostrils. The firelight danced on her scales. "A few burns, that's all. I'll be fine."

"I don't mean the burns."

She looked up at him, eyes like sapphires the size of apples.

"I don't know," she whispered. She lowered her head and nestled against his neck. "I miss him, Elethor. I miss him all the time. I keep thinking how... if Orin were still alive, he'd know what to do. He'd rally the troops, tell me how to fight, and..." A tear streamed from her eye. "And I wouldn't feel so lost, so alone."

Her words dug into him, a shard of ice. *Orin would know what to do. Orin would fight. Orin would save us.* But how could he, Elethor, the younger son, the lesser prince—how could he inspire such love from his people... from Lyana? How could he be a good king to Requiem, and a good husband to Lyana, if he too felt so lost, so afraid?

"I miss him too," he said, voice cracking. "But... it's up to us now. We must know what to do, how to fight, how save our home. And we will, Lyana. We will save Requiem."

His words sounded trite to him. As a king, he would have to inspire, to lead, to galvanize. He wanted to sound as wise as the ancient leaders of Requiem from the stories—the legendary King Benedictus who fought the griffins, or the great Queen Gloriae who slew the tyrant Dies Irae, or Queen Lacrimosa who led Requiem in the Battle of King's Forest.

But I'm not like them, he thought. *I'm just a sculptor. And I still miss and love Solina, the very enemy who attacks us.*

Lyana nestled closer to him, her breath hot against his cheek.

"I... I think I now know how you felt," she whispered. "When Solina left, I mean. You loved her. And you lost her. The pain must have been so great, tearing inside you. I cannot think of greater pain." She lowered her eyes. "I'm sorry, Elethor. When Solina left, I was glad. I scolded you for loving her. I mocked you for your pain." Her eyes glistened with tears. "I'm sorry."

They huddled in darkness as lava gurgled around them, fire rained, and the stone walls shook and cracked. A fountain gushed by the boulder, nearly spraying them with lava, then crashed back into the sea. They huddled closer, scales clanking, and wrapped their wings around them as a tent.

"Yes," Elethor whispered. "I hurt when she left. And I hurt when she returned. I loved her for so long, it's hard to switch to hating her, even now, even when I know that she killed my father, my brother, and so many of our people. I... I hate myself for it, that I once kissed her, wanted to marry her, spent years pining for her." He closed his eyes. "I'm the one who should be sorry. You were right, Lyana. You were right all along about her, and about me."

How had he come to this place? A moon ago, he would never have thought it possible. Solina, the love of his life, was now his greatest enemy. Lyana, the girl who always scorned him, now huddled at his side, his betrothed and future queen consort. Requiem lay leagues above them, past tunnels of terrors he had never imagined could exist. His life seemed so mad now that his head spun, and he could only cling to this rock and to Lyana, and he felt lost.

"Come, Lyana," he finally said. "We'll fly again. Maybe we'll find the Crimson Archway today... and the Starlit Demon who's locked behind it."

They flew over the fire. They flew for hours through the great caverns of the Abyss, down tunnels where lava rushed, over great forests of bones, through chambers where smoke blinded them and the howls of ghosts filled the darkness. Finally, when their lungs burned and their wings could barely flap, they emerged from a tunnel into a great cavern the size of a city.

"Stars," Elethor whispered, feeling sickness rise inside him.

The cavern was a league wide and tall, carved of craggy rock. Pillars of stone stood like ribs, and rivers of lava coiled. A mountain rose in the chamber's center, pale pink and knobby. When Elethor squinted, he saw that the mountain was made of bodies—thousands of them, maybe millions, naked and interwoven.

"Who are they?" Lyana whispered, flying at his side.

Elethor didn't know. He saw the bodies of men, women, and children, skin pale and hairless, eyes staring, mouths gaping. Were they dead Vir Requis? Were they but a nightmare? Nausea rose inside him, and the stench of death filled his nostrils, spinning his head. Suddenly he was sure he would see his father and brother there, dead and naked, eyes staring. He gritted his teeth, forcing down his sickness.

"Look, El, on top of the mountain!" Lyana said.

An archway rose atop the mountain of bodies, carved of craggy stones. When they flew closer, Elethor saw that blood seeped from between the bricks, painting them red. Mist and shadows swirled inside the archway, casting black light, like a portal to a storm.

"The Crimson Archway," Elethor whispered. "The path to the Starlit Demon."

They flew up the mountain. Countless bodies lay below them, famished and limp like discarded chicken skins. Elethor narrowed his eyes and soared toward the archway. It looked just wide enough that, if he pulled his wings close, he could shoot through it. Whatever shadowy land it led to, and whatever enemy waited there, he would face it.

He was only seconds from flying through the archway when a creature rose from the pile of bodies.

At first, Elethor thought that the bodies themselves were rising upon the mountaintop. Then he realized that the creature had lain there all along, but was as naked, fleshy, and famished as the bodies. Fifty feet long, its skin hung loose on knobby bones. It had the body of a great cat, furless and starving. Its head was the head of a woman, but much larger, the size of a carriage. Her face was pale and stoic, her eyes golden and feline. Her torso, nude and stitched from collarbone to navel, rose to block the archway.

Elethor thrust his claws forward, beat his wings mightily, and slowed to hover in midair. He growled. Lyana flew and hovered by him, fire flickering between her teeth. Elethor's heart beat against his ribs.

"Who are you?" he demanded of the creature. "Name yourself."

The beast watched them, a soft smile on her lips. Her eyes glimmered gold, and a trickle of blood dripped from her pale lips.

"I am Herathia," she said, voice hissing like wind, "the Guardian of Crimson, the Sphinx of the Abyss, the Protector of the Starlit Demon. You cannot enter, King Elethor Aeternum of Requiem, Son of Olasar. The way is forbidden to you."

Elethor flapped his stiff wings, refusing to land upon the mountain of bodies. The thrusts of air sent the smallest bodies, mere babes, tumbling down the mountain.

"Stand aside, or we will burn you," he said to the sphinx. "The Starlit Demon is a servant of Requiem; you will not block our way to him."

The sphinx tilted her head. The stitches running up her torso shifted, and blood seeped from them, trickling between her breasts to her feline paws. She snarled, baring sharp teeth stained with blood. Human heads filled her mouth, rotting, faces twisting in anguish.

"The old kings of Requiem placed the Starlit Demon here, long before the griffins attacked your halls, before your ancestors raised columns of marble, back in the days when your people lived feral, digging underground for shelter and knowledge. It was as a behemoth, devouring all, bringing evil upon the world; its starlight seared flesh and its wrath tormented and broke the minds of those who fought it. I am the Guardian of Crimson! I protect the evil of the beast. I move for none, not even for the spawn of those who placed me here. Leave this place of shadow. Return to your land and leave the darkness to rustle below the earth you till."

Lyana growled deep in her throat. "I know of you, Herathia! You lie. You are a riddler. We keep scrolls of your trickery in Requiem. You guard the way with riddles. I've read of them."

The sphinx turned her feline eyes to the blue dragon. "Lyana Eleison, daughter of Deramon, I do not merely ask riddles. I *kill* with riddles. If I ask you my questions, you will fail to answer. You will die. You will join the bodies at my feet, a million souls who thought they could answer me. They now form my bed. Turn back, Lyana and Elethor. Leave this place and do not tempt me; my words are poison and will cost you your souls."

Elethor stared at the bodies in disgust, still not daring to land upon them. "Do you mean... you asked these people riddles?"

The sphinx nodded. One of her stitches tore, and pus dripped from her. "They failed to answer."

Elethor growled. He had no time for this. His people languished underground while Solina attacked; he could wait no longer. He let fire grow in his belly.

"They did not have dragonfire," he said, roared, and blew a jet of flame.

The fire spun and slammed against the sphinx. Lyana howled and added her fire to Elethor's. The inferno roared, white hot. The bodies on the mountaintop burned. The heat blazed against Elethor's eyes, blinding him. He kept spewing his fire, wings fanning it, as much as he could muster.

Finally, after long moments, the flames died.

The sphinx stood upon seared bodies, unharmed. The stitches along her torso had melted, revealing a gaping cavern full of severed hands. The skin around her wound, however, was as pale and sagging as before.

"Do you think mortal fire can burn me?" she asked. She narrowed her feline eyes, bared her teeth, and raised her claws.

Black lightning blazed from them. A bolt slammed into Lyana. She gasped and fell. A second bolt crashed against Elethor's chest, and pain suffused him. He opened his maw to roar, but found no breath. Agony spread across him, clutching at his throat, crushing his innards. The pain was so great, he lost his magic. His wings and scales vanished, and he thudded onto the mountain in human form.

Black lightning raced across him, raising smoke, and finally he found his voice. He screamed in anguish. Lyana twisted on the bodies beside him, also back in human form, sparks twisting around her like serpents. She wept and screamed.

"Enough!" Elethor shouted, tears streaming down his cheeks, and with a flash, the lightning vanished. He doubled over, gasping for breath and trembling. Lyana coughed beside him, on hands and knees, head lowered and hair dangling in a red curtain. He crawled toward her over the bodies, his knees digging into their flesh, and raised a trembling hand to touch her hair.

"Lyana," he said, voice hoarse.

She coughed, struggled to her feet, and stood atop the bodies. Legs shaking, Elethor stood up beside her. The sphinx dwarfed their human forms. She towered over them, an implacable sentinel of bone and skin and stench. Her golden orbs, each the size of a human head, glimmered down at them.

"Turn back, children of starlight," the sphinx said, voice deep as the sky. "You will not pass my door."

"We will pass!" Lyana shouted up to her. "Ask us your riddles, Herathia, Crimson Guardian. We will answer them. We will not fail."

The sphinx bared her fangs. Blood rained from her mouth. "Very well. I will ask you my riddles. And you will ask me yours. We will take turns like the great riddle masters of old. If I cannot answer your riddles, I will let you pass." She licked the blood off her lips. "And if you cannot answer mine... your bodies will lie forever at my feet."

DERAMON

He stood, stiff and aching, and lowered his head. The smoke stung his eyes and his gut felt colder than the heart of winter. His men stood at his sides, staring at the ground. His wife stood ahead, eyes raised, praying to the ceiling as if stars could still shine upon them.

"May the Draco constellation bless their spirits. May their souls find their way to our starlit halls."

Adia closed her eyes, whispered last words, and nodded. Ten of Deramon's men began shoveling dirt into the ditch, covering the dozens of bodies. They had dug this crevice into the floor of a narrow, earthy tunnel, using makeshift shovels from broken axes and helmets.

This is no proper burial for warriors of Requiem, Deramon thought, jaw clenched. They deserved to be buried in a field of grass and flowers, or burned in a pyre like the great warriors of ancient days. Not this. He looked away, grimacing. And yet he knew they had to bury them somehow, and fast. If they began to rot, disease would spread, and more in these tunnels would die.

Adia sang softly as the dirt mounted, covering the bodies' limbs, then torsos, leaving the faces for last. Deramon had seen too many young men buried in his life, and they always buried the faces last. A bitterness caught in his throat, half a laugh, half a moan. *It's as if we hope that, as we shovel on the dirt, the dead might still awake and cry for salvation.*

His throat constricted. *Noela was wrapped in a shroud when I buried her,* he remembered. *At least I never had to see her face—the soft, innocent face of a babe—covered in dirt.* It had been thirteen years since his daughter's death, but the pain never lessened. If Noela truly waited among the stars, Deramon prayed that his fallen men would find her, protect her, and comfort her until the day they buried him too.

When the bodies were buried, Adia whispered, eyes damp. "As the leaves fall upon our marble tiles, as the breeze rustles the birches beyond our columns, as the sun gilds the mountains above our halls—know, young child of the woods, you are home, you are home. Requiem! May our wings forever find your sky."

Deramon mumbled the prayer with the rest of his men. Would they ever see sky again? He did not know. Did the souls of the fallen truly rise to the Draco constellation, dine in ghostly halls among the great kings of old? Deramon did not know that either. *When darkness surrounds you, belief in light comes hard.*

An image flashed through his mind, churning his gut: his eldest children lying dead in a mass grave, earth piling up upon them. Bayrin's face was pale, a gash running down his cheek. Lyana was as beautiful as ever, as beautiful as the day she'd been born. Finally earth would cover their faces too, leaving them to rot underground. Deramon gritted his teeth and clenched his fists, banishing the image.

They're still alive, he told himself. Bayrin was brave and clever; not as hardened as some guardsmen, but quick-witted, resourceful. He would know how to survive, how to protect the princess. Lyana was just as clever, and swift with the blade; if anyone could survive in the Abyss, that shadowy world beneath these tunnels, it was her.

Deramon rubbed his shoulder; it still blazed from where Solina had cut him. Worse was the shame of failing to kill her. *She was mine,* he thought, stomach roiling. He had only to swing his axe one more time, and he could have slain the Queen of Tiranor, ended this war, and sent the invaders fleeing. And yet he had failed. He had let her wound him, let her reach the armory, burn the wounded, claim the upper chambers. He lowered his head, eyes narrowed to slits.

"Deramon," came a soft voice. Adia approached and placed a hand on his shoulder. She stared at him, eyes soft. "You should rest. When is the last time you've slept?"

He sighed and held her hand. "Time? It has no meaning in the dark. It might have been a day, maybe three days, maybe a week." He turned away from her and nodded at two of his men. "Baras, Ilvar, follow. We will inspect the lines."

They walked through a narrow, clammy labyrinth. The tunnels were darker and rougher down here. In the upper levels, passageways were wide and sturdy, their floors cobbled, their walls smoothed, their ceilings held with columns. Up there, archways led into fine chambers: the library, the armory, the wine cellars, and more. All these had fallen to Solina. Here, in the deeper levels, only crude burrows wound. Some were natural caves. Others were abandoned mines where the ancients had dug for iron and gold. All were as cold and dark as wormholes.

His men lined the walls, holding spears and swords; most were bandaged, burnt, and bloody. Survivors sat and lay at their feet: frightened children, mothers holding babes, and old men and women who whispered and wept. Every Vir Requis over age thirteen now stood as a soldier, even those who'd never swung a sword. They bore the steel of their fallen comrades. As Deramon walked down the lines, inspecting them, they stared back with solemn, deep-set eyes. Many were mere youths—boys who had never shaved, kissed a girl, or dreamed of war.

So many gone, Deramon thought as they walked. Once, he had commanded a thousand men of the City Guard, warriors to defend Nova Vita. Two hundred of those men now stood here; the Tirans had killed the rest. Once, five thousand more warriors, King Olasar's Royal Army, had fought for Requiem; they had burned over King's Forest. Once, fifty knights had defended the realm; now only one remained, his daughter.

So many burnt. So many dead. Even if Bayrin finds the Moondisk, and even if Lyana wakes the Starlit Demon, how can we recover from such loss?

Soon Deramon turned around a bend and reached the barricade, a pile of boulders and pikes blocking the upper chambers. Fifty men stood here, clad in plate armor, swords drawn; they were as many as could fill this tunnel. Silence blanketed the darkness. No more screams rose from above.

Good, Deramon thought. *May our men who fell captive find some peace in death.*

"Garvon," he said to one of his captains—a gaunt man with one eye, a white beard, and a splintered shield. "How is the guard?"

The man bowed his head. A cut ran down his cheek, freshly stitched. "Quiet, my lord. The Tirans have made no attempt to break the barricade for hours. They're regrouping; many of them are wounded too."

"They will attack soon," Deramon said, voice hoarse. *Stars, if they have more of that dark magic that broke our first barricade, how will we hold back the tide?*

Garvon nodded, gripping his sword. "We are ready for them, my lord. We will hold them back. And if they break through, we will fight them in the tunnels and cut them down in darkness." He raised his chin. "The upper chambers are wide; they could burn us there. Here in the narrow depths, they will fall."

No, Deramon thought. *We cannot defeat them, even here. Not with so few men. Not against the wrath and fire of these southern demons.* They needed aid; Deramon knew that. They needed his children back.

Boots thumped behind him, running up from the deeper tunnels, and a man called out, "Lord Deramon!"

He turned to see Silas, a young soldier who had once guarded the eastern wing of Olasar's palace. Today half his face was burnt and bandaged, but he still carried a sword and shield. His eyes were wide and blood splashed his dented armor.

"What is it, Silas?" said Deramon. "Speak."

The young soldier reached him and bowed his head. "My lord Deramon, men are fighting at the silo. One stabbed another. Others are trying to grab the sacks of grain."

Deramon began marching at once, fists clenched. Silas followed. What guards lined the walls stood at attention, chins raised, hands grasping swords and spears.

Children of Requiem squabbling over grain like hens, Deramon thought in disgust. *I will have them flayed.* His anger bubbled in him. His king had fallen. The new Boy King had plunged into darkness. He, Deramon Eleison, was caretaker of Requiem now, an ancient and proud kingdom. He would not let it descend into madness on his watch.

He marched down sloping, twisting tunnels like the veins of a stone giant. Soon he reached the lower silos. The main pantries were higher up, in the chambers Solina had claimed; there Requiem stored its dried fruit, vegetables, smoked meats, salted fish, barley, and sacks of golden grain. Here in the depths was only what grain the upper chambers could not hold—a meager supply that Deramon doubted could feed the survivors for a moon. Ten guards stood at the silo's gateway, holding back a crowd of men who were trying to push through. One man lay dead in the corner, a knife in his heart.

"My daughter is starving to death!" a man was shouting, shoving a guard. "Starving! She has not eaten in three days. She is only four years old. How could you stand here like this, letting us die?"

Another man began shoving a second guard. "There is grain behind you! You are a man of Requiem, or do you serve the Tirans? Let us through."

The guards were scowling and shoving the men back. "The grain is rationed. Your children are not starving; they received grain like everyone else."

The first man had tears on his cheeks. "What grain? She hasn't eaten in three days! Where are these rations? Not all received them." He grabbed the guard's spear and tried to wrench it free. "I will hand out the grain."

Deramon stormed toward them, howling. "Cease this!"

His guards bowed their heads. The men who'd tried to break through cried of hunger, of famished children, of youths eating double rations, leaving others to starve. Deramon listened and scowled. He was a fighter; he knew how to kill an enemy with steel, claw, and dragonfire. Hunger was a foe he had never known, and it might be the foe that slew them here.

How long before this grain is gone? How long until we turn to eating one another? Two moons? One?

"Silas," he said to his guard, "organize another round of rations—one cup of grain per person. Take what men you need to make sure everyone eats. If you see anyone eating double rations, depriving another of food, I want them clamped in irons and brought before me."

Silas bowed. "Yes, my lord."

Sacks of grain were opened and gourds being filled when shouts rose from the tunnels behind. Steel clanged and cries echoed. A soldier came racing from around the corner, face red.

"My lord Deramon! Tirans are breaking through the barricade. They have a battering ram."

Deramon cursed, drew his sword, and ran. His soldiers ran with him. He raced up the tunnels, heart hammering.

Maybe it won't be hunger that kills us after all, he thought. He rounded a corner and beheld the barricade collapsing, sending boulders tumbling and dust flying. Through the wreckage, he glimpsed a battering ram slam into the rocks. Tiran troops stood around it, blades drawn and eyes full of bloodlust.

It is a blessing, Deramon thought and snarled. *We'll die of steel and fire. We'll go down fighting after all.*

A dozen Tiran troops broke through the wreckage, leaped over the boulders, and ran toward him. Deramon howled, swung his sword, and leaped into battle.

MORI

Her pain had faded into a daze. Her wings blazed with agony; she knew that, but could barely feel it. Her lungs burned, her muscles cramped, her heart thudded. The agony drove through her, but exhaustion drowned it like a gag muffling screams. She and Bayrin had been flying for a day and a night. Dawn rose around her, and still she saw no island, only endless leagues of sea.

She wanted to ask Bayrin how he was, but could find no breath. He flew by her, tongue lolling. Her wings felt like they could fall off. She could almost imagine it—one more flap, and they'd disconnect like sails torn from a ship, fly alone into the horizon, and she would tumble. Despite herself she laughed weakly.

"Bayrin," she managed. "Let's... let's swim for a while."

If she could no longer fly, perhaps she could swim, let her wings rest and her legs propel her onward. She began spiraling down, wings billowing, the smell of salt in her nostrils. When she reached the water, she nearly crashed into it. It stung her belly, ice cold, shocking her. She lost her breath and wanted to take flight again, but could not. Her wings hurt too much. Lashing her tail, she managed to flip onto her back, stretch out her wings, and float.

Bayrin spiraled down above her. He crashed into the water by her side, howled, and cursed.

"Stars, this water's cold!" He flipped onto his back and floated beside her. He panted, smoke rising between his teeth. "Gone is the hope for any future little Bayrins."

Mori smiled wanly, not sure she understood the jest, but thankful that Bayrin's spirit was high enough to attempt one. Though she shivered in the water, she was thankful for a break from flight; her wings cramped and blazed in pain. She lay upon the water, watching the clouds roil. They formed gray and blue shapes like swooping dragons which soon began to weep. The sleet pattered against her belly. Suddenly she found that she too was weeping.

"Mori!" Bayrin said. "I know you were hoping for little Bayrins, but... what's wrong?"

What was wrong? How could he ask that? Her world had fallen. Orin was dead and so was Father. Her city lay in ruin, Elethor was in the Abyss, and she lay here, a dirty and impure thing, floating in a sea that could never wash her shame. She wept for her fallen brother and father, for her soul that too felt dead. But how could she tell Bayrin that? How could she speak to anyone of the twisting guilt, grief, and agony inside her? How could she tell them that she still saw Orin's eyes, lifeless, staring at her from his burnt face as Acribus choked her?

Instead she only said, "Bayrin... I want to go home."

He sighed and his eyes softened. He reached out his wing and touched her shoulder.

"We will go home," he promised. "We'll fly over Requiem again, Mori. You and I, and Elethor and Lyana. We'll hunt in King's Forest, stargaze from Lacrimosa Hill, and lie in the palace gardens and watch the birds. We'll sit by the fireplace in Alin's Alehouse, drink sweet ice wine, and listen to minstrels play. You'll read your books with maps, and Elethor will whittle those little wooden animals of his, do you remember them? We will rebuild our city. We will go home again."

But was there a home? she wondered. Was there still a forest, and a garden, and an alehouse, or had they burned? Was there still a city to rebuild, or mere piles of ash and bodies? Did Elethor and Lyana lie dead underground, or twisted by black magic?

"I have to believe," she whispered. "Or otherwise let the sea claim me." She stared into Bayrin's eyes. "We will find the Moondisk. We have to."

Or else all this pain, this death, was for nothing.

Bayrin opened his mouth, as if about to speak, when suddenly his eyes widened. A cry of pain tore from his maw.

"Bayrin!" Mori cried.

He kicked and floundered. His wings fluttered, spilling water, and he rose from the sea.

Mori screamed.

A twisting lamprey clung to Bayrin's back, its mouth locked onto his scales. The creature looked like a great, writhing worm, tall and wide as an oak. Its tail lashed in the water. Hovering above the water, Bayrin tried to soar. His wings fanned the sea, sending ripples across it, but he was upside down, legs kicking uselessly at the air. He could not rise. The lamprey tugged, holding him down like a chain.

"Get it off!" Bayrin cried.

Mori flipped onto her belly, craned her neck forward, and blew fire.

The jet slammed against the lamprey, roaring hot. The creature opened its mouth, detaching itself from Bayrin, and screamed. Its mouth was a perfect circle, a foot in diameter, and ringed with several rows of teeth. Blood filled it.

Bayrin soared, teeth marks on his back. Below, the burnt lamprey crashed into the water and began swimming toward Mori.

Heart pounding, she leaped from the water, wings flapping. Waves rippled. She soared, dripping wet, and the lamprey leaped, soaring after her. It was massive—easily the length of her tail—its body slick and undulating. Its mouth opened wide. Wings thudding madly, Mori screamed, swiped her tail, and knocked it aside. It crashed into the water, writhing and screeching.

"What the stars was that?" Bayrin shouted, blood on his scales. He looked from side to side, as if seeking it.

Water rose in curtains. Two lampreys leaped from the sea and flew toward them. They had no wings, but they soared as if shot from geysers. Their maws opened wide, and their teeth glimmered.

Mori screamed and blew fire at one. The other slammed against her tail, and its teeth sank into her flesh. She cried in pain, lashed her tail, and began to fall. It tugged her down—she could barely believe its weight. She flapped her wings madly, struggling to rise.

"Bayrin!"

He swooped, leveled off, and shot forward. His flames baked the creature. It screeched and fell.

Three lampreys leaped from the sea.

Mori shouted, batted one aside with her tail, and flew high. A lamprey shot up to her right, dripping water and screeching. She flamed it and kept soaring, and soon the sea was distant below her. Ten more lampreys leaped from the water, and Mori was sure that she flew high enough. But the lampreys kept flying upward, as if they were mere fountains of water. Their mouths opened wide.

Bayrin blew fire at one. Mori blasted her flames at another. One flew up directly beneath her, mouth wide, tongue reaching out. She swerved, and the lamprey knocked against her side, mouth sucking the air. She tumbled, flapped her wings, and knocked into another lamprey. She clawed at it, beat it back, and flew higher.

"Bayrin, higher!" she shouted.

They climbed the sky. Soon they flew so high, the waves were mere ripples, and the air was cold and thin. When the lampreys crashed back into the sea below, they seemed small as earthworms. Mori blew out her breath in relief.

"Bayrin," she said, "you're hurt, I—"

Screeches rose below. She looked down to see a hundred lampreys, maybe more, shoot up from the water. *They must be mad,* she thought. *We're hundreds of feet in the air.*

And yet they kept soaring, tails flapping, propelling themselves through the air as if swimming underwater. Mori growled and flew even higher, but the lampreys were faster. Soon they were feet away, and she bathed them with fire. They kept shooting up, aflame. Several shot around her, so fast that she felt the whoosh of air. Another slammed into her belly, and she shouted, clawed at it, and knocked it off.

The lampreys who overshot her turned in midair and began to fall. One slammed onto her back, its teeth dug into her shoulder, and she screamed.

A growl pierced the air. Bayrin swooped, a lamprey clinging to his tail, and slashed his claws. He dug into the lamprey on Mori's back, and when it opened its mouth to screech, it detached from her flesh and fell.

"Bay!" Mori cried and blew flame, hitting the lamprey that tugged on his tail. It burned, writhed madly, and tumbled.

Dozens more came shooting up from the sea.

"Damn it!" Bayrin said. "These things could probably fly to the stars themselves. If flying up won't stop them, fly north! Come on!"

The lampreys soon soared around them, mouths sucking air, tongues seeking. The dragons flew forward on the wind, blasting fire at the creatures. They seemed endless. Whenever one crashed back into the water, three more shot up. The wounds on Mori's shoulder blazed; the lamprey's teeth had chipped her scales and dug down to the flesh. Blood trickled from her leg. She blew fire in all directions, but soon her flames dwindled to mere sparks; she would need rest and food to replenish them, and she would find neither in this sea.

"Mori, look, ahead!" Bayrin shouted. He slammed a lamprey with his tail and clawed another.

Mori stared ahead and gasped. Her heart leaped. Tears sprang into her eyes, and she howled.

"The island! The Crescent Isle!"

It still lay leagues away, but her eyes were sharp, and she knew this was the place. Green and misty, it formed the shape of a crescent moon. From here, it seemed as small and distant as the moon itself. She had never felt such hope, such joy and relief. Her body shook with it. She blazed toward her salvation.

A volley of lampreys flew at her. Several slammed into her belly, knocking her into a spin. Teeth dug into her. For a moment she saw only spinning sky and clouds.

She clawed the lamprey on her belly, but it wouldn't release her. More of the beasts flew around her, mouths peeling back, revealing their many teeth. They leaped from all sides, flew in arcs, and rained above her. One more slammed into her side and bit. Soon they were sucking her blood as she screamed.

"Bayrin!"

Three of the beasts clung to him, writhing as they fed. Bayrin howled. He tried to roast them with fire, but only sparks left his maw; he too was too tired, too famished, too weak. He clawed at the beasts, and one fell, but two others slammed into him and bit.

"Fly, Mori, to the island!"

She coughed and gasped for breath. Two lampreys clung to her, and dozens more leaped all around. She lashed her claws and tail, knocking them aside. She couldn't even claw the ones attached to her without letting ten more bite.

"Mori, fly!"

She flew. Her wings blazed. She howled in pain. She shot forward, dipping, rising again, tumbling. She managed to slash the lamprey on her belly, and it fell, but two more leaped. One attached its maw onto her leg, and the other replaced the one on her belly. She screamed and clawed but kept flying.

She dipped. Soon she flew a hundred feet over the water, then fifty. The lampreys kept tugging her down, drinking her blood, and she howled as she flew.

Please, stars, give me strength, let me reach the land alive.

She did not know how long she flew. Minutes seemed like hours. Her eyes blurred. She could barely hear Bayrin roar at her side, barely see him. Mist swirled around her. Pines rose ahead.

The island.

It lay a league away, maybe closer, its trees towering, dark green columns rising from fog. She flapped her wings with every last drop of her strength. Just to reach that island. Just to land. To rest. To sleep.

A lamprey leaped from the water, slammed into her, and bit her neck.

Her eyes rolled back, she tumbled, and icy water crashed around her.

Her head went under. Water filled her nostrils. She kicked, dazed, pain pounding through her. She screamed and bubbles rose around her, white orbs in the deep blue. Her blood rose like red ghosts. Weakly, she lashed her claws, pierced one lamprey, and saw ten more swim toward her.

Goodbye, Bayrin, she thought. *Goodbye, Requiem. I go now to the starlit halls... to Father and Mother. To Orin.*

Claws slashed. A tail swung. Fangs bit. Lampreys screeched and fled, and Bayrin grabbed her under her wings, pulled her up, and her head rose from the water. She gasped for air.

"Mori, fly! Fly, Mori, we're almost there. Fly!"

He tugged her, raising her from the water. Boulders jutted around them. A rocky beach rose ahead, appearing and disappearing as waves crashed. She flapped her wings once, rose from the water, flapped again. Pines rose ahead like the columns of Requiem. She growled and flew, a lamprey still on her shoulder. She knocked her feet against a boulder, flapped her wings again, and drove a dozen feet forward. She hit another boulder, flew again, leaped and soared and crashed onto a beach.

Bayrin landed beside her, three lampreys on his body. He thrashed and knocked them off. Mori leaped onto them and bit, digging her fangs into their flesh. They opened their bloody maws to screech, and the dragons scurried up the shore, coughing and hacking. Bayrin slammed his tail against the last lamprey clinging to Mori, and it too fell, wriggled down the beach, and disappeared back into the water.

The wet, wounded dragons pulled themselves forward, too weak to fly, until they crawled beneath the pines. There they crashed down upon fallen pine needles, panting, blood seeping.

"We made it," Mori whispered, staring up at mist that swirled between the evergreens. "We reached the Crescent Isle."

Bayrin coughed and smoke rose from his mouth. Their tails reached out, seeking each other, and braided together. Soft rain began to fall. Mori closed her eyes and slept.

SOLINA

She walked down the tunnel, sabres drawn, and entered the library. Her lips peeled back in a smile.

The chamber was as she remembered. Its ceiling curved high above, high enough that if she wanted, she could shift into a phoenix here too, burn all the books and scrolls upon the shelves. But she was no brute, no mindless killer. Unlike most of her men, she knew how to read and write—both Old and Common Tiran, the Dragontongue of Requiem, and the High Speech of eastern Osanna. She knew that books held power—a power greater than steel, as great as magic itself. She would empty these shelves. She would take these books and scrolls back to the desert, place them in her temples, and learn from their lore.

Requiem will remain bare of knowledge, she thought, *a wasteland of skeletons and dried blood.*

"My queen!" said one of her men, a captain with a bloody sunburst on his breastplate. He bowed before her, fist against his chest. "The prisoners await your inspection."

She nodded curtly and walked deeper into the library. At the back wall, twenty weredragons stood in chains. Solina snarled. When she had lived in Requiem, the weredragons would taunt her. They would shift into dragons, fly above, blow fire, and she would watch from below, a scared and weak girl with no magic. In chains, they were as helpless as she had been. They had been stripped naked. Their bodies were lashed, bloody, and broken. Three were men, supposed warriors; the rest were women and children.

"Reptiles," she said to them, voice dripping with disgust. "Look at you. Naked. Filthy. Weak." She laughed bitterly. "You call yourself a noble race, an ancient and proud people." She spat. "I see only wretches."

A few of the weredragons stared back, defiance in their eyes. Others moaned, blood seeping from their wounds. The chains chafed their wrists and ankles, digging into the flesh. One, a girl no older than the princess Mori, was trying to shift. She grimaced, and scales appeared and disappeared on her body, and wings sprouted and vanished from her back. When her limbs began to grow, the chains dug deeper, shedding blood, keeping her in her filthy human form. Tears ran down her cheeks.

Solina approached the girl, a soft smile on her lips. "Precious," she said softly. "Do you still try to fight?"

The girl looked up with teary eyes, opened her mouth to speak, and Solina swung her sword. Raem, her blade of dawn, sliced the weredragon's neck as easily as a fisherman gutting his catch. Blood gushed, the girl gasped and choked, and her head slumped back. She lay still, blood spilling down her body to pool around her.

Solina grinned, teeth clenched, as the other weredragons howled.

Five years ago, this girl would have taunted me, she thought. *She would have shifted, soared in the sky, mocked my lack of magic. She would have burned me too, burned me like Orin did.* She snarled. *They all would burn me if they could.*

She ran her fingers along her line of fire, the scar that split her face and body. It still burned sometimes. She could still feel the screaming agony of fire. The rage and pain pounded through her, spinning her head. She turned to another chained weredragon, an old man with one eye, and she lashed her blade across his stomach. She stared with cold eyes as he screamed, as his innards spilled.

She turned to the next one. Her blades swung. She moved from weredragon to weredragon, ridding the world of their evil, banishing their shadow with her light.

"For the Sun God!" she cried as she plunged her blades into the last one, a child clinging to the corpse of his mother. "For your glory, Lord of Light! I banish the weredragon curse for you."

Blood washed the floor, rivers of it, intoxicating with its scent. Blood had splashed her face, Solina realized. She wiped it with her fingers and licked them eagerly.

Soon I will drink Elethor's blood too, she thought. *Soon we will meet again, my love.*

"Clean this mess," she said to her men. "If the blood dirties the books, I will replace the parchment with your hides."

She turned and left the library, grinning savagely, boots sloshing.

ELETHOR

He stood upon the mountain of bodies, still in human form, and faced the sphinx. Herathia's feline body rose taller than him, draped in wrinkly skin. Her torso and head towered, a pale woman as large as a dragon. The Crimson Archway rose above her, leading into shadow and mist.

"Ask us your riddles," Elethor said to her, heart pounding. He reached out and clasped Lyana's hand. She squeezed back.

Behind that archway waits the Starlit Demon, he thought. *Behind that archway is the hope for my people, for Lyana, for my sister. I must pass.*

He swallowed a lump in his throat, remembering the pain of the sphinx's curse. If he failed to answer her riddles, how long would she torment him before letting him die? A minute? Hours? Moons or years? Eventually he and Lyana would join these bodies, a new peak for the mountain of them, and Requiem would fall. Everybody he knew would die.

No, he told himself and drew sharp breaths. *Don't think about that now. You will answer the riddles. You will pass through the archway.*

The sphinx regarded him, a soft smile on her lips, as if she could read his mind. A trickle of blood ran from her lips and trailed down her body, snakelike. She opened her mouth, revealing bloody fangs and chewed human heads, and spoke in a deep voice like wind through tunnels.

"All love me with full hearts
They visit me by day
Yet they cry around me
At night they stay away"

Elethor raised his eyebrows, considering. He turned to look at Lyana. She stared at the sphinx, frowning, lips scrunched together. She turned and met his gaze, thought a moment, then nodded.

"Seems easy enough," she said.

Elethor couldn't help it. Even here, wounded and famished, leagues underground upon a pile of bodies, he rolled his eyes.

"Of course it's easy for you," he muttered. "Everything always is."

She glared at him, fire blazing in her green eyes. "If it were up to you, Elethor, I think we'd grow old trying to solve it." She turned to look up at the sphinx. "I have the answer!"

The towering creature gazed down upon them, stars glimmering in her feline eyes. Her tongue licked her lips. "Answer! But if you answer wrong, your souls will be my prize."

Elethor winced, remembering the pain of her black lightning.

"Lyana, wait," he began. "What are you—"

But she ignored him and called up to the sphinx, "The answer is: a beloved's grave."

Herathia's lips curled back, showing teeth and gums. Elethor's heart pounded as if trying to escape his chest, and his palms dampened. A beloved's grave? He wished Lyana had consulted with him first, but by the stars, the answer did fit.

"Well?" he demanded of the sphinx. "Is that the answer?"

She shifted her claws, each one as long as his body. They dug into the corpses she sat upon, tearing through the pale flesh into bloodless cavities. Her tongue darted out and a hiss left her throat, a sound like steam. She was laughing, Elethor realized.

"You have," she said, "answered correctly."

Elethor breathed out a shaky sigh of relief. His hands tingled and he turned to Lyana. She looked at him, gasping and smiling. She hesitated an instant, then stepped over a body and embraced him. She clung to him, and Elethor realized that she was trembling and that tears filled her eyes.

"I was right," she whispered, voice shaky. "Thank the stars, I was right."

He tried to snort derisively, but only a weak puff of air left his nostrils. "Of course you were right. You always are, remember?" He turned to the sphinx. "Herathia! We answered your riddle. Will you let us pass?"

Her lips pulled back further, past the gums, showing veins and red flesh clinging to her skull. "You will not pass, child of stars. You answered one riddle, but did not ask one of your own. Ask me a riddle, Boy King. If I cannot answer, then you may pass my door."

He groaned. Ask her a riddle of his own? He knew no riddles. He was a sculptor, a stargazer, a reluctant king. He squeezed Lyana's hand.

"Any riddles under that mop of red curls?" he asked her.

She scrunched her lips, a line appearing between her eyebrows. She spoke in a low whisper into his ear. "The answer would have to be something Herathia wouldn't know. Something of sunlight, or sky, or trees... something foreign to this dark place."

Elethor looked around him. The mountain of bodies sloped into valleys of stone. Rocky walls surrounded the place, rising to form a dome above their heads. Rivers of lava flowed and clouds of smoke danced like demons.

"That pretty much includes everything other than fire, rock, and death," he whispered back.

They thought in silence for long moments. Elethor tried to remember riddles he had heard in childhood. He vaguely recalled reading a book of them in the library—he had shared a few with Mori—but could remember none.

Mori would have remembered, he thought. *She loves that library.*

His sister was always so sad, so frightened, but when reading in the library, she would smile, laugh, and her eyes would sparkle. She would run to him with a new book, show him a word that she loved, or a tale that moved her, and life and joy would overcome her shyness. At the memory of her eyes and smile, a lump filled Elethor's throat, and tears stung his eyes.

"El, how's this?" Lyana said. She leaned forward, hid her mouth with her hand, and whispered into his ear.

He thought about her riddle but could not guess the answer until she revealed it. Nodding slowly, he helped her fine-tune the wording, praying that Herathia could not hear whispers behind palms. Finally, when they were happy with their riddle, Lyana turned to face the sphinx.

"Herathia!" she cried. "We have a riddle."

The sphinx gazed down at them, eyes blazing, tongue licking the air. She seemed eager like a cat toying with a mouse.

"Ask," she said.

Lyana raised her chin, thrust out her chest, and called out her riddle.

> *"I sing as fairly as a bird*
> *I glide as gently too*
> *I comfort the most aching soul*
> *With a voice so clear and true*
> *I live on branches and windowsills*
> *Relishing the breeze*
> *Yet I don't live*
> *Just place me down*
> *You'll silence me with ease"*

The sphinx did not miss a beat. An instant after Lyana fell silent, Herathia calmly spoke: "Wind chimes."

Elethor's heart sank. She had solved it! She hadn't even thought for a second! Had the sphinx heard them whispering? Had she cheated?

"You heard us whisper the answer!" he shouted at her. "Your ears must be sharper than ours. Will you cheat at our game?"

She snickered, a bubble of blood bursting on her lips. "I cheat not, shapeshifter. Insult me again, and our game will end, and you will die. I would like that." She snarled. "Prepare for my second riddle, children of stars. If you cannot answer, you will join my nest of corpses."

Elethor steeled himself with a deep breath and waited. After a moment of silence, the sphinx spoke her second riddle.

"I sadden the sun
High in heaven
And the night's moon too
I follow the eagle in his flight
I lived wherever he flew
At a ball I slide away
In a crowd I'm shy
I'll sneak up when you're alone
I'll make you shake and cry"

Lyana frowned and tapped her cheek. Elethor thought long and hard, but his mind was blank. He tapped his thigh, pursed his lips, and ran a dozen answers through his mind, but none fit. When he looked at Lyana, she was pale and her lips trembled.

She doesn't know either, he realized.

"Answer, shapeshifters!" the sphinx demanded and her eyes reddened. A growl left her throat, stinking of rot. "Solve my riddle or my light will sear you." She raised her claws.

Cold sweat washed Elethor. Lyana gasped and clutched her sword.

"Wait!" Elethor said to the sphinx. "I will answer, I..."

What riddles would he read with Mori in the library? He summoned back the memory, seeing his sister again; she would huddle in the shadows between books, a single candle lighting the library, smiling to herself softly, fleeing the world that scared her into the realms of imagination.

He breathed out shakily. He knew the answer.

"Loneliness," he said softly.

Lyana gasped at his side and whispered, "Of course."

The sphinx's eyes sparkled with amusement and hunger. She leaned forward, sending bodies rolling down the mountain. Elethor nearly fell, and Lyana clung to him. A gutted child rolled by him, disappearing down the mountain into shadow.

"This game is getting interesting," Herathia said. "You have answered true. Now ask me a riddle." She licked her lips, cutting her tongue on her teeth, then sucked the blood. "Make it hard."

Elethor turned to look at Lyana. Her eyes were solemn as she stared at him.

"We'll think silently," she said. "No more whispering."

He nodded. He tried to think of riddles, brow furrowed. Lyana covered her eyes and her lips moved silently. The sphinx leaned forward, drooling and hissing.

"Ask!" she shrieked. "Ask me your riddle or die!"

Elethor clenched his fists, shut his eyes, and thought until his head hurt. Suddenly, in a flash, it came to him. He remembered! Mori had asked him the riddle two years ago, laughing when he could not answer.

"I have a riddle for you," he said. He opened his eyes and looked at Lyana. She nodded, and he looked back at the sphinx and recited from memory.

> *"Never leaves home*
> *Walks alone*
> *When in danger*
> *Turns to stone"*

The sphinx sighed, rot on her breath. "A turtle," she said, "entering its shell for safety."

Lyana stared at him, mouth open, eyebrows raised and head tilted.

"It was a tough riddle," he answered in a small voice. "I couldn't answer when Mori asked me."

Lyana's face turned red, and she looked ready to throttle him. She gritted her teeth as if stifling rage, breathed in heavily, and turned away.

"I will ask you a third riddle," said the sphinx. "Are you ready, children of stars?"

Elethor and Lyana looked at each other, took deep breaths, and nodded. The sphinx raised her head and spoke, voice echoing across the mountain.

> *"Young princess of sand*
> *Sad prince of snow*
> *Turned to queen and king*
> *From the desert*
> *With heat and blood*
> *The birds of fire sing*
> *When father falls and brother dies*
> *When flesh and fire burn*
> *When an ancient kingdom falls to ruin*
> *Why does our king still yearn?"*

Elethor clenched his fists and lowered his head. Rage and shame coursed through him. This was not fair. This was no riddle; it was an accusation, a cheat, a trick. He raised his burning eyes and stared at the sphinx.

"You speak of me," he said, voice raw. "And of Solina."

He did not know how the sphinx knew of life aboveground. Could she see through leagues of rock and flame? Was she a goddess like the stars of Requiem?

Lyana clenched her fists and howled. "You are cheating!" she said. "This is not a true riddle. I've read books of riddles before." She panted with rage, cheeks red. "Riddles follow a format. Their answer is simple, their hints obscure. The answer always snaps into place and seems obvious when you know it. This is just a question, not a riddle!"

The sphinx raised her brow. "This is the greatest riddle of his life. He must answer."

Elethor gritted his teeth and looked away. Did the sphinx want to cheat? Fine. He would answer. He would play her game.

"Because she was *mine*!" he said, digging his fingernails into his palms.

The sphinx growled and raised her claws. "That is no answer, Boy King."

"It is the only answer!" he shouted, eyes burning. "I'm not ashamed of it. You want to know why I still love Solina? Why, even after she butchered my family, toppled my city, and murdered my people, I still love her?"

His breath came heavy. He was aware of Lyana gaping at him, but paid her no mind. Blood pounded in his ears, and his heart thrashed as if trying to break his ribs. His head spun, and the sphinx eyes stared at him, boring into him, peeling his soul.

"Yes," he whispered. "I still love her, Herathia. When I think of her eyes, her hands in mine, the sunlit days when we lay upon grass, yes... I still love her, even now. Because she was mine." Tears burned in his eyes. "Orin had his inheritance, his sword, his betrothed. My father had his throne. Mori was adored by the court. But I had no room there; I was a lesser prince, a mere sculptor, no warrior or leader. But Solina..." He could barely breathe; his lungs ached. "She was beautiful, and strong, and wise, and from another world. She was a princess, a great light in her homeland. And she loved me. Me, the younger prince—not Orin, not my father, but me. She was mine, and proud, and beautiful, and I would share her with none. Earning her love was the greatest thing I could do; she was my crown, my throne, my golden pride."

He realized that tears ran down his cheeks, his chest rose and fell, and his fingers shook. Vaguely, he was aware of Lyana placing her hand on his shoulder.

"So yes," he whispered, "I still love her, and I hate her. The heart will still love those that broke it, like a drunkard loves the wine that ruined him, like a poor gambler still loves his favorite game." He looked up at the sphinx and smirked through his pain. "Does that answer your riddle, Crimson Guardian?"

The sphinx was grinning—a cruel, feline grin, the grin of a huntress.

"Yessss," she hissed. "That answered it well. I like this game. Ask me another riddle."

Rage flared in Elethor, turning the world red. This was all a game to her! He had spilled out his innermost secrets, secrets he had spoken to no one. His people were dying. Lyana probably hated him now, and always would, as much as he hated himself. And all this demon could do was grin! Anger made him tremble. If she would cheat, he could cheat too. If she could ask questions to trap him, he could do the same to her.

Without even looking at Lyana, he shouted out his next riddle. It was an old riddle Mori and he would laugh about as children. A trick. A game of words. A *cheat*.

"Why don't donkeys drink dawn's delicious dew?"

Beside him, Lyana gasped and spun toward him. Her face reddened, and she looked ready to shout, attack him, or faint. Elethor ignored her. He stared at the sphinx, chin raised.

Herathia hissed and glared. "That is no riddle." Her voice crinkled like old parchment. "What game do you play?"

"Answer me, Herathia!" he shouted. "Answer, or can you not? If you fail to solve my riddle, let us pass. These are the terms you agreed to, that the elders of Requiem bound you to. Answer!"

She tossed back her head and screamed, a sound so loud that Lyana covered her ears, and Elethor nearly fainted. Blood spouted from her mouth like a volcano. Her claws thrust, knocking down bodies.

Elethor refused to cow. "Can you not answer?"

She whipped her head down, spraying blood. "I should kill you, mortal. I should rip your head off and chew upon it for a thousand years as you scream in my mouth. Donkeys? Dew? What riddle is this?"

He took a step toward her. Blood filled her eyes, and he stared into them levelly. "That is my riddle. My sister told me this riddle years ago, when we were children. I could not solve it then. Can you?" He shouted over her screeches. "Why don't donkeys drink dawn's delicious dew?"

The wound along her torso split wider. Bodies spilled out, teeming with maggots. Skinned and bloody and headless, the bodies writhed, still alive, fingers groping.

"I asked for a riddle, not a trick, not a cheat!" cried the sphinx. Her voice rose like a storm. "Donkeys drink no dew, mortal! Donkeys in a field? They drink water, mortal. They drink water from a bucket or a stream. What trick is this? I do not accept your riddle. You cheat."

He stood firmly, even as she screamed so loudly, he thought his eardrums would burst. The bodies from her torso convulsed around him, nearly tripping him, but he managed to stay standing, to stare at her, to shout.

"Is that your answer? That donkeys drink from buckets and streams?"

Her skin peeled back, revealing rotten flesh crawling with centipedes. Her head caught flame and ballooned, boils growing across it.

"This is no riddle! He cheats, he tricks us! What is the answer? What is the trick?"

"Elethor!" Lyana cried. "We have to fly! She's going to kill us!"

No, Elethor thought. No, he would not flee. He had fled for too long. He had solved her riddle; he would answer this one too.

"Dawn's dew," he said, "drips from drunken dragons drooling." He smiled mirthlessly. "It's not much of a riddle. But it was enough to stump you."

Her head grew grotesquely, five times its previous size. Segments burst, revealing the skull within. Still she screamed, voice so high-pitched, it tore at Elethor's ears.

"Dawn's dew drips from drunken dragons drooling!" she cried. Her voice rose like steam. "He cheats! A joke! A trick!" Her eyes burst into flame. "You will suffer, Elethor of Requiem. You will suffer for this trickery. Requiem will fall! Her columns will crack and her skeletons will litter the earth. You will watch as she burns! You will watch as your people die. This I curse you with. This I vow to you. Your land will crumble as I do!"

The sphinx burst, shattering into a thousand pieces of flesh. They fell, chunks of meat, onto the bodies, turned to liquid, and seeped into the mountain like rain into soil. The screeching echoed through the chamber, then too fell silent.

She was gone.

The Crimson Archway loomed before Elethor, unblocked.

Slowly, blood on his face, he turned to Lyana. She gaped at him, wet and red. She opened and closed her mouth three times before she could speak.

"That was incredibly, inconceivably stupid!" she said. "Woolhead!"

He nodded. "That's the beauty of it."

She howled and hopped. "How dared you not consult with me first? How could you ask her a... a stupid tongue twister, not even a riddle?"

He shrugged. "It worked, didn't it?" He grasped her arms. "Lyana, that was the idea. The sphinx would have solved any real riddle. She lived here for thousands of years. She had heard them all, and if she hadn't, she'd heard enough to figure out any new ones. But a dumb tongue twister Mori invented? There was no chance she could have answered it." He swept his arm around them. "And it worked. It blew her apart." He sighed and looked into Lyana's eyes. "I do know what I'm doing sometimes, Lyana. I'm not always a woolhead."

She sighed, looked away, and blinked silently for long moments. Finally she looked back at him, leaned up, and kissed him on the lips.

"That," she said, "is the last kiss you'll ever get from me, so I hope you enjoyed it." She grabbed his hand and pulled him. "Now let's enter this archway and wake this Starlit Demon of yours."

They walked toward the bleeding archway. Shadows and mist swirled within it. With deep breaths and drawn swords, they stepped into the darkness.

BAYRIN

They slept through the night, holding each other as rain pattered against their scales. Dawn rose cold and so misty, Bayrin could only see several feet ahead: pines behind him, a rocky beach at his sides, whispering waves ahead. When he rolled onto his side, his scales clinked and his wounds blazed.

Mori stirred, smoke rising from her nostrils like more mist. Her eyes cracked open and gleamed. Dew glimmered on her golden scales, and lamprey bites dug red and raw on her shoulder, belly, and tail.

"Are we... are we on the island?" she whispered. "Or was it a dream?"

Bayrin struggled onto his feet, wincing as the bites across him burned. He unfurled his wings, flapped once, and tossed his head. His neck creaked. He was a lanky dragon, bones longer than most. And yet the island's pines dwarfed him; they must have stood two hundred feet tall, maybe more, as tall as Requiem's palace. Birds chirped, hooted, and cawed within them, and mist floated between the branches like ghosts. The piny scent filled the air, thick and heady. He breathed it deeply.

Mori rose to her feet, craned her neck back, and gasped. Her eyes lit up.

"Look at the size of them!" she whispered. "I've never seen trees so large." She turned to Bayrin, a smile showing her teeth. "These must be Mist Pines. Luna the Traveler wrote about them in her books. She said they're the largest trees in the world, and some are ancient, five thousand years old; that's older than Requiem itself."

Bayrin looked around at the mist. "How are we going to find the Moondisk here? Would it just be lying on the ground, hidden in a cave, stuck in a tree?" He snorted smoke. "Did Luna the Traveler write about that?"

Mori shook her head, scattering raindrops. "No. All I know is what I read in the book *Artifacts of Wizardry and Power.*" She quoted from it, chin raised. "In the Days of Mist, the Children of the Moon sailed upon ships to the Crescent Isle, built rings of stones among the pines, and danced in the moonlight. A Moondisk they forged of bronze inlaid with gold, and upon it the moon turns, and the Three

Sisters glow, and its light can extinguish all sunfire, so that the Sun God may never burn them."

Bayrin watched a snowy owl glide between the trees. He flapped his wings, rose in the air, and tried to grab it for breakfast, but it hooted and flew away. He landed back on the shore, claws digging ruts into the pebbly sand.

"So, we look for rings of stone," he said. "And we look for these Children of the Moon, whoever they are. That seems like a good start. Flying won't help us; the whole place is cloaked in mist and treetops." With a deep breath, he shifted into human form. When he stood upon his human feet, the trees seemed even larger, towering monoliths. "Let's walk and explore and find these Children of the Moon, if they're still around."

Mori shifted back into human form too. Her dress was tattered and damp, and tangles filled her hair. Her cheeks were pink and crusted with salt from the sea. Her eyes, however, still shone with hope, and Bayrin felt a jolt run through him, like a shot of strong rye on a cold night.

Stars, she's so beautiful when she's happy, he thought, and the thought surprised him. Mori—beautiful? How could Elethor's baby sister, a frightened girl who'd cry and run from him in childhood, seem so fair and kind and gentle?

He noticed that he was staring and looked away toward the trees.

"Let's go," he said and began to walk, leaving the beach and entering the forest. Mori walked at his side, head tilted back, gaping at the distant treetops.

They walked for a long time, though Bayrin could not judge how long. He couldn't see the sun; when he looked up, he saw only mist, branches, and leaves. His stomach twisted with hunger, but he found no food in this forest; birds hooted and cawed but remained hidden, and he saw no other animals. He rummaged through his pack, but found only moldy cheese and a soggy bread roll. As they walked, he scraped off the mold and shared the paltry meal with Mori.

A glimmer of white flashed between the trees.

"Bayrin, look!" Mori whispered.

He narrowed his eyes and stared. "I saw it."

Whatever it was, it was gone. Only mist remained between the branches, undisturbed. Bayrin cocked his head, listening, but heard only the distant sea, the wind in the pines, and the hooting owls.

"What was it?" Mori whispered. "Did you get a look? I saw only something white and flowing, like a silk scarf."

Bayrin sighed. "That's all I saw too. It was just another owl."

She shook her head. "No, it was larger than an owl. Let's go look for it."

They walked across a carpet of leaves, trunks rising around them. A stream gurgled ahead between mossy boulders. Across the stream, a boulder rose white and sharp upon a knoll, drenched in a sunbeam. On its craggy surface glowed a rune of three stars around a crescent moon. The moon glowed soft blue, while the stars glowed golden.

Bayrin and Mori approached the boulder silently, boots sinking into pine needles and crumbly earth. When Bayrin touched the stone, it felt unnaturally warm, like touching a mug of mulled wine.

"Bay!" Mori whispered and pointed.

He whipped his head around and saw the white flash again. It glowed a hundred yards away; it indeed looked like a silk scarf. In an instant, it was gone between the trees. Bayrin began to run, boots kicking up needles. Mori ran at his side.

"Come back here!" he called. "We're friends. Show yourself!"

He heard no reply, and after long moments of running, he stopped and breathed heavily. Mori panted at his side.

"I saw it!" she said. "It looked like an animal, a deer or a horse." Her eyes shone.

Bayrin rubbed his belly. "I could use a deer. I'd settle for a horse too."

He sighed and sat down heavily. His feet and back ached, and hunger gnawed at his belly. The lamprey bites had shrunk when he shifted into human form, but still burned. He wanted nothing more than to sleep, but how could he? It had been long days since they left Requiem. The survivors back home needed him, if they still lived. He placed his head in his hands.

"Bayrin, are you all right?" Mori sat down beside him and touched his shoulder.

He looked up at her soft, pale face, her gray eyes that melted with concern, her smooth brown hair full of leaves and salt. Could she be the last Vir Requis other than him? Were they doomed to be lone survivors from the slaughter?

"I don't know, Mori," he said and held her hand. "I don't know if we can find the Moondisk, or if it even exists. I don't know if anyone is alive back in Requiem. What if they're all dead already?"

A moon ago, he thought, Mori would have shivered and wept to hear his words. Today she stared back steadily, chin raised.

"Then they are dead," she said softly, "and we're the last ones. But I don't believe that, Bayrin. I can't believe it. Not yet." Her hand tightened around his. "When I was a child, I read stories of the great heroines who fought Dies Irae. I would dream of being brave like them—like wise Queen Lacrimosa, or like the warrior Gloriae the Gilded, or like the great Agnus Dei who burned her enemies with fire. I... I always felt so scared and weak compared to them. They were great fighters, and I... I was just a girl in a library, reading adventures to escape the world." A tear rolled down her cheek. "But now *we* face a war, Bayrin. We must be like those great warriors of old. It is our time to be brave, to believe, to fight for Requiem, to defeat the Sun God who burns us. Those heroes in the old stories... they never gave up. Even when things seemed hopeless, even when everyone died around them, they kept going. This is what courage means: to keep fighting even in the darkness, even when all but a sliver of hope is lost. An enemy can take your treasure, your land, even your life, but one thing he cannot take: your choice to fight back." She sniffed, tears in her eyes. "And I will fight back, Bayrin. I won't give up. Ever. Not so long as any of our people live, even if only you and I are left."

She trembled, and her tears fell, and when Bayrin reached out to wipe those tears, he found himself embracing her. Her eyelashes fluttered against his cheek, and his lips touched her forehead, and without knowing how, he was kissing her. Her lips were soft, warm, salty with her tears but sweet too. He cupped her cheek and kissed her for long moments, as if melting into her; he knew nothing but her softness, her scent, her hair around his fingers, and her body trembling against his.

Suddenly she gasped, pulled back, and gaped over his shoulder. A white figure, like a snowy animal, reflected in her eyes. Bayrin spun his head around and saw it there. The breath left his lungs.

It was no deer or horse, but a great white lion. Its mane seemed woven of moonlight, long and white, and its eyes shone silver, narrowed like two crescent moons. Its breath plumed and its tongue lolled, blood red. It met his gaze and held it for long moments, then turned and began loping away.

"It wants us to follow," Mori whispered. She rose to her feet and pulled Bayrin up too.

"She's scared of spiders," he muttered, "but vicious predators with dagger-like teeth? Those we follow."

They walked through the mist, following the white lion along palisades of pines. Its mane glowed like a beacon. When they fell behind, it would turn its head, stare, and wait. They followed for what seemed like leagues—over a cliff that overlooked the sea, along a fallen log that bridged a river, and into a valley like a bowl of mist. Dusk fell. Fireflies emerged to float through the mist, little moons behind clouds. The lion glowed ahead, and Bayrin and Mori followed in the shadows, crickets chirping around them.

As he walked, Bayrin touched his lips, still feeling Mori's kiss. Though Requiem burned in the south, and an island of magic rolled around him, he couldn't stop thinking of her lips against his, the softness of her hair, how her body had trembled against him. Bayrin had kissed girls before—Tiana, the kitchen maid in Requiem's palace, and Piri, the daughter of a winemaker, and a third girl who'd visited from the east and whose name he never learned. But none of them had felt so delicate in his arms, a flower he wanted to protect from the frost. He glanced at Mori as he walked, and when he saw her soft smile, again he felt it, that warm melting of his heart, like butter over fresh bread.

Mori... the girl he used to taunt, whose braids he would tug, whose tears he would mock. The girl who'd always tag along when he'd go hunting with Elethor, then cry whenever he caught a deer. The girl he'd scare at nights by squawking and pretending to be a griffin. How could he now feel this way toward her, the way he felt toward Tiana or Piri, but a hundred times stronger?

He realized that the lion had stopped walking, and Bayrin stopped too and looked ahead. In the darkness, a mountain rose from the pines, black against the stars. The lion stood at its feet, gazing up toward the peak, then turned toward him and Mori. Fireflies haloed around its head. Owls hooted in the darkness, crickets chirped, and wind rustled the trees, a night music like soft pipes in the temples of Requiem.

"Child of the Moon," Mori whispered, silver in the night's glow. She approached the lion and touched its head, gingerly at first, then warmly. She stroked it with a soft smile. "I am Mori Aeternum of Requiem, a child of starlight. I come seeking your help."

The lion's glow blazed, like a moon emerging from clouds. Mori pulled her hand back and gasped. The light coiled around the lion, a hundred fairies of silver, and it stood upon its back legs. Its back straightened, its front legs became arms, and soon it stood as a man. His skin was milky, his beard long and white. A broach, shaped as a crescent moon, glowed upon his silver robes. He seemed ageless, his face unlined, his eyes wise.

"You... you're a shapeshifter too!" Mori said, her breath catching. "Are you related to us Vir Requis?"

The man nodded and spoke with a deep, soft voice like waves and mist and the sound of light. "I am Aeras of the Crescent Isle, a child of moonlight." He smiled softly. "We have heard of Requiem, our sister land, whose children dance in the light of stars. We watched you fly over our sea, then become a man and woman upon our shore." He reached out his hands. "Welcome to our land, friends of the night."

Bayrin took a step forward, frowning. "If you saw us fly, why didn't you help us? Why did you wait and only show yourself now, when you knew we were hurt?" He looked around him, but saw only shadows. "And where are the rest of you?"

Aeras bowed his head. "We did not know if you were friends or foes; we have never met the children of Requiem's stars. Our only knowledge of your people comes from old songs and older whispers." His face darkened. "When we heard you speak of fighting the Sun God, we knew that we share a foe. Once our people covered many islands, but the cruel deity of sunfire burned us." He sighed and his eyes softened. "As for the others, you will meet them. We will give you food and healing herbs."

Bayrin had many questions. He wanted to ask about the Moondisk, and how many other lions lived here, and how they had managed to survive the Sun God's attacks. But before he could ask, Aeras turned and walked into the mist, robes gliding around him.

Mori took his hand. "Come, Bay, let's follow him." She smiled. "He'll help us."

They walked in darkness over fallen pine needles until they reached a gateway cut into the mountainside. Two statues flanked the opening, twenty feet tall, carved as owls. Their silver wings spread above them, forming a lintel. Aeras led the two Vir Requis under the wings and into a tunnel carved into the mountain.

Silver arches supported the tunnel, carved with runes of moons and stars. Jars of fireflies glowed in alcoves, lighting the way, and the air smelled of soil, deep water, and pines. They walked for long moments. Mori tilted her head back, gaping at the silver columns, the fireflies, and the glowing runes. A soft smile touched her lips, and on a whim, Bayrin reached out and held her hand. She squeezed his palm.

I used to mock her hand for its extra finger, he remembered. Now the feel of her hand in his felt warmer than mulled wine.

The tunnel began to widen, and cold air flowed from ahead, scented of wine and fur. Silver light fell upon them, like moonlight between summer clouds. A few more steps, and the tunnel opened into a vast, glittering chamber.

Mori gasped and tears filled her eyes.

"Beautiful," she whispered. "It's so beautiful, Bay."

Bayrin whistled softly.

"Stars," he said. "Now this is something."

He had been in caves before, but this was more like a palace. The chamber loomed, larger than Requiem's royal hall. Stalagmites and stalactites coiled and glittered, a hundred feet tall, like the melting candles of gods. Some formed shapes like dragons, others like knobby people, and some like trees.

These columns surrounded a silvery pool large enough to bathe ten dragons. Upon its water rippled the reflection of the moon, larger than Bayrin had ever seen it; he could see craters, valleys, and hills upon it. The moonlight filled the chamber. Bayrin looked up, expecting to see the true moon shining through a hole in the ceiling, but saw only a rocky dome glowing with runes.

Hundreds of white lions filled the chamber, he realized. Some lay between the stalagmites, eyes shut. Others whispered in nooks. Some stood around the pool of moonlight, drinking from its waters. When they saw Bayrin and Mori, the lions looked upon them, nodded, and whispered blessings.

"Welcome," said Aeras, "to the Chamber of Moonlight. Welcome to the heart of our realm."

He walked between the stalagmites, silks billowing. Bayrin and Mori followed, gaping at the melting stones, the glittering pool, and the lions who followed them with silvery eyes.

Aeras approached an alcove in the wall. The stone here was smooth, forming a rounded nook like a basket. Aeras gestured at it.

"Sit and rest," he said. "We will bring you food and song and healing."

Mori bit her lip and climbed into the nook. She leaned back against the smooth stone, pulled her knees to her chest, and smiled. She looked like a babe in a stone bassinet. Bayrin, however, remained standing. He ignored the ache in his muscles and wounds.

"Aeras," he said, "we can't rest. The Sun God attacks our home and we need your help. We seek the Moondisk—a weapon to defeat the phoenixes, great birds of fire that serve the Sun God and burn our people. Give us no food, no music, no healing—give us the Moondisk. We can't wait another hour."

The Children of the Moon looked at one another. Their eyes darkened and their glow dimmed.

Aeras sighed deeply. "The Moondisk will douse the fire of the phoenix; it has sent them fleeing from our island. But the disk has since been taken, and reclaiming it has failed us."

Bayrin felt the breath leave his lungs like air from a bellows. His shoulders stooped and his eyes stung. Ice seemed to wash his belly. Sitting in the nook, Mori gasped and her eyes dampened.

"So we failed," Bayrin said, voice choked. He felt like weeping, and it was all he could do to remain standing. "We've come all this way, and... the Moondisk is gone." He thought of his parents, his sister, and his friends, and his voice cracked.

Aeras raised his hands. "Not all hope is lost, child of stars! The Moondisk is not gone; it lies here upon this island, on the peak of this very mountain. Sit, child of starlight. Eat and drink, and we will tell you what you must know."

Warmth flickered inside Bayrin. The Moondisk, here on the mountain? What riddles was this man speaking? He wanted to throttle Aeras, to demand answers, but forced himself to sit by Mori. When more Children of the Moon brought him bowls of fruits, he ate, and when they served him jugs of water, he drank. Vaguely, he was aware that the fruit was fresh and sweet, the water pure and cool, but he could barely taste them. Famished as he was, he cared about no food, drink, or rest, only about one thing—getting the Moondisk.

"Speak, Aeras!" he demanded as two young women, pale Daughters of the Moon with silver eyes, bandaged his wounds. "I am thankful for your hospitality, truly I am, but our people are dying. They burn as we speak. We must bring them the Moondisk at once and cannot delay. How do we find it?"

Aeras stood before him, eyes dark. "It was five thousand years ago that we made the Moondisk, forging it from bronze and gold and the light of the moon. It protected us from the wrath of the Sun God for many generations, even as our people burned upon islands we could not reach. The Sun God sent many beasts and spies to steal our Moondisk, to cleave it with their axes of steel. As our numbers dwindled, we took the Moondisk to the mountaintop and raised there a champion, a great demon of wood and stone, and set him to guard our Moondisk."

Mori swallowed a bite of pear. "Is this demon still there?"

The Children of the Moon lowered their heads. Several shed tears.

"Yes," said Aeras, "he still lives upon the mountaintop, guarding the Moondisk from any who would claim it. We named him Ral Siyan, which means Beast of Wood and Stone in our tongue. He obeyed our ancestors, but many seasons of loneliness drove him mad, and he no longer serves us. He will not obey us. He will not surrender the Moondisk we set him to guard, not even when threatened with spear and arrow."

Bayrin rose to his feet, clasped his head, and sighed deeply. "Great. Just great. First phoenixes on our tails. Then lampreys the size of my sister's vanity. And now this, a beast of wood and stone that no spear or arrow can kill." He groaned.

Mori stood up and placed a hand on his shoulder. "Don't despair, Bayrin," she whispered. "We've come this far. We'll find a way."

"There is only one way to claim the Moondisk, children of stars," said Aeras. "You must defeat Ral Siyan in battle. Our people are blessed with moonlight, and we can become the white lions, creatures of the moon; we are beings of magic, of meditation, of wisdom. But you..." His eyes shone. "You are of Requiem. You are blessed with starlight, the light of the Draco constellation. You can become dragons, creatures of wrath and ruin. You can fight Ral Siyan and reclaim the sacred Moondisk of our ancestors." He squared his shoulders and raised his chin. "Fight him, Bayrin and Mori of Requiem, and you may take the Moondisk to your land, and defeat the servants of the Sun God, for we are your brothers and share your enemy."

Bayrin swallowed, looked at Mori, and clasped her hands. "Are you up for a good old-fashioned fight, Mori my dear?"

She trembled but bit her lip, raised her chin, and nodded.

"We fight," she whispered.

LYANA

Shadows and lightning swirled around her. Whispers rose like wind. She looked ahead but saw nothing, and her feet walked upon mist. Suddenly she was falling, tumbling through an endless storm, and she shouted and shifted. Wings burst from her back, and she flew, roaring fire. Wind and clouds whipped her.

"Elethor!" she called. She had stepped through the Crimson Archway holding his hand, but he was gone from her now. She whipped her head from side to side, blowing flames, but could not see him. Nothing but storm clouds flowed around her, charcoal and blue and deep purple like bruises. When she spun around, the Crimson Archway was gone; she saw only the endless storm.

"Lyana!" His voice rose somewhere in the distance; she could not tell from which direction. He seemed leagues away. She called for him again, but he did not answer.

Fly, Lyana, she told herself and tightened her lips. *Fly!*

Winds blasted her, billowing her wings like sails. She nearly tumbled. Shadows tugged her like chains, but she kept flying, one wing flap after the other. Stars streaked around her, countless lines of light. Lightning crashed. Thunderclaps deafened her. She blew fire and roared.

"Elethor, can you hear me?"

Rain of blood pattered against her. Faces of shadow and clouds swirled in the storm, mouths opening and closing, eyes appearing and disappearing. She saw Orin's face smiling, then screaming, then melting in lightning fire. She saw the face of her brother Bayrin, and of her young sister Noela who had died in her cradle. She saw her parents, Deramon and Adia, burning in a rain of acid and calling to her.

"Lyana!" they cried. "Lyana, why did you forsake us to die?"

She howled. *No. No, they cannot be dead! They cannot.* It was only a dream, a vision, a lie.

Her sister Noela wept in the clouds, a mere babe, crying to her. "Why did you not weep when they buried me? Why did you shed no tears?"

I wanted to! I wanted to cry like my parents, like Bayrin, but I couldn't, I couldn't, I had to be strong for them....

Her beloved Orin flew toward her, a dragon of cloud and lightning, bleeding and burnt. Half his face was a gaping wound, showing the crimson innards of the heavens.

"Why do you fly with Elethor?" he cried. "Why did you leave me to die and take my brother for your betrothed?"

He blew flames that washed her, red clouds that dispersed into rain.

"I should have been there," she whispered, wings roiling the clouds. "I should have gone with Orin to Castellum Luna, helped him fight the phoenixes, not stayed north and let him die... I let him die... Elethor, I let him die."

She tried to fly, to escape Orin's burnt face, his one eye that blazed, his dripping wounds. She beat her wings madly, shoving through the storm, but a gust of air caught her, and she tumbled through the sky. Lightning smashed into her scales, and they grabbed her, all of them—dead and burnt Orin, and her dying parents, and her dead sister Noela. They clung to her, begging.

"Don't fly, don't run, don't leave us, Lyana! Don't leave again. It's cold and dark in the Abyss, please save us, save us Lyana, don't leave us again...."

She wept and tried to flee, but could not; she knew that they would always follow her. She knew that no matter how far she flew, those eyes would haunt her—across endless skies and into her grave. She saw herself years in the future, a great Queen of Requiem upon her throne, her king Elethor at her side. Gold and jewels and peace surrounded her, but still at night she would curl up, weep, and try to flee them but find no peace.

For there is no peace for you, child, whispered a deep voice, and Lyana screamed and saw the black hill with the black flower. It rose before her between the clouds, a towering monument, larger than Requiem herself, woven of her terror. A great black bowl, it rose from a landscape of ink. A single black rose grew atop it, and Lyana tried to reach it. She knew she had to save that rose, to heal it, to stop the terrible pain of it, the horror that pounded. She screamed, for this mountain was larger than the world, larger than her mind could grasp. Her soul left her body and spread across the landscape, twisting with its fear, and everywhere she saw those petals.

"I have to... I have to save it," she whispered. "I have to *count* them. I have to *line* them. You have to keep the *numbers.*"

The Shrivel she had eaten laughed inside her belly, a coiling worm, forever inside her, forever mocking, forever counting. Its teeth gnashed at her entrails, and its claws dug, her eternal child, a parasite of her womb.

I am here within you, it whispered, taunting. *You cannot flee me, and you cannot flee those you let die, not until you climb the mountain and heal the black rose... until then I will remain and feast upon you.*

"Lyana!" cried a desperate voice. "Lyana, listen to me! Lyana, do you hear?"

She shouted and blew fire. "Leave me! Leave me! I killed no one. Please..." Tears streamed down her cheeks. "I am a soldier! I am a knight of Requiem. I have to save him, Elethor. I have to save the king, and Orin, and Noela... oh stars, Noela..."

She wept. Her body convulsed as she tumbled from the sky. Sweet Noela, little Noela, only a moon old, and they buried her, and Lyana couldn't even weep, she couldn't be weak, but now she wept and shouted. *I have to save her... I have to save her from this place. I have to save all of them.*

"Lyana!" the voice cried. Claws dug into her shoulders and pulled her. "Fly, Lyana!"

She could see nothing but her tears, but she outstretched her wings, and the wind billowed them, tossing her higher. She leveled off, banked, and flew upon the wind. The sky. She had to find the sky. Elethor flew beside her, brass scales shimmering, and she saw it, a hint of dawn ahead, a smudge of blue.

Requiem! May our wings forever find your sky. She remembered those words. She soared, howling and blowing fire. Though the storm blasted her and lightning smashed against her, she flew, tearing free from the grip of the dead. Her tail lashed and her claws reached out.

"Elethor!" she cried. "Fly with me, Elethor!"

They soared, cutting through the storm, smashing through rain and rock, until Lyana saw it. Tears filled her eyes again, but now they were tears of joy. *I see it... stars, I see it.* They were the columns of Requiem, white marble rising from fire and blood into good, healing starlight. They beamed from death to hope, from firelight to starlight, and Lyana flew like she had never flown, tears on her cheeks. *I will find your sky, Requiem... forever.*

The two dragons dived through the lightning, streaming toward the ghostly columns that rose among the storm of the Abyss, and soon flew between them. The pillars gleamed around them, palisades guiding them home. Flames blazed against their bellies, and starlight kissed their backs, and wakes of red and white light trailed behind them. They shot between the columns, through the storm, and dived into a great cavern of stone and starlight.

The storm silenced.

Lyana gasped.

She flew. She heard nothing but the thud of wings. Elethor flew at her side, panting, fire rising between his teeth. The chamber rose around them, the size of a kingdom, its ceiling of stone lit with countless stars. Lyana's heart pounded.

We made it, she thought. *We passed through the storm.*

A great boulder rose ahead like an island rising from darkness, and she spiraled toward it. She landed upon its top, so weak, and shifted into a human. Elethor landed beside her, shifted too, and they lay holding each other. Tears wet their cheeks and their chests rose and fell.

She clung to him. "What was that storm?" she whispered. "Did you see them too? Did you see the dead?"

His face was pale. His arms held her close as the stars gleamed above. "I saw my dead brother, and my dead father, and..." His eyes dampened. "I saw Mori dead too. She cried for me to save her, and I tried to, but I couldn't." He blinked and whispered. "Are they all dead, Lyana?"

"No." She clenched her fists behind his back. "I will not believe it. The storm... it showed us our nightmares, I think. It isn't real." She laid her head against his shoulder. "It can't be."

A shiver ran across her. Did that Shrivel truly live inside her, a coiling worm in her belly? Or was that merely her fear that nested in her soul? She did not know.

"El," she said, "thank you... for holding me. For pulling me from the darkness. I was drowning."

He stroked her hair and kissed her forehead. "I told you, Lyana. I will always fly by your side. I will always look after you. You can repay me later by smashing those statues I carved of Solina." He sighed and laid his head down against the stone. "You were right. I was a fool." He shook his head, grimacing. "When the sphinx asked me about her, I couldn't lie... I had to tell her that I still love her, even now. Lyana, she killed my father and my brother." He looked at her with haunted eyes. "How could I still love her?"

She held him close. "Love me instead," she whispered, "and hold me for a while longer."

He kissed her cheek and held her, and stroked her hair, and their bodies pressed together until the pain and fear faded, until their whispers and warmth could drive away the memories.

Lights blazed from below.

Lyana and Elethor rose to their feet upon the pillar of stone. They gazed into the darkness below. Two eyes like stars cracked open, shooting pillars of light like the starlit columns of afterlife.

"Stars," Lyana whispered.

In the new light, she saw great shoulders of stone and a rising tail, and soon a creature unfurled in the shadows, larger than a palace, a being of rock and light.

The Starlit Demon rose before them in the darkness.

MORI

As they flew up the mountain, heading toward its granite peak, Mori wanted to think about the task ahead. She wanted to steel herself for battle, imagine seizing the Moondisk from its demon guardian, prepare for a long flight over the sea and back to Requiem. Yet as her wings stirred the cold air over mountainsides of pines, she only thought of Bayrin's kiss.

Stupid love-struck girl! she scolded herself. *You think of kisses and love and romance while your people burn, while your brother and father lie dead?*

She looked at Bayrin who flew beside her, his eyes narrowed, mist swirling around his green scales. Mori felt a chill invade her.

No, she knew. This was not how romance felt. Lyana had told her about love—she said how when Orin was near, she would tremble, her heart would flutter, how warmth would spread through her, how joy bloomed inside her. This felt different. Mori felt no flutter, no warmth, no joy.

She lowered her eyes. She felt shame. She felt unclean.

Would Bayrin love me if he knew my secret? she thought, soaring over mountainsides of chalk and leaf. *If he knew how I let Acribus claim me, and how I didn't even fight him, how I... how his filth still clings to me? He thinks I'm just sweet Mori, the young princess, like from the fairytales... but I'm not her anymore. Not now. Not ever again.* Her shame burned inside her like a demon child in her womb. Was that Acribus's child, a babe with cruel eyes and a white tongue, that festered inside her?

"Mori, are you ready?" Bayrin called to her.

No, she thought. *No, I'm not ready to kill a demon. I'm not ready to fly over the sea again, to return home and find more dead. I'm not ready to face this world and keep flying.* She growled, thought about the old heroines from her stories, and nodded. *But I will do these things nonetheless.*

She gave her wings three great flaps, filling them with air like sails, and soared toward the mountaintop. Bayrin soared beside her. Smoke streamed between his teeth, and the thud of his wings blasted her. They cleared the mountain's peak, and Mori found herself looking down upon an ancient ruin.

Pillars lay fallen and chipped. Their capitals were shaped as bucking elks, but smoothed with centuries of rain. An archway rose from a tangle of ivy and bushes, the wall around it long fallen. Bricks lay strewn. Shattered wood, snapped branches, and boulders littered the ruins. Wild grass grew from a smashed mosaic. Whatever structure had once stood here, nature was overgrowing it; the fallen bricks were more moss than stone.

"There was a temple here once," Mori said, circling above it. She had seen enough temples in Requiem to know them, even when ruined; she could feel the old holiness of the place. The Children of the Moon had worshipped the night here.

"Where is the Moondisk?" Bayrin said, flying beside her.

Mori flew above the ruins, fanning the grass and mist. She squinted, seeking the glint of bronze and gold. Did the Moondisk lie hidden among these tufts of grass, fallen trees, and ruin of an ancient temple?

"And where is the demon who guards it?" she whispered. She saw no life here but for the plants; no call of birds, no chirp of crickets, nothing but the rustle of grass.

Bayrin grunted. "Maybe the demon left years ago, and the Children of the Moon had never bothered checking." He began spiraling down toward the ruins. "Come on, Mori, let's start overturning rocks, find this Moondisk, and get out of here."

Mori puffed out smoke, uncertain. This place was too quiet. Yet Bayrin was descending, and so she joined him, throat tight.

A moan shattered the silence.

The ruins shifted.

The fallen columns began to rise.

Mori screamed and banked, shot across the ruins, and soared. Rocks flew skyward. The fallen walls rose like a marionette on invisible strings. Columns formed legs and arms. The archway rose like shoulders, bedecked with a cloak of ivy and grass. The roots of fallen trees entwined, forming a great head with blazing eyes of blue crystal. Arms lashed out, ending with claws of leafy branches. Mori flew backward, gaping at the beast. The creature twisted and formed before her, and soon stood as a giant, three hundred feet tall, a behemoth woven of wood, leaf, and crumbled ruins.

Ral Siyan, Mori knew. *The demon of stone and wood.*

"Bay!" she screamed. She trembled and her heart thrashed. Where was Bayrin? She could no longer see him. Her wings thudded madly, billowing the demon's leaves. Its blue stare transfixed her, burning her eyes.

"Mori, it has the Moondisk!" came a cry, and Bayrin flew around the demon, eyes blazing.

He seemed so small compared to the creature, a mere bird flying around a tree. The demon of wood and stone howled, a sound like a collapsing dam. It lashed an arm at Bayrin. Its bricks creaked like joints, raining dust. Its branches twisted and groaned. Its fingers of wood missed Bayrin by a foot. The green dragon flapped his wings, blasting the beast with air, sending leaves flying.

When the demon turned toward her, Mori gasped. She saw the Moondisk! A circle of bronze, the size of a shield, it lay within the archway that formed the demon's torso. Vines and brambles held it like veins around a heart. Upon its dented and dulled surface, a golden moon and stars still glimmered.

Bayrin soared, turned, and swooped toward the beast.

"Time to burn," he said and blew fire.

"Bayrin, no!" Mori cried. She soared and slammed into Bayrin, pushing him aside. His flames rained upon the mountaintop, missing the demon. The beast of wood and stone roared, a sound like cracking boulders, and swung its arms. A log slammed into Mori, and she gasped for breath, head spinning.

"Mori, what are you doing?" Bayrin shouted, smoke billowing from his maw. He rose higher, dodging another blow from the demon. Mori flew beside him, panting. Her side blazed with pain where the beast had struck her.

"You'll burn the Moondisk!" she managed to say. "It's surrounded with branches. The bronze and gold would melt in dragonfire!"

Ral Siyan howled, a deep cry, the rage of forests and oceans and buried rock. The demon leaped, columns swinging. The two dragons scattered, and Mori found herself growling, anger pounding through her.

I won't let my family die, she thought. *I won't let Solina cut open Elethor too. I won't let Acribus rape Lyana like he raped me.* Her growl turned into a roar, and she swooped, claws outstretched. *I will grab the Moondisk.*

The demon spun toward her, all twisting roots and vines. Her claws glinted. She reached toward the Moondisk. Her claws almost closed around it... but the vines and brambles that encased the disk twisted. A branch lashed out, and its thorns slammed into her, each like an arrowhead. She screamed as they pierced her scales, fell, and her back hit the mountaintop.

The demon swung its arm like a hammer. The stone column came crashing down, as wide as an oak. Mori screamed and rolled aside, and the column smashed into the ground, shattering rock.

A roar pierced the air, and Bayrin swooped. His tail swung and slammed into Ral Siyan's head of root and leaf.

Wooden chips flew. A branch cracked. The demon turned. The stone archway—its torso—creaked and rained dust. The branches within the archway bound tighter together; Mori could barely see the Moondisk within them now, but she drove forward. Her howl rose. Her claws slashed at the brambles.

The Moondisk loosened. It fell a foot within the archway. Before Mori could grab the disk, the branches and vines wrapped around it again. The demon spun, arms lashing. One column slammed into a swooping Bayrin, knocking him to the ground. Another roared over Mori's head.

"Bayrin!" she cried. "Bayrin, get up!"

He lay on his back, wings flapping too feebly for flight. His tail flopped weakly and his eyes rolled back. The scales along his left side were cracked. Ral Siyan laughed—a grumble like an avalanche—and raised stony arms above the fallen green dragon.

Mori howled.

"You will not hurt him!" she cried and drove forward.

She slammed into the beast, cracking the stones of its archway. It tumbled forward and crashed down, and its leg—a column of stone and ivy—slammed into Bayrin.

Horror exploded inside Mori. *Stars, no, stars, please don't let Bayrin die, please please. I killed him, stars....*

Ral Siyan rose to its feet, the stones of its body shifting and rearranging themselves. The vines inside the archway coiled like a nest of snakes, wrapping tight around the Moondisk. The demon's mouth, a mere crack in wood, opened in a mocking grin.

Mori screamed with all her rage, all her pain, all her fear. It was the cry she could not utter when Orin died, when Acribus raped her, when her home burned and crashed around her. It was the cry of Requiem, of loss and wrath. She shot forward like an arrow, howling. Her claws reached out. Fire streamed from her maw, trailing behind her as a wake. A battering ram, she crashed into the demon, breaking through its archway. Roots and branches snapped against her. Her teeth closed around the Moondisk, and she shot out the archway's other side, scattering splinters of wood.

Howling, she spat the Moondisk into the air, where it spun and blazed in the sunlight. Before it could fall, Mori spun and blew her fire.

The stream of flame crashed into Ral Siyan. Its branches and leaves ignited. It howled, consumed with fire, a living torch the height of a palace. The mountain seemed to Mori like an erupting volcano.

"Bayrin!" she cried, tears in her eyes, and dived down. She saw him lying on his back, head drooping, wings limp.

Is he dead? Stars, please, let him live.

As the demon lashed its arms and howled, Mori grabbed Bayrin with her claws. She grunted with effort, pulling him back. Her feet dug into the mountainside. With a howl, she managed to drag Bayrin ten feet back, then twenty, until they were sliding down the mountainside. His eyes were still closed, and she wrapped her wings around them as they tumbled. Pebbles cascaded around them. With a thud, they slammed onto a rocky outcrop and lay still.

A hundred feet above her, Mori saw Ral Siyan still thrashing and burning. Smoke billowed from the demon. Its cry pierced the air, a cry of mourning, of endless pain. The cry was wordless, the cry of a wounded beast, but the more she listened, the more human it seemed to Mori. She thought she could hear words within it.

"Maaaa!" it seemed to cry. "Maaaa! Mother! Mother, please!"

It raised its hands to the sky, and Mori saw the moon there, a pale disk in the soft daylight. Blazing branches tore off the demon and fluttered, a thousand fireflies. It cried to the moon, its mother, a dying child. Mori wept for it; suddenly the creature was beautiful to her, a wonder she had slain.

With a great crack like snapping bones, Ral Siyan's archway crumbled. The stones crashed. Columns fell and shattered. Branches landed, crackling with fire. When the rocks settled, nothing remained of the demon but more ruins and scattered flames.

Tears in her eyes, Mori lowered her head toward Bayrin. He lay still, head tilted back and scales dented. Mori wept and shook him.

"Bayrin!" she whispered, throat tight. Her tears fell upon him. "Bay, wake up! Come on! Wake up, please!"

She cradled his head. He couldn't be dead. Couldn't! In death, Vir Requis returned to human forms. He was still a dragon. He had to live, *had to*, otherwise his magic would fail, he couldn't die like this, not in her arms, not like Orin had died. She sobbed and trembled.

"Bay?" she whispered.

As she held him, his scales melted. His wings pulled into his back.

He turned into a bloodied man.

Sobs racked Mori's body.

Dead...

She shifted into a human too. She sat upon the boulder, cradling him in her arms. Her hair covered his face, and she shook him.

"Bay, Bay, wake up!" she whispered, unable to speak any louder. "Please, Bay, please. I love you." She kissed his cold lips and held him tight. "I love you, Bay, please, don't leave me."

He moaned.

He moaned! Mori's heart leaped. Fresh tears fell and she shouted and shook him wildly.

"Bay!" She touched his cheek. "Bay, you're going to be all right. I'm going to take care of you."

His eyes fluttered and he moaned again. His lips moved, but only a hoarse whisper left his throat. Mori leaned closer to hear his words.

"What is it, Bay?" she whispered.

"I... I fell on my lamp." His face crinkled up. "Ouch."

Mori laughed as she cried, body shaking. She touched his cheek and kissed him again, a peck on his lips, and felt his hand in her hair.

She thought that they would kiss again, like last time, and she wanted to. She ached for it. But she pulled back, and once more her shame flooded her, ice inside her. But then his arms were around her, and she *was* kissing him, and she melted into it.

And it feels right, she thought. *It feels good.* Her tears streamed down her cheeks, mingling salty in their kiss. She lay down beside him, arms around him. When she looked up, she saw a glint. The Moondisk lay on the mountainside above them, a beacon of light for her home and her life.

DERAMON

He slew the Tiran with a downward swing, driving his axe into the man's head, through helmet into skull. Blood spilled and the man fell dead, joining his fallen comrades. When he hit the ground, his visor clanked open, revealing a young face.

A boy, Deramon thought. *Nothing but a stupid boy, fifteen if he was a day.*

He spat and gritted his teeth. He cursed under his breath, damning Solina for this slaughter, for killing his people, and for forcing him to kill hers.

"Bring the hammers!" he bellowed. "Break this tunnel upon them!"

The corpses of Tirans and Vir Requis rose in piles. They stank, blood and offal seeping from them. Severed limbs littered the floor. Years ago, Deramon used to read to his children stories of epic battle. In those books, the heroes smote the enemies with light and justice. *The books never mention the entrails and bones and human waste,* he thought. *They never mention the heroes cleaving the skulls of boys too young to shave.*

Men came running from deeper below, holding hammers still hot from the forge. As Deramon and ten soldiers swung swords at those Tirans who surged from above, the hammermen slammed at the ceiling and walls. Chips of stone rained. One Tiran leaped forward and slew a hammerman. The Tiran fell, face caved in like a red crater, when a second hammerman bashed his skull. Blood splashed and the screams of men echoed. The body of a slain child lay torn under the fighters' boots, limbs ripped off, her head a flattened ruin. Chunks of stone fell and cracks raced along the tunnel walls.

"Where are you, Solina?" Deramon grumbled as he swung his sword and axe. "Come and face me again."

Two more men died. Hammers swung. Stones rolled and cracks pierced the ceiling.

"Back, men!" Deramon shouted hoarsely. Dust flew. "Back!"

He slew another Tiran, cleaving his armor with an axe blow, and leaped back into the darkness.

Boulders tumbled. Men screamed and dust filled the air. The tunnel collapsed.

A boulder slammed down an inch from Deramon. A rock crashed against his helmet, another against his pauldron. He ran, leaped over a body, and fell. His men leaped around him. The sound roared like an army of dragons. For a moment Deramon thought that all the tunnels below Requiem would crumble, that every last survivor would die.

Bayrin and Mori will live, he thought as rocks pummeled him. *We've saved my son at least.*

For long moments, he lay on his stomach, rocks raining against him. The dust flew; he saw nothing but gray and black. It seemed the passing of ages before he realized that he could hear men moan. One cursed and spat, while another wept and prayed. The dust was settling, and soon Deramon could see again. Men shifted around them, coated in dust, their blood seeping through it.

His body ached and his head rang. Grimacing, Deramon sat up and turned around.

The tunnel had collapsed into a heap of boulders. He could neither see nor hear the Tirans. Blood seeped from under the wreckage.

"Good," he muttered. *May they all lie dead.*

He rose to his feet, leaning against the wall for support. His men rose around him. Behind them, the tunnel sloped deeper into darkness; the prayers and cries of survivors rose from the depth.

I've buried us alive, Deramon thought. *How long until we run out of air? How long until we all perish in the darkness? Will we ever find a way back to light?*

He did not know. But death was delayed. They had staved off fire, even if hunger, thirst, and suffocation still awaited.

"Their battering ram will not break this blockage as easily," said Garvon, the captain with the white beard and one eye. Dust filled a gash along his cheek, and a dent pressed into his breastplate, leaking blood.

"No," Deramon agreed and scratched his own beard, wondering if he'd live to see it as white as Garvon's. "Go see my wife, Garvon. Go see Adia. Get your wounds bandaged. Silas!" He turned to see the younger soldier struggle to his feet; blood seeped from under his helmet. "Silas, can you stand? Can you still swing a blade?"

The young man nodded, lips tight, and lifted his fallen sword. "My blade will always swing for Requiem."

He is younger than my son, Deramon thought. *But not as young as the boy whose skull I cleaved.*

"Good. Stay here and guard this pile of rubble." Deramon passed his eyes over the others who were rising from the dust. "Talin! Raion! Stay here with him. The rest of you too. I'll send up fresh men."

Leaving them there, he walked with Garvon down the tunnel. Soon they were stepping through crowds of women and children. If the survivors had been cramped before, they were now pressed together, a wall of flesh and tears and blood.

This place is a grave, Deramon thought. How much more of these tunnels could they lose? So much of the underground had fallen. All that remained was this—a few burrows, a few alcoves, thousands of survivors breathing and crowding together. How long until their air was gone? A day? An hour?

We cannot wait for you, Bayrin, he thought. *We cannot wait, Lyana. Return to us... or flee as far as you can, and never return to our tomb.*

Robes swirled, and Adia came walking toward them. The survivors around her bowed their heads and moved aside as best they could, letting her pass. She mumbled blessings to them. The priestess's face was pale, her eyes sunken, and blood stained her robes.

"Deramon," she whispered. She touched blood that trickled down his forehead.

"We held them back," he said, so hoarse he could barely speak at all. "We brought the tunnel down upon them."

And upon a dozen of my own men, he thought.

She stood for a moment, stern, the Mother of Requiem, the great Priestess of Stars... and then her lips trembled, and she embraced him and clung to him.

"Thank the stars," she whispered. "Deramon, I thought you had left me. Stars, so many are dead. So many I cannot heal."

He looked over her shoulder at the survivors. Here too people were dying. Some were sick, their wounds festering. The elderly huddled on the floor and babes wept.

Deramon wanted to comfort his wife. To be strong for her, to give her hope... but he knew that hope was gone. *We will die here. But we will die fighting.*

"Adia," he began... and his breath died.

Cracks raced along the ceiling, and with a crash and sound like crumbling mountains, boulders rained. A hole broke open above, and firelight blazed, like the sun breaking through clouds.

"Storm the tunnels!" rose Solina's voice above. "Slay them all!"

Tirans leaped from above, tossed down shovels, and drew swords. Solina landed like a cat, snarled, and swung her twin blades.

Vir Requis screamed and tried to flee, but there was nowhere to run; they fell dead at the Tirans' blades.

"Garvon, with me!" Deramon shouted and ran forward, shoving men aside. Behind him, he heard more of his troops rushing into the tunnel. He saw Solina stab an old woman who gasped and fell. Then a Tiran man charged toward him, thrusting a spear, and Deramon parried with his sword.

The Tirans' torches filled the tunnels. There were dozens, maybe hundreds. They kept pouring in from above. Cold winter winds came with them, shrieking through the tunnels, tasting of flame and night.

Deramon swung his blades. As soldiers, women, and children fell dead around him, he grimaced and thought: *At least we now have air.*

MORI

She flew on the wind, the Moondisk clutched in her claws, clouds streaming beneath her. When she saw the mountains ahead, their snow golden in the dawn, tears filled her eyes. Those were the mountains of Requiem.

"We're home," she whispered into the wind.

When she looked at Bayrin, who flew at her side, she saw his eyes gleam. Flames crackled between his teeth.

"Home," he said, voice streaming into the wind like the smoke from his nostrils.

The clouds obscured all but the mountaintops, and fear filled Mori. What would she find beneath that cloud cover? Smoldering forests? Nothing but ruin and skeletons? The city of Nova Vita still lay many leagues away. When she arrived, would the Moondisk bring hope for her people, or would her gift be given to the dead?

"Remember, Mori!" Bayrin called to her. "When we see the phoenixes, you point the Moondisk at them. I'll burn them with fire."

Mori nodded, clutching the bronze disk in her claws. Would it work? The disk seemed so small, no larger than a shield. How could it defeat the flame of Tiranor? The Children of the Moon had claimed its rays would extinguish phoenix fire, but what if they were wrong? What if that was only a legend? It had been thousands of years since the Sun God had attacked the northern isles; tales from so long ago also spoke of golems of clay, fairies that snatched the teeth of errant children, and other stories that could not possibly be true. Was this Moondisk just another myth?

"Bay, are you sure that—"

She had no time to voice her concern. Before she could complete her sentence, a ball of light flared on the horizon, like a sun rising from the clouds.

Bayrin cursed and bared his fangs.

"Stay near me, Mori," he said. "There's only one. It's time to test the Moondisk."

Fear pounded through Mori. Her limbs shook and flames danced inside her maw. She growled and showed her fangs, and smoke streamed from her nostrils. She glided upon an air current, diving toward the orange ball of light ahead.

Be strong, Mori, she told herself. *Be brave. For Requiem. For Bayrin.*

The ball of fire burst from the cloud cover, and Mori couldn't help it. She screamed.

The phoenix shot forward. It screeched, a sound like shattering mountains and typhoons. Its wings outstretched, a hundred feet in span, crackling with fire. Its body coiled, woven of liquid fire, and its eyes blazed like two suns.

It was him. She would know him anywhere. Acribus.

Every instinct inside her screamed to flee. Her heart thrashed. Her wings shook. She could barely breathe. *Turn and fly, Mori! Fly away and hide!*

"With me, Mori!" Bayrin shouted at her side, roaring fire. "Fly!"

Mori howled and blew flame. Heart thrashing, she shot toward the phoenix.

The Moondisk thrummed in her claws, vibrating. Soon it shook so wildly, she nearly dropped it. It felt so hot, hotter than coals, its heat shooting up her limbs. She clutched it tighter and screamed, driving forward along the wind.

The phoenix howled and its eyes met hers. Its beak, white hot shards of molten steel, opened to screech, revealing a maw of lava. It came surging toward her, wings flapping, raising fountains of light.

A ring of silver light exploded in her claws.

A shock wave shot out, the color of sky, its hum deafening. A beam of light coalesced and blazed forward, faster than arrows, wider than the pillars of Requiem, consuming Mori. She screamed with pain. She wanted to die. The light and sound vibrated through her, claiming her; she could see and hear nothing else. And yet she kept flying. She held the Moondisk. She raised it in her claws.

Wings flapping madly, she pointed the beam forward and heard the phoenix howl. The light washed it. Mori could see nothing but blue, but she growled, forced herself to narrow her eyes, to stare, to see her enemy.

Caught in the beam, Acribus howled. His wings flapped and his claws lashed. No more fire covered him. He flew as a great, naked bird, his flesh pale and wrinkled, his eyes black and beady. He looked to Mori like some plucked, starving vulture, a weak and wizened thing.

"Burn it, Bayrin!" she screamed, voice nearly lost under the deafening howl of the light. "Burn it dead!"

Through the silver beam, a dragon swooped. Bayrin's scales blazed under the light, a bright white tinged with silver. His claws outstretched. His maw opened. A stream of fire shot from his maw, spinning and crackling, and crashed against the naked phoenix.

Acribus howled. The fire engulfed him. His flew back, wings pounding the air. He clawed and burned.

Growling, Mori dived forward, the Moondisk clutched in her claws. She swooped. Rage filled her. Keeping the Moondisk's light upon him, she showered Acribus with fire.

Her flames cascaded against the naked bird. Acribus howled. His wrinkled skin burned, burst, and peeled off. Welts rose across his flesh, swollen like rotten fruit. His eyes melted. Soon he looked like a phoenix again, covered in burning flames—but this fire burned him.

He mewled, a high sound that chilled Mori, and she realized: *This is the sound I made when he hurt me.* She blasted him with fire again, tears in her eyes, a howl in her throat.

Her fire burst against him, and Acribus fell from the sky.

He tumbled, a burning bird, his skin crackling. Mori swooped above him, Moondisk in her claws, keeping the beam upon him. Wind and smoke stung her eyes. Acribus tumbled through clouds, a comet crashing toward the earth. Mori followed, screaming, holding him in the beam lest he became a phoenix again. Forests rushed up toward them. The earth spun. Mori screamed and dived.

The naked, burning bird crashed through the treetops and hit the ground.

His magic vanished. He shrank like a piece of meat crumbling under fire. Soon he lay upon the earth as a broken, charred man. Smoke rose from him.

Mori landed beside him and tossed the Moondisk aside. It thumped into dry leaves, its light dimmed, and its hum faded. Once more, it was nothing but a shield of bronze inlaid with gold. Mori turned her eyes toward Acribus, who lay at her feet.

He moaned and twitched, still alive. Burns covered him. His clothes stuck to his soft, red body, melted into his flesh. He gasped for breath and whimpered.

Mori shifted into a human, drew her sword, and held it above him.

She wanted to slay him, but her hand shook, and tears filled her eyes. She could only stand above this ruin of a man, this living piece of burnt meat. In the old books she read, stories of epic adventure, dragons always slew their enemies with fire and glory. But the books never told of this. They never told of flesh melting over bones and the stink of it.

This is what Orin looked like, she remembered. *It's how he looked when you raped me by his body.*

With the flap of wings, Bayrin landed beside her in smoke and fire. He shifted into a human too, came to stand beside her, and blanched. Shock and disgust suffused his face, and he gritted his teeth. When he drew his sword, his hand shook.

"Stars, Mori," he whispered. "Look away. I'll finish this."

He tried to turn her aside, but she would not move.

"No," she whispered. "I... I want to see him die. I have to."

She looked up at Bayrin. Ash and dirt covered his face. Blood still stained his clothes from the lamprey wounds. His red hair was now black with soot. Mori wanted to tell him, *needed* to tell him, to tell somebody the secret that burned inside her.

"Bayrin, he..." Tears caught in her throat, and her body trembled, but she had to do this, she had to speak now before her courage left her. "Bayrin, at Castellum Luna, after they killed Orin, he... Acribus, he grabbed me and..."

Bayrin winced. "Mori, it's all right. You don't have to speak of it. I think I know what happened. You don't have to tell me... if you don't want to."

A sob fled her lips, but she tightened her jaw and clutched her sword. *Stay strong.*

"I have to tell you," she said, "I have to, I have to speak to somebody. He raped me, Bayrin. He raped me by the body of my brother, and... I didn't even fight him. I let him do it. I'm sorry." Tears filled her eyes.

Bayrin shook his head, eyes damp and narrowed. "For what, Mori? Sorry for what?" He blew out a shaky breath. "Stars, Mori, it wasn't your fault. You didn't let him do anything."

Mori closed her eyes, sword wavering in her hand. She still felt so dirty, so ashamed, so impure. But a sliver of relief filled her, a dim ray of hope. She had told Bayrin, and he hadn't recoiled in disgust. He still stood at her side. For an instant fear swelled inside her, and she was terrified that he would try to embrace or kiss her, and she knew she would flinch at his touch, that the memories would flow through her. But he only stood at her side, sword in hand, and she loved him for it. It was all she wanted from him right now.

"Bayrin," she whispered and opened her eyes. "Can you... can you do it?"

He nodded, face pale, eyes haunted but determined.

Mori turned away and walked several feet, facing the trees. She clutched her sword so tight her fingers hurt. She closed her eyes. When she heard the cry behind her, a mewl like a kicked dog, she winced and a tear ran down her cheek.

She heard Acribus moan no more. It was over.

"He's gone," she whispered, trembling. "He's gone forever."

The sun began to set. They had flown for two days and a night, not resting, and Nova Vita still lay many leagues away.

That night they slept upon a bed of dry leaves, naked birches rising around them. Under their cloaks, Mori shifted until she lay against Bayrin, warm in his arms. She slept with her head against his chest, his hand stroking her hair, and for the first time in many nights, she did not dream.

ELETHOR

The Starlit Demon rose before him from the shadow.

A beast of stone, it rose two hundred feet tall, nearly as tall as the cavern that held it. Fissures ran across its bulky form, leaking starlight. Its teeth were white boulders, its eyes swirling pools of starlight. Its body shook and clanked as it grumbled, a sound that shook the chamber.

Elethor and Lyana stood upon the pillar of stone, still in human forms. Holding hands, they gazed upon the rising beast.

"Demon of Starlight!" Elethor cried. "I am Elethor, Son of Olasar, King of Requiem! I come to free you from your lair and call upon your help."

The Starlit Demon's head thrust forward, as large as Elethor's house in Nova Vita. Its mouth cracked open, a canyon in rock, and it rumbled with a voice like cascading boulders. The chamber shook with it.

"I serve no king... return to your sunlight... and let me sleep."

The behemoth of stone began descending into the shadows again, a mountain sinking into night. Its eyes began to close, leaving but glowing slits like crescent moons. A ridge of boulders rose down its back like a spine, creaking and shifting.

Elethor tightened his jaw. After all this—walking through the Abyss itself—would this creature refuse to help them? Floaters of light filled his eyes. His breath shook in his lungs. Lyana's hand tightened around his, squeezing it like a drowning woman.

"You will not sleep!" Elethor called to the demon. "Wake, Starlit Demon, and serve those you are bound to! You served my forefathers. You are still sworn to my house. Rise and serve Requiem, the kingdom your stars shine upon."

The demon raised its great head again. Dust and pebbles rained from its body. Its eyes opened again, blazing so bright Elethor snarled and looked aside, his own eyes narrowing.

"Sworn to your house!" the demon bellowed, voice echoing across the cavern, its waves thudding against Elethor's chest. "Your fathers imprisoned me here. Your fathers stripped me of fire to feast on." A growl left its maw, so powerful Elethor swayed and nearly fell. "Leave this place, lest I feed upon your flesh instead."

Clutching Elethor's hand, Lyana raised her chin and shouted to the beast.

"If it's fire you crave, we will feed you fire!" Her cheeks flushed and her eyes blazed. "Are you hungry, Starlit Demon? For years you slumbered here, and your light is dim. Will fire fill your belly?"

The Starlit Demon turned its head so quickly, its tail of stone lashed and hit a wall. A crack ran along the chamber, showering stones. The beast roared, baring its teeth. Its gullet blazed like swirling, molten stars.

"I have craved fire for longer than your mind can grasp," it said. "For two thousand turns of your seasons, I slumbered here, craving heat and flame to devour. The hunger in my belly is a forge you cannot fill."

Elethor and Lyana looked at one another and nodded. They shifted as one, flapped their wings, and rose as dragons. The Starlit Demon roared before them, maw open so wide, Elethor knew it could swallow even his dragon form.

"Here is a taste of the fire you crave!" Elethor shouted and blew his flames.

The stream of fire roared toward the Starlit Demon, and for an instant, fear filled Elethor. What if his fire burned the beast? What if it attacked them? But the Starlit Demon opened its maw wider, swallowing the flames. Lyana blew fire too, and the demon feasted.

The dragons let their flames die. The Starlit Demon roared.

"Is that all the fire you can kindle?" It made a deep sound like laughter, body shaking. "All the dragons of Requiem would not fill my belly. Ten thousand blew their fire upon me, but I knew no fill."

"If you follow us, we will grant you more fire!" Elethor shouted.

The demon's laughter deepened, cruel laughter that made the chamber shake. The pillar of stone upon which Elethor and Lyana had stood crumbled and fell. Cracks raced across the Starlit Demon's stone body, emitting beams of light.

"The armies of your fathers blew flames from their mouths into mine, but my craving was stronger." The Starlit Demon glared at Elethor, drenching him with light. "And so I toppled their halls, and feasted upon their children. Your kings were not pleased. How will you feed me when your fathers could not?"

Elethor hovered before the beast, his wings blowing rocks and dust off its body.

"I will not feed you dragonfire. I will feed you sunfire itself. Ten thousand phoenixes fly over Requiem, and each is woven from

the Sun God's flame. Emerge from your lair, Starlit Demon! Follow
me to Requiem, and you will feast."

The Starlit Demon rose, filling the chamber with its girth. Its
claws emerged from the darkness below, raining earth; each seemed
carved of flint, larger than a horse. It tossed back its head and roared,
and the sound crashed against the chamber walls, cracking them.
Lyana screamed in pain; the demon's howl knocked her back in the air.
Elethor grimaced. He felt like that roar could crush his scales and
snap his ribs.

"Will you follow, Starlit Demon?" he cried. "Will you fly to
Requiem and feast upon the phoenix fire?"

The demon leaped.

The chamber seemed to explode.

A fountain of stone and light, the Starlit Demon crashed into
the ceiling, claws digging, maw biting. Boulders cascaded. Dust filled
the air, blinding Elethor. He flew backward until his back hit a wall.
He saw nothing but raining rock, clouds of dust, and beams of
starlight.

"Lyana!" he shouted.

He could not see nor hear her. A boulder fell before him,
grazing his tail. Elethor flattened himself against the wall. Rocks
pummeled him. He tried to call for Lyana again, but dust and rocks
filled his mouth.

The starlight dimmed, and Elethor managed to blow fire,
lighting the darkness. Through the storm of debris, he discerned the
Starlit Demon burrowing into a hole in the ceiling, tail lashing. Soon
the beast disappeared into the tunnel it dug, driving upward like a great
earthworm.

"Elethor!" came a cry from across the chamber, and Lyana flew
toward him. Dust coated her blue scales, turning her gray. With three
great flaps of her wings, she soared toward the hole in the ceiling.
"Come on, Elethor, we follow!"

With that, she soared into the hole above, following the Starlit
Demon. Heart hammering, Elethor pushed himself off the wall. Dust
and rocks rained against his wings as he flapped them, but he gritted
his teeth, narrowed his eyes, and forced himself to fly. The tunnel
gaped above him, fifty feet wide. He saw Lyana's tail swish above and
he followed.

Tunnel walls blurred at his sides. The light of the Starlit Demon
fell in rays. Dirt and rocks cascaded, clanking against his scales.

He flew for what seemed like leagues. The Starlit Demon
burrowed and roared, crashing through the stone and dirt. Elethor

growled, slipstreaming in the beast's wake. If he swerved to the right or left, boulders would tumble against him, denting scales. Lyana flew above him, drafting behind the demon's tail. The behemoth dwarfed the two dragons, ten times their size.

The demon cut through the Abyss. The tunnel drove through craggy chambers, revealing the horrors of the underworld: nests of squirming eggs, rotten children coiled inside them; bloated worms, six feet long and bearing human faces; bodies that rotted, squirming with insects, yet still screamed in pain. But soon the tunnel grew colder, and Elethor saw bones, rocks, soil, and the buried ruins of old cities.

We are leaving the Abyss, he thought. *We are leaving this unholy underworld and entering the crust of the world.*

He exhaled a shaky breath of relief, and his eyes stung. How long would nightmares of this place haunt him? At once he knew the answer: for the rest of his life. He would not forget the sight of Nedath, a dead girl atop the body of a centipede. In the dark he would always see Lyana wrapped in cobwebs, turning into a shriveled creature. Every night, he knew that he would dream of the bodies upon the hooks, undying beasts that fed upon their own flesh.

He looked at Lyana, who flew above him, and his heart seemed so small, so cold, wrapped in ice.

Nobody else will ever know, he thought. *Only Lyana and I. We'll never be able to speak of what we saw... not to anyone above ground, maybe not even to each other.* He could barely see; his eyes blurred with tears. *But we still have each other. Lyana is saved... and I will always be with her, to hold her in the darkness when our nightmares swell.*

The thought of Lyana made his chest feel a little warmer. She kept the terror at bay. Elethor nodded as he flew, eyes damp. *We will live in peace again, together—we will save our people, we will stargaze on Lacrimosa Hill, and we will leave this darkness behind us. She and I.*

All his life, Lyana had been a thorn in his side, the sanctimonious girl who'd endlessly scold and lecture him. But today as he flew, he saw above him a strong, wise woman... a woman he wanted to spend his life with. A woman, he knew, that he could learn to love.

The Starlit Demon burrowed for what seemed like hours, roaring in the dark, until it crashed through a slab of stone, and screams rose above.

Elethor gasped.

As he shot up, he saw burrows running alongside the tunnel the Starlit Demon carved. His people—thin, bloodied Vir

Requis—cowered there like ants underground. They covered their eyes in the demon's starlight and cried.

An instant later, the Starlit Demon crashed through the topsoil and shot into the night sky, a geyser bursting into the world. An army of phoenixes burned above, screeching and flapping wings of fire. The world spun. The sound deafened Elethor. Boulders cascaded and the tunnels began to crumble. Several Vir Requis fell into the darkness, tumbling past Elethor. They shifted into dragons below him, howled, and flew behind him.

"Elethor!" Lyana cried above. She soared out of the tunnel and into the night, crashing into the army of phoenixes.

Elethor howled and shot into the night. The phoenixes swooped. Dragons flew up below him. Vir Requis still in human forms ran deeper into tunnels. Sound and light crashed.

SOLINA

She was flying with her troops, a phoenix in the night, when the demon burst from underground.

It looked like a great scarab made of stone, larger than a whale. Its claws tore through the earth, and its eyes blazed, two stars shooting beams of light. The earth crumbled around it, a sinkhole falling into darkness. Vir Requis screamed and fell from their burrows, now revealed to the night.

It looks, Solina thought in a moment of incredulity, *like a gopher bursting from an anthill.*

She spread out her wings of fire and shrieked. Considering its girth, she had expected this stone demon to crawl upon the earth, but it came soaring into the sky. Wingless, it flew toward her and her phoenixes. Its eyes nearly blinded her, and its roars thudded against her, fanning her flames.

"Kill the beast!" she shrieked, her voice emerging from her beak like typhoons of sound. "Sunspear Phalanx! Dragonbone! Bring it down!"

The two phalanxes swooped in formation, each a terror of fifty phoenixes. One fell upon the stone demon from the right, the other from its left. Their beaks and talons thrashed its hide.

They crashed against the beast like flaming paper against a cliff.

Solina watched, shrieking, the flames crackling with fury across her. The phoenixes attacked the stone demon again, wave after wave of them, only to crash against it. The demon's eyes blazed with starlight. Its claws lashed and its teeth bit, tearing phoenixes apart. Their flames filled its maw, ran down its throat, and blazed through the fissures along its belly. The demon seemed like a great, flying furnace.

And my men are stoking its fire, Solina realized. She howled, a sound that could shatter walls. Elethor had found a demon in the depths, a creature to eat the flames of her wrath. As she flew above, she saw the beast swallow three phoenixes. Other firebirds slashed at its body, only to die at its claws and fall, shredded, like burning leaves.

Solina narrowed her eyes and swooped, claws outstretched.

You think yourself clever, Elethor. But you have only doomed yourself.

Where the stone demon had burst from the ground, a chasm loomed, its rims crumbling into darkness. Alongside the cavern walls, Solina saw openings to a dozen burrows. Inside each burrow the weredragons still cowered, fragile humans not daring to fly, even now. She saw only several dragons flying behind the stony demon; the rest were too cowardly to shift and emerge to battle.

But I will bring the battle to them, Solina thought. *I spent a moon trying to break into these places... and now, Elethor, you have opened a dozen doors.*

She snarled, skirted around the feasting demon of stone, and swooped into the gaping chasm. A dozen burrows surrounded her, running from the chasm walls into darkness. Weredragons wept in their human forms and tried to flee deeper, but their burrows were packed tight; they could either become dragons and fly into the phoenix sky, or die as humans underground.

Men with swords were rushing to each tunnel's entrance, pushing back the women and children. But in one tunnel, a crumbly burrow like a wormhole, only children wept, torn from their mothers' grasps when the demon had crashed through their hideout. Shrieking, her flames crackling, Solina flew toward that tunnel.

The children screamed. Across the crater, men howled inside their own tunnels. A ball of fire, Solina shifted in midair, becoming a woman again. As she flew, she drew her twin blades. She tumbled into the children's tunnel, swords swinging.

Aknur, her left blade of nightfire, halved a young boy's face. Raem, her right blade of dawn, cut a girl from collarbone to navel. The other children were fleeing deeper, tripping over one another, wailing in fear. Solina grinned and walked deeper, blades swinging, showering blood and cutting down the vermin.

I will not let these creatures grow and breed, she thought as she sliced two girls who embraced and wept. *I will clear the world of their darkness, Sun God, for your wrath and glory.*

She stepped deeper into the tunnel, over bodies and severed limbs, leaving a trail of blood and sunlight.

I will kill them all.

Howls rose behind her. Flames crackled. Solina spun to see a brass dragon fly toward the tunnel she stood in. Solina's grin widened, her heart pounded, and she licked blood off her lips.

"Elethor!" she cried and raised her dripping swords. "You have come to me at last."

ADIA

She stood in the tunnel, comforting a girl whose hands had burned to stumps, when the world collapsed.

The floor cracked, and she watched children fall into the chasm. Boulders fell from the ceiling, crushing people around her. The tunnels shook, dirt rained, and a tower of stone jutted up before her. Great claws, larger than Adia's body, sliced before her. A creature as large as a temple, its eyes blazing beacons, rose before her, leaving ruin and blood in its wake.

As people fell and screamed, Adia thought she glimpsed two dragons—brass and blue—flying after the creature, following it through the tunnel it carved.

The Starlit Demon, she knew. Tears sprang into her eyes. *Lyana is alive. My daughter is alive!*

As dust flew and stones rolled, Adia clenched her jaw. She wanted to run through the people, shift into a dragon, and fly to Lyana. She forced herself to remain.

This is my station. These are my people to heal.

She moved from one to another, digging them from the rubble. One old man wept, clutching a fractured arm. Beside him a young boy lay, his leg buried under a boulder. How could she heal them all? How could she choose between them—grant death to one, life to the other?

Adia was kneeling over a pregnant woman whose head was bleeding when fire screamed. She looked up and saw phoenixes raining into the chasm the Starlit Demon had left. One phoenix flew to a tunnel that gaped open across the chasm, shifted into Solina, and leaped into a crowd of screaming children. Several other phoenixes swooped toward the tunnel Adia huddled in, shifted into Tiran men with blades and armor, and ran into the throng of survivors.

Adia found herself snarling. The time to hide was over, she realized; they would find no more shelter underground, not with the tunnels collapsing around them. They had to flee. Her heart ached to leave the wounded woman... but Adia left her.

"Vir Requis!" she shouted, running toward the Tirans at the entrance. "Vir Requis, follow! We shift! We fly! To the sky, children of Requiem!"

As she ran, she grabbed a sword from a fallen soldier, drew it, and swung the blade. Around her, living soldiers of Requiem swung their own blades. One Tiran fell into the chasm. Adia ran and barreled into another, shoving him into the darkness.

"Find the sky!" Adia shouted, leaped from tunnel into chasm, and shifted into a dragon.

Wings sprouted from her back with a thud. White scales clanked across her. Fangs sprouted from her mouth. She tossed back her head and howled, blowing blue fire. It had been so long since she had shifted, so long since she had felt air under her wings, flames in her gullet, the magic of starlight in her veins.

Beneath her, the falling Tirans shifted into phoenixes and soared toward her. Behind her, Vir Requis were leaping from the tunnel, shifting into dragons, and soaring. Adia soared with them. She flew up the chasm, following the path of the Starlit Demon, and shot toward a night sky strewn with firebirds. More tunnels gaped open along the chasm's walls, and hundreds of Vir Requis were leaping from them, turning into dragons, and soaring after her.

Adia shot past layers of rock, soil, and frost, and finally burst out from the underground. The ruins of Nova Vita spread below her, walls and columns fallen. Thousands of phoenixes flew above her. Hundreds of dragons soared around her. The Starlit Demon howled in the sky, a great slug of stone that flew with no wings. It crushed phoenixes between its teeth, and its belly bulged with their flame, a furnace in the sky like a sun.

"Rise, dragons of Requiem!" Adia cried. "Into the sky!"

Phoenixes came swooping toward her, crackling and raising sparks. More flew below. If death flowed underground, and death burned above, she would lead her people to die in the sky. The Starlit Demon could not consume all their enemies; its jaws bit many, but too many phoenixes flew. This creature of the underworld would not be their savior.

But maybe, Adia dared to hope... maybe in this chaos, a few dragons could escape. Maybe as the Starlit Demon devoured their enemies, some of her people could flee into the mountains, the forests, the southern swamps.

But I will stay, she thought. *I will stay until they are all fled or burned. I will die in the sky of my home under the light of my stars.*

Phoenixes dived toward her, lashing their talons. Adia shot between them, soaring through their wings of fire. The flames crackled against her, and she screamed but drove past them. More flew above. Around her, hundreds of dragons were rising.

"Fly to all directions of the wind!" she cried. "Fly to the mountains and forests. Flee into the wilderness, dragons of Requiem!"

Adia saw a group of young dragons, mere children barely old enough to fly, soaring into the air. They wailed, sparks left their throats, and their wings fluttered like the wings of hummingbirds. A crackling phoenix, thrice their size, began swooping toward them. Its howl tore the air and the young dragons wailed.

Narrowing her eyes, Adia surged. She flew straight up, roaring. She shot around the young dragons, spread her wings wide, and raised her front claws. The swooping phoenix crashed against her, and Adia screamed. The flames bathed her scales.

"Fly, children!" she shouted as the phoenix claws tore at her shoulders. "Fly north to the mountains."

She slammed her tail against the phoenix, but it was like clubbing a forest fire. Smoke filled her nostrils and she could barely see. She pulled her wings close, tumbled, and flew again. Welts covered her belly, where she had no scales to protect her. The scales on her back felt like stones in an oven, and lacerations covered her shoulders. She looked around madly, seeking the children, but could not see them, only countless firebirds. Had the young ones escaped?

The phoenix that had attacked her screeched above. It swooped, a comet of spinning fire. Adia closed her eyes, fearing the fire would melt them, and raised her claws. She prayed, ready to die.

A shadow fell upon her. A howl thudded in her ears. When she opened her eyes, Adia saw the Starlit Demon crash into the phoenixes above.

Stars, the size of him, she thought. She was a powerful dragon, her wings wide and her tail long, but beneath the Starlit Demon, she felt like a fish swimming under a ship. Flames crashed around the demon as dozens of phoenixes attacked it, but none could burn it. The creature's appetite knew no bounds; its jaws opened and closed, biting phoenixes like a wolf biting hens.

Blue scales flashed to her left.

A cry pierced the night.

"Mother!"

Adia looked and saw her daughter there. Lyana looked slimmer, the shine of her scales dimmed, but she was alive, she was flying, she was well. Tears filled Adia's eyes. *My daughter. My beloved.* She wanted to fly toward Lyana, hold her, never let her go again. But she steeled herself.

"Lyana!" she cried. "Lead the southern route!" Behind her daughter's shoulder, she saw a hundred dragons fly into a cloud of phoenixes. Many burned and fell. "Lead them to King's Forest and I will meet you there!"

Lyana looked behind her, saw the phoenixes swoop against the fleeing dragons, and nodded. With a growl, the sapphire dragon flew toward them.

"Dragons of Requiem, follow!" Lyana called. "We fly to the forests!"

Adia looked around her. Hundreds of dragons were fleeing to all directions of the wind. Thousands of phoenixes were swooping upon them or chasing them into the distance. Below, in the collapsed chasm, some Vir Requis still huddled in what shelter remained of the tunnels. The sounds of battle rose from the earth; Tirans and Vir Requis still fought there in human forms.

We are overrun, Adia realized. A chill ran through her. The Starlit Demon could not devour ten thousand phoenixes. It could not stop the fire that burned her people.

Our era ends here, she thought, tears in her eyes. *The Second Age of Requiem ends like the first... in blood and fire and destruction.*

Three phoenixes fell upon her. Their claws lashed, their beaks bit, and their fire blazed against her. Adia shouted and could barely hear her own voice. She called for the Starlit Demon, but could not see it. She saw nothing but fire.

No more pain filled her. Only warmth.

I die now, she thought. *I go to the starlit halls of my fathers. I will forever dine there with my parents, with the fallen men and women of my house. I am coming to you, stars of Requiem.*

She heard the glow of those celestial halls, a sound like harps. She saw their glow, silver and soft, bathing her with light. No more fire burned her, and Adia could smile, for she died as she had lived—fighting for the song of her people.

She raised her eyes, and looked to the stars, and saw the silver light blaze. Caught in the beam, the phoenixes still flew, but no more fire burned upon them. They were as naked vultures, black and wizened, exposed for their true ugliness and frailty.

Two dragons came coiling down from the light, tails whipping behind them, and Adia gasped.

"Bayrin!" she called. Her son flew there! She knew his great, lanky frame, his emerald scales, his bright eyes. Princess Mori flew by him, gripping a disk of silver light; she seemed to be holding the moon itself. Did they too die? Did they too now fly among the stars of Afterlife?

"Mother!" Bayrin called. He dived. His fire rained upon the naked vultures, and his claws slashed them. The beasts burned, bled, and fell.

Adia's heart thrashed, she gasped, and tears ran down her cheeks.

They were not dead, she knew. She laughed as she cried. *They found the Moondisk.*

She flapped her wings—three great thuds—and soared. Her fire roared, spun, and crashed against a naked phoenix that screeched in the Moondisk's glow.

The phoenix blazed. For a moment it looked like a firebird again, but this was dragonfire. This fire burned it. The creature squealed, cawed to the sky, and fell. As it tumbled by Adia, it became a man again... nothing but a burning man who thudded against the ruins of Nova Vita below.

Adia spread her wings wide, blew fire, and roared. Hope burned anew—hope of moonlight and dragonfire.

LYANA

She was rallying the fleeing dragons, driving them toward the southern forests, when the light blazed behind her. Lyana turned and saw her brother plunge through the light, blowing fire upon extinguished phoenixes. Princess Mori flew behind him, holding a disk like the moon, bathing the world with its glow.

Tears sprang into Lyana's eyes.

Bayrin and Mori are back. Hope is back.

"Fly to the forests!" she cried to the children who flew around her. "Wait for us there!"

As the small dragons flew off, Lyana turned, snarled, and soared into battle. Her fire bathed the sky.

Under the beam of Mori's Moondisk, the phoenixes lost their flames, only to ignite under dragonfire. Lyana saw her mother fly above, a great white dragon in the night, blowing her flame upon the enemy. Her father came soaring from below, a burly copper dragon, a hole in his right wing and fire in his maw.

Ten phoenixes flew toward Lyana from all sides. The Moondisk's beam blazed far in the north. The Starlit Demon howled and feasted to the west. Lyana flew alone against the enemy.

"Mori!" she shouted across the battle. "Mori, give me your light!"

Did the golden dragon hear? Phoenixes filled her vision. One crashed into Lyana, and she howled. Talons cut her. Wings of flame blazed against her. A second phoenix slammed into her right, and fire roared, and Lyana cried in agony, and—

Moonlight washed the world.

The flames vanished like a candle under a blanket. The light hummed. Caught in its glare, the phoenixes were nothing but naked birds, blinded and screeching.

Ignoring the pain of her wounds, Lyana howled and spun, blowing a ring of fire around her. The phoenixes kindled, welts rose across them, their skin cracked, and they crashed from the sky.

Howls of dying dragons rose to the north. The moonbeam left Lyana, its light rushing to extinguish a northern horde of phoenixes. Lyana looked around, panting. Hundreds of corpses rained upon the ruins of Nova Vita. Thousands of dragons were fleeing or fighting, and countless phoenixes still blazed. Above the battle, Mori was directing the Moondisk from left to right, pausing on each group of phoenixes just long enough for dragons to burn them. The Starlit Demon still moved across the sky, consuming phoenixes that fled from Mori's light.

"Yarin!" Lyana called to a red dragon who flew above. She remembered him well—a young man in the service of her father.

He turned toward her, fire between his teeth, a gash along his face. "My Lady Lyana!"

"Yarin, to me!" she called. "Bring your men. We follow that beam."

She shot under a swooping phoenix, soared above the Starlit Demon who dived by, and surged toward a group of young dragons. They were mere youths, no older than fifteen, but they would have to fight like men today. Welts covered them and one's wing was torn.

"Dragons of Requiem!" she called. "Follow—to blood and glory!"

They howled and blew flame, and Lyana soared, rallying more dragons as she flew. Phoenixes descended upon them. Three dragons fell, turned to humans, and crashed against houses below. Fire bathed her. Lyana narrowed her eyes and flew toward the light of the Moonbeam.

Silver light covered her. The phoenixes cried, naked. She burned them. Her dragons blew flames around her. They howled for death and glory, for Requiem, for their princess. The phoenixes fell dead.

The moonlight left them, shooting to the east. Lyana snarled, spun, and followed it.

"Stay in the beam!" she shouted. "Dragons of Requiem, behind me! Burn the enemy!"

They flew among the fire and moonlight, blood raining. As Lyana sounded her roar, she looked around the battle, seeking Elethor. Where was their king?

"Elethor!" she cried over the battle, but did not hear him. She gritted her teeth. Requiem needed their king, needed Elethor to rally them around his cry—not her, not Lyana, but King Elethor Aeternum.

"Elethor! Hear me!"

Rage boiled inside her. If he was not dead, she would kill him herself. He needed to lead his people, now more than ever. Where the stars was he?

She roared her dragonfire, bathing the phoenixes. They fell dead, thudded against the Starlit Demon as he dived below, then crashed to the city ruins. Requiem trembled with fire, blood, and light.

BAYRIN

A dozen phoenixes soared toward Mori.

Flying beside the princess, Bayrin roared.

"Mori, to your left!"

She spun in the sky, pointing the Moondisk to her left. The beam caught the phoenixes and they extinguished. Bayrin swooped upon them, bathing them with fire. They crackled and fell.

"Bay!" Mori shouted above him, fear twisting her voice.

The beam of moonlight left Bayrin, sweeping to the north. He turned his head and saw ten more phoenixes surge toward Mori. They shrieked, claws outstretched. When the beam hit them, they cried and lost their fire. Wings aching and wounds blazing, Bayrin soared toward them. He roared fire and burned them down.

He spared the battle below a glance. Phoenixes fell like rain. The dragons of Requiem were flying from side to side, staying within the moonbeam. He saw his sister, a sapphire dragon blowing fire. He saw his parents—Deramon flew as a burly copper dragon, crashing into phoenixes, while Adia soared as a white dragon, leaving a wake of flame. When Mori moved her Moondisk, those dragons too slow to follow burned in phoenix fire.

"Mori, phoenixes over the temple!" Bayrin shouted. A hundred of them were roaring from the marble roof, comets of fury.

Mori nodded and moved the Moondisk upon the enemy. The phoenixes screeched and Bayrin saw dozens of dragons swarm upon them, roaring fire.

More screeches sounded above. Bayrin looked up and cursed. Ten phoenixes had managed to flank the battle, fly over the clouds, and were now swooping upon Mori from above.

"Mori, fire above!" he shouted and soared. She banked, and Bayrin crashed upward. His wings brushed her, and he slammed against the phoenixes above.

Fire engulfed him. Talons tore him. Beaks of flame ripped his flesh. He howled and lashed his claws but cut only fire.

Silver light bathed him. Below, Mori was flying upside down, pointing the moonbeam toward him. He roared fire and the phoenixes fell.

"Point the Moondisk down!" Bayrin shouted to her. Welts blazed across him. He felt ready to fall from the sky, but forced himself to keep flying. "I've got your back. Protect the dragons below."

Mori looked as hurt and wounded as Bayrin felt. The lamprey bites still bled on her shoulders. Like him, she had not slept or eaten in two days. And yet she snarled and directed the Moondisk down, catching a formation of soaring phoenixes. Bayrin showered them with fire.

Three more phoenixes swooped from the clouds above Mori. Cursing, Bayrin drove toward them.

"Keep that moonbeam pointing down!" he shouted as he soared by her.

He crashed into the firebirds above. Their flames washed him. He screamed in agony. It felt like flying into a forge. He clawed blindly.

I will protect Mori. I won't let them burn her.

Moonlight bathed him. He roared fire. The phoenixes fell.

More flew at Mori's left. He drove forward and crashed into their fire. When she lit them with moonlight and he burned them, more flew from the right. Bayrin howled, scales blazing, and crashed into them.

Protect the princess. Don't let them burn her. Don't...

Fire washed him.

Talons ripped him.

Bayrin howled and blew flame, and his world was nothing but heat, screams, and pain.

ELETHOR

He flew toward the tunnel, shifted into human form, and rolled into the darkness. He leaped to his feet while drawing his sword. When his eyes adjusted to the shadows, his stomach churned. The sight was as sickening as anything from the Abyss.

Dead children covered the tunnel floor, cut with blades. One girl's face was slashed. A boy was missing his arm. A second boy lay in the corner, disemboweled. The sight and stench nearly made Elethor gag. He gritted his teeth and raised his sword.

Ahead in the darkness, before a crowd of weeping children, stood Solina.

Elethor's heart thudded. His head spun.

Solina. Flame of his life. Light of his soul. The woman he had loved with heat like dragonfire. Blood covered her armor, face, and blades. She stared at him, and he saw the same emotion swirl in her eyes. She gave him a sad, crooked smile.

"Elethor," she said softly.

He walked deeper into the tunnel, stepping over strewn limbs and corpses, his boots sloshing through blood. His eyes narrowed, he could barely breathe, and for a moment he only managed to shake his head and whisper.

"Solina... how could you do this?"

A snarl fled her lips, sounding almost like a sob. A shaky, toothy grin twisted her face; Elethor couldn't decide if she grinned like a wolf or a madwoman.

"They are vermin, Elethor," she said. "They are nothing but lizards. You saw how they taunted me." Her eyes blazed, narrowing to blue slits. "You saw how they would fly above me, mock me, roar fire down on me. They burned me." She took a step toward him. "I won't let them come between us again. I will kill every weredragon between you and me until you're mine again."

"I am one of them!" Elethor shouted. His eyes stung. "Solina, you have gone mad. You have lost your mind. This is not the woman I knew, that I loved. You were good once, Solina. You were—"

"I was weak!" she screamed. "I was scared." Tears fled her eyes. "I was an orphan, Elethor. Your father murdered my parents, slaughtered my brothers like animals, and made me live here, a prisoner, a cripple." She took another step toward him, tears rolling.

She let one sabre clang to the ground and reached out to him. "But you made it bearable, Elethor. You loved me, even though I could not become a dragon, even as everyone else in this land loathed me, saw me as less than human. But *they* are less than human. They are creatures. They are dead now; I killed them. I burned them. I did this for us, Elethor. Don't you understand? For me and you."

He shook his head, looking at the blood that covered the tunnel. "Killing children?" His voice was barely a whisper. "Stars, Solina, how could you think this would bring us together?"

"Because I know that you still love me." She stared into his eyes. "Because I remember. I remember your kisses. Your whispers. I remember how we would come here, to this very tunnel, and speak of our dreams. We would speak about how cruel your father was to me, how one day we would fly away and be together in some faraway land." Her eyes shone. "That day has come, Elethor! I brought it here. I made it happen so our dream could come true." Her body shook. "Don't you see?" She clutched his shoulder. "We can be together now like we always wanted, like we knew would always happen. We'll fly to Tiranor, you a dragon and I a phoenix. I've built a palace where we will reign, king and queen of a desert land. It's that magical place we've always dreamed of, Elethor. It's what we've always wanted."

"I did not want this!" he shouted. His pulse pounded in his ears, and his head spun. "You will not cast this blood on me. You've gone mad in your southern land, with this... this Sun God who corrupted your mind." He swept his arms around him. "Dreams? Magical kingdoms? Love? You drenched the world in blood! You slaughtered children!"

"For you!" she shouted hoarsely. "For us!"

"Not for me!" His eyes burned. "I did not ask for this. You—"

A child tore free from the group of survivors behind Solina. He ran forward, skirted around Solina, and made toward the tunnel exit, maybe hoping to fly outside. Solina cut him down. Her blade flashed and sliced his leg, then swung down onto his shoulder, cleaving him. The child fell, gurgled, and died.

Elethor sucked in his breath. Head spinning and heart pounding, barely able to see through the sting of tears, he swung his sword at Solina.

She stood only three feet away, but it seemed the longest distance his sword had ever swung. It seemed the longest instant of his life. He was cutting the roots of that life, the old memories and meaning that had forever filled him, driven him, defined him. In that instant that lasted hours, he realized how much Solina had shaped him—he had grown up in her light, in her arms, almost a part of her. Without her, who was he?

A king, a voice whispered inside him. *A betrothed to Lyana. A leader of dragons.*

A whole man—no longer a boy in his brother's shadow, no longer a sculptor who shied away from the court his fathers had built. If he cut her down, he would cut himself free—free to become this man of his own right, to sit upon the throne with a whole heart.

He had always felt like half a soul; a night to Solina's day, starlight to her fire. Now he became one.

The instant passed. His sword reached her. Her blade rose and parried, and steel clanged.

She thrust her sabre at him, snarling, a wild animal, no longer human. He parried. He thrust again. And they danced.

It was a dance like they used to love—of passion and rage and hope. Her sword bit his shoulder, like her teeth would as they made love in this tunnel. He bled and thrust again, slamming his blade against her armor. Her sword flew at him, he parried, swung again.

He felt no rage. No more sadness. When he looked upon her, he no longer saw the old Solina—the girl of golden hair, of bright eyes, of secrets only he knew. He saw only the rot inside her, and he slammed at her until he cut her down. His blade shattered hers, and she fell. His sword slammed against her armor, denting it, and she gasped.

She knelt before him, head tossed back. Blood poured from a crack in her breastplate. Her mouth opened and closed.

"El," she whispered. "El..."

He stood above her, his sword raised. He could stab her now. He could slice her neck. He could—

"El," she whispered, "do you remember the wooden turtle?"

Blackness clutched him. He could not help but lower his head, close his eyes, and feel the breath leave him. She spoke with a trembling voice; she sounded so much like the Solina who would hold him years ago. Her every word shot arrows through him.

"El, you carved it for me. I remember... I said how I wanted a pet, a friend in Requiem, and you made me a wooden turtle. Remember how we'd imagine that, in the magical kingdom we would find, our turtle would come alive? How—"

Pain blazed on his thigh, not the throb of memory, but searing agony. Elethor gasped. His eyes snapped open to see Solina twisting a dagger in his leg.

Blood spurted and Solina leaped. She drove her fist into Elethor's chin, and his head snapped back, and he saw nothing but light and blood and stone. He fell, stars floating before his eyes. Solina pounced atop him, baring her teeth.

"I will spare your life this night," she hissed, "so you may see the death I bring to your land. But I will give you this first."

She pulled the dagger from his thigh. He raised his arms, but could not block her strength. She drove her blade down his face. Pain exploded. Blood filled his eyes and mouth.

"I will kill them all, Elethor!" she screamed. "I will burn them all with my fire. You will watch! And then you will crawl to me and beg to be mine!"

She leaped past him, tossed herself outside, and shifted into a phoenix. Her flames crackled, and when Elethor turned his head, he saw her soar into the night. Her scream carried on the wind, high-pitched, a storm of rage.

"You will beg, Elethor! You will beg!"

He struggled to his feet. Blood washed his face and leg. He made to leap after her, but his thigh twisted, and he fell. His elbows banged against the tunnel floor. He crawled to the exit, stared up, and saw the Moondisk bathe the world with light.

He tried to shift into a dragon. He let the magic fill him. Light and agony flooded him, his eyes closed, and his head fell.

BAYRIN

Time swirled like stars.

Darkness clutched him, pulling him into slumber, and Bayrin dreamed. In his dreams, he lay in human form upon bloody earth. Mori was kneeling above, also a human, cradling him in her arms.

"Bay!" she cried and shook him. "Bay, please..."

He dreamed of his sister there too, weeping over him, and his mother praying, and soldiers bearing him on a litter into a temple of marble and candles.

"Mori," he whispered. "I have to protect her... I have to fly...."

His voice died and he slept.

He felt like he slept for years.

When his eyes finally fluttered open, he thought he was dead. Soft light bathed him, and marble columns rose around him. He lay in a bed, a white blanket pulled over him. It was supposed to be night, but dawn's light fell from the windows.

"Mori?" he whispered, voice hoarse. He raised his arm and saw that bandages covered it.

"Do I look like Mori?" a voice answered him. "Bay, if I look like my sister, you look like a phoenix. Actually, for a while up there, you did look like one."

Bayrin pushed himself up in bed, pain blazing. He winced. A figure sat at his bedside, silhouetted in the dawn's light. Bayrin squinted, bringing the figure into focus. His breath caught.

"Elethor?" he whispered.

His friend nodded, smiling softly, though his eyes were sad.

"El!" Bayrin cried. He tried to leap up, to hug his friend, but his head spun, and he fell back into bed. Everything hurt; he felt like he'd been dipped into a bath of coals.

"Take it easy, Bay!" Elethor said and squeezed his shoulder. "You got banged up pretty badly there."

In a flash, Bayrin remembered. *The phoenixes!* They had swooped toward Mori, and...

He pushed himself back up, panting. "I have to save her, El. The battle! Mori is..."

"Mori is *fine*, Bay!" Elethor said. "Lie down, for stars' sake, or I'll tie you down." His voice softened. "You saved her life up there. You saved all of us."

Elethor himself was wounded, Bayrin saw. Bandages covered his shoulder and leg. Fresh stitches ran along his face, from forehead to chin. The young king looked like he'd been to the Abyss and back—which, Bayrin supposed, he had been. He couldn't help but laugh.

"Look at us, El—a pair of beaten up patients." Suddenly he found that tears filled his eyes. "Stars, Elethor, I missed you. What happened? Is the battle...?"

"The battle is over." Elethor sighed and lowered his head. "Solina fled. So have those phoenixes who survived. Not many of them did, but some managed to flee into the south. After the Starlit Demon ate his fill, he vanished back underground; I imagine he'll sleep for a good long while to digest his meal." He winced. "It was bad, Bay. Many Vir Requis died. Too many." His voice dropped to a pained whisper. "Thousands are gone."

Bayrin's breath caught and horror clumped in his throat. "Is... my sister? My parents?"

"They're alive. Your father looks like he was dropped into a nest of weasels, and your mother has seen better days. Lyana is bashed up like an old leather ball after a thousand kicks, but she wouldn't admit it." He smiled softly. "They're here in the temple, wounds tended to."

Relief swept over Bayrin, but grief too. *Many Vir Requis died. Too many.*

Eyes stinging, he looked outside the window. He watched the morning light fall upon ruins. Clear skies rolled outside, blue without a tinge of smoke. A lump filled his throat, and he swallowed.

"Where..." His voice caught, and he blinked for a moment, unable to speak. "Where is Mori? I want to see her."

Elethor helped him up. Bayrin slung his arm across the king's shoulder, and they walked slowly. Step by step, they left the chamber and moved down a hallway. Wounded filled the hall, lying on makeshift beds. When they passed by chambers, Bayrin saw more wounded inside. Healers rushed back and forth, robes swishing. Many were hurt themselves, faces and limbs bandaged, but they still bustled about, carrying herbs and bandages.

Most of the wounded were Vir Requis, Bayrin saw, but some were Tirans with platinum hair and pained blue eyes. For a moment rage filled Bayrin. Why should they tend to wounded Tirans, the men who had tried to slaughter them? But he only sighed, his rage soon dissipating. *Let the bastards live. Let them see the mercy and goodness of those they thought mere reptiles.*

Finally they reached a narrow hallway, its wall smashed and its floor strewn with bricks. Two guards in breastplates stood before a doorway, clutching spears. They bowed to Elethor and pulled the door open.

"Go and see her," Elethor said softly. "I'm needed at court, and you two have a lot to discuss." He clutched Bayrin's shoulder, then pulled him into an embrace. "It's good to have you back, friend."

When Bayrin stepped alone into the room, he found himself holding his breath, suddenly sheepish. Their quest north, the battle with the demon of wood and stone, the inferno over Nova Vita... it all seemed like a bad dream to him now. He had kissed Mori on the Crescent Isle, had vowed to protect her, but... back home, in Nova Vita, would she mock him for it? Would they be as before the war—he the ne'er-do-well guard, she the timid princess who shied away at every touch? It felt like waking from a dream, not knowing what the dawn would bring.

She lay in a bed, wrapped in embroidered blankets, her wounds bandaged. When she saw him enter, she smiled wanly and lowered her eyes. The dawn's light kissed her pale cheeks, pink lips, and chestnut hair. She was so beautiful.

Bayrin stepped toward her, hesitant. She looked up at him, then down again, and her eyes dampened. His breath caught, he froze... and then he took three great strides toward her. He found himself embracing her, nearly crushing her in his arms, as she wept against him, soaking his shirt. As the morning's light fell upon them, they kissed with tears and laughter. She touched his cheek, and he couldn't help but cry too; joy and relief swept over him.

"Hi there, Mors," he whispered.

She smiled tremulously, tears on her lips. "Hi there, Bay."

He laughed and pulled her back into his embrace. He rocked her gently in his arms.

"I told you we'd do it," she whispered.

Still holding her, Bayrin looked outside. Burnt trees rose between ashy walls. Buildings lay toppled. But he saw people move between those buildings, lifting fallen bricks, collecting shattered weapons, and sweeping the ash away. It would be a time of pain, he knew, of mourning and grief. *But we will rebuild.*

He knew then—things would not return to how they had been. He had changed too much. He remembered himself before the phoenix fire—a lowly guard with great parentage. He had watched his sister rise in the ranks of the court, his father lead armies, his mother speak to the stars. And he would joke to hide his pain, run off with Elethor to escape his failed life.

But he had purpose now. He had Mori.

I may still be nothing but a lowly guard... but I guard the Princess of Requiem, the woman I love.

"I won't let anyone hurt you again," he whispered into her hair. "I love you, Mori. I know that healing will be long and painful—for you, for this city, for all of us. I know that some battles only now begin. But you have me. We'll go through this together."

She lowered her eyes, her lashes brushing his cheek, and clung to him. "I miss them, Bay. My brother. My father. I miss them so much, that... I don't know if the pain will ever end." She looked up at him, eyes sparkling with tears. "I love you too, Bayrin. Always. So much that it hurts, so much that... when you fell from the sky, I thought I would die, that light could never more shine in the world." She smiled shakily and nodded. "We will heal together, Bay, you and I. It hurts so much, but... we have each other. We'll do this together."

A robin took flight outside the window, rising into a clear sky. *Spring is here,* Bayrin thought, Mori in his arms. They sat together silently, embracing, watching the dawn rise.

ELETHOR

He stood above the twin graves, jaw tight, staring with dry eyes.

The stones rose tall and white, carved of marble and engraved with the Draco constellation. One bore the name of King Olasar. The second bore the name of Prince Orin.

My father. My brother.

Elethor lowered his head. Spring had come to Requiem, and grass grew where snow, blood, and ash had fallen. Bluebells bloomed upon the hill, and the air was sweet, but Elethor's heart was heavy. He found no peace here, only memories and grief.

He remembered the day of the funerals. His throat tightened to remember the coffins, their birch wood inlaid with golden leaves and stars. Elethor had looked upon them, unable to stop the horrible thoughts, the twisting imagination. Inside the coffin, was his father only a burnt skeleton? Was his brother just a severed head—the only part of him found? He had clenched his fists, praying to remember Father as the wise ruler, his brother as the handsome hero, to forget the blood and fire.

That had been a moon ago, but the blood and fire remained in Elethor's mind, and even the song of birds or the scent of flowers could not dull them.

How do you forget the sight of dead children, limbs severed and bellies slashed? How do you forget the demon Nedath, or the sphinx of the underground, or the shriveled bodies that lingered there?

He turned away from the graves, jaw clenched and eyes burning.

He walked that day through the city of Nova Vita, his guards at his sides. Requiem's crown, forged three hundred years ago by Queen Gloriae herself, rested on his head. He visited the temple and spoke to those who still lay wounded, healing or slowly dying. He visited buildings covered with scaffolding, where masons spoke of new walls, arches, and towers. He visited the barracks of soldiers, too many of them gone, and praised their courage and sacrifice.

The numbers spun through his head as he moved through the city. Fifty thousand Vir Requis had lived here under his father's reign. He now ruled thirty thousand haunted souls.

Everywhere he looked, he saw the wounds of battle. As he walked through the city, Elethor saw a child sitting upon a toppled wall, his face wrapped in bandages, his eyes peering and haunted. He saw a young woman sweeping her porch; her left arm ended with a stump. He saw a husband leading his wife down a street; a scarf covered her eyes, and a scar ran along her head.

Elethor greeted all those he passed, squeezed shoulders, whispered comforts. He tried to stand strong. To smile. To jest that wounded children were stronger than knights, that farmers missing limbs would be back plowing tomorrow, that women with burnt faces were still as beautiful as queens. His words tasted stale.

He turned to face a wall and shut his eyes. *Did I drive her to this?* he wondered, as he wondered every day, the guilt clawing inside him. He touched the scar along his face, a twin to the one Solina bore, her last gift to him. *Did I cause this death and pain?*

"My lord."

The gruff voice rose behind him. Elethor turned to see Lord Deramon. The burly man stood in burnished armor. His sword clanked at his side, and in his left hand, he held his axe. More white than ever filled his beard.

Elethor approached him, and the two stepped into a quiet, cobbled alley.

"So many lost limbs, eyes, faces." Elethor lowered his head. "Every wounded person mourns dead family and friends. Deramon, how do I give them strength? How do I comfort them?"

Deramon gave a low grumble like a bear disturbed in his cave. He blew out his breath and said, "Give them time to mourn. You walk among them. You stand tall. You smile rather than cry. This is well, Elethor. You are doing right."

Elethor nodded, eyes stinging. "I keep thinking... what would my father do?" He looked up at Deramon. "How would he lead today?"

Deramon's lips tightened and he clutched Elethor's shoulder. For a moment, Elethor was sure that the lord would admonish him, call him a callow boy, speak of how greater King Olasar had been.

But Deramon only stared at him steadily and said, "Your father watches from the stars, Elethor, and he's proud of you. *I* am proud of you. You will make a fine king, and a fine husband to my daughter." He growled and hefted his axe. "I'll be here to make sure of it."

Grumbling, the lord trundled out of the alley, barked orders at some wandering guards, and disappeared around a corner.

That evening, Elethor walked toward the gazebo in the city square, the place where she had asked him to surrender, and where he chose to lead Requiem to war. He stood staring at the columns and glass panes, then turned and looked south. Somewhere beyond forest, mountain, and desert, Solina waited.

Are you looking north now, Solina? Do our eyes meet across the endless leagues?

"Elethor."

Again a voice rose behind him, but this voice was high, fair, and soft. For a terrible instant, he was sure it was *her*, Solina. He spun around, saw Lyana, and slowly exhaled.

She stood in her silvery armor, the ancient armor of the bellators, the knights of Requiem; she was the only one of their number to survive. Her eyes were soft, and her sword hung from her waist. Her wounds had healed, the scabs peeling to show her pale skin strewn with freckles like stars. A year ago, the mere sight of Lyana would chafe him, like seeing a bee during a garden meal. Today she seemed so fair to him, so soothing, that his eyes stung.

This is how I let go of the ghosts, he thought. *With Lyana.*

"She offered me surrender here," he said to her, voice soft. "In this gazebo. If I had gone with her to Tiranor, how many would still live? How many lives would I have saved?" He shook his head. "Did I make a mistake, Lyana?"

She walked toward him, placed her hands on her hips, and glared at him. "Elethor, if you do not stop speaking utter nonsense, I will kick your backside across this square. If you had surrendered, she would have burned us all, and you know it." Her eyes flashed. "So will you please stop moping, and maybe grow some sense in your hollow head?"

He sighed. *Same old Lyana after all.*

"Would have saved me the lectures," he said and couldn't help but smile.

She shook her head, curls flouncing. "Just wait until we are wed, Elethor. If you think this is bad, you haven't seen nothing yet." She grabbed his hand and tugged him. "Now come *on*! Stars. We're meeting my parents in the court today, and the Prince of Osanna will be there, and if you are late again, I swear that I will..."

He stopped listening. He let her pull him across the square toward the palace, and as they walked, he looked at the flowers that grew in gardens, and the masons hauling bricks, and the doves that flew, and he felt something new, something he had never felt in his life.

He felt whole.

SOLINA

She stood upon the Tower of Akartum, a spire of sandstone and platinum. The wind billowed her hair, tasting of sand and palm oil. Tiranor rolled before her: the lush palms of her oasis, fluttering with cranes and ibises and falcons; the ships that sailed along the River Pallan, laden with spice and gems and treasures of distant lands; the towers of her city, shards of white capped with gold; and beyond them dunes kissed golden with her lord's light, rolling to distant yellow mountains.

"It is my realm," she whispered into the wind. "My magical world of secrets." She shook her head, hair billowing. "You could have been here with me. You could have stood here too."

She looked north past oasis, dune, and mountain. Did he stand there too upon a tower, looking south toward her? She caressed her shoulder where she bore a scar his sword had given her. And yet she loved him, even now.

She could have killed him, she knew. She had wanted to. In the tunnels of Requiem, the bloody dagger in hand, she could have plunged it into his heart. But no. Not yet. He had not suffered enough in life to escape her torment.

"I will bring you here, El," she said and licked the sand from her lips. "But first... first you will watch me slay your sister, and your betrothed Lyana, and all the people of your realm. You will stand and watch them die, and I will make you drink their blood." She nodded, a soft smile on her lips. "And then, El, then I will bring you here, a broken man. I will chain you to this tower, and let the vultures feed upon your living flesh and eyes. And then, El... then maybe I will grant you mercy. Then maybe I will kiss you and let you die."

Upon her tower, she turned around and faced south.

Her army spread across the desert.

A hundred thousand men stood in burnished breastplates, bearing spears, bows, and arrows tipped with poison. Ten thousand horses stood in armor, tethered to chariots of wood and iron. The sun fell upon them, and the golden suns upon her men's breastplates blazed. And behind her men...

Solina's smile widened.

Beyond the army, the dunes undulated, and grumbles rose from beneath. Something was buried there, something ancient and cruel. Beneath the sand waited her greatest champions, like the eggs of snakes waiting to hatch. Soon the desert was trembling, and a crack opened, a womb ready for birth. Sand fell into the crevice. The grumbles turned to roars that shook the city.

Solina raised her arms. Her heart thrashed and her blood thrummed in her ears.

"Arise, my children!" she cried. "Arise from the desert and serve your queen!"

As the beasts hatched from the sand, Solina snarled, tossed her head back, and howled at the sun and its glory.

BOOK TWO:
A DAY OF DRAGON BLOOD

SILAS

Three dragons flew in the night, seeing demons in every shadow.

The swamplands rolled below into darkness. Mist rose from the mangroves like ghosts, only to disperse in the flap of leathern wings. The clammy scents of moss, mud, and leaf filled the dragons' nostrils, mingling with the scent of fire that crackled inside their maws. No stars gleamed above; it was a night of cloud, of fear, of a quiet before the storm.

"Where are you?" Silas whispered, scanning the darkness. His scales clanked and his scars still blazed. It had been a year since the war, a year since the Tirans had flown over these swamplands, killed his king, toppled his home, and left his body a ruin of burnt flesh and lacerations. A year—and still the scars burned, those that covered his body and those that clawed inside him.

"My lord!" said Tanin, a young dragon who flew beside him. He was a mere boy, just turned sixteen, and green as his scales. "My lord, do you see something?"

Silas grumbled. "I'm not a lord, Tanin. And lower your voice; it could carry for a mile on this wind."

Farm boys, he thought and spat. *They send me farm boys to lead in patrol.* A year ago, Silas had served among a thousand true warriors, hardened dragons who fought for Requiem's glory. Nearly all had died in the war, burned in phoenix fire over the capital or cut with steel in its tunnels.

Yet I linger. Thousands of warriors died around me, in glory and fury, and here I am... a scarred, twisted old thing serving with the children of farmers and bakers. He was barely thirty, but he felt old beside these youths—his soul like ancient leather, crumpled countless times, and his bones brittle as rusted blades.

Wings churned the mist, and Yara flew up to him, her eyes bright. A slim silver dragon, a baker's daughter, she bared her fangs.

"Silas!" she said, panting. "I saw something! A shadow in the night." She pointed her claws south.

Icy fingers seemed to clutch Silas. He looked south but saw only leagues of shadows, swirling clouds, and mangroves that swayed over mud and water.

Scales clattering with fear, Tanin snorted a blast of fire. "Where, Yara? Where?"

Silas whipped his head around and hissed. "Silence, boy! Still your tongue and your fire."

He turned his head back south. He narrowed his eyes, seeking, barely breathing. Gliding silently on the wind, he sniffed the air.

Nothing, he thought. *Nothing but leagues of these swamplands. No enemy. No—*

Beside him, the two young dragons gasped. Silas cursed and filled his maw with flames.

Damn it.

A dozen shadows swooped from the clouds, not a hundred yards away. Red eyes blazed and fangs glinted; Silas saw nothing more of the creatures but shadow. He growled, spat a curse, and blew a jet of fire.

The flames spun and screamed, and for an instant Silas saw the beasts. His blood froze. They were large as dragons, their scales metallic, their wings wide, their jaws long and sharp as blades. Human riders sat astride them, faceless behind jagged helms. Then the fire crashed against the beasts, and their shrieks shattered the night. They screeched like smashing glass, like cracking bones, like storms. Their wings thudded and they crashed against him.

Claws tore at his scales. Fangs drove into flesh. Silas growled and slashed at them, his claws screeching against scales as hard as iron. Sparks showered. He saw Yara and Tanin fighting beside him, and blood sprayed through the mist.

"Yara, fall back!" Silas howled. "Send the signal!"

One of the beasts swooped again, scales rippling and claws lashing. Silas spun, swung his tail, and hit a head of scales and spikes. Another beast flew at his right, a mere shadow in the night, and fangs dug into Silas's shoulder. Pain blazed and in a flash, Silas was back in the tunnels, back in the darkness under Nova Vita, fighting the war that had left his brothers dead and him this burnt shell of a man. Fire once more raced across him, burning as his city collapsed and all those he knew fell dead around him.

He blasted more fire. It crashed into the creatures and showered, and Silas was back above the swamps, a year later, fighting to stop this war from flaring again. In the firelight, he saw Yara retreat. The young silver dragon puffed her chest, tossed her head back, and seemed ready to send the signal for aid—three upward blasts of fire.

Before she could summon her flame, the shadowy beasts turned toward her, opened their maws, and spewed jets of pale liquid.

Heat blazed and stench flared. Silas growled. The yellow projectiles slammed against Yara and she screamed—a sound of such agony that Silas knew it would forever haunt him. The liquid sizzled across the silver dragon, eating through her scales, melting her face, and digging into flesh. Her magic left her, the ancient magic of Requiem, the magic that let their people fly as dragons. She fell from the sky as a human, a young woman burning away into bones. She disappeared into darkness.

"Oh stars, oh stars!" cried Tanin, and the green dragon turned to flee. He flew not fifty yards before the metallic creatures roared and spewed their acid. The sizzling streams crashed against the fleeing dragon, and Tanin howled and wept.

"Please!" he cried, and his voice sounded so young, the voice of a mere boy. "I want to go home, please, I'm not a soldier, please..."

He turned to look back, and his eyes met Silas's gaze. For an instant—a cold, terrible instant that lasted for ages—Silas stared into the eyes of a young, terrified boy who had believed in him... whom he had led to death. Then the acid dripped into those frightened eyes and melted them like flames melting candles. Tanin too became human and tumbled, burning into a red, bubbling chunk of meat that disappeared into shadow.

Panting, Silas beat his wings and turned to face the creatures. In the darkness, he could barely see them—only the shape of their wings, the glint of their fangs, and the red of their eyes. They surrounded him, ten or more. The riders on their backs were mere shadows. Silas's heart pounded. He knew he had to send the signal, he had to blast his fire—three blasts into the air, a cry for aid—yet if he moved, they'd kill him. He had seen enough men die to know when his own death loomed.

He tossed back his head and began to blow his fire.

The creatures swarmed.

A jet of acid flew. Silas soared and swerved. The blast slammed against his wing and he screamed. The heat blazed, enveloping him. Holes tore open in his wing; he heard wind rush through them. He flapped madly, trying to shake off the acid, but it stuck to him, eating, digging, tearing his wing apart until it fell like burnt paper shards.

He began to tumble from the sky, beating one wing.

The swamps rushed up toward him. Above him the beasts swooped.

"Take him alive!" shouted a rider. "I want him *alive!*"

The wind roared. Silas craned his neck as he fell and blew fire upward. The flaming pillar crashed against one swooping beast. It howled and pulled back. A dozen others dived down, great falling shards of black. Claws reached out and grabbed him, digging past scales into flesh.

He crashed through mangroves into mud and moss. The beasts crashed atop him. Fangs dug into him, and chains swung and wrapped around him. He glimpsed the riders leaping off their mounts, the glint of golden suns on their breastplates, and an iron club swinging toward his head.

Light exploded and darkness fell like a cloak above him.

Rain pattered.

Wind howled.

Stars swirled and Silas wandered through endless tunnels, seeking his dead brothers, seeking a way out.

LYANA

Lyana stood on the winehouse roof, watching the square below where thousands roared for death.

It seemed every soul in Irys, this lush oasis city, had come to see the execution. Men, women, and children crowded the roofs of their mudbrick homes, peering between rooftop gardens of herbs, fruit, and vegetables. Soldiers, clad in pale breastplates and armed with spears, lined cobbled streets that snaked between palm groves, silos, vineyards, and workshops. Even the River Pallan, which coiled between the city's columned temples and villas, overflowed with ships—from the simple cogs of fishermen, to the great sailed ships of traders whose holds overflowed with spices, silks, and jewels from distant desert lands.

Tiranor, Lyana thought, the sandy wind in her hair. *Scourge of Requiem—gathered here in all her glory and might, as different from my home as sunlight from starlight. I stand in the lions' den.*

It was the Day of Sun's Glory, the pinnacle of the moon's cycle; tonight that moon would be black in the sky, and tomorrow the sun would rise victorious. The people wore white and gold to worship their fiery god, and the scent of myrrh wafted through the city, thick and heady in Lyana's nostrils. She had always loved the smell, but today it smelled like corpses to her. It was a day for all great things in Tiranor, this land of sand and stone—for war, for worship... and for death.

The crowd's roars swelled when five wyverns emerged from the Temple of the Sun, a sandstone edifice whose columns and towers rose above the city, capped with platinum. The scaly beasts dragged themselves from the temple's bowels and onto the hot, sun-drenched streets. Even in the glare of Tiranor's blazing sun, their scales were midnight black, their eyes red pools like fire underground. Riders sat upon them, their helms shaped as cranes' beaks, their whips ringed with gold.

Lyana grimaced and clenched her fists. The first time she had seen the wyverns, she had thought them some strange, southern dragons—they were large, scaled, and winged like the dragons of the north. But unlike dragons, they had but two legs—muscled and wide as their tails, with claws like great swords, twice the size of dragonclaws. Their jaws thrust out like blades, lined with teeth. Worst of all was the weapon that spewed from those jaws; Lyana had seen their acid burn only once, eating a condemned thief into bones, and it still filled her nightmares.

Chains dragged behind the wyverns. When they stepped farther from the temple, the shackles tugged their captive out onto the street: a bloody, lacerated dragon.

"Silas," Lyana whispered. Tears stung her eyes.

The wyverns grunted and trundled down the streets, dragging the chained dragon behind them. Silas breathed raggedly. His one wing was missing, burnt to nothing but a charred bone. His scales were dented, his horns sawed off. As the wyverns dragged him along the road, his blood trailed behind him. All around the crowds roared, stamped their feet, and pelted Silas with refuse and stones.

Lyana's legs shook, she panted, and her head spun.

"Oh Silas," she whispered.

She had fought alongside him in Nova Vita, battling the phoenixes over the city of dragons. He had served her father, the Lord Deramon; in her childhood, Silas often guarded her chamber at night and taught her swordplay during the day. She had to save him. She had to discard her disguise, shift into a dragon, swoop and grab him and fly with him to safety. She had to—

You have to serve your kingdom, whispered a voice inside her. *You have to stay at your post. You are a daughter of Requiem, and you serve all her people... even if you must let one die.*

It was the voice of her father, her king, and her ancestors—the voice of her honor and memory. It was a voice she hated this day.

She adjusted the silk scarf around her eyes. The loomers of Confutatis, ancient city of the eastern realms, had woven this scarf, and they had imbued it with all their skill and magic. From one side, the cloth was translucent as summer mist; from the other, solid and thick as wool. Through the scarf, the world shone clear to Lyana; to any observer, the silk hid her green northern eyes. To this city she was but Tiana, the blind dancer of the River Spice. Her hair, once a pyre of fiery red curls, now hung smoothed and bleached a platinum blond—the hair of a Tiran. Her skin, once pale and strewn with freckles like starfields, now gleamed golden, rubbed with dyes that would tint her for moons. Once she had worn the armor of a bellator, a knight of Requiem; today she wore but strands of white silk that revealed more flesh than they hid.

I was Lady Lyana, a defender of Requiem, a warrior who could shift into a dragon and roar to battle, save Silas, and burn my enemies. She squared her jaw, heart pounding. Now she must be only Tiana—only the blind dancer from the southern dunes, only a girl with a scarf over her eyes, a girl who could not even see this dance of blood before her. *How I wish that I were truly blind today.*

The five wyverns moved along the Palisade of Kings, a wide cobbled road lined with palms and obelisks capped with platinum sunbursts. Blood trailed behind the dragging Silas, and the multitudes roared. Cranes and ibises flew overhead, and soldiers on horseback rode behind the dragon, bearing the banners of Phoebus—a flaming sun upon a white field. The procession made its way down the palisade, under the great Queen's Archway whose stones were carved with sunbursts, and into the Square of the Sun where thousands roared and raised their hands to the heavens. The true sun blazed overhead, drenching the city, a god of light and heat and punishment.

Across the square lay the Palace of Phoebus, a towering edifice, greater even than the palace of Requiem where Lyana served her king. Its columns rose three hundred feet tall. Stone guardians, shaped as faceless warriors, flanked its great doors; each statue stood taller than three dragons. The wyverns began climbing the stairs to the palace gateway. Silas dragged behind them; the dragon thudded against each step, groaning, smoke leaving his nostrils.

Blow fire, Silas! Lyana thought. *Blow your flame and kill what bastards you can!*

Yet he was too weak; she saw that. He was barely strong enough to cling to his dragon form. She saw the marks of whips across him. They had tortured him, forcing him to remain a dragon, though surely it took every last drop of his strength.

Lyana clenched her fists. *Queen Solina wants the mobs to see him as a broken, bloody beast, not a man.*

The doors to the palace, wrought of gold and ivory, swung open. As if summoned by Lyana's thoughts, Queen Solina stepped out of shadows, stood above the stairs, and raised her arms.

The city bowed before her, a great wave of myriads. Jaw so tight her teeth ached, Lyana forced herself to bow too.

"Blessed be the Sun God!" cried Solina. She wore steel so pale it was nearly white. A golden sun glimmered upon her breastplate, and twin sabres hung from her belt. Her platinum hair swayed behind her like a banner, and a crown of jagged, golden spikes rose upon her head like claws.

You murdered my king, Lyana thought, a sandstorm of rage flaring within her. *You murdered my betrothed. One day I will kill you, Solina.*

"Rise, children of the sun!" Solina cried, arms raised. Across the oasis city of Irys, the people rose and cried her name. "A beast we found lurking along our borders. A demon of scale and claw!"

Upon the roofs and streets, the crowd roared. Lyana looked upon the people through the silk of her scarf. She had never seen such rage, such pure, storming hatred. It suffused the faces of the men and women of Tiranor, twisting them into cruel masks. It gushed from their throats in raw howls.

We are but demons to them, Lyana thought. *We, the children of Requiem, are a noble and ancient race—a nation that lives for music, for meditation, for peace. And we are nothing but monsters here.*

"The dragons burned your fathers and mothers!" Solina cried. "Thirty years ago, when they invaded our glorious land of sunlight, they toppled our towers and drank the blood of children." Her voice nearly drowned under the roaring crowd. "But we've rebuilt! Our palace stands anew and our people are strong!" She tossed back her head and howled her words to the sun. "We will never fall!"

The roars swelled so loudly that Lyana felt them thud in her ears, pound in her chest, and shake the River Spice Winehouse below her feet.

"We will never fall!" cried the people. "We will never fall! Hail the Sun God!"

Lyana lowered her eyes. The first Tiran War had raged before her birth. Solina herself had been only a babe. Its wounds had long washed away from this city; all the fallen buildings stood again, and once more trees filled this oasis with life.

"And yet the hatred we sowed then still blooms," Lyana whispered. "And it still burns our sons and daughters."

The wyverns flapped their wings and tugged the chained dragon to his feet. Soldiers climbed the towering statues that flanked the palace doors, attaching chains to hooks. Soon Silas hung shackled between the stone guardians, a bloody dragon with one wing, displayed in all his wretchedness to the city. Solina stood before him, her boots red with his blood.

"The dragons bring drought to our land!" the queen cried. "They drink the waters that should overflow the River Pallan! The dragons eat our grain, leaving our poor to hunger! The dragons mock our lord, the Sun God who gives us life, and worship the night!" With her every word, the crowd roared, and Solina spun toward the chained Silas. "Now Requiem will learn the price of its evil. Blessed be the Sun God! His fire shall extinguish all darkness. Soon we will burn all dragons and cast out their evil with light. We will never fall!"

Fly now! cried a voice in Lyana's head. *Toss off this silk scarf, discard your disguise, and fly as a dragon to save him. You are a knight of Requiem, no blind Tiran dancer!*

Her every breath was a struggle. Her head spun. Her fingernails dug into her palms. *Oh, stars.* Her king had sent her here as a spy—to dance, to listen, to learn. *Stars, not to watch my friend killed before my eyes.*

And yet she watched, trembling upon the roof.

Solina mounted a wyvern, the greatest among them, a behemoth of iron scales named Baal. The queen cracked her whip and her mount reared. The beast roared and spewed a stream of yellow, smoking acid onto the chained dragon.

Silas howled.

Lyana wept.

I'm sorry, Silas, I'm sorry. There was nothing she could do; she knew that. If she flew, she too would die. If she flew, all her work would burn with her bones. Yet still the pain and shame coursed within her.

The acid ate through the dragon's scales, blood boiled, and Silas turned back into a man. The body hung for a moment upon the chains, then fell and broke apart. Lyana turned away and closed her eyes, but she could still hear the screams.

The crowd's roar spun around her. Vaguely, she heard Solina cry of her glory, heard her scream of offering a burnt head to the crowd; all sounds were muffled. Struggling for breath, Lyana stumbled across the roof of her winehouse, fumbled to open the trapdoor, and stepped into the attic. Once inside, she all but fell against the wall, clutched her breast, and gasped for air.

Stars, oh stars.

She forced herself to take long, slow breaths, to count to ten, to calm the tremble of her limbs.

"You will not have died in vain, Silas," she whispered. "I vow to you. I will avenge you."

I will learn about the invasion of Requiem. I will report back to my king. And I will save Requiem from the wrath of this mad, murderous queen.

She leaned against the wall until her heartbeat began to calm. Soon her eyes regained focus, and she saw sacks of grain, jugs of ale, hanging strings of dried fish, and jars of fig preserves. In the corner lay her bed, a mere pile of straw topped with a canvas blanket. Once Lyana had lived in palaces, a great knight in the courts of Requiem. But those days lay long behind her; she had lived here in Tiranor as

Tiana the dancer for a year now. Today, more than ever, she missed her home and knew the worth of her sacrifice.

Downstairs in the common room, she heard the doors slam open, boots rush in, and hoarse voices cry for ale and wine. Those were the voices of soldiers; she would have recognized the gruff calls anywhere. She had heard such voices a year ago when the Tirans had invaded her realm, burned her city, and killed thousands around her.

"Come, come, sit and drink!" rose the voice of Peras, the kindly old owner of the River Spice. "Sit here, I—"

The soldiers roared below. "The dancer! Bring us the dancer! Bring us wine, old man, and bring us the girl!"

Lyana ground her teeth. Death made such men thirsty for her wine and hungry for her flesh. She would serve them wine. And she would dance for them. And one day, she swore, she would burn them all.

For you, Orin, my fallen prince. For you, Silas, whom I could not save. For the thousands of Vir Requis these soldiers killed. I will avenge you, Requiem.

She grabbed her walking staff. She stepped downstairs, silks swaying across her body, baring all but her most private parts. Staff tapping, she entered the common room. Soldiers filled it, clad in steel and leather. At the sight of her, they roared and slammed fists against the tabletops. How many of those men had slaughtered women and children in Requiem? How many more would they slaughter once the second invasion began?

Peras, kindly old keeper of the winehouse, was hobbling between the men, serving wine, platters of dates, and steaming rolls of bread. One soldier shoved the old man aside.

"Dance!" he cried to Lyana. "Dance for us, Blind Beauty! We've seen blood and death, and now we will see grace."

When they looked upon her, she knew they saw a blind girl, a scarf hiding her green northern eyes in a land of blue-eyed desert warriors. Tiana's hair was smooth and bright as beaten platinum, her skin golden as dunes—a desert daughter clad in silks, a walking staff in hand, as different from Lady Lyana as sand from snow. When she looked upon them through her scarf, she saw steel and bloodlust, a death for her people.

"Dance as we drink!" one soldier called. "Summer solstice approaches, a day of dragon blood, a day when we kill and die. Let us drink today for life!"

Her heart pounded. Today was the new moon, a day of sunfire and wine. But summer solstice was the holiest day of the Tiran year, as holy as the Night of Seven to the children of Requiem. What did this soldier mean? Would the second invasion of Requiem begin on that holiest of days, a mere eighteen days away?

"Dance!" they cried.

She walked forward and tapped her staff, feigning her blindness and meekness, and they cheered. Peras began to play his lute, and the soldiers joined in, singing and drumming upon the tabletops. When she reached the center of the common room, tables of drinking men around her, Lyana laid her staff aside. And she danced.

A year ago, when she had been a knight in Requiem, Lyana had learned to dance with her betrothed Prince Orin; they would sway among the lords and ladies of the court, lovers caught in the song of harps and pipes. Here, in this southern land of sunlight and sand and steel, she danced not like a noblewoman, but like the wick of a flame, like desert wind, like a bird of many colors rising among palms. She closed her eyes until she truly became blind Tiana, and she surrendered herself to her dance. The men roared around her like desert storms.

As she danced, she was Tiana; she forgot her true name, her true parentage, her true soul. She became the Blind Beauty, the Desert Rose, the wonder of Irys. Her body swayed and her silks flowed. She spun, arms raised.

I am a daughter of dunes, whispered her soul. *I have risen from the desert like a column of fire. I am kissed with sunlight and myrrh and pomegranate wine. I am a desert bird, flying, seeking the sky.*

At these moments, when she danced, she could almost love her enemy, almost love Tiranor for the beauty of her song, the sweetness of her fruits and wines, and the glory of her ancient towers and gold. She was Tiran. She was Tiana. She was blind and a thing of wind and sound. If Lady Lyana, a knight of Requiem, still lived inside her, she was now a scourge of cruel northern snow.

The music died.

Lyana gasped and opened her eyes behind her scarf.

Through the silk, she saw the doors of the River Spice open, and a shadow entered the winehouse and her life.

First two armored men entered the room, bearing shields and spears. Gilded masks hid their faces, shaped as the heads of ibises, the curving beaks a foot long. They moved to flank the doorway, metal sentinels, and slammed down their spears. They were the Gilded Guardians, Lyana knew—warrior priests bred to protect the highborn of Tiranor. A third man followed, entering the shadowy common room with a wind scented of sand.

He was tall—the tallest man in the room. His head was shaved bald, and his face was lined, hard, and handsome. He wore armor of pale steel, unadorned but for a golden sun upon the breastplate. A sabre and dagger hung from his belt, their scabbards simple leather, their pommels shaped as sunbursts. If not for the suns upon his pauldrons, denoting him a general of Tiranor's army, Lyana would have thought him a simple soldier.

But no, she thought. It was more than just the rank upon his armor or the Gilded Guardians who flanked him. This man did not have the eyes of a common soldier. When he stared over the room at her, she saw no lust for blood, flesh, or wine. She saw nothing at all—only blue ice, calculating and heartless.

"General Mahrdor," whispered one soldier, rising to his feet. His face paled and he slammed his fist against his breastplate. "My lord!"

The other soldiers in the room, a good hundred or more, stood at attention. Their fists all slammed against their chests. All sounds died: the music, the raucous calls, even the men's breath. Lyana stared at the general and her heart thrashed. He was staring right at her: not at her body, like the other soldiers would stare, but directly through the scarf and into her eyes.

He knows! she thought. *He knows I'm not blind. He stares through the scarf—into my eyes, into my soul.*

She dared not move, not even shiver. She struggled to calm her pounding heart; she felt that General Mahrdor would hear its beat across the room.

No, he cannot know, she told herself. *To others, the scarf is solid silk, white and covering my green northern eyes. He sees only Tiana. Only a blind dancer.*

Finally he tore his eyes away from her; it felt like he'd pulled a dagger free from her gut. He began walking through the silent winehouse, the soldiers frozen around him. He made his way to a table before Lyana. When he stared at the men who had occupied it, they bowed and retreated into the shadows.

General Mahrdor sat, poured himself a mug of wine, and stared at Lyana. The candlelight danced against his armor. When he spoke, the room remained silent. His voice was smooth as the wine, his accent highborn and meticulous; it flowed through the silent room, too loud.

"You must be this... Blind Beauty I have heard of." He took a sip of wine, sloshed it, and swallowed. "They call you the Desert Rose and say you are a dancer of much grace and beauty. I have always greatly admired and sought grace and beauty—from good wine, to fine art, and yes... though my soldiers might snicker to hear it, even dance."

Though a glimmer of amusement tweaked his lips, his eyes remained hard. Lyana barely dared breathe. A lump filled her throat, but she dared not swallow. She had heard stories of this General Mahrdor and his love of beauty. They whispered that in his villa upon the River Pallan, he collected items he found beautiful—jeweled skulls of men he slew, scrolls of human skin, and stillborn babes dipped in bronze. Lyana had always thought those mere stories, rumors told to spread fear of the great general. Now, looking into those cold blue eyes, she believed all those tales.

"Well?" Mahrdor said, staring at her. He leaned back in his seat. "Let us see the Blind Beauty. Dance for us, child."

She closed her eyes and she danced.

Old Peras played his lute, but the soldiers—who had clapped and pounded the tabletops—were now silent. She could hear the patter of her bare feet and the flutter of her silks. Her body swayed. She felt his eyes on her skin, skin dyed gold to hide her northern paleness. She was as rushes in the wind, as smoke rising from the desert.

When her dance ended and the music died, she bowed her head. Deathly silence filled the winehouse. General Mahrdor stared at her—stared through her scarf, stared into her skin, stared into her deepest dreams and fears. His eyes were bottomless and clutching.

Without a word, he stood up and left the winehouse.

Lyana felt like an empty bellows. Her limbs began to tremble. Around her, the soldiers breathed out shakily, emptied their mugs, and cried for more wine. Soon cheer and song filled the winehouse again, but iciness lingered inside Lyana.

This is what I've danced a year here for, she thought. *Stars, let him remember my dance! Let my painted body linger in his mind! Let him return. Let me learn what I can... if there is anything to be learned from icy, clutching eyes.*

Night fell, wine flowed, and music swirled. Platters of roasted fowls, served on beds of leeks and mushrooms, filled the winehouse with their scents. Men cracked open pomegranates and greedily scooped out tiny jewels of seeds. A few men began playing mancala, the great game of the desert, dropping seashells into pits in a board, then howling after every round. Lyana was standing in the corner, singing soft desert tunes to an old soldier with one leg, when a Gilded Guardian returned to the winehouse and approached her.

"Dancer," he said, voice echoing inside his ibis helm. The beak swooped, long and sharp as a dagger. "The General Mahrdor, may the Sun God bless him, has invited you to his villa tonight. He requests a private dance. In return he will pay you a handsome reward. Will you accompany me through the dark streets to his home of light?"

Around them, soldiers smirked and hooted.

"A private dance for the general!" one called, a man who wouldn't have dared breathe around Mahrdor. "I'd say you've charmed the old man, girl."

Another brayed laughter. "He'd like a private dance in his bed, I'd wager."

Lyana barely heard the laughter. Her innards leaped and her breath stung in her nostrils. She would enter the villa of General Mahrdor himself, chief of Tiranor's armies! Her head spun. In a year of work, listening to these drunken soldiers chatter, she had not achieved half so much. Her fingers trembled. What dark secrets would she learn in his home? Memories rushed through her: rumors of bronzed fetuses, severed heads, and parchments of human skin. But she dreamed of other treasures: of maps, of battle plans, of secrets whispered in darkness when her flesh intoxicated him and loosened his tongue.

Tiranor planned a second invasion of her home; Lyana did not doubt that. If anyone could reveal its time and location, it was General Mahrdor.

"I accept," she whispered to the Gilded Guardian.

They left the winehouse and walked through the night. On the night of the new moon, when the sky was darkest, the Tirans lit fires across the city and praised the Sun God, the banisher of darkness. Great braziers crackled atop the Palace of Phoebus, which rose to her left across the square. Torches blazed upon the columns of the Sun Temple, which rose upon a hill to the east. People crowded the streets, holding candles and chanting prayers to banish the night. Smoke rose and sparks swirled like fireflies, filling the darkness. Light and fire ruled; shadows fled.

We are shadows to them, Lyana thought. *We, the children of Requiem, who worship the stars and can fly as dragons—we are creatures of darkness for them to burn.* She swallowed a lump in her throat. These people who marched the streets, holding candles before them, did not lust for blood or death; they lusted for light. They had never met a Vir Requis, Lyana knew. They knew only the stories Queen Solina fed them: stories of wretched beasts called weredragons, demonic shapeshifters of the north who could grow scales and wings, who had toppled their temples thirty years ago.

They think us beasts, mindless killers, monsters of darkness, she thought. *They will burn us all if I cannot stop them.*

She could not stop Solina from spreading lies. But she could discover her plans. She could warn her home. She could save her people from the endless fire of Solina's wrath.

The Gilded Guardian walked silently, staring ahead through the holes in his helm; he seemed to Lyana like an automaton of metal. He took her to a dock upon the River Pallan where rushes swayed and water flowed over mossy stones, reflecting the light of lanterns like a thousand jewels. Frogs trilled and children knelt above the water, sending candles floating upon wooden toy boats, gifts to banish the darkness of the northern seas. In the water swayed a full-sized boat too, ten feet long, shaped as an ibis. Silver filigrees lined its hull, forming coiling shapes of phoenixes. The Gilded Guardian stepped into the boat, reached out his hand, and helped Lyana in. His hand was gloved in leather, icy even in the warm summer night.

He rowed. They floated down the river, soon passing the Sun Temple whose priests moved between columns, blowing ram horns. The smell of frankincense, palm oil, and charcoal filled the air. Past the temple, the river ran between the narrow mudbrick homes of tradesmen: scribes, masons, blacksmiths, and healers. Around a bend, the river flowed through a copse of palm trees, then into the wealthy quarters of merchants and nobles. Villas rose here upon the riverbanks, their gardens lush, their doorways flanked with statues. The greatest villa lay ahead, rising from a verdant paradise of palms, fig trees, and terraces of flowers. A palisade of columns led to its gates, each topped with a status of a desert animal; Lyana saw falcons, foxes, snakes, and gazelles.

They docked the boat. Three slaves waited there, clad in crimson livery, their hooded heads bowed. They accompanied Lyana through the gardens toward the villa. The song of frogs, owls, and crickets rose around her, and the heady scent of jasmine filled the air. Lyana's heart thrashed as she walked, tapping her staff before her. For a year in Tiranor, she had lurked in shady alleys, danced in rundown winehouses, and sought whispers among the common soldiers of the city's dregs. Now she walked toward the greatest house in Irys; what knowledge would she find here?

General Mahrdor waited at the villa's doors. At first Lyana did not recognize him. Instead of armor, he wore a white tunic fringed in gold, an iron circlet in the manner of Tiran nobles, and sandals. He smiled thinly, but his eyes remained cold. Again it seemed to Lyana that he could see through the scarf around her eyes, just as she could.

Again a chill ran through her, but she sucked in a breath and forced herself to keep walking toward him.

For Requiem, she thought. *For my family, for my king, and for my home.*

"Tiana!" he called to her, arms outstretched. "That is your name, is it not? Come, my Blind Beauty. Welcome to my home."

He dismissed his guards and slaves, and soon Lyana found herself tapping down a grand hall, its floor a mosaic of suns and stone vultures with jet eyes. She and Mahrdor walked alone. Great statues lined the hall, shaped as nude women with the heads of animals, their fangs bared and tongues rolling. Lyana had to struggle not to shiver, not to stare at them.

You are only Tiana, she told herself. *You are only a blind dancer; you cannot see this place.*

He reached out to her. She forced herself not to flinch, to feign surprise when he took her hand. His flesh was cold like a corpse's hand.

"Come, let me help you," he said. She stared forward but felt his eyes beside her, boring into her.

Past the main hall, they climbed a stairway and entered a wide, shadowy chamber. Lyana's jaw tightened, and it took all her will to stifle her gasp.

The stories were true. Sundry items filled this place, overflowing shelves, tabletops, and alcoves. Shrunken heads, their skulls removed, hung on strings from the ceiling. Pickled hands floated in jars. A chair stood in the corner, formed from human femurs. Old torture devices, their iron rusted and dulled, hung on one wall between paintings of bloodied, broken men.

Mahrdor stood still, holding her hand. "It is such a terrible malady, blindness," he said. "I have brought you to my chamber of wonders, the place of my most prized possessions. And yet... yet to you, the world is still a pool of darkness."

She lowered her head and whispered. "Though my eyes peer into eternal night, the Sun God lights my heart."

He nodded sympathetically. "Well spoken, child. He is a merciful god to those who serve him. If your eyes are blind, your fingers will see for them. Let me guide you."

He guided her deeper into the chamber, then raised her hand above a shrunken head. When he began to lower her hand, Lyana's breath caught and her eyes winced beneath her scarf. The shrunken head seemed to stare at her, no larger than a pomegranate. When Mahrdor placed her hand upon it, she gasped softly. The skin was smooth, leathery, and cold. Mahrdor moved her hand across it—the lips that were sewn shut, the empty eyes, the wispy hair.

Lyana gritted her teeth. *Think that you touch only old cloth,* she told herself. *Only an old, beaten tunic.*

"Do you know what this is?" Mahrdor said.

"A... a doll's head," she whispered.

He laughed softly. "Yes, child, only a doll. A doll I made myself. I have taught myself the skill, you see—to cut the neck, remove the skull, and stuff the skin with herbs. It is an art, much like dance. I am an artist too, child."

He wrapped his arm around her waist, pulled her away from the head, and placed her hand against a deformed skeleton, its bones twisted and bloated.

"I found this poor soul begging on the streets of Irys," Mahrdor said. "He was a swollen freak, his back twisted and his face bloated like a hippopotamus." He sighed. "Killing him was a mercy, but... he was such a wonder, Tiana! Such a wonder that I kept his bones. Feel them. Run your fingers across them." He forced her hands along the twisted ribs, the withered hip bones, the coiled femurs. "Do you feel the bumps, the grooves?" He sucked in his breath, seeming almost like a man in ecstasy. "They are exquisite."

She nodded, bile in her throat. "They are... fine bones, my lord."

He pulled her away from the skeleton, spun her around, and placed her hand against a mancala board. Instead of seashells or seeds, its pieces were made from dried scarabs. He made her caress the beetles.

"These scarabs ate the flesh off my skeleton," he said. "They are ravenous little beasts! Once they had their fill, and died of overeating, it was a shame to merely toss them out. Dried like this, and still stuffed with human flesh, they make such wondrous little marvels. Can you feel their claws?"

She nodded. "They feel wondrous, my lord."

Next he placed her hand upon a wide, curling scroll that covered a tabletop. Lyana gasped. It was a map! A map of Requiem! Her heart trembled like a bird trapped behind her ribs. Wooden wyverns, each the size of a thimble, stood upon the map. The miniature army was arranged as if flying out of Tiranor, across the sea, and into Requiem through Ralora Beach upon its southern shores.

The invasion plans, Lyana thought. *Stars, he's going to invade through Ralora Beach.*

Her head spun. This beach was undefended, a mere rocky shore leagues from any outpost. King Elethor had to be told. Requiem's army had to move, to defend its beach, to—

Mahrdor placed her hand upon the map, interrupting her thoughts. He moved her fingers across it.

"I made this scroll myself," he said, "from the skin of a weredragon I slew." When she tried to pull her hand back, he held it firmly. He forced her fingers across it. "Feel it, child! Do not be afraid. *Caress* it. *Luxuriate* in it. Enjoy the texture. Do you feel how smooth it is?"

Stars, the skin of a Vir Requis? Is this scroll made from one that I knew? One that I commanded in battle?

She nodded and whispered. "It is most smooth."

"Only human skin feels so smooth," he said. "It is superior to the skin of any animal. Sometimes, when I cannot sleep, I walk into this chamber and just... caress. I like to wrap myself in it sometimes, to feel close to the woman who once wore this skin." He touched her cheek, and she flinched. "Your skin is smooth too, my child."

She swallowed, heart pounding. "I would make a poor scroll, my lord. My... my skin dries easily."

He laughed softly, still holding her hand. "No," he said. "You, as you are, are a greater wonder than any scroll." He sighed. "Do you see, Tiana? Do you see why I brought you here? You are a dancer. You live for the dance! You breathe beauty, wonder, grace, the awe of art. I too am an artist. A collector." He shook his head wistfully. "The men I lead... Soldiers. Fighters. Brutes. They think I command them because I love war, love bloodshed, love killing as they do." He barked a laugh. "Love blood and killing? No. Any brute can slay a man; what is there to love of that? No. I go to war, Tiana, to *collect*, to bring back these wonders. Bones! Skin!" He sucked in his breath, eyes lit with fire. "I admire these treasures, Tiana. And you... you are among the most lovely, wondrous treasures I have seen."

He grabbed her waist with both hands and she gasped. He stared down at her, those blue eyes blazing. Through the silk scarf, he met her eyes.

No! she thought, trembling in his grasp. *No, it's impossible, my scarf looks solid from the outside, only I can see through it, he can't be looking into my eyes, can't be...*

Her limbs shook.

She had to leave this place.

She had to send word to King Elethor, to tell him of the map, to...

His fingers grabbed her silks, tugged gently, and unwrapped them like a gift. The fabric fluttered down, and she stood nude and trembling before him. She kept her chin raised, refusing to lower her head, refusing to cover her nakedness. She was only Tiana here, a dancer from the dunes, but she still had her pride.

He caressed her cheek. "So smooth..."

He led her toward a divan at the back of the room, pulled her down, and kissed her neck. His hands were confident but gentle. He knew what he wanted from her; he would take it, not with violence, not as a warrior... but as a collector. He acted, Lyana thought, as if claiming her—*owning* her—was his right, as if she would give herself to him as naturally as the night gives itself to dawn.

She had never lain with any man but Prince Orin, her betrothed whom Solina had slain. Her throat tightened and her tears burned to think of him. She closed her eyes as Mahrdor lay atop her, as his eyes closed, as he collected her. His breath was rough against her face, and she clenched her jaw.

For my home, she thought. *For Requiem.*

ELETHOR

Elethor, King of Requiem, stood upon Lacrimosa Hill before the leaders he had summoned to his council: A true dragon of the west, a griffin of the east, and a prince in armor upon his horse.

Around them, grass rustled and trilliums bloomed white. Burnt birches spread for miles, but new saplings grew between them. A flock of small, white clouds herded across the sky and distant geese honked. It was a beautiful day, but darkness lay upon Elethor's heart as he regarded his guests.

He stroked his beard as if he could draw strength from it. He had not shaved in a moon's turn, and the beard still felt foreign, too scratchy and hot and altogether not *him*. His father had worn a beard; so had his grandfather. Elethor joked that he was too busy to shave, but in truth, he had grown the beard to *feel* more like a king. On days like today, meeting these foreign leaders, it wasn't helping; he still felt too young, a mere sculptor, not a ruler of Requiem. He looked at his sister who stood beside him, a princess clad in a gown of green and silver, and drew comfort from her eyes.

If the beard doesn't help, at least I have Mori, he thought. The others might see him as too young, too callow, too weak—Elethor the sculptor, the young prince who had never wanted the throne, who had always shunned the court, and kingly beard be damned. But to Mori he was King of Requiem, as noble as their father; he could see that in her eyes, and that soothed him. He turned back to his guests.

"Friends," he said. "I have asked you to meet me here—a council of the great northern kingdoms. Thank you for taking the journey to my home in such a dark hour."

The true dragon, a salvana from the western realms, batted long white eyelashes. No wings grew from his back, yet he floated above the hill like a serpent upon water. A hundred feet long he was, with scales like disks of beaten gold. His beard was white and flowing, his moustache long, and his eyes like crystal orbs. Like all true dragons, he had no human form; the salvanae lived feral in the west, building no homes and forging no metal, but praying and singing in the wild. This salvana was the greatest among them: Nehushtan, a priest and leader of Salvandos.

"It has been three hundred years," the true dragon said, "since I flew above this place, child of stars. The seasons have turned, and once more Requiem calls for aid." When he blinked, his white lashes fanned the grass.

Elethor nodded to him, then turned to his right. A prince of griffins stood there, large as a dragon. His breast, head, and talons were those of a great eagle, noble and white as a winter sky before snowfall. His lower half was that of a great lion, larger than any true lion of the wild, and golden as bales of hay on a fall's sunset. His name was Velathar, son of King Vale, descended from the great Volucris himself, the griffin who had led his kin from captivity in Osanna back home to Leonis Isles. The griffin prince bowed his head to Elethor and gave a low caw.

Finally Elethor looked ahead. A man sat there upon a horse, his beard brown and flowing. A crown of gold sat upon his head, and he was clad in a brown robe embroidered with green trees. A sword hung upon his thigh, the scabbard filigreed with leaves. He was Prince Raelor of Osanna, son of King Aera, descended of the priest-king Silva who had raised Osanna from the ashes of its great wars.

"I have ridden hard for many days, King Elethor," said the prince. "I have answered your summons, though we in Osanna fight the darkness that grows in Fidelium. The dead rise from their tombs under the mountains, forge dark steel kissed with fire, and march across the plains. Already our northern forts have fallen. What urgent matter do you summon me here for in this time of war?"

Elethor rested his hand on his sword's pommel and raised his chin.

"It is a time of war for Requiem too. In the south, Tiranor musters a great army—twenty thousand wyverns fly for Queen Solina, mindless beasts that live for nothing but bloodshed. They are an ancient evil; for a thousand years, their eggs lay as stones in the sand, and now Solina has quickened them with the fiery seed of her lord. These beasts will fly over the sea, and they will invade Requiem, and they will burn this land with their acid. If Requiem falls, a hundred thousand Tiran troops, each armed with spear and crossbow, will follow the wyverns into this land. Solina's ambition goes beyond the destruction of Requiem; she will expand her empire here and build her forts upon your doorsteps. If Requiem should fall, no lands will be safe; not Salvandos to our west, nor Osanna to our east, or even the Griffin Isles across the sea."

Nehushtan blinked his glimmering orbs, fanning the grass with his lashes. His beard swayed and his floating body coiled behind him, golden scales chinking. He spoke in a voice like crumpling paper.

"Child of starlight, this seems to me a feud between Requiem and Tiranor alone. One might say this feud is between King Elethor and Queen Solina; a personal war. Why should we, the peaceful salvanae of the west, concern ourselves with conflicts not our own? We are a peaceful people; we true dragons live for meditation, for starlight, for prayer and wisdom. Not for bloodshed."

The prince of Osanna nodded upon his horse. "The wise salvana speaks truth. They say in my land that King Elethor and Queen Solina were once lovers, that the war between them has grown into a war between their hosts. You call us here for what—to ask for our aid? Why should Osanna fight your wars when our own borders are threatened?"

Elethor looked at his sister. Mori stared back silently. As always, her soft gray eyes could calm the storm in his soul. He took a deep breath, then turned back to his guests.

"This war is between Requiem and Tiranor, that is true," he said. "Solina does not yet threaten your lands. For years, Tiranor has remained in the southern deserts beyond sea and swamp, and she has grown strong. A great army now lurks there, greater than any in our northern realms. What if this army left the desert? Imagine this great host—so many men and beasts—here in the north, upon your very borders, with no desert or swamp between you and their wrath. Will Solina content herself with conquering Requiem alone? Perhaps. Or would she use this land as a base for further expansion? There aren't enough farms in Requiem to feed her troops; our land is rocky, mountainous, forested and wild. There are great plains of farmland in Osanna; Solina will crave them. There are great fallow fields in Salvandos; Solina will crave them too." He gripped the hilt of his sword. "We must band together to stop Tiranor from leaving her borders. This host threatens Requiem now; it will threaten you tomorrow. Let us join our armies. Let us keep Tiranor in the desert beyond sea and swamp."

He took a deep breath. At his side, Mori nodded, silently agreeing with his words. Elethor looked at his companions: a wise true dragon of the west, an eastern king, and a griffin from distant isles. They looked at one another, silent.

Prince Velathar the griffin broke that silence. He gave a series of caws and chatters, head tilted and wings ruffling. Elethor could not speak the language of griffins, but Prince Raelor of Osanna was descended from the great priest Silva, and he could speak the tongue of beasts. He listened, stroking his beard, and translated the griffin's caws.

"This is good and well for Salvandos and Osanna, says the Griffin Prince. But what of Leonis, the land of griffins? Its isles lie across many leagues of sea, and Tiranor is no threat to them, even should it conquer Requiem. Why should griffins fly to aid dragons?"

Mori approached the griffin, raised her arm, and touched the beast's great white head. For the first time, the princess spoke. Her voice was meek at first, but gained strength with every word.

"Dear Prince Velathar," she said, "I grew up reading stories of your ancestor, the great King Volucris, perhaps the greatest griffin who has lived. When I was a girl, I loved nothing more than hearing tales of Volucris flying to Requiem's aid, sounding his cry, and fighting alongside our Queen Lacrimosa in the Battle of King's Forest. That queen fell here, where we now stand, upon this hill that bears her name. King Volucris fell here too, and we in Requiem still remember his great sacrifice." She looked from companion to companion. "Our ancestors forged great alliances. They fought together against the evil of Dies Irae: griffins, salvanae, men, and Vir Requis. Our kingdoms joined hands then to defeat the evil that roamed this land. It has been many years since those days; have we forgotten the value of friendship since?" Tears sparkled in her eyes. "If you will not fight for the sake of your own realms, fight for that old alliance: for friendship, for justice, and for memory."

She finished her speech with a shuddering breath and stood, looking from one to another. Elethor moved to stand by her and placed a hand on her shoulder. If not for the solemnity of the council, he would have embraced her.

I love you, sister, he thought. *Our father would be proud of you today.*

The guests looked at one another, and Nehushtan spoke first. His scales clinked like a chest of coins as his body undulated above the hill.

"You have spoken well, daughter of starlight, and with much passion. It is true; our four realms fought together once. I myself flew here three centuries ago and fought in the Battle of King's Forest, perhaps the greatest battle this realm has known. Queen Lacrimosa, your ancestor, was a brave and noble queen; for many seasons I mourned her passing." The old dragon sighed. "Yes, I fought alongside Requiem then. But those were different days, long ago. Only seven Vir Requis then flew, the Living Seven whose statues still stand in your city; the rest lay as charred bones upon the land. We of

Salvandos could not let those last souls perish; we flew then with wrath, with lightning, with starlight. We were proud to fight at the side of Queen Lacrimosa and her daughters, the warriors Gloriae and Agnus Dei. But now, Princess Mori... now the descendants of Lacrimosa flourish. Thirty thousand dragons live in Requiem, a great host of fire and fang. We in Salvandos hate war more than anything under the stars; today you have the might to fight your war alone."

The priest tilted his head, blinked, and turned aside. He began floating down the hill, his serpentine body coiling behind him.

"Wait!" Mori cried. "Nehushtan, why do you leave us?"

He did not reply. Beard fluttering, the old salvanae rose into the sky like a plume of smoke. Soon he was but a golden thread in the distance, flying west to his ancient realm.

The Prince of Osanna spoke next. His horse sidestepped beneath him and nickered.

"The salvana speaks wisdom," he said. "Thirty thousand dragons fly here. Let them fight this war. Osanna is a great and ancient kingdom; our horses are swift, our steel is bright, and our hearts are brave. Yet when wyverns fly, let dragons fight them! We will fight our wars upon the ground." He shook his head sadly, and his voice softened. "Our kingdoms are allies; that is true. I grieve to see the blood that has spilled here... and the blood that will yet spill. Yet these are dark times, and we face our own threat in the north; we must fight our own enemies rather than yours. I am sorry, King Elethor of Requiem. We cannot help you."

With that, the prince kneed his horse, turned around, and galloped downhill. Soon he was but a speck in the distant fields, raising a cloud of dust as he rode into the east.

Elethor turned to the last of his guests, Prince Velathar. The griffin stared at him, tilted his head, and clawed the earth.

"Prince Velathar," Elethor said. He stared into the griffin's eyes. "My ancestors fought alongside yours. Will you fly with us again? Will you bring aid from your land, an army of griffins as fought here years ago? Let us join our great kingdoms again. Let us fight this evil from the south—for the sake of our old friendship."

Please, he added silently. *Without you, we are alone.*

The griffin lowered his head. He stared at the grass for a long time, perhaps thinking of his ancestors' bones that lay buried here alongside the bones of Queen Lacrimosa. The griffin raised his head and looked west at the distant golden thread—the retreating salvanae. He turned east and looked toward the horse that galloped there.

Finally he lowered his head again and nuzzled his beak against Elethor.

What does that mean? Does he mean to help us?

The griffin pulled back, and his eyes were sad. He gave a solemn shake of his head.

No.

With a great flap of eagle wings and talons that ripped the grass, the griffin soared. Soon he was flying into the horizon, a golden speck fading away.

Elethor and Mori remained upon the hill, alone in the forest. The only sound was the rustling grass. The siblings looked at each other. Mori's eyes were huge and round, the color of storm, and the wind ruffled her chestnut hair.

Elethor squeezed her shoulder. "We fought alone against the phoenixes," he said, "and we defeated them. We will defeat the wyverns too."

Mori lowered her head, held the hilt of her sword, and nodded. She did not need to speak; Elethor knew her thoughts. The same thoughts rattled through his skull.

The phoenixes killed nearly half our people. Only an ancient magic drove them away, not the heat of our fire, nor the sharpness of our fangs. Now a greater army flies against us... and we stand alone.

He pulled his sister close. She leaned against him, and the wind blew across them.

"We will fight alone," Mori whispered, "and we will defeat them. I believe. Deramon is a great warrior. So is Lyana and she will return to us. We will fight the wyverns in the air, and in our tunnels, and upon the mountains, and we will drive them back into the desert."

Elethor nodded. Deramon was a great warrior, it was true. So was Lyana. The rest of their army was composed of green youths, mere children torn from farms, bakeries, and vineyards. The wind seemed to invade his very bones, and he lowered his head.

A roar rose in the south, interrupting his thoughts. Heart thrashing, Elethor turned toward the sound. A black dragon was flying toward him and his sister, rising and dipping in the air.

When the dragon flew closer, Elethor recognized her. She was Lady Treale, the youngest daughter of House Oldnale which ruled the eastern farmlands. A youth of nineteen, Treale had begun squiring to Lady Lyana last year, training to become a knight. With Lyana away, Elethor had sent the girl to patrol the southern border; why did she now fly here outside Nova Vita?

"Treale!" he cried, pulled back from Mori, and shifted into a dragon. Brass scales clanked across him, fire filled his nostrils, and he flapped leathern wings. He took flight in a cloud of smoke.

The black dragon wobbled as she flew toward him, and puffs of weak smoke rose from her nostrils. Then Elethor saw what she carried in her claws, and his breath died.

Stars. Stars, no.

In each front claw, Treale held a body wrapped in a shroud.

They met above a forest clearing, spiraled down, and landed upon the grass. Treale placed the bodies down—the shrouds covered them from head to toe—then shifted into human form. She stood as a woman with smooth black hair, olive skin, and weary dark eyes. When she wobbled on her feet, Elethor shifted too and caught her.

"Treale," he said, examining her. Dirt and blood stained her armor. "Are you hurt?"

She shook her head, eyes haunted. "No, my lord. The blood isn't mine. It's... theirs." She looked at the bodies and her eyes dampened.

Mori came flying toward them, a slim golden dragon. She landed, shifted back into human form, and rushed to embrace Lady Treale; the two were childhood friends. Heart hammering, Elethor looked at the bodies. The shrouds hid their faces. They seemed so small, so frail.

"Who are they?" he whispered.

Treale looked at the dead and spoke softly.

"They are Tanin and Yara, a farm boy and baker's daughter. They served my father in our lands; they grew and baked our grains. They fell at the border." She looked at Elethor, and horror replaced the grief in her eyes. "When I found them, they were burnt with acid. Their commander, a soldier named Silas, was missing. Wyverns did this, my king." She clenched her fists and her voice shook. "Solina murdered them."

Elethor held her shoulders and stared into her black eyes.

"Did you see the wyverns, Treale?" he asked sternly. "Do they invade Requiem?"

She swallowed. "I saw a dead one on the ground, charred with dragonfire—a great beast all in iron scales like armor. I ordered my men to gut it and bring it to their king; they fly a day behind me. Three live wyverns flew there. When I arrived with my men, they retreated into the south." She snarled. "The cowards invaded, murdered, and fled. I wanted to chase them. I will find them and kill them still! But... I had to bring them back, my king. I had to see them buried. I had to..."

Pain overflowed her words, and she closed her eyes. A tear drew a line through the dirt on her cheek. Elethor held her, kissed her forehead, and looked over her head to the south.

Again you bring death to my door, Solina, he thought. Rage flared within him, so hot that he gritted his teeth. He held Treale close. *Our neighbors abandoned me, but I do not face you alone, Solina. You will find that every dragon in Requiem fights you with a great roar.*

BAYRIN

He limped along the docks, hunched over, cloaked and hooded in ratty old homespun. His hand, black with dirt, reached out in supplication.

"Suns for the poor?" he croaked as sailors walked by. "Spare coins for a poor old beggar, my lords?"

The sailors ignored him and walked on, speaking to one another of finding a winehouse, soft beds, and cheap women to warm them. These ones had not seen land for weeks; they had the hungry look of men too long at sea. Bayrin could not guess what ship they had come from; hundreds lined the docks of Hog Corner. Some were mere fishermen's barges, others merchant ships with embroidered sails. Some were wide and sturdy, built for sailing north, out of the delta and into the salty sea. Others were slim and long and lined with oars, made for rowing south along the River Pallan to distant jungles of spice, jewels, and slaves. Many ships—those farther along the docks, where soldiers patrolled and no beggars dared shuffle—were military machines laden with steel and Tiran fire.

If you wanted news, Bayrin knew, you came to Hog Corner. Centuries ago, it was said, pigs would wallow here in mud, giving the place its name. Squatted upon the northern fringe of Irys, where the Pallan turned from river to delta, Hog Corner still boasted as much mud and stench as ever. Upon its hundred docks, merchants, soldiers, prostitutes, and beggars all mingled and fought and shared their tales. There were no temples in this part of Irys, no palaces or villas or nobles. In the winehouses, brothels, and alleys of Hog Corner, far from the great gilded columns of the city south, Bayrin could hear tales of sea battles, songs of distant lands, and mostly gossip. If you wanted to know which lord bedded which noblewoman, which priest was caught stealing gold, or which officer was smuggling women into the barracks, you came to this place. If the River Pallan was the artery of Tiranor, here was its throbbing heart.

"Suns for the poor, my ladies?" Bayrin croaked in his best beggar's voice. "Spare some old copper suns?"

The young women walked by, faces gaunt and eyes sunken. These ones were the dust eaters, he knew; wretched souls addicted to the southern spice. They would sell their clothes, their bodies, and their souls for but spoonfuls of the stuff. They gave him dead stares and shuffled onward, always seeking, always hunting the next taste of their elixir.

Bayrin grumbled under his hood. When he brushed dirt off his cloak, his own stench wafted and sickened him. He still could not get used to smelling this bad. A year ago, only his cloak would stink; now it seemed to have permeated his hair and skin.

Being a beggar is not my style, he thought. He was a noble son of Requiem, the personal guardian of Princess Mori Aeternum herself. He should not *stink.* A sigh fled his chafed lips.

They send my sister to be a dancer, he thought bitterly, *in a winehouse far in the clean, safe city south—right outside the palace! But old Bayrin... he gets to wallow in mud and stink like the hogs that gave this place its name.*

"Come on, Lyana," he whispered into the night. "Bring me some news of this invasion, and let's leave this cursed city."

He missed home. The memory of Requiem pounded through him every night—the rustle of birches, the beauty of white marble columns, and the loving eyes of his princess. More than anything, he wanted to see Mori again, to hold her, stroke her soft hair, kiss her lips, and never let her go.

If you saw me now, Mori, you'd wrinkle your nose and shove me away in disgust. A smirk twisted his lips. *I should return to Requiem like this, in my foul disguise, and see if your love for me is true.*

"Come on, move it, ya wretches!" rose a voice ahead. Bayrin raised his hooded head, peered into the shadows, and saw three drunken soldiers stumble down the docks. They were leaving the Black Shell, the seediest winehouse in Irys, a place where drunkards and dust eaters spent their paltry coins. Their boots sloshed through puddles, and one drew his sabre and flailed it about haphazardly. A group of sailors and peddlers scurried out of their way, and the soldiers moved on, leaning against one another. They began to sing a slurred song.

> "Dragons fly
> And dragons burn
> Dragons scratch and bite
> But Tiran men
> With spear and blade
> Will bloody dragons smite!"

They began to sing a second verse—this one quite ruder, detailing different parts of dragon anatomy Tiran blades would slice—when the soldiers noticed Bayrin. One kept singing. The others scowled and nudged their comrade.

"What are you looking at, beggar?" one soldier said. "Bugger off, will ya? Go!"

He marched toward Bayrin and kicked, knocking him down. Under his cloak, Bayrin wore boiled leather inlaid with steel rings, but still the kick drove out his breath and spread agony through him. He lay on cobblestones damp with water, blood, and vomit.

"Spare a few copper suns, my lords?" he said, speaking with his grainy beggar's voice. "Spare a few coins for an old, limp beggar before you sail off to smite the bloody dragons?"

The soldier kicked him again. His boot, tipped with steel, slammed into Bayrin's hidden leather armor, sending blooms of pain spreading through him. He grunted.

I am a son of Requiem. I can turn into a dragon. I can kill these men and burn every ship in this port. He ground his teeth, coughed, and forced himself to lie still. He had to wait for Lyana; she met him here every three days, and he hadn't missed a rendezvous yet.

"Pardon, my lords, pardon," he said and began crawling away. Bayrin, the guardsman from Requiem, would have fought and killed these men; here in Tiranor, he was but an old beggar, feeble and groveling.

"He thinks we're lords!" said one of the soldiers, a brawny man with a stubbly face, dented armor, and flushed cheeks. "Do we look like lords, you scum?"

Another kick sent Bayrin crashing down. The soldiers laughed. Boots nudged him and spears poked him. Under his hood, Bayrin snarled. These men were weak. Cowards. They taunted an old, defenseless beggar, yet if they knew who he truly was...

"I say we cut off his head!" cried one. "A little killing to whet the appetite before we go slay some reptiles."

"Shove your spear up him!"

"Cut his guts out!"

The boots kicked, a spear scratched his thigh, and laughter rang. Bayrin crawled along the docks. Ahead rose the Old Mill—an abandoned mill now turned into a den of dust eaters. Coughing and grunting, Bayrin scuttled toward it on hands and knees. He crawled into the shadows behind its old bricks, leaving the sailors, dust eaters, drunkards, whores, and peddlers behind. The three soldiers followed, laughing and spitting upon him.

"He thinks the shadows can hide him, friends!"

"Good. Let's kill him nice and quiet in the dark."

Bayrin looked around him. He saw nobody but his three tormentors. Only the tallest masts of ships peeked over the roof of Old Mill. Only the loudest drunkards could be heard from behind its brick walls. Nothing but him, three Tiran soldiers, bricks, and shadows.

The soldiers raised their swords.

Bayrin stood up, doffed his cloak, and shifted.

Wings burst out from his back with a thud. Claws and fangs thrust forward. Scales rose across him. The soldiers gasped. Before they could scream, Bayrin slashed his claws. He cut through steel. Blood spurted. Two soldiers fell dead. The third tried to run. Bayrin pounced and bit, and the man's scream died between his jaws.

It took only seconds. The three lay dead and torn apart.

Bayrin shifted back into human form and looked around, heart hammering. Had anyone seen him? His palms sweated and he panted. He had never before dared become a dragon here in Tiranor, especially not after seeing what they had done to Silas.

Stars, if anyone saw...

He stood still, heart hammering, waiting for wyverns to descend upon him, for their acid to wash the flesh off his bones. When long moments passed and no enemies arrived, Bayrin breathed out in relief. From around Old Mill, the same miserable sounds of Hog Corner still rose: the squeals of the town's cheapest women, the grunts of drunkards, the songs of sailors, the creaking of ships on docks, and the peddlers crying out their wares.

With a grunt, Bayrin pulled the three bodies into deeper shadows, around a few barrels, and toward a wharf behind Old Mill. A young woman lay there on the cobblestones, deep in dust's sleep. Praying she would not wake—if she did, he would have to silence her too—Bayrin shoved the bodies into the water. They sank in their armor. With any luck, they would remain in the depths.

He stepped back toward the crowded docks, still lightheaded, to find Lyana waiting for him in shadow.

"Spare a sun for an old beggar, my lady?" he rasped, hunched over and hobbling.

His sister stood in her disguise—hair smoothed and dyed a platinum blond, her pale skin painted a Tiran gold, and her northern eyes hidden behind a scarf. A white cloak draped around her, and she held her walking staff in hand.

"A sun for a dear old man," she said, fished in her pocket for a coin, and held it out.

Bayrin approached her, took the coin, and bowed his head. He whispered. "What news, Lyana?"

Softly she said, "Not here." She raised her voice. "May I buy you a bowl of soup, old man? To warm your old bones?"

He bobbed his head. "Old Mill serves good fish and onion soup, my lady, if it pleases you."

Truth was Old Mill served the worst fish soup in Irys, possibly in all of Tiranor. That served Bayrin well; it meant the fishhouse was empty but for three dust eaters, their heads upon their tables. Soon Lyana and Bayrin sat in the shadowy corner of the common room, eating bland soup with week-old fish from clay bowls. The owner of the fishhouse, a deaf old man, sat in the corner playing mancala against himself; the board was shaped of cracked old clay, and the pieces were mere pebbles. The three dust eaters snored.

Bayrin took a sip of soup, wrinkled his face, and spat it back into the bowl. "Horrible stuff, this. I think I swallowed a few drops too." He leaned forward. "What have you learned?"

He could not see through her scarf, but somehow he knew her eyes were haunted. Her skin was dyed gold, but somehow he knew that beneath that dye she was pale. Her hand trembled around her spoon.

"Bayrin, I met him! General Mahrdor himself! I danced for him at the River Spice, and... in his home."

He slowly placed down his spoon. "You... what?"

She nodded.

Bayrin tasted the soup again and forced himself to swallow. "Lyana! For a year you've danced for a thousand soldiers, and you barely learned what hand they toss a spear with. Then one day you meet the general of Tiranor's hosts... and get invited to his house?"

She nodded. "He liked my dancing."

Excitement leaped in Bayrin. For a year, he had been sneaking between Tiranor and Requiem, delivering what paltry knowledge Lyana gleaned—what formations she saw wyverns fly in, what new names soldiers gave their phalanxes, or how many wagons of helms and spearheads she saw leave the forges. They knew Tiranor was mustering a great army, and they knew an invasion was near, but the important knowledge—the date of the invasion and its location—eluded them. Would Mahrdor deliver this knowledge to her?

Alongside his excitement, sourness spread. Lyana, his sister... dancing for Mahrdor himself in his villa. Bayrin had invited enough young women to his own home to know what Mahrdor wanted.

"Lyana, did he touch you?" he asked, eyes narrowed. He clutched his spoon like a sword. "If he did, I will... I will..."

"Will what, eat his soup?" He could feel her glare through her scarf. "Bayrin, unless you can cut through Mahrdor's breastplate with a wooden spoon, focus on what's important now. I saw a map in his villa. A map of Tiranor and Requiem with wooden wyverns arranged for invasion. Ralora Beach, Bay. That's where he's going to attack. It'll be on summer solstice; he talked of leaving that morning." She reached across the table and clutched his hand. "We finally found what we came for. Leave. Tonight. Tell Elethor the news. The invasion is only seventeen days away."

Bayrin looked around nervously. As blind Tiana, his sister was meek and quiet, but today bits of Lady Lyana flared—learned, lecturing, and *loud*. The dust eaters, however, continued to drool contentedly at their tables. The deaf cook was picking his ear while squinting at the mancala board. Bayrin let out a shaky breath and glared at his sister.

"All right, Lyana, we fly home tonight." He placed down his spoon. "Right now."

She shook her head. "You fly. I'm staying here."

He looked around again, leaned forward, and hissed. "Lyana! Forget it. You saw what they did to Silas. These people don't play games. Three soldiers attacked me tonight. Their bodies lie at the bottom of the Pallan, breastplates slashed with dragon claws. Mahrdor will notice three missing men. If he finds their bodies and sees the claw marks, he'll go hunting dragons."

His sister gave him a crooked smile. "What dragons? I am but Tiana, the Blind Beauty, the dancer from the southern dunes. And I've gained his trust—or at least his lust." She squeezed his hand. "Bay, I've spent a year working for this. I can't leave so soon. I will learn more. If I charm him, he might even take me on the invasion; generals have been known to take mistresses to war. He—"

"He wants to invade my kingdom, Lyana. I don't want him invading my sister too. No way. You agreed to dance for Requiem, not to... to..." He felt his cheeks flush.

"It won't come to that. He only wants me to dance; that is all I will do for him."

She patted his hand, but Bayrin heard the hesitation in her voice.

She's lying, he thought. *She will lie with the enemy for Requiem; she might have done so already.* The thought sickened him more than the stale soup.

"Lyana," he finally said, "as your older brother, I forbid it. You will not stay."

She scoffed, blowing out her breath so loudly it blew back a strand of her hair. "Do you? Bayrin, you might be my older brother, but I am a knight. You are not. I am betrothed to our king. You are not. And I will choose my path, not you." She rose to her feet, leaned forward, and kissed his cheek. Her voice softened. "Go home, Bayrin. Warn our people. Be safe. I love you, brother."

He stood up, still trembling. He wanted to grab her, to drag her with him, to take her away from this... this nightmare city that swarmed with hatred, blood, and acid. But before he could react, she spun and left the fishhouse, her cloak fluttering. He remained standing in shadow.

"Goodbye, Lyana," he whispered. "I love you too, sister. Be careful. Stars, be careful."

He stepped outside into a night of vomiting drunkards, sailors tugging whores, and dust eaters licking their desires with wild eyes. He stepped behind Old Mill where blood still coated the cobblestones. He leaped into the water where bodies still lay. He swam. Underwater, he could see torches flicker above, the hulls of ships, and the glint of fallen coins. He rose for air and sank again. His eyes stung and worry gnawed his bones.

Stars, Lyana. Be careful. Return to us soon.

The River Pallan flowed into a delta, thick with reeds. The lights of the city faded behind him. Flowing toward the sea, he summoned his magic.

Dark wings rose, spilling water. A shadow soared. A dragon flew in the night, flying north, flying home.

ELETHOR

He stood above the twin graves, head lowered, despair clutching at his throat.

"You fly now in our starlit halls," he said. His eyes stung. "Fly well, Yara and Tanin, warriors of Requiem."

A wave of tears spread over the crowd. Weeping rose in swells. Thousands had come to the funerals—soldiers, farmers, tradesmen, the old and the young. They covered Lacrimosa Hill where years ago Requiem's great queen had fallen in battle. They wore white robes—Requiem's color of mourning—fastened with silver birch leafs, sigils of beauty and peace. The families of the slain lay upon the graves, clutching the tombstones and crying to the sky.

Warriors? Elethor thought, looking at the families who wept—mothers gasping for breath, fathers sobbing, siblings barely old enough to fly. *No, they were not warriors. Tanin was but a farmer's boy, Yara the daughter of a baker—youths I sent south to die.*

True warriors had once guarded Requiem, thousands of men and women trained to defend their realm. They lay now in thousands of other graves, their tombstones dotting the hill like stone flowers. Grass rustled here but no more trees; the holy birches of Requiem had burned in the war last year, charred boles falling like so many bodies.

If she can, Solina will kill everyone who weeps here, Elethor thought. *If I cannot stop her, we won't even lie in graves. Our bones will lie charred among our toppled halls.*

Mother Adia, High Priestess of Requiem, stood at his side. Cloaked in white, she was a tall woman, cold and handsome as a marble statue. She raised her arms and sang above the cries of the crowd.

"As the leaves fall upon our marble tiles, as the breeze rustles the birches beyond our columns, as the sun gilds the mountains above our halls—know, young child of the woods, you are home, you are home." She raised her head to the heavens. "Requiem! May our wings forever find your sky."

Across the hill, the children of Requiem repeated the prayer. Elethor looked above to that sky and saw dragons there, hundreds of them. Nearly all the old City Guard had fallen last year. Lord Deramon had raised a thousand more recruits—youths from across the land—and they now roared above, wings beating and breath steaming. The sight of them soothed Elethor. They were perhaps merely the children of farmers and tradesmen, youths who had never held a sword or shield, but their breath was still hot, their claws still sharp.

When you invade us again, Solina, you will find us ready. You will find Requiem's roar still loud.

The people dispersed slowly, holding one another and shedding tears. Most still bore scars from the phoenix fire. Many had lost limbs, eyes, faces. Many had lost parents, siblings, children. Yet even now they mourned two more fallen. Even now they craved life and wept for its loss. Solina had not taken their humanity; that soothed Elethor as much as the dragons above.

Lord Deramon approached him, a white cloak of mourning draped across his chain mail and breastplate. His calloused hands clutched an axe and sword. The grizzled warrior, his flaming red beard streaked with white, bowed his head.

"My king," he said, "let us fly together."

Elethor nodded, summoned his magic, and shifted. He took flight as a brass dragon, flames trailing from his jaws. Deramon shifted too and flew beside him, coppery and clanking, a burly beast of a dragon. They left Lacrimosa Hill and headed toward Nova Vita, capital of Requiem, which rose white and pure from the charred forest.

"How are the new recruits?" Elethor asked him, the wind nearly drowning his words. He glided on a current.

Deramon snorted a blast of fire. "Mere youths. They are soft. They weep at night in the bowels of Castra Murus; I hear them." He growled. "But I will harden them, my lord. They will fly as warriors."

Elethor nodded, but his belly knotted. They had raised new forces for Requiem, but were they enough to hold back Solina? A thousand sentries now guarded Nova Vita, a new City Guard. A thousand more flew along the southern border, patrolling the wastelands of swamp and sea that separated Requiem from the desert. When he looked south of the city, he saw the remainder of their forces training in fallow fields—three thousand soldiers of the Royal Army drilling with swords or flying as dragons.

I lead a few thousand callow, frightened youths... against the might and wrath of a desert empire.

"Will it be enough, Deramon?" he asked. Wisps of cloud streamed around them. "Solina is raising a great host. Our spies speak of myriads of wyverns and men. Will you harden these youths in time?"

Our spies. He snorted to himself. Those spies were his best friend, Bayrin Eleison, and his betrothed, Lady Lyana. Aside from his sister, they were the people he loved most in the world, and yet he could not speak their names today. *To speak their names is too painful. Too dangerous. Today Bayrin is more than my friend, and today Lyana is more than my betrothed. They are the hope of Requiem.*

Deramon growled. Smoke rose from his nostrils, nearly hiding his head. "They will be ready, Elethor. They will fight to the death for you." The old warrior looked at the young king. "Requiem will stand, my lord... or she will fall with a roar that will echo through the ages."

Elethor grumbled under his breath. "I prefer the former."

They reached the city. Wings scattering clouds, Elethor looked down upon his home. Nova Vita's walls rose from burnt trees, a ring of white. Dragons perched upon the crenellations, wings folded and eyes scanning the horizons. Beyond the walls, the city rolled upon hills: the palace, its columns soaring; the temple, its silver dome bright in the sun; two forts that bookended the city with towers and banners; and thousands of homes and workshops built of craggy white bricks.

Every house lost a soul, Elethor thought. *Every house mourns.*

He parted from Deramon, leaving the old warrior to clank and snort his way toward Castra Murus, the squat barracks of the Guard. Wind whistling under his wings, Elethor dived toward Requiem's palace. Even now, over a year since Solina had killed his father and brother, it felt strange to rule here. He still did not feel like a king, only the young prince. Every time he flew toward this edifice of marble, Elethor wanted to turn tail, flee into the forest, and spend his days sculpting, stargazing, and forgetting this war.

And yet every time, he tightened his jaw, narrowed his eyes, and flew between the marble columns into the hall of his fathers.

Upon the marble tiles, he shifted back into human form and walked, boots thumping. The throne lay across the hall, woven of twisting oak roots. But today Elethor did not walk toward this ancient seat. He crossed the hall, stepped through a doorway, and entered the east wing of the palace. Here, in a great chamber of stone, hung a dead wyvern.

Elethor stood before the corpse and stared.

Stars, look at it, he thought.

Lady Treale had found the creature, burnt and bloated, in the southern swamps by the bodies of Tanin and Yara. Some had wanted to bury it, others to burn it. Elethor had refused.

"Clean it and stuff it," he had told them. "Hang it up for us to study."

More eyebrows had risen when he insisted they hang the creature in the palace. Surely a dusty courtyard, or a barracks, or even a temple could store the beast? But no. Elethor had insisted. He wanted this creature here, in his home, under the same roof where he slept, ate, and waited for fire. He wanted to look at this creature every day, to stare at its fangs, its claws, its dead glare. This thing had killed two of his people; he would keep it close.

He felt so small standing before the wyvern. It hung on chains thicker than his arms. It must have been fifty feet long from nose to tail's tip; longer than but the greatest dragon. Dark scales covered it, square and metallic like plates of armor. It had only two legs, not four like a dragon, but those legs ended with claws as long, thick, and sharp as the heaviest greatswords in Requiem's armories; they made dragon claws seem like mere daggers. The beast's jaw thrust out into yet another blade, this one longer and wider than a man; Elethor imagined that it could crush through a dragon's scales like a spear into a spring doe.

Last time Bayrin had returned with news, he had reported an army of these beasts, twenty thousand strong. He had claimed they could spew acid, burning flesh off bones like fire eats leaves off trees. Elethor clenched his jaw as he stared at the great, hanging corpse.

Wings thudded and emerald scales flashed outside the window. Claws clattered against marble tiles behind Elethor. He turned to see, through the doorway, a lanky green dragon land in the palace hall.

"Bayrin!" he cried out.

His friend had been gone to Tiranor for three moons. The green dragon looked exhausted; his tongue lolled, his chest heaved, and his ears drooped. With a snort of smoke, he shifted into human form. Where a dragon had panted now stood a gangly young man, his shock of red hair wild, his eyes green and weary.

"Hello there, El," Bayrin said and walked toward the east wing. "Good to be home, and... *stars above,* what's wrong with your *face?*"

Standing in the doorway, Elethor uncomfortably scratched his beard. "It's... a beard. I figured I'd grow one."

Bayrin squinted and leaned closer. "*That's* a beard? I thought a weasel was attacking you; I was just about to tear it off." He shook his head in wonder. "By the stars, you're turning into your father, El. And what the abyss is that behind you?" He elbowed Elethor aside and stepped into the east wing where the dead wyvern hung. "Are you hiding any mistresses here, or... oh *bloody stars.*"

Facing the hanging wyvern, Bayrin gaped. A strangled cry fled his throat, and he drew his sword.

"It's dead, Bay!" said Elethor and pushed his friend's sword down. "Don't cut my head off!"

Bayrin let out a stream of curses, slammed his sword back into its scabbard, and shoved Elethor back.

"Merciful stars, El! I just spent three moons in Tiranor counting those creatures. The last thing I need is to find one here!" He gave the beast a sidelong glance. "Even if it's dead, stuffed, and hanging from chains. Stars, they're ugly critters, aren't they? Almost as ugly as that hairy thing on your face." He shuddered. "Do you remember our old nurse, the one who once slapped me for stealing her wooden teeth and stuffing them into Lyana's skirts? This creature reminds me of her." He gave Elethor his own sidelong glance. "Come to think of it, so does your beard; I recall she had a bit of one herself."

Elethor embraced his friend. "Welcome home, Bay. Tell me the news! What did you learn? How is..." He swallowed, sudden fear twisting his heart. "How is Lyana?"

Bayrin sighed and looked back at the hanging wyvern. "She's in better shape that our friend here. But I'm worried. El, the invasion is near, and she thinks she knows where Solina will attack."

For long moments, Bayrin spoke, telling of his time in Tiranor: of the ships mustering for war in the docks; of the wyverns that drilled above Irys in battle formations; of Silas executed in town square; and of Lyana dancing for General Mahrdor, learning of a journey on summer solstice, and seeing a map of wyverns invading Ralora Beach.

When he was done speaking, Elethor stared silently at the hanging wyvern.

If Lyana is right, thousands of these creatures will fly into Requiem this moon. Memories of the Phoenix War pounded through him: burning homes, lacerated children, Solina's lips against his, and her dagger slicing his face. Her last words to him echoed.

I will kill them all, Elethor! she had screamed, his blood on her face. *I will burn them all with my fire. You will watch! And then you will crawl to me and beg to be mine.*

He left the wyvern and entered his throne room. He walked toward the Oak Throne, sat between its twisting roots, and gazed upon his hall. Bayrin came to stand before him, hair draggled and face smeared with mud.

"Am I a good king, Bayrin?" Elethor asked, voice low.

Bayrin raised his eyebrows. "You could give me a castle or two, command a few concubines to warm my bed, and I wouldn't mind a golden Bayrin statue in the city square... but otherwise you're doing fine."

Elethor sighed and looked upon the wide hall, the columns topped with dragon capitals, and the charred birches that creaked outside.

"I sent her into danger, Bay. They burned Silas in the town square. If... if they catch Lyana..."

Elethor's throat constricted. He had loved Solina for so many years, a love of fire, pain, and blinding passion. His love for Lyana was newer and had grown gradually, not a crashing flame, but warm embers that heated slowly. Would his first love kill his second?

Bayrin raised his chin and clenched his fists. "My sister outstubborns mules to pass the time. I'd drag her back in chains, if I had any." He sighed. "She will learn what more she can, and she will return. On the summer solstice our future will unfold: for Requiem, for Tiranor, for Lyana... for us. The war is coming, El. It flares again this moon."

War. Elethor's jaw clenched and icy waves rose inside him. His fingertips trembled. *How many more graves will I stand over? How many more families will I watch mourn?*

He nodded and rose to his feet. "I'll summon a council of the highborn. I'll fly to Oldnale Manor today. We will speak—the three great houses of our realm—of how to crush this threat."

Bayrin gaped at him, white showing all around his irises. "Fly to *Oldnale Manor?* Summon a council? Elethor! Solina is at our doorstep. Call the banners. Lead the Royal Army south—today, now, right after you shave your ridiculous beard. We meet Solina over the shore. We kick her lovely golden backside back into the desert."

"No, Bay." Elethor shook his head. "I will not lead Requiem to a rushed war—not without first discussing it with the highborn."

"What's to discuss?" Bayrin raised his hands to the heavens. "Stars above, Elethor, let's fly south now. We'll fly there together. You, me, and these three thousand toddlers you've trained into an army. It's war again and I'm not missing out on the fun."

Elethor laughed mirthlessly and traced the scar splitting his face, the scar Solina had drawn. "This is what the fun of war gave me." He sighed. "Bay, summer solstice is twelve days from today, isn't it? The flight south will take six days, seven if we're slow. That gives us some time." He bitterly twisted his jaw. "You know what Lord Yarin Oldnale thinks of me, what many of the people think too; that I'm but

a youth, inexperienced and irrational. I will not fly to war on a whim."
He raised his hand to silence Bayrin, who had begun to protest. "War
is here, Bay, I know that. And we will fight this war. But we will meet
first—House Aeternum, House Eleison, and House Oldnale from the
eastern farms—like the great councils my father would hold." He
clasped Bayrin's shoulder. "Stay here, Bay. Stay with Mori. I will
summon the farmlords and be back here in four days."

Bayrin's face changed like the sea in sunrise. "Mori," he
whispered. "Damn it, El, I missed her." He ran a hand through his
hair, sniffed at his clothes, and cleared his throat. "How do I look?"

"Slightly worse than the dead wyvern."

"Good enough!" He turned to leave, then looked back and
sighed. "If I weren't eager to see your sister, I'd drag you south right
now. You got lucky. Fly fast, El. Stars, you better be back here on
time. Twelve days, my friend. Twelve days until twenty thousand of
these buggers knock on our doors."

The two embraced—a long, wordless, crushing hug. Then
Elethor stepped outside, shifted into a dragon, and kicked off the
palace stairway. His wings billowed with air, and he soared over the
city.

"The wait is over, Solina," he whispered as the wind whistled
around him. He remembered the softness of her lips, the warmth of
her body, and the bite of her blade. "You were my love. You were
my life. You will die in my fire."

SOLINA

She stood in her chambers, twin blades in hands, clad in a robe of golden weave embroidered with tiny pomegranates. She stared into her tall bronze mirror and saw a queen, a scarred woman, a holy daughter of the Sun God, and a spurned soul lost in endless desert.

Around her glittered the glory of her dynasty: platinum chalices inlaid with ruby ibises, tapestries of jackals and falcons, jewelled sabres with pommels shaped as suns, and chests of gems and spices. Blankets woven of gold and silver adorned her bed of ivory. Outside her arched windows, her oasis spread to rolling dunes kissed with sunlight. By the brightest window stood the tools she had brought here for him: chisels, hammers, and three great blocks of marble.

"It was to be your nook," she whispered. "Your place to sculpt while I stood nude before you, watching you form me from stone." She touched her left blade to her lips where he would kiss her. "Oh, Elethor... this was a chamber for us."

She would bring him here. But now she would bring him in chains. Now she would hurt him. Now her soul would forever remained split like her face where the scars of fire ran.

"You could have sculpted me with hammers, but now these hammers will break your bones, Elethor. I will break your spine one segment at a time as you scream and beg me to kill you." She closed her eyes; they burned with tears. "Why did you refuse me, Elethor? Why did you drive me to this?"

She turned away from the marble and tools, walked to a window, and stood with the sunlight upon her. The steeples of Irys rose before her, carved of polished sandstone capped with platinum. Far in the south, past leagues of sand, she could just make out a distant patch of green: the oasis of Iysa, a twin to Irys, where the small oranges she craved grew in winter. Her kingdom rolled beyond the horizon, yet what were treasure and glory worth if she had none to share them with?

I could have shared them with...

A deep, dark memory stirred inside her, clawing at the prison she had buried it in. She felt its cold breath in the core of her being.

No.

She clenched her fists.

No.

That memory was still too raw, still too real, a demon inside her that she dared not awake. She placed her hand on her belly. She trembled, closed her eyes, and bit down hard.

That one will remain buried. That pain I dare not feel again.

She spun toward her chamber doors, intricate works of art carved of olivewood and embossed with silver falcons.

"Ziz!" she shouted.

The doors opened and her slave stepped inside, a demure young woman. Her platinum hair fell in braids, and her blue eyes looked up with fear, then down at her toes. She wore a dress the color of sand, its hems lined with blue tassels. She was a desert child, the daughter of nomads—a good slave.

"My queen," the girl said, eyes downcast.

"Come here, Ziz. Stand beside me."

The girl crossed the chamber and joined Solina by the window. The desert wind blew her hair. When Solina thrust her blade, Ziz gasped but did not scream. Red bloomed across her gown like a desert flower. She looked up, eyes huge blue pools, wondering, betrayed. Solina held her as she died, kissed her forehead, and laid her down at her feet. She had needed this, needed to kill, needed to feel the warmth of blood on her fingers, see the light of life extinguished from a pair of eyes. She pulled her blade free and licked the blood from it thoughtfully. *Blood kills the memories.* She gazed upon her kingdom.

"Soon the palace will be empty of slaves," spoke a deep, smooth voice.

Solina turned to see General Mahrdor at the doorway, clad in armor, his sword at his side. His face and bald head were tanned a deep gold, and his eyes glimmered as they stared at her. Solina realized that her gown was open too far, revealing more flesh than it hid.

"You come to make love to me," she said.

He raised his eyebrows, entered the chamber, and closed the door behind him. "I come to discuss our war. I come to report of our troops' morale. I come to ask for more armor and spears. Are you so vain that you think every man at your door comes to ravage you?"

She couldn't help it. She gave him a crooked smile. "You are not every man; the others would die if they entered this chamber." She doffed her robe and stood naked before him. "Love me. I know why you're here. Do it. Roughly. Make it hurt."

He stood staring in silence. Blood pooled at their feet. She raised her chin and stared into his eyes, refusing to blink first. Finally he stepped over the body and grabbed her. He pulled her to her bed, tossed her upon her blankets of silk and golden thread, and climbed atop her. He claimed her. He hurt her. He gave her sweet pain to shout with, and she drove her fingernails down his back, and she bit his shoulder until she tasted blood. When she tossed her head back and closed her eyes, she thought of Elethor and screamed.

When he was done, she shoved him aside, rose to her feet, and grabbed her gown of white silk. She pulled it over her body; it kissed her skin with a thousand kisses.

"Come," she said, "we will inspect the lines. Show me what you've done with my army."

She returned to the window and whistled—a long, loud sound like a bird of prey. The thud of wings sounded in the courtyard below. A growl rose into a screech. With a flash of scales, her wyvern ascended a hundred feet, from the cobblestones below to her window. The beast's wings pounded the air, bending palm trees below and billowing her curtains and hair. His scales clattered, thick plates like iron armor. His eyes blazed red, his teeth snapped, and smoke rose from his nostrils. His name was Baal, and he was the greatest of the wyverns, a forge of acid, a behemoth of wrath and muscle and bloodlust.

Solina shuddered to see him, a shudder of awe and delight. For a thousand years, the eggs had lain in the desert sands, hard and polished like obsidian. For a thousand years, the priests of Tiranor, and the kings and queens of the Phoebus Dynasty, had prayed and chanted and cast their spells... and the eggs still slept.

But I... I quickened them with the seed of flame, with the life of my lord the Sun God. Her lips pulled back in a grin, and she inhaled sharply, savoring the acrid stench of the creature. *My prayers were answered; my glory flies across the desert. I am a mother of beasts. I am a goddess of wyverns.*

With her foot, she nudged her dead slave halfway out the window.

"Eat," she said.

Baal tilted his head, regarded the dead woman, then thrust forward like a striking asp. He took the body into his mouth, tossed back his head, and swallowed. His neck bulged and his scales clanked as the body moved down his throat.

"Turn," Solina told him. "I will ride you."

He turned sideways, still clinging to the palace wall. Solina climbed out her window and into his saddle. She grabbed the pole

that was fastened there; it bore her banner, a golden sun upon a white
field. With a crooked smile, she looked over her shoulder at Mahrdor,
who still stood in her chamber.

"Ride behind me," she said.

Soon they flew upon Baal over the city. Solina gazed upon the
glory of her home. From up here she could see all of Irys. The Pallan
halved the city, a trail of silver-blue, a giver of life in the desert.
Countless ships sailed down its waters, from the distant lands of the
south, to the docks of Hog's Corner, and finally into delta and sea.
Along the riverbanks rose the villas of the wealthy, their gardens lush
and their columns tall. Beyond them coiled cobbled streets lined with
houses and shops of mudbrick. Her palace glittered behind her, a
glory of polished limestone and gold; only the great Temple of the Sun
stood as tall. All around the city, her empire rolled into sand and haze
and wonder.

Beyond the oasis, upon the rock and sand of her desert, her
army awaited. Thousands of chariots stood tethered to horses, their
wheels spiked, their riders armed with whips and bows. Thousands of
soldiers bustled between tents, armed with spears and arrows tipped
with poison. Greatest of all, twenty thousand wyverns stood upon the
sand that had hatched them, as large as dragons, as cruel as the desert
sun; they would lead the charge into Requiem, crushing the
Weredragon Kingdom and paving way for her ground troops.

As she flew above, the army saw her banner, and they cried for
her glory, a great cheer that rolled across the desert. Men raised spears
and wyverns screamed.

"Queen Solina!" they cried. "Golden daughter of Phoebus!"

"Elethor has only five thousand soldiers," she said to Mahrdor
as the wind whipped her hair. "Even if he summons every child and
old woman in Requiem, small and feeble dragons in flight, he cannot
stop us. We will crush them like the insects that they are."

Behind her in the saddle, Mahrdor grunted in approval. "My
collection will grow. After you kill the Boy King, may I have his
bones?"

She laughed. "You may have some before I kill him; I think
that would amuse me. Turn one bone into a flute, and I will play it for
him." She raised her banner high; it caught the wind and thudded.
She shouted to the army. "Soon you will feed upon weredragon flesh!
Soon you will bring light and fire to the world!"

They howled. Men clanged spears against shields. The wyverns
screeched, shaking the desert. The sun shimmered, a beacon of her

lord. Solina raised her head, closed her eyes, and let the light of the Sun God bathe her with glory.

MORI

She stepped into the temple, harp in hand, and took a shuddering breath. Her head swam, her lungs constricted, and the columns swayed before her. She forced a deep breath.

"Be calm, Mori," she whispered. "Be calm. Breathe. You can do this."

She took a step deeper into the temple. She had always feared this place—there were so many priestesses here, so many people come to pray, so many sick and wounded come for healing. The voices all echoed in the halls, and their feet all pattered, and the movements of robes danced like ghosts. One time all the sounds and figures had frightened Mori so much, she had run outside, shifted into a dragon, and fled the city for two days.

"But today they need me," she whispered, lips trembling. "Today I will face my fear."

She took another step.

The hall stretched before her, marble tiles white and veined with blue. Two children ran across the hall, chasing each other with wooden swords. A young priest walked between columns, carrying towels, and smiled at her. Mori's heart leaped into flight. Suddenly the priest's fluttering robes were burning. Before her eyes, they became phoenix wings, showering fire and flying toward her. Suddenly the children no longer played with wooden swords but lay bloody, steel swords buried in their bellies. Their eyes gazed at her, begging, bleeding.

"Princess Mori," said the swooping phoenix.

Mori gulped and blinked. Again she saw only a priest before her, a young man who smiled at her. She took a shuddering breath, clutched her luck finger behind her back, and managed to smile.

Only two children and a priest, she thought. *I'm safe here. I'm safe. There are no phoenixes anymore, no dead children, no war. Those days are gone.*

She kept walking.

Before the war, Mori could always retreat into the library, a great shadowy chamber underground. Only the royal House Aeternum carried the keys to the library; she could find solitude there, solace from the voices, from the movements of too many swaying cloaks, from all those crowds that spun her head. She would curl up underground with a good book, and she would read for hours. Inside the world of books, she was never afraid; she could be brave as a knight or wise as a wizard. There were no voices that were too loud, no movements too jarring, no crowds that spun around her and stole her breath.

"But now the people here need me, the people in this temple," she whispered to herself. "They need me just as much as the books do. I will comfort them however I can."

She swallowed and took another step.

Step by step, heart racing, she crossed the hall and entered the Chamber of Healing.

The domed roof towered above her, painted with scenes of stars and wise dragons of old. Columns surrounded the room, their capitals shaped as birch canopies inlaid with silver. Three rows of beds stood upon the marble tiles, and in them lay the wounded. They raised their heads, smiled at Mori, and those who still had hands waved them.

Blood rained. Fire burned. Tiran soldiers stormed the hall, plunging blades into flesh, and Queen Solina flew as a phoenix, burning bodies into ash, and...

No. Mori closed her eyes and tried to remember what Mother Adia had taught her. She breathed in slowly, filling her lungs top to bottom, held her breath, and exhaled it. She breathed deeply three times, then opened her eyes and saw no more fire, no more blood. She nodded, tightened her lips, and walked toward the wounded.

"Princess Mori," said one man who lay abed. The war had taken his four limbs; he lay wrapped like a babe in swaddling clothes. He smiled at her. "We missed you, my princess."

She smiled back. "Hello, Rowyn. I missed you too." She pulled a scroll from her pack, unrolled it, and showed it to him. "I painted these flowers for you."

He whistled softly. "They're beautiful. You know how I love sunflowers. I used to grow them before the war."

She placed the scroll by him and walked on. She reached a bed where lay Alandia, the daughter of a farmer. She had been burned so badly her face was still bloated, and her arms ended with stumps.

"Princess Mori," she whispered.

Mori knew that Alandia still lived with daily pain, even today, a year after the war. Mori produced another scroll, this one painted with horses. She knew how Alandia loved horses; she had owned two before the war.

"Here, Alandia, more horses!" she said. "See? I drew Clipper and Starshine."

The two horses now lay buried, two more victims of the war. Mori had painted them from memory a hundred times for the burnt girl. She placed the scroll on the bed.

She kept moving between the beds, handing out gifts. One child had lost his eyes and ears; she gave him a box of scented oils. If he was blind and deaf, she would let him smell a hint of life. Another man, once a soldier, had lost his sanity; he lay bound to his bed, mumbling and weeping. Mori kissed his forehead and recited old poems to him, poems he had once loved. As she whispered, she saw his face calm, and she stroked his hair until he slept. A hundred wounded filled this temple, still lingering in pain, and Mori knew these ones would stay here forever. Their bodies or minds were destroyed, their families were gone, and their houses had fallen.

Elethor can fight for them, she thought. *Bayrin can guard them. But I... I can soothe them. I can bring them some joy in their world of pain.*

When she had distributed her gifts, she began to play her harp. Lady Lyana was a great warrior, Elethor a sculptor, Bayrin a trickster; she, the young Princess Mori, had always found her talent in music. She closed her eyes as she played her harp, and she sang her song. It was an old tune of Requiem, sung among the birches for thousands of years, even in the Golden Age before the great wars had toppled Requiem's glory. It was a song of birch leaves in wind, of wings on the sky, of marble columns rising into the night... but as Mori sang, it became too a song of warmth over fear, of whispers into a pool of loneliness, of broken souls mending under a sky of fire. It was the song of her life: of her tragedy in Castellum Luna where she had lost her brother and her innocence; of her war over Nova Vita where she had seen so many slain; and of her hope for healing, her hope for a new dawn in Requiem. It was a song of starlight.

She played the last note, a haunting whisper and the flutter of dragon wings fading into nightfall, and opened her eyes. She saw that across the hall, clad in white silk, stood Mother Adia. The High Priestess looked upon her with soft eyes and smiled sadly.

"My princess," she said.

Mori approached the older woman and embraced her. "Mother Adia! I practiced the breathing you taught me last night, and I thought of birches in the wind, like you said I should, and I had only one nightmare."

A year ago, the wounds of war fresh, nightmares had twisted her nights. Until dawn, Mori would see Solina burn her brother, feel Lord Acribus grab and choke her, and see dead children strewn across Nova Vita. Slowly, moon after moon, she worked with Mother Adia to breathe, to think of birch leaves, to see stars and flowers in the night, not fire and blood.

Mother Adia kissed her cheek. "I'm glad, Mori. It will still be a while, but I hope that soon you'll sleep the whole night with no nightmares at all."

Mori nodded, feeling warm and safe in the embrace. To sleep the whole night through—without waking up breathless, trembling, and covered in cold sweat? She did not think it possible. Not now, with Bayrin and Lyana away in the south. Before Bayrin had left for Tiranor, she would sleep in his arms, and when nightmares woke her, she could huddle closer to him, kiss him, and feel safe. Now she slept alone, and she missed Bayrin so badly that her stomach ached.

"I hope so," she whispered into Mother Adia's robes. They were soft like the birch leaves she thought of at night.

Mother Adia took her from the Chamber of Healing and into halls and rooms throughout the temple. They spent an hour meeting healers in training, carpenters building new beds, and priests organizing chambers of supplies: bandages, vials of silkweed milk, needles and stitches, bone saws and scalpels, pots of healing herbs, and codices full of medical drawings that both scared and soothed Mori.

War will flare again. Bayrin spoke of armies mustering in the south, and she knew the second invasion could begin any day now. Her knees trembled, and she clutched her luck finger behind her back, the sixth finger on her left hand.

This time, when fire rains and steel bites, we'll be ready to heal the wounded. Adia will be ready with her herbs and bandages, and I'll be ready with my song and harp.

She stepped outside onto the marble stairs of the temple. The wind pinched her cheeks and played with her hair. She looked upon the city of Nova Vita, and peacefulness settled upon her like golden dawn upon storming sea. The forest was still charred, but new saplings grew between the blackened stumps. Many houses still lay in ruin, but masons were busy as ants, building new homes. Many graves covered Lacrimosa Hill beyond the city walls, but many dragons still lived, gliding overhead.

"Come back to us soon, Bayrin and Lyana," she whispered into the wind.

The flap of wings ruffled her hair. A brass dragon came flying toward her, scales clinking and breath snorting. Mori shielded her eyes with her palm. It was her brother, King Elethor. Smoke streamed from his nostrils in two trails. His claws clattered against the temple's marble stairs, and he folded his wings. He tossed his head, snorted flickers of fire, and shifted.

When he stood in human form, he looked *old* to Mori, older than she'd ever known him—not old like Lord Deramon perhaps, or like Father had been, but... he suddenly seemed closer to them in age, no longer a youth like her. Only last year, he had been merely her brother, the quiet Elethor who lived upon the hill. Today she saw a man clad in steel armor, a longsword strapped to his side, his face bearded and his brow showing the first hints of creasing. The thin, quiet prince she had known was gone; today she saw a king.

"Mori," he said, "Bayrin has returned from Tiranor... and he brings news."

Bayrin is back! Mori's heart leaped with joy. Bayrin—the boy who would tug her pigtails in childhood, who had grown into a man who would kiss her lips, hold her in his strong arms, and protect her. Bayrin—her guard, her guiding star, and the sky in her wings. She wanted to run to him, to kiss him, to hold him forever... but something in Elethor's eyes held her back. Her brother's gaze was somber and his voice low; Mori froze and stared at him.

The news is bad.

Cold, skeletal claws seemed to clutch her heart. She could barely breathe and her eyes stung. She grabbed Elethor's hands and squeezed them.

"El," she whispered, "is... is the war here again?"

Think of the leaves. Think of the wind in the birches. Think of stars at night. Don't let the nightmares rise.

He looked around him, then lowered his head and spoke softly. "Mori, do not speak of this to anyone. Not yet. I don't want the people alarmed. We think the invasion is near. We think we know where the enemy will fly." He stared at her steadily. "I need you to be strong. I need you to be brave."

Mori had expected to shiver, whimper, and see the world spin. Strangely no fear filled her, only a metallic resolve. She nodded.

"I will be brave," she whispered. "Elethor... I will be strong. I will fight."

She embraced her brother, laid her head against his pauldron, and held him tight. His armor was cold and hard against her. He kissed her head.

"Our forces are strong," he said, his arms around her. "We've trained them well. This time Solina won't catch us by surprise. This time we'll cast her back into the sea."

Mori closed her eyes. A vision flashed through her head—Elethor lying in the temple with the wounded, his limbs gone, his face burnt like Orin's face back at Castellum Luna. She held her brother tight.

"I know, El. I know we're strong. I love you."

He mussed her hair. "I love you too, Mors." He held her at arm's length. "I fly east now, beyond the mountains, to summon the farmlords. We will hold a council of Requiem's highborn—like the great councils Father would hold. It's two days to Oldnale Manor and two days back. Sit upon the throne while I'm away, Mori. You rule in Nova Vita in my absence."

A tear streamed down her cheek. Elethor turned, shifted into a dragon, and flew across the city. Mori stood upon the temple steps, hand raised, and watched until he disappeared into the east.

BAYRIN

Sea salt, sweat, and dirt covered him. He desperately needed a good, solid soak, but Bayrin remained in the throne room, waiting for Mori.

"If she loves me when I stink, it's true love," he said to a marble bust of an old king—he thought it was King Benedictus, the great hero from the legends—who stood upon a plinth. The bust merely glowered.

Old Benedictus must smell the stink too, Bayrin thought.

He rocked on his heels, anxious to see the princess. The night they had parted, she cried and held him tight; he had barely extricated himself. He had kissed her, promised to return to her, promised to always love her. That had been three moons ago, and now Bayrin thought he could burst—he wanted nothing more than to pull her back into his arms and kiss her again.

At the same time, a sliver of ice pulsed beneath those feelings. Worry for Lyana gnawed at him. His little sister—dancing for General Mahrdor himself! Like everyone who'd spent more than an afternoon in Tiranor, Bayrin had heard the rumors about Mahrdor. They said the man skinned humans to make scrolls, books, even upholstery. They said he collected shrunken heads, pickled hands, and bronzed fetuses he cut from living women's wombs. The thought of Lyana in his villa festered inside Bayrin so sourly that he barely noticed the palace doors open.

"Bayrin!" cried Mori. She ran across the hall toward him.

Stars, she's beautiful. Thoughts of Mahrdor's collection instantly left him. Whenever he returned from Tiranor, he realized what a beautiful woman Mori had grown into. The girl from a year ago, meek and skinny, was gone. Instead he saw a young woman, almost twenty years old, with billowing chestnut hair, wide gray eyes, and lips that smiled like all the sweetness of a fruit harvest. Despite this war and despite his worry for Lyana, he felt his heart melt, and he reached out his arms. She crashed into his embrace, and they shared a long kiss—a kiss that lasted the lifespan of oaks, the age of mountains, and the rise and fall of stars, and yet when the kiss ended, he felt it too short, like a harp's note that fades too soon.

He held her in his arms. She looked up at him, wrinkled her nose, and said, "Bay, you *stink*." She laid her head against his chest. "But I still love you."

I knew it, he thought.

"I think I got some of the stink on you too," he said. He held her hand and began leading her down the hall. "Come with me. I have an idea."

She looked over her shoulder at the throne, which was dwindling behind them. "Bay, Elethor flew to summon the Oldnales to a council. He said I must sit on the throne while he's away. I—"

"Did he say you can't sleep then, or eat, or bathe, or make love? Stars, I hope he didn't forbid that last bit." He guided her across the hall. "Come on, Mors, this throne has been here for hundreds of years. It will wait another hour for your lovely backside to warm it." He gave that backside a pat, nudging her outside the palace doors.

They stood on the palace stairway and gazed upon Nova Vita. Above the southern city wall rose Castra Draco, fortress of the Royal Army, in whose courtyard men and women dueled with swords and shields. The sounds of hammers on anvils rang; in the city's three smithies, blacksmiths were forging new breastplates, helmets, swords, and spears. For the first time, they forged armor for dragons too: great helmets the size of wheelbarrows, steel collars to shield necks from arrows, and massive breastplates to protect dragons' undersides where no scales grew. Above in the sky, Bayrin saw phalanxes of dragons swoop and blow fire, drilling great mock battles above.

War is coming, he thought. *But that is tomorrow. Today is my day with Mori.*

He shifted into a dragon and flew. With a snort of fire, Mori flew at his side, a slim golden dragon. They dived above the coiling streets. Soon they flew over King's Forest, wings bending the grass and saplings that grew from last war's ashes. They headed north toward the mountains of Dair Ranin where the Seven—great heroes of the olden days—had lived before founding Nova Vita.

They flew until the city disappeared behind, and the forests grew verdant and untouched by war. Oaks and birches spread for leagues below, their canopies an undulating green sea. The River Ranin rolled between the trees, spilling from distant misty mountains. In the old days before the wars, Bayrin would fly here with Elethor to hunt and fish and escape the court. He knew every boulder, meadow, and cave for leagues around.

"The air smells good here," Mori said, flying at his side. "Like trees and water, not... not like fear."

The two dragons, green and gold, flew around a stony mountainside and across a valley. Upon a cliff Bayrin saw the Stone Elder, a great, mossy statue of a dragon; it loomed twice his own size. They said the ancient, wild children of Requiem had carved this sentinel ten thousand years ago, long before the Vir Requis had forged iron, raised livestock, and plowed fields. The Ranin roared around the monolith and crashed down the cliff, a waterfall of mist and fury.

As Bayrin and Mori flew toward the waterfall, their wings rippled a reedy pond below, sending deer and cranes fleeing into a copse of birches. Bayrin dived and crashed into the pond, spraying a fountain.

"Come on, Mori!" he called into the sky. "It's not deep."

She circled above, looked down fearfully, then narrowed her eyes and dived into the water beside him. The pond swirled and the waterfall cascaded ahead, showering them. The Stone Elder glowered upon the cliff above. Bayrin could no longer see the forest around him, only mist and spray.

With a gulp of air, he shifted into human form. When he placed down his feet, the water rose to his chest. The waterfall seemed greater now, an angry liquid demon, and the spray pounded his weaker human form with countless watery arrows. After a moment's hesitation, Mori shifted too; the lake rose to her neck, and the spray drenched her hair.

"I'm scared," she said, voice nearly lost under the waterfall's roar. "The water is rough. Won't we drown?"

Bayrin shrugged. "Oh, I'm sure we will." He pulled off his shirt, then his boots, and finally his pants; he let them float away. He took a step through the swirling pond, moving closer to the waterfall. The spray pummeled him, turning the world white and blue.

"Finally you won't be stinky," Mori said.

He nodded. "Finally maybe you'll kiss me properly."

He pulled her toward him and kissed her—quite properly—for long moments. When he pulled off her gown, she shivered and clung to him, and he kissed her again. She was so small against him; her head only just reached his shoulders. Their naked bodies clung together underwater, and he kissed her ear while whispering to her—endless whispers that made her laugh, and blush, and kiss him again.

War is coming, he thought, *but that is another day. Today I am happy.*

When their love was spent, they waded to the lakeside, lay upon the grass, and let the sun dry them. He held her, kissed her head, and wished he could stay here forever. The sun began to set and he closed his eyes.

Twelve days, he thought. *Twelve days until acid rains and blood washes us.* He held Mori close, shut his eyes, and clenched his jaw with the pain of old wounds and memory.

LYANA

The old man reached out and touched her bruised cheek. He clucked his tongue and shook his head sadly.

"Savages!" he said and sighed. "Beasts in armor. To strike a blind woman..." He shook his bony fist at the ceiling. "If I were a younger man, I would have given them a bruise or two!"

Lyana smiled softly. Over the past year, she had come to love old Peras, keeper of the River Spice. She lowered his hand and squeezed it.

"It doesn't hurt, Father Peras," she said. She leaned forward and kissed his stubbly cheek. He smelled of flour and dried figs. "I'm fine, and I can take care of myself."

"I saw!" he said and laughed, showing gums with only five teeth left. He shook his head in amazement. "I never would have thought a blind girl could kick so swift and hard. Now the soldier is missing a few teeth too."

She smiled softly. *But I am not a blind girl,* she thought. *I am a bellator, a knight of Requiem, a noble warrior of the north. And if I kick swiftly, and kick hard, I show a piece of Lyana, and that is more dangerous than any soldier's fist.* She took a deep breath. *I must be more careful. I will not let my cover slip and my people down.*

The crescent moon had crossed the sky outside. Dawn was near. The last of the soldiers had left the River Spice, stumbling down the street, singing the songs of their phalanxes. A dozen candles lit the winehouse, and moths danced around their flames. The orange light flickered over toppled mugs, a shattered clay plate, a half-eaten figcake, and stains of blood. Walking stick tapping, Lyana approached a broom in the corner, grabbed it, and began to sweep the floor. Peras moved around the room, collecting mugs and polishing tabletops.

Lyana loved this time of night; they were her favorite times in Tiranor. The sounds of the crowd died outside, and she could hear the wind through the palm trees, the crickets, and the frogs that trilled. She glimpsed the stars shining outside; later tonight she would climb upon the roof and try to count them all.

The Draco constellation shines here too, she thought, *even in hot, cruel Tiranor. The stars of my fathers bless me even so far from home.*

"You have fought men before, I think," said Peras, examining a crack in a mug.

Lyana smiled, broom in hand. "I am a winehouse dancer. Of course I've fought men."

I have killed men, Father Peras, she thought. *I killed them in tunnels, and in the sky, and I will kill ten thousand more if I can before this war ends.* She continued sweeping and said no more.

Peras shook his head and blew out his breath. "Men can be cruel creatures, Daughter Tiana. I have seen too much cruelty in my years... too much blood, too much hate. But not all men are cruel." He righted a fallen chair. "You should find a good man, not a soldier, not a drunkard... find yourself an honest trader or craftsman. You don't want to spend your life dancing here, do you?"

She smiled softly, sweeping shards of clay into the corner. "Dear Father Peras! I would be happy if I could forever dance in this place... though beauty does fade, and no man wants to see an old crone dance." She laughed. "I have a good man, neither a soldier nor drunkard." Her voice softened. "Back in my home far away."

Rubbing a tabletop with a rag, he looked up at her, his eyes sad. "You must miss him."

She sighed. "I was betrothed to his brother at first, a great desert warrior, the strongest man in our tribe. My betrothed was son of our chief. He owned many goats and sheep and three horses—horses that could rival those from Queen Solina's stables." She laughed softly. "It does not sound like much here in Irys, this light of the north, but in the southern dunes, a herd of livestock is worth more than gold and jewels."

She lowered her head, remembering her Orin, Prince of Requiem, a tall and handsome hero, the love of her life... a love she had buried. She took a deep breath and continued, broom still in her hand.

"One day black horses emerged above the dunes," she said. "Brigands in black rode them, sabres bright. My betrothed fought them. I did too, but they were too many. My betrothed fell and the sand ate his blood. I remember only a flash of a blade, blood on my face, and when I woke, I found that I had lost my love... and lost my eyes."

All light dimmed when you died, Orin, she thought. *All starlight faded from my nights.*

With a shake of her head, she kept sweeping. "After that, well... by the laws of our tribe, I became betrothed to his younger brother. It's an old law passed down through generations; without it, widows would be cast aside, left destitute in the desert. So as I mourned, I found myself promised to a young man named Rael." It was a common name in the deserts south of Irys, Lyana knew. She smiled softly. "Rael is nothing like his fallen brother; he is not a warrior, but a stargazer, not a hero, but a scribe of scrolls. At first I mourned, and scorned him, and wanted to flee him, but as time went by, he showed me great love—not fiery, passionate love like his older brother and I had shared, but a quiet caring, a deep respect, an ember that grows to flame. And I miss him, Father Peras."

He placed down his rag, approached her, and patted her arm. "How did you end up here, Tiana? In Irys, this city so far from your home?"

She closed her eyes behind her scarf. *Your people burned my city, killed nearly half my people, and plan to kill the rest. You are kind, Old Peras, but your queen is cruel, and her soldiers lust for blood and death.*

"A storm from the desert," she whispered. "Sand that buried our tents. A drought that killed our livestock. Brigades that murdered half our tribe. Pain, death, starvation... and so I am here. To dance. To fill my purse with bronze and copper and what silver I can earn. To return some day with life. Here in Irys, I am the Blind Beauty, a dancer from the dunes. At home, I am a shepherdess and a leader of my tribe."

Peras looked outside the window into the night. The street was silent and dark. The old man's voice was soft. "We all wear masks. I was a soldier once, did I tell you? Fifteen years I fought for Tiranor; I was an archer in the Steelmark Phalanx. Back then we used good, honest *bows*, not these clumsy crossbow contraptions the soldiers use today. I fought thirty years ago when the dragons of Requiem flew over our land, toppled our towers, and killed my king and queen. I shot poisoned arrows at them, watched the fire burn my brothers, and saw my home fall." He shook his head and closed his eyes. "The wounds I saw, Tiana... They told us war is glorious, that our light would drive out darkness with the song of the Sun God. I saw no glory. I saw blood, I saw women aflame, and I saw children burned into charred corpses. After the war ended, my family was gone. My phalanx was gone. My home was a pile of rubble. They gave me some medal of gold." He snorted. "I sold it and bought this place, named it The River Spice, and now instead of being a soldier, I serve soldiers wine and figcake." He held her arm. "We all wear masks, and we all flee our past, child. Sometimes it's all we can do to survive."

An owl hooted outside, and Peras moved his arm so that a mug slipped off a table. Instinctively, Lyana reached out and caught it.

Her heart nearly stopped.

Her breath caught.

She stood, mug in hand, eyes wide behind her scarf. She stared at Peras. He stared back, the kindly old winehouse keeper gone from his eyes. She saw the soldier there again.

He knows. Stars, he knows.

"Please," she whispered.

Never breaking his stare, he took the mug from her, placed it back on the table, and nodded.

"We all wear masks," he repeated. "Sometimes we wear scarves." He stared at her silently for a moment that seemed to last an age. Then he laughed and swept his arms around him. "Look at this place! Clean as new, and it's not yet dawn. Let's find some sleep, Tiana. Soon it will be a new night, and there will be more soldiers to intoxicate."

He left the common room and climbed upstairs, humming an old desert song.

Lyana stood alone, heart still hammering. Suddenly she felt exposed, nearly naked in her silks. She missed her armor of Requiem, missed her sword and dagger. Clad in steel, she felt so strong, so brave, a great warrior. Who was she here? A girl. Fragile. A flower to be trampled.

I want to fly home, she thought. *I want to become a dragon in the night, fly over the sea, fly back to my armor, to my city, to Elethor and Mori and everyone else.* Yet she only tightened her lips and stood in place. She had a duty here. She would remain Tiana a while longer. She had served her home with steel and flame; now she would serve Requiem with silk and skin.

As if summoned by her thoughts, the door opened, and General Mahrdor entered the winehouse.

He walked alone this night; no Gilded Guardians stood at his sides, steel birds of prey. He wore a white robe over his armor, and his head was hooded. He smiled at her thinly, but his eyes were blue shards, cold and scrutinizing. Again she felt like he could see through her silks, through her dyed skin, into her very soul.

"Tiana!" he said. "I apologize for the lateness of my visit and delight to find you still awake. I myself could not sleep. When I closed my eyes, I saw visions of you dancing; I knew I must see you dance in the flesh before your phantom twin abandoned me. Will you come to my villa, Tiana? Will you dance in the dawn?"

We all wear masks, echoed the words in her mind. *May my mask shield my pain. May the horror crash around me like a river around a boulder.*

She nodded. "I will dance for you, my lord."

The Draco constellation shone overhead as they sailed a boat down the Pallan. A crescent moon grinned. Mahrdor held a lamp before him, and the light danced upon the water like jewels.

Only eleven days until summer solstice, Lyana thought. *Eleven days until the hosts of sunfire spread to my home. Eleven days until I must kill or flee this man.*

He took her to his villa on the hill and into a hall lined with columns. Between the pillars, Lyana saw palms and rushes slope toward the Pallan, and the lights of distant homes glimmered. A hot wind blew over the water, ruffled her hair, and filled her nostrils with the scents of river and grass.

Mahrdor sat on a giltwood divan, placed his sandaled feet on a footstool, and leaned back.

"Dance for me," he said.

Again she danced for him with no music. Again her body swayed to a whispered song, the music of stars above, wind in palms, the flow of water in darkness. Her body flowed for him, and her bare feet tapped upon limestone tiles, and her eyes closed. She danced until wisps of purple dawn spread across the sky, and then Mahrdor stood and approached her, and held her, and stroked her cheek.

He leaned her against a porphyry column, kissed her neck, and made love to her there in the light of the dawn, as the River Pallan slowly awoke below them. She closed her eyes, leaned her head back, and thought of her home as he filled her. She thought of the dragons that flew above King's Forest, so high she could barely see their colors. She thought of the marble columns of Requiem's palace where she lived with Elethor, the smell of her morning bread, the calls of chickadees that always seemed to mock her. She gasped as Mahrdor loved her, and she knew she was yet another land for him to conquer, yet another trophy for him to claim, and a tear streamed down her cheek.

When he was done, he kissed her tear, stroked her hair, and whispered to her.

"You are more beautiful than this dawn, Tiana, and you are more precious than our short lives under the sun. You are like the River Pallan, a gift from the desert, and your lips are oasis fruit." He took her hand. "Come with me, Tiana. I have a gift for you, a gift as rare and beautiful as you are."

He held her hand. He took her across the hall and into a towering, domed solarium. The dawn shone through the narrow windows; they were made from true glass, a priceless rarity in Tiranor. Ferns filled the room, and a hundred cages hung between them, holding hundreds of birds: finches, macaws, conures, lovebirds, and many others Lyana could not name. They all squawked and fluttered in their cages.

In the center of the solarium stood a great, golden birdcage. It rose six feet tall, maybe taller, and its bars curved to form dragons aflight. It was empty, its door open.

"I am, as you know, a collector," Mahrdor said. He swept his arm around him. "Smell the air, Tiana! You will smell a thousand plants from all the lands of the world; I collect them. Listen to the song of birds! You will hear a hundred different species; I collect them." He turned to face her. "And you, Tiana... you are the rarest, most beautiful of birds."

Suddenly his face changed.

Rage overflowed his eyes.

He raised his fist to strike her.

She flinched and raised her hand in defense.

As her heart hammered and her mind spun, Mahrdor nodded and slowly lowered his fist.

"I thought so," he whispered.

Terror shattered inside her.

Lyana summoned her magic and began to shift into a dragon.

He clutched her throat and squeezed, and she gasped for breath, and his fist now did strike, and pain exploded. White light flooded her. Her magic fled her. His fingers dug into her neck, and he dragged her and threw her into the cage.

His hand freed her throat. She sucked in breath and tried to shift. He slammed the cage door shut, trapping her inside. Scales flowed across her, and her body ballooned, becoming the dragon. She slammed against the cage bars and howled in pain. Her magic fizzled. She roared and clutched at it and tried to shift again, to break the cage bars, to blow fire. She felt wings sprout. Fangs lengthened in her mouth. Her body grew, hit the bars, and again her magic vanished.

She fell onto her knees, panting, a caged woman. She snarled, tore her scarf off, and glared at Mahrdor.

He stood before her, arms crossed, smiling sadly.

"Oh, Tiana," he said. "Did you truly think I did not know? Did you truly think you could fool me like you fooled the common soldiers at your winehouse?"

"My name is not Tiana," she hissed and bared her teeth as if she were a dragon. She slammed against the cage bars. They were thick and strong; gilded iron, she thought.

He shrugged. "Your name matters not. You are my pet, my trophy, the crown of my collection; that is what matters to me." He looked over his shoulder. "Come, Yarish! See her without her scarf."

Out from the shadows stepped a tall, gaunt man with white hair. Lyana growled, heart hammering. She knew this man; he was the deaf innkeeper of Old Mill in Hog Corner, the fishhouse where she would meet with Bayrin. Today the man wore no rags but donned the armor of a soldier. He gave her a blank stare; he seemed almost bored.

"Are all weredragons as stupid as this one?" he asked Mahrdor. "If so, we should have no particular problem facing them in battle."

Weredragon. Lyana growled and slammed against the bars. She hated that word—a dirty, foul word of hatred, of blood, of scorn.

"I am a Vir Requis," she said, "a daughter of ancient Requiem blessed with starlight. You will find us very problematic to kill." She snapped her teeth as if she were a dragon who could tear into their flesh; she craved to taste that flesh. "When you attack our land, you will find us ready to fell you from the sky."

The two Tiran officers looked at each other and laughed. Mahrdor shook his head. He patted the cage bars, then pulled his hand back when she tried to bite it.

"Oh, precious weredragon pet," he said. "Do you refer to the army of your King Elethor, which heads to Ralora Beach? Yes, weredragon. I know you saw the map in my chambers; I placed it there for you. I know you spoke of it to your brother, that he flew over the sea to sing the news." He gave a sad, theatrical sigh. "I think... when your King Elethor and his army arrive at Ralora, they will find only seagulls and crabs to fight."

Lyana stared, her insides trembling. Her eyes burned and she felt tears gather. She could barely breathe and her head spun. It was a ruse, had been a ruse all along. How could she have been so stupid? How could she think this disguise could fool them?

Please, stars, do not let this be... do not let my kingdom fall.

With a growl, Lyana reached out of the cage, trying to grab his arm, to pull it toward her, to bite it off. He took a step back, stared at her sadly, and shook his head.

"I will kill you," she whispered, eyes narrowed and glaring.

He smiled thinly and hunger filled his eyes, the hunger of a wolf for its prey. He licked his pale, thin lips.

"No," he said softly. "No, you will not kill me, Lyana. Nor will I kill you." He fingered a dagger that hung on his belt, its pommel shaped as a sunburst. "No matter how much you beg me to."

His grin widened.

Lyana roared and slammed against the bars.

ADIA

Without her children, her house seemed empty as a barren womb, a hall of ghosts. Most days since the Phoenix War, Adia spent her time in the temple, healing and praying; or in the tunnels stocking bandages, herbs, and supplies for siege; or in the streets of Nova Vita, visiting and comforting grieving families. But today, for the first time since the phoenixes had burned this city, Adia had taken a day for her own home.

She knelt now in her garden, stubbornly fighting a losing war against dandelions which had invaded her rows of herbs. *Even the plants fight their wars,* she thought wryly. She kept tugging at the weeds until her fingers were raw and her robes covered with soil. When she surveyed her work, she saw that she had put but a small dent into the yellow invasion.

Once children had run across this lawn, she thought. Once Lyana and Bayrin had fought here with wooden swords, their feet tearing up whatever she had planted and dragging mud into the house. Once the stray dogs Bayrin would adopt—Adia had never understood where he found so many—would dig through her flowerbeds and eat her herbs. Once laughter and light had filled these gardens. Today this was all that remained: weeds and silence.

Abandoning her floral war for another day, Adia left the garden. Sunflowers and lilac grew around her door, wild and untamed, their leaves perforated with insect bites. They too needed care she could not give them. Her door was painted green and silver—some in Requiem thought them blessed colors—and when Adia stepped through this doorway, more silence greeted her.

She walked through her house and began to aimlessly work—sweeping a corner here, polishing a mug there. As she wandered the halls, she found the silence unbearable; it engulfed her like a white demon. There were too many rooms in this house upon the hill, too many halls, too many corners where memories whispered.

Three children had once filled this house with light, she thought. But Bayrin now lived in the palace, guarding his princess; Lyana now spied in the south, in such danger that Adia lay awake most nights, struggling for breath; and her sweet youngest child, Noela, still slept under her grave upon Lacrimosa Hill. No more laughter. No more clacking of wooden swords. No more muddy footprints, or scraped knees, or nights of stargazing with cider and roasted walnuts. Only this: empty rooms and silence.

Why had she come to this place? She had work to do in the tunnels: jars of preserves needed to be labeled, and swords needed to be hung on racks, and scrolls needed to be placed on shelves. She had healers to train at her temple, young and frightened girls who had never stitched a wound, sawed through a crushed leg, or comforted a dying man. She had stars to pray to: the constellation Draco, stars of her fathers, guardians of Requiem.

And yet today she had chosen this place, this home she had shared with her husband for... how long had it been? Adia shook her head in amazement when she counted the years. Twenty-nine summers had gone by since she had married Deramon and moved into this house on the hill. She had been only a youth then, not yet twenty, and the world had seemed so bright to her, Deramon so strong, her house so full of warmth and wonder.

Empty rooms and silence; it was all that remained.

But no, she thought. Memories remained, moving through these halls like ghosts: Bayrin as a young boy, wild and impossible to tame, scratching his name into every wall; Noela first laughing, a mere moon before she had laughed no more; Lyana squealing as she tugged her brother's hair and fled when he pretended to be a griffin. Adia could still see Bayrin's name upon the walls, though it had been twenty years, and she could still hear the echoes of her daughters laughing and crying and calling for her.

She entered her bedroom, a sparse chamber of unadorned walls, a simple bed topped with white sheets, and no ornaments but for a basket of dried flowers upon a table. Adia walked to a window and looked outside at the burnt forests. She smiled softly. Those memories were kind, yet they too were fragile. Should Queen Solina fly to this hill, she would topple these empty halls and silent rooms, and then those memories too would die. Nothing would remain of this place but bricks and ash, and all the dandelions that plagued her would lie as charred dust.

She looked at the city outside; from here, she could see half of Nova Vita roll across hills to the walls and forests. She was High Priestess, the Mother of Requiem, and all those souls below were as children to her. All those memories would perish, and all those lights would fade.

"It is madness," she whispered. "Five thousand Vir Requis soldiers, most of them mere farmers, bakers, and shepherds... against myriads of wyverns and a hundred thousand desert warriors."

And yet what else could they do? Stock their supplies. Train their warriors. Pray.

"And walk through our homes," she said softly. "Relive the memories. Savor the light of life for one last day."

She heard the door open across the house, the clink of armor, and the heavy footsteps of her husband. Soon Deramon stepped into the bedroom. When Adia looked at him, she marveled at how more white now filled his beard; only last year, that beard had been bright red, and only a few white strands had invaded it. Now for every red hair, a white one grew.

Adia touched his cheek. "Deramon," she said softly and kissed him.

He removed his breastplate, then hung sword and axe upon the wall. She helped him unclasp the rest of his armor: vambraces upon his arms, greaves upon his legs, pauldrons like shoulders of steel, and a coat of chain mail. When finally he stood in nothing but a woolen shirt and pants, he looked so small to her, his arms scarred. Once she had thought him a bear of a man, a mountain of muscle and grit.

The years had softened him; they had done the same to her. For a few years now, Adia had allowed no mirrors in her home. She did not want to see the lines that grew under her eyes, the white that invaded her own black hair, and the new weight that coated her bones. When she first moved into this home—*twenty-nine years, stars!*—many called her the fairest woman in Requiem, a tall and willowy beauty with midnight hair and eyes like magic. Today her hips were wider, her legs blue with veins, her mouth less likely to smile.

Does he think me ugly? she wondered as she looked at Deramon. She knew that some lords, when they crossed their fiftieth year, took concubines—young, pretty things for secret nights. On days like these, when death loomed, would he seek out last comforts?

"It has been nearly thirty summers since we moved into our home," she said to him. "The years have kissed my hair with white, softened my flesh upon my bones, and drawn lines of memory upon my face. But today I will love you like we used to love—with all the fire we would kindle in our youth. I will take you once more into my bed, like the first time, for this may be the last time."

She doffed her robes, stood naked before him, and saw his face soften.

"The years did not mar your beauty," he said, "but deepened it. When we wed, I called you the fairest flower in Requiem; that you are still." He cupped her cheek with his large, rough hand and kissed her lips. "Now and always."

She took him into her bed. She made love to him—with the fire and passion of their youth, and with the slow burn of what they had grown for so many years. She cried out to him. Today was a last day; she savored every breath, every touch, every whisper. When their love was spent, she lay against him and kissed him.

"I love you, Deramon," she whispered. "After Noela died, I know that I forgot that. I know that my love fled you then; all love fled from me. But I love you deeply, fully; I am yours always, and I will be yours in the starlit halls. I am yours in our life and death."

The sun began to set and she slept in his arms. Tomorrow fire would burn; tonight she lived twenty-nine years of laughter and starlight.

LYANA

She slammed against the cage bars and howled.

"Mahrdor!" she shouted. Her voice filled the solarium. "Mahrdor, free me! Open this cage or the fire of Requiem will rain upon you!"

The birds that filled the aviary shrieked and fluttered. Finches bustled in their hanging cages, beeping. A macaw squawked and bit at the bars of its own prison. A horde of green conures flew from perch to perch, their cages swinging. All had smaller, humbler cages than her own. All hung upon walls or between plants in corners. Lyana's own cage stood in the center of the chamber, the golden centerpiece of Mahrdor's collection. She was his prize pet.

"Mahrdor!" she shouted.

No one but the birds answered. Lyana kept slamming against the bars, but they would not dent. When she scratched at them, the gold peeled back to reveal iron. She tried to shift into a dragon again, but as soon as scales began to cover her and her body grew, the bars shoved her back into human form.

Finally, when her body was bruised from banging against the bars, she fell to her knees. She lowered her head, letting her hair cover her eyes, and gritted her teeth. A deep terror festered inside her. Mahrdor had known—he had known all along—and now Elethor would be flying to Ralora Beach... flying to nothing but waves and sand.

He will leave only the City Guard in Nova Vita, she knew. *Only my father. My brother. A few green youths they had trained. They will die.*

The fear rose in her like flames would rise in her dragon's maw. She snarled and glared through the bars at the glass panes above. The sun was beginning to set. How long until Solina's army flew?

"I have to escape," she whispered. "I have to warn Elethor. I will not be the one who lets Requiem fall."

She slammed against the bars again. They bruised her skin. She howled in frustration and fell back down. Her eyes burned and she clenched her fists to stop them from trembling.

"I have to escape," she whispered again. "I won't let Solina murder my family. I won't let Mahrdor imprison Princess Mori like he imprisoned me." She growled. "I will escape!"

She kept slamming against the bars until the sun sank, darkness filled the solarium, and she saw nothing but a faint glimmer of moon through the glass ceiling. With a wordless shout, Lyana sat down, pulled her knees to her chest, and lowered her head.

"I'm sorry, Elethor," she whispered.

She tried not to think of home. Remembering would be too hard. Yet in the darkness, she could not stop the memories from rising like dreams. She saw the gardens of the palace, a lush haven where she would walk with Elethor and talk to him of politics and warfare and heraldry, then catch him giving her a warm look and smile. He would pull her close and kiss her cheek, and she would struggle and call him a blockhead for ignoring her words, but then capitulate and let him kiss her under the trees. She saw Bayrin again, her oaf of a brother, sneak into her chamber to draw rude pictures on her shield, place frogs in her bed, and once—she shook her head to remember it—hide a snake in her drawer of undergarments. She thought of her parents, and of her friend Mori, and her squire Treale Oldnale, and a lump filled her throat. She could not stop a tear from falling.

In the darkness, she saw the acid coat them—Elethor, her family, and her friends. Like Silas at the palace, they would scream, and their flesh would melt, until they lay as sticky bones with anguished skulls.

She placed her head against her knees. She tried to stay awake, but sleep still found her, and dreams emerged in the darkness. She no longer huddled in a cage, but hung in a cocoon of cobwebs. Nedath, Guardian of the Abyss, scuttled toward her—a rotting girl with the body of a centipede. The demon licked and bit her, and Lyana screamed and wept. She swung on the cobwebs, and dozens of creatures swung around her, shriveled skin clinging to spines, their heads shrunken like those in Mahrdor's chambers, their toothless gums smacking. *Count the screws! Grow sideways like the little hairs of skeleys.*

Cold wind blew.

A sun raced between clouds.

She walked through King's Forest outside her city, stepping daintily between conifers ancient and gnarly, her feet as snowflakes upon a carpet of fallen needles. As ten thousand magpies sang, she traversed the hilltops, and there she came upon a lion of the woods. A noble creature was he, with soft fur the color of light and paws that left no prints. She reached her fingers into his mane, and when she looked upon herself, she saw that her armor had become a pixie homespun of grass and fur, old leaves and strings of golden hair.

"O, King of all Beasts," she whispered into his ear, and lay beside him, and there he licked her lily hands and chanted blessings upon her.

"Climb onto my back, fair maiden of these pines, and lay your head upon mine," he said, and Lyana climbed onto him. He ran across the hills and took her to a faerie court where stone balustrades surrounded a pool of twigs and cyclamen petals. A sword of stone lay upon an old shield there, encrusted with kings' blood, and on its blade silver runes told of want and lacking.

King Lion laid his head upon the shield, and kissed the stone blade so that his lips bled, and anointed Lyana with a kiss. He sang.

Queen of blood
Lie upon the grave of kings
Child of shattered metal
And light

He seemed as though he would sing more. He forgot the words.

In the woods...

In the woods Lyana wept. In the woods she prayed for life, she who had been marked to die. In the woods a giant boy with the head of a moose disassembled her methodically, neatly unscrewing arms, legs, her head, laying the pieces out before him. He blinked his eyes, wet eyes the size of saucers, long lashes like oily curtains.

"Daughter of Eleison," he said, his voice like a grunt, the groan of a rutting beast. She was a tiny doll to him. His furry hands would not leave her, arranging and rearranging her pieces upon the earth of this land. This land...

So beautiful an animal...

Her blood seeped into the pinecones.

Through her city she walked, houses like boxes, stained hands, snarling teeth and fear so thick in the air she coughed, choked, and fell to her knees.

O, King Lion! King of all beasts!

She ran from door to door, but each was barred to her. She sought her mother and father, but she found only puddles on the ground full of floating teeth. In the puddles she saw the face of her dancer—hair platinum, eyes hidden behind a scarf, face dyed gold. Tiana. Her eternal twin.

The boy awaited them both, and Lyana shivered and hated and feared. She lowered her head, let her hair cover her face, and wept as men with swords marched and shouted around her, and wyverns flew over the eastern hills.

When she awoke, a cruel sun seared her through the glass ceiling. When she touched the bars of her cage, they burned her fingers. Her limbs were stiff, her head aching, her throat parched.

"Stars of Requiem," she whispered, but her lips were so dry that they cracked, and she tasted blood. She fell silent.

The birds woke, squawked, chirped, and beeped around her. The flowers growing from their vases and baskets bloomed toward the light. The room soon sweltered, and Lyana's throat ached for water, and her head began to spin. She rose on stiff limbs and began slamming against the bars again, a rhythmic beat. She threw herself against them until the gold peeled off the iron, her shoulders were raw, and bruises spread across her. She kept slamming, again and again, jaw clenched, mind blank, just to do something—anything.

"Mahrdor!" she shouted, hoarse. "Come and see me, Mahrdor! Come face me. I will kill you!"

The birds shrieked, her only answer.

He would arrive soon, she knew. He would arrive to see her, to bring her water and food, to taunt her, maybe to demand she dance, or demand she lie with him. He would not just leave her here. She kept attacking the cage as the sun moved across the sky and began to set again, and orange and red light filled the aviary.

She sat, knees pulled to her chest, and watched the sunset. Was Elethor watching the sunset too, flying toward Ralora Beach? Was Mori watching the sky, ruling alone in Nova Vita, awaiting the fire?

Her head spun and her skull seemed too tight. Her lips bled. Her throat blazed. Her stomach clenched with hunger. How long could she survive here? He would arrive soon, she knew. He would bring her water. If he did not, she would perish; he did not encage her in gold, his prize pet, to let her die. He would arrive soon—before darkness fell. He would bring sweet, cool water from deep wells, water to soothe her throat, cure her spinning head, and give her strength to fight him. The cage spun around her. She gagged and coughed.

Darkness fell.

She sat against the bars, shivering, arms wrapped around her.

He wants me to die. He will let me die here. I will die tonight. Goodbye, Requiem. I will fly to your starlit halls.

She closed her eyes and saw the pillars of afterlife.

Boots thudded across the hall.

She opened her eyes and winced. Lamplight filled the aviary, and three shadows approached her. They wore armor and helmets; she could not see their faces. When they reached her cage, one tossed a waterskin, a loaf of bread, and a wheel of cheese past the bars.

She glared at the soldiers. She wanted to shout curses at them, to try and break the bars again, to reach out and try to scratch them. One more glance at the water and food, and she chose them instead. She drank first. The water was brackish, and there was not nearly enough, but it was the best thing she had ever drunk, sweeter than wine from Requiem's vineyards. She stuffed the food into her mouth until her cheeks bulged.

Before she could swallow, the guards lifted her cage. They began to carry it toward the doors. Lyana swallowed hastily and shouted at them, voice hoarse.

"Fight me like men! Open this cage and face me in battle, cowards!" She banged against the bars. "Are you so weak that you fear to fight a woman?"

They kept walking, carrying her through the doors and into a corridor. These were no Gilded Guardians, she saw; they did not serve the General Mahrdor. Their helms were not shaped as ibises, but as falcons. Their armor was not golden, but pale platinum with sunbursts upon their breasts.

Palace guards, Lyana knew. *Queen Solina's men.*

She reached out the bars and scratched at their armor; a feeble gesture. She tried to snag one's helmet off, hoping to claw his eyes, but he caught her wrist and twisted so hard that she yelped. He released her just before her bone could crack.

"Where are you taking me?" she demanded, cradling her wrist and glaring. "I am a soldier of Requiem. You will answer to the wrath of our king."

One guard turned his head, and his falcon helm faced her. When he spoke, his voice was gravely and high-pitched, truly the sound of a steel bird. Through his visor's eye holes, she glimpsed a face hideously scarred; his eyelids were raw and hairless. This one had been lax around wyverns, she wagered.

"Queen Solina is... borrowing you for a while," the guard said, his voice as raw and twisted as the skin around his eyes. He made a sound halfway between a chuckle and a clearing of the throat. "She will return you to General Mahrdor eventually. Whether you'll return the same creature, well... that I doubt."

A hissing sound rose from his helm, and it was a moment before Lyana realized: it was laughter. The sound sent a chill through her; she couldn't help but shiver.

Solina.

Lyana had seen the queen's work in Requiem—bodies cut, burnt, killed in agony, even children. *She tortured my Orin to death. Will she do the same to me?*

She screamed in her cage and slammed against the bars.

The palace guards carried her out of Mahrdor's villa and into the gardens, where fig and carob trees rose from pebbly earth. Braziers stood in palisades, lighting the night and filling the air with scented smoke. A wyvern awaited in a cobbled courtyard, snarling at the stars. When it saw the approaching guards, it howled and bucked, scales clacking and tail lashing. Acid dripped from its maw to burn holes into the cobblestones. Its metallic scent filled Lyana's nostrils and seared her tongue.

The guards hoisted her cage onto the wyvern's back. She rolled against the bars, clenched her jaw, and snarled. They chained the cage down, and the deformed guard climbed into the beast's saddle. He grabbed a whip, cracked it, and the wyvern took flight.

The beast soared so fast, Lyana's head spun, black shadows spread across her eyes, and she nearly passed out. Her ears throbbed and her insides sank. Even as a dragon, she would never soar so quickly. She gasped for air and clenched her fists, struggling not to faint. The wyvern's girth blocked most of her view, but she could see the rims of the city around it, from the southern dunes where the torches of soldiers crackled, to the northern delta where ships sailed to sea, lanterns glowing upon their hulls. She stared across that sea, squinted, and tried to see Requiem's shores; she would draw comfort from them. Those shores were too distant and dark for her eyes, and she lowered her head.

I am alone here.

The wyvern began to descend. Streets snaked in labyrinths below, crowded with houses, palm trees, and people carrying tin lanterns—thousands of ants from up here, thousands of lives, thousands of worlds, all unaware of her pain. Lyana glimpsed the Tower of Akartum, which rose upon Phoebus Palace; they were heading there. To *her*. To the woman Elethor had loved, the woman who had murdered Orin, the woman Lyana vowed to kill.

The wyvern landed in a courtyard surrounded by walls and towers. A gateway led into the palace—a quiet backdoor. The soldiers carried her into a corridor and down a stairwell, its walls carved with suns and falcons. Their boots thudded and a thousand candles lit their way, wax melting like men under acid.

The air grew cool and musty as they descended. It seemed like they plummeted forever; the stairway coiled like a worm digging toward a man's heart. Lyana couldn't help but shiver. She crouched in her cage, snarling between the bars.

Don't dig so deep! she wanted to cry. *You will wake the creatures of the Abyss. You will free the Shrivels who hang there. You will wither with them.*

Yet a different horror dwelled in this underground. After countless steps deeper into darkness, the staircase ended and they entered the palace dungeons.

A tunnel stretched before Lyana, hewn of craggy stone. Cells lined the tunnel walls; blood trickled from between their bars, and screams rose from them, twisting in the air like demons of sound. The stench of disease, nightsoil, and fear filled Lyana's nostrils, so powerful that she gritted her teeth to stop from gagging.

The guards carried her cage down the tunnel. As they walked, Lyana stared into the cells they passed. Her stomach clenched and she could barely breathe. Inside one cell, guards were slicing pieces off a chained man as if carving a roast boar; the man screamed and writhed with every slice. In another chamber, guards smirked as they let rats feast upon a chained woman's legs; her feet were already gone. In a third cell, children hung from hooks, still alive and mewling, their bodies twisted with acid and their eyes pleading.

Lyana closed her own eyes. She did not want to see more. As the guards kept carrying her down the hall, however, she could still *hear* the torture: whips landing, hammers breaking bones, and mostly screams, horrible screams like those of the Abyss.

"I am a knight of Requiem," she whispered to herself, arms trembling. "I am a warrior. I am strong. Whatever they do to me, I can bear it."

And yet she knew that was a lie.

I cannot bear it.

If they broke her body here, they would break her mind too. If she ever returned to Elethor, she would be a shell of a woman—a cowering, mindless wretch, a fool for his court. A tear streamed down her cheek.

"I'm sorry, Elethor," she whispered. "I'm sorry, Mori."

Would they too end up here? Elethor had told her that Solina had spared his life in Requiem's tunnels; she wanted him a prisoner, not a corpse. She would bring him here, Lyana realized; she would bring Elethor to this place, and the Princess Mori, and Bayrin, and her parents, and their flesh would be sliced like roast boar, and rats would eat their legs, and...

Lyana shivered, fists trembling and tears flowing from closed eyes.

The hall seemed to stretch forever. If the Abyss loomed below Requiem, here was Tiranor's buried realm of darkness. After what seemed like hours—hours of screams, of blood, of the *crack* of bones and the *rip* of flayed skin—they reached an empty cell.

My own corner of pain, Lyana thought. *My own place of madness.*

The guards carried her cage inside and placed it on the floor. The walls closed in around her; the cell was no more than five feet wide. Its walls were carved of living rock, and manacles hung from its ceiling like iron Shrivels. In the guards' torchlight, Lyana saw that blood splashed the walls, floor, and chains. In a corner, a rat feasted on severed human fingers.

"Remove her from her cage," said the scarred guard to his comrades. He hissed a laugh. "Hang her from the manacles."

The guards snarled, lifted chains from the floor, and began slinking them through the cage bars. Lyana snarled, grabbed the chains, and tugged them.

"Hands down!" said the guard with the burnt face. He thrust a club into the cage and rapped her fingers. She yowled and tried to grab the club, but he pulled it back. Her fingers blazed. She grabbed at the chains again, and the club slammed down a second time. Pain blazed up to her shoulder, and she thought her fingers might be broken. When the chains were slung through the cage bars, the guards tugged them. They wrapped around her body, tightened, and clutched her like iron pythons. She writhed in the trap. When she tried to tug the chains loose, the guards pulled them tighter, and the links dug into her torso.

When they opened her cage door, she tried to leap at them. The chains crushed her. She floundered like a fish in a net. When they grabbed her arms, she screamed and kicked and tried to bite them. Clubs descended; one hit her shoulder, another her wrist. A guard backhanded her twice, so that her lips split, and her jaw screamed in pain.

She howled, blood in her mouth. She tried to summon her magic, to shift into a dragon. Fire tickled her maw. Scales began to appear across her. As her body grew, the chains tightened further, cutting off her breath. She gasped for air and her magic left her. Hands grabbed her wrists and bent them. She roared; she thought the guards would snap her bones. A knee drove into her stomach and she gasped. Pain was all she knew.

They yanked her arms up, and manacles closed around her wrists. Chains tightened, pulling her toward the ceiling. She screamed. Her heels left the floor; she remained standing on her toes. The guards pulled the gilded cage outside the cell, leaving her hanging from the ceiling.

Her captors shuffled outside. All but the scarred guard with the hissing laughter remained. He stared at the hanging Lyana; his eyes were red behind his helm. She stared into those eyes and bared her teeth.

"I will kill you some day," she said softly. There was no emotion to her voice, no rage, no fear; she was not speaking a mere threat, but a cold fact.

The guard stared at her for a moment longer, then began to slowly remove his helm. Lyana grimaced and disgust swelled inside her. His head was nothing but a scar; it looked like a clump of wet, white cloth. He hissed through a toothless mouth; it looked like a mere slit in leather.

"Kill me?" he said. He laughed, a sound more like a cough. "I used to hang in this cell, girl. I hung here as they doused me with wyvern acid." He coughed and spat. "For a year I served my sentence. Now I watch others suffer like I did. Kill me? Soon you will want to kill yourself more than me."

He turned around, left the chamber, and slammed the cell door behind him.

Darkness filled Lyana's world. She heard nothing but a hundred screams.

ELETHOR

They sat in the palace war room, a towering chamber with brick walls, a shadowy dome, and an oak table so wide and heavy a dragon could sleep upon it. Torches flickered in the walls and thick curtains hid the windows. Seven seats, taller than warriors, stood around the table.

Elethor looked around the room, eying each person in turn. The highborn of Requiem sat before him.

"We have word from the south," he said. "Lady Lyana reports that armies muster, that Tiranor plans to strike at summer solstice." He jabbed his finger against a parchment map that lay across the table. "Solina will strike here, at Ralora Beach, southeast of Castellum Luna. The invasion is eight days away."

The seated highborn looked at one another, brows furrowed. At the head of the table sat House Aeternum: himself and Princess Mori. Once three more chairs had stood here: one for his father, one for his mother, and one for Prince Orin. Now only he and Mori remained, the last survivors of their ancient dynasty.

To their right sat the great House Eleison: Lord Deramon, captain of the Guard; his wife Adia, High Priestess; and their son Bayrin, guard to the princess. One seat stood empty like a missing tooth in an aching gum: Lyana's seat. When Elethor looked upon that chair, ice filled him.

At the table's left side, a man and woman shifted uncomfortably. Both wore green fabrics embroidered with the sigil of their house, a golden stalk of wheat. Both were graying, thin, and shrewd. The man was Lord Ferenor Oldnale, the woman his wife, the Lady Alyn—the parents of Lady Treale who had returned the bodies to Nova Vita. Young Treale herself sat at their side, clad in armor, her hair hidden beneath her helm. The Oldnales owned great lands outside the city; they ruled farmers and shepherds, and in the war room, they stared at one another somberly, then at their king.

"My lord," said Lord Ferenor. He rose to his feet, bowed his hoary head, and stared from under his brows. "We have suffered greatly in Requiem. Two wars against Tiranor already... I fought in the first one thirty years ago. My two sons fell in the second last year." He shook his head, his voice cracked, and tears filled his eyes. "We cannot bear a third war. Fly out to Tiranor! Meet its queen. Sit with Solina at her table and treat with her. The time has come for peace."

Lord Deramon, burly and bearded, rose to his feet so roughly his chair nearly toppled over.

"Treat with the woman who burned our city!" he blustered. "Make peace with... with that devil who slew our children underground?" He pounded his fists against the tabletop. "Lord Ferenor, your sons were honorable men. I mourn them. But your mind has gone soft with your grief! Let warriors speak here tonight, not farmers."

Ferenor stiffened and his cheeks flushed. "Lord Deramon, calm yourself. Warriors have ruled over Requiem for long enough. What have you warriors brought us? Not surprisingly: war. Perhaps now is the time for farmers' counsel." He smoothed his tunic. "Yes, Solina burned our city and slew our children. Did we not do the same to Tiranor thirty years ago? She is an enemy, yes. You make peace not with friends, but with enemies."

Deramon growled so loudly he could have been standing in dragon form. "Where were you, Ferenor, when Solina's men poured into our tunnels? Where were you when she was burning our children, when I was swinging my axe and sword into the skulls of her men? I did not see you in the battlefield. After you've faced ten thousand men with hatred in their eyes and blades dripping Vir Requis blood, come to me and speak of making peace."

"And I suppose you want to face ten thousand more men!" Ferenor said, pulling himself as tall and straight as he could. "I suppose you want to see more blades dripping our blood! Put down your sword and axe, Deramon. Lift a plow and a pitchfork; our people need them more than your weapons."

Deramon reached for that sword and axe, which hung on his belt. Bayrin leaped to his feet and grabbed his own sword's hilt. Treale cried out in horror and tried to pull her father back into his seat. Before steel could be drawn, Elethor rose to his feet and raised his hands.

"Calm yourselves!" he demanded. "Deramon, Bayrin, sit down! Ferenor, you too. We've come here to talk, maybe to shout, but not to fight. Down, all of you."

Their eyes shooting daggers, they sat down, though Deramon kept his hands clenched around his weapons. Bayrin sat grumbling, his face nearly as red as his hair. For a moment, everyone sat stewing and staring at one another. Elethor continued.

"Three thousand warriors of the Royal Army train here in Nova City," he said. "Most are young and green, yes, but they will fight bravely. I will lead them to Ralora Beach and meet Solina in battle."

Again the room rose in shouts.

"This is madness!" said Lord Ferenor, leaping to his feet again. "Three thousand warriors? They are mere boys and girls!"

Bayrin actually jumped onto his chair, pounded the air, and shouted. "Boys and girls with more courage than you, Ferenor!"

Ferenor's wife, the Lady Oldnale, was shouting at Bayrin to sit down and stop making a fool of himself. Deramon was growling. Mother Adia raised her hands and cried for calm. Mori cowered in her chair and whimpered, and Treale rushed over to comfort her. Elethor clenched his fists at his sides and closed his eyes. The voices rang through his head, spinning like the voices of the creatures he had seen in the Abyss.

We must turn the screws, skeleys! the shriveled creatures had said, mere spines wrapped in skin. *We must count the hairs that grow sideways!* They all spun around him, laughing and smacking their gums.

No one will know, Elethor thought. *No one will know of those nightmares Lyana and I saw. No one can know the true darkness of the world but me and her.*

He felt a hand on his shoulder. He opened his eyes to see Mori at his side, looking at him in concern. He patted her hand and looked back at the council.

"Lord Ferenor," he said to the blustering lord. "I understand your concern. Truly I do. Your daughter serves in the Royal Army. My betrothed does too; so did my brother. But I know Solina. She will not offer us peace. She comes to kill us. She comes to kill every last Vir Requis and topple our halls. There is only one thing we can do against the tide from Tiranor; face it in battle."

Bayrin shouted approval and slammed his fist into his palm. Ferenor, however, seemed unswayed. He raised his nose and snorted.

"Solina cares not about my daughter, nor my farms, nor your fine halls of marble." He pointed a shaking finger at Elethor. "She hates *you*, Elethor. You alone, you and your family. Why should my farms burn and my daughter fight for a feud between you and her?" He raised his voice above the shouts around him. "She killed your father and you want revenge! That's all this is about. And the sons and daughters of Requiem will die for your pride!"

Everyone shouted so loudly Elethor could only make out random words. Deramon shouted something about Ferenor being the greatest coward in Requiem, while Lady Oldnale cried that Deramon was a bloodthirsty brute. Robes swaying and hands trembling, Ferenor was shouting at Elethor; he could hear only "warmonger!" repeated over and over.

Rage boiled in him. Elethor clenched his fists, wishing Lyana were here with him; he thought that his betrothed could outshout them all. *But for now you are away, Lyana, so I'll have to do the loudest shouting.*

"Settle down!" he cried. "Sit down, everyone! Deramon! Bayrin! Sit down and take your hands off your swords. Ferenor, calm yourself! *Warmonger* you call me? War is coming whether we like it or not. A host flies to Requiem; what would you have us do rather than face it? Cower in our holes and wait for death?"

"I would have you make peace!" Ferenor shouted. "I would have you solve your conflict with Solina using words, not fire and steel. You will doom us to more death! When children die, their blood will be upon you!"

With that, Ferenor Oldnale kicked his chair down. It crashed to the floor. With a flourish, he wrapped his cloak tightly around him, spun on his heels, and marched out the door. His wife followed, snorting and giving the council a last dirty look before disappearing outside. Lady Treale bit her lip and lowered her eyes as she trailed after the pair; she looked back at the council guiltily, whispered an apology, then followed her parents outside. Bayrin shouted after them, shaking his fist and cursing their house, and it was long moments before those remaining in the room settled down and stewed silently.

Peace, Elethor thought. *Could he make peace with Solina? Could he meet her at Ralora Beach, treat with her, and avoid this war?*

He looked at Mother Adia, who had mostly remained silent. She stared at him, her eyes deep pools. Again she reminded him of the marble statues he would carve, stoic and pale and strong.

"Adia," Elethor said, "you are a priestess, a healer, a woman of peace. What do the stars tell you? Can we truly avoid this war?"

She stared at him steadily, and starlight seemed to swirl in her eyes. She stood straight and tall, then spoke in a voice like the song of the sky.

"I saw the bodies of children torn apart. I saw the men who slew them. I saw Solina burn the wounded I tried to heal. Elethor, there will be no peace with this queen. She flies here with one purpose: to kill us all." She reached across the table and grabbed his hands. "You must stop her from reaching this place. You must meet her in battle, crush her host, and cast her back into the desert."

"Stars yeah!" Bayrin said and pounded the tabletop. "It's wyvern killing time."

Elethor looked at the map on the table. He ran his fingers across the mountains, valleys, and seas. *Ralora Beach. That is where I'll see her again—Solina, love and bane of my life. The woman I kissed so many times, the woman I sculpted and pined for... the woman I must kill.* He looked up at what remained of his council.

"Deramon and Bayrin. Stay here with the City Guard. Protect Nova Vita." He turned to Adia. "Adia, pray for us. Prepare to heal us." Finally he looked at his sister, and his voice softened. "Mori, while I fly to the south, you will be the only Aeternum in Nova Vita. Sit upon the throne until I return. You rule in my stead."

She nodded, lips trembling but eyes staring at him steadily. He turned to leave, but Mori caught his arm, then pulled him into an embrace.

"Be careful, El," she whispered. She looked up at him with wet eyes. "Please, El. Please be careful. Be strong. I will pray for you. I will protect our city while you're away."

He held her tight and kissed her forehead. She felt like a trembling leaf in his arms. She was his last living family, his most precious soul.

"I'll be back soon, Mori. I promise you." He held her hands tight and looked into her eyes. "I promise."

Long arms wrapped around them and squeezed—Bayrin joining the embrace, tall and knobby, his shock of red curls pressed against their faces. Elethor was short of breath before he freed himself from the crushing hug. When he did, he and Bayrin clutched each other's shoulders.

"Fly high, El," his friend said, eyes somber. "And if you see Solina, by the stars, this time just kill her quickly."

He sighed, remembering the time he had let her scar his face, let her escape from him. "I will." He squeezed Bayrin's shoulder. "And you, Bay, guard my sister well. If you don't, I'm going to hang you up beside that dead wyvern."

Next he shared a crushing handshake with Deramon; the burly lord grumbled something about killing a few dozen Tirans for him. Finally Elethor embraced Mother Adia, who was as soft and warm as Deramon was cold and steely. The priestess kissed his forehead and whispered a prayer.

"May you always find Requiem's sky, my king." Adia smiled and touched his cheek. "I will await you upon the walls of your city, son of Draco, and I will pray for you."

Her embrace was like starlight wrapping around him in a cocoon, forever warm and guiding his way. He ached for it when they parted.

His throat tightened and his eyes stung. He turned and left the chamber.

Outside the palace, he shifted into a dragon and soared into the night. He let flames fill his maw, and he shook his body to hear his scales rattle. The city rolled beneath him, silver under the moonlight. Elethor looked upon the rows of homes and workshops, the palace below him, the temple ahead, and the white walls like a crown rising from King's Forest.

"I won't let you fall again, Nova Vita," he swore into the wind.

He descended toward Castra Draco, fortress of the Royal Army, whose four towers rose white and tall, their banners undulating. Elethor flew above the battlements and roared his call.

"Warriors of Requiem!" he cried. "Soldiers of the Royal Army! The time has come to spread your wings, to blow your fire, to fly to war. Sound the horns of battle! Arise, warriors of Requiem!"

Atop the four towers great horns blew. The sound keened across the city, deep as the years of Requiem—a peal of ancient song, of runes in stone, of the age and light of stars.

"Arise and fly, dragons of Requiem!" Elethor called as the horns of Requiem blew.

Armored men and women began streaming from the fortress. In the courtyard, they shifted into dragons and soared, firelight dancing between their fangs. Elethor growled and began flying south, wind roaring beneath his wings. He blew flame in the night, a beacon of war. Behind him, hundreds of dragons flew, soon thousands.

"Fly, Royal Army! We fly south! We fly to war."

The dragons soared. Flames rose in pillars. The city turned orange below them, and people emerged from their homes to wave and sing prayers.

Elethor dived into the night. Behind him, thousands of dragons flew and roared their song.

SOLINA

As she descended the stairs, rage simmered in her, a white-hot forge. She clenched her fists, gritted her teeth, and her breath hissed.

"Lyana," she whispered, almost able to taste the name's foulness on her tongue; it tasted like congealing blood.

At the bottom of the stairway, a doorway led into her tunnel of triumph. As she walked, boots clanking, she smiled to hear the screams, to see the twisting bodies, to smell the acid that ate through flesh and bone. Her enemies twitched and begged for death in every cell: those nobles foolish enough to oppose her plans, and those soldiers too weak and slow when she had drilled them. Their families too hung here, flayed and whipped and cut and burnt, wives and children alike.

Good, Solina thought, smiling as she walked by cell after cell. *They suffer for their disobedience, and Lyana the weredragon will suffer most among them.*

A child screamed from one cell; he hung from the wall, body blackened.

"Please, my queen," he begged. "Please."

She nodded to him as she walked by. "I will give you mercy, child. I will let you die once your body can bear no more."

The child was a fellow Tiran. Even if his father was a traitor, his blood was pure, and he deserved eventual death. But Lyana... Solina snarled and dug her fingernails into her palms. Lyana was a weredragon, a filthy shapeshifter. She deserved no such mercy. She would live to a ripe, miserable old age.

Finally she reached the weredragon's cell, the smallest and darkest cell in this dungeon. Solina opened the heavy, blood-stained door and stepped inside. Her snarl turned into a smile.

A single torch flickered upon the wall, casting orange light against the beast. Lyana hung from the ceiling on chains, head lowered, her hair dangling. More chains wrapped around her torso and legs, keeping her in human form. She stood on her toes; her shackles would not let her heels touch the floor. Tatters of a silk garment covered her, barely concealing her bruised flesh.

"Lyana," Solina said softly.

The weredragon raised her head and stared. A bruise spread across her cheek, and her lip was swollen, and yet she glared with blazing hatred.

Solina's smile widened. "You still have your spirit," she said and drew a razor from her belt. "That's good... that's good. I will enjoy breaking it."

Solina inhaled deeply, savoring Lyana's scent of fear. The memories swirled in the darkness like ghosts. *Can't you fly, Solina? Can't you fly?* The little girl with red curls laughed and danced around her. *Look, I can become a dragon! Can't you fly too?*

Solina clenched her jaw and raised her razor. The torchlight blazed against it, and a flicker of fear filled Lyana's eyes.

Good, Solina thought. *Good.*

"Your hair," she said. "You have straightened your curls. You have dyed them platinum. You try to appear as a Tiran, but we smelled your dirty blood. You mock our pure, noble race with your treachery." She took a step forward, razor raised. "I will strip you of this mockery."

She grabbed Lyana's hair, pulled it, and began shearing. She gritted her teeth as she worked, tearing nearly as much hair as she cut. She moved the razor roughly against Lyana's head, scraping her scalp; blood beaded upon it. Lyana glared and snarled, but said nothing. Rage simmered in her eyes, amusing Solina; she smirked when she examined her work. Lyana stood bald before her, head bloodied.

"Much better," she said, nodding. "The world will see you for what you are: a filthy creature. I've stripped you of the hair that mocks us. I will now remove that glare from your eyes."

Solina reached into the pouch on her belt. She withdrew a glass vial. The liquid inside swirled, milky white tinged with green tendrils. She broke the wax seal with her thumb, and a scent like vinegar and apples filled her nostrils, sour but not unpleasant. Lyana, however, winced and bit down hard, and her fists clenched.

"Do you know what this is, Lyana?" Solina asked, holding the vial out. When it neared the chained Lyana, the weredragon hissed and turned her head aside. "It is a rare herb, one that grows in Osanna across the sea. Laceleaf, they call it there; they use it in their cooking. The weredragons have a different name for it, don't they? *Ilbane* you call it, I am told. A poison to your wretched kind. They say just the touch of its leaf can burn you; here I carry its pure latex."

Lyana snarled and looked aside, eyes reddening. "Ilbane has not grown in the world for hundreds of years."

"Then this should not harm you in the slightest."

She splashed the vial onto Lyana's face.

The weredragon clenched her jaw and growled. Her fists shook and her body writhed. Her skin reddened where the liquid touched her. She hissed, sucked her breath, then finally tossed back her head and howled. Solina watched, smiling softly.

"It burns, does it not?" She shook her head sadly. "I would use acid on you, child, were not my Lord Mahrdor so smitten with your pretty face." She caressed Lyana's cheek. "For now I will leave your face pretty... but I will hurt you. I will hurt you badly. You will scream for me like nobody has screamed before."

She pulled another vial from her pouch. A dozen more clinked inside. Lyana saw the collection, paled, and closed her eyes. A tear flowed to her lips.

"Solina, please," she whispered.

Solina laughed. "You are begging so soon?" She shook her head sadly. "I begged too as a child when you mocked me, when you called me a stranger. I begged the Sun God to free me from your prison. I begged too as a woman when your betrothed burned me and left me scarred. And I begged Elethor. I begged him to be mine, to rule with me in Tiranor... but he chose you instead." She broke the seal off her second vial. "From my childhood until today you hurt me, weredragon. You mocked me. You stole my love. And now you spy on my kingdom. And yes, you will beg now. You will beg all night and for every night hence."

She smiled and raised the second vial.

For an hour she worked—spilling the sap across Lyana, watching it burn her, hearing her scream. She forced it down her throat. She splashed it into her eyes. She smeared it across her until the weredragon shook and wept. When finally her vials were empty, she unlocked the chains that bound Lyana to the ceiling. She watched the wretched creature fall to her knees, trembling and smoking.

"Guards!" she cried.

She stood smiling, hands on hips, as her guards entered the room and lifted the weredragon. Solina began walking upstairs, out of shadow and into sunlight. As the guards dragged Lyana behind her, the chained wretch barely struggled. Her feet dragged and blood trickled down her chin. Even if chains were not still binding her, Solina doubted the girl could muster enough strength to become a dragon now.

They dragged Lyana out of the palace, through a garden of fig trees, and into a courtyard. A snowy mare waited there—White Flame, Solina's favorite mount, the finest beast from her stables. The horse nickered and tossed her head, chinking the golden rings that filled her mane. Lyana slumped, the guards holding her up. She coughed weakly and spat blood.

"Chain her," Solina said.

The guards pulled Lyana's arms forward, manacled her wrists, and ran a chain between them to White Flame's saddle. Solina mounted her mare, stroked her mane, and kneed her.

White Flame began to walk. Solina smiled upon the saddle. Lyana shuffled behind, coughing and struggling for breath.

"Weredragons think themselves a noble race!" Solina said. Her guards marched at her sides, spears thudding against the cobblestones. "Look at this one. Look how she walks behind me, chained and bruised. How noble she is!"

They crossed the courtyard, rode through a vineyard, and entered the sun-drenched streets of Irys.

Thousands of men, women, and children roared—they crowded the streets, covered the roofs, and stared from their windows. They howled at the sight of Solina and the chained weredragon. As Solina rode and Lyana limped behind, the people shouted and jeered.

"Weredragon!" one cried.

"Murderer!"

"Monster!"

Somebody tossed a rock. It struck Lyana's shoulder and drew blood. Another tossed a soiled swaddling cloth. Soon hundreds were tossing refuse at the chained, limping weredragon. Solina smiled as she rode, keeping the chain tight; it was long enough that none of the trash could hit her. She kneed her horse to a faster clip. Lyana fell, was dragged several feet, and barely struggled back onto her feet. Blood trickled down her elbows.

She is no longer screaming, Solina thought in distaste. Her lip curled. *She will scream more before this day is over. The entire city will hear it.*

As she rode, she thought of Elethor—her pure, handsome prince, the love of her life, the fire of her youth. He had rejected her, swung his sword at her, cast her out... and chosen this Lyana, this filthy weredragon, instead. Solina growled. She was a great queen, a beautiful monarch clad in gold and splendor and sunlight. Behind her dragged a bloody, filthy wretch, half alive, a mere creature, not a woman to love.

"You will see, Elethor," she whispered. "I will bring this Lyana with me to Requiem, and you will see her filth, her monstrosity. She will be broken when you see her again, a crushed insect, and I will be glorious."

She rode all morning as the crowds jeered. Lyana coughed and struggled for breath, her feet bloody, her eyes rolling. When the sun hit its zenith and her lord's fire burned brightest, Solina rode across the Square of the Sun, heading back toward her palace. The Palace of Phoebus, her ancestral home, loomed above her—an ancient edifice of towers and battlements. A limestone staircase, fifty feet wide and glittering white, led from the courtyard toward the palace gates, where two faceless stone warriors stood, a hundred feet tall. At the foot of this staircase she halted White Flame and dismounted.

Lyana collapsed onto the cobblestones. Thousands of people filled the square, howling in rage, tossing rotten fruit onto the weredragon.

"Stand her up," Solina said to her guards. "Take her up the steps to the Faceless Guardians where we burned the last one."

A smile on her face, Solina began walking up the steps of her palace, heading toward its gates. Behind her, her guards grabbed Lyana under her arms, hoisted up the bloody creature, and dragged her upstairs. As Solina climbed, her smile grew, and her lord's light filled her eyes. The glory of Tiranor and the Phoebus Dynasty rose above her, stone kissed with gold. Sunbeams flared around the Tower of Akartum, the tallest steeple in Tiranor, blessing her.

Finally they reached the Faceless Guardians, two statues of stone that protected her home; they had stood here for three thousand years, and even the dragons of Requiem had been unable to topple them. The guards chained Lyana between the two statues, one arm bound to each, so that she stood stretched between them. The weredragon's head hung low, and blood trickled down her chin.

Solina approached her captive, touched the blood on her cheek, and leaned close.

"This is where we killed your friend Silas," she whispered. "Are you frightened, Lyana?"

The weredragon looked up. Pain filled her eyes... but rage too. Deep, simmering rage, two forge fires. Blood and bruises covered her face, but Lyana managed to growl.

"You may kill me," the weredragon said, "but the wrath of Requiem will fly upon you, Solina. You will burn forever in the flames."

Solina laughed. "So much spirit still left to break; it is a wonder. You are making this day more enjoyable than I could have imagined." She whispered into Lyana's ear. "And your spirit *will* break, Lyana. It will break today. I was merciful to Silas; I let him die.

You will receive no such mercy, not for many years." She turned toward her guards. "Beat her. Beat her so the city hears her screams."

She stepped back. The guards stepped forward, whips in hand. And they beat her. And she screamed. And the city heard.

The crowds howled. The whips lashed. Blood fell upon the stones of her palace.

When Lyana fell unconscious and her guards lowered their lashes, Solina glared at them.

"You will beat her until I tell you to stop."

The beating continued. The sunlight flared across them, a blaze of glory and justice.

ELETHOR

As sunset spilled over the field, the sounds of the camp rose like music: soldiers talking and coughing, spoons clattering in bowls, and ravens cawing as they circled overhead. Three thousand Vir Requis sat upon boulders and grass, eating and drinking, boasting of how many Tirans they'd kill, laughing at rude jokes, and remembering their homes. One man began to sing Old Requiem Woods, an ancient song; others soon joined him, and the song swept through the camp, and even the most dour and frightened hummed and smiled.

"Two days from Nova Vita," Elethor whispered. "Four days from the sea where I'll meet Solina again."

He stood upon a hillock, apart from the others. He was not much older than these soldiers—a young king of only twenty-six summers, his father fallen too soon. And yet he felt decades more ancient, an old man with the weight of an ancient race upon his shoulders. The wind tousled his hair and filled his nostrils with the scents of cooking meats, strong ale, sweat, and grass. He looked upon this camp and thought about Lyana, and the summer night felt cold.

"Fly back to us," he whispered. "Be safe."

A young woman detached from the camp and came walking uphill toward him. She wore a breastplate engraved with a stalk of wheat, and a sword hung from her hip. When she came closer, Elethor recognized her smooth black hair, olive skin, and dark eyes: the Lady Treale Oldnale, squire to Lyana. When she reached him, she held out two steaming bowls of stew.

"My king," she said and bowed her head. "I thought you might be hungry. Please, would you eat with me? I have some bread in my pack too and a full wineskin."

She looked up at him expectedly. A short and slim girl, Lady Treale was of an age with Mori—not yet twenty—and a friend to the princess. As Elethor watched her, he remembered fighting Tiran soldiers in the tunnels—towering men twice Treale's size, bloodlust in their eyes. How long would Treale last in battle against them, and if they let her live, would she beg them for death? An image flashed through his mind: young Treale trapped underground, sliced with swords, screaming as desert warriors mounted her. He clenched his jaw, banishing the thought.

He sat down and patted the grass beside him. "Come, Lady Treale. Sit beside me. Let us share a meal and wine."

She sat beside him in the grass and wriggled until she was comfortable. They ate silently for long moments, watching the camp. The singing below died, soon replaced with gales of laughter over rude jokes.

"Not much like my father's army," Elethor said with a sigh. "Those were hard men; they ate with grim purpose, fuel for battle. I rarely heard them laugh."

Treale chewed a crust of bread. "These ones are nervous. I lead a phalanx of a hundred warriors; they are younger than me, and I'm not yet twenty. Most have only held plows until this year; others have only held quills. Several of my warriors are fifteen years old; some of the boys are too young to shave." She heaved a sigh. "Let them boast of the Tirans they will kill, my lord. Let them laugh at their jests and sing their songs. It drowns their terror." She looked at him, and he could see her own fear behind her eyes. "It is better than terror."

Elethor sighed too. He placed his spoon down in his empty bowl. "Your father thinks me a fool. He tells me to make peace with Solina, not lead these youths to war. When we meet Tiranor's army, we will not face the children of farmers. We will meet hard men from a cruel land, bred to kill for their Sun God; women too, brides to the blade, desert warriors who shave the sides of their heads, pierce their lips with rings, and lust for the blood of dragons." He looked at Treale. "They do not tell jokes around their campfires this night. They do not laugh nervously to hide their fear. They do not sing old folk songs. They sharpen spearheads and howl for blood. Each of these warriors will ride a wyvern, cruel beasts with scales harder than ours and acid crueler than our fire. They will fly in perfect formations. They will not scatter in battle. They will each fight to the death."

Treale paled and clutched her spoon as if it were a sword. She tightened her lips and raised her head.

"Do we stand a chance?" she whispered.

Elethor looked down at the camp. Two boys were chasing each other around a fire, swinging swords in mock battle. They laughed, the high laugh of youths; they were barely old enough to even be called youths.

"I don't know," he said softly. "Your parents think not. What do you think, Lady Treale? Your father calls for me to make peace; by that, he means me to surrender. And yet you are here, clad in armor, fighting for your king. Tell me your thoughts."

She placed down her empty bowl, uncorked her wineskin, and drank deeply. "I'm frightened," she finally said. "And I don't know if we can win this war. But..." She looked into the night, for a moment lost in thought. She looked back at him. "My lord, my brothers fought for King Olasar. They died over King's Forest. It broke my father's heart; mine too. It's been over a year, and I still weep for them most nights. They were raised to be farmlords, not warriors, yet they fought for their king." The firelight danced in her eyes. "I will fight for mine."

He reached out and clasped her hand around the wineskin. His eyes stung. "You are brave, Lady Treale. You are brave like the knight you squire for. I am honored to fight by your side."

She smiled and rolled her eyes. "Brave like Lady Lyana? That I am not. She is a great warrior and a true bellator! The last of her kind. My brothers were knights too, and they often spoke of her courage; they said she could best any man in swordplay. You walked with her through the Abyss itself! A land of horror." She shivered. "I can only wish to be as brave; my insides quiver now to think of it. You are most lucky to be her betrothed."

Elethor took the wineskin from her and drank. It was good, strong wine from the southern vineyards on the coast; dry and warm in his throat.

"Lyana is strong," he said, "and wise, and brave. She is our greatest warrior. My brother Orin was such a warrior; his men adored him. I did too, as did Lyana." He drank again.

Treale reached out, hesitant, and touched his arm. Her eyes were soft. "You are a good man for her, my king. You too are strong and brave; you will be a fine husband to Lady Lyana."

He raised his eyebrows and blew out his breath. "Oh, Lyana needs no good man, nor fine husband; not since Orin died. But the land has its laws; I am to care for her after Orin fell. Do you know why such laws exist, Treale?" When she shook his head, he continued. "In the old days, the women of Requiem had less power than today. They could not serve in the army, nor own land, nor possess wealth. They were dependant on their fathers and then their husbands. Widows could become destitute, and so living brothers took them as wives—to protect them. Lyana does not need my protection—she's always been strong—but the old laws remain. We both respect them. And I love Lyana; I can think of no better queen."

She kept her hand on his arm. "And yet... you once loved another," she whispered.

Her eyes were soft, her lips parted. Elethor knew then that she too had once loved and lost; perhaps a young man fallen in the war.

"Yes," he said softly. "I once loved another."

I loved Solina like wine, like sunrise after darkness, like fire in the cold. For years she lit my life; for years after she left Requiem, the pain of losing her hollowed me.

Yet he could not tell these things to Treale, just as she would not speak of the lost love that filled her own eyes. She gazed at him softly, then shook her head wildly and rose to her feet. She brushed crumbs off her as if trying to brush off memories.

"I'm betrothed in an arranged marriage too," she said, "to some horrible, pompous farmlord." She thrust out her chest, swung her arms, and walked in an exaggerated swagger. Then she sighed and her arms drooped. "And he's nearly twice my age! Oh, my stars; sometimes I wish I were a commoner, not the daughter of a highborn father." She gave him a sidelong glance. "Don't you ever wish the same, my lord? To... to marry whoever you truly loved, not whoever the laws of the land require you to love?"

He thought of Solina: the flame of his youth, the light he had carried for so many years. She had been passion and sweet unending pain. She had been forbidden and banished. Lady Lyana... did he feel the same toward her?

It had been a year since he'd seen Lyana, and he missed her, and he loved her—he knew that he did—and yet... he could not stop the doubts from whispering. As Requiem's ancient laws decreed, men inherited the wives of fallen brothers—to protect and provide for them. Yet Lyana needed no protection from him; she was wiser than him, stronger in battle, and just as wealthy. How could he defend her, be a strong man she could depend on? He respected Requiem's laws, and he would marry his dead brother's betrothed, and Lyana told him that she loved him, but... did she truly? Before Orin's death, Lyana had glanced his way only to lecture him; was her love for him now true, or forged by ancient creed?

As these thoughts filled him, he couldn't help but notice Treale's beauty; her lips were full, her skin smooth, her hair a cascade of midnight. Her armor fit snugly against her body, hinting at the curves beneath. She looked at him with huge, admiring eyes, a young woman in the presence of her king. What would it be like, Elethor wondered, to choose a bride himself—a bride like Treale, a pretty young maiden who looked up to him? Could he have been happy with her? Treale saw him as a great king, a leader, a strong man, not the younger brother of a fallen prince, not some... consolation prize.

He thought of Bayrin, his closest friend. Bayrin had such a love—he had Mori, a woman who adored him, a soft and loving woman to protect. With somebody like Treale, could Elethor have that too? With Lyana, he always struggled to appear strong enough, wise enough, noble enough... and he always felt like he failed, like no matter what he did, he fell short of Orin, fell short of the hero Lyana deserved. As Treale looked at him with her large eyes, he understood how Bayrin felt with Mori; he felt strong, a powerful man with a woman to defend.

And she wants me, Elethor thought, staring into Treale's eyes; she stared back, lips parted, chest rising and falling. *I can see it in her eyes. If I want her, she is mine.*

He lowered his head, tearing his gaze away. Guilt flooded him. Lyana was spying in Tiranor, risking her life for him; how could he think such thoughts? And yet he thought them, and he could not speak of them—not to Treale, and perhaps not to anyone.

He looked back at the young squire. "I love the Lady Lyana. She is strong. She is wise. She will be a fine queen."

Treale bit her lip and nodded. She sat back down and lowered her eyes. "Yes, she is all those things. I love her too! Truly I do. It's an honor to squire for her." She looked back up at him. "I'm sure she will be a fine queen for you and that your love will grow. You both deserve it, my lord; I know how much you suffered."

He leaned back and let his fingers play with the grass. He watched the campfires below, hundreds of flickering stars.

"I never wanted to be king, you know," he said. He laughed softly. "Shocking, I'm sure; the whole kingdom knows it, I reckon. I wanted to be a sculptor. I *was* a sculptor. But Lyana... this is what she was born for. I've known her all her life; from the time she could talk, she spoke of being a knight, and a heroine, and a queen someday. She is those first two things already; she will be the latter soon enough." He turned his head and looked at Treale. The firelight painted her face and danced in her eyes. "What of you, Lady Treale Oldnale? Did you always dream of being a knight?"

She smiled softly. "Oh stars, no. I never held a sword until a year ago. Not what you want to hear on the eve of battle, I'm sure, but it's the truth. I always wanted to be... oh, it's terribly silly." She blushed and stared at him pleadingly. "Promise you won't laugh if I tell you. Will you promise? All right. I always wanted to be... a puppeteer." She made a soft squealing sound and covered her face. "Horrible, isn't it? But..." She peeked between her fingers. "I've always loved puppets. I used to watch them as a child at the farm fairs—the puppet shows with Kyrie and Agnus Dei, who would always fight and bicker, but loved each other dearly. My mother used to tell me I looked like Agnus Dei—the real one from the stories, not the puppet. Do you know? Our family is descended from her and Kyrie, that's what Father says."

Elethor nodded and sighed. "Oh, I had to spend many painful hours studying lineage in my youth, tracing the lines of the families from the Living Seven. My teachers used to bore me half to death with tales of Agnus Dei's grandson moving east, settling the plains, and founding your house. Dreadfully dull lessons."

She snorted a laugh. "They are less dull when puppets perform them at farmers' fairs. I still remember the taste of blackberries, and the sound of the flutists, and how my brothers would insist we go see the cattle. But I always wanted to watch the puppets. I was only eight years old when I sewed my own Kyrie and Agnus Dei dolls—I made them from my old dresses and pillows—and my parents roared with pleasure when I put on a show. I knew then that I wanted to do nothing else. I wanted to make puppets—rooms of them, *castles* full of them—enough for countless fairs." She sighed and her eyes saddened. "But then... then the war broke out. The phoenixes invaded, and my brothers fell in battle, and... well, it seemed wrong to sew puppets when war raged. So I took my oldest brother's sword and shield, flew to the capital, and well... here I am today." She played with a blade of grass. "It's not much of a story, my lord, not as impressive as yours or Lyana's. I did not walk through the Abyss nor fight in the tunnels. I switched a needle for a sword, farmlands for barracks; that is my tale."

The sun had disappeared beyond the horizon while they spoke; only a dim glow now painted the west. The stars winked between clouds; Elethor could see only the tail of the dragon, the last few stars of the Draco constellation.

Below in the field, the soldiers were unrolling their blankets and lying down to sleep under the stars. The night's first guards shifted into dragons, took flight, and began circling over the camp. Weariness crept over Elethor; they had flown hard for hours and his body ached.

"This hill is a good place for sleep," he said. "The grass is soft, the air fresh, and guards patrol above us." He yawned and stretched. "If you've not found a place to lie down, share the hill."

Treale yawned magnificently, a yawn that flowed across her body from toes to outstretched fingertips. She unbuckled her breastplate, unclasped her sword, and kicked off her boots. She hesitated for a moment, looked down and up again, then leaned forward and kissed his cheek. Her lips were soft and warm. Then, blushing, she lay down at his side, placed her cheek upon her hands, and was soon asleep.

Elethor watched her for a moment, smiling softly. He remembered a day long ago when Treale and Mori—mere children then—had placed a toad on his dinner plate, then fled the hall giggling and shrieking.

Mori would always delight in the Oldnales visiting Nova Vita, he remembered. *She would speak for days of her friend Treale coming to see her and would cry whenever Treale flew home.*

It did not seem so long ago; the years had gone by in a daze, and now Mori sat upon the throne, and Treale flew to battle at his side. Elethor lay down beside the young noblewoman, looked up at the stars, and found that his weariness had left him. How could he sleep with all these souls—his sister, his soldiers, and his people at home—depending on him? How could he lead them to war like his father had?

He rolled over so that he faced Treale. He drew comfort from the peacefulness of her slumber—the smoothness of her face, the rise and fall of her breast, and the breeze in her dark hair. He closed his eyes and finally sleep found him too, and he dreamed of hot desert winds, thrusting spears, and sandstone towers rising from dunes.

MORI

Whenever Lord Deramon entered the palace hall, Mori felt faint. Today he stormed in with all his usual bluster, bowed curtly, and stomped toward her. Sitting on her brother's throne, Mori cowered and wished the chair's twisting oak roots could swallow her. Her heart thrashed and she felt a trickle of cold sweat trail down her back.

"My princess!" Deramon called, a great bear of a man, his beard a red flame, his axe and sword clanking against his armor.

Mori's head spun as he approached. It was not that Deramon was a bad man—and after all, he was father to Bayrin and Lyana, two of the people she loved most. It was just that...

Oh stars, does he have to walk so fast? And do his eyebrows need to be so red and bushy? She tried to imagine those eyebrows not as flames that could burn her, but as two friendly caterpillars crawling above his eyes. The thought calmed her, and she even managed a tremulous smile.

"Lord Deramon," she said in a small voice.

He had soon crossed the hall and bowed, hands on his weapons. "My princess, the work on the tunnels is complete. Come with me; I will show you the fortifications."

Mori didn't want to go with him. She wanted to stay here, in the safety of the palace, with only columns of marble around her and Bayrin at her side. She looked over at Bayrin now; he stood as always by her throne, his armor bright and his sword at his side. He placed a hand on her shoulder and spoke softly.

"Are you ready, Mors? I'll be with you."

Mori looked between him and Deramon and shuddered. The city was just so... so *busy*, all bustling with masons and healers and carpenters. There would be wagons of bricks, and mules carrying lumber, and peasants storing food, and the sights and sounds would spin her head. She knew they would; they always did. Here in the palace there was silence, there was safety, there was soothing marble and the song of harps. She gave Bayrin another pleading look, but he only patted her shoulder and smiled comfortingly.

Mori lowered her head, bit her lip, and nodded. "I'm ready," she said in a small voice.

I am Princess of Requiem, she thought. *I will do my duty. With Elethor away, I rule here. I must protect my people, even if the city sounds will make my knees shake and my belly twist.*

They left the hall, stepped outside the doors, and stood for a moment on the hill. Mori gazed upon the city that rolled around her. She heard the sound of hammers on anvils, forging armor for men and dragons. Smoke plumed from smelters and dragons dragged wagons of iron ore from the mountain mines. Farmers wheeled carts down the streets, carrying preserves, wineskins, and dried fish into the tunnels. Dragons perched upon every wall, and men-at-arms guarded every street. The smells of smoke, oil, and sweat filled the air.

War, Mori thought. She took a deep breath, clutched her luck finger behind her back, and began walking downhill. *I will be brave. I will stand strong for my people.*

As they walked through the city, people bowed their heads and whispered blessings upon them. Hands reached out to touch Mori's gown; she knew these were signs of respect for their princess, but their touch frightened her. So many still bore the scars of last year's war. So many had burnt flesh, missing limbs, haunted eyes that spoke of their pain, or no more eyes at all. They spun around her, and her breath felt tight, and her chest ached, and again she saw him—Orin, charred and dying, his innards spilling, and Acribus grabbing her, and—

No, Mori, she told herself. She shut her eyes and forced a deep breath. *Don't think of that. Breathe. Just breathe.*

She forced herself to focus only on that breath—good, healing air entering and leaving her lungs. She focused on the feel of cobblestones beneath her feet and the light breeze on her face, and slowly her heartbeat slowed, and she opened her eyes. Once more the city was steady, and no more fog covered her vision.

Soon they reached Benedictus Archway, which rose from a cobbled square, leading into the tunnels. Two guards stood before it, spears crossed. They bowed their heads and parted for Mori. She stepped between them onto a steep, narrow staircase that plunged into darkness.

Deramon walked at her side. "The staircase is too narrow for wyverns, my lady. We made damn sure of that." He gestured at his feet. "And the stairs themselves are narrow, as you can see. If any Tirans charge down, they will crash in their armor."

As Mori descended and shadows spread, she found herself soothed. Her head cleared and her fingers no longer trembled. There was safety here underground, surrounded by stone. She kept walking, a hundred steps or more, until she reached a doorway. The doors towered above her, carved of oak banded in iron.

"If the Tirans invade, this is the first obstacle they'll face," Deramon said. "No battering ram will break through these doors; they're solid oak and iron, a good foot thick."

"Almost as thick as Lyana's head," Bayrin spoke up behind them.

Deramon pounded on the doors. "Open up, men!"

As the doors began to creak open, Bayrin muttered, "Solina won't need a battering ram; she just has to knock."

When the doors had opened, Mori saw five guards bearing pikes and shields. Longswords hung at their waists, their pommels shaped as dragonclaws. Deramon nodded to them and turned to Mori.

"If the Tirans invade the city, I'll place a hundred of these pikemen here. Even if Solina does break through these doors, she'll face blades of sharp, cruel steel."

"Almost as sharp as Lyana's tongue," Bayrin said. "And just as cruel."

Past the doors and pikemen, they walked down a tunnel. Its walls were craggy, and Mori ran her hand across the stone, drawing comfort from its cold roughness. Candles burned in alcoves, and pikes and swords hung from hooks. As they walked, Mori imagined thousands of people fleeing here into darkness, and she took deep breaths and bit her lip.

This is a safe place. A safe place.

The tunnel stretched two hundred yards, maybe more, before it reached another staircase. The steps were so narrow, Mori had to hold the wall for support. Finally they reached a portcullis, its bars shaped like dragon teeth. Beyond these iron jaws she saw more guards; they wore plate armor and bore crossbows and swords.

"If the Tirans claim the top level, they will be stopped here," Deramon said, voice a low rumble. "If war reaches this city, I'll place two hundred men here armed with enough crossbows and bolts to slay an army. The Tirans will pile up dead."

Bayrin tapped the jaw-like portcullis. "I like it. Judging by how crooked these iron teeth are, Lyana obviously modeled for them. Let's see what's next."

Deramon gestured at the guards, who pulled the portcullis open. Beyond the iron teeth, they walked down more tunnels, these ones so narrow they had to move single file. Mori walked between the two men, barely as tall as their shoulders. She wished she could spend her life here underground, Bayrin at her side, maybe with a good book too, one with maps. The air was cool here and the noise of the city gone.

If ever this war ends, she thought, *I will fill this place with books and scrolls and come here to read every day. Nobody can hurt me here.*

As they walked through this second level of tunnels, Deramon gestured at walls stocked with spears, crossbows, and shields. He spoke about filling this place with guards who would slay any Tiran warrior who reached this deep. Finally they reached a third barrier: great doors carved of solid bronze. More guards stood here, and when they pulled the doors open, Mori saw a cavern that plunged into darkness.

She entered and looked around, hands clasped behind her back. The cavern loomed around her, nearly as large as the palace throne room. Its walls and ceiling were craggy, still showing the claw marks of dragons. A hundred candles burned here. Alcoves in the walls held supplies: jars of apple preserves, strings of sausages, jugs of wine and ale, skins of water, and sacks of grain. Other shelves held more weapons: arrows and bows, swords, and spears. Through narrow passageways, Mori glimpsed more chambers, similarly sized and stacked.

"And this chamber," Bayrin said, "is as big and hollow as Lyana's head."

Mori explored the chamber. She ran her hand over the supplies and weapons, peered into the other chambers, and drank from an underground stream she found. It reminded her of Crescent Isle's great caves, the place where she had met the Children of the Moon last year; it seemed lifetimes ago. She knew what this place was for. The soldiers would guard the top two levels. Here the young, old, and wounded would hide.

"Here we will survive," she whispered.

She closed her eyes. She remembered fleeing into the dungeon of Castellum Luna as the phoenixes flew; they slew her brother there. She remembered fleeing into these very tunnels as the phoenixes burned the city; Solina had shattered their defenses and slain thousands. When she opened her eyes again, Mori's heart nearly stopped.

Twenty thousand bodies filled the chamber, twisted with acid, their skin like wet cloth. A few twitched and begged for death; most already lay dead. Blood sluiced her boots and Solina laughed, hands on her hips, like she had laughed when killing Orin. The dead reached out to Mori. Melting hands clutched at her gown, and faces like dripping wax begged her.

"Please, Mori, please, save us, kill us, please..."

They pawed at her, their skin melting, sticking to her, and dripping off their bones to stain her gown. Mori closed her eyes again.

No. I won't look at them. I will breathe like Mother Adia taught me.

She opened her eyes again and they were gone. She saw only Bayrin and Deramon standing several feet away, pointing at a blade and arguing about whether it was a longsword or a bastard sword. Finally Deramon snorted in disgust, shook his head at his son, and turned to Mori. He called her over, and she approached hesitantly.

He took her to a tapestry upon a wall, one she had sewn throughout her sixteenth year. Upon its blue fabric, embroidered dragons flew between silver stars, and white birches of glistening thread rose below them. Mori remembered working her fingers raw on the tapestry; it had taken her countless hours to make, and she had given it to Orin to hang in his chambers. She remembered how his eyes had widened to see it, how he had hugged her, and how they had flown that night to Lacrimosa Hill to gaze upon the real stars.

And now my tapestry too hides underground like all the memories of my life.

When Deramon pulled the tapestry aside, Mori's own eyes widened. A narrow tunnel gaped there, just wide enough for a man to crawl into. Mori peered into it; she could not judge its length, but when she called out, her voice echoed deep.

"My men have been carving this tunnel since the winter," Deramon said, standing behind her. His voice, normally booming, was strangely soft. "If all else fails, Mori—if the wyverns slam at the doors of these chambers—you will crawl into it."

She pulled her head out from the tunnel, turned toward Deramon, and shivered at the sight of his eyes; she had never seen the gruff old warrior look so sad.

"Where does the tunnel lead to?" she whispered.

Still holding the tapestry back, Deramon stared into the tunnel's darkness. "To the wilderness. To hope and exile. To life." He shook his head softly. "It will save you, Mori; it will take you from this city, from war, from death. You will spend a long time crawling through its darkness. When you emerge, you will fly... fly as far as you can and never look back."

Mori stared into the tunnel. The darkness seemed to stare back, an abyss peering into her soul. Bayrin came to stand beside her, placed his arms around her, and held her close.

So that would be my fate, Mori thought. *Should the Tirans break through, I would be doomed to forever flee, to hide, to survive in pain while my people lie dead behind me, their ghosts crying to me.*

Deramon seemed to shake himself from a dream. His armor clanked, he grumbled something under his breath, and he let the tapestry fall to hide the tunnel.

"But it won't come to that," he grumbled, all the grit back in his voice, and again he was the same gruff old lord. "If the Tirans are foolish enough to invade, we'll smite them dead."

The lord turned aside with another grumble, marched toward a rack of swords, and stared stubbornly at them. Bayrin went to his side, and soon the two were arguing again. Mori remained by the tapestry. She stared at it: the lush blue fabric, the dragons of golden thread, the thin silver birches, the stars she had stabbed her fingers so many times to sew. As she looked upon the scenes, the embroidered dragons almost seemed to fly and the stars to shine: a scene of Requiem in the night, peaceful and glittering.

But now a new night falls, she thought, *and when its darkness spreads, will I dare do what I must? Will I dare enter this tunnel, crawl to life, leave the others to die? With Tirans in the hall, their steel slaughtering us, how many would flee behind me? Five? Six? Would the rest remain here in their tomb?*

She shut her eyes and turned away. She walked toward Bayrin and Deramon, stood at their side, and listened to them argue about steel and forging and the shapes of crossguards. She missed Orin and Father and Lyana, and she could not shake the trickling, icy fear that filled her belly.

MAHRDOR

He walked through the night, flanked by guards. Alongside the alleyways, the walls of workshops and winehouses closed in around him like a prison cell—craggy, hard, unyielding. Lord Mahrdor hated walls around him. He hated these narrow burrows of the commoners.

This city is a prison, he thought, mouth twisting bitterly, *and I am a hunter of the desert.*

He gritted his teeth as he walked, as around him soldiers marched, as before him commoners scuttled into their homes. He yearned to leave this cesspool, to mount his wyvern, to fly across sea and plain, to hunt in the great northern wilderness. He licked his lips, imagining it. So many creatures there to catch! So many bones to study. So much skin to peel, and screams to hear, and jars to fill.

"Let Solina crave her glory," he whispered into the night, the walls closing in around him. "Let her worship the sun. I will have my prizes of the night." He looked up at a sky strewn with stars. "The sun fades in the dark, but my collection never dies."

In his left hand, he carried a sack with three dripping lumps. With his right hand, he reached into the pouch on his belt. He fingered the treasures he kept there, teeth he had collected from the old man's sons. How they had screamed! The memory of those screams warmed his blood, and the cold, hard feel of the teeth steadied his head. Soon the alley walls no longer seemed to trap him.

There is power in my trophies. There is glory in the night. There is safety.

The alley opened into shadow, and soon they walked across the Square of the Sun, boots thudding against its cobblestones. Lingering peddlers and wandering youths saw the soldiers and scurried into shadow. Clouds flowed across the moon. Mahrdor took sharp, deep breaths, as if he could inhale the night itself. Soon, he thought, he would carry more teeth in his pouch—the teeth of Lyana. He decided to take her treasures slowly, to savor them: first a toe, then a finger, eventually her foot in a jar. He would keep her alive for as long as he could; for decades. She was his greatest prize, his rarest of birds, and he would make her last.

Finally he saw the winehouse again. It rose tall and narrow, built of rugged mudbrick. A sign hung above the door, painted blue and gold, featuring an oared ship and the words "The River Spice".

Mahrdor turned toward his men. The Gilded Guardians stood frozen, staring at him through their ibis helms. They gripped their swords.

"You know what to do," he told them.

They moved forward, automatons of steel and gold. One kicked down the door, and they streamed into the winehouse. Mahrdor stood at the doorway, smiling softly, watching them smash jugs of wine, crush tables, and shatter plates and mugs. Wine thick with clay shards sluiced around his boots.

"What are you doing?" cried a crinkly voice from the second story. "What do you want?"

The old winekeeper rushed downstairs into the common room, hair wild. Peras was his name, Mahrdor remembered.

Foolish man, the general thought. *You should be fleeing across the rooftops, not charging into your death.*

One Gilded Guardian grabbed the old man. The other drove a gauntleted fist into his stomach, then backhanded him. Blood filled the old man's mouth, and his scream faded into a gurgle. The guards shoved him down, and one kicked him. Coughing blood, Peras crawled into the corner and shivered. He tried to reach for a fallen knife, but a guardian stepped on his hand, then raised a fist above him.

"Enough," Mahrdor said.

The Gilded Guardians froze. The winehouse lay in ruins, and the only sound was Peras's hacking breath. Mahrdor approached the fallen, bloody man and opened the sack he carried. He held it upside down, and three heads rolled onto the floor.

When Peras saw the toothless heads of his sons, he tossed back his own head and howled. He leaped up and clawed at Mahrdor, crying in agony. Blood stained his tunic and tears filled his eyes.

"My sons! My sons! They were winemakers, only winemakers." He grabbed the fallen knife and slashed the air. His eyes were red, his face torn. "Damn you, Mahrdor! May the Sun God burn you!"

Mahrdor stepped back, dodging the knife, and drew his sabre. He thrust the blade. Steel gleamed in candlelight. The sabre drove into Peras's belly so smoothly Mahrdor barely felt any resistance; it was like skewering a slab of butter. He stepped closer, driving the blade down to the hilt, smiling softly. Peras gasped and blood trickled down his chin.

"You harbored a weredragon," Mahrdor said to the dying man. "I do believe it will be *your* soul that burns."

He shoved Peras back and pulled his sword free. The old man fell, whispered a last prayer to his god, and died between the heads of his sons.

Mahrdor stared down at the body and the heads. His lips curled in disgust. The remains looked to him like crushed worms. Briefly he considered taking a trophy from Peras too, but the man had only several teeth, and the rest of him was wretched. Bile filled his throat, and Mahrdor turned away.

"Burn them," he said to his guards. "Burn everything inside this place. It sickens me."

He stepped outside into the night and sucked the air. When his head stopped spinning, he spat and walked into darkness.

I don't need that old, shriveled body in my collection, he told himself. *Soon we fly to Requiem. Soon I will have Lyana. Soon I will have all the trophies of a god's dreams.*

DERAMON

"Into the tunnels!" he shouted, flying above the city. "Single file! Walk, don't run. Keep moving!"

Below him, the people of Nova Vita shuffled down the streets. Youths were snickering with their friends; Deramon saw one boy pinch a girl's backside, making her squeal. A few old women stood chatting in the corner. Deramon fumed and smoke blasted from his nostrils. Only a year had passed since Solina had burned this city, and already these people forgot the horror of war?

"Into the tunnels, come on, you lazy bastards!" Bayrin shouted, flying beside Deramon. The young dragon blasted fire across the sky. "If this were a real invasion, you'd all be charred bones by now. Move it! Move!"

The people below hastened their step and moved down the streets. They began snaking into the three archways that led underground: one marble archway at Benedictus Square, a second by the temple, and a third behind a copse of trees by the city walls. Clad in steel, men of the City Guard lined the streets, guiding the people into safety.

As Deramon flew above the city, his belly knotted.

"They're too slow," he muttered. "Damn too slow."

Beside him, his son sighed and shook himself, clanking like a bag of dice. "They'll move faster next time, or I swear, I'll start roasting people from above." He looked at Deramon. "Father, I've seen these wyverns fly. They're fast. Damn fast. Faster than Mori with a snapping turtle chomping her tail. If any show up here, the people will have to do better."

Deramon cursed under his breath, and so much smoke left his maw it nearly blinded him. Over the past few moons, every mason and carpenter in town had been working in the tunnels. After Solina had destroyed the underground labyrinth last year, Requiem had rebuilt it stronger and safer, but that wouldn't help if the people couldn't enter fast enough.

"Move it!" he shouted at the streets below where a few stragglers shuffled toward the tunnels. Finally—it seemed like ages—the last laggard disappeared underground.

"City Guard!" Deramon shouted; a thousand of the guards still lined the streets. "Shift and fly! Battle formations!"

At his order, a thousand men and women shifted into dragons and soared. Their roar shook the city. Four phalanxes—each with a hundred dragons—moved to perch upon the city walls. Four more phalanxes landed upon the palace, the Temple of Stars, and the city's two forts. The remaining dragons circled above Nova Vita, howling and roaring fire.

It wasn't perfect. Some dragons bumped against one another as they flew, and some seemed hopelessly confused, not sure if to perch upon a building or soar. Some phalanxes flew in tight formations, divided into battle flights of four dragons—two leaders flanked by two defenders. Other phalanxes flew in a confused cloud.

Bayrin grunted. "They're bloody farmers, Father. Look at them. Half of them look like they've never flown in their life." He sighed. "The wyverns will tear through them like Lyana's cooking through my bowels."

Deramon was busy howling commands. "Dragonclaw Phalanx, bloody stars, form rank! Flights of four, go!" He whipped his head around. "You! Where are you flying? What phalanx are you? Go, down there, guard the temple, girl!"

The groan that escaped his son's throat was loud as a roar. "Merciful stars, we're in trouble. Look at that one, Father. She's barely fifteen if she's a day, I reckon. And she's in the City Guard?" He panted and glared at Deramon. "Father, if Solina reaches this city, she'll be flying with thousands of wyverns—tens of thousands—each bearing a seasoned rider. How are these... these farm girls and bakers' boys going to stop her?"

Deramon was wondering the same thing. Last year, he had commanded a thousand tough, gruff men. All but two hundred had burned, and half of those survivors now guarded the southern border. *Damn it, I need more time,* he thought. *I need another year to turn these youths into warriors.*

"It'll have to do," he said. He flapped his wings, rising higher, and waited until his guards finally manned their posts. "It's what we have, Bayrin. And they will fight when the time comes. They might be youths. But they can still blow fire. They can still slash claws. They will fight and they will protect our city." He cracked his neck. "At least, Bayrin... let me pretend. It's better to have hope than to despair." He blasted fire and howled to the city. "Drill's over! Return to your homes! City Guard—shift and regroup in the fortress courtyard!"

The tunnel doors opened and the people began streaming back into the streets. A few looked around nervously, possibly imagining the coming war. Others still laughed and gossiped as they went. Many were wounded, still carrying the scars of the phoenix attack; these ones limped and stared with haunted eyes. Others ran and laughed, the scars of war gone from their bodies and souls.

As the people returned to their homes and workshops, the dragons of the City Guard flew to their garrison, the squat Castra Murus by the northern wall. The thud of two thousand wings sent saplings bending, cloaks fluttering, and dust flying across the fort's battlements. When the dragons landed in the courtyard, they shifted into armored men and women bearing swords; they would need their steel should the battle move underground. Finally, after long moments of bumping into one another and Deramon shouting himself hoarse, they stood in formation—ten phalanxes, each commanded by a survivor of the old City Guard. They stood in rows, stiff, heads raised. One man scratched himself, then froze when Deramon scowled.

Finally, when all stood at attention, Deramon shifted too and stood before them in human form. Bayrin stood at his side, shaking his head sadly.

"Farm girls and bakers' boys," the young man repeated and sighed.

Deramon grumbled as he stared at his warriors. Elethor had drafted every healthy Vir Requis over fifteen years old, but some here looked younger. A few girls were so short and skinny they looked barely old enough to fly, let alone fight a wyvern. Some boys looked so green, Deramon half expected them to be chewing straw and herding sheep right here in the courtyard. Some were scrawny, others fat. A dozen or so were old graybeards with bent backs. Some had the pale look of scribes or priests, others the tanned look of farmers. They all had but one thing in common. They all looked scared.

"They sent me boys and girls!" Deramon shouted at them. He spat noisily. "They sent me the sons of farmers, boys who had never held a sword. They sent me the daughters of seamstresses, girls who had only wielded needles. They sent me weak, frightened children!"

They stood at attention, stiff, a few trembling. Deramon growled and continued.

"But now war is coming. Now you are no longer youths." He raised his voice. "Now you are men and women of the City Guard! Now you are warriors of Requiem!" He stared from one to another, scowling. "I once led a thousand seasoned fighters; they fell. You are here to continue their fight. You are here to honor their memory." He paced the courtyard, moving across the lines. "But when Queen

Solina invades our city, you will not fight for honor. You will not fight for glory. You will not fight for gold, because I'm not going to pay you." He stood still and faced them. "You will fight for farmers and seamstresses, for scribes and masons, for winemakers and shepherds. You will fight for your fathers, your mothers, your siblings, your grandparents. You will fight for your homes, because if you don't, Solina will destroy those homes and kill those families." He drew his sword and raised it. "Today you are warriors! Today I am proud of you. Raise your swords, City Guard!"

They roared. A thousand blades rose like a steel forest. At his side, Bayrin was grinning wildly and raising his sword so high, his arm looked ready to dislocate.

The roaring continued for long moments. When Deramon stalked off to his chambers, he heard the guardsman swing blades, cheer, and speak of slicing Solina to ribbons. They laughed. The fear had left them.

But fear still dwells inside of me, Deramon thought. He closed the door to his small, shadowy chamber in the heart of Castra Murus. The air was cold and damp, and Deramon poured himself a mug of strong spirits. He drank; it burned down his throat. When he closed his eyes, he saw the faces again—the faces of his dead men, staring up at him as he shoveled dirt into their graves.

"They're only youths," he whispered in the dark. "Only children. Stars, don't let them die under my command." He lowered his head and his shoulders shook. "Stars, don't let me lose these boys and girls too."

He looked out the window at the sky. Night was falling. War was near.

ELETHOR

"Come on, Elethor!" she said. She tugged his hand and they ran through the forest. Solina laughed. "Come on, you turtle!"

Leafy branches slapped them. Moss and dry leaves flew from under their boots. Finally they emerged from behind alders thick with lichen, beams of sunlight fell, and they beheld the waterfall. Solina gasped and squeezed Elethor's hand so tightly she nearly crushed it.

"Beautiful," she whispered.

The water crashed down a cliff into a pond, spraying mist and foam. A great, mossy statue of a dragon perched atop the cliff, guarding the waterfall. The ancient children of Requiem had carved it, legends said, thousands of years before King Aeternum had raised the palace of Requiem.

Solina spun toward Elethor, teeth sparkling in her smile, her eyes glittering blue. Her chest rose and fell as she panted.

"Come on," she said, "let's get closer!"

Elethor stood before the pond. The waterfall's spray wet his face. "Why don't we just admire it from here, we can—"

With a snort, she leaped into the water, dragging him with her.

Water flowed over him and entered his nostrils. He thrust his head out and took a breath, only for Solina to splash him, filling his mouth with water.

"Elethor, come on. Closer! Right under it." She pointed at the waterfall that crashed ahead into the pool. Her hair turned dark gold with water, and her freckles shone like stars. She turned and began swimming toward the waterfall's wrath.

"Solina! Can't we just swim here?"

She turned back toward him, gave him a toothy grin, then began to swim toward the waterfall again. With a sigh, Elethor followed. The spray soon rose so thickly he could see only a foot ahead. The water crashed so loudly, his ears ached. Water kept filling his mouth, eyes, and nostrils.

"Solina, where are you?" he shouted and spat out water.

He looked around but saw only the mist. Currents swirled around him, and when he put his feet down, he could no longer feel the pool's floor.

"Solina!"

A hand reached out from the mist, grabbed the back of his head, and pulled him forward. He found himself pressed against Solina, her mouth against his, her hands in his hair. They kissed for long moments. The water crashed around them.

She shoved him back. "Get *off*. Come on, follow me." She mussed his hair, then vanished into the spray.

He caught her on the lakeshore. She stood before him, dripping wet, her tunic clinging to her. With a crooked smile, she stripped off her clothes and shook her hair. They made love there in the sunlight, until dirt and grass and dry leaves clung to their wet bodies, then lay holding each other and watching the water. She nestled against him, and he kissed her head. The autumn leaves rustled and the blackbirds sang.

"I don't ever want to go back," she whispered. She tightened her arms around him, laid her head against his chest, and closed her eyes. "I don't ever want to return to Nova Vita. I want to stay here with you, Elethor. Just you and me here in the forest. I love you so much. I hate all the other ones. I hate them!" She opened her eyes, revealing tears. "I hate Lyana, and I hate her father, and I hate all the rest of them." She growled, then sniffed, and her tears fell onto his chest. She held him tight. "I love you so much, El. You are the only one I love. Let's never go back."

He kissed her head and held her close. Her naked body was warm against him.

"Lyana can lecture a lot; I know it! She does the same to me, but she means no harm. Mori can seem to pity you; I know that too. But she only tries to comfort you, not hurt you. You know this, Solina; I've told you many times. Please let go of your anger." He pulled back an errant lock of her hair. "Never go back? Requiem is our home; it's your home too now. Will we live as beasts in the wilderness? Hermits clad in leaf and fur?"

"I don't need any leaf or fur." A deep light filled her eyes. "I am no beast, no hermit. I am the last survivor of the Phoebus Dynasty. Let us flee Requiem! Come with me to Tiranor, El. I will rally my people. I will raise the palace anew, that palace your father destroyed. We will rebuild the desert, El! You and I. We will become great rulers, an empress and emperor in a magical realm." She clutched his shoulders, digging her fingernails into them. "It will be our secret world, a world of steel, spice, and sunlight." Her eyes shone.

Elethor sighed. "Solina, I wish I could go there with you. Truly I do. But... what lies there for us? A ruined, toppled city. A desert of sand and death." He shook his head. "How could I leave my family? How could I leave Orin and Mori and Father and the rest of them?"

She snarled. Her fingernails drove deeper into his shoulders, so painful that he winced.

"To the Abyss with them," she snarled. "I don't care about them, El. They don't understand us. They don't know what it's like to be us. They don't know how much we love each other." She rose to her feet, walked toward the lake, and stood with her back to him. She gazed at the waterfall. "One day they will see, El. They will see my strength, and they will see our love, and we will no longer have to hide."

He walked toward her and embraced her. She laid her head against his shoulder, and they stood holding each other, watching the water crash.

He turned around.

Below the hill, his army stood—three thousand dragons clad in armor, snorting fire and smoke. They covered the valley, scales chinking, the heat of their flames filling the air. Elethor stood above them, still in human form—no longer a skinny youth, but a bearded man in armor, a sword at his side, his face scarred with war.

It's been eight years since that day, he thought. And even now he missed the touch of sunlight, the kiss of her lips, and her hair between his fingers.

She was different then. I was not wrong to love her then.

He lowered his head and closed his eyes. The guilt clawed inside him, clutching his innards. She had been his love—his life. *It's me she wants. It's our war—hers and mine.* He gritted his teeth. *And thousands will die for us.*

He turned away from his army and looked south. Mountains spread into a horizon of dark clouds. Ralora Beach lay beyond the shadows; from there she would emerge.

Is Lord Oldnale right? Do I lead us to destruction? Will Requiem burn for the love and hatred of me and her?

Staring into the southern clouds and rain, he remembered Solina killing the children in the tunnels, burning the city, screaming that she would slaughter them all. He clenched his fists.

No. Oldnale is wrong. Solina would destroy us—for the death of her parents, for her captivity, for her madness.

He shifted into a dragon, flapped his wings, and rose into the sky. He roared a pillar of fire.

"Dragons of Requiem!" he called. "We fly! We fly to war!"

They howled behind him. Their wings beat like war drums. Their flames rose. The Royal Army of Requiem took flight. Elethor soared into skies of cloud and rain, and his army followed with howls and fountains of fire. As he dived through the storm, Elethor remembered swimming after Solina as the water pounded him, chasing her, seeking her through mist and spray. He had caught her and kissed her that day; now he would meet her again... and kill her with steel, flame, and blood.

SOLINA

She stood upon the Tower of Akartum, the tallest spire of her palace, and caressed the chains embedded into the limestone.

"Soon you will hang here, Elethor," she whispered. She imagined caressing his face like she caressed the chains, kissing him, and leaving him to wither in the sun. "Soon you will scream here upon the city your father burned."

At her feet, five vultures cawed in an iron cage. They bit at the bars, screeched for food, and clawed the air. She had been starving them, tossing them enough raw meat to keep them alive but always hungry, always vicious. She cooed to them.

"Soon, my darlings. Soon, when he hangs here, you will feed upon his flesh."

The smiled softly, imagining it. How he would writhe! How he would beg! When the vultures tore into his flesh, he would weep for forgiveness. When the vultures tore out his eyes, he wouldn't even be able to do that. But he would scream.

"Oh yes, you will scream, Elethor." Solina licked her lips. "The entire city will hear it."

She swept her arms around her, spreading her light across Irys. The city rustled around her, the palms and figs swaying, the cranes and ibises singing, the River Pallan flowing like a string of silver. The sandstone temple rose before her, kissed in sunlight. The villas of the wealthy lined the riversides, while behind them stretched thousands of brick homes, silos, and shops. Far north, the city melted into Hog Corner and finally to delta and sea.

"I will fly across this sea for you, Elethor," she whispered. "And I will bring you home."

The vultures bit at their cage, screeching for blood.

Smiling softly, Solina turned south and faced the desert. Upon the dunes stood her army. Twenty thousand wyverns screeched and clawed the sand, a host such as the world had never seen, twice the size and might of the phoenix army she had led last year. Men and women sat upon them, clad in steel, their shields like twenty thousand suns, their spears like rising sunrays. Solina raised her arms and cried to them.

"You will slay dragons!" she shouted, and her riders raised their spears and howled. The wyverns tossed back their heads, jaws rising like blades, and roared. The city shook with their cry. It was a cry of war, of death, of light and victory and her eternal glory. It was a cry that thudded in her chest, blazed with light across her eyes, and filled her mouth with the taste of blood.

"You will topple the lizard courts, avenge your fallen brothers, and bring the Reptile King in chains to die in sunfire!"

Their howl swept over her like wind from the desert, like the breath of her lord. She whistled, a sound like a bird of prey, and her wyvern took flight from the courtyard below. The beast's wings thudded, bending palm trees and sending sand flying across the palace. His scales, square plates like armor, clanked and glimmered. His eyes blazed red, his black teeth snapped, and smoke rose from his nostrils. Baal, the king of wyverns—a forge of acid, a deity of wrath and muscle and bloodlust.

When he reached the tower's battlements, Solina climbed into his saddle. She grabbed the shield and spear that hung there and raised them—sun and sunray. She dug her heels into Baal, and the wyvern's wings beat like a storm into sails. The beast soared, wind streamed Solina's hair, and she snarled.

"To war!" she cried and raised her spear higher. The tip glinted, a beacon of fire.

"To war!" howled twenty thousand riders behind her, and wyverns screeched, and wings thundered. The city streamed beneath her, trees bending and leaves flying under the blast of leathern wings. When she looked behind her, she saw her army following, a sunlit host, a light upon the desert, a fire to burn out the darkness of dragons.

"To Requiem!" she shouted.

"To Requiem!" rose the cry behind her.

They streamed over delta and sea. To war. To Requiem. And to Elethor.

"We will meet again, my love, my life," she whispered, remembering those days long ago when she would love him in darkness. Soon no more darkness would hide him. Soon he would hang upon her tower, and her lord's light would strip him bare, and his bones would be her toys.

The wrath of Tiranor flew, and Solina smiled.

LYANA

Pain burned across her like scarabs ripping flesh from bone. Every flap of the wyvern's wings shots bolts of fire through her. She sat in the saddle, chains clutching her in an iron embrace. All around her, the army of wyverns flew, a storm of scales rising and falling. Wind gusted, rain fell, and the wyverns soared. Lyana winced, her stomach rising and falling like a dead jellyfish on a storming sea. She felt a stitch on her back open and blood trickle to her tailbone. She closed her eyes and let out a soft moan.

"Silence," said Mahrdor. He sat in the saddle behind her, his arms reaching around her as he held the reins. "Make another sound, and I'll cut off your hand and gag you with it."

She fell silent. They had stitched the raw, bloody lashes across her body, but not before rubbing ilbane into them. The poison still burned, spreading through her. Every jostle in the saddle felt like whips beating her anew. She opened her eyes once more, saw the wyverns rise and fall in the rain, and swallowed to stop from gagging.

Oh Elethor, she thought and her eyes stung. *I failed you.*

He was waiting at Ralora Beach, she knew—hundreds of leagues away. Because of her... because of her. She grimaced and cursed herself, the anguish a claw inside her. She had fallen into Mahrdor's trap so easily. She had doomed her people to death—sweet Princess Mori, her dearest friend; her family, whom she loved more than life; Elethor, her betrothed and king. *I doomed them all.*

A gust of wind blew rain across them. The wyvern bucked and howled, and Lyana dug her fingernails into her palms. She felt another stitch open, and she trembled with the pain. *What I must look like now...* Her face felt swollen; she could barely see through her puffy eyes. Her torso bore a network of long, raw welts still oozing blood between the stitches. The chains dug into her, working their way through her skin. Her scalp still felt raw and bare. If her family saw her now, would they even recognize her, or see only a bloodied, beaten wretch?

A thunderbolt crashed and the wyverns screeched. A few spewed acid into distant forests below; where the foul liquid landed, the trees crumbled. Lyana looked around her, trying to place her location. She could see almost nothing through the storm: trees below, the shadow of mountains ahead, a river to her west. They had crossed the Tiran Sea yesterday, but Lyana did not know this land.

This is not Requiem, she thought. She had flown over Requiem countless times, traversing it north to south, east to west. She knew every mountain, river, and forest in Aeternom's Kingdom. She breathed out sharply through her nose.

Of course.

She shook her head. How had she not guessed it? Solina's army would not invade Requiem's southern border; a thousand dragons patrolled it, from Gilnor's swamps in the west to Ralora Beach in the east.

"We're flying over Osanna," she whispered as thunder rolled.

Osanna. Ancient realm of men. Empire of steel and stone. Its soldiers rode horses, unable to become dragons like Requiem's children; they could not stop an army of wyverns. Osanna's border stretched across the east of Requiem, from the snowy mountains of northern Fidelium and down hundreds of leagues to the southern sea. Not with every dragon alive could Requiem patrol that great wilderness of forest, mountain, and plain.

Lyana gritted her teeth. She had to escape. She had to warn Elethor. Images of the Phoenix War swam before her: burning people in the streets, children torn in two, severed limbs littering the underground. *I can't let my city burn again.*

The fear and anger pounded through her, overpowering her pain. She looked down at the irons binding her: they wrapped around her torso and clasped her wrists behind her back. Her armor and sword were as parts of her; they could shift into a dragon with her. But these manacles were foreign constraints. If she shifted now, they would dig through her enlarged body, shoving her back into human form.

Her mind worked feverishly. Mahrdor would have the keys. She knew such men; he wanted to control her, to own her, to have power over her enslavement and freedom. Even if he intended to never unlock her, he would keep the keys on him. *Part of owning someone is having the power to free them... and refusing to.*

She would kill him, she swore. Even if they flew at full speed, it would take several days to reach Nova Vita; she would kill him before that time. She would kill him tonight, or next night, or while they rode this wyvern, or outside the very walls of Nova Vita, but she would kill him. She would not let him reach her city. She would not let him bring death and blood to her people.

He will pin me down tonight, she thought. *He will shove himself inside me as I lie chained, as he proves his dominion. And I will bite out his throat.* She snarled into the rain. She could not grow dragon fangs while chained, but her teeth could still shed blood.

They flew for hours. They flew through wind and lightning, over forest and glen, over forts and snaking walls where men scurried like ants. They passed out of the storm into a red sunset, and the wyverns screeched, a sound like cracking mountains, like dying worlds. Thousands of the creatures howled in the red light, flies bustling in a puddle of blood. Solina rode at their lead, all in gold, her banner raised. The queen began to descend toward a field of rocks and wild grass, and the others followed. Air shrieked around Lyana, her head spun, and her stomach lurched. She had flown for countless hours as a dragon; flying in human form was new, and she gritted her teeth to stay conscious.

The ground rushed up to meet them. The wyverns filled their wings with air and landed, claws kicking up earth and grass. They tossed back their heads and shrieked to the sky, and the world seemed to shake. Mahrdor landed atop a hill, and when his wyvern bucked, Lyana fell back against the general. Her back blazed, an inferno of agony. His breath filled her ear, scented of wine and the honeyed scarabs he ate.

"Tonight you will dance for me again," he whispered.

His wyvern lowered its wing, forming a ramp to the ground. Mahrdor dismounted, grabbed Lyana, and pulled her to the field. She stood chained beside him, watching the army set camp, and tried to judge their location. Bayrin had said that, flying as hard as he could—pushing himself to the very limits of his strength—he could travel from Irys to Nova Vita in five days. If these wyverns flew as hard, they were in south Osanna now, somewhere west of Altus Mare port, but still south of the great city of Confutatis. The plains rolled for leagues around her, fading into mist and the shadows of jagged mountains.

Soldiers bustled about, their steel red in the sunset. As darkness fell, they lit torches and fires. Commanders marched around the camp, shouting orders as lower ranks unpacked supplies from their wyverns. Tents began to rise, squat and tan for the common soldiers, tall and embroidered for the officers. Around the campfires, the troops began to eat their battle rations: flat breads dipped in palm oil, dried fish, tangy cheeses, and dried figs and dates. Where the officers camped, cooks prepared more lavish meals: water fowl brought live in cages, slaughtered fresh, and roasted upon coals; platters of pomegranates, olives, and small hard apples; and soft breads cooked upon iron disks. Wine and beer flowed through the camp, and as darkness fell, soldiers sang of the conquest to come. The wyverns fed from sacks of rotten meat bustling with flies, and they too shrieked as if singing for war.

At the far side of the camp, upon a boulder the size of a house, stood a tall shadow—a woman holding a banner, her hair flowing in the night.

Solina. Queen of Tiranor.

Lyana gritted her teeth, staring at the queen over the army of man and beast. Was Solina staring back at her from the darkness? Lyana thought of how Solina had seduced Elethor in his youth, kissed him, made love to him in Nova Vita. The rage simmered inside her. This desert tyrant had tainted Lyana's betrothed, burned her home, and killed so many of her people.

I will kill you too, Solina, she thought, fists clenched behind her back. *I will kill you and Mahrdor. I vow it. I vow it by the stars of my people.* She raised her eyes, seeking those stars, but clouds covered the night. *First night from Tiranor. How many more nights are we from my home?*

Armor creaked and Mahrdor placed a hand on her shoulder. His fingers closed around it, too tight, driving pain through a welt that rose there. He gazed upon the camp with her. His face was blank, the face of a golden statue. Lyana stared at his belt where hung a ring of keys.

Those keys are for my shackles, she knew. *And he wants me to see them. He wants me to know his power over me.*

"You will dine with me tonight," he said. "Come, my tent is ready for us."

He gestured at a lavish tent, as large as a commoner's house, which rose upon a knoll. Its black canvas walls were emblazoned with golden suns. Gilded Guardians surrounded the tent, bearing spears and shields. Despite her fear and wounds, Lyana found that her belly grumbled. She could not remember when last she had eaten.

Clutching her shoulder, Mahrdor led her into the tent. Inside, his men had set an oak table, a bed topped with embroidered blankets, and iron candelabra holding a score of candles. A meal steamed upon the table—a honeyed roast duck on a bed of sliced limes, a platter of flat breads dipped in oil, stewed greens topped with sliced garlic and almonds, and a bowl of miniature oranges from the southern city of Iysa. A golden jug of wine stood by two jeweled cups. Two chairs stood at the table, their olivewood engraved with scenes of ibises flying over rushes.

"Sit," he told her, led her to a chair, and shoved her into it. "Eat."

He sat across the table from her, took a knife, and began to carve the duck. The skin *cracked* when he cut into it, and the meat's scent filled Lyana's nostrils. Despite herself, her mouth watered. She sat, wounds blazing, wrists bound behind her back. When he placed morsels on her plate, she leaned forward and ate. The meat was fatty and tender, the bread still steaming and dripping olive oil, and the stewed greens so soft they almost melted on her tongue. When he poured wine into her mug, she grabbed the rim with her teeth and drank; it was strong, dry wine that spun her head.

For a long while, they ate silently. Mahrdor watched her during the meal, eating little himself; he merely nibbled the odd morsel. His eyes never left her, but Lyana didn't care. She was famished and she ate whatever he gave her. She would need her strength to kill him. She would need her strength to flee this place.

Finally, when the duck lay as barren bones, Mahrdor sighed.

"It is a pity," he said. He reached across the table and caressed her raw scalp. "You had such beautiful hair. Dyed a Tiran platinum, I presume? Do I detect red stubble growing?"

She swallowed a bite of bread, glared at him, and said nothing.

He sighed. "Lyana, you misjudge me. That is your name, is it not? Lyana Eleison, a lady of Requiem's court?" He sipped his wine. "I care not that you are a weredragon. I knew you to be one the very first night I saw you. Did I hurt you then?" He shook his head. "I am not Solina. I wish not to torture you, nor beat you, nor parade you through the streets as the commoners pelt you with their trash. I did not give you your wounds; the queen did that. I did not place these manacles around you; she did."

She growled at him. "You caged me."

He raised his eyebrows. "Caged you? Yes, that I did. I caged you in a gilded work of art, its bars shaped as dragons—a home for a rare bird, for a beloved pet. Manacles of iron? Crude things. They do not befit one so fair."

"Then remove them from me."

"And see my rare bird fly away? No, I dare not. Not here in this camp." He picked an olive from a dish, placed it in his cheek, and sucked it. "I do not crave war, Lyana; it is a barbarous thing. I do not crave blood, nor the torture of my enemies; those are things for brutes, for lesser men. I am—"

"A collector, yes. So you have said."

He laughed—a cold, brief sound. "I do repeat myself, don't I? A fault I should remedy. But yes, Lyana, I am a collector of fine things. The map you saw in my chamber was set there to trap you; my other prizes are true trophies. Oh, I could make some trophy from you too; a shrunken head, perhaps, or a chair from your bones and skin. I would enjoy carving you into a piece of art, but I think you, Lyana, are a greater prize when living. I will modify you; a few changes here and there with knife and hammer. But aside from those, I will keep you as you are—a rare bird, a pet for a golden cage. Surely that is a better fate than what Solina can offer you; she would offer you only the dungeon, the lash, and the poison." He caressed her cheek. "I will protect you from her, Lyana, and you will be mine. A true weredragon noblewoman—the crown of my collection."

She raised her chin and glared. "You will not call me that word. I am a Vir Requis. I am descended from Terra Eleison himself. I am—"

"...in no position to make demands," he finished for her. He spat his olive pit into a handkerchief, folded it neatly, and placed it by his plate. "Are you done eating? Good, Lyana. Good. The food has done well with you; the color returns to your cheeks and the fire to your eyes. Soon your wounds will heal, and your hair will grow, and you will be as fair as before. I will see to it."

He rose to his feet and began to remove his armor. He placed his breastplate, vambraces, pauldrons, and a dozen other pieces of steel upon a table. When he stood clad in nothing but his tunic and breeches, he moved to stand by the bed.

"Now," he said, "dance for me. Dance like you danced in my home. Dance and you will see that home again—and never more Solina's dungeon."

She stared at him. He stared back, digging his gaze into her. *For Requiem.*

She rose to her feet so suddenly her chair fell back and nearly knocked over a candle. Her chains clanked. Never removing her eyes from his, she danced.

Once she had danced in silks; today she wore chains and tatters. Once she had swayed like a desert wind; today she moved like a trapped bird fluttering against the bars of its cage. He eyed her hungrily. As she swayed near him, he tugged at the rags she wore, tearing a strip of cloth. He bared his teeth, a rabid wolf eyeing his prey.

As she danced before him, chains chinking, he reached out like a striking asp, grabbed her, and pulled her onto the bed. He shoved her facedown onto the mattress, and when she looked over her shoulder, she saw him undoing the laces of his breeches.

When he mounted her, she closed her eyes, gritted her teeth, and buried her face in the bed. She wanted to do it now, but forced herself to endure him. He was lustful now. He was strong now. He would be weak soon. He had known her twice before; she could endure it again. She closed her eyes and thought of the skies of Requiem, the sound of harps in marble temples, and the thousands of dragons who flew like shards of colored glass under the stars.

When he was done with her, he rose to his feet, breathing heavily. He approached the table, yawned magnificently, and began to pour more wine.

"By the Sun God, Lyana," he said, "you do take the strength out of a man."

Quick as a juggler, Lyana shoved her bound wrists under and around her legs; her arms were now bound before her, not behind her back.

She leaped toward him.

She wrapped her chains around his throat and pulled.

The jug of wine fell and shattered.

Their lovemaking had weakened him; it had strengthened her. He made a choking sound, struggling for breath and finding none. She dug her heels into the floor, growled, and pulled back with all her might, willing the chains to dig into his neck. He reached over his back, and his fingers grazed her scalp; he could have grabbed her hair, had Solina left her any. She tugged the chains with all the strength she still had.

"I am Lyana Eleison, daughter of Lord Deramon and Mother Adia," she hissed into his ear. "I am a knight of Requiem. I am a daughter of starlight. You will die today."

He stumbled back to the bed, clawing at her. He was a tall man; she was slight. She clung to his back, tugging, grinding the chains. Blood dripped down his chest. He croaked for breath. They slammed into a candelabrum; the candles fell onto the rug. He stumbled toward the tent walls. She dug her heels and pulled him back.

Die already! She gritted her teeth and hissed as she pulled the chains. He took a step toward his armor and sabre. Snarling, she tugged the chains mightily; they dug into his throat. He kept walking. Another candleholder fell and the rug began to blaze. His hand reached for his sword. He grabbed the hilt.

Lyana twisted the chains and gave a mighty tug. Mahrdor drew his sword, gasping for breath. She pulled him back. He raised the blade. His bare feet stepped onto the burning rug, and with a choked mewl, he fell forward.

He crashed to his knees, and Lyana tugged backward, growling and straining, until he gave a last gurgle, and his head slumped forward.

Crouched above him, Lyana snarled and looked around the tent. The flames had spread to the walls and crackled, raising black smoke. Shouts rose outside. She heard soldiers clanking toward the burning tent. She straightened, panting and growling, a feral animal. Her arms and legs were still manacled. Gilded Guardians burst into the tent.

With a shout, Lyana slammed her fists against a burning chair, sending it flying. It crashed into the guardians and blazed. There were three of them, their blades only half-drawn.

Stars of Requiem, be with me.

Lyana crouched, grabbed Mahrdor's sword, and wrenched it free from his grip. Was he dead or merely unconscious? She had no time to check. Wrists bound, she swung the sabre with both hands. She drove the blade down, hitting one guardian where his pauldron met his neck; her blade drove several inches down his torso. She pulled it free, swung again, and cleaved the neck of another guard.

The third managed to draw his own sword. Lyana swung, parried, and drove the blade forward. It clanged against the guardian's armor. The tent blazed. Lyana swiped her sword across the tabletop, sending burning scraps into the guardian's face. When he fell back, she drove her blade down hard, cleaving him.

Outside, she heard more soldiers shouting and running uphill. Smoke filled the tent now, so thick that she coughed and could barely see. She leaped over a flaming rug, knelt by Mahrdor, and grabbed the keys from his belt. Frantically, she twisted her fingers; with her wrists bound, she could not fit the key into the manacles' lock.

Soldiers burst into the tent.

Lyana swung around, lashed her sword, and tossed a flaming table against them. Key in hand, she leaped over fire, through tent walls, and out onto the hill. She rolled in the night, still chained, toward an army.

Soldiers came rushing up toward her. With her mouth, Lyana thrust key into lock and twisted. The manacles around her wrists clanked open, revealing bloodied flesh. The soldiers ran, shouted, and began drawing their blades. Teeth bared, Lyana thrust the key into the chains around her legs. The lock clinked. The chains fell. The soldiers reached her.

She swung her sword, parrying one weapon. A second sabre nipped her shoulder, and she screamed. She raised her blade, parried, and thrust. Blood splashed. Lyana leaped back.

Pain exploded when she summoned her magic. Her head spun. She could barely cling to it. She was too wounded, still coughing, still too weak. Scales appeared and disappeared across her. A sabre swung down, and she raised her blade, barely parrying. Wyverns shrieked around her and the clouds above swirled. Two of the scaled beasts came swooping toward her. The world burned and spun.

Requiem! May our wings forever find your sky.

Her mother's words spoke in her mind, deep and strong, comforting her.

This is not me. I am not a wounded creature who lies in the mud. I am Lyana Eleison. I am a knight of Requiem, daughter of a great priestess. I walked through the Abyss itself. I fought in the Phoenix War. I am Vir Requis and I will find my sky.

Blades lashed down toward her.

They clanged against scales.

Her wings beat like war drums, sending smoke and dirt flying. With a great roar, a *dragon* roar, she soared. Her claws lashed men. She flew higher. Wyverns swooped toward her, and she blew her fire. The jet of flame roared, lighting the night, and slammed into the beasts. They howled and bucked, and Lyana shot between them.

She flew straight up, moving so fast that her head spun. She dared not look behind her. She crashed through clouds until the stars burst into light above. The Draco constellation shone, the stars of her fathers. She flew toward it.

Shrieks sounded below her. She looked down to see wyverns—a hundred or more—burst from the clouds toward her. Riders sat upon them, and their crossbows fired. Lyana howled and banked, and the bolts shot around her. One scratched her shoulder. Another pierced her wing, and she roared in pain. She rained her fire, hit one wyvern, and flew southward.

The beasts shrieked. Jets of acid flew.

Lyana soared, neck craned back, so fast she nearly blacked out. The acid flew beneath her; she flapped her wings mightily, but drops still sizzled against her tail. She howled. It felt like a hundred arrows slamming into her.

I am a bellator of Requiem. I am a warrior. I walked through the Abyss. I will fly!

In the south, she saw the storm still brewing. Lightning burst inside the clouds, stains of light. Lyana growled and flew toward the tempest. An army of wyverns flew behind.

Acid sprayed. Lyana swooped and shot forward, narrowly dodging it. A drop splashed her wing and ate a hole through it, only coin-sized but blazing with agony. Wind whistled through the opening. She roared and flew forward, straight as a javelin.

When she looked over her shoulder, she saw more wyverns; hundreds now flew behind her. Their bolts and acid flew. Lyana gritted her teeth, beat her wings mightily, and shot into the storm.

Thunder boomed. Lightning blazed around her. Rain pounded her, aching against her wounds. The winds billowed her wings; she nearly tumbled. She narrowed her eyes and gritted her teeth. Despite the agony, she flew on. Lightning crashed and the clouds roiled like smoky demons.

I will never stop flying. Not until I reach Elethor.

If Bayrin had delivered the message, Elethor and his Royal Army waited at Ralora Beach. It lay hundreds of leagues away.

I must find him. I must summon him back to Nova Vita. If the wyverns reach the city before us, Requiem will fall.

Lyana snarled and flew.

MORI

Silence filled the royal hall.

Beyond the marble columns, silence filled the city.

Mori sat upon the Oak Throne, barely wanting to breathe, and prayed for some sound, anything to break this emptiness. She wanted to hear armor creak as soldiers rushed outside, or dragons roar above, or minstrels play, or children laugh, or... anything other than this silence that rang in her ears.

Outside, the guards manned their posts, perched upon wall and roof. Their family members, those too young or old or wounded to serve, huddled in their homes. Barely a breath stirred across Nova Vita, jewel of the north, capital of Requiem.

We all wait, Mori thought, *with bated breath, with tight hearts, with tingling fingers. We wait for the storm to strike. Stars of Requiem, look over my brother. Bring him home to me safely.*

She turned to her left, and the fear in her heart softened. Bayrin stood there, the only other soul in the hall. Her guardsman held the hilt of his sword, and a helm covered his head of shaggy red curls. When he saw her looking at him, he tilted that head to her, gave her a crooked smile, and winked.

"You look quite comfortable in that throne, little one. I think when Elethor returns, he might find a contender for the crown."

She gave him a shaky smile; the sound of his voice was desperate relief, a breath of air for a drowning woman.

"I wish I never had to sit upon this throne," she said. Her smile faded and she looked at her feet; she was short enough that they did not reach the floor. "I miss the days my father sat here. I miss the days Orin filled the seat when Father was away. I..." She sighed and clutched her luck finger. "I never thought Elethor and I would be the ones ruling here."

Bayrin cleared his throat theatrically. "*Elethor and I*, is it? Mors, my sweetness, dear old El rules alone; he is our king and tyrant, as tragic as that is. *You* are a seat filler." He gave her a penetrating stare. "At least you are quite prettier to look at than Elethor; guarding him is a real eyesore."

Mori lowered her eyes. She wished she could laugh at Bayrin's words. More than anything, she wanted to lie in his arms in some fluffy bed, to watch the clouds outside the window, to laugh at his prattling until her cheeks hurt. She wanted little else from this life; not a throne to fill, not gowns, not power... only a warm bed, an open sky, and a man who loved her. She sighed. If Solina reached this city, even those humble dreams would be lost. Solina would burn them with the rest of this city.

Before her eyes, she saw the Phoenix War again: Solina raining fire upon the city; children running burning through the streets; men crawling through tunnels, bleeding, missing limbs; and more painful than all, she saw her brother burnt and cut on the ground, entrails spilling, as Lord Acribus hurt her. She closed her eyes, as if she could banish those visions in darkness, but they still danced.

Breathe, Mori, she told herself. *Like Adia taught you. Breathe and be brave.*

Standing at her side, Bayrin took her hand and squeezed it. "Don't be scared, Mors. If any wyverns enter this room, I'll give them a taste of my fire. It doesn't taste quite as bad as my mother's porridge, but it'll do the trick."

But Mori wasn't scared for herself; she had fought in a war already, and she was ready to fight another one. She was scared for her people: the farmers and tradesmen, the merchants and miners, the children and elderly. If Elethor did not return—she trembled to think of it, but knew that she must—she would lead what remained of Requiem. Could she and Bayrin truly fight Solina and all her hatred?

She looked at Bayrin. He smiled at her, hand on the hilt of his sword.

And if the time comes, she thought, *will he draw that sword for my last mercy? If our city walls lie fallen around us, and Solina's men pound at our doors, would Bayrin find the strength to plunge his sword into my breast, then fall upon it?*

She left her throne and walked across the great hall of Requiem's kings. Its marble columns towered, the tallest structures in Requiem. As she walked, Mori touched every pillar she passed. She had studied many scrolls about their history. Three hundred years ago, Queen Gloriae had risen from the ashes of war and built forty-nine of these columns. The fiftieth, which Mori now approached, was thousands of years old; the first King Aeternum, father of the dynasty, had carved that column in the days when Vir Requis still lived wild. In the books, it was written that even Dies Irae the Destructor, who had killed a million Vir Requis, could not topple that column.

When Mori reached the ancient pillar, she placed her palm against it, lowered her head, and closed her eyes.

"Please, King Aeternum," she whispered, willing her voice to travel past the ages, through generations of monarchs, to the first king of her land. "Please, my king, give us strength. Watch over us this hour. I will not let your column fall."

She tried to imagine the old monarchs of Requiem standing here and praying: King Aeternum who raised this column millennia ago; King Benedictus who led Requiem in war against the griffins; the great Queen Lacrimosa who fell in the Battle of King's Forest; Queen Gloriae who raised Requiem from ruin and founded Nova Vita; Queen Luna the Traveler who had written many books and scrolls; and her father, King Olasar, the greatest man she had known.

And now Elethor and I, the young prince and princess, are the last of our dynasty. Now we must pray, and we must fight.

She opened her eyes, left the column, and approached the doors of her hall. They stood open before her, revealing the city. Mori stepped under the gateway, stood above a great marble stairway, and stared upon her realm. Cobbled streets snaked among young birches, spreading to white walls; beyond lay forests, mountains, and an orange sky. The wind billowed her hair.

Bayrin came to stand beside her and held her hand. They stood together, silent, watching the long night fall.

ELETHOR

They perched upon the cliffs of Ralora Beach, three thousand dragons with smoke in their nostrils, fire in their maws, and fear in their hearts. Smoothed stones and seashells, white and indigo and deep purple, formed a mosaic upon the shore below, appearing and disappearing as the waves raced, crashed against the cliffs, and retreated in an eternal assault. Beyond this shore of stone and shell, the sea stretched into the horizon, a gray carpet patched with metallic blues and greens. The sky above mirrored the waters, roiling with clouds that veiled the sun.

"Where are you, Solina?" Elethor whispered. He stood atop a towering boulder, the highest point on the cliff. Around him, his army spread like scaled crenellations—a dragon on every patch of bare rock. Behind them, where the cliff sloped to a landscape of hills, more dragons waited. Their eyes all stared. Their nostrils all smoked. Not a tail flapped nor a wing shrugged. Their bodies were tense, their scales silent, their fire simmering and ready to blow.

"Come on, Solina," Elethor spoke to the sea. "You wanted to see me again. I'm here, waiting for you."

When he narrowed his eyes, he saw nothing but the endless sea. The waves crashed. Foam sprayed. Clouds swirled. No wyverns, no Tirans, no old lover and desert queen.

It was the summer solstice. If Lyana had been right, the Tirans would invade here today.

When the sun dipped toward the horizon, the dragons began to move restlessly. A few blasted snorts of smoke, and Elethor heard scales clink. He grumbled and dug his claws into the cliff.

"My lord, what should we do?" said Lady Treale, who perched upon a boulder beside him. The black dragon was staring into the horizon, her fangs bared. She was young, but she was of noble birth and a knight in training, so he had stationed her at his side. With every knight but Lyana slain in the Phoenix War, Elethor could not afford to turn squires away—not even the youngest daughters of farmland lords.

It's not because of how she kissed my cheek, he thought. *It's not because of her soft face smiling by my side at nights, nor the starlight in her hair, nor the light in her eyes.* He grumbled low in his throat. *Lyana is away—my betrothed, the woman I love. Treale is the closest thing here to a knight, and I need her near. That is all. That is all. And her pretty smile be damned.*

"They'll be here," he said to the young dragon, trying his best to ignore how large her eyes were. "I trust Lady Lyana. She's never let us down. If she says Solina will invade here today, it will happen."

Treale shifted her lower jaw. "My lord, the sun begins to set. What if..." She swallowed a puff of smoke. "What if we're in the wrong place?"

Then Requiem is defenseless, he thought. *Then nothing but a small, green City Guard stands between Solina and Nova Vita's fall. Then we are cursed, and only dusty old scrolls will remain to tell of our glory.*

He said none of this.

"I trust Lyana," he repeated instead.

But did he trust her? Lyana was his betrothed, his love, the woman who had walked through the Abyss with him. To him she was a paragon of strength, wisdom, and courage. Was he blind to her faults? Maybe Treale's father had been right. Maybe he should never have flown to war, but instead met with Solina, treated with her, maybe even surrendered to her. Every wave that crashed sounded like the moan of a dying man, and as the sun set, every sunbeam looked like a bloody spear.

Whispers rose behind him and voices cried out.

"Lyana!" cried one of the dragons upon the hills. Others echoed his call.

"The Lady Lyana! Lyana returns!"

Elethor spun toward the hills, heart thrashing. A blue dragon was flying from the north, roaring fire.

Lyana.

"Stars," Elethor whispered. He took flight, wings beating so mightily, the air bent down Treale's neck. He soared over his army, away from the sea and toward the flying blue dragon.

"Elethor!" Lyana cried to him.

She was hurt, he saw. He gritted his teeth. Blood covered her scales, and she flew with a wobble.

"Elethor, they're behind me! Wyverns!"

She still flew over a mile away. Before she could reach him, a dozen wyverns plunged from the clouds into open air. More followed until a hundred swarmed after Lyana, their stench carrying on the wind. The beasts screeched, blew jets of acid, and shot toward the Royal Army.

Stars. Fear, sharp and cold, thrust into Elethor like a spear. For an instant he froze, wings still, staring at the creatures. Teeth bared, he forced the fear down and roared.

"Dragonbone Phalanx!" he shouted to the dragons below him, a group of farm boys with wide eyes. They would have to fight as men today. "Fly, to my left!" He looked to his right where stood a hundred slack-jawed dragons, the sons and daughters of traders. "Firespear, fly! To my right!"

The wyverns shot toward him with blazing eyes, a mile away, then a hundred yards. Riders sat upon them, clad in steel and clasping crossbows and shields. They were but a drop from the sea of Solina's army, but they were a drop of acid.

Lyana reached him, bloody and panting, and spun to fly by his side.

"Dragonbone!" Elethor shouted hoarsely. "Firespear! Fly! Fly!"

Two hundred dragons clumsily took flight. A few yelped in fear, and others blew fire too soon, scattering their flames into empty air. Dragons from other phalanxes soared too and came to fly behind him, a jumbled crowd. Treale shot forward to fly at his side, roaring fire, and Elethor growled and summoned his own flames.

The wyverns crashed against them.

Elethor had never seen a living wyvern, only a hanging corpse. Now a horde howled before him; it was like facing charging bears after studying a harmless rug. A jet of acid flew toward him and Elethor banked. The spray hit a dragon behind him, and the young soldier screamed. Elethor saw his scales bubbling, and then the dragon lost his magic; he fell, a screaming boy, his clothes and skin sizzling. Crossbows fired and bolts flew; one slammed into Elethor's leg and he yowled. Ten more wyverns swooped above him, and acid rained. Elethor reared, flew backward, and hit a dragon behind him. With a roar, he shot flames in a fountain. They crashed against the wyverns. The creatures screeched, heads tossed back, and Elethor soared toward them. He blew more fire, then lashed claws and fangs.

He howled. It felt like biting iron; the beasts had scales like the thickest armor. When he clawed them again, sparks rose; he could not reach their flesh. One of the creatures thrust forward and bit, a striking asp. Fangs dug into Elethor's shoulder, just missing his neck, and he roared. He lashed his tail madly, hit the beast, and its jaw opened. Elethor roasted it with fire.

The wyvern's rider blazed, screamed, and fell from the saddle into the night. The wyvern itself roared, confused, consumed with bloodlust. Without its rider, it was but a mindless beast. Elethor clubbed its head with his tail, again and again, until it fell from the sky.

"Aim for the riders!" he shouted to the dragons around him. "Kill the riders!"

He looked around wildly, surveying the battle. He could not see Lyana. Far to his right, Treale was shooting between wyverns as fast as a scurrying bee, blowing flames. Hundreds of dragons flew haphazardly, abandoning all the formations he had taught them; they fought not as an army, but as a mob. Wyverns crashed between them, clawing and biting and blowing acid. Dragons turned into young men and women all around and fell screaming, acid eating through them. Bodies littered the hills below.

A fountain of acid poured toward him. Elethor growled, banked, and crashed into a second wyvern. Droplets blazed against his wing, and he howled. He flapped that wing madly, shaking the acid off, but already holes were tearing open. The wyvern he'd crashed into clawed his shoulder, drawing blood. With a growl, Elethor bit into its neck. He thought his fangs could break off, yet he grimaced and shoved them deeper, until he bit through the wyvern's scales and tasted flesh. The creature roared, and Elethor pulled his jaw back, a scale in his maw like an iron shield. He spat it out and blew fire in a curtain, holding back the other wyverns; a dozen flew toward him, eyes red and maws dripping.

"My king!"

Treale swooped from above, claws outstretched, and slashed at the wyverns. She joined her fire to his. Ten more dragons flew from below, showering flame. Atop the wyverns, riders burned and screamed. A few were still firing crossbows even as they blazed. Elethor soared, swooped, and lashed his tail. He tore one rider near in half, showering blood like red mist, and roasted another. Their riders dead, the wyverns fought wildly, driven by pure instinct. The dragons crashed against them. Fire and acid filled the air. Claws and fangs lashed. Bodies fell.

Finally only a handful of wyverns remained. Screeching, they turned and began to fly north.

"Don't let them flee!" Elethor shouted. He looked around, seeking Lyana, but couldn't see her. Fear gripped him, but he growled and began flying north in pursuit; seeking Lyana would have to wait.

Treale and several of her troops, dragons from her father's farmlands, flew with him. They were young, fast dragons, grown strong from hunting over the plains. They caught the wyverns a league from the beach, slew them with fire, and roared in triumph.

When the beasts hit the ground below, their acid spilled like juice from cracked melons, eating into the earth.

When the last wyvern was dead, Elethor found himself trembling.

Lyana. Stars, Lyana, where are you?

As Treale and the others howled around him, he spun and began flying back to the beach.

Stars, Lyana, if I find you dead, I'm going to kill you.

He returned to hills littered with death: bodies charred black, their bones peeking from cracked skin; strewn limbs and severed heads, ripped from torsos with claw and fang; and clumps of raw flesh leaking from blackened armor, mere vestiges of humanity. Blood soaked the grass. Among the dead, wounded men and women screamed, some missing limbs, some burnt black and red, some futilely clutching at their spilling entrails. Elethor saw one girl, sixteen if she were a day, weeping in blood; her legs were gone, burnt away to stumps.

Nausea rose in Elethor. His head spun. Lord Oldnale's words returned to him. *The sons and daughters of Requiem will die for your pride!*

Elethor clenched his jaw, lungs tight, barely able to breathe. The death and blood whirled around him.

They had brought a dozen healers from Nova Vita—young women trained by Mother Adia in the temple. These healers now rushed among the wounded, pressing bandages to cuts and burns. Dozens of dragons still flew above, having abandoned their phalanxes; they looked like headless chickens flapping around a coop. The rest of the army perched atop the cliffs, some staring back at the hills, others still watching the sea.

A hundred wyverns nearly tore through us, Elethor thought, stomach churning. *What will twenty thousand do when we meet them?*

Then he spotted Lyana, and all thoughts but of her faded from his mind.

He had not seen her in a year, and he barely recognized her. She lay on the ground in human form, wearing tatters of silk. Lashes covered her body, stitched but still raw and red, and her head had been shaven so roughly scratches covered her scalp. Her eyes were closed, her body limp. Several soldiers surrounded her, staring down with pale faces. Elethor landed by them, nudged the young men aside with his wings, and shifted into human form.

Stars, oh stars, Lyana, what did they do to you?

He knelt above her and checked her pulse. Her heart still beat, and she still breathed, but that breath was shallow. Bruises covered her face, and fresh blood beaded along her stitches. They had beaten her within an inch of her life. One of the lashes looked particularly raw and swollen; Elethor thought it might be infected.

"Lyana, I'm here," he whispered. He lifted her head gingerly, leaned down, and kissed her forehead. "You're safe now. We'll heal you."

Along with his worry, shame filled him. How could he have doubted his love for her? How could he have spoken to Treale of being forced into marrying Lyana... thought of Treale herself as a woman to love? He clenched his fists and his head spun. Here in his arms lay Lyana—imperious, headstrong Lyana, beautiful and sad Lyana, the woman he loved more than the sky, than the rustle of birches, than the stars themselves—a new light in his life.

Healers soon knelt above her, rubbed herbs into her wounds, and let her drink medicine from a vial. Still Lyana slept. She was barefoot, Elethor noticed in a daze, her soles cut and red. He touched her forehead and his eyes stung.

"Lyana," he whispered as healers tended to her. "Do you remember what I told you in darkness, when we walked through nightmares we thought we could never wake from?" His memories returned to the Abyss and the disease that had infested her there. He caressed her cheek. "I told you that I would heal you, that I would bring you home. I told you that I'm always yours. I still am."

Treale approached in human form, damp eyes peering from an ashy face. Mud and soot covered her armor. She knelt by Lyana, touched the knight's cheek, and then looked up at Elethor. Worry filled her eyes.

"My lord, the wyverns... they flew from the north," the squire said. She looked at the storm clouds whence the beasts had emerged. "Where did they come from? What does this mean?" She looked back at him, eyes haunted. A bloody cut ran down her arm.

Still holding Lyana, Elethor looked at a dead wyvern that lay a dozen yards away, burying its rider. His belly knotted and an invisible claw clamped his skull. He looked back at Lyana.

"Wake up," he whispered to her. "Wake up, Lyana, and tell us what you know."

She lay in his arms, eyes closed, breath shallow.

"The Lady Lyana will sleep for a day and night," said one of the healers, a young woman with dark braids and white robes now blood-red. "We gave her silverweed wine. It will heal her, but she will not wake until tomorrow."

With a stab of memory, Elethor recognized this healer; she was Piri, the daughter of a winemaker, a girl whom Bayrin had boasted of kissing in the forest three years ago. He remembered her brother too; the man had fought by his side in the Phoenix War and fallen underground. Elethor closed his eyes, his belly sinking. His breath felt like smoke in his lungs.

"Place her on a litter, Piri," he said. "We fly with her."

Piri looked at her fellow healers and nodded. Two of the robed women fetched a litter, placed Lyana gently upon it, and strapped her down. Piri shifted into a slim, lavender dragon with silver horns; the litter was fastened onto her back like a saddle. Elethor ached to see his betrothed lying there, so small upon her mount.

He turned away to face Treale and hundreds of other soldiers; they stood in the dirt, watching him, awaiting orders.

"These wyverns were but a drop from the sea of Solina's army," Elethor said. "Lyana was their prisoner; her wrists and ankles are chafed from chains. She escaped them. She flew here; the wyverns we slew were sent to catch her." He looked south toward the crashing sea. "Solina will not invade from the south." He clenched his fists. This beach lay only a league from their eastern border. *Bloody stars, how could I be so blind.* "She already flies in Requiem. She invaded from Osanna... from the northeast."

Ash covered Treale's face, but he could still see her blanch.

"Stars," she whispered. "The border with Osanna... My parents..." She shifted into a dragon and took flight, her wings raising clouds of dust. "She will be burning Oldnale Farms. We must fly!" The black dragon blew fire. "Fly, dragons of Requiem! Fly!"

Elethor shifted too, flapped his wings, and took flight. Night had fallen. He soared higher until the air grew thin and cold and the hills became mere lumps across a rolling land. He tossed his head back. He roared the signal: three diagonal blasts of fire. A pause. Three more blasts tilted like falling columns. A pause. Three more. All dragons across the border, which stretched from here to Gilnor in the west, were trained to know this signal.

Fall back.

Fall back to Nova Vita.

He stared to the west. The next guard post lay several leagues away; three dragons patrolled there. Elethor stared, barely daring to breathe. What if they could not see him through the clouds? What if they had fallen? Finally, in the distant darkness, he saw the signal returned.

Three diagonal blasts of fire. Fallen columns.

Fall back.

Fall back to Nova Vita.

Even farther away, so far he could barely see, the next outpost raised the signal too. The alarm would stretch across the border for hundreds of leagues, from soldier to soldier, until it reached the swamps of Gilnor where the last dragons flew.

Fall back.

Fall back home.

Elethor descended until he flew a hundred yards above his army. Men were already digging graves for the fallen. Elethor roared to the army.

"Fly, dragons of Requiem! Shift into dragons and fly! Into your phalanxes. Fly in formation. Leave your dead. We fly to war!"

Fire streamed between his teeth, impossible to contain; he blew a stream into the sky. He began to fly north, eyes narrowed and belly roiling. Soon three thousand dragons flew behind him, their wings and howls a storm. Treale flew at his side, panting and snarling.

"We must fly to Oldnale Manor, my lord!" she said to him, eyes flashing. "It lies on the border with Osanna. If Solina invades there, she will burn every farm my family owns."

Elethor cursed himself. He cursed the wyverns. He cursed Solina and all her men. He had left the dead to rot behind him. He would now leave the living too, and the fires of sacrifice burned through him.

"We do not fly to Oldnale Manor. If wyverns flew there, Treale, we must trust that your family fled. Twenty-five thousand souls live in Nova Vita; that is where Solina heads. That is where we head too." He growled and blew a blast of fire. "We failed to block her passage into Requiem; we can no longer save the countryside. We fall back to the capital."

Treale gasped and tears filled her eyes. She shook her head mightily and roared her fire.

"My king! I cannot abandon my family. I cannot leave them to die." She glared at him, fire sparking between her teeth. "I must fly to them, my king."

He glared back at her, eyes narrowed. "You are a soldier of Requiem, Treale Oldnale. You train for knighthood. Your duty is with your king." He lowered his head, chest aching, and his voice softened. "I lost my family to Solina; I know the pain of loss. But our duty now lies at the capital; it is Nova Vita we must defend now. And you will fly there with us."

Treale gave him a long stare, rage and tears mingling in her eyes. Then she blasted fire, spun around, and began flying east.

"I go to warn my family!" she said. "That is where my duty lies. Goodbye, King Elethor! We will meet in our starlit halls of afterlife!"

With that, she disappeared into the clouds, roaring fire.

Elethor watched the clouds, throat tight.

Her family will die, he knew. *She will die. Her home and people will burn. All of Requiem will rise in flame again.* He howled, letting rage overflow his terror. *But I will save my city. If Requiem burns around us, I will save our last bastion.*

"Fly!" he cried. "Fly with all your speed!"

They flew through the night, three thousand strong, sons and daughters, a young king, a bloodied knight. The darkness spread endless before them and the winds of war screamed.

SOLINA

He entered her tent clad in armor, clutching his throat and still wheezing. He took slow, confident paces and held his back straight and shoulders squared—a pathetic attempt to restore some pride. He had lost their catch; no steel armor nor strong stance could save his pride today.

Solina sat in her chair, feet upon a footstool. Around her draped the walls of her tent—thick red cloth embroidered with golden suns. Candles burned upon giltwood tables around them. Solina sipped wine, then placed her goblet down. She gave Mahrdor a long, silent look. He stared back steadily, blue eyes emotionless, but his fingers still clutched his throat, and his lip gave a twitch.

Solina sighed. "You let the bird fly."

When he spoke, his voice was but a hoarse whisper. "A dragon, my queen, not a bird; a dragon who nearly clawed my throat out." He pulled his hand back, revealing a neck scratched red and raw. Blood still dripped from it.

Solina laughed. "The Lady Lyana Eleison. I grew up with her, Mahrdor—a pampered girl born into splendor. I saw her cry once when a bee stung her in the gardens. And this rich, spoiled spawn of a lordling, born with a silver spoon up her backside, nearly clawed out the throat of mighty General Mahrdor, Lord of Tiranor's Hosts?"

As stiff as he stood, he managed to stiffen further. "My queen, the girl you knew has grown. She is a vicious beast now, a creature, a—"

"Was she a dragon in your tent?" Solina asked.

Mahrdor began to say something, then closed his mouth. He inhaled sharply through his nostrils. "My queen? I—"

"You claim she is no bird, but a creature, a... how did you call it? A vicious beast? Your tent still stands, does it not? Charred, yes, but still standing. I saw it from the hill. Surely a vicious *dragon* would have torn your tent to shreds."

Something cold and dangerous filled his eyes. She had never seen him stare at her like that. Quick as it kindled, the blue fire in his eyes died. He raised his chin. "She shifted into a dragon outside my tent."

"And yet..." Solina crossed her legs upon the footstool. "And yet you were found gasping and croaking *inside* your tent, clutching at your throat. You were dragged from the smoke nearly dead. Curious thing, is it not? One could almost think—it's a long stretch of imagination, to be sure, but hear me out—one could almost think that a chained, pampered, utterly defenseless girl choked you... not a dragon." She raised her palms, as if weighing one enemy in each. "Vicious dragon? Chained girl? Which was it, Mahrdor? Which of these horrible enemies did this to you?"

His lips pulled back in but the slightest snarl, and his hands formed fists at his sides. "A girl who can *become* a dragon, a—"

"A girl who became a dragon *after* choking you." She rose to her feet and approached him. "Mahrdor, you lead this army. You command the hosts of the Sun God himself. You are, supposedly, the greatest soldier in my kingdom. And this..." She touched his neck. "The work of a chained, pampered girl from a soft northern land."

He stared at her silently. She could see his emotions: rage, shame, and finally... finally the blank duty of a soldier. He lowered his head, jaw clenched.

"I failed you, my queen." Fists clenched at his sides, he knelt before her. "Forgive me, your highness."

She sighed again, stepped aside, and looked at the back of the tent. A clay jug sat there, a cloth atop it. When she sniffed the air, its scent tingled her nostrils. She turned back toward her general. He looked at the jug, paled, and returned his eyes to her.

"My queen. I..." He breathed sharply. "I beg you."

"Beg me?" she said and snorted a laugh. "I begged too, Mahrdor. I begged the weredragons to spare my parents' life. I begged them to release me from my northern captivity. I begged so many times." She touched her line of fire, the scar that ran down her face, neck, and chest. "But they scarred me, Mahrdor. They deformed me. It was Lyana's betrothed who gave me this scar, the lover of the woman you freed." She pointed at the jug. "Now you will carry scars too. Do it silently. Your left hand; the one you tried to conceal your neck with. Make not a sound. If you scream, your right hand will follow."

His lip curled. "And if I refuse?" he rasped.

She shrugged. "Refuse then. Storm out of my tent and try to escape; we will hunt you. Try to kill me. You could not defeat a chained girl; you will not defeat me."

He took a step toward her. His eyes blazed. "If I escape, you will hunt me, but you will not catch me."

"Perhaps." She sat back down and sipped her wine; it tasted of berries, oak, and a hint of spices. "You could perhaps evade us for a while. You could seek exile in some distant land, a sojourner. Instead of your villa upon the River Pallan, you could squat in alleys in Confutatis, or live feral in Hostias Forest, or become a hermit in some western mountain in Salvandos. You could forsake your servants and fine meals; you could eat squirrel dung if you like. It bothers me not; it would, in fact, amuse me. Then, a few years down the line, I will find you with a long beard and some ratty cloak—a pathetic disguise—and I will dip your head into my vase. Or..." She raised her left hand and flexed the fingers. "You can do this quickly, you can do it silently, and we can keep flying to Nova Vita."

He stared at her. Their eyes locked for what seemed the turn of seasons. She saw the madness there, that madness he kept hidden, that drove him, that would have him prove his loyalty today. She herself would have run, but he would be too stubborn, too proud.

He tore his eyes away, walked toward the jug, and thrust his fist into the acid.

His jaw clenched and his body shook, but he did not make a sound.

ELETHOR

They flew through the night, thousands of dragons with blazing eyes. Clouds hid the stars and rain fell. Only the fire in their maws lit the darkness. Their wings glided upon the wind. Below them, red firelight raced against mountaintops and cliffs.

"Be strong, Mori," Elethor whispered into the wind. "I'm coming home."

When he looked northeast, he saw the distant red glow. It still lay many leagues away, but rose like a dawn. Firelight. The wilderness of Requiem burning. *Solina flies there.*

He looked over his shoulder. His army stretched for a league behind, the slower dragons dragging like a wake. Elethor cursed. They were only as fast as their slowest soldiers.

"Fly, dragons of Requiem!" he shouted in the night. "Fly with all your might!"

He looked back into the northern darkness. Nova Vita lay there beyond mountains, forests, lakes, and fields. Hundreds of leagues still lay between them and their home. Elethor had been flying for a day and night, and his wings ached, and his lungs burned, and dull pain throbbed in his chest. He forced himself onward.

Soon true dawn rose in the east, as red as the distant fires. Clouds stretched across the sky like bloody fingers. When Elethor looked at his army, he saw dragons panting, wobbling, and falling out of formations. Behind him, the stragglers were nearly too distant to see. Many of the dragons who had guarded the border—those who had been stationed closest to Ralora—had joined them. The others were making their own way to the capital; it could be days until they began to arrive. Elethor ground his teeth, spat flame, and cursed some more.

"We must rest, my lord," said a lavender dragon who flew by him—the young healer Piri. Like all healers, she wore a litter over her back; upon it, fastened with ropes, Lyana lay in human form. The knight's eyes were still closed, her wounds still raw.

Smoke rose from Elethor's mouth, nearly blinding him. He wanted to keep flying. How could he stop when Solina burned the farmlands, when her army flew toward Nova Vita, when the last Vir Requis faced the wrath of twenty thousand wyverns? He growled and forced his wings to keep flapping. He had to save Mori. He had to save Treale if he still could. He had to stop Solina from felling the city his ancestors had built.

"My lord!" said Piri. Her tongue lolled and her eyes rolled back. She wobbled as she flew, jostling Lyana upon her back. "Please, my lord, we must rest."

The lavender dragon looked ready to fall from the sky; if she fell, Lyana would fall with her. How long had they been flying? A day and night, or was it two nights? Elethor could no longer remember; he could barely form thoughts. All he knew was pain—the blaze in his lungs, the throbbing of his wings, the stabs in his chest. Exhaustion overwhelmed him, numbing even this pain. He felt like he could fly forever until he collapsed at the gates of Nova Vita.

"Solina," he managed to whisper. "Solina, I am coming for you."

Yet how would he fight her, sapped of strength, his army close to collapsing? Piri was right. They had to sleep, eat, and regain their strength. Even if they could reach Solina without rest, they would reach her exhausted; she would crush them.

He nodded and tossed his head to scatter the smoke from his nostrils. "We set camp." He raised his voice. "Dragons of Requiem, we land."

He began spiraling down toward a valley between rolling mountains. A river pooled there into a lake, its shores grassy. A few feet above the lakeshore, Elethor filled his wings with air, reached out his claws, and landed with a groan. As soon as his wings stilled, pain blazed across them, down his chest, and into his jaw. He felt like he would never fly again. He looked above him to see thousands of dragons land around him, moan, and collapse.

Elethor shifted into human form. At once sweat covered him. He wiped it from his eyes, approached Piri, and helped unload the litter Lyana lay on. He laid his betrothed upon the grass and knelt over her.

"Lyana," he whispered and held her hand.

Her eyes fluttered opened; she seemed just now to be rising from her long silverweed sleep. She blinked at him, then gasped and tried to rise, but straps still held her to the litter.

"Elethor!" she said. "El, the wyverns, they—"

"I know, Lyana." He touched her forehead; it was hot. "We've been chasing them north for two days. You drank silverweed and have been sleeping." He began unbuckling the straps that held her onto the litter. "We're in Cela Mountains, a third of the way to Nova Vita."

As soon as her straps were opened, she sprang up, crashed into his embrace, and held him tight. She sniffed and her fingers dug into his back.

"Oh, Elethor," she whispered. "I'm sorry. I'm so sorry."

He closed his eyes and lowered his head. She felt so thin in his arms, frailer than he'd ever known her. He held her awkwardly, daring not touch the stitches that ran across her back. He wanted to stroke her head, but her scalp was still raw; red stubble covered it. He gently kissed her forehead.

"You need not be sorry, Lyana," he whispered. "*I* am sorry, though. I sent you into danger. I let this happen to you. I'm sorry, Lyana. I will never send you away again." He raised her chin with his finger and kissed her lips. "I'm not letting you get into any more trouble."

She laughed weakly and tears sparkled in her eyes. "My parents could never keep me out of trouble; you won't either." Then she sniffed again and touched his cheek. "Did you grow a beard, Elethor? It suits you. You look like your father."

He snorted. "You lose hair, I gain it." Then he pulled her close again, nearly crushing her against his chest. "You scared me, Lyana. Stars, I'm glad you're back. I—"

I love you, he wanted to say. *I love you like a new spring after winter. You are the strongest, bravest woman I know.*

Yet as he held her, he could say none of those things. He could still feel the touch of her lips on his. And he still thought of Orin, the man she had loved, the man they had lost. He still thought of Solina, whose kisses never felt like this, warm pecks of the lips, but like spirits shooting through him. He loved Lyana; he knew that. How could he not? Lyana was wise and strong and beautiful. And yet... and yet...

I hold her because Solina left. I hold her because my brother died. He looked away.

Soldiers approached them, carrying battle rations: dried meats, kippers, bread rolls, and jars of apple preserves. Elethor accepted the food gratefully, both for his hunger and the awkwardness of his embrace with Lyana. He released his betrothed, and for long moments they ate in silence.

The commanders of his phalanxes approached. Most were survivors of the old City Guard—seasoned warriors. A few were minor nobles—one an Oldnale, an uncle of Lady Treale, another a distant cousin of Bayrin and Lyana. Elethor gave them their orders:

"We sleep for five hours. Then we fly again."

Within moments, the soldiers of the Royal Army lay with closed eyes; those who had followed him to Ralora Beach, and those who had joined them from the border stretching west. Elethor lay upon the grass, looking up into the clouds. Lyana nestled in his arms, her head against his chest, her breath soft. She slept, mumbling and holding him. He kissed her cheek.

Dawn rose around them, blood red. In the northeastern horizon, distant fires glowed.

Be safe, Treale, Elethor thought, staring to her distant home. *Come back to us.*

As he held Lyana, he thought of Treale's soft hair, her dark eyes, and her warm lips against his cheek. He thought of Solina, the love of his youth, who flew from the north. He wanted to think about nobody but Lyana, nobody but this perfect woman in his arms—and she was perfect, even with her hair sheared and her body bruised. And yet his belly knotted, and his thoughts swirled like ghosts rattling in his skull. Finally he slept, Lyana warm in his arms.

TREALE

She had left the Royal Army two days ago and soared over the wilderness. She was young and slim and fast as roaring wind. The army had long disappeared behind her; the plains lay ahead, rolling green toward distant fires.

Oldnale Farms. Burning.

Her wings, lungs, and chest blazed with pain. She howled and blew fire. She had forced herself to sleep last night and to hunt a deer, but exhaustion still tugged on her like chains. The thought of the two graves outside Oldnale Manor—the graves of her brothers, slain fighting the phoenixes last year—rattled through her mind. She would not let her parents lie dead beside them.

The plains spread beneath her for leagues. Wild grass and reeds swayed. A river cut through them, bustling with cranes and geese. Hills rose every league, bristly with elms and beeches and maples. In the distant northwest, Treale could just make out Amarath Mountains, a white hint upon the blue sky. When she looked east, she saw red and black clouds claw the sky; her home lay there.

"Mother," she whispered, eyes stinging. "Father."

Her shadow raced across the grasslands below; she had never flown faster. Memories flowed through the mists of pain. Treale saw the great, scarred table in the manor hall where she and her brothers would play with wooden soldiers; the apple pies her maid would bake, and how Treale would sneak into the kitchens to steal a slice before dinner; the spears and arrows she would carve from fallen branches in the grove outside their home, pretending to be a warrior; and the hundreds of puppets she had sewn and placed upon a dozen shelves.

"My home," she whispered into the wind. "All my memories, my heartbeat, the sky of my wings."

Did the fires now claim it?

She flew, plains racing beneath her, wind howling across her scales. She blew fire. She flew for hours, a small black dragon in an endless world of grass and distant flame.

The sun hung low and red in the west when she saw the Tiran army.

A cry fled her throat.

Treale knew then: There was no hope for her family, for her king, for her army, for her race. Requiem would fall, and her children would burn or scatter in the wind. There would be no victory against these invaders from the south, only acid, blood, and death.

They covered the sky like a black cloud. Countless wyverns swarmed there; from this distance, they were mere specks, but Treale had seen enough up close to imagine their metallic scales, their red eyes, their chins that thrust out into blades. Upon their backs, she saw the glint of armor and streaming banners. Even from leagues away, she heard the shrieks and war drums, a song of death. Smoke unfurled above them, turning the sky black, and shadows spilled across the land like ink. Behind them fires blazed across the prairies. As Treale flew, she saw wyverns dipping from the mass, swooping to the lands below and kindling them. The fires raced across field, meadow, and forest. As every new blaze crackled to life, the wyverns shrieked with new vigor.

They did not come here to conquer, Treale thought. *They did not merely come here to kill. They came to destroy the very land that bred us.*

She dived down so fast her head spun and her belly lurched. She landed in swaying grass, shifted into human form, and knelt. The wild grass rose around her, five feet tall. Grasshoppers and crickets bustled. Treale pulled her knees to her chest, shivered, and whispered prayers.

"Please, stars of Requiem." She hugged herself so tightly her arms ached. "Please don't let my parents lie dead; they are all I have left. Don't let these wyverns reach our city; it is all Requiem has left. Don't let King Elethor lose his courage; he is our last hope."

She looked up at the sky. Smoke was spreading above, blocking the sun, turning blue to black. The wyvern shrieks tore across the land. She could hear men now too; they shouted orders to one another, voices as cruel as the wyvern cries. Would they fly here too? Would they burn this grass she hid in?

She sat shivering, peering between the blades of grass, until the cries of the swarm moved westward and dimmed. Treale stood, only her head rising from the tall grass. The wind streamed her hair, and when she stared west, she saw the wyverns flow into the distance.

"They're heading for Nova Vita," she whispered. "Fly fast, Elethor. Save whoever you can... and flee this land."

She leaped, shifted, and flew east. A wall of fire rose before her.

Treale dived through smoke, coughing, eyes narrowed and watering. Soon flames were racing below, baking her belly. She swerved, rose, and dipped, seeking pockets of air. The fire crackled and roared. The sky churned black and red. She felt as if she flew through a furnace, and she yowled. She wanted to rise higher, to escape the smoke, but dared not. She had to stay here near the ground, seeking her home.

Soon the land below her changed. These were no wild grasslands that burned, but ploughed fields. The wheat and barley—lush green when she had left her home—now blazed. Barns rose in flame and collapsed. Treale could not even cry; the heat seared her tears dry. She howled. She kept flying.

Finally she saw it ahead, red on black—Oldnale Manor burning.

"Mother," she whispered.

She shot between columns of smoke. She swerved between walls of fire. A blast of flame from trees below licked her claws, and she screamed and drove onward. She crashed through fire, dived toward the hill Oldnale Manor rose upon, and landed in the courtyard outside the manor gates.

Cobblestones covered the courtyard, searing hot against her claws. Three guards lay dead before her, flesh charred black; if not for their armor, the wind would have scattered them into ash. Around the hill, trees crackled and flames blazed. Before her, the doors of the manor stood burning. She saw more flames through the windows above.

"Mother!" she cried. "Father!"

Still in dragon form, she ran toward the doors and slammed through them. The wood crashed with a shower of burning splinters. Inside the main hall, tapestries and rugs burned and smoke swirled. Treale crawled, head against the floor where less smoke flowed. If she became human now, the heat would bake her flesh; even her dragon scales felt close to melting. She coughed and kept moving.

"Mother! Father!"

She could see barely a foot ahead. She reached out her claws, scratching the floor. She hit a fallen chair, shoved it aside, and kept moving. Her tail flapped behind her. She coughed and roared for her parents.

She crawled another foot through the smoke... and found herself staring at a burnt body.

Treale screamed.

The flesh had blackened and shriveled, clinging to bone. The skull gaped and the fingers thrust up like burnt twigs. Shreds of charred cloth clung to the body, and around its neck hung a talisman shaped as a sheaf of wheat.

It was her mother.

Tears filled Treale's eyes. She shivered. She froze for a moment, then with a cry, she scurried two feet away. Her throat burned. She could barely breathe. She hit something soft and hot, turned her head, and saw a second body. It too was charred black, little more than crisp flesh clinging to bones in armor. She knew the breastplate it wore; this was her father.

Treale howled. She wept. She had to take the bodies from here; she had to bury them. Weeping, she clutched her father with her claws. His body came apart in her grasp, falling from his armor like ash from a pipe, and Treale closed her eyes and trembled.

A rafter cracked above. Flames showered. The beam crashed before her and fire roared. Treale coughed and had to close her eyes against the heat. She pushed herself back, spun, and ran toward the doorway. She burst outside into the courtyard and took flight.

"I'm sorry, Mother," she whispered. "I'm sorry, Father."

She soared until she burst from smoke into clear sky. She coughed and trembled in the air. When she looked below her, she saw nothing but the inferno. A chunk from Oldnale Manor's roof collapsed, and soon nothing remained but brick walls, a shell of death and memory.

A fiery trail led west, stretching from the manor across the land. The flames trailed behind the wyvern army, moving fast, moving to Nova Vita.

When they reach our city, all there will die, Treale knew. *My friend Mori will lie charred in the ruins of the palace. Twenty thousand dragons—children, elderly, the wounded of the last war—they all will die.*

Treale tossed back her head and roared, a great howl that seemed to tear the sky, a howl of rage and loss. She was but a small black dragon, a single voice in the flame, but she thought her howl could rise to the stars.

If they die, I will die with them. I will go down fighting like my brothers did. She snarled and blew flame. *And I will take some wyverns with me.*

Roaring, she flapped her wings and drove through the air, following the wyvern army. The lands burned behind her, and tears flowed from her eyes—tears of farewell for her home, her parents, and the green lands she had loved.

BAYRIN

He was flying over the eastern forests, the city walls a distant crown behind him, when he saw the shadow. Bayrin cursed and spat fire.

The darkness spread over the mountains, a hundred miles away—as far as his eyes could see. At first he thought it a cloud, but it moved too swiftly. It looked more like a great flock of ravens, but ravens would be too small to see from here. Bayrin growled deep in his throat.

Wyverns, he thought. When he sniffed the air, he caught a hint of their stench; they stank like vinegar and sulfur.

"Damn it, Elethor, where are you?" he muttered, gliding on the wind. His king had gone south to stop these beasts from invading; now they flew from the east. A chill ran through Bayrin, rattling his scales and rippling his tail. Had these beasts skirted the Royal Army... or crushed it?

"Well, the fun begins," he said, turned around, and began flying back to Nova Vita. "El, if you're alive, you better get back here soon to join the party."

As he flew, he tossed his head back and blew blasts of diagonal fire—the shape of falling columns. Patrolling several leagues around the city, his fellow outflyers blew their own blasts and began to fall back to the walls. The walls themselves brimmed with dragons, a good five hundred of them, wearing the armor their smiths had been forging all year.

Will the acid eat through steel as through flesh? Bayrin wondered. He growled again. *We'll soon find out.*

As he approached the city, he roared the call. "Enemy at the gates! City Guard, man your posts!"

Roars and blasts of fire rose from the dragons upon the walls. The city erupted into chaos. Guards streamed out of craggy Castra Murus, shifted into dragons, and flew to perch at their posts: fifty dragons upon the palace, fifty on the Temple of Stars, and hundreds more spread across the walls. A hundred guards marched down the streets in human form, clad in breastplates and holding swords and shields. Their faces were hard as iron masks.

"People of Nova Vita!" Bayrin cried as he circled above the city. "Evacuate into the tunnels. Walk calmly in single file—like we drilled. Into the tunnels!"

Families began leaving their houses, frowning at the skies. A few children were laughing and elbowing one another; they thought this too was a drill. Others sniffed the air, seemed to detect the distant stench of the wyverns, and their eyes darkened. The people began to snake down the streets—some limping, others moving on crutches, the stronger helping the weaker. Soon they were filing into the three archways that led underground.

Bayrin looked over his shoulder toward the east. He flew too low to see the shadow now, but the acrid stench still wafted on the wind. He thought he could hear a distant buzzing like a cloud of locusts. He cursed under his breath as he flew over the city.

"Damn it, Elethor, where are you?"

As people streamed through the streets below, Bayrin flew toward the palace. He landed outside its doors, shifted into human form, and ran into the main hall. Several guards stood upon its tiles; behind them, Mori sat upon the Oak Throne.

The princess looked at him over the guards, and Bayrin's breath caught and his heart twisted. *Stars,* he thought. Her eyes seemed to drown him, gray pools of infinite depth. Mottles of sunlight kissed her pale cheeks, and her chestnut hair cascaded. Such sadness clung to her that Bayrin ached; with only a look across the hall, her eyes spoke of Orin's death, of the fall of Castellum Luna, of their kiss in the mists of northern isles, and of the wildfire that raced toward them. For the length of her stare he froze, unable to move or speak or breathe. A guard in the hall stirred and his armor creaked, drawing Bayrin's gaze. He cleared his throat and scowled.

"Men!" he barked. "Into the tunnels. Guard the people underground. Move! I'll lead the princess to safety."

The guards bowed their heads. "Yes, Lord Bayrin," they said and raced outside, drawing their longswords.

Bayrin looked back at Mori; they were alone in the palace. She rose from her throne, face blank. She wore a gown of bluish gray—the color of her eyes when she cried—and a sword hung from her waist, its pommel shaped as a dragonclaw. Bayrin crossed the hall, walked up the marble stairs to the dais the throne stood on, and reached out his hand.

"Come, Mors," he said softly. "Let's get you into the tunnels."

She stood frozen before her throne. Between the eastern columns, she could see the city where dragons perched upon roofs and walls. The sky was turning red; distant fires blazed.

"Where is Elethor?" the princess whispered. "Where is my brother?"

Bayrin took her hand. He spoke softly. "I don't know, Mori. Come, we must go."

She turned to meet his gaze, and again the sadness of her eyes flooded him. Her lips parted, pink in her pale face like a flower in snow. Her hair swayed in the wind that blew between the columns. She seemed to him almost a figure of starlight, a ghost in the hall. He tightened his hand around hers, and she raised her head, took a slow breath, and nodded. He helped her down the stairs of the dais, and they crossed the hall in silence. The columns rose around them, and Bayrin wondered if this was the last he'd see them standing.

Outside he found a sky the color of burnt flesh. Hundreds of dragons of the City Guard perched atop roofs and walls, staring east with narrowed eyes. Smoke rose from their nostrils in hundreds of plumes. On the cobbled streets, people were still moving toward the tunnels; guards in armor guided them. Bayrin saw an elderly woman limp forward, leaning against her daughter. One child pushed a wheelbarrow where lay his legless brother. Many people still bore the scars of last year's war, limbs and faces twisted with old fire.

Stars, haven't these people suffered enough? Bayrin thought, sudden rage finding him. He clenched his fist around the hilt of his longsword. *We barely survived Solina once; now she comes to burn us again.* He wanted to shift into a dragon, fly into the wyvern army, and slay Solina with all his fire and fury. For a year now, sadness had filled this city—had filled Bayrin too—as they healed, as they rebuilt, as they still wept for the dead and wounded.

Now this desert queen brings her steel and fire here again. Bayrin growled. *Now she seeks to undo all our healing.*

How could such cruelty exist? How could one queen feel such hatred, such rage, that she would seek to crush an entire race? Bayrin could not understand it. This felt like something from the old stories, the ones where King Benedictus fought as the tyrant Dies Irae slew all but the Living Seven. Bayrin had never imagined such terrors could truly exist outside of dusty old books, yet now he smelled them on the wind, and he heard their shrieks in the distance coming closer.

They reached a tunnel entrance. People were moving under the archway, down the stairs, and into shadow. The archway guards bowed their heads.

"Princess Mori," they said. "Lord Bayrin."

Mori bowed her head to them. She touched each guard on his shoulder and kissed his cheek. Their eyes were solemn, strong but frightened.

"Thank you, my friends," Mori whispered. "Thank you for your strength, for your steel, and for your courage."

Bayrin led the princess onto the narrow, candlelit staircase. Last year, the people had rushed into these tunnels, burning and terrified. Today they walked somberly, and every few feet, guards stood with spears, crossbows, and shields. At the bottom of the staircase, a heavy door waited, and more guards stood here to usher them through. Down the tunnels Bayrin and Mori walked, passing more and more guards, under the portcullis, and past doors of bronze.

Here spread a network of chambers where Requiem's people hid. Thousands of men and women—those too young, old, or wounded to fight—huddled here. Word had spread that the war had truly come, that this was no drill. Tears filled eyes, mothers embraced children, and whispers rose like maelstroms. In every chamber, three guards stood armed with steel.

"The Princess Mori," whispered a few people. More whispers rose through the tunnels. "The Princess Mori! Stars bless you, my lady."

Bayrin led Mori to the deepest chamber. The walls and ceiling loomed, carved with dragon claws. The air smelled of moss, soil, and fear. They moved to stand by a wall where candles burned in alcoves. Mori looked at Bayrin, held his hands, and her lips parted as if she would speak but could not find words.

"Mori, I return to my post," he said softly. "I will watch upon the walls, and I will fight in the sky above our city." He looked at the wall where hung a tapestry, its threads forming scenes of dragons flying under stars. "Mori, if I fail... if they break down the doors... you know what to do."

She looked at the tapestry and clutched the hilt of her sword.

"I know," she whispered.

He nodded, throat tight. "It will not come to that. Not so long as there is fire in my maw, strength to my claws, and wind in my wings. I promise you, Mori."

She lowered her head and nodded, bit her lip, and looked up at him. Tears trembled in her eyes, and she touched his cheek, then wrapped her arms around him. She held him tight.

"Be careful, Bay," she whispered. "I love you."

She looked up at him, and he cupped her cheek and kissed her—a long kiss that melted into rivers of mist. Bayrin closed his eyes, and again he lay upon grass in the Crescent Isle, the place where he had first kissed Mori. He could smell the pines and mist. He could feel the cool, damp air against his skin and Mori's soft hair in his fingers. She had been a mere girl then, frightened and meek, and he a lowly guard; the past year seemed like a lifetime of healing.

"I love you too, Mors," he whispered and held her close. He kissed her forehead. "I will come back to you. Always. Always."

He left the tunnels, her kiss still warm on his lips and the softness of her hair still tingling his fingers. When he emerged onto the city streets, he found them deserted; every last guard aboveground perched as a dragon upon the walls and rooftops. He shifted and took flight, wings raising demons of dust. He landed upon the eastern wall and stared into the distance.

The shadow was closer now. Fire raced below it, consuming the countryside, and smoke unfurled like wings. Bayrin could just make out the glint of distant armor and spearheads, just hear war drums on the wind. He shifted his jaw and fire sparked between his teeth.

Twenty thousand wyverns, he thought. *A thousand dragons of the City Guard. Stars, Elethor, where the abyss are you?*

Wings beat like more war drums, air blasted Bayrin, and his father landed beside him. Lord Deramon was a burly beast of a dragon, all clanking copper scales. The stone walls moaned below him, and so much smoke rose from his maw it hid the landscape.

"Any sight of the Royal Army?" Deramon asked, voice a grumble like gravel under boots.

Bayrin shook his head. "Nobody has seen Elethor. No word from him." He looked at his father and his stomach knotted. "We are alone."

Had Elethor fallen? What about Lyana? Bayrin's eyes burned and terror swelled inside him. He clutched the battlements, his claws digging into the stone. He forced himself to think of Mori's eyes, her lips on his, and the softness of her hair. If his king and sister were dead, he still had to fight—for Mori and for all the others underground.

The smell of smoke and acid filled his nostrils. The eastern shadow shimmered and grew.

SOLINA

Night began to fall when she saw the City of Dragons ahead. She bared her teeth and snarled. Her wyvern howled beneath her and clawed at the sky. Baal's scales clanged and as his tail lashed, Solina bounced in the saddle, pushed her knees against it, and smiled.

"Nova Vita," she whispered and licked her lips.

A year ago, she had ravaged this city—ripping dragons upon the streets, crushing houses, and burning the holy birches of Requiem. And yet these walls still stood. *Now is the time to finish the job.*

"Mahrdor!" she shouted, voice rising on the wind. "Divide them up! Invasion formation. Go!"

When she looked over her shoulder, she saw him flying there upon his wyvern. His left hand was wrapped in leather, and his right hand clutched a sabre. Behind him flew two hundred phalanxes, each a hundred wyverns strong. Every wyvern howled for blood and clawed the air. Every rider raised a spear and cried for glory, for Tiranor, and for Queen Solina. The roar shook the sky. Every phalanx flew in formation, their banners sporting their sigils: bloody claws, flaming hearts, crossed sabres, blazing suns, and dozens of others.

"Phalanxes!" Mahrdor shouted, voice hoarse and deep in the wind. "Invasion formation! Sunfire! Bloodspear! To my right, move. Wyvern Claws, Heartflame, Sabre Steel—fan out, go!"

The general flew between the lines, arranging the phalanxes for invasion. From the border, the army had flown in a line—an arrow of glory. Now they spread out like a claw opening to clutch the city. They would encircle this pathetic Nova Vita, crush it in their grip, and claim its spoils.

"Soldiers of Tiranor!" Solina howled, riding at their lead. She grabbed the banner pole from its ring on her saddle and raised it high. Her standard blew wide and long—a golden sun upon a white field. Her soldiers howled for their queen.

"Queen Solina! Queen Solina! For the glory of Phoebus!"

Even in the wind, their voices reached her, so loud and deep they thudded in her chest. They gained speed. Below them the lands streamed, and the wind shrieked, and the clouds swirled, and Solina howled for the glory of her lord.

"Soldiers of Tiranor!" she shouted again, banner held high. "Tonight your wyverns will feast upon dragon flesh!" The riders howled and the wyverns shrieked. "Tonight the light of the Sun God will banish the darkness of reptiles!" The soldiers roared and brandished their sabres. Solina screamed hoarsely. "Tonight every phalanx will prove its glory and strength! The phalanx that kills the most weredragons will enjoy the greatest spoil: the Weredragon Princess for its men's pleasures!"

The riders howled their approval. The phalanx commanders raised their banners high and chanted their names.

"Sunfire!"

"Bloodspear!"

"Sabre Steel"

Two hundred banners flew. Two hundred phalanxes roared for their glory.

"We fly to war!" Solina howled, raising banner in one hand, sabre in the other. She cried out the Old Words of her people. "We will never fall!"

They answered her call. "To war! To war! We will never fall!"

The city loomed near now—so near that she could see the dragons upon its walls.

"Destroy this city!" she shouted and the army roared. "Bring me the king and princess alive! Slay every other reptile you find!"

They shot through the wind. Their banners streamed. Their wyverns cried. They crossed fields and flew over burnt forests, moving closer, until the city loomed three leagues away, then two, and Solina snarled. She reattached her banner to her saddle and grabbed her shield. She held sword and shield before her. *Soon I will lick blood from this steel.*

She was snarling, already tasting the coppery sweetness, when roars rose in the south.

She turned in the saddle and saw him there.

My love. My youth. My sunfire.

"Elethor," she whispered.

She knew it was him. From here the dragons were but a distant cloud, a shimmering shadow of color and flame, but she knew that he flew there. She could feel him on the wind, hear him in the distant roars. Once more she heard his cry—echoing from eight years ago—as he stood upon the walls of Nova Vita, calling her name.

"Solina!" His voice had been raw and torn. "Solina!"

She had wept that day, burnt and bleeding and alone. She had left him, going into her exile. She had fled into the sand, raised her kingdom from ruin, raised this army, raised this glory to light the world. And now he would shout again above the walls of Nova Vita. Now again fire would burn and blood spill.

"Elethor," she whispered again, "you have come to me."

How many times she had kissed him! How many times she had loved him in the dark! Today he would be hers again, not a lover, but a prisoner. Today he would cry her name again, not in love, but in agony as she ripped into his flesh.

"Elethor..."

She clutched her sabre between her teeth, grabbed the reins, and pulled her wyvern around. The beast banked, tilting so steeply that Solina nearly fell from the saddle. She snarled and began flying south.

"Riders of Tiranor!" she cried. "Assault formation! Form rank! Follow me—we fight in the sky!"

The other riders noticed the distant cloud too. From here the dragons were a mere smudge in the sunset, a shimmer of scales, blue and red and green. Fire rose from them like sunbeams. Their howls rolled upon the wind. Solina led the charge, sabre raised, shouts ringing hoarsely. When she looked over her shoulder, she saw her army change formation; now they formed a great fist in the sky. Her strongest phalanxes flew at the vanguard, armed with spears and crossbows. Their wyverns filled their maws with acid; the sharp stench filled Solina's nostrils and burned her lungs. She inhaled deeply, savoring it.

"For the Sun God!" she cried and her army echoed her call. "Banish their darkness with our light!"

The two armies streamed toward each other. When the dragons came nearer, Solina bared her teeth in a grin. At most four thousand dragons flew toward them—probably fewer. *We outnumber them five to one.*

"For Requiem!" rose their distant cries, deep and echoing against the stony mountains below. "Requiem!"

The sunset blazed red, casting beams across the land like spilling blood. The mountains below kindled in the light. Dragonfire rose in pillars. Wyverns screeched. Soon only a league separated the armies, and Solina raised her blade and cried to her love.

"Elethor! Elethor, we meet again!"

He flew at his army's lead, a brass dragon with fire in his maw. He sounded his roar, and his dragons answered the call.

"For King Elethor!" the dragons cried. "For Requiem!"

Fire blazed toward her. Her wyvern's acid blew. Above the mountains, the armies clashed with blood and screams.

ELETHOR

Roaring fire, he flew at Solina.

Sunrays blazed around him. His fire streamed forward, crackling and spinning. From the inferno, a stream of acid hissed. Elethor howled and banked, dodging the acid. The drops sizzled against his side, jabs of agony like arrows tipped with poison.

"Elethor!" rose her voice from the smoke and flame. She laughed maniacally. "We meet again, Elethor, King of Lizards!"

He growled and flew toward her; he could just make out her form among the smoke. All around them, dragons and wyverns clashed. Fire and acid sprayed, blood spilled, crossbows fired, and bodies rained. Elethor blew fire and Solina raised her shield. The flames bathed it, white-hot, and Solina screamed.

Her wyvern, the great beast Baal, lashed claws the size of men. Elethor pulled back, dodging the blows. Baal's neck thrust forward, jaws snapped, and a fang tore at Elethor's leg. Blood splashed, and Elethor soared just as the beast spewed acid.

He swerved, dodged the sizzling fountain, and swooped. Before he could muster fire, Baal barreled into him. Fangs drove into Elethor's shoulder. He roared. Acid filled Baal's mouth, spilling across Elethor; he screamed in agony.

"You scream like a sow in heat, Elethor!" Solina shouted, grinning wildly. She raised her crossbow, loaded a bolt, and aimed. "You will scream for me in Tiranor soon."

Nearly blind with pain, Elethor swiped his tail.

The crossbow thrummed and a bolt glanced off Elethor's horn.

His tail hit Solina and she screamed.

The blow knocked her sideways—nearly off her saddle. The reins tugged tight, and Baal released Elethor and fell into shadow.

"Elethor!" Solina screamed, and then a horde of dragons and wyverns rolled between them, and she vanished into clouds of fire and blood.

Elethor's shoulder blazed; acid drenched it. He slapped his claws and blew his breath at the foul liquid. The last drops fell, revealing a steaming wound; the acid had eaten through three scales and left his flesh raw and red.

He looked through the flames, seeking his fellow dragons. They flew all around him, four thousand strong; nearly all the dragons who had guarded the southern border, from Ralora to western Gilnor, now flew with him. They were roaring battle cries, blowing flames every which way, and scattering and reforming in chaos. Some howled in fury; others wailed in fear. As he watched, acid sprayed several dragons. They became men and women in midair, screaming and clutching at their melting faces; they fell into darkness.

"Dragons of Requiem!" Elethor cried. "Form rank! Into your phalanxes. Fight them! Kill the riders! Burn them down—"

Two wyverns crashed into him. Their fangs and claws tore at his scales. Acid sprayed and Elethor howled.

He soared, claws lashing, and crashed between them. Above them, he shook himself and bellowed. The acid was already eating at his scales; as he shook, it rained upon the wyverns below. Their riders screamed as the acid seeped through their armor.

Even as they burned, the riders raised crossbows. Bolts flew. Elethor swerved. One bolt shot through his wing, and he crashed into a wyvern at his side. Another beast dived above. Elethor could see no end to them. He spun in all directions, spraying fire and holding the creatures back.

"Solina!" he shouted.

Where was she? He dived between raining bodies, seeking her. Smoke blinded him. Wyverns and dragons shot in every direction, flashes of scales. Human bodies thumped against him, rolled off, and hit the mountains below.

"Form rank!" Elethor shouted. "Dragons of Requiem! Fight them!"

He looked from side to side, panting. Acid coated them. They screamed. Their magic left them; they became men and women and tumbled. *No, not men and women,* he realized. They were mere boys and girls—farmhands, weavers, and shepherds. They cried for their mothers. They fell, flesh melting, screams echoing in Elethor's ears.

This is no battle, he thought. *It's a slaughter.*

The wyverns flew in perfect formations, attack flights of four—two attackers flanked by two defenders—swarming from phalanxes of a hundred. They undulated into the distance; Elethor saw no end to them. Most had not even fought yet, but howled for blood, awaiting their turn to kill. They formed a ring of metal and acid around the dragons, picking them from the sky one by one.

"Dragons, fly in your phalanxes!" Elethor cried. "Kill the beasts!"

Blue scales flashed below. From a ball of fire and smoke soared Lyana. Flames streamed from her maw and crashed against a wyvern above her. She spun, lashed her tail, and tore off a rider's arm; it tumbled with a spray of blood. She looked from side to side, clawing the air. Elethor flew toward her, roared, and flamed a wyvern. Soon the two dragons, brass and blue, fought side by side. Wyverns flew from all sides.

"This is a bloodbath!" she shouted at him. "Elethor, we must retreat!"

Crossbows fired. One bolt glanced off Lyana's back, and another pierced her wing. A spear slashed Elethor's burnt shoulder and he howled. Wyverns dived from above and acid rained. Elethor and Lyana scattered, dodged the burning rain, and soared. They blew fire, slashed claws, and felled wyverns from the sky.

The bodies of Vir Requis tumbled all around them, returned to human forms. One girl slammed onto Lyana's wing, still alive and screaming, then plummeted into darkness. A boy fell before Elethor, a writhing mass of flesh that twisted and steamed with acid. His screams died before he could hit the mountains below.

"We cannot let them reach the city!" Elethor shouted. He lashed his claws, blew fire, and tried to find Solina. Was she dead? Did she still fight?

Wyverns dived toward him. Blood and acid filled the sky. The sun disappeared behind the horizon, and dragonfire lit the night. Screams and shrieks rose, and the dead fell in darkness.

DERAMON

He stood upon the walls, a coppery dragon spewing smoke, and growled at the distant battle. From here, he could see nothing but bursts of fire, fluttering shadows, and glints of steel. He could hear only distant screams and muffled commands. Deramon fumed and gripped the crenellations.

"It's a bloodbath," Bayrin whispered at his side, tail slapping the wall. He snorted a flicker of fire, then looked at Deramon. "Father, let us fly to them."

Deramon grumbled under his breath. He was commander of the City Guard; never had his force left Nova Vita to fight the battles beyond the walls. For three hundred years—under his father's command, and his grandfather's, and his ancestors' going back to Terra Eleison himself—the City Guard had manned its post.

"We have our orders," he said gruffly. "We protect the people of Nova Vita. We will not leave them in the tunnels."

Bayrin fumed. Smoke rose between his teeth in curtains. He shook his head wildly and slapped his tail. "Father, I can hear them screaming from here! Those are our men screaming. Stars, they're dying out there. They need us."

Deramon glared at his son, a gangly green dragon. "The people of this city need us. Twenty thousand seek shelter in the tunnels; we'll not abandon them. This is our post."

Snorting and shifting his claws, Bayrin looked back and forth between his father and the battle. A separate battle seemed to rage within him. Finally he leaped from the wall, filled his wings with air, and began flying south.

"To the Abyss with my post!" he called back to Deramon. "I'm flying to Elethor."

The young guard growled, blew fire, and soared into the night. Soon he was but a sliver of scales flying toward the storm of battle. Deramon watched from the walls, growled, and cursed. He shook his head mightily, scattering fire, and his claws dug ruts into the battlements. Finally he let out a string of curses, flapped his wings, and rose into the air.

"Stars, I'm going to regret this," he muttered. He looked over his shoulder and howled to his men. "Temple Guard! Palace Guard! Northern Wall! Barracks Guard!"

The dragons of those posts stared at him, eyes glowing in the night—three hundred warriors in all. *Damn buildings are empty anyway,* Deramon thought with a grumble. He raised his voice again.

"Fly—with me! We fly to war." Deramon roared fire and glared at the rest of his Guard, those who manned the remaining walls and streets. "The rest of you miserable lot—man your posts and don't let any bloody wyverns in, or I'll flay your hides!"

With that, he flapped his wings, howled to the sky, and flew into the southern darkness. Behind him, four hundred dragons roared and followed. The wheat and barley below bent under the beat of their wings, and their flames lit the darkness.

"For Requiem!" one guardsman cried behind. The others answered his call. "Requiem!"

They cut through the night. The wind roared around them. Four hundred dragons—flying toward a storm of fire, acid, and death. The fire of battle lit the night. When they drew closer, they saw thousands of wyverns—tens of thousands—surrounding the Royal Army. Their scales clattered, their claws shone, and their acid felled Vir Requis from the sky. Bodies rained and slammed into the mountains below.

Deramon growled. Ice seemed to spread through his gut like the fingers of ghosts.

My men don't know I too feel fear, he thought, jaw clenched and eyes narrowed. *Not I, the great Lord Deramon Eleison.* And yet as he flew, his belly twisted with terror, and he howled to let his fire melt the ice.

He flew for glory. He flew for death. This would be the last battle of his life, the battle where he fell, where his son fell, where his men fell with a roar to enter legend. He sounded that roar now.

"Requiem!" he called to the sky.

The wyverns ahead spun to face the new dragons, reforming rank in the clouds. They bared teeth like swords, their eyes burned red, and their riders fired crossbows. Bolts streamed through the night, shards of lightning. Two dragons howled, turned to humans, and fell from the sky. With shrieks and battle cries, a thousand wyverns flew toward the City Guard.

The sky exploded with fire, acid, and blood. Deramon roared his flames, burning three wyverns. He lashed his tail, slamming its spikes into another's eyes. His dragons roared around him, and fire spouted and rained to the mountains below. The wyverns filled the night. Sprays of acid rose and fell around him. Deramon skirted between them, growling and beating his wings, trying to fan the acid aside.

One spray glanced off his side and he roared; it felt like spears slashing across him. He growled and swooped toward the wyvern that had burned him. The beast reared and bit the air. Deramon lashed its head, but his claws glanced off scales, raising sparks; those scales felt harder than the thickest breastplate in Requiem's armories. The wyvern shrieked, a deafening sound, and shot more acid. Deramon dropped in the sky, flew under the beast, and rose behind it. He snapped his jaws at the rider, catching the man as he spun to aim his crossbow. Deramon's teeth punched through armor and tore the Tiran in two. He spat out half a corpse, then bathed the screeching wyvern with flame.

Still the beast flew and roared. Deramon clutched its back, bit its neck, and clawed its flanks. It bucked beneath him. Deramon was among the largest dragons in Requiem; this beast made him seem like a scrawny child just learning to fly. Its tail lashed and slammed into Deramon's back, cracking scales. Shrieks sounded above, and more wyverns dived, maws opening to reveal pools of acid.

Deramon cursed, tugged sideways, and flipped the wyvern over. He held the struggling beast above him, and the acid cascaded onto its belly. It roared. Its legs kicked the air. The acid seeped through it scales, and its blood rained.

"Father!"

Bayrin's voice rose through the battle. The green dragon shot through fire and smoke, roared, and slammed into the wyverns above Deramon. They howled. More dragons flew into them, showering them with fire.

Cursing, Deramon tossed off the mewling wyvern he clutched; it tumbled from the sky. He flew up and joined Bayrin, and they lashed their claws, felling another beast. When Deramon looked around him, he saw a sea of wyverns; thousands encircled him, his son, and what remained of the dragons he had led to battle. Perhaps fifty still flew; the rest lay dead on the mountainside.

"Elethor!" Deramon howled. He stared south over thousands of wyverns and dragons, clouds of fire and acid, and spraying blood. "Elethor, get your dragons out of here! We fight underground!"

A brass dragon rose from fire, perhaps a mile away—Elethor Aeternum, King of Requiem. Blood stained his muzzle, and he spat a legless Tiran rider from his mouth. He nodded at Deramon and shouted to those of his dragons who still lived.

"Royal Army!" he cried. "To the city! Fall back to Nova Vita. To the tunnels!"

Dragons began rising from the fray and flying north. Deramon cursed and felt those old, icy fingers reach through him. Four thousand dragons had flown south with the Royal Army; he saw several hundred who still lived.

It's a massacre, he thought. His innards burned and shook. He saw the images again: his men dead underground, his king burnt, the bodies of children strewn around him—children he had vowed to protect. Beyond those shadows, he saw an older ghost: the body of Noela in her crib, a mere babe. He had shaken her, pleaded with her, raised her above his head and howled in grief. He had buried her. He had wept for days, mourned for years.

How much death can we endure? he thought in a haze. He could barely hear the battle anymore. The screams were muted. The acid and fire gave no heat. The bodies on the mountains below gazed up at him—young eyes, scared, the eyes of sons and daughters, husbands, wives.

You failed us, Deramon, those eyes said to him. *You vowed to protect us. Won't you save us?*

Deramon shut his eyes. The children in the tunnels would die too. They would die like Noela. But he would not bury them; he would die in acid at their side.

"Father, fly!" rose a voice. Deramon opened his eyes to see Bayrin hovering before him, his scales burnt with acid, his flank slashed and bleeding. His son slapped him with his wings. "Father, fly with me."

With a howl, Deramon flew.

The dragons of Requiem raced over the mountains.

The wyverns chased.

When Deramon looked behind him, he saw Elethor leading ragtag survivors in flight. Wyverns dived all around them, spraying them with acid, picking them off one by one. With every flap of dragon wings, another Vir Requis turned human, screamed and clutched melting skin, and tumbled into darkness.

"Fly, dragons of Requiem!" Deramon shouted. He dived back toward Elethor, roasted a wyvern, and flew by his king. The lands streamed beneath them. The wind roared. All around them, countless wyverns shrieked, and riders chanted, and acid flew, and crossbows fired, and everywhere—everywhere in the night Vir Requis fell dead. Wherever he looked, he saw them burning, saw their pleading eyes.

Deramon! You vowed to protect us!

"Fly, dragons of Requiem!" cried King Elethor. "To the city! To the tunnels!"

Deramon sought Nova Vita in the darkness. He could not see the city. Flying to battle, the flight had seemed so short, a mere dash across field, forest, and mountain. Now the miles stretched endlessly. Now the fields and forests drank the blood of dragons.

"Father!" rose a pained cry, and a blue dragon streamed toward him.

Pain drove through Deramon like a spear in his chest. His eyes stung. *Lyana!* Lyana flew there, his daughter, the light of his life. She was wounded, her scales chipped, her eyes narrowed with pain, and her body thin.

"Lyana," he whispered.

Again he held Noela's body, his youngest daughter. Again he wept over the babe. *Stars, don't let me lose Bayrin and Lyana too. If you have any mercy, stars of Draco, let me die before them.*

A phalanx of wyverns, bearing banners of red swords, swooped from above. Crossbow bolts ricocheted off Deramon's back and he roared. Acid rained. He banked, knocked into Lyana, and shoved her aside. The acid streamed around them. Deramon howled, raised his neck, and flamed the beasts. Lyana soared and slashed at the wyverns' bellies, tearing saddles loose and sending riders tumbling. Yet for every Tiran they slew, three Vir Requis screamed, burned, and fell.

It seemed like hours before they saw Nova Vita ahead. The city rose from a scorched forest, crackling with torches. Deramon howled and flew as fast as he could.

"To the tunnels!" he shouted. "Flee to the tunnels, flee underground!"

He looked around him; only dozens of dragons still flew. He looked behind him; the wyvern army filled the night. Countless red eyes blazed and countless fangs glistened in the firelight.

The surviving dragons, burnt and bloody and roaring, flew over the city walls. Those dragons still on the battlements and roofs took flight, roared fire, and crashed into the wyverns. A few died. A few fled north.

"Into the tunnels!" Deramon cried. "City Guard, we fight undergrou—"

Three wyverns crashed into him, cutting off his words. Acid doused his scales and fangs bit. He howled and spewed fire, driving them back. All around him, dragons and wyverns crashed above the city, fangs biting, claws lashing. Death rained. Claws and tails lashed at buildings and walls, and bricks fell. Columns crashed. Screams filled the night as the city of Nova Vita, fair capital of Requiem, crumbled below.

SOLINA

Her hand blazed. She snarled. When she raised her fist, her glove was charred and torn. Through the rents, she could see raw, red flesh. She clenched her fist tighter.

You did this, Elethor, she thought. She howled in rage. Ignoring the pain, she twisted her burnt fingers around her banner pole. She lifted it high, letting her standard unfurl. She flew above the battle, watching the wyverns and dragons clash above the city below.

"Level this city!" she shouted. "Leave no building standing! Bring me King Elethor alive."

Nova Vita was a small city—a backwater village compared to the glory of Irys. Her cloud of wyverns covered it entirely, a black fist from above. Barely a hundred reptile warriors still lived; more fell dead every moment. Some were landing on the streets, shifting into human form, and racing into the tunnels.

"Where are you, Elethor?" Solina whispered.

She dug her heels into her wyvern. With a scream, the beast swooped so fast that Solina's stomach lurched. She narrowed her eyes, snarled, and grasped her sword and banner tight. In the rushing dive, the wind lashing her, she could barely feel her burnt hand.

Wyverns parted to let her dive until she flew mere feet above the city's roofs. Below in the streets, weredragons clanked in armor, racing toward the tunnels. Solina howled, tugged her reins, and flew above them.

"Burn them, Baal!" she cried.

Her wyvern sprayed the street with acid. Weredragons screamed and fell. They tried to slap the acid off, but it seeped through their armor and began eating their flesh. One man clawed at his face; his eyes were already gone. Solina grinned, soared upon her wyvern, and flew across the city amphitheater and public baths; beyond them more weredragons were racing down the streets toward a second tunnel entrance. Solina swooped, splashed the street with acid, and soared as the men below screamed and fell. Baal's claws crashed against the tunnel archway, and its stones cascaded and crushed weredragons. The beast's wings beat, sending debris flying across the city.

Solina soared higher, seeking more dragons. She could see none. With their fire gone, the night was dark; she could barely see fleeing shadows. Her wyverns spread around her, flying in rings. Their riders held torches and howled for blood.

"Destroy these buildings!" Solina cried. "Let no column stand!"

The wyverns roared, dived, and began lashing the city buildings. A year ago, she had led ten thousand phoenixes to this place; their bodies had been woven of fire, and they had burned many trees and doors and bodies, but left the city's masonry standing. Today she had brought twenty thousand wyverns, each a behemoth of rippling muscles under metallic scales. Buildings collapsed under their blows like houses of cards.

"Level this city! Bring it down!"

Bricks tumbled and columns cracked. Dust rose in clouds that flowed across Solina. She dived toward the Temple of Stars, which rose upon a hill. She tugged the reins left, and her wyvern spun. His spiked tail—wider and stronger than a battering ram—cracked a column. He lashed the column again and again until it shattered. Soon the entire temple was collapsing. Solina soared higher and smiled as the dust flew and the bricks fell.

"You prayed here to your stars," she said. "But they cannot save you now. Not from the glory of my lord."

The weredragons cowered in their tunnels, daring not fight. Solina spat in disgust; they were vile creatures, too craven to defend their home. Truly they were shadows of the night, slinking things that wilted in the light of her lord.

She tugged the reins, directing Baal to fly over the Weredragon Palace. The edifice rose three hundred feet tall, its marble columns capped with dragon capitals. Solina snarled to see it. Eight years ago, the Weredragon Prince had burned her here. The scar blazed across her body now, a searing memory. The line of fire ran from her forehead to leg, from that year to this day. This cruel palace, disguising its evil with marble grace, was where the weredragons had torn her apart from her love, exiled her, and sealed their doom.

"You burned me here," she whispered through clenched teeth. "Now these ruins will scream for ten thousand years."

She reached into the pouch that hung across her saddle. She withdrew two clay balls wrought with red runes. A smile spread across her face.

Tiran fire.

The liquid inside these clay balls burned brighter than streams of dragonfire, than pools of acid, than the smelters of southern Iysa where her blades had been forged. For a year, a thousand men had labored in her barracks, distilling this liquid ruin and blessing it with the wrath of the Sun God. Today their work would blaze in glory.

She circled around the palace, rose high above its roof, and dropped two clay balls. As they fell, she saw the runes upon them glow red. Then they hit the palace, and her glory covered the city.

The Tiran fire exploded with blue light. The inferno burst out, great disks of white flame. Bricks shattered, columns cracked, and smoke filled the sky. Solina screamed to the Sun God, pulled out two more clay balls, and dropped them too.

The explosions rocked the city. Two columns shattered and fell, and then the roof caved in. Solina could barely see through the smoke and dust and flame. Laughing madly, she wrenched the pouch off her saddle and held it upside down. Ten more clay spheres tumbled onto the palace.

The air itself seemed to crack.

Ringing filled her ears over a sea of muffled susurration.

Fire thrashed the sky, and columns fell, and clouds of smoke rose; she could hear nothing but the ringing, a song of angels. She laughed, though she could not hear her own voice, and soared higher. Wind blew, kissed her cheeks, and streamed her hair. Below, the dust rolled across the city, burying the houses, the amphitheater, the barracks, and the collapsing temple. When the dust settled, Solina howled and laughed.

The Weredragon Palace was gone. Only a single column remained standing, rising from rubble.

"There is only one monarch of Requiem, Elethor!" she cried, her voice but a dim, distant whisper under the ringing in her ears. "I am queen of this land. You are but a cowering reptile. Emerge from your hole and face me!"

Thousands of wyverns howled below her, flying across the city and tearing it down. A hundred of the beasts slammed into the towers of Castra Draco, garrison of the Royal Army; the towers tumbled. Claws tore down homes. The walls crumbled, and beyond them in the farms, acid poured across the crops, until nothing but scorched earth remained.

"Tear down every last wall!" Solina howled. "I want to see nothing but rubble!"

All night the wyverns flew, screeching and destroying. Their riders chanted and laughed and sang the songs of their phalanxes. The weredragons remained hidden underground, if any still lived. It was a night to banish all nights, a battle to end all darkness.

When the sun rose, it rose upon glory. Its beams lit a world cleansed of evil. Solina raised her sword to the light and cried to the Sun God, and tears streamed down her cheeks.

"We bring your light to the world, Sun God!" she cried. "Hail the Light of Tiranor!"

Her army roared the prayer. Sunlight glinted on bright armor, spears, and swords. Their banners streamed in victory. Below them, where a city had stood, a single column rose from a ruin of rubble, dust, and bones.

TREALE

As she flew toward the city, she watched it fall.

Her eyes stung, her lungs ached, and a cough still lingered in her throat. Her scales and wings were singed, and it was all she could do to keep flying. The lands of Requiem burned around her in the night: farms, grasslands, forests, all crackling and raising red pillars in the night. Before her, across the leagues, she saw Nova Vita, and she saw its towers fall.

The cloud of wyverns clutched Aeternum's City, a black claw from the south. The beasts kept swooping and knocking down homes. A great wyvern, bearing the banner of Queen Solina, unleashed balls of fire that rocked the city. As Treale flew, she watched the Temple of Stars shatter—the place where she'd been born. She watched the palace crumble until only one of its columns remained. She watched the walls themselves—the fabled white walls of Nova Vita, which Queen Gloriae herself had raised to defend her city—collapse.

"Requiem," Treale whispered. "Land of dragons. Realm of Aeternum. I watched your towers fall, and I shed tears, and I cried to the stars for your glory lost."

In her old books, King Benedictus had spoken those words—centuries ago when the griffins had toppled their forest halls. King Benedictus had borne the rare, black scales Treale too possessed. She was descended from him through his daughter, Agnus Dei, who had survived the slaughter.

And now I fly here, and now I watch the slaughter, and now I watch your towers fall, Requiem.

Treale flew closer to the city, then paused and hovered. Tears stung her eyes. The shrieks, war cries, and booms of shattering stone rose ahead. They slammed into her. The smell of acid burned her nostrils.

"What do I do?" she whispered, head spinning. Her breath quickened into a pant. Her chest ached. The cries slammed against her: the roars of wyverns, the chants of Tiran men, and beneath them... could she hear screams of pain, of her dying brothers and sisters?

What do I do?

Dawn began to rise around her, red and gray, and her eyes blurred. Hovering in midair, she looked aside. What would her ancestor Agnus Dei have done? In all the stories, Agnus Dei was a great warrior, a fiery dragon who charged recklessly into the hordes of the enemy. In old paintings and statues, she looked like Treale too—with dark fiery eyes and black hair.

"She would not run," Treale whispered. "She would roar her fury, blow her fire, and charge at the enemy. She would kill many wyverns until they finally tore her down."

And she would have died, whispered a voice inside her. *She would have died and never given birth to her son Ben, and House Oldnale would never have been. I would never have been.*

Treale turned and began flying north, heading toward the distant forests beyond fire and death. She could hide there. She could try to find other survivors. She could continue the battle from the wilderness. Her throat tightened as she flew, and tears flowed from her eyes.

The faces of her parents, charred and gaping, filled her eyes. Thousands of souls now burned in the city, crying out to her, begging for aid.

With a yelp, Treale spun and began flying toward the city again. *They need me. I can't leave them. I must save them!*

She howled as she flew, a black dragon in the blood-red dawn. Soon the city was closer, rising from inferno. The eyes of the wyverns burned. Their banners flapped. Their songs rose—songs of glory, light, and death. No more dragons flew. The wyverns were swooping and tearing down the last trees, homes, and statues. The sun rose, its red light falling upon little but rubble.

They're all dead, Treale thought as she flew over blazing farmlands. *Stars, they're all gone, they're all fallen.*

She mewled and spun around again. Once more she began flying north. She had to hide. She could no longer help her people. If she died with them, her bones would lie here forever, useless. In the forests of the north she could survive, she could seek survivors, she could...

I am a coward. She growled and her eyes burned. *I am a soldier, yet I flee from battle.* She looked up, seeking the stars of Requiem, seeking their guidance. Yet she could not see the sky, only smoke and ash, black and red. No more starlight fell upon Requiem. Voice torn, fire in her maw, she cried out the prayer of her people.

"Requiem! May our wings forever find your sky." She howled as she flew. "I will find your sky again, Requiem. I vow to you."

Shrieks of rage flared behind her.

She turned to see a dozen wyverns tear themselves from the army over Nova Vita, howl at the sky, and fly toward her.

Treale cursed. She cursed Tiranor, she cursed the Sun God, and she cursed herself for her stupidity. They had heard her cries, seen her fire, and now she too would die, and her bones would not even rest among her comrades, but burn in the wild.

She could charge at them, she knew. For death! For Requiem! For eternal starlight—to die in battle, to rise to the starlit halls in a final blaze of glory.

Instead, she kept fleeing toward the northern forests.

King's Column still stands in the ruins of our palace, she thought. The legends whispered that it would stand so long as a single Vir Requis lived. If she was the last one alive, she would not die here, she would not let that ancient column fall.

The world burned. She flew over the ruin of her home. The wyverns howled behind her. When she looked over her shoulder, she saw their eyes blaze, their riders aim crossbows, and their maws gape, full of acid. A dozen flew there, maybe more, black and red and golden in the clouds of smoke.

She shot through ash until the cries of the city faded behind her. She burst through flame and flew through smoke, coughing, blinded, the heat searing her belly. When she looked behind her, she saw only black and red swirls, a nightmare world, the Abyss itself risen to fill Requiem. Yet still she heard the wyvern cries. Still they followed her. Crossbow bolts whizzed through the smoke around her, and one grazed her tail. She bit down on a scream.

They can't see me. If they can't hear me, they will lose me.

She swallowed. She blinked. She shoved down the horror that filled her. She flew.

Treale no longer knew north from south. She saw nothing but smoke around her, smoke above her, and fires below her. The world spun. Was she still flying to the forests, or had she changed direction in the inferno, and was flying back toward the ruin of her capital? She heard the shrieks behind her, distant and echoing.

Just keep those shrieks behind you, she told herself. *Just fly away from them as fast as you can.*

She trembled. Her scales felt hot enough to melt; they expanded in the heat so that she could barely move. Her lungs and throat blazed as if she had swallowed lava, and she did not know how much longer she could fly. Yet she forced herself to keep flying, one flap of her wings after another. She tried to keep her body slim, to leave no wake through the smoke. Yet she must have been leaving a trail, for the shrieks still sounded behind her, and more bolts flew toward her. One lashed her side, and she bit down on a yelp. She gritted her teeth, blinked her eyes, and flew onward.

"I'm sorry, Elethor," she whispered. "I'm sorry I could not fight by your side, could not die by you."

In the haze of smoke and fire, she lay by him again upon the hill. She talked to him of their pasts, and kissed his cheek, and slept by his side—young and scared, but feeling safe by her king. It was a last, kind memory and she let it fill her. If nothing else—if all the halls of Requiem fell, and she died here in the wilderness, and jackals ate her bones—she still had that memory. She had still lain upon a hill with her king, and talked to him of old manor halls and puppets and dreams. She still had one dream of soft, quiet camaraderie to soothe her in the flames.

It seemed like she flew for hours. Her head was muzzy, and a deathly haze had begun to drown her pain, when finally she emerged from the smoke. An ancient forest rolled before her, spreading into red dawn, a tangle of shadows and secrets.

Before the wyverns could emerge from smoke behind her, Treale swooped. She all but crashed into the forest, snapping branches and slamming, half dead, onto the hot earth. She shifted into human form at once. In her smaller, weaker body, she trembled so violently that she could only lie shaking. Ash covered her. Welts rose across her skin. She coughed on the ground, gasping for breath.

"Please, stars," she prayed. "Let me live. Let me *live*. I cannot die here, away from my people, shameful. Please don't let me die."

She could not stop shaking. The trees rose above her, labyrinths of wood. She coughed and sucked the hot air for breath, and her eyes rolled back, and the haze of death spread across her. *No! No.* She clawed the ash. She bit her cheek and pain flared. She forced a deep, raw breath, and her lungs screamed in agony. She tried to remember that night—the night she had lain by Elethor upon the hill—and draw strength from it, to once more taste the clear air and feel brave.

The wyverns roared. Their cries nearly shattered her ears.

"Stars, give me strength."

Burnt and shaking and gasping for air, Treale Oldnale pushed herself to her feet. The forest spun around her, and she had to grab a bole to stop from falling. She looked south and saw a wall of smoke like a shimmering tapestry. The wyverns shrieked within it. As she stood trembling, she saw them burst from the inferno and fly above the forest.

Treale ran.

She ran between the trees and leaped over roots. Above in the canopy, the wyverns overshot her. They appeared only as shadows against the smoke and clouds, black against black. Their cries rang out.

"Find the weredragon!" cried one rider, voice distant and echoing. "Tear down the trees! The creature shifted and runs as human. Find it!"

Treale's boots hit a root, and she fell. Her cheek slammed against the earth. She lay trembling, eyes burning. The wyverns soared overhead, bending the trees. She felt the blast of their wings. Droplets of their acid pattered around her, raised smoke, and began to eat into the earth. A few droplets hit Treale's boot, and she winced and gritted her teeth, struggling not to scream. She kicked the boot off, pulled her knee to her chest, and slapped at her foot. The flesh felt hot and raw.

"Please, stars of Requiem, please. Let me live. Shine on me this red dawn."

She looked up but saw no stars, only the canopies of trees, a sky of ash, and the shadows of wyverns that circled and screamed.

Tears of pain streamed down her face. She did not know if any other Vir Requis still lived, or if she was the last. Her body shook so badly, she did not think she could rise. She gritted her teeth so hard they ached. She growled. Arms like wet towels, she managed to grab a branch. She pulled herself up. Her lungs burned and her knees shook wildly; she did not think she could still run.

But Treale ran. She ran through the forest, not knowing what direction she moved. She could see only several feet ahead, and the trees rose like twisted goblins around her, their branches reaching out to snag her, to tear her clothes, to scratch her face bloody. She tasted the blood and sap on her lips. Still she ran, the forest spreading endlessly and the scourge of her people howling above.

ELETHOR

They stood behind the doors, swords drawn, and waited.

The tunnel walls rose around them, craggy and black. Only several candles upon the walls lit the darkness; their light flickered and cast shadows like dancing demons. Elethor gripped the hilt of Ferus, his ancient sword. With narrowed eyes, he stared at the doors before him. He tightened his lips. He breathed slowly. He waited.

His warriors stood around him. Lyana stood at his right, sword drawn in her right hand, dagger in her left. A helmet hid her stubbly head, the Draco stars carved onto its brow, and the candlelight danced against her breastplate, the ancient breastplate of a bellator. At his left stood Bayrin and Deramon, clad in the armor of the City Guard and clutching their own blades. A hundred other warriors—survivors of the battle over the mountains—filled the tunnel behind them, blades orange in the candlelight.

A hundred souls stood in silence, staring at those doors. A hundred souls waited for death. Beyond those doors, a staircase rose narrow and steep toward the fallen city. The candles flickered with their every breath. Not a piece of armor clanked.

Stars, be with us today, Elethor prayed silently.

The doors before him were a foot thick, carved of oak bolted with iron. Great beams stood in brackets. No battering ram would break these doors, Elethor knew. A wyvern's tail perhaps could shatter them, but Elethor had ordered the doors built a hundred yards down the narrow staircase; no wyvern could fit down here to reach them.

Behind him, the tunnel sloped into silent darkness. Beyond tunnel, portcullis, and more doors loomed the chambers where his people waited, where Mori waited, where the last light of Requiem glowed.

All that separates them from their fall is me, my warriors, and a whisper of starlight.

He flexed his fingers around the hilt of his sword, reminding himself that he had prepared for this day.

We are safe here, he told himself. *They will not claim these tunnels. We will hold back the enemy.*

A smaller, cold voice whispered in his head. *But for how long?* They had food and water for a year. It was a long time, but eventually their supplies would run out. What then? Would they starve here underground? He squared his jaw and clutched his sword tighter. Had he led his people into a tomb?

A great boom shook the tunnels. The candles flickered and dust fell. Above, through many feet of stone, he could hear the distant cries of wyverns. Elethor narrowed his eyes and sucked in breath. A second crash shook the tunnels, and again the wyverns wailed, a distant sound like ghosts. Elethor snarled. When he looked at his sides, he saw Lyana, Bayrin, and the others clutch their swords tight. More booms sounded. More dust rained and the candles danced. Muffled voices rose in song: the battle songs of Tiranor, songs of triumph and bloodlust.

For the first time somebody spoke. "Bloody stars," Bayrin muttered and spat. "They're destroying the city. Bastards."

Lyana looked at her brother, then turned toward Elethor. Their eyes met. Any other day, Elethor would have expected to see Lyana roll her eyes, scold her brother, and launch into a lecture. Today she only stared silently, and new ghosts haunted her eyes. Elethor remembered holding her in the Abyss as Nedath's curse spread across her, as her body wilted and her teeth fell. They had emerged from darkness. They had defeated ancient evils underground. The memories pained Elethor but comforted him too; they had faced darkness before and defeated it. They would face this new darkness together too.

"Elethor," she said, pale. "Bayrin is right. I know he rarely is, but... they aren't leaving one building standing."

Elethor nodded, fist clenched at his side. He spoke in a low voice. "I know. But I would rather them crush buildings than bodies." He shook his head, struggling to drown panic. "Stars, Lyana, they ripped through our army. They were like hawks in a cloud of sparrows."

Lyana looked behind her where warriors filled the tunnel. "There are twenty thousand wyverns above us. They outnumbered us over the forest." She looked back at him, eyes dark. "Elethor, we have twenty thousand Vir Requis in the lower chambers. One dragon for every wyvern." She bared her teeth. "Let us fly! Let us fly in battle, the great last stand of the Vir Requis. Let every child, grandparent, and wounded son of Requiem fly to war today. We will make such a roar."

Her eyes glistened in her pale face, and her hands gripped her weapons. *She is a warrior,* Elethor thought, *raised on tales of knights and epic battle. But I am a king.*

"Lyana, these wyverns crushed soldiers—dragons trained to fly in formation, to blow fire from above, to slash claws, to lash tails. My soldiers trained for a year, and these wyverns tore through us." He shook his head. "Thousands of survivors hide below us, it's true. Children. Mothers and babes. Old men and women. Cripples." He sighed. "Even as dragons, their fire is weak, their claws soft, their hearts frightened. Many of them have lost their fangs to old age; many others haven't even grown theirs. No, I will not lead them out to die in the skies. There is safety underground."

Her eyes flashed. "Elethor! Last year they tore through these tunnels like—"

"Last year this place merely stored grain and wine. Last year no doors stood here. We have thick doors now and strong men to guard them; three levels stand between the Tirans and our people. They will not break in so easily this time."

Bayrin, who had watched the exchange with dark eyes, let out a slow breath. Dirt smeared his face and hair, and a wound spread across his arm.

"Famous last words, El," he muttered. "Bloody stars, but for the first time in my life, I'm going to agree with Lyana. We—"

Battle cries surged behind the doors, cutting off his words. Armor and weapons clanked above, and soon Elethor heard boots thudding down the staircase, rushing from the city into the tunnels. The cries of Tirans rose, hoarse and crude. Above them rose a shrill voice; it made Elethor close his eyes, grind his teeth, and cringe with old pain.

"Kill the weredragons!" cried Solina behind the doors. "Bring me the Reptile King alive! Slay the others."

The boots thudded and the Tiran voices rose in wordless, enraged shouts. With a boom that shook the tunnels, they crashed against the doors.

Elethor tightened his grip on his sword. His hand was sweaty. Why hadn't they carved this tunnel wider, wide enough for a dragon to blow fire? Why hadn't they made the doors thicker, or carved them with arrow slits? They hadn't had enough time! Not enough time to dig, to prepare, to—

The Tirans slammed against the doors again. They creaked, and Elethor found himself snarling.

Deal with this now. You cannot change the past. Face them down as you are.

He looked to his left at Bayrin and Deramon. They stared back and nodded.

"We fight with you, my friend," Bayrin whispered.

Deramon growled. "We kill for you, my king."

When Elethor looked to his right, he saw Lyana glaring at the doors, blades raised. She spared him a quick glance, eyes blazing with green fire, and smiled crookedly.

"I'm ready to spill blood," she said. "Keep count, El; I bet I can kill ten times more than you."

Elethor nodded at her, silent. *Good.* This was the Lyana he wanted to see, not the Lyana with sad eyes, but the knight with the fiery stare.

The doors shook again and splinters cracked. The Tirans howled behind the oak and iron. Again and again the doors shook, and every boom rolled through the tunnel, louder than thunder. *Thud. Thud.* The Tirans howled. Solina screamed. *Thud. Thud.* Splinters flew.

"Break them down!" Solina shouted.

Her men roared. *Boom. Thud.* Splinters flew. Candles fell around Elethor. He stood still, staring at the doors, waiting. His warriors stood around him. *Boom. Thud.* Again and again. Screams and shrieks. *Thud. Thud.*

"Requiem," Elethor whispered. "May our wings forever find your sky."

His men repeated the words around him. The Tirans screamed for blood. Their shadows danced under the doors. *Boom. Thud.* Screams and splinters.

And then... silence.

Ragged breath, curses, and grumbles sounded behind the doors. Boots stomped upstairs and Solina's shrieks faded. Soon the sounds of her men faded too, moving back to the city above.

Elethor released the breath he hadn't realized he was holding. He squinted at the doors.

What are you doing, Solina?

"Stars yeah!" Bayrin said at his side. He grinned wildly. "The doors stood! The bastards couldn't break them. This time we were ready for them!" He growled at the doors. "Pity, almost; I was looking forward to shoving my sword up Solina's backside."

When Elethor looked at Lyana, he saw less hope there. The knight was still staring at the doors, her eyes narrowed and her lips tightened.

"I don't like this," she whispered.

Bayrin snorted. "Why, Lyana? You were worried you couldn't kill as many men as me? The cowards gave up! They thought they'd find undefended tunnels like last year. Well, they—"

Elethor interrupted his friend. "They'll be back, Bay. Keep your sword drawn. Get ready. Wait."

Silence fell.

They stood, gripping weapons, breath soft.

Above, the sounds of collapsing buildings faded, and even the wyvern shrieks died.

Elethor caught his breath. In the silence, his ears rang.

With a swell like a typhoon, a thousand wyvern shrieks rose above. Elethor grimaced. The sound was so loud and shrill he couldn't help but cry out. Bayrin snarled and winced, Deramon cursed, and Lyana growled. It sounded like the entire army of wyverns cried above the stairs. Acrid stench flared, so hot it burned Elethor's nose, eyes, and throat.

Lyana straightened and her face paled. Her eyes widened and she shouted, "Back! Everybody back!"

Confusion reigned. Lyana began retreating, trying to herd soldiers back into darkness. Elethor stared at her, then back at the doors. The stench of acid intensified. His eyes stung so badly, he could barely see. The wyverns above howled. A sound like a river roaring plunged beyond the doors.

Smoke and stench exploded, and the doors began to sizzle. Acid seeped around and under them.

"Stars," Elethor whispered. He spun and began running. "Back, everyone! Deeper into the tunnels—move!"

Acid sluiced around his boots. The soles began to sizzle. He cursed and ran. A hundred soldiers raced before him. Bayrin and Deramon ran cursing at his side. When he looked over his shoulder, Elethor saw the doors splintering. A hinge fell. Acid burst through a hole and shot into the tunnels. The doors looked like a dam holding back a river—a dam about to collapse.

Elethor looked back ahead and ran, teeth bared and eyes burning. The darkness swirled. Behind him, he heard the doors shatter.

MORI

They huddled in the chambers of the third level—twenty thousand souls, weeping, shaking, and praying. Mori stood by the tapestry she had woven, struggling to calm her beating heart. The sea of people rolled around her. Wounded soldiers, survivors of the battle, writhed upon the floor, their flesh twisted with acid. Children screamed and clung to their mothers. What soldiers could still stand manned the doors, swords drawn and faces hard. From above, Mori heard faded echoes of battle: wyverns screeching, buildings collapsing, and men howling. With every boom of a collapsing tower, the people shivered; some wept and trembled.

"Be strong, Elethor," Mori whispered, clutching her luck finger behind her back. "Be strong, Bayrin and Lyana."

She missed them. Her chest ached for them. She wished she could be with them now, guarding the upper tunnels, a sword in her hand. She was no warrior, but surely anything was better than this—waiting here in the darkness, only a few candles lighting the chambers, surrounded by tears and wails and the stench of burnt flesh.

One wounded guard moaned only several yards away, his face melted away, his eyes gone; he gaped with empty sockets. Mother Adia knelt above him, her robes stained with blood and death. Younger healers, her pupils, were moving between the other wounded, applying ointments to wounds, pouring silkweed into mouths, and praying. Yet even the healers trembled, and even their faces were pale.

They are all scared, Mori realized—healers and guards, the wounded and the strong. So many, even those untouched by acid, still bore the old scars of the Phoenix War. *There is no hope here, only fear.*

Mori tightened her lips. No, she was no warrior, but she was a leader to these people. She was a princess of House Aeternum, an ancient dynasty that had ruled in Requiem for millennia. She would help her people in her own way.

"Children of Requiem!" she called. Her voice was small at first, nearly drowned under the sounds of battle and weeping. She called out louder. "Vir Requis! Hear me, my people."

They looked at her—children, the elderly, guards, healers and wounded. Many still wept and trembled. Mori forced herself to stay strong, to calm the thrashing of her heart. So many eyes upon her spun her head, but she clutched her luck finger, and she spoke loudly so that her voice carried through the chambers.

"My brother, King Elethor, protects us. His sword is sharp, his armor thick. Our soldiers stand at his side; they are brave and strong. We are safe here." She turned to look at Adia who still knelt above the blinded man. "Mother Adia! May I lead the people in prayer?"

Holding the wounded guard, Adia stared across the people at Mori. Her eyes were deep, dark pools reflecting the candlelight; the shadows of memory and loss danced in them. She nodded silently. Her lips twisted but she said nothing.

Mori began to sing. She was no priestess, but she loved the temple services; she would always sing the prayers along with Mother Adia, voice quiet and shy, but pure. Today she let her voice sing out loudly for all to hear; it still sounded high to her, too high, not deep and sonorous like Adia's voice. Yet it carried through the chambers, and the people sang with her.

"As the leaves fall upon our marble tiles, as the breeze rustles the birches beyond our columns, as the sun gilds the mountains above our halls—know, young child of the woods, you are home, you are home. Requiem! May our wings forever find your sky."

As they sang, the fear seemed to leave the people; their trembles eased, their tears dried, and their backs straightened. They had sung these songs a year ago in the Phoenix War. The Living Seven had sung these songs three hundred years ago, fighting Dies Irae and his griffins. Three thousand years ago, King Aeternum himself—the first king and Mori's ancestor—had carved these words into King's Column, which still rose above them.

In generations to come, Mori thought, *the Vir Requis will think of us—of me and my people—singing our words underground. We will survive. We will pass our song on, a torch of starlight, a dream to forever find our sky.*

Screams echoed through the tunnels above.

Mori's voice died.

The people began to whisper and weep again. The guards at the doors clutched their swords and looked around with narrowed eyes. The screams rolled above them, torn in anguish. The stench of acid hit Mori's nostrils, so sharp it burned through her nose down to her throat and lungs.

"Stars," she whispered. She looked over the crowd of survivors at Mother Adia. The priestess met her gaze, eyes wide with terror.

Boots thudded outside the doors. Men screamed. The smoke and caustic stench swirled. Voices cried in anguish. Fists began pounding at the chamber doors. She heard them cry of Requiem, cry for starlight, cry for their king.

"Open the doors!" Mori cried to her guards. "It's our men! Open the doors!"

Her guards, faces pale and jaws clenched, lifted the bar from the doors' brackets. At once the doors slammed open. The smell of acid flared. From the darkness, a Vir Requis guard ran into the lower chambers, screaming. His flesh twisted with acid. Mori screamed too. He looked, she thought, like tallow melting in a suit of armor.

The burnt man ran five paces into the chamber. His eyes had burned away. His mouth screamed, a gaping hole in his ravaged face. People scurried aside, wailing. The guard fell to his knees, gave a last cry, then fell forward and lay silent.

Through the doors, acid began to trickle into the chamber.

Mori stood frozen for an instant. In her mind, she saw everyone in these chambers—thousands of them—melting and burning, screaming, pawing at her, weeping as they died around her. For that instant, her heart froze and no breath found her lips.

She clutched her luck finger.

Panic later, Mori. Fight now.

She ran toward the shelves of supplies. "Grab sacks of grain!" she cried. "Pile them at the door! Soak up the acid!"

She grabbed a sack of wheat, dragged it toward the doors, and tossed it down. She drew her sword, slashed the sack open, and grain spilled. The wheat began to soak up the flowing acid. Some sluiced around her shoes, and her soles began to steam.

"Grab the grain!" she cried. "Stop the acid!"

Around her, some people wept and shivered, curled up into balls. Others began to pull more sacks of grain, slash them open, and spill their contents onto the acid that trickled from above. As they worked, more guards began running into the chambers. Some were so burnt, they were unrecognizable; they were but living wounds. Others suffered milder burns; they too began slashing open sacks of grain.

Stars, where is Elethor? Where are Bayrin and Lyana and Deramon?

Mori growled and kept working. Why had they not foreseen this? Why had they not carved drainage holes into the tunnels? She winced, cursing herself but knowing she could not change the past. *Fight now. Save these people now.*

The acid flow strengthened from trickle to stream. Mori dragged more sacks, slashed them open, and spilled more grain. People wailed around her. Some acid flowed around the grain and began eating at people's boots.

Elethor, where are you?

As she dragged a sack forward, she saw Adia dragging the dead man away, the one who had first burst into the chambers. His flesh dangled through his armor, and sudden horror pulsed through Mori. Was that... was that Elethor? Was that wounded, wreck of a person Bayrin or Lyana?

No. No! It can't be. Tears stung her eyes and she slashed another sack open. The acid was pouring more powerfully now. People were screaming. Several children shifted into dragons—they were but the size of horses—and clung to the ceiling.

"Do not shift!" Mori shouted. If they all became dragons, they would crush one another and breathe all the air. "Move into the deeper chambers. Go!"

They began to move through the network of chambers, pushing deeper, but acid kept pouring. More and more grain spilled. The acid began to eat through Mori's shoes; they were falling apart. She grimaced and kept working even as her soles began to blaze.

"Mori!"

She looked up and tears filled her eyes. Bayrin came running through the doorway. Behind him ran Lyana, Elethor, and Deramon. Acid was steaming on their boots and armor, but their skin was still smooth. Mori cried out to them, a tremble seizing her.

They leaped over the sacks of grain, which were still soaking up the acid, and began kicking off boots, unclasping armor, and removing gloves. They tossed the steaming leather and steel aside, then began slapping at their bodies.

"Merciful stars, this stuff is hot!" Bayrin cried. He pulled his tunic off and tossed it aside, remaining bare-chested. He slapped at his torso, searching for droplets of acid.

Mori rushed toward him. "Bayrin! The Tirans! Are—"

Eyes dark, he spat. "They haven't entered the tunnels, but they've got every last bloody wyvern flooding us with acid, I reckon."

Lips tightened, Mori turned to look at her brother. Elethor's shoulder was burnt, his jaw was tight, and his eyes blazed red and hard. He clutched his longsword Ferus.

"Keep stacking the grain!" he shouted to the people. "Every last sack—I want it blocking the doorway!"

They kept working. Soon a great pile of sacks—enough grain to feed hundreds—filled the doorway and half the chamber. The survivors huddled deeper against the walls, pushing into the further, deeper chambers, a sea of living flesh filling this labyrinth of stone. Mori stood huddled between Bayrin and Lyana. She reached out and clasped their hands—Lyana with her right hand, and Bayrin with her left hand, the one with her lucky sixth finger.

If we die, she thought, *I die with those that I love.* A bitter smile touched her lips. *That is not a bad way to die.*

She looked up at Bayrin. He met her eyes and squeezed her hand tight. They stood together—a king and princess, healers and wounded, nobles and commoners. They watched as the sacks began to melt, as the heat and stench rose. One man began to sing, voice hoarse, the old songs of Requiem. Hesitant, a woman joined him, and soon they all sang together—thousands of voices rolling through the tunnels, thousands of voices calling out the cry of starlight, the song of dragons.

Acid saturated the grain. The sacks melted away. The distant shrieks of wyverns sounded, and the acid grew to a river... then came gushing into the chambers.

MAHRDOR

Pain.

Pain tore through him like a horde of scorpions in his veins.

He twisted his left hand into a trembling fist. The black leather glove he wore clung to the ruin of his flesh, sticking to blood, fat, and muscle. The pain flared from fingers to elbow and coursed through his body. Blood pounded in his ears. A red veil seemed to cloak the world.

She did this to me.

He sat upon his wyvern, a beast named Phel born with four leathern wings, having absorbed her sibling in the egg. One eye, one nostril, and three teeth of that twin thrust out from Phel's cheek, twitching with anguish; the rest of the parasite rotted inside her. The twisted wyvern perched upon a hill, claws digging into a fallen column. From his saddle of leather and steel spikes, Mahrdor stared down across the ruins to the archway; Solina sat there upon her own wyvern, goading the beast to spew more acid into the darkness below.

She burns the weredragons like she burned me.

He snarled. Even the movement of baring his teeth sent pain blazing, and he nearly lost consciousness. He clutched the reins.

I should kill her now, he thought. Rage crackled through him. Fire blazed across him. *I should slay her with my sword. I should peel back her skin, eat her flesh, and carve her bones with my name.* Blood and fire painted the world. His head spun. His fingers trembled, and he gritted his teeth so hard he chipped a tooth and spat out the chunk. He licked his lips and imagined the taste of Solina's organs bursting between his teeth.

He tugged the reins. His wyvern cawed, leaped over a pile of bodies, and landed ten feet closer to Solina. Mahrdor glared at his queen. She sat upon her mount, her back to him, her hair billowing, a banner of gold in the dawn.

Mahrdor grabbed the glove on his left hand. He peeled the edge back, snarling. The pain exploded like Tiran fire inside him. Through the veil of red, he stared at the flesh beneath: twisted, soft, barely clinging to the bone.

I will burn her too, he swore. *Slowly. Inch by inch. Year by year. She will grow old in my dungeons, screaming for me. She will live a long life.*

Why had he taken the ancient punishment? Why had he dipped his hand into the acid? He could have killed her then. He could have slain her in her tent; he was strong enough, and she was but a woman, weak of flesh and mind. And yet... and yet he had shoved the hand in. He had taken the pain. He had drunk it up eagerly, savoring it, a pup begging for forgiveness.

For what? The mercy of a queen? The honor of his post, a lord of hosts? He snarled, choked, and coughed. He spat a glob of phlegm and blood. What did he care for honor or power?

"All I ever craved was my collection," he said through a tight jaw. "All I ever wanted was to *create*."

He was an artist first, a warrior second. How he would have created art from Lyana, a true knight of Requiem! He would have molded her body, painted and pierced it, broken and healed it, shattered her bones and reshaped them until they mended into the forms he desired. And he would have molded her mind. He would have turned her from a proud, strong warrior into a mindless slave, a cowering creature, an animal that knew nothing but fear and pain and drool. She would have been his greatest creation, his gilded bird.

That is why, he knew. *That is why I drove my fist into the jug. Never forget. Never forget why you are here.*

He growled at the sky where red clouds churned. He would find his Lyana again. He would return her to his villa in Tiranor. He would break and reshape her. If he had to sacrifice a hand, well... let his hand be as a work of art too.

He ripped off the glove.

He screamed.

He held the deformed hand before him in the dawn. When he flexed the fingers, flesh tore and pain blinded him, rivers of red and white. He found himself laughing through his screams.

It is beautiful, he thought.

His queen had done this to him, and he laughed, realizing his folly. How could he have hated her for this? She had made his hand beautiful. She had molded him. She had *collected* him. She had turned his flesh into a work of art, into rivulets of scars, into *beauty*.

Maybe one day he would return the favor. He would scar her with beauty too. But not yet. Not yet. First he would take what was his: a horde of weredragons to collect, a knight, a princess, a king too if Solina would allow it.

"They will all be my treasures," he whispered to his ruined hand. "They will all be beautiful like you, my love."

He tugged the reins, pulling his wyvern away from Solina. He dug his heels into the beast and Phel soared, four wings beating in unison. Soon Mahrdor was circling above the city, nostrils flared, taking in the scent of death. In the dawn, the devastation rolled below him, a tapestry of triumph. The walls of Nova Vita lay fallen, bricks strewn across the smoldering forest like scattered teeth. The temple lay shattered, its columns snapped like bones. The palace lay in rubble; only a single column, hundreds of feet tall, rose from its ruin. Homes, shops, statues—all lay smashed, white with ash and red with blood.

Such pathetic creatures, the weredragons, Mahrdor thought. He had fought in the war thirty years ago, a mere youth clutching a spear for the first time. He had watched the dragons destroy Irys, kill his parents, torch the palms and boil the River Pallan. How they fell now! They had not lasted a day.

Mahrdor thought back to that war thirty years ago. He remembered finding his family crushed and burnt in the ruins of his house. He remembered lying by their bodies for days, staring at their gaping wounds, watching the flies feast, smelling them rot, admiring their beauty. When finally priests had found him in the ruins, they had thought him mad, had shaken their heads at his smile, at the blood on his lips.

But is it not better to smile than weep? Mahrdor thought as he flew above, admiring the death and destruction. *Is it not better to admire beauty than mourn loss? To collect art rather than cry over blood?*

He began circling down toward the city square, where Tiran warriors guarded a pile of wounded, whimpering weredragons. Some Tiran soldiers stood afoot, aiming spears or crossbows at the prisoners. Others sat upon their wyverns, ready to spew acid. The weredragons lay in human forms, clad in chains and splashed in blood.

Mahrdor landed his wyvern in the square. The beast's claws dug ruts into the cobblestones. She tossed her scaly head back, nostrils flared to inhale the scent of weredragon blood, and howled to the sky.

"Be calm, my girl," Mahrdor said and stroked Phel's nape. "Soon you will feast upon their bodies. Once they tell me all they know, their flesh will be yours."

The wyvern mewled, slapped her tail, and beat her four wings. Her drool splashed the cobblestones and began eating through the stone. The third eye on her cheek blinked and shed tears. Sometimes it seemed to Mahrdor that this absorbed twin, only hints of it showing, craved flesh and blood just as much.

Stroking the beast, Mahrdor dismounted. When his boots hit the cobblestones, pain flared through him, racing through his bones to the fingers of his ruined hand. As he walked toward his men, he saw their eyes shift to that hand, saw horror and disgust fill them. When he gave them cold stares, they stiffened and saluted, banging their fists against their breastplates.

"How many prisoners are there?" he asked one of the soldiers, a phalanx captain with golden skulls upon his pauldrons.

The man looked at the pile of chained, bloody weredragons and snarled. He was missing a tooth, and a scar ran across his head, cleaving his platinum hair like a red snake.

"Fifty in that pile, my Lord Mahrdor," he rasped. "Ten of them are dead already. A dozen more will be dead by nightfall." The captain snorted. "The rest will live a little longer if you wish it, my lord, though they will envy their dead."

Mahrdor stood and examined the creatures. One looked like a pile of rotten cornmeal, moaning and still smoking with acid. A few were children. A few were dead. Chains bound them in a pile of flesh, blood, and tears. Mahrdor pointed at one.

"There, bring me him, the brute with the black hair. That one is a soldier."

The weredragon sat hulking, head lowered, his wrists and ankles bound with manacles. Burns spread across his arms, and his left eye was swollen shut. He wore a breastplate emblazoned with the Draco constellation; a man of the City Guard, Mahrdor knew.

Two Tiran soldiers approached the pile of prisoners and jabbed the burly guard with spears.

"Up, weredragon," one said with a grunt. "On your feet."

The wounded guard grunted and remained with his head lowered. His helmet had been knocked off in the battle, and blood matted his head. One of his ears was a lacerated mess.

"Can you hear, lizard?" the Tiran said. "Get up, damn it."

The two Tirans grabbed the weredragon and began pulling him up. Finally the beast seemed to awake. He tossed back his head and howled, the wordless cry of an animal. He spun, lashing his chains at the Tirans. The men cursed and thrust their spears. One spearhead slashed the weredragon's leg, and the creature howled and swung his chains again. More Tirans rushed forward. It took ten men to subdue the weredragon, chain his wrists to his sides, and shove him forward. When finally the brute stood before Mahrdor, blood stained his teeth and dripped down his leg.

Mahrdor stood, examining the weredragon. Held in the grip of two Tirans, the weredragon stared back from his one good eye; that eye blazed with hatred.

"Good," Mahrdor said. "Good, you have spirit. That means you'd have risen high in the Weredragon Guard. You'll have the information I need."

He reached out his burnt hand. When he uncurled his fingers, they blazed with pain and made a sickening, crackling sound like old parchment unfolding. He caressed the weredragon's bruised cheek and swollen eye, letting wound touch wound.

"My hand," Mahrdor said, "is a work of art, a landscape of pain and punishment. I will turn you into a work of art too. Piece by piece, I will make you beautiful."

The weredragon growled, but fear filled his one good eye. Mahrdor nodded. Smiling thinly, he turned to his men. "Bring me jugs of acid. We will see if he learns to speak."

Two men brought forward the acid.

Two others shoved and held the weredragon down.

Mahrdor began to work.

As the weredragon screamed, Mahrdor smiled. As flesh burned, he licked his lips. He created. Even here, in the rubble of battle, he was an artist. He shaped flesh. He wove symphonies from screams.

"There is an escape tunnel underground," he said as he worked, trickling acid against flesh. "The Weredragon King would have carved one. Where does it lead?"

The weredragon only screamed. His left leg was gone already, a sticky mess of flesh barely clinging to bone. Behind him, the other weredragon prisoners wept and wailed. Mahrdor clucked his tongue and kept working.

"Speak and your pain will end," he said. "Speak and I will create something from your corpse rather than your living flesh. It would be easier for you, I think." He poured more acid and the man's howls rose. "I have escape tunnels in my villa in Tiranor. My queen does in her palace. Every ruler of importance has some path to flee an underground tomb. Where does the Lizard King's tunnel go?"

Mahrdor worked and the man screamed.

He screamed of his phalanx.

He screamed of his commanders.

He screamed for his wife and mother.

He screamed until he was a useless, burnt chunk of flesh, and Mahrdor kicked him aside. He licked his lips and grinned.

"This one knows nothing," he said. He pointed at a second chained weredragon—a young woman in the steel armor of a soldier. "Bring me that one."

He cracked his neck and kept working. Soon this one was screaming too.

It was three more weredragons before one finally screamed, face sizzling under acid, of the escape tunnel underground.

"It leads to the eastern hills!" the creature cried, its eyes eaten away. "It emerges between three boulders on a hillside—five hundred yards east from the walls. Please... please..." The creature sobbed. "Please kill me. Give me death. Give me mercy."

Mahrdor kicked the wretch aside.

"Give you mercy?" he said to the twisted beast. "But you already gave me what I want. Why should I dirty my sword?"

He turned, leaving the burnt weredragon to writhe and wail on the ground. He mounted Phel again and soared, smiling thinly.

From behind him rose the screams of the prisoners and the laughter of his men. Below him rolled the destruction: piles of rubble, smashed columns, and the corpses of wyverns and weredragons. Two archways still stood, the entrances to tunnels; at each one, wyverns lined up to spew acid underground.

By nightfall the tunnels will be overflowing, Mahrdor thought. He licked his lips, imagining the beautiful screams and stench and death below. He looked at his left hand and shuddered to imagine all the flesh that was now sizzling below the earth, hidden like the curves of a woman under a dress.

He spotted Solina in a square, still sitting atop Baal, her behemoth of a wyvern, the greatest of the beasts. She had moved aside, allowing a lesser wyvern to spill acid underground. The fumes stung Mahrdor's nostrils and eyes. His arm blazed in pain as if remembering the heat of acid. Gritting his teeth, he landed his wyvern upon the smashed cobblestones by his queen. He bowed his head to her.

"Queen Solina."

She looked at him, amusement in her eyes. She raised her eyebrows, stretching the scar that halved her face.

"Your hand," she said. "Will you not bandage it? I do not wish to look upon this thing."

Phel grunted and sidestepped beneath him. The twisted beast was smaller than Baal, but Mahrdor thought his girl just as mean. He patted her scales until she calmed.

"You created this hand, my queen," he said and raised it in salute. "Don't you wish to remember your power over me? Don't you wish me to always remember my sin and your might?"

"I care not," she said. "You are a soldier. A tool. That is all." She looked at the tunnel entrance. Heat and distant screams rose from it. "I care about the Weredragon King. I care to see his body burned and writhing, not yours."

Mahrdor allowed himself a thin smile. "I can give you the Weredragon King. You may burn him yourself if you please."

She snarled at him. "I asked you to bring me the whore Lyana, and you let her free. What nonsense do you spout now?"

Upon his wyvern, he sketched an elaborate bow. "No nonsense, my queen, only information. I persuaded our prisoners to impart it. There is another doorway to these tunnels; it lies outside the city. The weredragons carved it as an escape route." He looked at the acid pouring underground. "They will be escaping now, I presume. Your Weredragon King, his sister, and probably the lords and ladies of the Reptile Court—including my beloved bird—are likely crawling out from the city as we speak."

She reeled Baal toward him. The beast snarled and his drool spattered. Solina herself looked nearly as beastly, her eyes blazing and her lip curled back.

"Where does this tunnel lead to?" She raised her sabre. "Speak, Mahrdor, or by the Sun God, your right arm will burn too."

Mahrdor laughed and flexed his ruined fingers. The pain flared, turning his laughter into a grimace. He coughed blood and smiled. "I will lead you there, my queen. I will lead you to the Weredragon King." He kicked Phel, driving her closer to Solina. He glared into his queen's eyes. "But I want my Lyana. And I want the Weredragon Princess. Give me those two rare birds, so that I may reshape them and turn them into pets of my own. You can keep the king and do with him as you please."

Staring at him, her eyes blue ice, she tugged Baal's reins. She spun the beast around until wyvern pushed against wyvern. She leaned sideways in the saddle toward Mahrdor, sword drawn and eyes narrowed.

"Show me there." She kicked her wyvern, soared, and howled. "If the king is mine, his women will be yours! Now fly!"

Mahrdor smiled and flew.

ELETHOR

The acid kept pouring. Wails rose through the chambers. Acid pooled and people huddled atop boulders and clung to walls. More acid streamed from above and sizzled. Droplets splashed onto flesh and burns spread. Feet melted. Children wept. An old man cried to the stars and leaped into the stream, a vain attempt to hold it back with his body; the acid ate through him and kept pouring.

"Elethor!" said Deramon, face red. He moved through the crowd, grabbed Elethor, and pulled him toward the wall. "This is it, Elethor. It's time to leave—you and Mori."

Eyes somber, Deramon gestured at the tapestry Mori had woven, which hung upon a craggy wall. Elethor knew what lay behind it—the escape tunnel carved for his family, a snaking pipe that led outside the city.

He looked back at the crowd of survivors. Many had begun to dig, forming holes for acid to fill and mounds to stand on. Others stood upon corpses. The acid kept flowing around them, moving from chamber to chamber.

"There are thousands of people here," Elethor said. "I won't leave them to die."

Mori stood by his side, face pale but lips firm. She nodded, head raised. "I'm not leaving either, Deramon," she said with a voice soft but steady. "I am princess of this realm; I go down with the ship."

Deramon scowled, looking from king to princess. His eyes darkened and his lips curled back in a growl. "You and Mori are the last Aeternums, a dynasty that has ruled in Requiem for three thousand years. I loved your father, Elethor, and I loved your brother. I won't let you and your sister die too. I am sworn to guard your house; I will not let it fall."

Elethor glared at the older man. "And I am sworn to guard this realm, and I will not let it fall." He grabbed the tapestry and pulled it free, revealing the tunnel. He turned to the survivors and called out, voice echoing. "Mothers and babes—to me! Mothers and babes only—through this tunnel! It will lead you to safety. Mothers and babes only!"

The people wailed. At once it seemed that everyone was charging toward the tunnel. One man slipped and fell into streaming acid; he screamed and burned. Bayrin stood in the crowd, holding men back, shouting for mothers and babes. Adia was praying and guiding mothers forward. People were weeping.

Elethor clutched Mori's hand. He looked into her wide gray eyes. She stared back steadily, clutching his hand.

"Are you sure, Mori?" he whispered. "I will send you through this tunnel if you wish it. There are thousands of people here; it would take hours for everyone to crawl out, and we have only moments before the acid overflows us."

Her eyes flashed. Her lips tightened. Suddenly Mori looked as fierce and strong as Lyana.

"I stay," she said. "With you. With my people. If we go to the starlit halls, we go together." She raised her voice to the crowd. "Mothers and babes only! Move, to us!"

Soon the first mother appeared at their side, weeping and clutching her newborn. Adia, her white robes tattered and burnt, helped guide the young woman and her babe into the tunnel. Soon they disappeared into the darkness.

"Keep crawling!" Elethor called into the tunnel. "Crawl for an hour—until you reach the forest—then fly! Fly east and don't return."

Bayrin and Deramon were moving through the chambers, guiding mothers and babes through the crowd. Adia helped each pair enter the tunnels and prayed for them. Some older men tried to shove their way through, to enter the tunnels themselves; Bayrin and Deramon held them back.

"Mothers and babes only!" Elethor shouted. Only ten pairs had entered the tunnel so far; countless still remained. "Into the tunnel. Crawl and then fly!"

Wyvern shrieks echoed above with new vigor. The flow of acid intensified. People screamed and scrambled onto one another. The holes they had dug filled up, and the mounds began to melt. The acid began to consume Elethor's boots and sting his feet. He breathed sharply through clenched teeth. Mori clasped his hand so hard she nearly crushed it. In the far side of the tunnel, where the floor sloped, people wailed. The acid rose past their ankles, then reached their knees. They began to fall and burn away.

"Into the tunnels, go, my child!" Adia cried to a mother and babe, helping them climb into the darkness.

We're not going to last another moment, Elethor realized. How many had they saved? Thirty people? Forty? *The rest of Requiem will die in these tunnels, the end of our Second Age.*

Lyana moved through the crowd toward him. Her face was pale, her eyes wide. She clung to his arm.

"Elethor," she whispered. "Elethor, I will fly with you. I will roar by your side in the starlit halls. We fly there together." She growled at him. "Don't you leave me there!"

Elethor growled too. The acid blazed against the soles of his feet, and he pushed himself to the wall. Panic swelled in his lungs.

No. No! I won't let Requiem fall on my watch. Not for my war with Solina.

People fell and screamed and melted before him. They reminded him of the bodies he had seen last year in the Abyss, but back then, hope had awaited them. He and Lyana had freed the Starlit Demon. They had driven the beast through the earth, carving a great shaft out into the sky.

What I would give for such a tunnel now! I—

Elethor froze.

He snarled. He looked at Lyana who clung to his left. He looked at Mori who clung to his right. He loved them both so much that he shook with it. He nodded. His eyes stung.

For my father. For Orin. For the light of our stars and the sky in our wings.

He looked at Mother Adia. "Adia, I need you to stay here. I need you to keep leading the mothers and babes through the tunnel; once they've all escaped, you will crawl after them, and you will lead them to safety." He turned to Deramon. "You too, Deramon; they will need your strength. You and Adia will lead the survivors."

They all stared at him. Adia sucked in her breath.

"What are you planning, Elethor?" the priestess whispered.

He turned away from her. He looked between Lyana and Mori, who both clung to him, and at Bayrin, who approached with somber eyes.

"Fly by my side, Lyana and Bayrin," he whispered. "Fly by me, Mori. Whatever happens, we fly together."

They looked at him, lips tightened. They said nothing.

If we die, we die together, Elethor thought. *If today I fall, I fall with those whom I love.* He squared his shoulders and raised his head. *But I won't fall without a battle for the poets to sing of.*

He faced the crowd and roared.

"People of Requiem!" he shouted. "Hear me, Vir Requis! I am your king, Elethor Aeternum, Son of Olasar. Hear me today!"

They turned toward him, and he saw the fear in their eyes. *I am their king; let me be a pillar to them.* He raised his head and spoke in a voice deep and clear.

"We are in darkness," he said. "We are in the pit of despair. But I do not lose hope. I do not stop fighting. Even in the most dark, hopeless cave a light shines somewhere; we will find that light and crawl toward it." He pointed to the tunnel behind him. "Mothers and babes—Adia will lead you to safety. She will lead you to light. Follow her through darkness and into the wild."

The mothers kept moving toward the tunnel, clutching their infants. Some moved on burnt, twisted feet. Adia and Deramon continued helping them into the tunnel, blessing them with prayers. Elethor raised his voice louder.

"The rest of you!" he shouted. "We will find our light too. We will find our sky. I promise this to you. Today you are soldiers! Today you are all warriors of Requiem. Young and old, children and elders, you now fight for the Royal Army! You can fly as dragons. You can blow fire. You can slash your claws. Today we all fight with one roar! Today we are all warriors of starlight! Stand back, people of Requiem, hear my roar and answer my call!"

He let go of Lyana and Mori.

He leaped through the people toward the flowing acid.

In the chamber of stone, he shifted into a dragon.

People screamed and scurried back. Elethor's claws reached out, hitting the walls. His wings hit the ceiling. In dragon form, he nearly filled the chamber, nearly crushed the people beneath him. They ran and leaped over acid. With a great dragon roar, Elethor began to slam his tail against the northern wall.

This is where the Starlit Demon flew, he remembered. He had seen the tunnel maps. This was the place—beyond this wall. Here had the Starlit Demon carved its cavern. Here awaited their sky. He slammed his tail and chunks of rock fell.

"Requiem!" he cried, fire in his maw. "Our wings will find your sky!"

He slammed his tail again. Cracks raced. Rocks plummeted. The wall collapsed outward, revealing a gaping shaft—a hundred feet in diameter—full of wind and rain and echoing wyvern cries.

"Fly, dragons of Requiem!" Elethor shouted and leaped into the great shaft. He beat his wings and soared toward the sky. Walls of stone raced at his sides. "To death! To blood! To glory! Today we all fight; today we roar as one!"

With a roar that could deafen gods, the dragons of Requiem soared behind him—out of darkness and into the light of battle and song.

SOLINA

Outside the city the forests burned. Solina flew upon her wyvern, savoring the smell of smoke. It was a dry summer; Solina had kindled these flames only yesterday, and they now raced across Requiem, eating all in their path. She smiled thinly as she flew over the burning landscapes. Should any weredragons escape Nova Vita, they would find little sanctuary here. No places remained for them to hide. All the weredragon lands now blazed with the light of her lord, casting out the reptilian darkness.

She looked behind her. Lord Mahrdor flew there upon his own wyvern, and behind him flew fifty of his men, each armed with crossbow, spear, sword, and shield. Their wyverns screamed and their wings roiled the smoke from the blazing lands below. Behind them, Nova Vita lay as a black smudge upon the land, bustling with wyverns like flies over a carcass.

Her smile widened. *You will flee that rotting carcass of your city, Elethor,* she thought. *You will flee into my arms.*

Mahrdor flew up beside her. He pointed his ruined hand below.

"There, my queen. Three boulders by a hillside. That is where the weredragons will emerge." He licked his lips. "That is where Lyana and I will meet again."

Solina imagined what he would do to Lyana, and laughter bubbled in her throat. She had seen Mahrdor's work before. Truly, the man was an artist. She had seen the scrolls he made from human skin, the chairs of bones, the shrunken heads, the pickled hands. And she had seen worse: the sniveling, pathetic creations he kept in his deeper chambers. Those ones were his greatest treasures, living works of art that he had created—breaking and reshaping bones, sewing flesh to flesh, twisting and burning and molding his prisoners into creatures of haunted beauty.

That is what awaits you, Lyana, Solina thought. *That is what awaits you, Mori.*

She began spiraling her wyvern down toward the boulders. Her men descended around her, wings fanning the forest flames.

"But you, Elethor," she whispered. "You will be *mine* to torment. I will break you myself. I will wield the hammers that nail you to my tower, that shatter your bones, that make you scream and weep and beg. I will stand there, glorious in the light of my lord, and watch my vultures feast upon your living flesh." She clenched her fists. "The entire kingdom will watch, and the people your father orphaned will cheer!"

She landed in a patch of burnt grass and hot stones. Baal screeched at the flames that surrounded them; the wyvern was skittish, bucking and whipping his tail. Solina patted his scales.

"Hush, Baal!" she said. "The fire of our lord cannot hurt us. Hush! Lower your wing."

The beast calmed, though his eyes still blazed red and his tongue still lolled, dripping acid that burned holes into the earth. When he lowered his wing, Solina climbed down to the forest floor. Grass smoldered beneath her boots. Before her in the hillside loomed the black mouth of a tunnel.

Solina grabbed the crossbow that hung across her back. She loaded a bolt and twisted the crank, pulling the string taut.

"Load crossbows, men," she said over her shoulder. "We enter the darkness."

Mahrdor and the others were dismounting their wyverns. The firelight blazed against their armor. They grabbed their own crossbows, and the sounds of twisting cranks filled the forest. Swords hung from their waists and spears hung across their backs.

"Let us slay some dragons," Solina said.

She turned back to the tunnel, and was prepared to enter it, when she saw two weredragons emerge. A grin split her face.

The female weredragon was halfway out the tunnel when she noticed the Tirans, paled, and froze. She held a babe in her arms; the little beast began to wail. Solina loosed her crossbow into the spawn; its wails died at once.

The mother screamed. Mahrdor's crossbow thrummed. Its bolt slammed into the mother's throat, and the wench fell, gurgling, still clutching her babe as if it still lived. Solina drew her sabre and landed two blows, finishing the job.

"Where is the Weredragon Princess?" Mahrdor demanded. "Where is the Lady Lyana?"

As Solina was loading another bolt, a shadow stirred in the tunnels. Solina saw a second mother and babe crawling forward. When the mother began to flee back into darkness, Solina shot her crossbow again, hitting the creature inside the tunnel. Her men shot their crossbows too, until the wailing babe inside silenced, and blood trickled out.

Solina sighed. "Oh, Elethor. You fool." She shook her head sadly and looked at Mahrdor. "The weredragons carved an escape tunnel... but send mothers and babes out, rather than their monarchs." She spat onto the body at her feet. "Noble halfwits. It will be their death."

Mahrdor cleared his throat and stared down at the bodies in distaste. "I care not for mothers and infants. I want a knight. I want a princess. I want my birds of paradise."

Solina loaded another bolt and stepped toward the tunnel. "You will have them, and I will have my king, though their feet might be a little burnt. They still cower inside as our acid flows." She entered the tunnel; it was only four feet tall, forcing her to crawl. She held her crossbow before her. "Follow, men! We slew them in the sky, and we will slay them underground."

She had crawled a dozen feet when she saw candlelight ahead. Yet another mother crawled there, clutching her wailing offspring. Solina shot them, loaded another bolt, and wriggled over their bodies. The babe was still alive and squirming; she slew it with her dagger. Every ten or twenty feet, she had to shoot another spawning beast and her get. The blood flowed across the tunnel.

She had crawled for what seemed like an hour, and she was down to only three crossbow bolts, when she saw firelight and heard screams ahead.

She grinned.

When she crawled closer, she saw a scene of ruin. A great chamber loomed ahead; in its walls, she saw passageways to other chambers. Bodies littered the floor, nearly covered with acid; most were nothing but bones now. A handful of survivors—more spawning mothers—crowded upon a mound of earth, waiting to enter the escape tunnel.

Solina licked her lips, leaped from the darkness, and landed among them.

The babes wailed. The mothers screamed. Behind her, her men began leaping from the tunnel, and crossbows fired, and mothers fell dead.

A roar echoed.

Solina spun around to see a great, coppery dragon in the chamber. She inhaled sharply. Lord Deramon! The beast stood before a wall that had collapsed. Through the gaping hole, Solina saw a shaft leading upward; she recognized the passageway the Starlit Demon had carved last year. Wyverns were flying down the shaft; Deramon was holding them back and blowing flames. Acid blazed across him, eating through his scales, but still the dragon howled, blew fire, and lashed claws. The wyverns were trying to enter the chamber, to attack the mothers and babes; the dragon flamed them.

Solina smiled, raised her crossbow, and pointed it at Deramon.

"Goodbye, old friend," she said with a crooked smile.

When she pulled the trigger, a white figure leaped forward and slammed into her. The bolt whizzed and ricocheted off a wall. Solina snarled and fell several steps, nearly crashing into the rivers of acid. She spun to see Mother Adia, the woman's eyes wild and her teeth bared.

The priestess was unarmed and still in human form, but she looked every inch a beast. Her eyes blazed with condemnation. Her hair flurried. Her fingers curled as if they bore dragon claws. She leaped again at Solina.

"Stars of Requiem!" the priestess cried and drove her fingernails toward Solina—her only weapons. "You will die here, Solina, and may your Sun God forever burn your soul."

Solina sidestepped, amused. With a snort, she drew her sabre. The curved blade flashed, arcing out of its sheath and into Adia's flesh.

The priestess froze.

Solina's smile widened.

With a snarl, Solina pulled the blade back. It emerged bloody from the priestess—a giver of hot, intoxicating blood, the blood of her enemies, the blood of her glory and triumph.

Adia stared silently, red spreading across her white goan like a field of poppies growing in snow. Her eyes were deep pools, emotionless. Her lips whispered silently.

"Weredragon," Solina said to her, disgust dripping from her voice. She spat. "Fall at my feet and beg for a quick death."

Adia held the wound that sliced her belly; she was calm, like a mother holding her babe. The priestess stared at Solina, and still no pain filled those eyes, no fear, no anger... and as Solina stared into those eyes, it seemed to her that starlight glowed inside them, not blazing and furious like the light of her lord, but soft and mysterious like the night sky. And suddenly Solina herself was afraid, for she saw a power in those staring eyes, in those pools of night—a power she could not understand or burn.

"Child," Adia whispered. Blood stained her lips. "Poor, wayward child... what have we done to you? How did we hurt you so? Why does such pain fill you?" She reached out a bloody hand. "Would you forgive us, child, for the pain we gave you?"

Solina sucked in her breath. That pain danced inside her, gripped her, and spun her head. Her eyes stung with it. Suddenly she was a youth again, frightened and lonely, seeking comfort in Elethor's arms. Suddenly the courts of Requiem seemed so large to her, the dragons so cruel, their fire so hot, their stars so beautiful and foreign to her—stars that would never bless her, a lost desert child. She wanted to weep. She wanted the priestess to embrace her, to pray for her, to be her mother too, as she was a mother to all of Requiem.

No! No.

Solina's fist trembled around her sword. *No, that is not me. It was never me!* She snarled. Her flesh burned with hatred. She did not need their pity. She did not need their love.

She howled in the chamber. "May your pathetic stars burn your soul, Mother of Reptiles!"

Screaming, she thrust her sword. It drove into Adia's chest. Hot blood stained Solina's fingers. When she pulled her sword free, the blood sprayed her, and Adia fell to her knees.

The priestess gave Solina one last look—a look of sadness and of love. The starlight in her eyes dimmed and she fell.

A howl rose behind Solina, deafening, filling the chamber like a storm.

Blood on her hands, lips curled back, Solina turned to see Deramon. The dragon roared—the roar of hearts rending, of forests burning, of towers crashing. It was a roar like the ghosts of a drowned city calling from the ocean depths, like a dying race that would forever cry from lost graves, like children lost in flame, like the sound her own heart had made when they tore her from Elethor. It was the roar of a man for the woman he loved, of a grief and pain too great for any mortal body to hold, too wrenching for any mind to contain. It was grief itself—primal, pure, and deeper than all the seas and tunnels in the world.

Solina froze in wonder, in fear, in awe. Tears filled her eyes.

I made him roar this sound, she thought. *I had the power to create this.* Here in this cave, before this dragon and this howl, it seemed to her a greater triumph than all the towers she had raised, the armies she had led, and the dragons she had slain.

I made something pure. I created this roar and it is the greatest, saddest, and most perfect thing I ever did.

The great dragon's scales blazed with light. His claws rose like swords. His fangs shone like the whetted blades of demons. The wyverns outside the cavern, freed from his flames, spewed acid. The streams crashed against Deramon, drenching him, eating away at him.

His scales began to shrink and twist, revealing raw flesh beneath them. Yet he did not fall. He rose tall in the chamber until his head nearly hit the ceiling. His wings unfurled like a dark sky. And he roared his fire.

The stream crashed toward Solina.

She screamed.

She remembered Orin's fire—the fire that had scarred her body and soul, that tore her from Elethor, that placed this flame in her heart. The old pain clawed inside her. Solina leaped aside. She nearly crashed into the acid. The flames blasted the rock where she had stood.

"Your soul will burn with hers!" Solina shouted and fired her crossbow.

The bolt slammed into the dragon's flaming maw.

The dragon reared. His fire hit the ceiling and rained. With a cry, Solina drove forward. She shoved into a mother and babe, knocking them into a stream of acid. She leaped onto their bodies, sprang toward the dragon, and swung onto his leg. She scurried up the scales until she clung to the beast's back.

He bucked and roared. His wings flapped. Solina snarled and clung to him. The dragon leaped, slammed against the ceiling, and Solina screamed. If not for her armor, she'd have been crushed between scale and stone. Acid sizzled across the dragon, eating at her breastplate, her boots, and her gloves.

"Die with your whore, reptile," she said. Tears stung her eyes and she could not breathe. "You tore me from Elethor. You told your cruel king of our love." Suddenly she was that youth again—afraid, angry, and weak. Her tears streamed and she roared, her own roar of pain and fury and loss. "You drove me to this, Deramon! You brought this death upon your land! Look around you. Look at the dead. Look at the corpse of your wife. Die knowing that you did this, beast! Die knowing that you killed her!"

Blinded with tears, strong with her fury, Solina reached around the dragon's neck. She swiped her sword. His scales were weakened with acid; her blade tore through them and into the flesh.

His roar died upon her steel.

The beast fell.

With a shower of blood, fire, and acid, the great Deramon Eleison—Guard of Requiem, slayer of many Tirans, Lord of Dragons—fell in darkness and light. His head hit the floor, and his wings fell limp, and the fire drained from him. Bloodied, he returned to his human form—a grizzled man clad in armor, body scarred and eyes dim.

Solina stood and stared down at the man. In her youth, he had always seemed so frightening to her, a mountain of hair and muscle and steel, all booming shouts and clanking weapons, twice her size and ten times as loud. Now he seemed so small to her—too thin in his armor, his beard more white than red, his booming voice silenced. He was still alive. He crawled across the mound of earth and stone. He reached out to the body of his wife.

His hand, bloodied and scarred, clasped the hand of Mother Adia. The priestess's hand, pale and lifeless, seemed so small and fair in Deramon's grip, a white flower in the paw of a lion.

"Adia," he whispered, voice hoarse, nearly silent. "Adia, my love. Do you see them? Do you see the white columns, the starlit halls of our fathers?" He clasped her hand, his eyes dampened, and a smile trembled on his lips. "We fly there together; we will dance and sing there always, my love. We will see our Noela again."

Solina drove her blade down into his back.

He gave a last gasp.

His eyes closed and he lay still, holding the hand of his wife.

Solina stared down at their bodies. Her lips curled back in disgust. When she looked up, she saw her men staring, silent. The last bodies of mothers and babes lay strewn at their feet, pierced with bolts. When fighting above Nova Vita, her men had cheered and howled for every dragon slain. Now they only stared.

She ignored them. She skirted a pool of acid and approached the shaft the Starlit Demon had carved last year. Wyverns fluttered up and down the chasm. Solina placed her fingers into her mouth—they tasted like sweet blood—and gave a loud, long shriek of a whistle.

A screech above answered her. Wings blasted air, each flap a thunderbolt rank with death. Baal, the King of Wyverns, dived down the tunnel and faced her. The beast hovered before the collapsed wall. Acid dripped between his teeth. Solina leaped through the opening, swung around Baal's neck, and climbed into his saddle.

"Grab those bodies," she told the beast. "Grab them and fly."

The wyvern reached into the collapsing cavern. He grabbed the body of Adia with one clawed foot, the body of Deramon with another. The beast licked his lips and looked over his shoulder at Solina.

"No, Baal," she said and stroked him. "You will not feast upon these ones. Not yet. We will first flaunt them before the city." She kneed him. "Fly! Into the sky!"

They soared.

Walls of stone blurred at their sides. They rose from underground into a city of ruin, then into a sky of smoke, ash, and fire. Twenty thousand wyverns screeched and spat their acid. Twenty thousand dragons flew around them—children, old toothless beasts, and cripples missing limbs. The mob of Requiem, an untrained mass, bustled and roared fire and slashed claws. Solina inhaled sharply.

It's beautiful, she thought. *A great tapestry of glory.* She had never seen so many beasts flying and killing under one sky; it seemed to her like the great stories of old, the ones where griffins toppled the mythical halls of Requiem's golden age.

Blood rained. Blood coated her. She licked blood off her lips and sword, savoring its coppery taste, the taste of her might. It was a day of dragon blood, a day of sunfire, a day of triumph. When she looked across the battle, she saw him there—her king, her love, the jewel she sought.

"Elethor!" she cried and flew toward him.

MORI

The battle was lost. Mori could see that. She shot through the chaos, eyes burning. Blood and acid rained. Everywhere she looked, clouds of wyverns and dragons fought above the fallen city. Bodies crashed down into the ruins, and their blood flowed across the strewn bricks, smashed mosaics, and shattered columns of her home. Wind roared and clouds of ash roiled above her.

Only a single column rose from the devastation, a great pillar of white marble, three hundred feet tall and kissed with a beam of sunlight: King's Column, raised by King Aeternum himself millennia ago. Swarms of wyverns were attacking it, lashing their claws and tails, but could not break it. Mori knew the legends. The old scrolls wrote that so long as a single Vir Requis lived, King's Column would not fall. Looking around the battle, Mori realized with a chill: the column might fall this day.

The wyverns were everywhere. Two swooped toward her, the sun at their backs. Mori screamed, dodged their streams of acid, and soared above them. She roasted their riders with fire. The Tirans screamed and burned, and the wyverns crashed down. Three more wyverns flew to her right, and Mori shouted and dived under them, then spun and blazed them. She had always been so fast, the fastest dragon in Requiem; these burly wyverns were clumsy around her. Yet other dragons were faring less well. So many were elderly, wounded, or young. Dozens were mere toddlers, no larger than ponies, their wings weak and their fire mere sparks. They fell around Mori, burning with acid and peppered with crossbow bolts. When they hit the ruins below, they returned to human forms and lay dead—slashed, burned, torn apart.

Mori growled. She flamed another wyvern. Acid splashed her tail and she howled. She soared higher, crashing through wyverns and dragons, and surveyed the battle. Barely any soldiers of Requiem now flew; their army was now comprised of the old, the weak, the frightened. The wyverns were tearing through them like a pack of wolves in a chicken coop.

She looked around for Elethor, Bayrin, and Lyana, but could not see them. Had they fallen too? Did she now lead these ragged, dying remains of her people? She growled, eyes stinging, fear an inferno in her belly.

We cannot win, Mori thought. *We must flee.*

"Dragons of Requiem!" she cried to the battle. "Flee! Flee into the forests! Flee to the east and west. Leave this city!"

When she looked below her, she saw a group of young dragons flying over the ruins of the temple. Wings batting madly, they cried out for their mothers. A wyvern shrieked and shot toward them. Acid streamed, crashed against one young dragon, and the child fell dead and twisted. Three more wyverns charged, their own projectiles spraying. The young dragons wailed and another fell, the acid eating through her scales like a swarm of ants on meat.

With a growl, Mori swooped.

She crashed between three wyverns fighting a few older, toothless dragons. With a howl, she rained fire upon the beasts that burned the children. They shrieked and turned toward her, acid sputtering. Their riders burned and screamed.

"Flee, dragons!" Mori cried down to the children. "Flee to the forests!"

Two of the wyverns began soaring toward her, their riders flaming. Several young dragons wailed and began fleeing, only for wyverns to pursue them. Crossbows fired. Another dragon fell dead.

Mori roared her fire. The flames crashed against streams of acid that rose toward her. The blasts exploded, spraying flames and acid. Mori howled, dived, and closed her jaws around a rider. She tore the man in two, then spat out his top half. It tumbled, entrails dangling like the tail of a comet. The second wyvern rose toward her, a crossbow thrummed, and a bolt slammed into Mori's shoulder. She blew her fire and swiped her tail. She knocked the rider half off the wyvern; the reins pulled taut and the wyvern banked. Mori bathed it with fire until it fell.

"Flee, dragons of Requiem!" she cried to the children. They were flying around confused, calling for their parents. Wyverns were tearing them down one by one. Mori flew, flamed a wyvern, and herded the children forward, wings spread wide. When wyverns shot toward them, she blew a ring of fire, lashed her tail, and thrust her claws.

"Together, here, with me!" Mori cried to the surviving children. Her wings opened wide, as if she could shield them all. She drove them forward, nipping at them with her teeth and goading them with her tail. "Fly! Fly into the forests and hide! I will find your parents and send them there too. Now fly!"

Wailing, tears in their eyes, the children fled. Soon they flew over the fallen walls of Nova Vita and headed toward the burning forests. Three wyverns began to chase them, and crossbows fired upon another child, sending the girl falling into the flaming trees.

Roaring, Mori flew over the crumbling walls. She crashed against the three wyverns. Fangs bit her tail. Acid blazed against her wing. She blew flames against the riders, soared higher, and swooped again, raining more fire. The wyverns fell.

"Fly!" she cried after the children; the survivors were distant now, mere specks over the blazing landscapes. "Fly and never return!"

She panted. Blood trickled down her scales, and wind roared through a hole in her wing. She turned back toward the city and grimaced. The wyverns flew like storm clouds over the ruins, raining their acid. Only a handful of dragons were fleeing over the toppled walls, wyverns in pursuit. Some dragons still fought but were falling fast. Mori growled. She began flying back to the city. Her wing ached and she wobbled. Her body burned, and she realized that acid had eaten through the scales on her back leg. A bolt thrust out from her shoulder, a demon of steel eating away at her.

Yet still Mori flew, eyes narrowed and breath blazing. She had to save whoever she still could. She had to find her brother, to find her love Bayrin, to find her dearest friend Lyana. And so she flew back to the inferno, blood and fire streaming behind her, death blazing before her.

She flew over the ruins. The battle raged around her. A great wyvern soared ahead, the largest she had seen, rising from darkness like a demon from the Abyss. Its rider glittered, a deity of gold holding a banner of a blazing sun. The rider's cry rang out above the battle, high and beautiful like the cry of a goddess.

"Elethor!"

Mori snarled.

It was Solina.

The Queen of Tiranor rose higher. Her wyvern's wings thudded, two hundred feet wide, spreading debris across the ruins below. Her gilded armor shone, a second sun in the sky. Her hair streamed behind her, a second banner of gold.

"Elethor!" she called again. "Your city is fallen, Reptile King! Fly here and beg me to spare those of your vermin that still live."

Mori wheeled her head around. Across the city she saw her brother, and tears filled Mori's eyes. Elethor rose from smoke, a great brass dragon roaring fire. Mori remembered him as a gaunt youth, a dragon barely larger than herself; now muscles rippled beneath his scales, his flames burned white-hot, and his eyes blazed with the fury of a king. Suddenly he was not merely Elethor, her sad brother, but a great king of Requiem, as powerful and noble as her father.

Wyverns surrounded him—hundreds of them—a fortress of iron scales and spraying acid. Inside the ring, two more dragons rose from smoke: Bayrin, his green scales splashed with blood and ash, and Lyana, her blue scales dented but her wings still beating strongly. The three dragons fought back to back, blowing rings of fire, holding the wyverns back.

Mori wanted to fly to them. They were the people she loved most; without them, there was no reason to live. She wanted to fight by them, to die by them if she must. She took a deep breath, flapped her wings, and prepared to charge and fall with them in the ring of iron and acid.

Before she could flap her wings again, she saw from the corner of her eye that Solina's wyvern clutched two bodies.

Mori's breath died.

She looked closer and felt her world collapse.

Solina's wyvern held the bloodied bodies of Adia and Deramon.

A mewl left Mori's throat, a cry of pain soon rising to a roar. Tears filled her eyes. Fire blazed in her maw. Mother Adia—her greatest teacher, her guiding star, the Mother of Requiem and like a mother to her. Lord Deramon—greatest warrior of Requiem, the bright blade of her people. Fallen. Their lights dimmed.

That day returned to her, that day worse than any other, a cold day in a far southern fort. She again saw Solina smile as Orin lay burnt at her feet, again saw the queen slash her blade, slice Orin open, savor his screams. Again Mori lay upon that table as Lord Acribus invaded her, and again Solina watched and laughed as Mori's body and soul and innocence shattered. That had been over a year ago, but now it bloomed within her, and rage filled Mori, a rage hotter than dragonfire, a rage that spun her head and overflowed her grief.

I was a child then, Solina, she thought. *I was scared, young, and alone. But now you will find my fire bright and my soul hardened. You gave me this pain. You gave me this strength.* Her dragon roar pealed across the city. *Now you will die in my flames.*

She drove through smoke and over ruin toward the Queen of Tiranor.

Solina spun toward her. "Mori!" the queen cried in delight. "My sweet little bird!"

The queen's crossbow thrummed.

Mori snarled and banked. The bolt grazed her leg, and she kept flying. The devastation blurred below her. Wyverns flew at her; Mori shot above, beneath, and around them.

Orin always said I could fly like a bee, she thought. *He always said nobody could catch me. You killed him, Solina. Now you will die here—in the city where he lies buried.*

She soared over the shattered Temple of Requiem and roared her fire.

Solina's wyvern, the great beast Baal, howled and reared. A sizzling jet spewed from his mouth. Acid crashed against flame. The streams exploded and rained upon the ruins.

Mori beat her wings madly. The left one throbbed, holes spreading through it, but Mori ignored the pain and growled. She shot over the crashing inferno and rained her fire upon Solina.

The queen raised her shield. The flames engulfed her, exploding around the shield and cascading upon her wyvern. The beast screeched and bucked, and more acid spouted, a geyser of heat and stench. Mori banked, dodging the stream. Drops splashed her and she roared, swooped, and lashed her tail.

Solina still lived, clasping her charred shield. With a howl, Mori slammed her tail down.

Light flashed. Solina's blade rose. Steel slashed Mori's tail and blood sprayed.

She screamed. The pain leaped through her, a striking asp. She blew more fire, but Solina flew beneath her, and her wyvern rose higher, a wall of scales and claws. The beast dwarfed Mori, twice her size. Its maw opened and its cry shook her, and its maw boiled like a smelter. Acid spewed toward her.

Mori soared. Acid splashed her back legs. She cried. She tried to blow more flame, but only sparks left her maw. The pain tugged at her magic like hands trying to rip off a gown; she struggled to stay in dragon form.

No! Don't fall. Fight her! Kill her! For Orin. For your people who lie dead beneath you.

Mori drove toward Solina and lashed her claws.

One claw slammed against the queen's shield and shattered it. Splinters showered. Mori's second claw slammed against Solina's blade. Steel rang and Mori howled. She leaned down to bite the queen.

Solina rose in her saddle and thrust up her sword.

The steel sliced across Mori's cheek, screeching and shedding sparks.

Mori screamed, pulled back, and heard wyverns swoop behind her.

She spun to see them. Their claws reached out and their riders shot crossbows. Bolts slammed into her.

"Take her alive!" Solina screamed somewhere below. "Chain the beast!"

Mori could barely see. For an instant she lost her magic, tumbled as a woman, then regained her dragon form and flew again. Smoke and fire and cloud swirled around her. Her wounds blazed. She tried to flap her wings, but a spear shot through the left one, where a hole already spread from the acid. She spun and did not know up from down. Blood flowed into her left eye.

"Elethor!" she called out. "Bayrin!"

She could not see them. She saw nothing but the blazing eyes of wyverns, claws that clutched her, and chains that swung around her.

"Bring her down!" rose Solina's voice from the haze. "Chain the beast!"

A claw slammed into Mori's back, driving through scale into flesh.

A cry fled her lips—a cry of pain, of fear, of a girl who was lost in Castellum Luna and breaking apart in the darkness.

Her magic left her.

She plummeted through the sky, a human girl, until claws caught her. The great shards wrapped around her, nearly crushing her ribs. More wyverns rose and chains swung around her.

"El!" she tried to cry, but her voice was only a hoarse whisper. "Bay... Lyana..."

She tried to shift into a dragon again, but could not. The wyvern claws nearly crushed her, keeping her in human form, and the chains tightened around her limbs. Wyvern scales surrounded her; between them, she could catch only glimpses of fire and ruin.

"Take her south!" rose Solina's voice. "Take her to Tiranor and chain her in my dungeon. I will come to her soon. Fly now! Fly south with the beast!"

A stream of scales flowed beneath her. Wyvern wings flapped around her. Mori struggled in the grip. She tried to cry out, but she could barely breathe. Soon the wyverns parted below, and she saw fallen walls and then flaming farmlands. She looked up to see a burning horizon flowing to distant, shimmering light.

The cries of dying dragons faded behind her. The lands streamed below. Mori's eyes closed and she knew nothing but pain, smoke, and the cry of wyverns.

LYANA

No. Stars, no. Please stars, let this be a dream. Let me wake.

She saw Queen Solina rise over the ruins. She saw the queen smirk. She saw the bodies of her parents fall from the wyvern claws.

Mother. Father. Tears filled Lyana's eyes. *Stars, please stars, no. They're dead. She killed them.* Her body trembled and she could barely keep flying.

A roar sounded behind her, torn with pain. Bayrin howled and blew fire.

"Solina!" he cried, voice hoarse. He soared, slashing and biting, a wild beast wreathed in flame. Lyana had never seen her brother like this. Blood and cuts covered him, and everywhere wyverns flew around him.

"Scream for me, beast!" Solina called across the battle. The queen laughed. "Die screaming for the reptiles that spawned you!"

Lyana's head spun. The grief seemed too great to bear. She howled to the sky. Around her, so few dragons still flew—a mere scattering of survivors. There were almost none left to save. Lyana sounded her cry: the cry of a warrior, of a knight, of a daughter grieving.

You took everything from me, Solina, she thought, tears in her eyes. *You took my city. You took my Orin. You took my parents.*

Even her rage could not rise above this grief, this great cry of loss, this falling of a kingdom and race. She howled with her grief and she flew toward Queen Solina through fire, acid, and blood.

I will kill her. I will kill our nemesis, then fall dead upon the ruins of the city I loved. My bones will rest forever by my parents, and I will walk with them in our starlit halls.

She saw the queen ahead. She narrowed her eyes. She flew with an empty, cold shard in her chest. She flew to kill and die.

A storm of wyverns rose from the ruins below. Bolts flew. Acid sprayed. Solina's voice rang across the battle.

"She is yours, Mahrdor! Enjoy my gift to you."

Lyana snarled. She saw the lord there. Mahrdor flew upon his four-winged wyvern, leading five more beasts. He clutched a crossbow in one hand; the other hung scarred at his side. Disgust flooded Lyana to remember how she had lain with him in his villa upon the Pallan, letting him invade her among his trophies of flesh. She drove toward him and blew her fire.

Mahrdor banked, and her jet of flame hit a wyvern behind him. Lyana soared. Fire and acid exploded. Crossbow bolts slammed into her; she barely felt them. She shot toward the sky, then swooped with the sun at her back, claws outstretched and fire raining. Another wyvern fell. Lyana howled.

For Requiem. For my parents. For the souls of my ancestors who watch from above. For the glory of our fallen columns and our stars.

Her fire bathed the battle. Her fangs bit through armor. Her claws painted the city with blood. She was Lyana Eleison, a knight of Requiem, a broken woman. She was a girl running through glittering halls to her parents. She was a youth gasping in wonder under blankets at old books of adventure. She was a glowing woman, betrothed to her prince, a lady of the courts. She was a warrior. She was a killer. She was flame and fang, claw and blood. She was Lyana Eleison and she was the wrath and agony of an ancient, fallen kingdom, the shattered notes of a dying song.

The wyverns fell around her, torn and burnt. Only one rider and beast remained before her: Lord Mahrdor.

Around her, the battle for Nova Vita raged in a haze. Some dragons were still fleeing, others still fighting and dying. Wyverns still swarmed around them. But here, in this pocket of silence above the ruins of her temple, it was just her and her enemy, her and the man who had invaded her body, caged her, and destroyed her home. She drove toward him, howling and blowing her flame.

Dragon crashed against wyvern. Fangs bit. Acid and fire roared. They tumbled, clawing and biting, and crashed into the ruins below. A fallen column cracked beneath them, and the wrath of Tiranor shrieked above.

Pain exploded through Lyana. Her back leg blazed; she thought the bone might be broken. Growling, she pushed back, untangling herself from the wyvern that writhed and snapped its teeth. Mahrdor rose from the saddle and drew his sword. Bricks, corpses, and puddles of blood spread around them. The stub of a column rose twenty feet beside her, ending with a crown of jagged marble.

Her head swirled. Lyana flapped her wings once. She struggled to her feet. She summoned fire into her maw.

Mahrdor's crossbow fired.

The bolt slammed into Lyana's neck.

She fell back, gasping for breath. The pain tore her magic from her like claws pulling her heart from her chest. As she shifted, the bolt clanked bloody to the ground. She found herself gasping in human form, on her knees, clutching her neck. She looked up, wincing and dizzy, to see Mahrdor walk toward her. Ash covered his armor, and half his face was gone, burned into a mess of red and black clinging to his skull. Eyes blank, he raised his sabre above her.

Lyana could barely move. The pain twisted through her bones like a horde of demons. With clenched teeth, her gloved hand closed around the hilt of Levitas, her ancient sword. She drew the blade as Mahrdor's sabre drove down. Steel clanged against steel.

The battle still raged above, but its sounds seemed muffled to her, the beasts blurred. Vaguely she heard her brother howl, heard Elethor cry for Requiem, heard Solina scream—but their cries seemed to rise from beyond distant dreamscapes she could not grasp. Her world had become this stage: half a column, bricks, and a cruel desert lord.

His blade flashed down again. Lyana parried. She pushed herself up, parried again, and thrust her blade. Steel clanged.

They moved in a slow, lumbering dance of pain. His flesh sizzled, dripping off his cheekbone. No emotion filled his eyes; they were blue ice, the eyes of a corpse. He swung his blade. Sparks showered.

"I will twist you," he said, lips bloody. His voice was gravely, a sound like bones crushed under boots. "I will shape you into a treasure. You will be the jewel of my collection, and you will *live*." He swung his blade. "I will never let you die. I will never let your pain end."

His sabre slammed against her breastplate, knocking the breath out of her. She swung her sword down and cleaved his pauldron. Blood spilled down his shoulder. He snarled, revealing a mouth full of shattered teeth. Their blades clashed again.

"No, Mahrdor," she whispered; it was as loud as she could speak. She felt blood trickle down her neck into her breastplate. "You will never more hurt anyone. You destroyed us, but you will fall with us. The one you sought for a trophy will be your death."

Her blade flashed. Levitas was an ancient sword, borne by Terra Eleison himself, a knight of Requiem, the hero of the great war against Dies Irae. Today she, his descendant, was the last of the bellators—perhaps soon the last of all dragons.

I still swing your sword, Terra, as you did. I still wear the armor of our order. I still fight for the bellators, even as they have all fallen, and I still swing Levitas for Requiem, even as she lies in ruin. I will soon dine at your side among our celestial columns.

She howled as she swung that old blade. She howled for her ancestors and for her king—a last battle cry. Levitas shone with starlight. The ancient steel drove through Mahrdor's breastplate, into his heart, and crashed through his back. With light and blood and metal, she drove her fury through him. She screamed with the might of her stars.

He gasped. He stared at her, skewered on her blade. They froze, eyes locked.

"I am Lyana Eleison," she whispered, clutching the sword inside him. Her voice trembled. Tears and blood ran down her face; she tasted both on her lips. "I am a knight of Requiem. I am a daughter of starlight. May your lord burn your soul in his fiery halls."

With a scream, she pulled her sword back. The blade retreated from him with gushing blood. He remained standing for but a moment longer, then fell forward. He lay dead at her feet.

Lyana shifted into a dragon. She took flight. She soared above the ruins. Thousands of wyverns howled, flapped wings, and dived toward her.

ELETHOR

Children lay dead upon the fallen palace. The corpses of elders, their white hair stained red, lay broken upon the shattered amphitheater. The body of a mother huddled under an orphaned archway, clutching the charred remains of her babe. As he flew between wyverns, searching for survivors, Elethor saw only death—thousands of corpses, extinguished stars.

"Mori!" he cried. "Mori, where are you?"

He could not see her. Night was falling, a sunset of fire and smoke and cloud. Shadows cloaked the city like a blanket. It began to rain. The drops pattered against the ruins, washing away the blood and acid. Distant thunder rolled and countless wyvern eyes burned red in the darkness.

"Mori!" he shouted. He had not seen her since bursting from underground in a shower of light. Had she fallen upon the city? He dived and flew between shattered columns, seeking his sister. So many dead—he saw corpses everywhere. They lay upon bricks, in puddles of acid, upon fallen walls. Some were mere skeletons, flesh eaten away and ribs cracked like the city's columns. Others were torn apart, limbs scattered. *Is one of those charred remains my sister?* Elethor's eyes burned as he called for her.

The rain fell in silver curtains. Nothing but bodies. Nothing but ruin.

And so it ends, Elethor thought in a haze. *So does Requiem fall, as it fell in the days of King Benedictus.* His eyes stung and smoke streamed between his teeth. *I'm sorry, Requiem. I'm sorry, Lyana. I failed.*

"Fly!" Bayrin cried in the distance. "Go, into the forest, fly!"

Elethor looked up to see his friend. Blood covered Bayrin's scales, but he still flew, herding a group of ragged, lacerated dragons. The survivors—there were a dozen or more—were taking flight from a collapsed house like crows rising from a disturbed tree. Wyverns spotted them, shrieked, and began to chase.

Growling, Elethor flew toward them. His body ached. The bolts of crossbows dug inside him, and burns stung across his scales.

Some still live. Some I can still save.

King's Column rose before him, a pillar of moonlight rising from darkness. It glowed in the rain. So long as it stood, there was hope, Elethor knew. So long as that column rose, he would fly. He would fight. He would seek the sky beyond wyvern and cloud.

He flew around that column, heading toward Bayrin and the others, when a great wyvern rose before him from the ruins. Its wings unfurled, black shrouds for the death of a god. Its eyes blazed, two red torches. It blocked the sky, a demon of darkness and iron. Atop its back rode a deity of gold, her banner streaming, her sword raised. The Queen of Tiranor cried out to him in the night.

"Elethor! Elethor!"

He reared before her, wings wide and fangs bared. "I'm here, Solina."

She raised her sabre high. Lightning flashed and slammed into the blade. Solina laughed—an echoing laughter that rang across the city like funeral bells.

"Hello, my love! Hello, my king!" Wyverns rose around her, black ghosts in the night. Solina pointed her blade at Elethor and called to them. "Grab the Reptile King! Bring him to me in chains."

The wyverns surged.

Elethor soared.

He rose through rain and cloud. Lightning crashed around him. Thunder blasted him and he howled in the darkness. Wyverns shrieked below him, and pillars of acid rose around him, a temple of corrosion. The clouds covered them. Elethor could see no more than several feet in any direction. He kept flying higher through the storm. The wind howled and shards of lightning exploded. One lightning bolt hit a wyvern; the beast screamed and fell.

"Catch the reptile!" Solina's voice stormed somewhere below him. "Chain the—"

Thunder boomed over her words. Elethor leveled off and dived through the clouds. He tried to fly north, to head into distant forests where he could hide between smoldering trees. He could only guess the direction. He saw nothing but clouds, heard nothing but thunder, rain, and shrieks. Acid sprayed to his left, nearly searing him. He banked right and flew higher.

He had to find Mori. He had to find Lyana and Bayrin. Were they still alive? Was anyone still alive? He ached to cry to them, to roar their names, but dared not; wyverns flew everywhere in the clouds. One appeared before him, emerging from darkness ten feet away. Elethor dared not even blow flames lest the other wyverns see; he drove forward and lashed his claws, tearing the rider apart. The wyvern fell. The rider's limbs tumbled.

Pain drove through Elethor. His eyes stung. Smoke blew around him, searing hot. He wanted to still his wings, to fall upon his realm, to lie forever as charred bones.

I failed my kingdom. I failed Lyana. I'm sorry, Father. I'm sorry, Orin.

He looked at the sky, seeking the halls of his fathers, but saw only cloud and rain. He rose higher. His wings blazed and wind howled around him. Ice began to spread across his scales, and the thin air spun his head, and yet still he soared. *Requiem. May our wings forever find your sky.* The clouds broke, and he emerged from the storm. Below him, the clouds and rain and lightning swirled, an orchestra of water and fire. Above him spread the night, ablaze with countless stars. The Draco constellation shone, glittering so brightly it nearly blinded him. He flew, caught between storm and star.

"I fly to you, Father," he whispered. All sounds faded; he could barely hear the storm beneath him. He looked up at the stars. "I fly to you, Queen Gloriae. I soon will dine in your hall, King Aeternum."

Will Mori await me there? Will Lyana forever sit by my side as the celestial columns rise around us? Will the great kings of old scorn me for my failure, for our ancient realm that fell under my reign?

A voice spoke behind him, clear in the night, as if answering his thoughts.

"You did not fail, Elethor."

He turned to see Solina upon her wyvern. The beast flapped its wings languidly, hovering before him. The golden queen regarded him, a visor hiding her face.

Elethor wanted to rage. He wanted to howl. He wanted to blow fire, to fight, to kill Solina and then crash dead with her to the ruins below. Yet no rage found him now, only grief that dampened his eyes, churned his gut, and swelled in his throat.

"I let Requiem fall," he said. He hovered before her. The night seemed so silent; only dim rumbles of thunder rolled below. No more wind blew. He hovered before his old love in soft darkness and starlight.

She shook her head. "No, Elethor. You could not have stopped me. Your father and brother could not stop me either; they fell before my flame. You fought me for many days, Elethor, and you led your people with honor. They are not ashamed of you, Elethor. You fought nobly and you are stronger than you know. Your father and brother were worshipped as warriors; they saw you as a sculptor, a stargazer, a lesser prince. But I knew who you are, El. I always knew. You showed your strength to me and to your people."

She lifted her visor. Her eyes were solemn. He remembered those eyes. With stabs of agony, he remembered marveling at their beauty, staring for hours into their depths. This was the woman he would kiss, the woman whose naked body he held under blankets, whose hair he would stroke—the woman who had claimed his soul and even now, even here, held it in her hands.

"My people are dead," he said. "Solina, what strength can I show them now?"

She pointed above to the Draco constellation. It seemed impossibly distant, impossibly large, great suns of distant fire.

"They watch over you, Elethor. The souls of your people whisper there; so do the souls of your father and brother. I sent them there, but I need not send you." She reached out to him. "It's not too late, Elethor. I love you. I've always loved you. Requiem is gone; I crushed it so we might be together again. Return with me to your home. Return with me to the desert; we were always meant to rule there together." Tears sparkled in her eyes like more stars. "Elethor... I hate you. I vowed to destroy you. But now I look upon you and I love you." She reached toward him. "You and I were always meant to fly here, to hurt each other, to love in pain. Blood and fire have always been ours; we have beaten blood and fire before, and I returned to you. It's time to go home."

Soft light glowed around her, and she seemed to Elethor not the Queen of Tiranor, not the tyrant and slayer of his people, but the Solina who would hold him in caves and forests, whisper of secret magical kingdoms, and cry onto his shoulder, then laugh and kiss him.

"I never wanted anything but this," Elethor said softly. "A quiet place. The light of stars. You and I. For years that's all I dreamed of."

Her wyvern's wings rose and fell like a silent midnight sea. Solina reached out toward him from the saddle. "That is what you have! That is what I brought us. Let your magic go, Elethor. Turn into the man I love, ride with me in my saddle, and we will live like this forever. No more fire or blood—just you and me."

He laughed weakly. Smoke rose from his nostrils. "That is not what you said last year when you drove your dagger down my face. You spoke of torture then. You spoke of making me beg for death." He sighed. "Solina, the days when we could have been like this, here in solitude, are gone. Too much blood has spilled. Too many stones have shattered. Too many lights have gone out."

She shook her head. "There is only this, Elethor. Don't you understand? There is no more Requiem for you to return to." Her wyvern lowered its head, its dark body nearly disappearing into shadow. Solina seemed to float before him, a golden queen in the night. "All has fallen. All has been laid to waste. The land where we grew up is gone, Elethor, swept away in this rain like the last snows of winter. Let spring rise from its ashes. With me, Elethor. With me."

He looked below him. The storm swirled silently, a sea of gray and red and blue, flaring every moment with the faded glow of lightning. Requiem had fallen; there was no more home beneath those clouds. All was gone: the temple where he would pray with his people, their song rising between the columns to the stars; the house where he would sculpt and whisper Solina's name in the night; the gardens and hills where he would laugh with Bayrin; the palace where he had grown up with Orin and Mori.

Gone. All is gone.

He looked back up at Solina. "Where is Mori? Where is my sister?"

Something crossed Solina's eyes, the flicker of deep fire. Her voice hardened. "I spared her life. I did not kill her. She lives, Elethor. She lives. She will be allowed to live in our realm."

Yet there was no warmth to her voice; the shadow of her rage now filled it. He looked into her eyes and saw the madness there. The old Solina still lurked inside her, crying out to him—the Solina he had loved for years, the Solina whom he still loved, even now. But that fire burned now across her soul, the fire that had burned her body and twisted her mind, that perhaps had always simmered deep within her. He could not rid her of it, he knew. He could not undo her deeds, could not cleanse her of her crimes.

A peace settled upon him then, and the starlight warmed him. He knew, perhaps for the first time, that she was gone from him; like never before, he knew that Solina—*his* Solina, the one he had loved—had fallen too, as ruined as the city below them.

"I will not join you in your desert court," he said. "You may fight me; you may try to chain me. I will die fighting you above the earth of my home, in the light of my stars." He smiled softly. "It will be a good death."

Solina stared at him a moment longer, silent. Tears flowed down her cheeks.

"Goodbye, Elethor," she whispered.

Lightning flared and thunder boomed.

Solina screamed.

She drove her wyvern toward him.

Elethor spread his wings and bathed her with fire.

She screamed. The fire flowed across her. He shot forward and his claws lashed. She swung her sword; the steel sliced his claw. He tried to bite her, to crush her between his teeth. Her wyvern swooped. Elethor followed, lashed his tail, and tossed Solina from her saddle.

She tumbled.

Her hair burned.

"Elethor!" she screamed, falling into darkness. "I carried your child, Elethor!"

She laughed and wept, hair blazing, arms reaching out toward him. Elethor inhaled sharply and dived after her, eyes narrowed.

"Solina!"

She laughed as she fell through cloud and rain, hair alight.

"I carried your child when Orin burned me!" she shouted, tears streaming. "I lost the babe in his fire. The kingdom you fight for, the family you love—they murdered your child!"

He reached out his claws.

He tried to grab her.

Stars of Requiem, stars, no. Please, stars, no.

He screamed, diving as fast as he could. He stretched out his claws. He grazed her fingertips. Screaming and laughing, her hair crackling like a torch, she vanished into cloud and rain

"Solina!" he howled and roared fire.

Stars, our child... stars, no.

He roared for her, voice torn, like he had called for her eight years ago from the walls of his city.

"Solina!"

He dived through the storm. Rain pounded his face. A lightning bolt slammed down by him. Wyverns rose from darkness and crashed into him. He tumbled. Scales flashed.

"Solina!"

My child.

"Elethor!"

The voice rose below, muffled and distant. A bolt of lightning slammed against a wyvern's rider and exploded. Fire burst. The beasts screeched. Elethor drove upward and through them.

The distant voice cried again. "Mori! Mori, where are you? Elethor!"

Lyana!

Elethor howled. He flamed two wyverns, clawed a third, and drove through the storm. Wind pushed against him, and rain lashed him, but he kept flying. He wanted to seek Solina, to dive through the clouds, to slay her if she still lived—but Lyana needed him.

"Lyana!" he shouted into the storm.

Lyana—his betrothed. Lyana—of steel and fire. Lyana—of red hair that would never fall the way she wanted; of green eyes that would mock him one moment and love him the next; of wisdom and strength, of softness and joy. A knight. A betrothed. A woman who had walked with him to the Abyss and back. She cried to him now. *Let me seek her now. Let Solina go.*

"Lyana!" he cried again. The wyverns streamed around him. "Lyana!"

Her voice called from the distance. "Elethor! Stars, Elethor, where are you?"

He dived lower. When he emerged from the clouds into rain and smoke, he cried out to her, and she answered his call, and he flew over ruin, over fallen walls, over charred forests. He saw blue scales ahead and he drove toward her, eyes stinging.

She flew and all but crashed against him. A green dragon emerged from shadows by them, the rain washing blood from his body: Bayrin.

Wyverns swarmed upon them. The three dragons blew fire, holding them back. A stream of acid fell, and they scattered, blew more flames at the beasts, and regrouped.

"Lyana, where's Mori?" Elethor demanded. Spears rained, and one lashed across his shoulder.

"We thought she was with you!" she said.

With a chill, Solina's words returned to him. *She lives, Elethor. She lives.*

More wyverns emerged from the clouds. Elethor cursed. He flapped his wings and soared back into the cloud cover. Bayrin and Lyana flew by his side, blowing fire at the wyverns.

"Bayrin, fly north!" Elethor shouted. "Lyana, fly east! I go south. We must find Mori."

A wyvern shot between them, showering acid. They scattered and Bayrin slew the beast with claw and fang.

When it fell, the green dragon cried, "And what then, El? The whole bloody kingdom is burning!"

Acid rained. They rose higher in the clouds. Lightning flashed and thunder boomed.

Stars, she was carrying my child...

"When the sun sets again, fly to Sequestra Mountains!" he shouted. "If you find Mori, bring her there. Now go! Find her, Bayrin!"

The green dragon cursed. His wings were charred and his scales bloody, but still he blasted fire. He turned and began flying north, calling her name.

Lyana remained at Elethor's side. Acid had spilled down her left flank, withering the scales. She stared at Elethor, her eyes haunted. She hovered before him.

"Oh, El," she said softly.

He growled. A lightning bolt crashed, illuminating a sky full of wyverns; thousands still flew.

"Go, Lyana!" he shouted. "Fly east! Fly now!"

She looked ready to weep. Her eyes watered. A howl left her throat. Her fire blazed. She spun around, roaring Requiem's call, and flew into the east. Soon she vanished into the clouds, wyverns in pursuit.

Stars, Mori, where are you?

He roared her name. He flew south. The fury of Tiranor flowed around him, and the bodies of his people littered the farmlands below.

TREALE

"Please let them fly away," she whispered, shivering on the ground. "Please, stars. *Please.*"

The charred trees rose above her, their leaves burnt white, their branches like fingers groping at the sky. The rain pattered down, swaying in the wind. Beneath the clouds flew the wyverns, grunting and screaming like rutting beasts.

"Don't let them see me, stars," Treale whispered.

She huddled in the mud between the trees. Ash and rain covered her hair. A glob of acid sprayed down ahead and began eating through a tree. Burns spread across her thigh and she grimaced; she had not imagined any wound could hurt so much. Her lungs still ached with smoke, and she wanted nothing more than to cough, but forced herself to hold her breath. She pushed herself down into the mud under the trees.

The wyverns flew in formation above; there were eight. When Treale peered between the branches, she could see that their riders bore banners sporting a golden sun on a white field—Solina's personal guard. The lead wyvern carried a bundle in its claws, and Treale glimpsed flashes of muddy blue.

She gasped.

Despite the ache in her wound, and the fear in her breast, she pushed herself up against the bole. She peered between the charred branches and leaves.

"Stars," she whispered.

The beasts overshot her, but Treale had seen enough. The wyvern held a woman in its claws, her blue dress tattered and bloody, her limbs chained.

Blue fabric was rare in Requiem; it came all the way from the southern sea, where divers collected the mollusks which leaked the indigo dye. Even House Oldnale, the wealthiest family in Requiem after the royal Aeternums and noble Eleisons, owned no blue fabrics. That was the color of royalty. That was a gown of a princess.

"Mori," Treale whispered.

The wyverns vanished overhead, flying... Treale did not know which way. How could anyone tell north or south with these clouds and this rain? Gritting her teeth against the blazing pain, she clutched the tree and began to climb. Soot covered her hands. The tree was wet but still hot from the fire. She grimaced. Her wounds burned like ten thousand suns, shooting pain through her limbs, into her fingertips, even into her teeth. She groaned and kept climbing. When she reached the treetop, she straightened. So much mud and soot covered her, she imagined that she looked like yet another branch. Squinting, she stared after the retreating wyverns. The blue gown flapped in the leader's claws, and Treale thought she could hear a muffled cry—the cry of a young woman. The rain kept falling, and even the shrieks of the wyverns sounded dim.

It's her. It's Mori.

Treale trembled and nearly fell from the tree. She clutched its branches so tightly her fingers bled. Mori had been her dearest friend since childhood; the two had been born mere days apart. Treale had grown up yearning for every harvest, when she could travel to Nova Vita and spend several joyous days with Mori—reading books in the library, teasing the princes with giggles and secret words only she and Mori understood, and going to the warrens behind Castra Murus to feed the rabbits. Every winter, when the Aeternums visited Oldnale Manor for the Feast of Stars, Treale would let Mori sleep by her side in her great canopy bed; the two would stay up nearly all night, whispering of the knights they would marry someday, what new pups they would adopt, and all the other secrets of youth.

Lyana would often spend time with them too, but Lyana was two years older and so much wiser, so much stronger; the knight had always seemed closer to the adults, more like Prince Orin. *But Mori and I were always as sisters—two young girls of great families with great older brothers.*

Now none of that remained. No more canopy bed or farms or... maybe not even any more Vir Requis.

"But you live, Mori," Treale whispered, eyes damp.

Shame burned inside her, as cold as her wounds were hot. She had defected from King Elethor's army. She had fled from Nova Vita at the sight of its ruin. Tears burned in Treale's eyes. *I am a coward. I wanted to be like Lady Lyana, a brave knight, but I fled from battle.*

She growled low in her throat. She narrowed her eyes and watched the wyverns flee.

"I abandoned my king, my lady, and my kingdom," she whispered, a lump in her throat. "But I won't abandon you, Mori."

The wyverns were soon distant specks in the storm, and she could no longer hear their calls. Treale knew what fate awaited Mori if she could not save her: the princess would be imprisoned and tortured, and when her body was broken, she would be burned in the city of Irys among the dunes.

I won't let that happen.

In the treetop, Treale shifted and tested her wings. She rose into the storm, a black dragon with dented, charred scales. The wind and rain lashed her, and she could barely flap her wings, but she growled, she snorted fire, and she flew.

"I will find you, Mori." Smoke streamed between her teeth. "I will follow you to the desert itself if I must."

They had no home to return to. Requiem lay in ruins, her halls fallen like so many old stones. But so long as Mori lived, there was hope. Treale sniffed and realized that tears filled her eyes.

We will flee into the wilderness, Mori, you and I. We'll find a cave to live in, or a green forest that no fire has touched, and we'll whisper and laugh together again. If everyone else is fallen, we will still have each other.

The wyverns flew ahead, flecks on the horizon. Fire flickering in her mouth, her wings roiling the clouds, Treale Oldnale followed through the ash, rain, and ruin of the world.

SOLINA

She stood at a towering window in her chambers, its archway large enough for a wyvern to fly through. A wind from the desert blew, billowing her white silks and platinum hair. Her golden jewels chinked, and the coppery taste of sand flickered across her lips. She gripped the hilts of her twin sabres and gazed upon her home.

Cranes and ibises flew above her oasis, singing to the sun. Date and fig trees rustled. Men labored across the city of Irys, sweat glistening on their golden skin: tending to vineyards, hammering swords on anvils, and raising statues and columns for her glory. Ships sailed up the River Pallan, overflowing with spices and gems from Iysa, Jewel of the South and a twin to Irys. From the north, wyverns were flying over the delta and landing in Hog Corner. Upon their backs, they bore the trophies of Requiem: longswords of filigreed steel, statues of marble from Requiem's temples, sacks of golden coins, and chests full of books and scrolls and artifacts.

"All your glory is mine, Elethor," Solina whispered into the desert. "All that you had is gone from you."

She winced in sudden pain. It had been a moon's turn since she had fallen over Nova Vita, since her wyverns had caught her tumbling and burning. Her chest still hurt sometimes, though her healers insisted her cracked ribs had healed. Her hair had burned; she had shaved it off that day, and it was still short under the wig she wore.

"And soon I will bring you here too."

Ten thousand wyverns still flew over Requiem, burning what forests remained, slaughtering whatever dragon they found cowering in the wastelands.

"All but you, Elethor," she whispered. "They will not slaughter you, no." She drew Raem, her blade of dawn, and held it aloft. "They will bring you here alive, and it will be this blade that you scream for, this blade that I will hold above you, as you weep and beg me to stab your heart." She snarled. "But I will not, Elethor; I will not show you any more mercy. You turned down my mercy. Now you will *live*."

She shut her eyes and winced.

I spoke to him of my secret. I spoke of our child.

She clenched her jaw so hard she felt her teeth could crack.

No. No. That will remain buried. She clutched her swords so tightly, her fists trembled. *I will never remember that pain again.*

She turned from her window. Trophies of her conquests filled her chamber. The sword of Lord Deramon, its blade engraved with the Draco constellation, hung upon her wall. The brooch of Mother Adia, a silver birch leaf, shone upon a plaque carved from the Weredragon Temple's marble. Below these spoils stood the Oak Throne of Requiem, the soot sanded off the twisting roots that formed it. Around the throne, covering the tiles of her floor, lay jugs of weredragon gold and jewels, helms of fallen knights, and blades of northern steel.

"I will sit upon this throne as I watch you scream," Solina whispered. "I will place my feet upon the helms of your warriors, and I will laugh as my vultures feed upon you."

Still clutching her swords, she left her chamber. Her sandals thumped against the stairs leading down her tower. She walked across corridors with tiles so polished her reflection walked beneath her, clad in white silks and gold. She crossed her grand hall where a hundred guards stood armored in platinum, their visors shaped like the heads of falcons, and her throne rose glittering, a monolith of ivory and jewels. She descended dark stairs into the underground, where the air was cold and damp even as the sun pounded the desert above. She walked down tunnels, sloping ever deeper, until all scent and sound and memory of the world faded into darkness.

She grabbed a torch that burned upon a craggy wall. Dust carpeted the floor. Cobwebs, old blood, and chained skeletons covered the walls. Still she walked, going deeper, until the tunnel narrowed to a mere burrow, and the air was so cold even the Sun God could not warm it.

She approached the chamber that lay ahead. Her torchlight flickered. She stepped through the doorway and snarled a grin.

The creature hung there from the ceiling, wrists chained. The pathetic, beaten thing did not even look up. Blood trickled from its wrists, and cobwebs filled its dangling hair. It was a wretched being, emaciated, its skin lashed and raw. When Solina approached and the torchlight blazed against the beast, it gave a low mewl and swung on its chains; it was too weak to do anything else.

Solina caressed the creature's cheek. It shivered under her palm. She stroked its hair and kissed its forehead.

"Hush now," Solina whispered. "Soon he will be with you, my sweet Mori. Soon your brother will be with you again."

ELETHOR

He stood inside the cave and stared out upon the forest. The trees rolled into misty horizons, their leaves golden and red. A cold wind blew, ruffling his hair, and ravens circled under the veil of clouds. A drizzle fell, deepening the colors of the world until all became a smudged painting of brown, orange, and silver. Elethor held Ferus's hilt. He could barely see Requiem from here, only a distant haze of smoke. The burnt lands of his fathers lay beyond the leagues, ravaged and swarming with wyverns.

Elethor lowered his gaze to the camp below the mountain. Men and women moved between the trees, clad in leaf and fur and mud. A few men were skinning a deer, and two children ran around a tree, banging wooden swords they had carved. A mother nursed her babe, and an old man sat upon a boulder, reading from a scroll of prayers. Four Vir Requis stood in dragon forms, guarding each corner of the camp; mud covered their scales to dull their shimmer.

Ninety-seven souls, Elethor thought. *Fewer than a hundred survivors from a realm of fifty thousand.*

As he stood in the cave upon the mountainside, looking down at this ragged camp, he thought of Mori.

"Do you too hide in some distant camp beyond our borders?" he whispered. "Do you have someone with you, someone to protect you?"

He looked over the forest, as if she could emerge any moment from the distance, a golden dragon—haggard but smiling, *alive.* Every day he waited here in this cave, watching the horizon for wyverns, watching for Mori. They had lived here for two moons now, and still she did not arrive.

Elethor lowered his head. *Maybe you lie among the ruins of Nova Vita, resting by the bones of Orin and Father. Maybe you now sing with them in the starlit halls. I love you, sister. I miss you.*

A blue glimmer flew upon the horizon. Elethor stood watching, the wind in his hair, until the sapphire dragon emerged from the distant mist and flew toward the cave. Lyana landed on the mountainside and looked up at him. Smoke rose in curtains from between her teeth.

"Lyana," he said. He approached as she shifted into human form. She stood before him with somber eyes, still clad in the silvery armor of the bellators.

"I'm sorry, Elethor," she whispered. She removed her helm, embraced him, and laid her head upon his shoulder. "I'm so sorry, my king. I searched Fidelium in the north, and the plains of Sequestra, and sought her among the cities of Osanna. None have seen the princess."

He held her. Her hair had grown an inch, and the fiery curls brushed against his face. He cupped her cheek and kissed her forehead. Her eyes were deep green pools.

"Maybe Bayrin found her," he said softly, but heard no hope in his voice and saw none in Lyana's eyes.

They stood upon the mountainside, watching the forest until emerald scales shimmered in the north, and Bayrin flew toward them. The green dragon landed outside the cave, panting and cursing. He spat a flicker of fire.

"Bloody stars!" Bayrin said. "The north is swarming with those wyvern bastards." He raised his tail; an ugly welt rose across it. "One gave me this before I roasted him." He whipped his head from side to side, then lowered his eyes. "I... I was hoping Lyana had found her. Oh, stars."

He shifted into human form. Red rimmed his eyes and ash filled his hair. His gangly frame was thinner than ever, stubble was thickening into a beard across his face, and soot covered his breastplate and scabbard. He looked down, tightened his jaw, and clenched his fists. Elethor saw a tear on his chin.

He approached his friend and held his shoulder. "We'll find her, Bay. We won't rest until we do. For as long as it takes, I will send out dragons to every corner of the world, and we will find her."

Yet in the cold pit of his stomach, Elethor knew there was only one more place they could search, one more hope to save her... to save everyone who still lived here among the trees.

He turned to look south. The forests rolled for countless leagues, finally fading into a yellow haze and blue mountains against a silver sky. Standing to his right, Lyana clasped his hand and held it tight. At his left side, Bayrin placed a hand on his shoulder and stared with him, solemn and silent. The wind blew their hair, cold and wet with rain, but Elethor thought he could scent the distant sands.

"What do we do now?" Bayrin said. "Do we stay here, hidden in the wilderness, and continue our search from this camp? Do we fly to Salvandos and seek sanctuary among the true dragons of the golden mountain? Do we fly east to Osanna and live among the men of the white halls?"

Elethor shook his head, watching the forest rustle and the rain sway in sheets.

"No, Bayrin," he said softly. "We will not flee. Not yet." He turned to look at his friend. "We collect what dragons we can still find among the ruins of Requiem. We fly to Tiranor. We rain fire upon them. If Mori is captive there, we will save her."

Bayrin nodded, lips tight. Elethor turned to look at Lyana; she stared back with green eyes that spoke of her loyalty, her love, and her fire that would forever light his darkness.

He squeezed her hand and whispered. "And we kill Solina."

They stood upon the mountain, holding one another, and gazed upon the southern horizon of forest, mist, mountain... and beyond them the cruel, endless desert.

BOOK THREE:
A NIGHT OF DRAGON WINGS

ZAR

The ropes chafed his wrists, and the blindfold squeezed his head like a vise, but Zar kept walking. He must have been walking for hours. A spearhead goaded his back, and he stumbled forward, breath rattling in his lungs. They had stabbed his back so many times, he imagined that it looked raw and red like minced meat. He could smell his own blood.

"Move it, scum!" said the guard behind him. Again the spearhead goaded him, a thrust too weak to puncture his flesh, but strong enough to shoot pain through him. "We haven't got all day!"

So it's still daytime, Zar thought. He would have thought night had fallen hours ago. The gravelly road stabbed his bare feet. His calves, his back, his head—they all throbbed. The wind blew hot and sandy against him. His throat was parched, his lips cracked; he wondered if thirst would kill him before the guards could.

Around him, he heard a hundred boots thumping, armor clanking, and scabbards clattering against greaves. A grunting sounded to his side, then a whip lashing flesh and a croak. Zar wanted to call out to his friends; even just speaking their names would comfort him.

They're taking us to die, he thought. *They will whip and stab and march us until we perish, and our bones will lie in the wilderness for crows to pick on.*

"Move, damn it!" cried the guard behind him, voice as gravelly as the road. "Faster!"

A whip cracked and pain exploded across Zar's back. He bit down on a scream. If he screamed, they would hurt him further. He had learned that lesson in the bowels of Solina's palace. *Never scream. Never make a sound. If you show pain, they will laugh, and they will crave more.*

He tried to remove his thoughts from this march, this thirst, this pain. He thought of his wife, a demure desert daughter, her hair so pale it was almost white, her skin deep gold, and her eyes blue like sky over dunes. He thought of his son, a suckling babe who would never know his father. He had done it for them. *All my crimes—for you.*

He had left his phalanx only for his family, only to be with them. He had abandoned his barracks to squeeze his wife's hand, to soothe her, to help the midwife guide his son into the desert. He had left for but a day, that was all—a dawn, an evening, a night of stars.

That was all. The barracks guards had caught him holding his son, wrenched the babe from his arms, and dragged him back in chains.

But I saw my son. I saw him. I will die with a memory of his eyes.

He thought of those eyes as they walked the road, moving higher and higher, climbing a mountain that seemed to never end. As his feet bled and his back blazed, he thought of his son's eyes and his wife's smile, and Zar knew that no matter how much they hurt him, he had a pure memory. This memory they could not take away, not with all the blades and whips in the desert.

The wind lashed him. They marched. They marched endlessly.

Finally, after what seemed the ages of empires and the lifespan of mountains, he heard the guards inhale sharply.

"The tower," one man whispered.

Cold sweat washed Zar.

There was only one tower—*the* tower—which men spoke of with such reverence, such fear. The Ancients had called it *Tarath Gehena*—Tower of the Abyss—but few dared speak that tongue now. In his childhood, his grandmother would whisper that demons punished errant children in this tower. His friends would point at steeples in the city of Irys, trying to convince one another that here stood Tarath Gehena itself, the place of whispers and screams.

The tower. The place of the key. Sun God, the queen seeks to open the Iron Door.

Zar's knees shook and his breath rose to a pant. In the dungeon, he had prayed for death, comforted himself with the thought of thirst or injury sending him to eternal rest. In the shadow of Tarath Gehena, no such comfort could find him. No pure memory or hope could soothe him here.

Here there were only screams, terror, and undying agony.

They kept walking, quiet now. Zar could barely hear the clank of armor, the thud of boots, or the moans of his fellow prisoners. Until now every step had seemed an eternity; now Zar wished time would slow down. Too soon, far too soon, they stopped. Rough hands ripped the blindfold off his eyes.

Sun God save us, Zar thought, blinked in the sunset, and trembled.

They stood upon a mountain that rose from the desert: three haggard prisoners, bloodied and clad in rags; fifty soldiers in pale armor, golden suns upon their breastplates and their helms shaped as falcon heads; and a desert queen all in gold and platinum, twin sabres drawn in her hands. These soldiers of steel had tortured him, and this desert queen had ordered him broken, yet as night fell around them,

Zar did not fear them. They were mere mortals. Before him it rose, a skeletal finger reaching into a crimson sky. The tower.

Zar had never before seen this place, not with his waking eyes. But he had dreamed of it countless times, then woke up in a cold sweat. He had seen it in his mind—when his grandmother whispered of its secrets, when his childhood friends bragged that they would climb it, and when Queen Solina's guards whipped him until the pain exploded into dreamscapes.

"The tower," he whispered, lips chapped and bleeding. "The place of the key."

Tarath Gehena rose knobby, black, and twisting like a melted candle of stone. The sun set behind it, spilling rivers of blood across the sky, the mountain, and the desert below. The tower's jagged crenellations rose like the crown of a demon king. At its base loomed a doorway, gaping and black like a cave. As the crimson clouds moved, the tower seemed to tilt. A shadow stirred between the battlements, and Zar's heart thrashed. He expected to see demons swarm toward him, but then the shadow vanished, leaving his heart racing and his clothes drenched with sweat.

Tarath Gehena, he thought. *A shattered bone of the Abyss risen into the world.*

Queen Solina walked forward, shoving her guards aside. Her eyes gleamed and a smile twitched across her lips, those lips twisted with an old scar. Despite the long march, she seemed unwearied, and little sand or dust clung to her breastplate and silken cloak. Her hair billowed, a pale banner.

"This is the place," she whispered, eyes alight and teeth bared in a grin. "This tower holds the key."

The sunset blazed against her, painting her blood-red, and madness shone in her eyes.

"You cannot open the door!" The words fled Zar's mouth, hoarse and shaking. "You will unleash something you cannot contai—"

A whip lashed his back, and a soldier kicked him, driving a steel-tipped boot into his side. Zar fell to his knees, gasping for breath. Tears budded in his eyes.

"Please," he whispered, trembling, remembering the stories his grandmother would tell: stories of demons peeling the skin off children, of reptiles writhing, of a horde of chaos with tarry wings and fangs to suck the souls of men. "Please, my queen, do not enter this tower. Do not take the key from within."

The soldiers raised whips and spears above him, and Zar winced, expecting the blows, but Solina held up her hand. The soldiers froze, weapons raised.

The Queen of Tiranor walked toward Zar, head tilted and lips still smiling, though no mirth filled her eyes, only cruelty like a scourge. She stood above him, a golden queen and him a wretched, bleeding shell of a man, wrists bound and body emaciated and broken. She spoke, voice soft and smooth like a morning breeze stirring the desert sands.

"You fear the tomb the key can unlock." She reached down and touched his forehead. Her hand was gloved in white moleskin, soft and warm. "You fear the creatures that dwell beyond the Iron Door."

Zar shivered on the ground. He feared this tower, this jagged sentinel; his stomach clenched and his skull seemed ready to crack. Yet this tower, for all its evil, merely contained a key.

But the door this key unlocks... The fortress it will allow her to enter...

He found himself weeping. "Please, my queen, please. Listen to the priests of the Sun God. Listen to the whispers of desert tribes, to the tales of grandmothers, to the horrors in old scrolls. Do not take this key."

Her face softened, the face of a woman seeing a wretched, kicked animal. She caressed his forehead, dirtying her gloves with his sweat and grime.

"Oh, dear miserable beast," she whispered. "*I* will not take the key from this tower. You and your friends will."

Sun God. Oh, Sun God, please no.

He flattened himself on the ground and kissed the dust at her feet. His body shook.

"Please, my queen, forgive me, I only... I only wanted to see my son, to—"

She spat on him. "Stand this wretch up," she said to her soldiers. Disgust now suffused her voice. "Let him enter last. I want him to watch his friends suffer first."

Guards grabbed Zar and yanked him to his feet. He writhed and kicked, heart thrashing, but could not free himself. After moons in Solina's dungeon, he was too weak, his arms thinned to the bone, his head always spinning, his heart always like a wild hare caught in his ribcage. To his right, he saw his fellow prisoners, two more souls who had languished in the queen's dungeons. They too were struggling in the grip of soldiers. They too were pale and emaciated, mere shells of humanity, their hair wispy and their eyes bulging.

"Send the first one in!" Solina shouted, voice echoing across the mountain. Zar thought that even the desert below, for leagues around, could hear her voice, the cry of a gilded goddess.

The soldiers dragged forward a prisoner—a cadaverous, bare-chested man named Rael, his back lashed and his left eye swollen shut. The man struggled, whimpered, and begged, but he could not free himself from the soldiers' grips. These were Queen Solina's personal guards, towering men—they stood near seven feet tall—bedecked in steel and platinum, automatons of metal, their faces hidden behind visors shaped as falcon beaks. Sometimes Zar wondered if any flesh lived beneath that metal, or if inside their armor they were nothing but godly flame.

"Please, my queen," Rael pleaded. As the soldiers dragged him toward the tower, he looked back, and his good eye met Zar's gaze.

Zar froze, his breath dying in his chest. He saw such horror, such grief in the man's one eye—a soul crumbling.

"Rael," he whispered.

"If you make it back, Zar, tell my wife I'm sorry," the haggard prisoner said. Blood flecked his lips. "Tell her I love her and I'm sorry."

Zar nodded, throat constricting. Rael had stabbed the man raping his wife; he had been caught, knife bloody in his hands.

"I'll look after her, Rael," he said, knowing that he was lying, knowing that he would never make it back home. "I promise. I—"

With a grunt, a soldier kicked Zar's back, sending him facedown into the dirt. His cheek hit a rock; he felt it pierce his skin. He coughed and spat blood, raised his head, and saw the soldiers shove Rael into the dark doorway of the tower.

"Find me the key and you will have freedom!" Solina shouted into the darkness, voice echoing. A grin played across her lips, twisting her scar, the old burn the weredragons had given her. "Find the key and the jewels of Tiranor will be yours!"

Zar lay on the ground, staring at the twisting pillar of stone. The red clouds swirled above it like pools of gods' blood. Was it possible? Could one of them—even Zar himself—find the key and receive freedom?

He clenched his jaw and winced when his shattered teeth touched.

"No," he whispered. "There will be no freedom if she unlocks the door this key can open. There will be no place to hide in the world."

He watched the tower.

Silence fell.

Solina stood before Tarath Gehena, hands opened at her sides, fingers twitching over the hilts of her sabres. Her soldiers stood like statues; not a piece of armor clinked. Zar pushed himself to his feet and watched. At his side, the second prisoner—a gaunt dusteater caught licking the forbidden spice in Irys's dregs—stood watching with sallow eyes; those eyes seemed dead, and her skin was already pale like a corpse. Even the wind stilled; the land itself seemed to be watching the tower with bated breath.

A deep, gravelly sound rose from the tower.

Again sweat drenched Zar.

Sun God, oh Sun God, save us.

His body trembled with new vigor. At first he thought that sound the creaking of stones, but then he realized: it was laughter—an inhuman, impossibly deep, demonic laughter.

A shrill scream pierced the air, cascaded down the mountainsides, and echoed across the desert.

"We must flee," Zar whispered. He turned to run, but soldiers grabbed him. Gloved fingers dug into his arms.

The deep laughter rolled, a sound of ancient evil, of pure malice, a sound like a parasite feasting as it bore through its host toward the heart. Wincing, Zar turned his head away from the tower; he could no longer look.

His gaze fell upon Queen Solina. He expected to see his queen shaken or remorseful, to see her skin pale and her eyes fearful, to hear her order them away from Tarath Gehena and back to their city. What he saw in his queen's eyes, however, terrified Zar as much as the laughter that rose from the tower.

Solina's eyes were wide, her grin toothy. Her chest rose and fell with excited breath. She seemed like a woman in ecstasy.

The deep laughter rose to a shriek, a sound so loud that Zar wept and even the soldiers cursed. Zar whipped his head back toward the tower and saw it shaking. The screams rose from it: the screams of demons and the anguished scream of a man.

Blood seeped from the doorway, so thick and dark it seemed almost black.

The human scream died, and the laughter of demons rolled across the mountain.

"Rael," Zar whispered. "I'm sorry, my friend."

A shadow stirred on the tower's top, moving between the crenellations. Zar froze and stared, heart hammering. He wanted to look away. He wanted to close his eyes. He wanted to do anything but stare at that shadow. And yet the darkness that stirred there held his gaze, as powerful as the soldiers who held his body. It seemed a human figure, Zar thought—a man cloaked in black, a hood hiding his face. The cloaked sentinel moved atop the tower, a thing of darkness; Zar saw no head within the shadows of that hood. The figure raised its hand. Zar's throat tightened and he winced; the hand was long and deathly gray, the fingers tapering into crimson claws.

A thing of darkness, Zar knew and wept. *A demon of the Abyss.*

The demon knelt and rose again. In its claws it held a bloody, lacerated corpse. The demon tossed the body from the parapet. It tumbled and thumped against the ground only feet away from Zar.

He couldn't help it. Zar screamed.

It was the corpse of Rael, gutted like a fish. They had cracked open the man's chest, scooped out his innards, and tossed aside this bloodied shell. Rael's dead eyes stared into his own.

Please, the eyes seemed to say. *Please, Zar, tell my wife I love her. Tell her that I'm sorry.*

Finally Zar could close his eyes. A tear streamed down to his lips.

"Goodbye, my friend," he whispered through chafed lips. "May your soul rise to the Sun God's courts of eternal light."

Solina walked toward the body, stood above it, and shook her head ruefully.

"Sad fool," she said. "He could have had his freedom; he was too weak." She turned toward her soldiers and raised her voice. "Send the next one in! Send the woman! Give her a sword; she can slay whatever evil lies inside or fall upon the blade."

The gaunt woman's eyes barely flicked as the guards untied her wrists, shoved her forward, and placed a sabre in her hands. After so many years crouched in alleys, licking the dust of the south, could she even feel pain and fear? Her eyes were sunken, already dead. She clutched the sabre before her; the blade reflected the red sunset as if already bloodied. Her only sign of life was sweat upon her brow and a tremble to her arms. Her lips, pale and dry, finally opened to speak.

"If I slay the evil inside," she rasped, "and if I find your key, I want the dust." She looked at Solina and her eyes reddened. A tear streamed down her cheek. "Please, my queen, if only a spoonful, if only a taste. I will find your key not for freedom, not for jewels, only for a sprinkling of the dust, my queen."

Solina sighed and shook her head. "Pathetic creature. You are a daughter of the desert! You are the stock of a noble breed, a warrior race of steel and sand and glory. And all you crave is that southern spice that twists you into a beast?" The queen spat. "But I will grant your wish. Bring me the key, and I will give you not a spoonful of dust, but great barrels of the stuff, so you may lick your desire for all your remaining days."

The dusteater's eyes widened, and she wept and trembled. "Thank you, my queen!" She could barely speak; her chest rose and fell as sobs racked her body. "I will find your key. I promise you, my queen."

With that, the dusteater turned, stepped toward the tower, and entered the darkness.

Zar stared, not daring to breathe. Queen Solina and her men stood frozen, eyes upon the tower. A single crow circled above, the only movement in the desert.

A scream rose.

Clashing steel rang.

Cruel, deep laughter bubbled.

Zar closed his eyes. *Sun God, oh Sun God.*

When a screech shattered the desert, Zar looked up to see the dark, cloaked figure reappear atop the tower. Once more, no light pierced its hood. Once more, its crimson claws rose. In its grip, it held a twisted corpse.

The creature tossed the body down, then disappeared back into the tower. When the body thumped against the ground, Zar stared for an instant, then doubled over and gagged. Whatever paltry scraps they had fed him—dry old bread and cheese—he now lost.

Please, Sun God, please, how can you let such horror exist under your light?

The dusteater had entered the tower a gaunt, nearly cadaverous woman. Now her body was bloated as if waterlogged. Her head bulged, twice its previous size. A twisted, parasitic creature melted into her body like a conjoined twin. Red eyes blinked upon her chest, and a shriveled hand thrust out from her belly, grasping at the air. A mewl rose from the wreck of a body; she was still alive.

Solina stared down in disgust. Even the queen finally seemed shaken, and her face paled. Her lips curled back in a snarl.

"Kill it!" she hissed to her soldiers. "Sun God, kill this thing."

The soldiers approached the twisting, gurgling creature. The parasite writhed across it, molded into the bloated body. The dusteaster's eyes twitched and shed tears, and her lips whispered. Zar could not hear her, but he could read her lips.

"Please," she begged. "Please kill me."

The soldiers thrust down their swords. Blood spurted. The creature convulsed, then lay still.

Solina shouted. "Send in the last one!"

Zar's knees trembled so badly, he'd have fallen had soldiers not grabbed him. When they began dragging him toward the tower, he kicked and struggled; it was like trying to break iron chains. As the tower grew closer, Zar saw shadows stir beyond its doorway, and he screamed and kicked and wept.

"Untie him!" Solina ordered. "Give him a sword!"

A soldier drew a dagger, pulled Zar's arms back, and sawed through the ropes binding his wrists. His arms blazed with pain as he raised them, and he found his wrists chafed raw and bloody. His fingers trembled and throbbed as the blood rushed back into them. Before Zar could even gasp with the pain, the soldiers shoved a sabre into his hands.

"Go on, you wretch," said one soldier, voice echoing inside his falcon helm—the man who had whipped and stabbed his back so many times. "Fetch us the key, maggot, and you'll have your sweet freedom, and you can return to your whore and miserable whelp."

Zar's eyes stung, the memories coursing through him: his son, his beautiful son with the blue eyes, fingers that clutched his, and soft hair like molten dawn. He could see him again.

All I must do is be strong, be brave, find the key... and I can go home.

Before him loomed the shadowy doorway. When he looked over his shoulder, he saw the queen there, her armor bright in the sunset, her eyes like sapphires. He saw her soldiers, fifty men clad in steel, swords in hand.

Or I can fight them, he thought. *I can swing my sword at them. I can try to cut them down. I can't kill them all, but maybe I can kill enough to run between them, to flee into the desert.*

He gritted his teeth, sending pain blazing down his jaw. Even if he did escape them, what then? They would hunt him. They would catch him. They would return him to the dungeon—to the whips, the pincers, the rats, the endless agony and screams. Here at least, in this tower, death could relieve him. It would be a gruesome death; the creatures inside could gut him, or mangle him, and he would scream... but at the end, they would kill him. That was more than Solina's dungeon offered.

And maybe... Zar swallowed a lump. *Maybe I can find the key. Maybe I can return home to my wife and son, a hero bearing jewels and glory.*

He squared his shoulders, swallowed again, and stepped into the tower.

Darkness swirled around him. Wind whispered like voices. He walked, step by step, sword trembling before him.

"Find the key!" Solina shouted behind him, but her voice was muffled and distant, an echo from a different lifetime. "Find the key for your freedom!"

He kept walking. His knees shook. The shadows engulfed him, then parted like a curtain, and Zar found himself standing in a round chamber.

His breath died on his lips.

The walls and floor were built of rough gray bricks. The room was empty but for a large, obsidian table engraved with a peering eye.

A creature sat at the table, fork and knife in hand. Zar nearly gagged; he had never seen a creature so grotesque. It looked like an obese, naked man, its folds of pale skin hiding its features—a creature like a great slab of melting butter. It seemed to have no eyes, only two slits. Two white folds opened to reveal a raw, red mouth and a wet tongue.

Zar wanted to stab the creature. He wanted to turn and flee. He wanted to close his eyes, curl up, and pray. Yet he stood frozen in disgust and terror as the creature raised its hand. Its fingers were fat as bread rolls, pale and glistening and ending with small claws. It pointed at a staircase behind the table; the stairs seemed to rise to a second story.

"Do I..." Zar's voice cracked, and he swallowed and tried again. "Do I climb? Is the key upstairs?"

The obese, pale creature said nothing, only kept pointing at the staircase. Its wrinkled slits stared at Zar like eyes. Its mouth opened again, revealing small sharp teeth.

Zar took a step toward the stairs, keeping one eye on the creature. Sword trembling in his thin hands, he began to climb. The stairs corkscrewed up, craggy under his bare feet, until they emerged into the second floor of the tower.

Zar felt himself blanch. He raised his shaking sword.

"Shine your light on me, Sun God," he whispered.

Fight it, he thought and clenched his jaw. *Kill it or your body too will fall from the tower.*

The second story looked much like the first, round and rough and empty. A creature lurked here too. At first Zar thought it a dog with two heads. But this canine creature was larger than a dog—closer in size to a horse—and its two heads were humanlike, bloated and staring with beady eyes. The two mouths opened and tongues unrolled, each a foot long and oozing.

"Stand back!" Zar said and sliced the air, blade whistling. He had been a soldier once. He had languished in Solina's dungeon for long moons, maybe for years, and his limbs were thin and shaking now, and his head spun. But the old soldier still whispered inside him, the soldier who had swung his blade in battle, fighting the weredragons in the tunnels of their northern lair. He could still wield a sword, and he could still kill.

As his blade swung, one of the creature's heads growled—a deep sound like thunder. The second head screeched—a sound like ripping skin. The dog bared sharp teeth, its muscles rippled, and it leaped toward him.

Zar screamed and swung his blade.

For the Sun God. For my wife. For my son.

His blade slammed into the creature's shoulder. Black blood spurted and clung to the steel, and Zar screamed again. The blood raced up the blade like a black, sticky demon. When it reached his hand, it drove into his flesh, and Zar realized: This was no black blood but a swarm of ants. The insects burrowed into his hand. He saw them crawling under the skin of his arm, racing to his chest.

His sword clanged against the floor.

The canine creature yowled. Its mouths opened wide. Its tongues reached out, red serpents, growing longer and longer. Zar stumbled back, and the tongues caught him, wrapped around him, and began to constrict him.

"Sun God!" he shouted. "Blessed be your light! Bless—"

A tongue twisted around his throat, squeezed him, and his voice died.

Blackness began spreading across his eyes. He fell to his knees, and the tongues pulled him closer, and teeth shone, and eyes blazed, and Zar wept.

The blackness overcame him, and he fell into a deep, endless void.

In the night, he walked through tunnels in a cold, northern land. His brothers walked behind him and fire roared ahead. The weredragons—shapeshifters of the north—filled the underground, and they *knew* these caves, they knew every tunnel and every bend, and they cut Zar's brothers down at every turn. Their blades thrust from shadows, and his brothers fell, and blood sluiced their feet, and everywhere he turned, he saw their pale skin and shining eyes. Zar wanted to flee, to find his way back into the light of the world, to let the heat of the Sun God warm him, yet more Tiran soldiers surged behind him, and his queen screamed for death and glory, and Zar kept moving deeper into darkness. Finally a weredragon all in armor, his beard fiery red and his eyes wild, thrust his sword into Zar's leg. He fell. His comrades pulled him back. So much blood poured from him; Zar had not imagined the human body could store so much. He knew that he would die here. He tried to crawl back but saw only darkness, only stone walls, only wild eyes and shadows and his blood pooling beneath him.

When his eyes opened, he found himself back on the ground floor of Tarath Gehena. He lay upon the obsidian table, bleeding across the engraving of the great staring eye.

Zar screamed and blood filled his mouth.

The obese, pale creature sat before him, fork and knife clutched in its hands, bloodied. More blood smeared the creature's slit of a mouth and rolled down the folds of its skin. When Zar looked down at his own body, he wept and begged and closed his eyes.

Please, Sun God, please, no, make him stop eating me, make him stop, make him give me my legs back.

Claws dug into his shoulders. He slid across the tabletop and thumped against the floor. When he opened his eyes, he saw a hooded creature clutching him, dragging him across the floor and onto the staircase. Zar's body thudded against each step, dripping, spilling, eaten away, so much of it gone, so much blood. Zar screamed and wept and begged, but still they climbed and climbed until they emerged onto the tower top.

The sky roiled red above, whirlpools of ash and blood and shadow. The hooded creature raised Zar above his head, half a man, still weeping. The creature screeched to the sky, a sound rising and shattering in Zar's ears until it cracked something inside him, and Zar could hear no more, nothing but ringing.

The world spun around him.

Wind whipped him.

He tumbled from the tower and crashed down, shattering, at Queen Solina's feet.

She looked down upon him, and her lips tightened sourly, and she turned to speak to her men. *She is beautiful,* Zar thought. *She is my beautiful queen, a deity of gold and purity.* He wept to see such light and beauty at the end.

He closed his eyes, thought of his wife and son, and walked toward the fiery halls of his lord.

ELETHOR

He lay in his bed—a mere pile of furs—and held Lyana close but could not forget the pain. She lay naked and sleeping against him, her head of fiery red curls upon his chest, and as he held her he thought: *She is beautiful, and she is all I ever wanted, and I should be happy now but this hurts too much. This is all the sadness in the world.*

He looked up at the cave's ceiling, rugged stone carved by dragonclaw into the mountainside. He looked at the walls where candles burned in alcoves. He looked back at Lyana and marveled at the milky pallor of her freckled cheek, the flame of her hair, and the warmth of her breath against him. He held her under the furs, his one hand on her thigh, the other on the small of her back. He never wanted to let her go. She was an anchor to him, and all around roiled a sea of blood and tears.

One thousand and fifty-seven.

Such a small number—a mere few trees from what once was a forest. Such a multitude—so many souls to lead, to defend, to give hope to. One thousand and fifty-seven. They survived the fall of Nova Vita. They slept in these caves and in the forest around it. They wore furs, and they ate what they caught, and they needed him, they needed their King Elethor to bring them hope, to lead them home, to defeat their enemies and bring new life to Requiem.

They need me to be my father. To be like the great kings of old. He closed his eyes. *They need me to be a man I am not.*

Lyana stirred against him. She mumbled something of poison that burned, crowds that chanted, and whips that lashed. When Elethor opened his eyes, he saw her wincing and biting her lip. She kicked under the furs, and he held her tight like holding a flouncing fish, and he kissed her head and whispered to her until she calmed. Lyana too, for all her strength in battle and fierceness by day, was afraid, was haunted, and was dependent on her king.

Sometimes Elethor envied her for her nightmares. They meant that she could sleep. He himself lay awake most nights, staring at this ceiling, holding his wife, whispering to her, trying to swallow the pain that filled his throat. Some nights the wyverns shrieked outside, seeking them as they hid under rock and leaf. Other nights his own demons called inside his head, memories of the Abyss, memories of children dead beneath him, memories of seeking his sister among the bodies.

He finally slept, but it felt like only moments passed before dawn's light fell upon his eyelids, and he opened them to see Lyana blink, the candles melted to stubs, and rain falling like silver curtains outside the cave. The sounds of the camp rose outside: soft voices, feet shuffling, and leaves rustling under boots. Lyana moaned, stretched under the blankets, and touched his cheek.

"Did you sleep?" she whispered. "You still look so tired."

I don't want to leave this bed, he thought, *and I don't want to leave this woman, and I don't want to fight this war.*

Yet he was Elethor Aeternum, King of Requiem, Son of Olasar, and he knew that he would still fly, still bleed, still roar his fire, even if he died upon the sands of Tiranor. But not yet. Not yet. This morning he lay in warmth, his wife pressed against him, the beauty of rain and leaf outside the cave that had become their home.

"Elethor," Lyana said, propped herself onto her elbow, and made to rise from the bed, but he held her fast. He pulled her back toward him and kissed her, and she closed her eyes.

They had been married for a moon now. They had wed in this forest, among leaf and rock, for the people to see, for the survivors to know that a king and queen led them, that there was still hope in the world, still light to follow. A moon had turned, a moon of waiting, of pain, of more love than Elethor had thought his heart could ever feel again, not a flame like the love of his youth, but a strong wine in autumn and warm blankets as rain fell outside. He made love to her now. They kissed as the light of dawn poured over them, and gasped, and he held her tight as she moved above him, her eyes closed, her cheeks flushed. He rolled her onto her back and lay atop her, and she felt so frail and thin, this woman who had fought in wars, survived the desert, and slain her enemies with steel—here in his bed, she felt like a doll, a flower he could trample. She buried her hands in his hair, moaning, her eyes closed, a fragile white thing, her hair still short, her every freckle as familiar to him as the stars of his fathers' constellation. Those stars seemed to burn around him, and all the lights of the heavens to flare, and he closed his eyes and tightened his fists and could barely bear this blend of joy and pain that still clawed inside him. His eyes stung.

He lay beside her, and she nestled against him. She kissed his cheek and played with his hair.

"You should have done that last night," she said. "You would have slept better."

He snorted a weak laugh. "Maybe I will sleep all day. You go lead them, Lyana."

Yet he rose from the bed. He dressed and donned his armor—old armor forged in dragonfire, dented and unpolished and feeling more heavy than ever. He clasped Ferus to his side, his old longsword his father had given him, and stared into a small mirror they had found and hung here. He barely recognized himself these days. It had been only two years since Queen Solina had led the phoenixes into Requiem, yet he seemed to have aged twenty. Where was the soft-cheeked sculptor he had been, a youth with sad eyes? He saw a hardened man in this mirror, his face gaunt and bearded, his eyes deep set.

Lyana walked up beside him, leaned her head against his shoulder, and whispered to him. She had donned her own armor—the silvery steel plates of a bellator, a knight of Requiem. Her sword Levitas hung at her side, slimmer and faster than Ferus, but just as strong and sharp.

"Let us face the day, Elethor," she said. "Let us see our people. Let us give them another whisper of hope."

They exited the cave into a forest red and gold with autumn. Dried leaves carpeted the forest floor, and moss coated the trunks of birch, maple, and ash trees. Requiem lay but a league east from here; the forces of Solina dared not yet burn this land of Salvandos, still fearing the wrath of its leaders who dwelled far in the west, guardians of this forest.

Yet if her power grows, Elethor thought, *she will burn this place too.* Birds called overhead, flying south for winter, and Elethor watched them. *They are heading to Tiranor. To Solina. Soon we will fly there too.*

People moved about the camp, clad in furs and old cloaks, leaves in their hair and mud on their cheeks. Some wore armor; these ones guarded the palisade of wooden stakes that surrounded their camp. Others wore bandages, still wounded from the war. Some lay in carts, limbs missing, flesh scarred, eyes anguished or burned away. A few men stood around a mossy boulder, praying and chanting from old scrolls. A girl was weaving blades of grass into dolls, which she then handed out to younger children.

One thousand and fifty-seven.

They had set camp here nearly three moons ago—Elethor, Lyana, and fewer than a hundred others. Their scouts had since been combing these forests, seeking more survivors. At first they would find bloodied and bedraggled Vir Requis every day, and their camp had swelled rapidly. By now few other survivors remained; Elethor's scouts had found only two—young twins, a boy and girl—over the past ten days.

Is this all there is? he wondered, looking down upon the camp. *Are these all who live from our nation?* He grasped the hilt of his sword, and his throat constricted. *Where are you, Mori?*

Once more, Solina's words returned to him, echoing through his mind as they did every day and night.

She lives, Elethor. She lives.

He closed his eyes, and his fist trembled around Ferus's hilt.

"I will fly to your desert, Solina," he whispered. "I will rain my fire upon you. If you took my sister, I will free her, and you will burn forever in my flames."

One thousand and fifty-seven. He opened his eyes and looked at them again—frightened children, wounded women, tired old men. Yet he would lead them in flight, and they would blow their fire—like the great last stand of Lanburg Fields where legendary King Benedictus had led Requiem's survivors against the griffins.

He turned to look at Lyana. She stared back with huge eyes like green wells, and he knew that she was thinking the same thing.

"Will it be enough?" he whispered.

She squeezed his hand. "I don't know." Her voice was soft, almost a whisper, but deep and haunting like ghosts in an ancient forest. "Maybe not, Elethor. But we will lead them nonetheless, and we will burn the enemy upon her towers, even if we fall in flame too."

"For the glory of our stars," he said. "For Requiem."

Her eyes dampened. "For Mori."

A scream rose from the camp, and Elethor sucked in his breath and spun his head around. He stared at the forest and the scream rose again—a scream of such terror and pain, for an instant he thought the Abyss had risen into the world.

The camp below stirred. Requiem's survivors rose to their feet and spun toward the sound. Steel hissed as Elethor and Lyana drew their swords. His heart hammered and his old wounds blazed.

She found us. Stars, Solina found us.

The trees stirred, and Elethor prepared to shift into a dragon, to blow his fire, to burn and die. Yet it was no Tiran troops who burst from the trees, but a single, haggard man with wild hair and wilder eyes. At first Elethor thought him some mad woodland hermit; he was shirtless even in the cold, his ribs showing beneath his skin. His teeth were missing, and dried blood caked his hair. He ran barefoot toward the cave, fell to his knees, and howled to the sky.

"Stars," Lyana whispered and gasped, and then Elethor recognized the man, and his breath caught.

This man was no wild hermit.

He was Vir Requis.

He was Leras Brewer and three moons ago, he had been strong, somber, a warrior of Requiem. Elethor had sent him south to spy in Tiranor before Requiem's survivors attacked.

He returned to us a broken beast.

Jaw clenched, Elethor sheathed his sword and marched down the mountainside toward the fallen, wailing man. Lyana rushed at his side, and guards of the camp, clad in armor and holding spears, hurried forward too. Soon a ring of people surrounded Leras.

The young man—*Stars, he looks old now,* Elethor thought—lay trembling, knees pulled to his chest. Tears filled his eyes, and his toothless mouth smacked open and shut. A memory flashed through Elethor's mind, a vision of shriveled beings of the Abyss, sucking the air and smacking their gums.

Elethor's head spun. He knelt by the trembling man and touched his shoulder. Leras cowered and wailed.

"Please," he begged, "please don't touch me, please don't hurt me. No more. No more."

Lyana stood above them. She raised her head and coned her palm around her mouth.

"Piri!" she cried. "Piri, we need you and your healers! Bring silverweed!"

Elethor looked down at the trembling man. Burn marks stretched across his chest. They had tortured him—burned him, broken his teeth, maybe broken his mind. Bile rose in Elethor's throat, thick with guilt.

I sent him south. I sent him to this.

"Nobody will hurt you here, Leras," he said softly. "You are safe here. You are home. You are home. We will heal you."

Leras stared with wild, red-rimmed eyes. He reached up and clasped Elethor's cloak, fingers bony and digging. His breath trembled and his ribs rose and fell like twigs upon a stream.

"You... you must flee!" he said, voice slurred with pain. "You cannot fly south. You cannot. She... she is freeing the nephilim, my king. The... stars!" Tears rolled down his cheeks. "Flee, King Elethor! Take these people and flee north—as far as you can—and never return."

Feet stomped through the crowd, and Piri Healer came walking forward, clad in the white robes of her order. With Mother

Adia fallen and the Temple destroyed, young Piri had become the closest thing Requiem had to a new High Priestess. Her dark braids were stern, her eyes sterner. Behind her trailed her pupils, a dozen young women in white silks, baskets of herbs and bandages in their hands. Piri knelt beside the wounded Leras, reached into her robes for a bottle of silverweed, and broke the wax seal with her thumb.

"Drink," she said, holding the bottle forward. "Drink and you will sleep and heal."

Elethor raised his hand, blocking the bottle from reaching the wounded man.

"Wait, Piri," he said softly. He kept his voice steady, but his insides roiled.

The young healer's eyes flashed. "My king! I—"

"Wait." His voice was harsh. He looked back at the trembling, wounded man. "Does Solina fly north? What do you know? Speak, Leras. Tell me everything."

The man's raw fingers groped at Elethor's armor, smearing blood. His eyes widened and his body shook.

"She is sending men to fetch the key. The key from..." He coughed and shook for a moment, then spoke in sobs. "From the tower! I saw the bodies. Stars, the bodies that fell from the tower. Cut, mangled, twisted. She wanted to send me in too. She pulled me from the dungeon. She wanted me inside. Please. Please! I shifted. I flew. I came here. She will free them!" His voice rose to hoarse, anguished shouts. "She will find the key and she will unlock the Iron Door. The nephilim will fly. You cannot fight them. You must flee! Fly north, King Elethor. Fly north. Never return!"

Leras's tears flowed, and sobs racked his body, and Elethor only held the man, unable to speak, barely able to breathe. His fear pulsed through his chest, and he felt the blood leave his face.

Herself pale, Piri poured the silverweed into the man's mouth, but he sputtered, unable to swallow. He hacked and laughed and wept.

"Fly," he whispered, "and never return."

His eyes rolled back, and he fell limp in Elethor's arms.

"Leras!" Piri cried. She pulled him from Elethor's arms, laid him upon the ground, and tried to revive him. She pounded his chest, poured more silverweed into his mouth, and shook him, but he would not wake. He lay with a smile—a last smile of peace—and staring eyes.

The people of Requiem stood all around, whispering to one another. Many trembled. Elethor rose to his feet and turned toward them.

"You have nothing to fear!" he called out. "Vir Requis, return to your tents and caves. You are safe here. I promise you this. You are safe."

Yet as the crowd dispersed, Elethor heard them whisper, and a few wept. As Elethor stood above the body, he realized that he had drawn his sword. Cold sweat drenched him and his breath quickened.

Lyana looked at him, eyes wide, her own hand around her sword's hilt.

"He spoke of the nephilim," she whispered. Her face was ghostly white. "The Fallen Ones. I've heard of them, Elethor." She spun and began walking through the forest. "Come. I will show you. Stars save us if he spoke truth."

Teeth clenched and sword drawn, he followed, and the man's dying words echoed in his mind.

Fly, King Elethor! Fly and never return!

LEGION

He howled in the depths. He screeched and laughed and banged against the walls until the pain twisted through him, and all around him swirled his brothers with fang and claw and horn and tongue.

"I am Legion!" His voice rose like steam. "I will bite, I will feast, I will serve. Free us! Free us, Goddess. Free us, Savior. I will serve! I will bring chaos."

His brothers and sisters filled the court around him, so thick he could barely see the walls, barely see these bricks that entombed them. Their eyes dripped pus. Their maws opened, drooling, screaming, seeking man-flesh to feast upon, craving sweet blood to suck. The nephilim climbed and twisted around the columns, scuttled across the ceiling, bled and screamed and flapped wings. A bloated, crawling nephil bit into a smaller beast, cracked his spine between his jaws, and fed and licked and laughed and screamed.

"Wait, brothers and sisters!" Legion rose among them, climbing upon scales and flesh and rusted armor. He raised his claws and howled. "Do not yet feast! Do not feed upon us, brothers and sisters. I am Legion! I will lead you to the world. I will lead you to man-flesh and sweet red blood. I will serve! She will come."

The thousands surrounded him, a sea of tooth and claw and blood, milky eyes blazing, drool dripping, hisses rising. They howled at him and climbed atop one another, mad in their pen, shaking the columns with their screams. They had been mad for so long.

"We must feast!" cried one, a lanky beast with moldy flesh, one wing torn off, and a scar that rent his rotting head.

"We must drink blood!" cried another, a shriveled twig of a creature, teeth running across her head and torso like stitches.

"No more, no more!" wept a swollen creature, flesh bubbling and sores seeping. "The pain! End the pain!"

Legion flapped his wings. Those wings blazed with agony; they had been cramped for so long, atrophying in this prison, their leather brittle and old, their bones like rusted blades. Yet he flapped them, screamed, and rose in a wake of fire until he hit the ceiling. He slashed his claws and wings, beating his brethren aside. He scuttled and descended onto his throne of bones, rusted spikes, and mummified flesh.

"See my burning crown!" he shrieked. "See the blaze of my fire! Hear my words, for I am Legion your lord!"

Around his head, his halo of fire crackled. He alone among the Fallen bore this flaming crown, for he was Legion; his mother had been the mortal Priestess Queen of the Old God, and his father had been Sharael, Demon King of the Abyss. Legion's blood swarmed with maggots, with pus, and with royalty, and upon his brow his birthright of lordship blazed. The beasts around him reached out to his crown, hissing and wailing, the firelight painting them red.

"Your pain will end!" Legion cried. "One day she will come—our savior. Hear me, Fallen Ones! Hear my howl. I am Legion! I am Prophet! One day she will open the Iron Door. One day a goddess of platinum and light will free us, and I will lead you to serve her. I will lead you to freedom! We will feast upon sweet, living blood and bones and skin and organs."

They roared around him, chanting his name, screaming for blood, spraying drool and pus and smoke. They crashed against the walls and columns, mad with hunger and thirst, eyes spinning, teeth biting at their own flesh. Not all believed him. Many roared and flew toward him through the mass, snapping teeth and lashing claws, until his servants beat them down.

"You lie!" the rebels cried, weeping blood. Their hearts beat madly beneath their brittle flesh, deep red and black. Their veins pulsed and their wounds dripped. "We hunger! We must eat one another. We must eat you!"

Legion rose tall upon his throne of the dead. He was so thin here, so frail, his skin clinging to his bones like old flesh on discarded blades of war. All around him, filling the stone court, his brothers and sisters spread and writhed and bled.

"No!" Legion cried, halo blazing. "No. We must wait. Do not weaken us. We are strong! We are Fallen. We are Chaos. We will remain strong and we will feast! She will free us. One day she will open the door, a goddess of platinum, a deity of steel." He shook his fists above him, claws digging into his palms. "I have foreseen it. I am Prophet. I will lead you out the Iron Door that seals us. I will feed you flesh and blood! We will crush the world and devour those who imprisoned us."

They roared and flew and clawed and bit and wept around him. Myriads filled this prison, crushing one another, clawing uselessly at the walls. Sometimes Legion thought them a single, writhing mass, many merged into one creature over the millennia. Behind them stood the Door, towering, solid iron, never rusting, forever sealing them here, forever burning their flesh, forever containing their madness.

"The door will open! I am Legion! She will free us, and we will crush those who sealed us, we will destroy the world, we will bring chaos and terror, and their spines will snap between our jaws, and their blood will be our wine. Hear me! Follow me, nephilim. We will be free!"

They roiled like a boiling sea and howled and begged and roared. Fangs and claws rose, red with blood, and eyes blazed, and snorts of fire burned, and wings beat as his brothers and sisters climbed one another, gasping for air to howl. Upon his throne of mummified flesh, Legion bared his fangs and laughed and screeched. He could already taste the hot blood and bones, and he shrieked so that the chamber shook—a great cry to his goddess... to Solina.

TREALE

She sailed into Irys wrapped in cloak and hood, the desert wind kissing her lips with the taste of sand.

The boat was long, narrow, and oared, and she stood upon its prow and watched the city. Her heart thrashed and she clenched her fists under her cloak's long sleeves. The delta teemed with ships around her, hundreds of them: trundling cogs laden with chests of grains, fruits, and iron ore; military longships where soldiers shouted orders as they rowed, shields and spears strapped across their backs; the creaky barges of leathery-faced fishermen, their hulls speckled with barnacles; and towering merchant ships with sunbursts upon their sails, their decks bearing bundles of silks, sacks of gems, and exotic beasts in cages. Everywhere Treale looked, sails creaked, oars rowed, men shouted, and gulls flew to nest upon masts and ropes. Reeds swayed everywhere, a field of them rising from the waters, and Treale saw at least two rafts entangled among them. Cranes, ibises, and birds she could not recognize flew overhead, squawking in a chorus. The smells of salt, seaweed, fish, and spices filled the air so thickly Treale could barely breathe.

"Please, stars of Requiem," she whispered in the shadows of her hood. "Watch over me here in this southern land of sun."

And truly a land of sun it was; Treale had never felt such heat, never seen such shimmering light. The sunlight seemed to bleach the world, fading all colors. Treale was used to the northern light of Requiem, a soft light that fell gently upon the green of summer, the orange of fall, and the white of marble columns. Here in Tiranor the sun pounded her cloak—she felt trapped in an oven—and doused the world with blinding whites and yellows. Even the water seemed barely blue, but more a bright white reflecting the sun's wrath.

Behind her, the old peddler coughed, grunted, and spat noisily. She turned to see him squinting at her and scratching his privates. His face looked like beaten leather, and his hair hung in scraggly white braids. Between her and him rose sacks of Osannan silk and wool, treasures he'd claimed to have been shipping into Tiranor for forty years now.

"Welcome to Tiranor, girl," he rasped and spat again. "It's hot and it's crowded, and if you're lucky, you'll last a day. They like

Osannan silk here, but not Osannan refugees who stink of the sea. And darling, you smell like fisherman's feet and catfish guts. Now toss me that second silver coin of yours, unless you want to swim the last hundred yards to the docks."

Treale was noble born; she had spent her youth in Oldnale Manor studying dialects of distant lands. Today she spoke with the eastern lilt of Osanna, great realm of men north of Tiranor and east of her fallen land of Requiem.

"I thank you for the ride, old man, and for your warning. But I will not heed it. I survived the wars in north Osanna, even as the undead warriors who rise there slew my family and burned my village. I can survive the desert too."

The old silkmonger scratched his stubble, hawked, and spat overboard yet again; Treale did not know how any man could produce so much spit.

"The desert is crueler than any undead host," he muttered. "You should have stayed in Osanna and faced its ghosts. There you can fight on the ground with sword and shield; here weredragons swoop and rain fire from above."

Treale looked across the water at fish that leaped between barges. *Weredragons.* It was a foul word, a slur she hated. She was a Vir Requis, a daughter of noble Requiem, a child of starlight, not some filthy beast. Yet she bit her tongue and swallowed her anger. Here she must not be Treale Oldnale, a lady of Requiem, but Till the refugee from Osanna, the humble daughter of weavers come to seek her southern fortune.

But I will not seek fortune here, she thought. *I will seek you, Mori. And I will find you. And I will free you. And we will escape this cursed desert and fly away together.*

The city docks spread before them, great cobwebs of wood and rope upon the water. As the boat rowed closer, Treale watched, cloak wrapped around her and hood pulled low despite the heat. Hundreds of people, maybe thousands, scurried upon the docks and boardwalks. Treale saw sailors in canvas pants, golden rings in their ears and sweat glistening upon their bare chests; wealthy merchants, bellies ample, sauntering in plumed hats and priceless purple robes; dockhands lifting caskets, sacks of grain, barrels of wine, and cages holding exotic birds of many colors; women swaying in silks that barely covered their flesh, their navels jeweled, accepting coins from sailors and leading them into alleys; and soldiers clad in pale steel, sunbursts upon their breastplates and shields, their spears bright. Above the docks loomed five craggy towers connected with a wall. Arrow slits peered from each tower like eyes, guarding the entrance to their realm.

Tiranor, Treale thought and clasped her hands behind her back. *Scourge of Requiem. Land of sun and heat and steel. I will find you here, Mori, and I will bring you home—wherever we find a home now.*

Soon she had paid the old monger and climbed off his boat onto a rickety dock. She took two steps, her head spun, and she reeled for a moment before taking a deep breath and walking on. Her legs felt like boneless chickens. How long had she been at sea? Treale could no longer remember. It had been three moons since Requiem had burned, maybe four. The days all blended into a great nightmare of running through forests, hiding in fields, finally reaching the great plains of Osanna in the east, then hitching rides with wagons to the southern port of Altus Mare. From there, Treale only remembered countless hours in a tottering boat, gagging into the Tiran Sea and baking in the southern sun. Three moons, maybe four; was that all? It seemed ages to her.

But I still remember your columns, Requiem, she thought. *And I still remember you, Mori. If all of Requiem lies fallen, and all her people but us lie dead, I will still save you.*

Children ran across the dock, carrying baskets of oysters, and nearly knocked Treale into the water. She tightened her lips, steadied her legs, and walked on. The planks creaked beneath her, and between them, she saw silvery fish whisk between weeds. When she raised her head, she saw the city of Irys before her, a great hodgepodge of sandstone and wood.

She walked between two guard towers, following a troupe of merchants riding donkeys. Soon she was walking along cobbled streets. Multitudes of people crowded around her; even before the wars, fewer people than this had lived in all of Requiem. Women walked bearing baskets of fruits and fabrics upon their heads. One man led a small, leashed monkey, an animal Treale had only seen in books. Priests walked in white robes, chanting and bearing lamps even as the sun blazed overhead. Mudbrick buildings and wooden stalls covered the roadsides. Shops and carts sold vases, fabrics, fruits and spices, dried meats and fresh seafood, iron tools and golden jewelry, and even—Treale gasped to see it—slaves in chains. Everywhere wafted the scents of freshly caught fish, wine and beer, a hundred spices, and beyond them all the sandy smell of the desert.

"Where are you, Mori?" Treale whispered.

She walked along the streets, leaving the docks behind. She found herself between brick homes whose roofs overflowed with gardens. Palm trees lined the streets, heavy with dates, finches, and scurrying monkeys. In gardens between the houses grew fig trees and grapevines on lattices. Treale had grown up in northeast Requiem, a land of pines, birches, and maples—cold and stately trees. *This* place was lush, the hot air thick with the scents of fruit and leaf and soil.

A child ran by her, racing a barrel hoop, and nearly crashed into a group of maidens bearing baskets of grapes upon their heads. Three priests rode down the street upon white horses, swinging bowls of incense and blowing ram horns in prayer. Soldiers marched around a silo, spears clacking against the cobblestones, their faces hidden behind ibis helms. Treale's head spun. She had never seen so many people crammed into one labyrinth; the city of Irys was like a great book overflowing with countless characters.

It seemed that she walked for hours. Treale had grown up on farmlands where only a couple hundred people lived. Whenever she would visit Nova Vita, the capital of Requiem where fifty thousand had dwelled, she would think it massive; her head would spin to see those crowds. This place dwarfed Nova Vita; beside it, the old capital of Requiem had been but a humble town.

Did we ever stand a chance in this war? Treale wondered. *Was there ever a hope to defeat this southern empire where millions live?*

As if in answer, shrieks sounded above, and Treale raised her eyes to see a flight of wyverns.

There were four of them; they flew in battle formation, two attackers flanked by two defenders. Treale leaped, driven by instinct, and crouched behind an abandoned cart. Her heart hammered, her head spun, and her hand closed around the hilt of her dagger. The wyverns screamed overhead, and once more Treale was running through the forests of Requiem, bleeding and burnt, seeking a place to hide and a hope to cling to. Then the wyverns disappeared over the roofs of the buildings, flying north to sea, and Treale breathed shakily.

"I'm safe here," she whispered to herself. "I'm only Till here, Till the refugee from Osanna, not Lady Treale of Requiem. These wyverns will not hurt me."

She released her dagger, and was about to stand up, when a shout rose.

"Girl! Girl, you, behind the wheelbarrow. Come over here."

Treale's heart hammered. She rose to see soldiers staring at her from their ibis helms; she could not see their faces. Each bore a spear, a sabre, and a round shield emblazoned with a painted sun. Each wore steel plates. There were twenty of them, automatons of metal, and Treale clenched her fists to stop them from trembling. She realize that her hood had fallen off, revealing her black hair, olive skin, and dark eyes, foreign colors in this realm of platinum hair, golden skin, and eyes like glimmering sapphires.

As the soldiers approached her, Treale struggled not to tremble or flee. She thought of King Elethor, and of Mori, and of the courage of Requiem's warriors, and she bowed her head.

"My lords," she said. "I am new to this city, and I seek work. Would you know of any seamstresses looking for help?"

One of the soldiers marched up to her, grabbed her arm, and stared through his visor. She could see his eyes—blue and shrewd. He grumbled deep in his throat.

"Osanna scum," he said over his shoulder to his comrades. "I know the accent. The bastards have been overflowing the port since their Undead War started."

Treale couldn't help but breathe out in relief. Her accent, learned from flying across the border into Osanna many times in her youth, had just saved her life.

If they knew I am Vir Requis, a daughter of their sworn enemies, they would execute me here on the street.

"Aye, my lord," Treale said and curtsied, as the daughters of Osanna were wont to do. "The undead rise from Fidelium's mountains and march across our realm. They slew my father; he was a weaver. I can weave too! Would you be so kind as to direct me to a seamstress? I will work for room and board."

The soldiers grumbled, and one laughed and whispered to his friend; Treale caught something about how she would better serve as a whore than a seamstress, which was all Osannan women were good for. Treale bit her lip. Osannans were perhaps scum to these tall, noble sons of Tiranor; scum could be spat upon, cursed, and allowed to live. That was more than they would offer her if they knew her true parentage.

The soldier who had first addressed her drew his sabre, and Treale gasped, sure that he would slay her after all. When he swung his blade, however, he slammed its flat end across her backside. She yelped; the pain bit her like a whip.

"Be gone, scum!" he said. "Seamstress? Find a brothel with a bed to warm, or find a gutter to clean of nightsoil. That's all you Osannans are good for. If I see you on these streets again, my sword will slice your neck."

He gave her a second lashing, this one against her legs, sending her scurrying down the street. Treale gritted her teeth, and sudden rage flared inside her. She clenched her fists. A brothel? A gutter? She was a lady of Requiem. She could shift into a black dragon and burn these men dead in a heartbeat. She felt the magic crackle inside her, the ancient power of Requiem's stars. Her fingernails began growing into claws, her teeth lengthening into fangs.

No.

She swallowed, forcing her magic down. It fizzled away, leaving her a mere human. If she became a dragon now, she could kill these men, it was true... and then a thousand wyverns would descend upon her.

Find Mori first. That is what you must do now. Even if you must swallow some pride.

Shame burning across her, her backside and legs blazing with pain, she gave another curtsy.

"Thank you, my lords, you are most kind, and your generous lashing reminds me of my place."

With that, she scurried around a corner, hoping she would never encounter those men again. She walked down a narrow street and pulled her hood down again. She would be wise to keep herself concealed, she decided, especially if she met other refugees from Osanna; she could fool brutish Tirans, but if other refugees of the Undead War encountered her, she doubted her accent was accurate enough to trick them too.

As she kept exploring the city, Treale kept waiting for it to end. And yet, as she walked south, Irys kept sprawling. Was she walking in circles? When she found stairs leading up a temple wall, she climbed up, looked around from a height, and gasped. Irys spread around her for miles.

I've been walking for hours, yet I've only explored the northern port, she realized. Most of the city still lay south of her, a jumble of walls, towers, squares, and countless winding streets. *Stars, a million people must live here!*

She climbed down the wall and kept walking, barely able to grasp one place with so many lives. Wagons trundled down the street before her, their horses tossing midnight manes. Stalls selling dates, apricots, figs, and spices lined the road, and lush gardens filled the air with a perfume. Children scurried everywhere, peddlers haggled with shoppers, and a woman in motley juggled daggers.

A statue rose in a square—a sandstone man with a crane's head, twenty feet tall. In its shadow, an old man performed with wooden puppets—one puppet of a phoenix, the other of a dragon. Treale's eyes widened. She had sewn hundreds of puppets in her youth; they were her greatest love. Yet when she approached the puppet show and stood among the children who watched it, sadness crept into her. The wooden phoenix, painted bright orange, soon slew the ebony dragon, and the children cheered. Treale lowered her head.

Even the puppets here hate us, she thought, and the silliness of her thought twisted her lips into a smile. With a sigh, she turned away from the show and moved through the crowd.

Besides, I won't find Mori watching a puppet show, Treale thought. She had seen the wyverns carry Mori south. They would have come to Irys; Treale was sure of that. Solina would want the princess of Requiem imprisoned here, in the capital, in the jewel of her empire. How many dungeons would a city this size hold? Or was Mori imprisoned in Solina's own chambers, kept in a cage like some trophy pet?

She would start by searching for the city prisons, Treale decided; it seemed the most likely place to look. She was not sure how she would enter those prisons; she would have to figure that part out next.

She approached a man hawking apricots from a cart. She was about to launch into a story of an imprisoned brother, then ask for direction to the dungeon. Before she could speak, however, great horns blew across the city, a peal that hushed the crowds.

Treale felt like an icy snake was crawling down her back. She did not like this sound; it was a keen like columns crashing, like a fallen race crying from graves, the sound her heart had made when Nova Vita fell. Around her, the people stood hushed for a moment, then roared to the sky. Their faces changed; anger and fear suffused them, and they pounded the air and chanted to the Sun God. Thousands began to move down the streets, catching Treale in their flow; she could not help but move with them.

The crowds swept forward, a simmering sea, and pulled Treale along the cobbled street. They passed under a great archway embossed with golden suns; it was large enough for three dragons to fly through abreast. Beyond the archway, the crowd swept Treale into a great square where myriads roared.

Treale stood in the throng, head spinning and breath panting. The sun beat overhead. She had never seen a square so large; it seemed larger than all of Nova Vita. She could not guess how many people filled it; they were an ocean of rage, a hundred thousand strong or stronger. A temple rose to her right, columns soaring and topped with platinum. Before her, across the square, rose a palace; it was easily the largest building Treale had ever seen, dwarfing even the fallen halls of Requiem. Its towers scratched the sky. Faceless statues guarded its doors, standing above a staircase with hundreds of steps. Soldiers surrounded the square and covered the roofs of the buildings; some sat upon wyverns, whips in their hands. Above in the sky, phoenixes circled the sun, screeching.

Treale wanted to flee this place. She wanted to shift into a dragon and fly from here, fly as fast and far as she could. Something was happening here, something dark and horrible, something she desperately wanted to escape. The square felt like a boiling pot about to overflow. And yet she stood among the crowd, hood pulled low.

If you shift now, you die, she told herself. *A thousand wyverns surround this square, and phoenixes fly above. Stay. Hide. Whatever happens in this square, you must live.*

The palace doors ahead, towering things of gold and ivory, began to creak open. The crowd roared even louder. The faces of the people swam around her, red and howling and twisted with rage. Fists pounded the air. Several people were climbing the base of a great statue of Queen Solina; Treale elbowed her way toward them, climbed onto the statue's pedestal between howling youths, and stared ahead.

When the temple doors were opened, the real Queen Solina emerged.

The crowd roared to the sun. Solina raised her arms, a deity of platinum. Soldiers in gilded armor flanked her. The procession marched across the palace's dais, stood above the stairway, and looked down upon the city. One of the soldiers held a leashed, haggard creature, perhaps a beaten dog. As the crowds roared, the soldiers lifted the creature and chained it between the towering, faceless statues that flanked the palace doors.

"Behold the weredragon!" shouted Queen Solina. "Behold our victory! We will never fall!"

All around Treale, the people of Tiranor pounded their fists and roared the call. "We will never fall!"

Treale stared, eyes dampening. This was no chained animal, no creature.

It was Mori.

Memories floated around Treale: childhood summers in Nova Vita when she played with Mori in the palace gardens; the royal family visiting Oldnale Manor in winters, and Mori sleeping at Treale's side in the great oak bed upstairs; stargazing with Mori and her brothers on autumn nights, then sneaking away from the boys to whisper of future husbands, wedding gowns, and all the other dreams of youth. And now... now this: Treale hidden in a cloak among a crowd of rage, and Mori in chains and rags, her skin sallow and lacerated.

"I will save you, Mori," Treale whispered as the crowd roared. Her knees shook. Her belly roiled. She dug her fingernails into her palms. "I swear to you, I will save you."

As the phoenixes circled above the square, leaving wakes of flame, Solina cried to the sky. The queen appeared to be in rapture, head tossed back and arms raised. Her raiment of gold and platinum shone upon her, reflecting the sun and fire.

"The weredragons burned your homes!" she cried, and the crowds roared. "They slew your sons and brothers and fathers, brave men of Tiranor who flew to banish their darkness. But we defeated them! We toppled their courts and we captured their vile princess. Tiranor lives, Tiranor grows strong, Tiranor lights the world!"

The crowd chanted, fists pounding the air. "We will never fall! Hail the Sun God! We will never fall!"

"Hail the Sun God!" cried Queen Solina. "Today is the Day of Sun's Glory. Today the light of our lord banishes the night." She turned to her guards. "Let the reptile taste our glory."

The soldiers raised whips.

Treale winced and her heart wrenched. "No..."

The whips fell and Mori screamed.

"No!" Treale cried, but nobody heard her; the crowd shouted around her.

The whips fell again, and Treale bit her lip and looked aside. Her fists trembled. Tears ran down her cheeks. She wanted to shift, to turn into a dragon, to fly to Mori and save her. Yet how could she? How could she fly with a thousand wyverns around her, with phoenixes covering the sky?

"Please," she whispered, as if Solina could hear her across the crowd. The whips fell again and again, and Mori finally stopped screaming. Her chin fell to her chest, and she hung limp in her chains.

The crowd roared as the soldiers dragged the unconscious princess back into the temple. Treale shook and wanted to turn away, wanted to run, wanted to fly, wanted to race toward the temple and leap in after Mori. She tried to elbow her way forward, but the crowd was too thick, suffocating her. She could barely breathe. Her limbs trembled, and she'd have fallen were the people not pressed against her.

"See how the weredragons suffer for their crimes!" Solina shouted, arms raised. "See how the cruel scream in pain! They tried to kill us. They tried to extinguish the sun itself with their darkness. We shall beat the creature every Day of Sun's Glory! We will find their king, who hides like a coward in the wilderness, and flay him for the sun to burn his naked flesh." As the crowds roared, Solina raised her hand high in salute, and the sun itself seemed to glow within it, a beacon of her might. "Tiranor is strong, and Requiem's last children will die under our heel!"

Treale panted, belly roiling and eyes stinging, as Solina vanished back into her temple. The doors of gold and ivory closed, sealing the queen, her men, and Mori within. As the crowd began to disperse, growling about the evil of the weredragons, Treale stood in place. She lowered her head, fists clenched at her sides. She tasted a tear on her lips.

"I'm sorry, Mori," she whispered. "I'm so sorry I left you, that I flew from battle, that I abandoned you." She trembled, remembering seeing the fall of Nova Vita... and fleeing it. "I will never find absolution from my shame, Mori, but I will save you. I promise you."

She stood in the square until the sun set and all but a few stragglers remained. Then Treale turned, walked in silence, and entered an alley between shops and taverns. The sun fell and darkness spread. Between the roofs of the buildings, Treale saw the Draco constellation, the stars of her home, and they soothed her. She missed her parents and her brothers so badly; they lay dead. She missed her king Elethor; she did not know if he too had fallen. She missed her home, Oldnale Manor; it had burned to the ground.

But Mori still lives. A last light shines. I am not alone.

Treale curled up in a shadowy corner, placed her head against her knees, and quietly wept.

NEMES

As the rain fell and the sun set, Nemes was digging a grave.

He was not a gravedigger; Requiem had employed three, and they had fallen in the war. Nor was he strong; his arms had always been thin, and others of the camp—surviving soldiers—were better suited for manual labor. But Nemes had volunteered to bury the tortured spy, for he had always loved three things above all else: solitude, corpses, and Lady Lyana.

"I have two here with me," he said softly among the trees, shoveling dirt. The camp lay far behind, and the dead spy stank beside him. "And if my Lord Legion wills, I will have the third soon enough."

He tightened his pale, bony fingers around the shovel's shaft. In the fading light, his flesh seemed gray to him, rubbery and old despite his youth; he was not yet thirty. Strands of his hair hung over his eyes, prematurely silvered—the hair of an old man. But Lyana was fair. Lyana's skin was smooth and pale like the silks Nemes's mother would dream of owning. Lyana would regret her words to him; Nemes vowed that. They would all regret how they'd hurt him; he swore that to the rain, to the worms, and to the body rotting beside him.

His arms shook. He was tired. He had never been so tired. He turned away from the grave—it was deep enough—and knelt by the body. It was a famished, scarred thing, barely better than the worms that crawled across it. Nemes touched the body's cold cheek, closed his eyes, and thought of Lyana.

"How sweet it would be to touch your cheek," he whispered. He licked his lips and imagined licking her skin. "Someday I will bring you here, Lyana, into this forest, and I will tear your clothes so that I can touch all of you, see all the pale flesh of your body, and know you here upon this grave."

Eyes closed and breath fast, Nemes caressed the corpse's hair. The rain pattered around him. When a worm crawled across his fingers, he opened his eyes. The corpse stared up at him, mouth open in a toothless grin, flesh a pasty white—as white as Lyana's. This dead, decaying thing was not as beautiful as Lyana, but it was close. It was close. It could soothe him for this night.

Nemes looked around him, a snarl on his lips. And why not? The weaklings were back at their camp—lying down to sleep, or to pray, or to hug and whisper their pathetic, weakling dreams. But he, Nemes, was strong; not of arm perhaps, but of spirit, of mind, of tooth. He was a scavenger of the night. He was a vulture, tall and dark and proud. He pulled his Iron Claw from his cloak, a curved obsidian blade. He thrust it into the body's neck and pulled down, gutting the torso. His nostrils flared, inhaling the sweet smell of death.

The light faded, and Nemes lit his tin lamp. In the red light, he studied. He dissected. He placed organ by organ. He clutched the heart in his palm and breathed in ecstasy. This felt almost like that first time, years ago, when he'd been only a boy in the woods. Back then he would catch only squirrels, crush their heads, skin them, and study their innards. But squirrels were for boys, and Nemes was a man now, a vulture, a future lord to Lyana. He craved the *humans*, and he savored this human. Every piece he removed sent shivers through him.

The others, he knew, would not understand. King Elethor had always craved the beauty of sculpture. The Princess Mori had always craved the beauty of music. Lyana, his eternal love, craved the beauty of marble columns and steel blades. Their minds were so small, their worlds so dark. *This* was beauty: a smell of blood, a glimmer on bone, and the secret worlds that pulsed under skin. Nemes inhaled sharply, imagining the beauty of the organs Lyana hid under her pale skin. He vowed to someday see them too, to touch them, to study them.

He buried the man and his organs. He covered the grave in darkness. He cleaned his hands in a stream. His work was done.

He wrapped his black cloak around him, clutched his staff, and whispered the words he had learned—the words of Lord Legion. Shadows rose from the earth like serpents of smoke. Nemes welcomed them. He let the wisps caress his legs, then rise and swirl around him, until he inhaled their clammy scent. Soon the shadows cloaked him and he vanished into the night.

A thin smile twisted his lips. He had learned the words from the Old Books, the ones buried deep in Requiem's library. Only the noble house carried the keys to that chamber, filigreed works of art they bore on chains around their necks. Knowledge was power, Nemes knew, and he craved it—the power in corpses and the power in books. On many cold nights, he had crept into Princess Mori's chamber, watched her sleep, and gently lifted the key off her breast. He would spend the night in darkness, surrounded with books, studying the ancient scrolls of Lord Legion, the nephil whose voice still whispered in the night, the child of a demon king and his human bride.

"Now your shadows cloak me, my lord," Nemes whispered. "Now I slither in darkness, hidden, like you."

Nemes's fists and jaw tightened in anger. Lord Legion had fallen; he languished in a tomb, sealed from his true glory, and only his whispers crawled across the land. One day, Nemes swore, Lord Legion would rise again and spread wings in the night. One day the cruel stars of Requiem would extinguish, and their worshippers would be those crawling. Then he, Nemes, would be lord over them. He—who had emptied their chamber pots, served their wine, and swept their floors—would make them bow.

He walked through the forest, robed in shadow, snarling.

In the darkness, the memories rose again. He saw his grandfather, a bent old man, sweeping the halls of Requiem's kings, then returning home to his bed of straw. He saw his father, a meek sickly man, toil to wash, to mend, to clean, to finally die of the cough. And he saw himself, and that memory stung worst of all. He saw a lanky boy, the child of a long family of servants, a boy raised to sweep floors and wash outhouses and pick fleas from dogs, a boy who dreamed of the power and beauty of those above him.

As he poured wine at feasts, how he had dreamed of sitting at the high table with Princess Mori, with Lord Bayrin and Lady Lyana, with the beautiful and mighty! At the Nights of Seven, how he had begged to join the nobles in their gardens, to sing with them, to watch the stars... and yet he would always enter the gardens last, to clean the mess those above him had left. He remembered one night, a night of a black moon, when he dared approach the Lady Lyana, dared ask her to a ball. How her eyes had pitied him! He never forgot that look of pity; it still burned him. He could still feel her hand on his shoulder. He could still hear her soft voice rejecting him, explaining that Prince Orin had already invited her, and how sweet and lovely Nemes was, and how many girls would someday adore him.

Walking through the forest now, nearly a decade later, rage still flared inside Nemes. With a growl, he punched a tree so hard his knuckles tore and his blood sprayed. He snarled and watched the blood drip, imagining tearing Lyana's flesh open too, seeing her blood, ripping out her heart like she had done to his.

"You will regret your words," he swore in the forest as he swore most nights, as he had been swearing for ten years. "You will scream for me to forgive you. And I will not, Lyana. I will not. Not until you are fully mine—your body, your organs, your very soul." His fists trembled. "You will be mine."

He reached into his cloak and grabbed his serpent amulet, the sigil of Lord Legion. He let his blood cover the talisman. Lord Legion loved blood, he knew; Nemes was glad to give some of his.

"With your power," he vowed, "they will all bow before you. I swear it, my lord. I will make them bow."

The lord's shadows swirled around him with fury, and Nemes kept walking until he reached the camp. Most slept on the ground, bundled in blankets. Some had built huts of branches and leaves. Nemes walked between them, silent and dark. Some of Requiem's survivors were still awake, huddled together and whispering; they could not see through his cloak of shadow. Nemes moved between them, a ghost. As a servant in Requiem's palace, he had always been as an invisible man; Lord Legion let him have the true power, no longer a mere mockery.

And once you are freed, Lord Legion, your true might will bless me. They will cower before us.

The shadows danced around him, a raiment of demons. He climbed the mountainside until he reached the cave where King Elethor and Queen Lyana now ruled. A guard stood there, a young woman with golden hair, a spear and shield in her hands. Nemes walked past her; she saw nothing. He entered the cave, walked down a tunnel, and entered the chamber of his beloved.

Lyana lay there upon a bed of fur, naked in candlelight, so pure, so pale, so fragile. Her skin like marble glimmered orange in the candlelight. Tiny scars like cobwebs covered her back; others had cut her before, but Nemes would cut her deeper. Her hair burned red and wild. Elethor lay beside her, rolled toward her, and touched her cheek.

Nemes stood in the corner, silent and shadowy, and watched the two make love. His lips peeled back, baring his teeth, as the naked bodies moved together, as Lyana moaned, as the foul King of Requiem invaded her purity.

You will bow before me too, Elethor, Nemes thought, fingernails digging into his palms. *My family has served you for too long, but a new power will rise. You will watch me dissect Lyana, and I will dissect you next. You will both live through it; that I swear to you. You will both live to see your shiny, wet organs in my hands and mouth.*

He watched as they made love. He watched as they fell asleep. He then turned, left the cave, and swallowed a lump in his throat. His eyes stung and his fists shook.

No, he told himself. *No. You cried too many times as a youth. You watched your father, bent and old, die of his work, and you cried. You watched Lyana marry the cruel prince, and you cried. No more tears. No more pain. You will never weep again, Nemes.*

"But you will weep, Requiem," he whispered in the night. The rain lashed his face. "You will."

Wreathed in his lord's shadows, he shifted. He took flight as a gray dragon, his snout long and thin and sniffing, his claws pale like shattered femurs. He rose between the trees, silent as a spirit rising to the afterlife, and pumped his wings. The rain whipped him, and he flew through the night, breath pluming before him.

He flew south.

He flew to *them.*

Before him in the clouds, he could see the smoke again. In the trees below, he could imagine the fallen columns of Requiem. He remembered standing outside the city, watching the Tirans invade, attack, destroy. They were a tall people, strong and noble. In the eyes of Vir Requis, Nemes always saw pity—pity like that which Lyana showed him. He saw haughtiness—like in the eyes of the princes when they gave him his commands. He saw tears—tears like those that had filled his own eyes in his youth. But none of those had filled the Tiran eyes. In *their* eyes nothing shone but cruel strength.

"Requiem is weak," Nemes hissed as he flew, smoke rising between his teeth. "But Tiranor is strong, and I am strong, and she is the greatest among them."

Queen Solina! He had stood in the tunnels, watching as she sliced children apart, as she gutted them and spilled their precious organs upon the floor. Their blood had splashed her, and she had licked it from her blades, and Nemes knew then, knew he had been a fool to ever worship the princes, to ever crave power in Requiem. Watching her lick the blood, he knew: Solina was the only mortal worthy of worship, the only leader of strength in this world.

"I will find you, Solina," he spoke into the night. The rain swayed and he flew until the forest vanished below him. The southern horizon stretched dark and endless ahead. "I will find you, Solina, and I will give you King Elethor, and I will give you his people, and I will take Lyana for my own. Together we will free Lord Legion. Together we will rise."

He blew fire. He roared. He licked his chops and snarled and dreamed of Lyana's pulsing heart in his hand.

MORI

She sat on the sticky floor, lowered her head to her knees, and whispered soft prayers.

"As the leaves fall upon our marble tiles, as the breeze rustles the birches beyond our columns, as the sun gilds the mountains above our halls—know, young child of the woods, you are home, you are home." Her voice trembled. "Requiem! May our wings forever find your sky."

Chains bound her arms to the wall. More chains wrapped around her ankles, pinning her legs to the floor. For the first week here, they had chained her standing; now at least they loosened the chains enough for her to sit, but her limbs still ached, and whenever she leaned backward, her lashed back blazed. Three moons had passed, and they had whipped her three times in the Square of the Sun, beating her bloody and then returning her here, to darkness, to languish and shiver and weep and pray.

And Mori prayed. She prayed to her stars. She prayed to King's Column, which she dreamed of, a pillar of marble and light rising from ruin. She prayed to the spirits of her parents, her fallen brother Orin, and all those who had died around her in Nova Vita.

"Look after me, dragons of starlight," she whispered through cracked lips. Her voice was weak and hoarse, the voice of a ghost. "I will soon fly by your side."

Her head spun, and she felt unconsciousness clutching at her. She had fainted so many times here in darkness as hunger twisted her belly, as blood seeped down her back to trickle around her feet. In her long dark dreams, she kept seeing it again and again: Solina slicing her brother open, Solina slaying children underground, Solina toppling the city Mori had loved. And she dreamed of Bayrin: her sweet, strong Bayrin, the love of her life, flying bloodied and scarred in battle, surrounded by wyverns.

Do you still live, Bayrin? Do you dream of me too?

Worse than the hunger, worse than the whips, worse than the darkness, was Mori's worry for them. Did Elethor still fly? What of her friends Lyana and Treale and all the others? Did any Vir Requis still live, or was she the last, a lingering relic of Requiem's glory, a princess shriveled into an emaciated wretch?

She swallowed a lump in her throat, twisted her fingers, and struggled to stay conscious. Keeping her eyes open was so hard here in the dark. They gave her no light in this chamber of craggy bricks, rusted iron, and blood. Torches flickered outside the door; what red light seeped around the doorframe was all she had. It was enough for her to witness her decay. Her knees were knobby now, and her thighs, which she had once thought far too rounded for Bayrin to like, now seemed skeletal to her. She wore only a tattered rag, and through it she could see her bones thrusting against her skin.

How many days had passed since they'd last whipped her? Mori did not know. Three? Ten? Days and nights lost all meaning here in the dark. Sometimes it seemed hours between the meals they fed her—cold gruel thrust roughly into her mouth with a splintered spoon. Sometimes it seemed days went by without food, and her head swam and her belly clenched before more gruel arrived. When the moon ended, they would drag her out again, and the sunlight would burn and blind her, and the whips would tear her skin.

Footsteps thumped outside the door. Shadows stirred. Keys rattled in the lock, and when the door creaked open, torchlight flared. Mori whimpered and looked away, the light blinding her. How long had she sat here in darkness, alone? It felt like ages.

"Meal time," rumbled her jailor. "You no spit up this time, lizard whore, or Sharik cram it back into your mouth."

Mori blinked, raised her head, and winced in the torchlight. Sharik, the brutish jailor, stood above her. He looked more troll than man, wide and pasty and lumpy like a bag of spoiled milk. He wore but a canvas tunic, barely better than her own rags, and carried a ring of keys on his belt. He held a club in one hand, a wooden bowl in the other.

Mori did not want to eat. The gray slop he fed her, full of lumps and hairs, left her stomach churning and her limbs shaking.

"I'm... I'm not hungry," she whispered.

Sharik grumbled and raised his club. "Club or spoon. Your choice, weredragon."

He slammed down that club now, rapping her hard on the shoulder. Mori winced, pain pounding through her. Sharik knelt, dug his spoon into the gruel, and held it out. The slop trembled, gelatinous and sludgy. Sharik glared at her above the bowl. His eyes were beady and red, moles covered his face, and stench wafted between his rotting teeth. Hairs filled his red, veined nose.

"I—" Mori began.

With a grumble, Sharik dropped his club and grabbed her jaw. His fingers, fat and pale as raw sausages, dug into her, forcing her mouth open. She gasped and sputtered. He shoved the bowl forward, slamming its edge against her teeth, and tilted it. The gruel began spilling into her mouth, and Mori coughed and sputtered.

"No spilling!" Sharik grumbled. "For every drop you spill, Sharik break one of your fingers."

Mori could barely swallow fast enough. The slime rolled down her throat, and she coughed but forced herself to keep swallowing. His fingers dug into her jaw so painfully, she thought he would snap it off. Her throat kept working. She spat out a bit, whimpering. Sharik growled and she kept swallowing, letting the sludge keep pouring. She could barely breathe and her belly roiled.

Finally the bowl was empty. Sharik pulled it back and Mori swallowed, gasped, and coughed. Her limbs, still chained to floor and wall, trembled.

"Hope you enjoyed meal," Sharik rumbled and smirked. "Sharik cook. Special recipe."

He chuckled, a deep sound, then slapped her face. Pain flared, and Mori felt her lip split. She tasted blood.

"Next time you eat silent," Sharik said and growled. "No more coughing. No more choking. Or Sharik hurt you more. Sharik cut your fingers and feed you them."

With that, he left the chamber and slammed the door behind him. Mori heard the keys jangle in the lock, Sharik chuckle, and his boots thump away.

For long moments, she could think of nothing but breathing; every breath that entered and left her lungs was a struggle. Her belly ached and her limbs would not stop shaking. But whatever foul concoction he fed her, it had kept her alive thus far; Mori tried to draw comfort from that.

Food gives me strength. Strength will let me escape. Strength will let me kill him.

Her hands were too weak to form fists, but she curled her fingers as far as they'd go.

"I will escape," she whispered. "I will kill him. I will find Solina and I will kill her too."

She kept inhaling deeply, struggling to calm the shaking of her limbs. She breathed in and out, focusing on the flow of air—rancid as it was—into her lungs, into her fingertips, into every part of her. She thought of the leaves on the birch trees back home. She thought of her friends and family. She thought of harps playing in Requiem's marble temples and of her stars. She nodded.

"All right, Mori," she whispered to herself. "It's time to try again."

Pain flared in her belly and spun her head. Every time she tried to shift in these chains, she ended up weaker, her wrists and ankles bleeding. She had come to dread these attempts, but she tightened her lips, inhaled sharply, and nodded again.

I must keep trying. I must. If I give up hope, I can only wait to die. Even if escape is impossible, even if my magic will forever fail me, I will keep trying. I will keep hope alive. Even a fool's hope is better than no hope at all.

With a deep breath, she summoned her magic.

It rose tingling inside her, bright as starlight, warm as mulled wine. She let it flow through her chest, into her limbs, and into her head, smooth and soothing like her breathing.

Help me, stars of Requiem. Light my way here in darkness.

Wings began to sprout from her back; she felt them scrape against the walls. Her fingernails began growing into claws. Her teeth began lengthening into fangs. Across her frail legs, golden scales began to appear.

I will find your sky, Requiem! Help me fly.

Her body began to balloon, and a tail began to grow beneath her, and Mori could taste the sky and starlight, and—

As her limbs grew, the chains dug into her flesh. Pain burst. Her magic began to fizzle.

No. No! Clutch it. Shift! Break the chains!

She clenched her jaw, growled, and clutched her magic, tried to keep shifting, to keep growing, to—

A yelp fled her throat.

Her limbs grew too fast. The chains tore into her. Blood dripped, and her magic vanished like birds fleeing a disturbed tree.

Her scales disappeared, her claws and fangs retracted, and Mori lowered her head. She sat shaking, and blood dripped from where the chains had bitten into her. She shivered for long moments, head spinning.

Try again. Shift! You can break the chains, you...

Yet the darkness clutched at her. She was too weak, too hurt. Too much blood had spilled. Her forehead hit her knees and Mori gagged, losing the gruel the jailor had fed her. She could not stop trembling, and she could barely breathe.

I'm sorry, Requiem. I'm sorry, stars.

She closed her eyes, wept quietly, and let the long, dark night draw her into its embrace.

SOLINA

The palace doors opened, and her guards dragged in a lanky man
robed in muddy black. A hood covered his face; Solina could see only
strands of dangling white hair. Sitting upon her ivory throne, she
narrowed her eyes and watched as her guards, tall men bedecked in
steel, shoved the man down upon the floor of her hall.

"My queen!" said a guard. His voice echoed behind his falcon
visor. "We found this one skulking outside the palace, muttering
strange spells. He claims he's a weredragon."

Fifty guards, ten generals of her army, and three Sun God
priests filled her throne room. They all sucked in their breath. Solina
leaned forward in her ivory throne. The fallen man coughed; the
sound echoed in her silent hall.

"Stand up!" she barked. She rose from her throne, her jewels
jingling, and walked down the stairs of her dais. Her sandals clacked
against the gold and white tiles of her hall. Granite columns rose
around her, the stone a mosaic of reds and blacks and whites, their
capitals coated in platinum.

"My Queen Solina!" said the robed man.

He pushed himself to his feet. His hood had fallen back,
revealing a smooth face that belied his long white hair; that face
looked no older than her own. His eyes were shrewd, his nose thin,
his mouth a red line across his pale skin. His hands, which peeked
from his robes, were long and skeletal; in one, he clutched a staff.

A guard kicked the man's leg behind his knee, forcing him to
kneel.

"Kneel before Queen Solina, scum!" the guard said.

The other guards goaded the man with spears. Another kick
sent him facedown upon the tiles, and a boot pressed against his nape.
The man coughed and hissed but did not struggle to rise.

"My queen!" he said, voice serpentine. "I only seek to serve
you. I come from Requiem, I—"

Solina waved her guards back and glared down at the
weredragon. Her chest rose and fell. She knew this one. She had
seen him during her captivity in Requiem. He had been but a youth
then, a scrawny boy who always seemed too pale, the son of the palace

servants. Twice she had caught him peeking through a keyhole, watching her bathe.

"Nemes," she said, voice twisting in disgust. "I know you. On your feet."

Solina was a tall woman, but when Nemes stood, she felt short; he towered above her, thin and long and pale as a bone. His lips twitched in a mockery of a smile; those lips looked more like crawling snakes to her. She remembered the stories whispered about Nemes in Requiem: the animals he skinned and dissected in the forest, the books of dark magic he read, and the women he would leer at, Lyana foremost among them. Yes, she remembered this youth, now this man before her. She remembered him and he disgusted her.

"Queen Solina!" he said and sketched a bow, struggling perhaps to reclaim some of his lost pride. "I remember you a beautiful maiden, a rose in the thorny court of dragons; your beauty has only grown, and here I find a golden deity, a—"

Solina drew her twin sabres with a hiss, crossed them, and thrust both blades against Nemes's neck; if she pushed them but a hair's breadth closer, she'd cut his skin. He froze and his voice died.

"Silence, slithering snake," she said. "What does a weredragon, a beast of night, seek in the courts of the Sun God?"

He tried to step back from her blades, but her men held him fast. He licked his lips, tried to speak, and when his neck bobbed, her blades drew a drop of blood. He whispered hoarsely.

"I do not serve the stars of the night, those petty gods of Requiem," he said. "Mine is a different, older lord. I will help you wake him. I will help you slay the weredragons."

Solina snarled and took a step nearer. She bared her teeth and glared at him closely; her nose was but an inch from his. She drove her blades but a whisper closer, and another drop of blood dripped down his neck.

"Perhaps I shall begin with slaying this weredragon," she said.

What game did this reptile play? Surely he knew he would die in this court. She knew he was mad; all of Requiem knew that. But she had not known the depth of his madness, if he was truly so keen to abandon his life.

He licked his lips again; his tongue was serpentine, a snake emerging from its lair. He hissed his words.

"I am, my queen, but a humble servant, the son of a servant. The weredragons themselves cared not if I lived or died; why should you? But I can give you their king, the cruel Elethor. Why kill me when I can deliver him to you? For three moons now, your men have sought him in the wilderness, burning forests and fields, scouring mountains and plains—and still the weredragons evade you. I was part of their camp. I can lead you there."

Solina growled. She lifted one of her blades, keeping the other on his neck, and placed it against his cheek. A red line of blood appeared. He hissed and dared not move.

"Why?" she whispered. "Why, Nemes, do you betray your filthy kind?"

A throaty chuckle rose from him, then died when the blades cut deeper.

"They are filthy, my queen, you are right. I cleaned their filth. I watched my grandfather sweep their floors, chop their wood, empty their chamber pots, wash their clothes... and all the while, they never invited him to a feast, or a hunt, or a ball. He died alone, thin and overworked. The same happened to my father. The same would have happened to me, had you not burned their cursed court to the ground." He hissed a laugh. "The weredragons speak of their justice, their pity, their wisdom, yet they are cruel. They are weak. In Tiranor I see strength! When you invaded Requiem, I saw a proud, noble people, a strong race, a beautiful race, a race where the powerful can rise, where pity and weakness are crushed. This I seek to serve, not Requiem's cruel lords. Allow me to serve you, my fair queen, my goddess of pride and strength, and I will deliver you the Weredragon King and what remains of his court."

She stepped back and sheathed her blades. Nemes gasped and clutched at his throat and cheek where lines of blood ran. Solina nodded at her guards, and they promptly kicked Nemes down again. He lay on the floor before her, a boot pressed against his neck, spears against his back.

"Empty words," she said and spat. "Do you think I will trust you? Your kin are reptiles; you are merely a worm. I should kill you now. Guards! Hang his head upon Queen's Archway. Let the city—"

"You seek the nephilim!" cried Nemes, cheek pressed against the floor.

Her men had drawn their swords and raised them. Solina held up her hand, stopping them from landing the blows. They stood frozen, sabres held above the worm.

Solina's heart raced. She sucked in her breath and snarled. He knew. Sun God, the worm knew of the key. He knew of the Iron Door and the creatures who lurked behind it. She knelt above him, grabbed a fistful of his hair, and raised his head. She glared into his eyes.

"What do you know of this?" she hissed.

Blood covered his cheek. He still managed to grin.

"One of Elethor's spies made it to our camp," he said. "A man you took to Tarath Gehena. He babbled. The weredragons knew not what he meant. But I do." He licked blood off his lips. "I know of the dark arts. I know of the Palace of Whispers where the nephilim languish. I know of the tower where the key to the palace is guarded." His lips pulled back, revealing crooked teeth. "I studied their art. I studied the books of Legion, their demon lord. If you free the nephilim, I can help you tame them; I speak their tongue and know their lore. With the nephilim's power, you can crush not only the weredragons, but the world itself. I ask only to stand by your side and serve you as you reign, and to serve Lord Legion. Will you accept? Will you let me serve your glory, let me watch you crush the world under your heel? I will have my revenge. You will have the greatest empire this world has known."

Solina stared down at him. What game was he playing? What weredragon trick was this? The dangers raced through her mind. He could be a spy sent by Elethor, hoping to win her favor. He could be planning to lead her into a weredragon trap. He could be an assassin, waiting to catch her alone. He could be insane. Solina knew enough of weredragons to never trust them; she would not trust this one.

Unless...

Unless there was some way he could prove his loyalty, prove his worth. Solina narrowed her eyes and nodded.

Yes, she thought. *Yes, a weredragon would do nicely. If he dies, he dies. And if he lives... I will be too strong for an empire of reptiles to hurt me.*

"Stand him up!" she shouted to her guards. "Chain him. Collar him. We leave for Tarath Gehena—right now." As Nemes struggled, and as her men clasped him in chains, Solina smiled. "The weredragon will prove his loyalty. The weredragon will retrieve the key."

At once Nemes began to object, sweat upon his brow. "My queen! I... I am not a warrior, merely a priest of Lord Legion. I can help you speak with the nephilim, but to fetch the key, perhaps a soldier or—"

"Gag him!" Solina said. At once her men silenced him.

She walked across the hall toward her towering doors of gold and ivory. When she snapped her fingers, more guards stepped from between her columns to march behind her. The weredragon's chains rattled, and a thin smile twisted Solina's lips.

When her guards opened the doors of her hall, she stepped outside and stood above the palace stairway. The Faceless Guardians, the great statues of her dynasty, towered at her sides. She gazed down upon her realm. The Square of the Sun spread below her, its cobblestones golden in the sunset. The Sun God's Temple rose to her left, scratching the sky, while Queen's Archway rose before her across the square, golden sunbursts shimmering upon its bricks. Beyond the square rolled countless houses and streets, finally fading into desert and delta. And there in the west, beyond dune and mountain, rose the tower. There awaited her glory.

The sun dipped in the sky, a melting ball of orange. Its light caught the platinum capitals of the columns surrounding the square. They burned like a ring of torches, like the light of her heart, and like her glory that would soon bathe the world.

BAYRIN

He rocked on his heels, rolled his eyes, and blew out his breath.

"Lyana!" he said. "You've been reading for ages. Will you tell us what the book says?"

She sat before him on the rug, huddled against the cave wall. The ancient codex lay open before her, a tome the size of a suckling pig. Lyana raised her eyes from the pages, glared at him, and held her finger to her lips.

"Shh!" she said and returned her eyes to the book.

Bayrin groaned. "Lyana! Merciful stars, you heard what the spy said. War and destruction. End of the world. Toes stubbed left and right. Will you *please* quit your pleasure reading, stop shushing everyone, and tell me what the book says about these Falling Ones?"

Lyana groaned too, an enraged sound like a mother bear disturbed in her cave. She bared her teeth at him.

"Bayrin!" she said. "It's the *Fallen* Ones, or *nephilim* in their tongue. And maybe if you had spent fewer years chasing tavern wenches, and instead learned to read and write, you could study this book too."

He raised his hands in incredulity. "I know how to read and write!"

"Scribbling rude limericks on alehouse walls doesn't count, Bayrin. Now *please* shut that blabbering hole in your face and let me read."

Bayrin let out the longest, loudest sigh of his life. He turned to face Elethor, who stood at his side in the cave.

"Do you see, El? Do you see what I've had to put up with all my life? Bloody stars, since becoming queen, her tongue's only grown sharper; you could slice a wyvern to ribbons with it, no sword necessary."

He expected Elethor to laugh; his friend would always laugh whenever he'd mock Lyana. And yet today Elethor only stood solemnly, face frozen, staring down at the book.

Stars, Bayrin thought, *you can barely even see his face anymore behind that dreadful beard of his.*

Where was the Elethor he had known, the young man who'd laugh or groan at his jokes? Where was the Lyana who'd leap up to punch him, not just glare and bury her nose in a book? Bayrin would welcome groans and punches over this tense silence, this... this wait for an evil he didn't understand.

Stars, Mori, I miss you, he thought and closed his eyes. A lump filled his throat. He would have given the world to have her here now—to hold her, kiss her, never let her go. The beauty of silver rain on autumn leaves, of stars in purple sunset, of Requiem's fallen columns; all paled by the love, beauty, and goodness of Mori. He thought of her pink lips that would kiss him, her gray eyes looking up at him in wonder, the smoothness of her hair, and the purity of her heart as he held her against him.

Where are you now, Mori? Do you too have a cave to hide in, somebody to talk to?

Elethor believed her a prisoner in Tiranor; others whispered that the princess lay dead among Nova Vita's ruins. Bayrin knew that she lived; he refused to believe anything else. And if she *was* Solina's prisoner...

Bayrin clenched his fists. *If you hurt her, Solina, I will crush you in my claws, and I will burn down your city with my flames.*

He shook his head wildly.

"That's it!" he said. "I've waited long enough. I want to fly. I want to burn." He walked around the book, sat down by Lyana, and shoved her aside. "Let me see what this storybook of yours says."

"Bayrin!" she began and launched into a lecture, but he ignored her.

He stared down at the cracked old parchment. A baker's boy had saved the book, an ancient tome titled *Mythic Creatures of the Gray Age*, when fleeing the city. Upon its pages appeared illustrations of a thousand beasts: griffins, dragons, undead warriors, and every other creature that had ever walked, slithered, or flown. Lyana had the bestiary open to a chapter titled "Nephilim".

On the left page sprawled an illustration of a battle. In a valley stood an army of knights and archers. Toward them swarmed a host of rotting, twisted giants. Each stood thrice the height of a man. Each wore motley pieces of armor over rotten, scaly flesh. Some were bloated, their skin oozing; others were lanky and covered in spikes and horns. All bore tattered wings tipped with claws. A crimson serpent appeared upon their shields and helms, their sigil.

"Merciful stars," Bayrin said. "Ugly bastards, aren't they?" He leaned down and squinted at the opposite page. Lines of text appeared there, nearly too small for him to read. "What's it say here, Lyana?"

Sitting beside him, she groaned. "I thought you said you could read, Bayrin."

"I can! But these letters are so small and faded, and they're written in the tongue of Osanna, which only old priests and shriveled-up scribes can read anyway."

"Well *I* can read it, and the only thing shriveled up here is your brain. I'll read it for you; if you squint any harder, your eyes will be sucked into your skull." She shoved him aside, cleared her throat, and began to read from the page, translating the words as she went.

"Ten thousand years ago, the children of darkness emerged from their Abyss, crawled upon the earth, and took human wives. Thus were born the nephilim, the Fallen, the spawn of darkness dwellers and human wombs. Tall as giants they grew with rotted flesh, blazing eyes, and wings like black banners. They roamed the land, and their cries shook the mountains, and their claws tore down the walls of cities.

"The Ancient Ones, the desert dwellers whose daughters birthed the nephilim, raised a great host. They drove the nephilim into the Palace of Whispers, their great fortress in the desert, and sealed them in a deep chamber. An iron door they wrought for the prison, which they locked with an iron key.

"The fathers of the Fallen, demons of the Abyss, raged at the shame of their children. They took the iron key into Tarath Gehena, a dark tower, and placed guardians around it, so that none will see the shame of their fallen spawn."

When she finished reading, silence fell upon the room. Elethor stood frowning down at the book; he had not spoken all day. Lyana hugged herself.

"I don't get it," Bayrin said and furrowed his brow. "If you wanted to seal these critters, why even make a key? Why not just... build a door that cannot open, or destroy the key—why hide it in some tower?" He sighed. "Of course some madwoman like Solina would eventually seek this key. Didn't the Ancients have any sense?"

Lyana glared at him. "They had more sense than you, Bayrin, and so do most bricks. They didn't use a regular door. The nephilim would smash through it. They used a magical door, a Door of Sealing; nothing can break through those. The Ancients lived ten thousand years ago, before Tiranor and Requiem even existed, and they crafted many magical artifacts. If you had ever paid any attention to your tutors, instead of scribbling naked ladies into your books, you'd have known that." She reached into her pocket and drew a filigreed key, identical to the ones Elethor and Mori wore around their necks. "Seen this key before, Bayrin? That's right. The key to Requiem's library,

Chamber of Artifacts, and... the Gates of the Abyss." She shuddered and pocketed the key. "Doors of Sealing exist in Requiem too, though their history predates our own. Without a key, they're forever closed."

"Somebody should have used one of these keys on your mouth," Bayrin muttered. "Seal it shut forever." He sighed. "So, what do we do now? Fly south and try to grab the key before Soli? Or do we fly north and hide like our spy Leras politely opined?"

For once, Lyana had no answer. She looked up at Elethor; so did Bayrin. The young king stood above them, silent, staring at the book as if he hadn't heard the conversation. Dark circles hung under his eyes, and his brow was creased.

Damn it, Bayrin thought, *he's too young for wrinkles, too young to look so tired.* His friend was not yet thirty but lately, with that ridiculous new beard of his and long sleepless nights, he looked ten years older.

"What do you think, El?" he asked softly. He rose to his feet and stood by his friend. "What do you make of all this mess?"

For a long moment, Elethor remained silent and stared at the book. When finally the king looked up, Bayrin lost his breath; a deep, haunting pain lived in Elethor's eyes, a demon's shadow twisting underwater. For three moons now, Bayrin had never stopped thinking of Mori, and her memory tore at him; looking in Elethor's eyes, he knew that the king felt the same pain for myriads of souls, for all those who had died in Nova Vita under his reign.

"We cannot run," Elethor said. His lips were pale, his voice ghostly. "We cannot run now, or we will always run. If Solina awakes the sleeping nephilim, her wrath will flow across the world; there will be no more places to hide." He gripped the hilt of his sword. "We must fly south. We must burn her land and topple her court. But not alone. With the nephilim, Solina will crave the world entire, and the world entire must fight alongside our banners. Dragons. Salvanae. Griffins. Men. We must fight as one or the world will fall."

Lyana sighed, a deep sigh that clanked her armor. "Elethor, the world abandoned us," she said and touched her husband's arm. "We tried to rouse them. We begged for aid when wyverns flew. Our friends forsook us. Where were the salvanae when acid flowed? Where were griffins when Solina murdered our children? Where were men when our columns fell? We are Vir Requis; we have no friends in this world. All we have is our fire, our claws, and our roar."

Bayrin nodded and pounded his fist into his palm. "Damn right! We fly alone. To the Abyss with everyone else. I'm going to roast Soli's backside myself."

Elethor turned away from them, walked toward the cave's entrance, and stood staring outside at the rain. From below rose the sounds of the camp: babes crying, children playing, and elders praying. The soft light limned Elethor and silvered his armor. He stood silently, one hand on the pommel of his sword.

"No," he said finally, not turning back to face Bayrin and Lyana. "Too many died. Too many voices are silenced. A thousand live here, a last light for our race. How many more hide in the wilderness? Another thousand? A hundred? Even if Solina empties her land of wyverns, if she wakes the nephilim, they will slaughter us in the desert. We cannot face this threat alone." He turned back toward them. "Bayrin, my friend, fly west from here. Fly west, take this book with you, and raise the salvanae to our cause. Lyana, my love, fly east and rally men and griffins to our banner. Our neighbors did not fight the wyverns, it is true. They will fight to stop Solina from unleashing the nephilim, or the world will burn—their lands too."

Bayrin bit his lip and tugged at his hair. "I don't know, El. I don't know. Flying to raise help will take a while. If Solina is working to find this key, we can't waste time." He blew out his breath. "But I'll fly west if you ask me."

Mori might be hiding out west. Will I find her in the golden halls of the salvanae?

Lyana gripped her sword and raised her chin. "And I will fly east—to the courts of men and the isles of griffins. If aid lies in the east, I will bring it here."

They left the cave. They stood outside above the forest, and the rain pattered against their armor. Bayrin looked at his companions: his friend and king, tall and gaunt Elethor, all the joy and life gone from his eyes; his sister, now his queen, her hair fiery and her fists clutching her sword and dagger. A lump filled his throat.

I love you, Elethor, he thought. *I love you, Lyana. More than I can ever tell you.*

He opened his arms. They crushed him in their embrace. For long moments the three stood silently in the rain, holding one another. The rain was cold and their breath plumed warm against their cheeks. The lump refused to leave Bayrin's throat and his eyes stung.

If you hide in the west, Mori, I will find you. Wherever you are in this world, I will bring you here. I promise, Mori. I promise.

Nemes

They had left their wyverns below the mountain. This was holy ground; they would not profane it with beasts that drooled acid. They walked. It seemed like they walked for hours. The trail coiled up the stony mountainside; they must have climbed a league high. All around them rolled the desert, lifeless and golden, nothing but endless sand and rock.

The sun dipped below the horizon, a shimmering drop of blood, then vanished. Only their torches now lit the night, and still they climbed: a golden queen, fifty men in steel, and a prisoner robed in black. Step after step. Mile after mile. And still the mountain loomed.

They had chained his arms. The rusty iron chafed his skin, and Nemes bit down hard against the pain. He could endure some pain, some humiliation. For a hundred years, the weredragons had shamed his family, forcing them to clean plate, floor, and chamber pot. What was one more night of chains for a lifetime of glory?

I will fetch you your key, Solina, he thought and gritted his teeth. *I am no weakling, no craven like Leras. I will fetch the key, and I will stand by your side as you release the nephilim, as you crush the weredragons, as you rule the world. I will be no servant then, but a lord of your court.*

The night and trail stretched on.

It must have been midnight when they reached the mountaintop. Clouds covered the sky. A hot wind blew and their torches crackled. There above them loomed the tower, a coiling shard of obsidian like a rotten nerve. The torchlight flickered against it, and Nemes bared his teeth and hissed.

The night was hot, but an iciness flowed from this tower; it invaded his cloak, cut his skin, and froze his very bones. He felt his talisman burn against his chest; the iron serpent cried out for its lord. This tower itself, Nemes realized, was like a serpent of stone, rising from the earth to scream at the sky. His breath came fast. His blood pounded in his ears.

"Yes," Nemes whispered. "Yes, my lord! I come to serve you here. I come to seek your treasure. I am Nemes! I am your dark blade to thrust."

His head spun. For years in the Weredragon Court, he would study the books of Lord Legion. He would twist the animals of the forest to please his lord. He would suck and chew their innards to taste Legion's truth. He would study the Old Words and learn the dark magic: to cloak himself in shadow, to move in silence, to see where others were blind. And all the while, the stars of Requiem burned him, the cursed Draco Constellation that had doomed him to servitude. Yet here... here no stars shone. Here the power of Legion reigned.

Nemes fell and kissed the ground. Tears filled his eyes.

"I serve you, Fallen Lord!" he cried. "For years I sought you, Lord Legion, and now I kiss your holy earth. You will rise!"

Somewhere behind him, Solina spoke in disgust. "Stand him up. Toss him in. I'm tired of his whining."

Hands grabbed Nemes's shoulders and tugged him to his feet. They yanked his arms up, unlocked his chains, and shoved him forward. Nemes stumbled, looked over his shoulder, and hissed at the men. His wrists blazed with pain as the blood flowed back into them.

"You will show this place respect!" Nemes said. He snarled at the soldiers; fifty of them stood behind him, clad in steel, faces hidden behind their falcon visors. "You walk on holy ground, and I am the servant of Lord Legion. One day you will bow before me—and before him—or your bones will be his feast."

For an instant the guards hesitated. Nemes hissed again, savoring the taste of power, the scent of their fear. Then Solina marched toward him. Her eyes flashed, and her scarred lips twisted in a snarl. She grabbed a sabre from a guard and thrust it into his hands.

"Fetch me the key and you can hiss like a snake," she said. "For now you are still a worm. Go! Enter the darkness."

He stared into her eyes; he guessed that few men dared to. For a moment the two stared in silence, neither one blinking—a desert queen and a dark priest, for a moment locked in silent struggle.

Finally he snorted and tossed the sword down. It clattered against the ground.

"I need no blade," he said. "Return me my staff; it is more powerful than any shard of steel."

Still Solina dared not break the stare. Silent, she walked toward a soldier, grabbed the staff from him, and tossed it at Nemes. He caught it in one hand. Only then did he looked away, bowing theatrically.

"I shall see you again, my queen, with the key in my hand and the power of Lord Legion at our doorstep."

The guards made to drag him into the tower, but Nemes glared at them, a glare of all his simmering pain, rage, and lust. It held them back. Nemes straightened his back, smoothed his robes, and raised his head. He walked toward the tower. The doorway loomed before him.

Heart thrashing, he stepped inside.

He walked through darkness. The sounds of wind and men faded behind him, leaving only silence. Shadows parted before him, wisps like serpents of smoke. Nemes found himself in a round, stone chamber.

An obsidian table stood here, piled high with platters of raw, bloody ribs. The bones looked human and flesh still clung to them. An obese, naked man sat at the table, his back to Nemes. As the man feasted, grunting and huffing, blood and gobbets of flesh flew.

Nemes gripped his staff tight, lips curling in disgust, and a grunt fled his lips. The feasting man froze, squealed, and spun toward him.

Nemes gritted his teeth, struggling not to faint.

This was no man, he saw, but some creature of pale, fleshy rolls, his eyes mere slits. The creature's mouth opened, revealing sharp teeth and chunks of half-chewed flesh. Blood smeared his cheeks. He gave a shrill cry that Nemes thought could shatter glass.

"The key!" Nemes demanded. He gripped his staff, hand shaking. "Where is the key?"

The creature stared at him, blood dripping from his mouth. Slowly he raised a pudgy, clawed hand and pointed to the shadows, where Nemes could just make out a second doorway. With that, the creature returned to his meal. When Nemes looked at the table, he grunted in disgust. The bones *were* human; a severed head rotted among them.

Nemes stared, sucked in his breath, and found that his mouth was watering. He craved a taste. He craved to crack the bones in his mouth, suck the marrow, and feast. But there would be time for that later. Once he freed the nephilim, the earth itself would be his table, and the flesh of the world would lie rotting before him, ripe for the feeding.

Nemes turned away. He stepped through the second doorway and onto a staircase. The stairs wound upward, a corkscrew of bloodied bricks, and brought him into a second chamber.

A pile of raw, writhing flesh lay curled up here, draped in sagging gray skin. Nemes raised his staff, stepped forward, and frowned down at the wriggling mass.

The creature leaped up. Teeth shone and eyes blazed.

Daniel Arenson

Nemes leaped back, swiping his staff. The wood *cracked* against bone. The creature fell into the corner, scampered up, and howled with two bloated heads. It looked like a furless, muscular dog, but its two heads were humanoid—the wrinkled heads of waterlogged corpses. Black drool like ink filled its mouths. The creature raced toward him again, claws clattering against the floor.

Nemes snarled and swung his staff. It hit one of the dog's heads. The second head latched onto Nemes's shoulder, and teeth drove into him, stinging like a thousand fires.

He screamed. He drove his staff into the biting head. The creature squealed but would not release him. The second head bit his left arm, and blood spilled to the floor.

No. No! I have not flown through fire and rain and sand to die here.

He looked around the chamber. Would there be room enough? Would the tower collapse around him? The teeth drove deeper and he screamed again. He had no choice.

Nemes summoned his magic, the ancient magic of Requiem that blessed even him, the kingdom's lost son. He shifted into a dragon.

Gray scales rose across him, hard and smooth as bones. The canine creature howled and fell to the floor. Wings sprouted from Nemes's back and slammed against the walls. He ballooned like a leech sucking blood. Horns grew from his head and hit the ceiling. A tail flailed beneath him. He filled the chamber, barely able to move. The two-headed dog whimpered below him; it now seemed no larger than a rat.

Nemes spewed his fire.

The white flames crashed against the dog, and the creature screamed, a scream like children dying, like demons burning. It writhed. Its skin melted. Its blood boiled. Nemes kept blowing his fire, and the creature blazed, but still it squirmed and screamed and begged. Soon nothing remained of it but bones, but it would not die.

Nemes snarled. He let his flames die. He slammed down his claws and crushed the burnt, bony remains. He felt them moving under his foot, and he ground them down. Bones snapped and finally the creature's screams died to a whimper... then went silent.

When he shifted back into human form, Nemes groaned. His shoulder and arm were a bloody mess. He doffed his cloak, examined the wounds, and felt faint. As his heart thrashed, the blood pulsed and spurted. Head spinning, Nemes rummaged through his cloak's pockets, produced his old leather pouch, and pulled out string and needle. He had used these tools often: sewing little creations from the animals he caught in the forests, mismatching heads and bodies and

legs, creating new animals that were stronger and more beautiful.
Today he sewed himself, fingers coated with blood. When his wounds
were sewn shut, they reminded him of his creatures, of the snakes with
the heads of squirrels and the ravens with bat wings. He tore off strips
of his cloak, bandaged the stitched wounds, and licked the blood off
his fingers.

He looked around the room, seeking the key. Nothing but
blood and burnt remains were here, staining the brick walls and floor.
A doorway led back to another staircase; the stairs wound up into
shadows. Nemes left the room and kept climbing.

When he entered the third floor, he felt the blood leave his face.
Disgust rose in him. The stench of rot filled his nostrils and roiled his
belly.

Rusted blades rose from the room's floors, walls, and ceilings
like iron brambles; old blood coated them. Among this rusted maze, a
woman's corpse sat in a chair, swarming with worms. Nemes had
once dug up a week-old corpse; this woman reminded him of that
maggoty old flesh. Her head hung low, the flesh so rotted, the skull
peeked through. Her eyes were gone; larvae squirmed in the sockets.
Jagged growths sprouted from her like horns, mimicking the spikes
that rose from the floor; they were colored a sickly green and sprinkled
with white splotches.

The woman was dead, but her belly was slashed open, revealing
a fetus that squirmed and sucked for air. The coiled, red creature
raised his eyes, stared at Nemes, and let out a wail. Sharp teeth lined
his mouth, and his eyes burned red. The fetus tugged dangling veins
inside the womb, and his dead, rotten mother rose to her feet. The
fetus grabbed and tugged other veins; his dead host began to shuffle
forward.

Nemes wanted to shift into a dragon, to burn the aberration
down. Yet he could not; the blades thrust out from every direction,
filling the room with rusted metal. If he shifted, they would pierce
him like an iron maiden. He hissed and raised his staff. The fetus
screamed, eyes blazing, and moved his dead mother forward like a
puppeteer. The fetus tugged a vein, and his mother swung a clawed
hand.

Nemes parried with his staff. The corpse's claws scratched
grooves into the wood. The fetus shrieked and drove his host
forward. The rusted horns that grew across the mother, diseased
tumors like blades, thrust toward Nemes. He leaped aside, dodging
the mother's growths, only to scratch his thigh against a blade that
rose from the floor.

A throaty, bubbling chuckle rose from the fetus. The little beast licked his lips in delight. He tugged the veins mightily, and the mother lurched toward Nemes, claws swinging and horns thrusting.

Nemes sidestepped, sliced his cloak on another blade, and swung his staff. The wood cracked against the mother's head. The corpse's neck ripped and centipedes fled from it. The head dangled. The fetus howled in rage. The babe drove the corpse forward, and a rusted growth—one that sprouted from the mother's chest—drove into Nemes's shoulder.

Nemes grunted, wound blazing, and kicked. His foot hit the fetus inside the sliced womb. The creature screamed, bit at his boot, and Nemes screamed too; the small teeth pierced his skin. He swung his staff again, hitting the mother's dangling head. The blow tore the rotted head off, and the mother crashed down. The rusty blades that rose from the floor pierced her chest. Blood gushed. The fetus screeched.

"You *killed* her!" cried the parasite inside the fallen body. His voice was shrill, demonic, a voice like wind through canyons and demons in the deep. "You *killed* my mother!"

Nemes could barely move. He stood panting, wounds blazing and blood dripping. Around him spread the brambles of blades. The fetus rose from the womb, dripping mucus. His umbilical cord ripped. The red, writhing creature leaped up, flew through the air, and grabbed onto Nemes's torso.

"You will be my new host!" the fetus screamed. He began slashing at Nemes's stomach, ripping his cloak and tearing his skin. "I will enter you. Let me in. You will be my mother!"

Nemes screamed. He grabbed the slimy parasite. He tried to rip it off, but the beast was too slippery, too squirming. The fetus began to bite at him. With bloody fingers, Nemes held the snapping head back. Such strength filled the creature; he was strong as a grown man.

"I will live inside you!" the aborted fetus screamed.

Nemes stumbled toward a wall bristly with blades. He pitched forward toward the spikes. A blade impaled the fetus and blood poured.

"Mother!" the babe cried. "Mother, it hurts, it stabs us! Why does he kill us?"

Nemes stumbled backward, clutching at his wounds. The fetus remained upon the wall, skewered on the blade. The creature writhed. He wept. Suddenly he seemed to Nemes not a demon spawn, but a human child, scared and hurt and dying.

"Mother," the babe whispered... and then his head slumped. He hung still like a slab on a meat hook.

Nemes limped toward a door in the back. His head swam and he trembled with blood loss. He trudged upstairs, holding the wall and smearing blood across it. He entered the fourth floor of the tower.

A choked gasp fled his lips.

No horror—not the obese diner, not the twisted dog, not the fetus in his host—could prepare Nemes for this.

Tears filled his eyes.

"No," he whispered and fell to his knees. "Please, no."

Lying on the floor before him, gasping and bleeding and pale, was his father.

The old man opened his mouth. His teeth were gone. His lips were dry. He tried to speak, sputtered, and whispered.

"S-son." He lifted a skeletal hand. Sweat covered his brow. "Son, please... please save me."

Nemes crawled toward his father and touched his forehead. It was blazing hot. His father was feverish, so frail his skin draped across his bones. His eyes were sunken, and a dry cough rattled in his chest. He wore only canvas breeches and he trembled.

"Father!" Nemes said. He doffed his cloak and wrapped it around the old man. "I'm here. Your son is here."

His father tried to smile, then coughed and grimaced. Blood stained his lips; more speckled his chest. He touched Nemes's cheek with shaking, twisted fingers.

"My son. You must take the key. You must take it from me. You—"

Coughing seized him, and he spat more blood.

No, Nemes thought. His fists clenched. *No! This cannot be. Cannot!*

"I saw you die!" Nemes said, tears burning in his eyes. "You died in the courts of Requiem. You died with a broom in your hands. The cruel king and princes did not even know; they did not care. I buried you! I buried you myself." He raised his head and howled at the ceiling. "What cruel mockery is this? How dare you show me this illusion!"

Tears burned down Nemes's cheeks. His father wiped them away, smiling thinly. His hair had once been dark and thick; now it was white and wispy, nearly all gone from his scalp.

"I live again," the old man said. "I died; it is true. He brought me back to life. Lord Legion. The prophet of the Fallen. He breathed new life into my lungs, and filled my heart with blood to pump, and placed me here. For you, Nemes. For you. To give you the key so you may free him."

Nemes shook as he held his father. The man felt so frail in his arms, his bones so brittle, likely to snap in an embrace.

"I will take you out of here, Father," he said. "I promise. Once we give the queen the key, she will reward us. We will be powerful, no longer servants. You will never serve again, I promise you." He let out a sob. "You will live in a palace of gold, and King Elethor will serve you, a slave in irons."

Nemes snarled, imagining it. With the gold Solina gave him, he would build a great hall, a palace larger than the fallen court of Requiem. He would build a throne for his father and force cruel Elethor to kneel before it, to clean the floors, to beg for mercy from the whips. He would build a dungeon for Lyana, chain her underground, and invade her body whenever he pleased. He would hurt her—like she had hurt him—and make her beg. The key would give him that.

"Where is it, Father?" he whispered. "Where is the key?"

The old man struggled to speak. Only a hoarse gasp left his throat. His body trembled and his veins pulsed. Nemes could feel the man's heart fluttering like a trapped bird. His father's skeletal hand rose, then pointed down at his belly. He tried to speak again, but only coughed and trembled.

"What is it, Father?" Nemes whispered.

His father pulled open the cloak, revealing his pale torso. He grabbed Nemes's hand, pulled it down, and placed it against his stomach.

Nemes sucked in his breath. His eyes stung.

"Please, Nemes," his father whispered. "Take it out. Cut it from me. Take the key."

Beneath his father's skin, hard inside his belly, Nemes felt the outline of the key.

"No," Nemes whispered. Tears blurred his eyes. "I cannot."

"You must." His father clutched his wrist. "Lord Legion will bless you. Cut the key out. Let me die again. My death will free me from this prison; I will die in your arms, knowing that you will rise to glory." Tears streamed down his wrinkled cheeks. "My son—the first of our family to rise to greatness."

Nemes clenched his jaw. His breath shook. *No. No!* He could not. How could he? To kill his father? The vile court of Requiem had killed his father! The man lived again; how could Nemes kill him for his vainglory?

He howled to the ceiling. His roar shook the tower.

"No! I cannot. I will not!" He shook his fists. "Do not ask me this! Please, Lord Legion. I beg you. I serve you. Anything but this! Do not ask me to prove my loyalty this way."

A low, rumbling laugh rose from the floor, bubbling up from the depths like tar. The walls trembled and dust rained. The tower itself was laughing, Nemes realized; it was a living thing, a demon of stone and dark magic and blood.

"Please," Nemes whispered.

A rumble shook the floor. The bricks creaked. A screech ran through the walls, rising as a voice, a shriek, a cry of endless darkness and wonder.

"You will prove your loyalty, Nemes of Requiem!" rose the cry of the tower, a sound like steam from a kettle. The walls pulsed. Blood dripped between the bricks. "You will slice him open. You will dissect him. Why do you think, Nemes, that you spent years in the forest, spent years cutting open your animals? For this! For this day. To free me. To free Lord Legion and his Fallen Horde. Slice him! Dissect him! Cut the key from his innards and raise it in glory!"

Nemes's breath shook. His hands trembled. His eyes burned with tears. He reached to his belt and drew the Iron Claw, the blade he'd used in the forest so many times.

"Forgive me, Father..."

He sobbed as he drove the blade down.

His father screamed.

Nemes wept as he worked.

When his father lay dead, Nemes stood and raised the bloody key and screamed.

"I passed the test!" His tears mingled with his blood. "I have the key! I am Nemes, a servant of Legion! The nephilim will swarm again, and the weredragons will die. They will beg and weep and I will crush them for their sins!"

He left the chamber, laughing and weeping, key held high. As he descended the stairs, he uttered the Old Words, and the shadows of his lord cloaked him. The smoky serpents writhed around him, a new cloak, a mantle of his glory. Soon the nephilim themselves would flow around him.

He passed the chamber where the mother lay dead, her babe impaled. He passed the chamber where the dog lay crushed and burnt. He entered the ground floor where the obese diner hissed and glared and smacked his lips. Nemes approached the demon, thrust his Iron Claw forward, and sliced the creature open from collarbone to navel. He laughed as bloody snakes fled the beast, leaving its sagging skin like creatures hatching from an egg. Now it was Nemes who feasted at this table. Now it was Nemes who ruled this tower and its secrets.

He stepped outside into the night, laughed, and raised the key. Lighting crashed into it, lighting the desert. Nemes saw Solina, her men, the endless leagues of sand and rock. Wind shrieked, blowing back his hair.

"The key, Nemes!" Solina shouted in the storm. She reached out for it. "Hand me the key and the trophies of Tiranor will be yours."

He stood in the tower doorway, laughing, the wind roaring. The shadows swirled and laughed around him.

"The key!" he said. "You want the key."

And why should he share it? Why should he, Nemes, give this desert queen her prize?

I can free the nephilim myself! This power can be mine, not hers. Why should I still serve? For years I knelt! For years I groveled. Now Nemes can rule; with the nephilim, no power could oppose me.

"The key, Nemes!" Solina demanded.

He laughed and snarled. "Why should I give it to you? Will you beg me, Solina? Will you kneel and—"

She leaped toward him.

Her blade flashed.

Nemes tried to pull back. She was so fast. She was a streak of gold and steel.

He screamed.

When her blade severed his arm, blood sprayed in a mist. His arm tumbled. His hand still clutched the key when it hit the ground.

"You will die for this!" Nemes screamed, clutching the stump.

Solina knelt by his severed arm. She wrenched the key free from his fingers.

"Chain him up!" she shouted to her men. "Drag him in irons to Irys. He will see the glory of the nephilim before we hang him to die upon the walls."

The guards stepped toward him, chains in their hands. Nemes hissed and turned to flee. He fell. His blood spurted. Hands grabbed him, yanked him up, and Nemes screamed before his eyes rolled back and darkness spread across him.

My glory... my power... I promised it to him.

"I'm sorry, Father," he whispered. "I'm sorry..."

Demons laughed, and dark claws grabbed him, and his soul sank into a long black night.

TREALE

"Pomegranates, fresh pomegranates, grab one to eat!" cried the boy.

He stood upon the banks of the River Pallan, a scrawny thing with deep golden skin, holding a basket laden with the red treasures.

"Grab a pomegranate, a copper a fruit!" he shouted.

Around the boy, a dozen other children stood upon the boardwalk, hawking their own wares from baskets. Behind them, longships rowed up and down the river, laden with more baskets and crates of goods.

"Carobs, dried carobs!"

"Fresh oysters, grab them while they're fresh!"

"Seashell bracelets for fertility! Wear them in bed for healthy babes!"

Treale stood upon the cobbled boardwalk, shaded under the awning of a chandlery. She wore her dark cloak draped around her and hid her midnight hair and eyes—foreign in this land of platinum hair and blue eyes—under her hood. The scents of the foods filled her nostrils. Her stomach growled and her mouth watered. She had not eaten in... how long had it been? She could barely remember; certainly she had eaten nothing since landing in Irys yesterday. Fingers trembling with hunger, she reached into her pocket, fished around, and produced a single copper coin. It was all the money she had in the world—not enough for a nice fish or crab, even if she had a place to cook them—but perhaps enough for a pomegranate.

She walked onto the boardwalk, leaped back as a peddler came trundling down upon his donkey-drawn cart, and kept moving. When she reached the boy hawking pomegranates, she held out her coin in her palm.

"I'll have one if you please," she spoke from the shadows of her hood.

The boy took the coin, squinted at it, and Treale felt faint. This was a coin from Requiem; she had smoothed its surface, effacing its image and lettering, but would the boy still recognize its origin? Would he sound the alarm and shout "Weredragon, weredragon!" for the city to hear?

"It's good copper," Treale said. "An old coin, but solid metal and pure. Feel its weight. That's worth two pomegranates. You have to sell me two."

Her legs trembled with hunger as the boy squinted at the coin. Treale had never felt so lowly. Only moons ago, she had been a lady of Requiem's courts, and now... now she trembled before a boy half her age, so weak with hunger she nearly wept.

Finally the boy nodded, pocketed the coin, and offered her the basket of fruit. Not a moment later, Treale crouched between a brothel and a shoemaker's shop, scooping seeds from a split pomegranate and eating so fast she nearly choked. When her meal was done, she stuffed the second pomegranate into her cloak's pocket. Though her stomach still rumbled with hunger, she would save the second fruit for later.

"It might be a while until you find more food, Treale Oldnale," she whispered to herself. "The days of feasting at the side of kings are over."

She rose to her feet, pulled her hood low, and began walking down the street. People crowded around her: loomers bearing baskets of fabrics, barefoot children scuffling with wooden swords, mothers nursing their babes, and bare-chested masons lugging packs full of bricks. Shops and stalls lined the roadsides. A child on a donkey knocked into a stall, spilling a thousand live crabs that scurried across the cobblestones. The crabmonger shouted and began a futile chase for his catch; Treale managed to grab one crab and stuff it into her pocket for later. The clang of hammers on anvils rose from smithies, laughter and grunts rose from brothels, and screams rose from surgeons' shops where tongs pulled teeth and needles stitched wounds. The sun pounded the city; the air felt like thick soup rank with the scents of fish, oil, tallow, and dried fruits.

Treale's head still spun to see so many people; they seemed to her like ants scurrying through tunnels. She missed the open spaces of Oldnale Farms: the rolling fields, the sunset over the forests, and the clear skies where she would fly with her brothers. And she missed Nova Vita, capital of Requiem where her friend Mori had lived: its wide streets, its marble columns that soared between birches, its music of harps that rose from silver temples.

That land is gone, she thought and her eyes stung. *The farms have burned, and the city has fallen, but you still live, Mori. There is still some starlight in the world.*

She made her way through the crowds, her black robes searing hot and swirling around her, until she reached the mouth of an alley, and before her spread the Square of the Sun.

The cobbled expanse stretched out like a sea of stone. Columns surrounded the square, and upon each capital, a wyvern perched and snarled. Soldiers marched here, their helms shaped like cranes and falcons and eagles, their breastplates glimmering with golden sunbursts. Their spears clanked against the cobblestones and their songs echoed inside their helms. Beyond the soldiers rose the monuments of Tiranor's glory: the great Queen's Archway, two hundred feet tall, its limestone engraved with sunburst reliefs; the Temple of the Sun, its columns capped with platinum; the great statue of Solina, fifty feet tall, from whose pedestal Treale had watched Mori beaten; and the Palace of Phoebus upon a great dais, its doors flanked with stone guardians, its glory tapering into the Tower of Akartum, the tallest steeple in Tiranor and perhaps the world.

Treale swallowed. *This is the most dangerous place upon this world,* she thought. *This is the heart of Tiranor's wrath and might. This is where I must walk.*

She took a deep breath, wrapped her cloak tight around her, and entered the square.

After only three steps, she held her breath and looked around, ready to scurry back into the alley. Yet the soldiers kept marching, and the wyverns kept their vigil upon the columns, and crows circled above and cawed as ever. Treale swallowed again, reached under her cloak, and grabbed the amulet she wore—a golden sheaf of wheat, the sigil of her house. That house had fallen, but Treale was still an Oldnale, and the touch of the gold soothed her. She kept walking.

She moved along the outskirts of the square, staying near the columns that ringed it. She tried to keep staring ahead toward the palace, but couldn't help it; as she passed near a column, she peeked up at the wyvern that perched upon its capital. The beast glared down, and a glob of its drool fell to burn a hole into the ground. Its tail flapped, but its wings remained still.

Sweat dripped down Treale's back. She remembered those wyverns swarming across Nova Vita, felling dragons from the sky. She wanted to shift into a dragon, to burn them, to kill as many as she could before they took her down.

Requiem will have its revenge, she swore. She clutched her amulet so hard it nearly pierced her palm. *That I swear to you, Solina. I will not forget your crimes. But not now. Not this day. Today is for Mori.*

She was halfway to the palace when the guards spotted her. Falcon helms turned toward her, creaking together. Spear shafts slammed against cobblestones. Perhaps sensing the men's unease, the wyverns atop the columns shifted and ruffled their wings. Treale froze, hood pulled low. Her heart thrashed and she clutched her amulet tighter.

Be brave, Treale, she thought. Her throat constricted and she could barely breathe. *Be brave like King Elethor. You fled the last danger; today you will be strong.*

A guard detached from his phalanx and came marching toward her. He bore a round shield, and a red cape fluttered behind him. Treale fought down the urge to flee, though her knees shook and she had to force her breath through clenched teeth.

"What do you seek here?" the guard called.

Treale curtsied in the manner of Osanna. "I seek the weredragon, my lord." She spoke with her best Osannan accent, knowing she would never pass for a Tiran. "I come to see the beast."

When the guard reached her, he tugged her hood back. He cursed, and behind his falcon visor, his eyes narrowed. Her black hair, olive skin, and dark eyes were as foreign in this land as hippopotamuses—beasts that filled the Pallan—would be in Requiem.

"Osannan dog," the guard said. "You scum have been washing up on our shores and swarming our streets."

Treale let out a shaky breath. *Thank the stars.* Her accent had fooled him; he thought her a daughter of Osanna, that war-torn land of eastern men, and not a child of Requiem. Tirans perhaps hated the former, but they slaughtered the latter.

"My lord." She gave another quick curtsy. "I might be scum from the sea, but even scum hates the wretchedness of weredragons." She forced a snarl. "The weredragons burned my village in Osanna. They killed my father. He was a jailor in our land. Now I seek to be a jailor too—not in the ruins of my Osannan town, but here in this land of southern glory. You keep a weredragon imprisoned beneath the palace; I saw it chained and whipped yesterday. If you'll have me, I will join your rank. I will help you guard the beast, shackle it, and whip it too." She clenched her fists. "I would enjoy beating it bloody."

The guard widened his eyes, silent for a moment, then burst out laughing. Treale stood, barely daring to breathe. It was a long moment before the guard could speak again.

"You!" he finally said. "You—a dog from Osanna, a land of flea-ridden woolmongers—want to serve in the Palace of Phoebus?"

He raised his spear. "Find yourself a brothel to spread your legs in. That is all your kind is good for, whore. Be thankful we even let you do that much; I say we should butcher your kind like weredragons." He raised his visor, revealing a leathery face, and spat at her feet. "Kneel and clean the cobblestones of my spit; that's what you Osannan scum are worth."

Treale stood frozen, rage flaring within her. She was a daughter of a great lord. She had flown by the King of Requiem in battle. She was a warrior, a woman of starlight, a—

You are alone, a voice whispered inside her. *Your home is gone; your father is dead and probably your king. Whatever nobility you once claimed is lost.*

She bit down on her anger. If saving Mori meant giving up some pride, well... she had enough of that pride to give.

She knelt. She cleaned the cobblestones with the hem of her cloak. She clenched her jaw and tried to ignore the burning in her eyes.

When she rose to her feet, she bowed her head and spoke softly.

"I will clean for you in the dungeon, if you let me. If I cannot stand there as a guard, let me serve you as a maid. I can clean. I can cook for jailors. But one thing I insist upon." She raised her eyes and met his gaze. "I want to work near the weredragon's cell. Her people burned my village. I will watch her suffer and I will hear her scream."

The guard looked over his shoulder at his phalanx, then back to Treale. He reached into her cloak, cupped her breast, and squeezed hard. Treale sucked in her breath and froze, daring not move. She wanted to shift, she wanted to burn him, she wanted to run... yet she could only stand here frozen between her pride and Mori.

"Yesss," the guard said slowly, crushing her in his hand. "Yes, I think we might just find you some work underground. There are many cobblestones there for you to clean."

He released her, and Treale gasped with the pain, and her legs shook.

Think of King Elethor, she told herself. *Think of how you lay by his side, kissed his cheek, and flew with him. Think of the courage he gave you.*

"Th-thank you, my lord!" she said to the guard. "I... I will serve Tiranor as best I can."

He snorted. "Yes, we'll make sure that you do. Quite often and quite well."

He grabbed her arm, digging his fingers so deep Treale gasped and thought he'd tear her skin. He began dragging her across the square, moving closer to the palace. Treale struggled to match his wide strides; when once she fell, he dragged her until she could walk again.

Think of King Elethor. Think of how you kissed his cheek. Think of the stars of Requiem; they shine here too.

Soon the palace loomed above them. The staircase rose hundreds of steps, ending with towering doors of ivory flanked by faceless statues, each larger than a dragon. Above this gateway rose walls and towers of limestone; the steeples clawed the sky. Treale was expecting a long climb, but the guards dragged her past this staircase toward a pathway alongside the palace. They walked along walls lined with archers. Fig and carob trees rose to her left; to her right rose the stone of Tiranor's center of power.

Finally they reached a small archway filled with a wooden door; a back entrance. More guardsmen waited here, spears crossed. The leathery-faced guard dragged Treale through the doorway and into the palace.

They moved through chambers and halls. The tiles gleamed white, and golden filigrees covered granite columns. Treale was hoping to see more of the palace; if any in Requiem still lived and hoped to fight, they would need the layout of this place. The guard, however, soon dragged her onto a staircase that plunged underground.

They descended for what seemed like miles, coiling deeper and deeper into darkness. Candles lit the rough walls. The steps were so narrow and craggy Treale nearly fell. Outside the palace, the sun had pounded her, and the heat had coiled around her like serpents. Here, as they descended, the air grew so cold that Treale shivered. Stairs led to tunnels, then stairs again, then doorways and more tunnels. This place reminded her of the labyrinth beneath Nova Vita where she and Mori would read books; these halls were just as dark and twisting. But Requiem's tunnels had also been warm and dry and safe. This place reeked of mold and echoed with distant screams.

Finally, after what seemed an hour of plunging, they reached a hall lined with cells, and those distant screams exploded like demons of sound.

Solina's dungeon, Treale thought and shivered.

"Sharik!" shouted the guard who held her arm. "Sharik, damn you. Come, boy. I have a treat for you."

At first Treale was sure the guard was calling his dog. When a burly, bald man came trundling up the tunnel, Treale realized: This was Sharik, and she was the treat.

"Sharik here, Sharik want treat," rumbled the man. "Give to Sharik!"

He had but three teeth, and moles covered his pasty lump of a head. He was wide and fierce-looking as a bull; a golden ring even pierced his flat nose. He wore a tattered canvas tunic, and a ring of keys jangled on his belt. His flesh was lumpy and pale like old turnips; Treale doubted the man had seen sunlight in a year.

The guard shoved Treale toward him, and Sharik caught her. The brute dug yellow, cracked fingernails into her arm. His breath assailed her, scented of rot. His nose sniffed at her cheek, and his tongue thrust out. Treale pulled back an inch, narrowly dodging the wet appendage.

"Give this one a job, Sharik," said the guard and laughed. "Have her empty your chamber pot, mop the blood off the floors, or even warm your bed at night if you please. I'll come for her some nights; on those nights she's mine. Do you understand, Sharik?"

The bullish man drooled and huffed. "Sharik likes treats."

He reached into Treale's cloak and tried to grope her. She struggled in his grasp, and he shoved her, then backhanded her. Pain exploded. White light flashed. She hit a wall, and Sharik raised his fist again.

"Sharik, no!" said the guard. "I want her beautiful. Do not scar this one. She is my gift to you; keep her pretty."

Sharik snarled, but when the guard reached for his sword, the jailor lowered his gaze and grumbled under his breath. His fingers still dug into her arm, so strong she thought he might break her bone. When the guard turned to leave, Treale almost wanted to call after him. *No, don't leave me here, don't leave me with this man, with these screams, with this smell of blood.* Yet she remained silent. Mori was somewhere here in this nightmare; Treale would stay, and she would save her.

"Come," Sharik grumbled, his voice like cascading stones. "Follow Sharik. Work for you."

He pulled her down the hall, trundling like a bear. Treale dragged behind him, and as they passed along the cells, she nearly gagged. She bit down on a scream.

Stars, no... how could such terror exist? Stars, how could such evil lurk in this world?

Prisoners filled the cells, broken and shackled and turned into wrecks of humanity. One man hung from chains, his legs cut off and the stumps still dripping. In another cell, children hung upon the walls, their skin burned off, their eyes pleading and their mouths gagged. In a third cell, a jailor was busy stretching a man on the rack;

the prisoner howled, his arms dislocated. Treale wanted to close her eyes. She wanted to weep. She wanted to fall and curl up and never look at these horrors again. Yet she forced herself to look. Somewhere, in one of these cells, Mori languished.

Stars, Mori, I'm so sorry. Now Treale could not help it; tears streamed down her cheeks. *I'm so sorry you are here.*

Yet where *was* the princess? Before Treale could find her, Sharik pulled her into a cell. This one was empty. Chains hung from the ceiling and fresh blood and hair covered the floor. For a moment, Treale was sure the jailor would imprison her here, and she made to flee, but he grabbed her and grunted.

"Clean!" he said. "Clean cell. Clean floor."

He stepped back into the hall, grabbed a bucket and rags, and shoved them at her.

"Clean! Clean and you eat later. Clean floor."

When Treale hesitated, Sharik grabbed a whip from the wall. Before Treale could react, he landed a blow across her shoulder. She yelped. The whip lashed through her cloak and tore her skin.

"Clean!" Sharik said. "Clean floor. Make clean for next prisoner."

Her welt blazing, her eyes still damp, Treale knelt. She grabbed a rag and dipped it into the bucket of water. She began to scrub.

"Faster!" Sharik said and his whip landed again. Treale yelped, her back blazing, and cleaned faster.

"When I'm done cleaning," she said and dared to look up, "I want to see the weredragon. I—"

The whip landed a third time, blazing against her from shoulder to tailbone. Treale arched her back and yowled with the pain. Sharik grumbled and clenched his fists.

"Speak again and Sharik take your teeth. Clean. Faster."

Treale cleaned. She did not speak again.

When the cell's floor was clean and the rags bloody, Sharik grabbed her by the hair. He yanked her up and dragged her out into the hallway. Treale yelped, her hair tearing in his paws, but he only tugged harder. He dragged her into a second chamber, closed the oak door, and locked it behind them.

This must have been his home, though it was barely better than the prisoners' cells. The chamber was rough and bare. It contained only a straw bed, a table laden with candles and dirty dishes, a chamber pot, and a chest of old rags.

"You sleep on floor," Sharik said. "Sleep!"

He raised his whip. Treale clenched her fists behind her back. She was a slight woman, thin and short and not very strong, and he was thrice her size. But she was young, she was fast, and she could fight him. There was no room to shift here, but she could grab his whip and strangle him, or gouge out his eyes, or....

No, she told herself. *Even if you can defeat him, Treale Oldnale, he'd holler and guards will swarm here. Save Mori. Even if you must give up some pride. You might sleep on a floor this night, but Mori sleeps in chains.*

She lay down on the floor like an obedient pup, hugged her knees, and looked up at Sharik. He stared down at her, his feet by her head, their nails cracked and moldy. Finally he grunted in approval, lolloped toward his bed, and climbed in. Soon the man was snoring like a saw, his drool seeping.

Treale rose to her feet. Her heart raced. The candles still burned upon the table, casting soft light. She tiptoed toward the bed and stared down at Sharik.

His keys.

They still dangled from his belt, each one longer than her hand. If Mori languished in this prison, one of these keys would open her cell. Holding her breath, Treale reached toward the ring of them.

Sharik snorted and rolled over, burying the keys under his girth.

Treale cursed this dungeon, cursed the gods, cursed every grain of sand in this desert and every brick in this dungeon. She reached around the brute, but he would not stir. She tried to roll him over; he would not wake or move. He kept drooling, and his snores kept rising, and the keys remained trapped.

Finally Treale fell to the floor, closed her eyes, and trembled. She was so weak, so tired; she could barely summon the will to breathe. Her belly ached with hunger. Sharik had never fed her as promised, and she felt too weak to crack open her second pomegranate. Her wounds blazed. Worst of all, the images of the prisoners would not leave her: their anguished eyes, their broken flesh, their seeping blood. Again and again, she saw Mori outside the palace gates, frail and screaming as they beat her.

"I will find you, Mori," she whispered into the darkness. "If not tonight, then tomorrow, or the day after, but I swear to you, I will find you, and I will free you."

She looked up at Sharik again; he had not budged, and his snores rose louder than ever. Treale wanted to try to move him again; with all her strength, perhaps she could roll him onto the floor, but what if he woke and beat her? He would soon roll over on his own,

Treale told herself. After all, how comfortable could it be, sleeping on his keys? She had to wait but a moment longer. Maybe two moments. Maybe...

Her eyes closed. Blackness tugged at her. She lay, curled up and shivering, and slumber pulled her into a deep, dark nightmare of mangled bodies and shrieking falcons of steel.

SOLINA

She flew through the night, a phoenix of crackling fire and claws of molten steel. The desert streamed below her. She opened her beak and cawed to the darkness. She was fire. She was gold. She was might. She called to her lord the Sun God, and his glory rose from the eastern dunes to kindle her empire. The sand and clouds burned with his might. She flew through the dawn, a bird of beauty, a light to banish the darkness.

She had brought this fire to Requiem; the weredragons had doused it with their dark magic. She had brought wyverns and acid to their halls; they had fled.

But they cannot fight the nephilim. They cannot flee my long arm. Their halls are fallen; their skulls will be mine.

She had left her men in Irys, her oasis jewel. Today she flew alone. Today was a day of her glory.

I was born for today. You will see my power, Elethor. You will see my light.

The agony rose inside her, twisting like demon claws in her womb. A child had grown there, a life she had created with Elethor. The small light had died; her soul had extinguished with it. In her dreams, he cried to her, her son of golden skin and blue eyes, a paragon of light, a holy son—a gift to the world.

For you, she thought. *For you I burn. For you I conquer. They killed you, my son. The weredragons killed you, and I will slaughter them all, and it will not be enough. For you I raise this army; in your memory the nephilim shall rise.*

She screamed to the sky, wings showering flame.

The mountain rose before her in the south, an edifice of stone under a yellow sky. It rose taller than the peaks of Amarath Mountains where she had crushed the Weredragon Army. It rose taller than the great mountains of Ranin where she would make love to

Elethor in their youth. It rose like her empire, undying, eternally strong.

When she flew closer, she saw that towers, archways, and walls covered the mountain, ancient beyond reckoning, faded into mere hints of their past glory. Steeples, once topped with battlements, now rose crumbling like melted candles. Archways, once gleaming in welcome, now rose craggy like the mouths of caves. Walls, once bright with soldiers and banners, snaked across the mountain like the faded trails of goats.

This had been a great fortress once—an entire city, a palace that had housed myriads. Thousands of years had passed since the Ancients had raised it. This was all that remained: rugged boulders, snaking trails, echoing chambers. In the rains and winds of time, the fortress had melted into the mountain like a corpse's flesh melting into the earth.

The sun crackled overhead. Heat waves rose from the endless dunes. Solina flew toward the mountain, a comet of fire. As a phoenix, her wings were two hundred feet wide; she was a beast of wrath. And yet the mountain dwarfed her. She felt like a mere spark by this stone edifice.

A great archway loomed upon the mountainside, as tall and wide as Queen's Archway back in the capital. Shadows loomed beyond. When Solina flew near, her flames lit a hall carved from living rock.

She shrieked—an eagle's cry that echoed down the mountainside—and flew through the doorway.

Walls of stone streamed at her sides. Her flaming wings beat, sending dust flying to reveal chipped mosaics of coiling serpents and manticores. The firelight leaped against the walls. The hall drove into the mountain, its ceiling a hundred feet tall.

The nephilim will emerge from this canal like a child from its mother's womb. I will be their mother.

She landed upon the dusty mosaic. She shifted into human form. Her flames writhed around her, then gathered into the amulet she wore around her neck. She clutched the amulet in her hand and raised it, casting its light against the grand hall of the Palace of Whispers.

Once this place had been beautiful. Once the Ancients had lived here, a people of golden light. Statues rose here, faded now with the years, showing a people slim and fair, their heads oval, their eyes almond-shaped, their hair flowing. Once the limestone statues had held blades; today but stumps of rusted metal remained.

"Once you ruled this world," Solina whispered to the statues. "But you sinned. You lay with the demons of the Abyss. You birthed the nephilim. They destroyed you, but I will rule them." She clenched her fist around her amulet. "You buried and sealed them. You tried to hide the shame of your spawn. They were your children and you shackled them. I will free them. I will rule what you imprisoned."

She walked deeper into the hall and entered a doorway. A dark corridor loomed before her, and she walked upon limestone tiles, her sandals clattering. Her light shone upon walls covered with silver runes and faded murals. The Ancients had drawn their wars here, a hundred feet tall upon the walls of their palace. The murals rose around her, painted in faded blacks, golds, and reds.

Solina saw hordes of men, great armies in steel, tossing spears and shooting arrows at their enemy. Painted nephilim charged across the walls, life-sized, thrice the height of men. The giants lumbered, bat wings spread wide, fangs and claws painted a faded blood red. Men died between their teeth and under their feet, crushed and devoured. Solina raised her amulet high, shining her light. The painting of a great nephil covered the ceiling, spines dangling from its jaws, a flaming halo around its head. Solina smiled to imagine the nephilim walking again, feasting upon the weredragons' backbones.

She explored the Palace of Whispers for hours. She climbed staircases and gazed upon shadowy halls. She moved through chambers where stood hundreds of statues, stone armies of sandstone and gold. She walked down winding halls lined with dozens of doors, labyrinths like the veins of a giant. The palace seemed endless. Solina thought that all the people of Tiranor, two million souls, could reside within these halls and think them roomy. This was not merely an abandoned palace, but a city.

No, not even a city; an entire kingdom, she thought. She walked through chambers where thousands of sarcophagi rose, tombs for ancient kings and warriors. She moved deeper and deeper into the mountain. She thought that the sun outside must have set. She thought that she could walk here for days—for years.

Finally, after what seemed like eras of wandering, a shriek shattered the silence.

Solina froze.

The scream was mournful, echoing, a cry like a dying star. It rolled through the palace, torn in agony, a call of ancient pain, of lingering torment, of fallen ones begging for revenge. She had heard such screams in Requiem when toppling her halls. She herself had screamed that way when the weredragons murdered her child.

Now the nephilim screamed, and Solina smiled.

"I am coming to you, my children," she whispered.

The scream died and echoed. A hundred screams then rose together, a chorus of screeches, groans, and wails. The palace reverberated. Dust rained as bricks shifted. A column cracked.

"I come to you, fallen children!" Solina shouted.

Her voice echoed down dark halls. She walked under vaulted ceilings, her light shining in the dark. The screams rose.

"Free us!" they screeched.

"The pain! End the pain!" they cried.

"Enough, enough!" they howled. "The pain must end!"

Solina raised her arms as she walked, casting her light upon halls as large as her entire palace in Irys. A grin spread across her face. She followed the screams through the darkness.

"I have the key, twisted ones!" she called. "Your savior comes to you!"

The screams swirled. The creatures wept and laughed and roared and shrieked.

"Savior! Savior!"

"We will crush bones, we will drink blood!"

"Legion will lead! Legion will kill!"

The Palace of Whispers trembled around her. A statue of a priest fell and shattered. Cracks spread along the ceiling. The screams of the nephilim raced like demons through the halls, so loud Solina could barely hear her own cries.

"Ten thousand years you languished here!" she shouted. "Today I free you, Fallen Ones. Today you will drink the blood of the world that tortured you!"

The palace echoed and shook with their cries.

She descended a coiling staircase. The screams rained against her. She crossed a dark hall lined with statues. The voices wept and begged. She reached an iron door that shone a deep gray; it towered taller than dragons. The screams crashed like falling empires.

"I have come, nephilim!" she shouted and laughed. "I come to free you!"

Red light and shadows scurried around the door. Claws reached under the doorframe, scratching at the iron. Blood dripped through the keyhole and between the hinges.

"Free us, free us!" they begged.

"End the pain!"

"End the hunger!"

Solina drew the key from her belt. It thrummed and gleamed in her hand, so hot it nearly burned her. A force was tugging it toward the lock; Solina barely kept it in her hand.

"I am Solina Pheobus!" she howled above the screams. "I am Queen of Tiranor! I am the Destroyer of Requiem! I free you, nephilim. You will follow my light to flesh and bone and blood!"

The red light streamed across her. Her key flared like a rising sun. Screaming and laughing, Solina placed the key into the lock.

She twisted.

Light and blood and sound exploded.

The Iron Door blazed like sunrise, then shattered into a million shards. Howls and stench rose. Shadows leaped. From the darkness, the nephilim swarmed.

Solina raised her arms above her, dwarfed by the giants, but shining bright with the light of her lord.

"Serve me, nephilim! I am Solina! I free you."

They spilled into the hall, weeping and shouting and swirling. They stood fifteen feet tall, giants of shriveled flesh, patches of scales, and diseased eyes. Their fangs tore at the walls. Their claws slashed. Their great wings, wide as the wings of dragons, beat the air. Their armor was rusted, their blades chipped, their chain mail hanging in shreds, yet still Solina knew: This was the greatest army the world had seen.

"We rise!" one shouted and wept tears of blood.

"We walk again!" cried another, a bloated beast with lines of teeth like stitches crossing its face.

They kept spilling from their prison, filling the halls, swarming across the caverns. A cry rose among them, a cry shriller and louder than all others, a screech like boiling oceans.

"Bow before Queen Solina!" The voice echoed. "I am Legion! I foresaw the savior. Bow before the Queen of Light!"

All around, the nephilim fell to their knees, wept, clawed the air, and screamed. They trembled. They kissed the floor.

"Hail Solina!" they cried. "Hail the prophet Legion! We rise!"

From the shadows of the prison, a great nephil emerged, taller than the others, reeking and rotten. He was an androgynous beast, a thing of ruin, but Solina deemed him male. A halo of fire burned around his brow; he alone among the beasts bore this crown. Solina knew this one from the old, whispered tales. He was Legion, spawn of a mortal priestess and a demon king—ruler of the nephilim.

Beneath his burning halo, strands of yellow hair dangled from his scarred head, caked with blood. Milky-white eyes burned in his face between oozing boils. He had no nose, only two slits for nostrils. Drool, blood, and sharp teeth filled his maw. His skin was rotten and torn, but muscles shone and rippled beneath it. His claws were long as swords and jagged black. Rust covered his armor and a great blade, taller than two men, hung at his side. He howled to the ceiling, arms raised and drool spraying.

"Hail Solina!" he cried. "I am Legion. I am Leader. I am Prophet. I serve you, Golden Queen! We are nephilim; we were fallen. We rise! We rise!"

They swarmed through the palace. They carried Solina upon their shoulders. They flapped wings, and clawed at walls, and shattered columns, and wept and praised her name. They flew to daylight. They flowed from the palace like a swarm of wasps from a nest. They filled the desert sky and howled at the sun. The land shook beneath them, the palace trembled, and the sand burned.

"Rise, nephilim!" cried Solina, caught in the storm of them, flying upon their glory. "Fill the world with your might! I will lead you to food. I will lead you to dragon bones and scales and blood to drink. Fly, nephilim! Fly north, fly to Requiem, and you will feast!"

The roared and sang and wept.

They flew.

Solina laughed and raised her arms and the sunlight bathed her.

MORI

She walked upon marble tiles, fallen birch leaves crunching underfoot and scuttling before her like orange mice. Marble columns rose around her, glowing like moonlight, and beyond them Mori saw the forests roll across hills, kindled red and gold and yellow with fall. She walked in Nova Vita, she thought, but she saw no houses, no snaking streets or smithies or forts, only mist, birches, and gliding leaves.

"Requiem," Mori whispered. Tears stung her eyes at the purity of her home.

These were the courts of Requiem. Mori knew these marble tiles, these columns, and the Oak Throne which stood before her in a beam of light. Here had her father ruled, and Elethor after him, yet Mori heard no flap of dragon wings beyond the columns, no sounds of mothers calling for children, no clank of armor or song of harps. She heard only the crunch of leaves, the distant song of birds, and the wind through the trees. The marble seemed purer than Mori had ever seen it; no scratches marred the floor or columns, and the letters engraved into them—spelling old prayers of Requiem—appeared crisp as if freshly chiseled.

Mori kept walking, approaching the beam of light where the Oak Throne rose upon a dais. Her breath caught. A figure stood before the throne! Though daylight shone through the mist, strands of starlight seemed to cloak the figure ahead. Mori clutched her luck finger and kept walking, and the figure of light descended from the dais and moved toward her.

When the figure drew nearer, emerging from the light, Mori saw a woman in golden armor, her hair a cascade of blond curls. Mori recognized the sword that hung from her side, its hilt jeweled and its scabbard filigreed with silver leaves; this was Stella Lumen, the sword Mori's father had borne, the sword Solina had broken.

"Queen Gloriae's sword," she whispered.

In her childhood, Mori had spent many hours praying in Gloriae's Tomb to the great marble statue of Requiem's legendary queen. Gloriae had defeated Dies Irae, the tyrant. Gloriae had raised Requiem from ruin and rebuilt this temple. Gloriae was her ancestor, the heroine of her childhood. Gloriae—not a statue or a legend from scrolls, but a woman of flesh and blood—now stood before her.

Mori knelt.

"My queen," she whispered.

Then she knew: This was not Requiem, or at least, not the Requiem she had known.

I died in the darkness of Solina's dungeon, she thought. *My body hangs from chains underground. My soul has risen to the starlit halls of my ancestors, and now I kneel before the soul of my great queen.*

She felt a hand on her shoulder, soft and warm as spring's morning light. Mori rose and stood before her queen, the woman who had founded Nova Vita three hundred years ago. Gloriae's eyes were green as deep forests, and her face was pale.

"Fly," the queen said.

Mori lowered her head. "I cannot."

Gloriae placed a finger under Mori's chin and lifted it. Her face was blank, the face of a statue, but an urgency filled her eyes.

"Fly," she whispered.

Mori looked up, expecting to see the vaulted ceiling she had always known. Instead she saw the sky awhirl with white clouds, a painting all in blue and white. A few of the columns were missing their capitals, and Mori realized: These were not the starlit halls of afterlife after all. This was the court of Requiem long ago, back when Queen Gloriae was rebuilding it, before the roof had even been raised. The sky of Requiem still shone upon the new Oak Throne. This was not her afterlife; this was a whisper of her past.

Mori turned to the east, looked between the birches, and saw two figures cloaked in light. Here were the other heroes of the great war, the founders of Nova Vita: Agnus Dei, clad in green, a woman of black curls and kind brown eyes; and Kyrie Eleison, Prince of Requiem, a young man of yellow hair and winking eyes, Mori's ancestor. They stood in the starlight, smiling softly upon her, waiting for her.

We will fly together through starlit halls, their voices whispered in her mind. *But not this day. Your tale does not end here.*

"Fly," Gloriae said again, and the queen held Mori's hands, sending warmth and love through her. "Become the dragon. You bear the golden scales like I do, a color of royalty and dawn. Become the golden dragon and fly. Find our sky. Find the light of stars in the dark."

Mori tried to shift here in the temple, to soar toward the sky, but pain blazed around her wrists and ankles, and her breath rattled in her lungs. She was so weak. She was so hungry, so hurt.

"I can't," she whispered. "I am chained. Iron binds me."

"And I wear steel and gold," said the queen, gesturing at her armor, "and I bear Stella Lumen, a shard of metal and light, the sword of my mother Queen Lacrimosa. And yet I can shift."

Starlight cascaded, the song of harps played, and the woman of golden curls was gone; instead a golden dragon stood before Mori, eyes green and sad.

A golden dragon, Mori thought. *Like me.*

"But... your armor is a part of you," Mori said, standing small and thin before the great golden beast. "I can shift with my gown too, and with a good book that I love, if I hold it close to my breast. But I could never shift with armor, nor a sword, not like Lyana can." She placed her hand upon the golden dragon's head. "You are a great warrior, Gloriae! You fought the armies of Dies Irae himself and slew so many. You can shift encased in steel; I cannot."

Yet why could Lyana shift in armor? Mori wondered. She had seen the knight shift with sword, shield, and helm; they all melted into her dragon form, then reappeared when Lyana became human again. Yet Mori had seen the knight once try to shift while holding a harp, a musical instrument she had never mastered; Lyana had become the blue dragon, and the harp had clattered to the floor.

Gloriae nodded, as if she could read Mori's thoughts.

"We can shift," the golden dragon said, "with what is *ours*, with what is *us*. My armor is a part of me, a steel skin. A book is a part of you, a piece of your soul upon parchment."

Mori stood in the court of Requiem, clad in a white gown, yet when she raised her wrists, the skin was red and raw; she could feel the chains around them, even here in this hall of light and ghosts.

"Will these chains be a part of me?" she whispered.

With silver light, Gloriae returned to human form. Softly the queen embraced Mori; her armor was cold, but her hair and arms were warm.

"We are part of you," Gloriae whispered into her ear. "We are with you. Always, daughter of Requiem. We fly with you even in your darkest hours. Surrender to the shackles. Let these chains become like arms of steel. They imprison you. They will let you fly."

The queen kissed Mori's forehead, lips warm and soft, and white light flowed, and for a moment Mori saw nothing but the glow of stars.

When the light cleared, she saw the dungeon again: the bloody floor, the brick walls, and the door before her. Once more she sat here in shadow, her arms shackled to the wall behind her, her ankles chained to the floor.

"Was it a dream?" she whispered, throat dry and voice raspy. Had she truly seen the spirit of Queen Gloriae and the great Kyrie Eleison and Agnus Dei? Had she seen a light from the starlit halls or a light from the past?

Mori lowered her head; it felt too heavy to hold up. Her stomach clenched, her back blazed with pain, and her eyes stung. She missed that hall of marble. She missed those birches. All lay burnt now, all was fallen.

We are with you, their voices whispered in the darkness, and Mori thought she could feel the warmth of starlight. *Always, daughter of Requiem. We fly with you even in your darkest hours.*

Mori closed her eyes, tightened her lips, and tried to shift.

Pain racked her body. She trembled. Golden scales began to appear across her. Her limbs began to grow, and claws sprouted from her fingers. Wings unfurled from her back. She could almost imagine the sky of Requiem, all blue and white and cold around her.

The chains bit deep, shoving Mori back into human form.

She sat trembling, head lowered, and coughed and blinked and gasped for breath. She could not stop shaking, and she tasted blood on her lips. Her eyes stung.

"I can't do it," she whispered. "I'm sorry, Gloriae. I want to fly with you. I want to go home."

She shook for long moments, ravaged with pain and weakness. Her skin felt hot; perhaps she was feverish. She closed her eyes and tried to breathe like Mother Adia had taught her: a slow breath in, a moment of healing, a slow breath out. She breathed again and again, letting the air—even the fetid air of this dungeon—flow through her body, soothe her trembling, and ease her pain. She imagined that she breathed the air over Requiem, the sky of her youth, a sky she vowed to find again.

She took one more great breath, filling her lungs, and tried to shift again.

She could see the sky. Clouds trailed across blue fields. Dragons flew there, hundreds of them—blue, green, gold, and a dozen other colors, all undulating on the wind, smoke trailing from their nostrils, wings gliding. She felt her own wings move behind her, and she raised her head, ready to soar.

Once more, the chains bit, and her magic fizzled.

She sat chained and trembling.

She thought of her books from the library of Requiem—books of adventures about brave knights, beautiful maidens, and dragons who flew to distant lands of wonder. She thought of her gowns, her harp, her dolls—the things she could always shift with, draw into herself, extensions of her body and soul.

She thought of these chains, things of cold metal, of pain. *They imprison you. They will let you fly.*

How long had she lingered here in the dungeon, shackled, wasting away? Several moons? Several years? These chains were parts of her now; she could barely remember a time without them.

They've become extensions of my arms. They've become like steel wings. They are part of me.

She tried to imagine that she'd been born shackled, that she would live and grow old and die in these chains. They were as parts of her as her clothes, as her old books, as her very bones.

They are me. They will shift into me, and I will take these irons into myself.

With a deep breath, she mustered her magic.

Wings thudded from her back.

Scales clanked across her.

With a pain like thrusting daggers, the chains flowed into her body.

Mori screamed.

The walls cracked. Her body ballooned and her head hit the ceiling. The chains snapped from the walls and molded into her, driving like steel demons as her magic spun. Smoke filled her nostrils, and her tail flailed beneath her, and she was a dragon, a frail and thin golden dragon trapped in the cell, freed, unchained, fire in her maw.

Always, daughter of Requiem. We fly with you even in your darkest hours.

Mori shook. She clawed at the door, again and again, until the hinges tore. She was weak, but her claws were still sharp, and the door splintered and tore apart.

Frail and wheezing, the golden dragon tumbled out from the chamber into a hallway. Shouts echoed and boots thudded. Mori could barely raise her head. She looked up to see Sharik rushing her way, a club in his hand.

Always, daughter of Requiem. We fly with you...

She tried to blow her fire; she could muster none. She was so weak. Only sparks left her maw. Sharik reached her, and his club swung, and Mori raised her claws. The jailor howled and Mori once more was flying over Nova Vita, wyverns all around her, as crossbows fired and spears dug into her flesh.

BAYRIN

Bayrin stood in the forest camp, stuffing his supplies into his pack, when Piri Healer marched up toward him, raised her chin, and announced: "Bayrin, I'm flying with you to find the salvanae."

The camp bustled around them. Over a thousand Vir Requis had been hiding here in Salvandos, several leagues west of the border with Requiem, since Nova Vita's fall. The forest spread around them, leaves red and gold and crunching underfoot, giving way to a chalky mountain that rose like a wall. Elders were tending to pots of simmering stew, children ran playing with wooden swords, and guards in muddy armor patrolled the palisade of sharpened spikes that surrounded the camp.

They had been living here for several moons now, and Bayrin had done his best to avoid Piri during this time. Packing his things today, he had congratulated himself on avoiding her until his very last day here... and now as she stood before him, chin raised and arms crossed, he cursed under his breath.

"Piri," he said and glared, "I fly alone."

She glared back with those lavender eyes he used to marvel at, and which he now hated. She was a tall woman, taller even than most men, and Bayrin had always felt uneasy around women this tall. She wore the white robes of a healer, the hems muddy, and her dark hair fell across her shoulders in two braids. When she scrunched her lips, Bayrin couldn't help but remember kissing those lips four years ago, and the memory sickened him.

"Bayrin Eleison!" she said and placed her hands on her hips. "You know the old saying: Those who fly alone die alone. I'm not letting you fly alone to seek aid from the salvanae. I'm going with you, like it or not."

Bayrin groaned so loudly he blew back a curl of his hair. It had been *four years* since he'd kissed her, and since then, it seemed Piri followed him everywhere. Before the wars, she would sneak into Castra Murus, barracks of the City Guard, and try to slink into his bed at night. Whenever he would pass her in Nova Vita, she would gaze at him lovingly, sending him fleeing. Even here, in this camp, she had been giving him longing looks for moons now, and he had barely avoided her.

Looking at those flashing, lavender eyes, Bayrin sighed. It was not that he hated Piri; truly, he did not. But stars, why did she have to pursue him so urgently?

So I kissed her. So what? They had rolled around in the hay a few years ago, and she had demanded marriage. Not a week had gone by since their first kiss, and Piri had already planned what they'd name their children. Bayrin had tried telling her he was too young for marriage—and certainly too young for children. He had tried to avoid her since. Yet year after year, she pursued him, tried to kiss him again, even tried to lie with him, and nothing could dissuade her.

"Piri," he said and frowned. "No. Just no. I know why you want to fly with me, and it won't work."

It was her turn to snort. She rolled her eyes. "Bayrin, don't you get a big head. Do you *truly* think I'm still infatuated with you? I'm long over what happened between us; not every girl in camp loves you, Bayrin Eleison, despite what you might think." She raised her nose at him. "I want to fly with you because I know Salvandos. I've visited Har Zahav before, the mountain where the salvanae live, to train as a healer. You need me as your guide. I've spoken to King Elethor about this, and he quite agrees. Ask him if you like; he will command you fly with me."

Bayrin sighed. He could just imagine Elethor's grin. On many nights back in Nova Vita, Bayrin would complain about Piri's onslaught, and Elethor would howl with laughter. Whenever Elethor—just a young prince then—would see Piri in the city streets, he would point her toward Bayrin and wink as the young woman began her pursuit. One time, when Bayrin had been hiding in an alehouse, Elethor had smuggled Piri inside under his cloak, then laughed for days about the mugs Bayrin had broken trying to flee the place.

"Of course Elethor would say that," he muttered.

He grabbed his longsword and buckled it to his belt, careful avoid Piri's gaze. As he was packing his pan, cutlery, and tinderbox, she kept standing with hands on hips, merely staring. As he was counting his rations—strings of sausages, sacks of oats, and jars of preserves—she began tapping her foot.

"Are you quite ready, Bayrin Eleison, or are you going to wait until the nephilim kill us all?"

He groaned, slammed an apple into his pack, and sealed it shut. He straightened, slung the pack over his back, and glared at her.

"I'm ready," he said. "Are you ready? To shut your mouth, that is?"

"Very clever, Bayrin." She nodded at his sword. "Why take a blade? Surely you could slay an enemy without it; they'll groan to death at your jokes."

She hefted her own pack, which hung across her back. Bayrin grumbled. He couldn't help but notice how the pack's straps pulled her silk robes taut, exposing her curves, or how her lips twisted as she smiled. A memory pounded through him: Piri four years ago, sneaking into his chamber and doffing her cloak to stand nude before him. They had made love three times that sweaty summer night.

With a grunt, Bayrin shoved the memory aside.

It's Mori I love, he thought, and sadness flowed over his memories of Piri's kisses. Mori—pure and beautiful, the love of his life. *Stars, Mori, I won't forget you, not now, not ever. I will find you, and when I do, I'll never let you go again.*

Eyes stinging, he shifted into a green dragon. He kicked off the earth, crashed through branches, and soared into the sky. He began flying west and shouted over his shoulder.

"If you want to fly with me, Piri, you better fly fast. I wait for no one."

The trees shook as she soared, a lavender dragon with silver horns. Her body was long and slim, her scales were bright, and fire flicked between her teeth. She flew like an arrow. Bayrin cursed, turned his gaze back west, and flapped his wings mightily.

He'd always been a fast dragon—not as fast as Mori, perhaps, but close. He flew now with every last bit of strength, determined to lose Piri over the wilderness. The forests streamed below him, an endless sea of red and gold. Mountain peaks rose ahead, white against the sky and cloaked in clouds. Bayrin dived between them on the wind, the scents of autumn in his nostrils. He flew toward a valley and streamed over a lake. His reflection raced across the water; the reflection of a lavender dragon raced there too.

Bayrin looked over his shoulder to see Piri close behind. Blasts of smoke rose from her nostrils. She snarled at him and beat her wings mightily.

"Bloody stars!" he cursed, turned his head back west, and flew with new vigor.

For a healer, she's damn fast.

"You can't escape me, Bayrin!" she cried behind him. "I'm just as fast."

She had the speed; Bayrin had to admit that. But did she have the endurance? He snarled and flew faster than he'd ever flown. The lake ended and forests of oaks and maples rolled below him. He flew until his wings ached, and his lungs felt ready to collapse, yet whenever he glanced over his shoulder, he saw Piri mere feet behind him. She panted, and her eyes were narrowed to slits, but she kept flying.

How many leagues did he fly? Bayrin couldn't tell; dozens perhaps. His body ached. He remembered flying across the northern sea with Mori, seeking the Crescent Isle, and the memory stung his eyes.

I wish you were flying here with me, Mori. We will fly together again. I promise you.

The sun began to set, and still the blasted lavender dragon flew behind him. Bayrin wanted to keep flying, but smoke rose thickly from his maw, and he was weary, so weary he wanted nothing more than to crash down and fall asleep.

Bloody stars, I'll lose the damn girl tomorrow, he thought and began to dive down. He spotted a clearing between trees where grass grew along a stream. He spiraled down, landed upon the grass, and shifted into human form. It was cold—damn cold—but still sweat drenched him. He knelt by the stream and drank deeply.

Piri landed by him, claws digging into the grass, and shifted too. She panted, and sweat dampened her hair and robes. She too approached the stream, knelt so close by him that their bodies touched, and also drank. She glanced at him, mouth dripping, and flashed a grin.

"Good flight." She reached up and tousled his hair.

He turned aside with a grunt, trudged away from the stream, and lay upon the grass. He was too weary to eat supper, and besides, eating meant having to stay awake around Piri. He turned his back toward her, placed his head upon his pack, and pulled his cloak over him as a blanket. He paused long enough only to kick off his boots, then closed his eyes.

Her voice spoke softly beside him. "Bayrin?"

He ignored her.

She spoke softly again, and he felt her fingers in his hair. "Bayrin, are you sleeping?"

He grumbled under his breath, keeping his eyes stubbornly shut, though he could feel her looking at him. The woman was a leech! He had never met anyone so clingy. He did not want to speak to her. He did not want to remember her kisses, those warm kisses that used to intoxicate his youth. He did not want to remember her lithe, naked body pressed against him, the warmth of her as they made love, her teeth biting his shoulder, or...

Stop it. He ground his teeth. *Stop thinking about her, Bayrin. It's Mori you love. It's Mori you are sworn to protect. Just ignore Piri.*

He lay still for long moments, pretending to sleep, and she did not speak again. Finally he heard her lie down behind him. She wriggled in the grass, and he felt her pressed up against his back. Her arm reached over him, and she nestled close under his cloak.

He groaned.

"Piri!" he said. "What are you doing?"

She cuddled against him, arm draped over him. He could feel her breasts press against his back, and her hand strayed down, moving dangerously close to the very last parts he wanted her near. He sucked in his breath.

"I'm trying to sleep," she whispered, her lips touching his ear. "I thought you were sleeping too."

He wriggled in the grass, moving away from, placing a good foot of space between them.

"Well, sleep away from me!" he said and closed his eyes tight.

He heard her stand, walk around him, then lie down on his other side. When he opened an eye, he saw her facing him. She wriggled closer to him, so close that she pressed against his chest. She sneaked under his cloak, draped an arm and leg over him, and cuddled.

"But I'm cold and I forgot my cloak at the camp," she said.

"Not my problem, Piri."

His cheeks flushed. *Stars damn it.* Her body against his was affecting him, like it or not. She pressed close against him, felt his arousal, and smiled.

"Please, Bayrin? I don't want to freeze to death." She closed her eyes, still smiling, and nuzzled her cheek against his cheek. "I'm just going to sleep. I know you still love Mori. I'm not going to do anything, I promise. Just... sleep..."

Her voice softened, and soon she was breathing deeply, sound asleep against him.

Bayrin cursed inwardly. He cursed Piri. He cursed Elethor for sending her here. He cursed the desert of Tiranor, and he cursed his own blood for boiling. Piri mumbled in her sleep and cuddled even closer, pressing hard against him. Stars, how would he possibly sleep like this?

He sighed. It would be a long night. It would be a long quest.

TREALE

She was stoking the fireplace in Sharik's small, craggy chamber when she heard shouts, ran into the dungeon corridor, and saw the golden dragon.

Her breath died and for an instant Treale froze, eyes stinging and fingers trembling.

She had been working in this dungeon for six days now, serving her master, Sharik. For six days she had swept his floor, stoked his fireplace, cooked his meals, and—she cringed to think of it—emptied his chamber pot and washed his foul tunics. For six days she had cleaned up after his work, mopping blood and gore from under the bodies he tortured. For six days he would grumble, fondle her, slap her if she met his eyes, and spit upon her. For six days she had tried to grab his keys—but whenever she inched close, she earned another smack that left her head ringing, and at nights his girth would cover his treasure.

And Mori was so close! Treale had heard the princess whimper down the hall, and she longed to run to her, to whisper under the door, to comfort her, to let Mori know she was here. And yet how could she?

During the days, Sharik kept her at his side. She would mop blood from cells where prisoners hung, their flesh lacerated, their skin peeled. She would collect the fingers he severed and burn them. She would bring water and food to whimpering or screaming mouths, trying to keep these broken bodies alive.

And yet the chamber at the hall's end where Mori lay... that was forbidden. In that chamber lay Tiranor's greatest prize, the Weredragon Princess herself. Only Sharik brought food and water to that chamber. Only Sharik mopped the blood from that floor. Even at nights when Sharik slept, Treale could not approach Mori's shadowy cell. During those long cold nights, Treale languished in her own prison—locked with Sharik in his room, forced to sleep on the floor by his chamber pot and gobs of drool.

And now—after six days of blood and screams that would forever haunt Treale—Mori's chamber door lay shattered across the corridor, and Sharik ran toward the frail dragon that emerged from it.

With a gasp, Treale began running too.

This corridor was narrow, but the golden dragon was frail enough to fit, her scales dulled and her wings limp. Mori tried to blast Sharik with fire, but only sparks left her mouth, and only wisps of smoke left her nostrils. She tried to lash her claws, but Sharik's club swung down, and Mori whimpered and fell against the wall.

Sharik raised his club again, prepared to shatter the dragon's head.

With a scream, Treale leaped and clung onto the jailor's back.

"Treale!" Mori cried.

Sharik howled and bucked beneath her, and Treale screamed and clutched his throat, trying to choke him. His club flailed and slammed against a wall. He swung the club backward, and pain blazed across Treale's shoulder. She yowled. She thought the blow might have shattered her bone. She slid off Sharik's back and slammed against the floor. The club swung down, and she rolled aside. The club cracked the floor by her, and Treale kicked, hitting Sharik's leg.

He crashed down atop her, and Treale gasped and yelped. His weight was immense; he was thrice her size. His hand reached out, fingers thick and clammy, and clutched her throat.

Treale gurgled for breath. She clawed at his hand, but it was like clawing a slab of ham. She drew blood but could not break his grip. Stars floated before her eyes. She thought her neck would snap. Sharik snarled above her, drooling onto her face; his eyes were mad. Treale kicked, again and again, hitting his belly; it was like kicking a soggy old mattress. He seemed not to feel the pain, and his fingers kept clutching her throat, and blackness spread across her vision.

Her eyes rolled back.

Goodbye, Mori, she thought. *Goodbye, Requiem. I'm sorry. I failed you, Mori. I failed.*

Sharik howled.

The fingers loosened around her neck.

Treale gasped for breath, a gasp she thought could swallow the world. The blackness pulled back from her eyes like curtains, and stars exploded across the dungeon. She struggled to her feet, clutching at her throat and hacking, and saw Sharik howl. Mori's horns had gored him; they pierced his back and emerged bloody from his chest. The blood soaked his tunic and sprayed Treale's face.

His club lay fallen. Treale grabbed it and swung. The wood *cracked* against Sharik's skull. She felt the blow reverberate up the club, up her arm, and into her shoulder.

Sharik tilted, head caved in, and crashed to the floor. He lay still, dead eyes staring, blood pooling beneath him.

Behind him, the slim golden dragon mewled, and her magic left her. Where a dragon had stood, pressing against the corridor walls, now lay a frail, scarred woman with pale skin and wispy hair.

Treale leaped over Sharik's body and knelt over Mori. She cradled her princess in her arms, and her tears splashed against Mori's cheek.

"Mori," she whispered, holding her princess close. "Mori, I'm here. I've come for you. I'm going to get you out of here."

Mori felt so thin in her arms, barely more than skin and bones. The princess smiled softly, a ghostly smile, and her eyelids fluttered.

"Treale," she whispered. "Are you really here? Is this a dream?" She reached up with a frail arm—stars, it was nothing but skin and bone!—and clung to Treale's shoulder. "Treale, I saw them! I saw Queen Gloriae, and Kyrie Eleison and Agnus Dei—the heroes from the old scrolls. They fly with us."

Treale's throat still throbbed with pain, and her arms shook with weakness, but she gritted her teeth and struggled to pull Mori to her feet. Other guards often patrolled these dungeons; they could appear any moment.

"Come, Mori! Stand. We have to go now. We have to run."

She looked around, waiting for guards to appear. Boots thumped somewhere above and screams echoed through the chambers. She growled as she pulled Mori to her feet. The princess could barely stand; she leaned against Treale, her arms around her shoulders.

"You have to walk as fast as you can," Treale said. She began to take slow steps down the hall. "Lean on me and let's get out of this nightmare."

Yet Mori did not move. She looked back at Sharik's body, a lump of warty white flesh and oozing blood.

"Wait," the princess whispered. "We need to free the others."

Treale hissed between gritted teeth, whipping her head back and forth. *Stars damn it!* she thought. The shouts of guards still echoed above; no doubt they had heard the fight, and they would burst into this corridor any moment. And yet... Mori was right, she knew. Other screams echoed here: the screams of prisoners who filled the cells, hanging from the walls, skin lashed and bodies broken.

We can't leave them here, Treale thought.

She moved back to Sharik's body. For six nights, he had lain snoring upon his keys; it took dying for him to lie upon his other side, the keys exposed. Still holding her princess, Treale grabbed the ring of keys and wrenched it off Sharik's belt.

"Come on, Mori!" she said, keys in one hand, club in the other. "Hold onto me and walk, and we're going to get everyone out of here."

She began moving down the corridor, heels digging into the floor, breath rattling and body aching. The screams rolled above, and boots still thumped, and steel clashed. Yet still the guards did not appear. What was happening in the upper chambers? Treale did not have time to guess. It sounded like a hundred soldiers were clanking above her; she knew she had only moments before they arrived.

Mori limped by her, arms around her neck, and Treale stumbled toward one cell. She thrust the keys into the door's lock. The lock clanked, and the door opened to reveal a cell with three prisoners.

The men lay upon the floor, bloodied and whimpering. Sharik had dislocated their arms upon the rack. They trembled, pale and sickly and coughing, blood upon their backs. For a moment Treale could only stand, breath wheezing, head spinning.

How can we do this? Guards shouted above. Hundreds filled the palace, and thousands filled the city. Scores of prisoners filled this dungeon, and most were too ill, frail, and wounded to walk; she could not carry them all.

Did I travel to Tiranor only to die in darkness? Did I survive the fire over Requiem, and fly through smoke and blood, to fall with my princess underground?

Treale tightened her lips. *No. No, I will not die here.* She knelt by the prisoners, somehow holding her club, her keys, and Mori. She growled. *We will not die like rats in Tiranor's bowels. We will find our sky. We will fly over Requiem again.*

"You must stand!" she said to the prisoners. "Stand and flee! Move, now, before guards arrive."

The prisoners crawled, struggling for breath, struggling to rise. One managed to stand, leaning against a wall, then fell and mewled. The others could not even do that. More wails rose from the other chambers, and voices cried out to her, begging for freedom, begging for death. Tears stung Treale's eyes, and she let out a frustrated yowl.

"How can I do this, Mori?" she whispered. The princess still leaned against her, so frail she could barely support her own weight. "How can we free them? There are so many... so many wounded..."

The prisoners were crawling toward her, bloody hands outreached, when a shriek pierced the dungeons.

It was a shriek like shattering glass, like rending souls, the primordial cry of ancient evil. It was so loud, the dungeon shook and dust rained, and Treale dropped club and key and covered her ears. The prisoners moaned and fell. The floor shook and cracks raced along the wall. Mori winced and also covered her ears, and the shriek kept flowing, rising to an impossible pitch, so shrill Treale thought her eardrums might rip.

When finally the shriek ended, Treale turned to face the cell door. She raised her club. Outside in the hall, a shadow was stirring.

Stars of Requiem, be with me.

The torchlight flickered madly outside, casting shadows and red light across the floor. Something was moving in the hall. Snorts rose and a stench like rotten flesh and mold invaded Treale's nostrils. A long shadow fell across the corridor outside the doorway, and the shriek sounded again, so loud Treale fell to her knees and winced and thought her skull might crack.

"Treale," Mori whispered. She trembled against her.

"Be strong, Mori," Treale whispered back. Her heart thrashed and her chest rose and fell. "Whatever walks outside, we will face it."

Was a wyvern crawling in the corridor? No, impossible; wyverns were too large to fit down here. Was it a phoenix? No; she would have felt the heat. Some beast, some evil, crawled outside the cell. Its breath snorted as if sniffing for flesh, and claws clanked against the floor, and the shadow neared, and finally the creature appeared at the doorway.

Treale froze. Such terror pounded through her she couldn't even scream.

She had faced wyverns in battle over Ralora Beach. She had seen the death of her parents. She had sailed from Osanna to Tiranor and survived for days in these dungeons, witnessing the blood and gore and agony of Tiranor's torture. Yet she had never seen anything that filled her with such pounding, twisting, screaming terror. Her teeth clenched, sweat drenched her, and her knees felt soft as wet cloth.

"Stand behind me, Mori," Treale whispered. Without removing her eyes from the creature, she knelt, placed Mori upon the floor, and straightened again. She raised her club with shaking, clammy hands.

The creature regarded her, one eye bright yellow, the other milky white and swollen. It crawled on hands and knees, body long and lanky, its bones thrusting against leathery skin. It looked almost like a man, but far too large; Treale guessed it would stand fifteen feet tall, if it had room to straighten. Leathern swings sprouted from its back, and its claws were long and thin. As it stared at her, its lips pulled back to reveal fangs like daggers. When its tongue lolled, drool dripped and sizzled against the floor.

"Stand back!" Treale warned and raised her club. Her knees shook, but she snarled and stayed standing. "You will not enter this place."

Its tongue licked its chops, long and wet like a sea serpent. Its white eye spun madly, the size of a melon, oozing pus.

"Fleshhhh," it hissed, eyes blazing. "We must eat, yes, we must lick blood, we must suck marrow. Fleshhh."

Quick as a spider, it scuttled on hands and knees into the chamber.

Treale yelped and leaped back. She swung her club, and it clanged against the demon's shoulder. The beast barely seemed to notice. Its head whipped from side to side, taking in the cell, like a starving man stumbling upon a feast and for a moment overcome, not sure which dish to devour first. Mori crawled into the corner, face pale, and Treale stood over her, club trembling in her hands. The beast gave them a stare, then looked back at the prisoners who mewled upon the floor. It finally seemed to make up its mind.

It pounced onto one prisoner, a man with dislocated arms and severed fingers, and began to feast.

Treale winced and Mori yelped. Blood and entrails splattered. The prisoner gave a last scream, then died as the beast fed. It ate greedily, claws lashing and teeth ripping flesh, then turned and pounced upon a second prisoner. The man screamed as the creature sucked up his entrails. The third prisoner, back lashed and legs broken, whimpered and began crawling away, but the demon leaped upon him too, and more blood splashed.

"Come on, Mori!" Treale cried. She grabbed the princess and pulled her up. "Run, Mori!"

As the demon feasted upon the third prisoner, crunching bones and sucking organs, the two young women stumbled out into the hall.

A second shriek, coming from ahead, tore through the dungeon. Walls cracked and dust rained. Treale screamed and Mori whimpered. More shadows stirred, and a second beast scuttled into the dungeon, licking its chops. This one's flesh was so rotten, it hung in tatters, revealing white bones. It crawled forward, long and rail thin. Its nostrils flared, and with a howl, it burst into a cell where children hung from a wall. The beast began to feast, splattering blood. The children screamed and died between its teeth.

"Nephilim," Mori whispered, her arms around Treale's shoulders. Her voice was weak, and her arms shook.

"Demons?" Treale whispered.

"Half demons. I read about them in my books. Their fathers were demons from the Abyss who took human brides; these are their spawn." She began to limp forward again. "Hurry, Treale!"

They rushed down the corridor as the nephilim screeched and slurped and feasted behind them. As they passed by cells, they saw that the prisoners had already been devoured. The doors lay shattered, and only bits of hair and bloodied chains remained beyond them. More screeches rose above; the dungeons were swarming with these creatures.

"More flesh!" rose cries behind them. "We must drink more blood! We crave more bones, comrades, and marrow to suck."

Treale's feet slogged through blood. The nephilim screeched behind her. Every step seemed a mile long. The staircase rose ahead; it would lead them out of darkness. It was only ten paces away, but seemed the distance of seas and forests. She walked on shaky legs, Mori leaning against her.

The shrieks swirled behind her, louder now. "More blood! More flesh to suck!"

Shadows danced. The torches flickered madly. The staircase was only five paces away now. When Treale looked over her shoulder, she saw the nephilim emerge from the chambers, maws bloody. They tossed their heads back and howled, and the dungeons shook.

The prisoners had only whetted their appetite, she realized. *And we're the main course.*

She yowled, clenched her jaw, and kept trudging forward. Mori was frail, but she seemed so heavy now; Treale's limbs were too weak, too thin. The creatures began scuttling behind them, claws clanking against the stone floor. Treale yowled and tried to run, but her feet slipped in the blood, and she crashed to her knees. Mori whimpered and fell beside her.

"Blood! Flesh! Fresh sustenance, comrades, fresh bones to snap!"

The two nephilim came charging toward them. Treale screamed and leaped to her feet. Was this corridor too small? Would the walls crush her? Would she crush Mori?

The nephilim snapped their teeth.

"Stand back, Mori!" Treale shouted, summoned her magic, and shifted.

Her body ballooned, becoming the dragon. Flames crackled in her maw. Her scaly flank shoved against Mori, pinning the princess to the wall. Treale howled, a black dragon trapped in the corridor like a clot in a vein. The nephilim screamed before her, and Treale blew her fire.

The flames exploded through the dungeon, crashed against the nephilim, and roared into the cells lining the corridor. The half demons shrieked, stones shattered, cracks raced along the ceiling, and bricks tumbled. Treale kept blowing her flames, and the beasts kept screaming. A chunk of the ceiling crashed against Treale's back, and she howled. More stones slammed against the nephilim, and she heard one's spine snap. She kept roaring her fire, emptying every flame inside her, until the beasts lay burnt and broken and still.

Panting, head twisting with pain, Treale shifted back into human form. Smoke and flame filled the dungeon; she could barely breathe. She knelt above Mori, and tears filled her eyes. The princess lay on her back, eyes closed.

"Mori!" Treale called, lifted the princess in her arms, and shook her. "Mori, wake up. Stars, Mori!"

The princess lay still in Treale's arms. *Stars, did I crush her? Did I kill her?* She placed her ear against Mori's lips. A shaky sob fled Treale's own lips. Mori still breathed! Some life still filled her.

"I'm going to save you, Mori," she said.

She wrapped Mori in her cloak, then roared with pain as she lifted the princess. She was not much larger than Mori. And yet here in this dungeon, weakened and wounded, she slung Mori across her shoulders and began to climb the stairs.

Step by step, growling with effort, Treale carried her princess out of the dungeon. Screams rose above her: both the shrieks of nephilim and the cries of men. Treale kept climbing. The stairs seemed to twist forever, finally leading to corridors that twisted and chambers where blood flowed. Down one hall, she glimpsed a nephil scuttling and shrieking for blood; she heard more racing through the palace above her.

It seemed hours before Treale found the back door that led outdoors into sunlight.

The sun nearly blinded her, and for a moment Treale saw nothing but light; she had been underground for six days now. When she blinked, she saw the sky swarming with nephilim. Hundreds flew there, maybe thousands, lanky bodies twisting and coiling, black wings flapping. They shrieked and howled at the sun.

"Hail Queen Solina!" they cried. "Hail Legion! We are free! We will feast! We will devour dragons!"

Treale stared, frozen, and her eyes burned.

The world is overrun. Can we ever flee such evil?

She sniffed and tightened her grip on Mori; the princess still hung across her shoulder, wrapped in a cloak, unconscious and breathing softly.

"We're leaving this city," Treale said.

She began to trudge away from the palace, and soon she walked down an alley where people fled, pointed at the sky, and whimpered in corners. If anyone even looked Treale's way, they saw her carrying only a thin bundle wrapped in cloth, perhaps some kindling for a fire.

"We are leaving this cursed desert, Mori, and we are never coming back."

Her legs shook, her back blazed with pain, yet Treale kept walking—step by step, breath by breath. She would cross the desert afoot if she must. Soldiers raced around her, shouting and pointing at the nephilim who swarmed above. Children wept and families rushed into their homes and peered from windows.

Treale kept walking, Mori across her shoulder, the screams of the nephilim shaking the sky.

MORI

The world spun around her.

Mori remembered little of leaving Irys, capital of Tiranor: only the scent of sand, the shriek of beasts above, and Treale carrying her across her shoulders. The young squire was a slight woman, and yet she had carried Mori through the entire city of sprawling squares, cobbled alleys, and throngs of people.

Stars, I'm so thin, Mori remembered thinking in a daze. *I'm skin and bones.*

Beasts of claws and fangs soared overhead, scuttled down the streets, and cried to the sun. Soldiers ran and somewhere above Solina laughed, flying upon the king of the Fallen, a twisted beast crowned with a flaming halo. Treale was sweating beneath her as they sneaked outside the city walls. The desert sands swirled around the squire's feet, and finally they rested beneath an ancient, smoothed statue of a falcon that rose from the dunes.

"Here," Treale said, reached into her pack, and handed her a waterskin. "Drink."

Sweat, sand, and blood coated Treale, and she panted and wiped damp hair off her brow. When Mori held out her arms to grab the waterskin, they seemed so thin to her, mere twigs compared to Treale's arms. Her hands trembled as she clutched the skin, and Treale had to help her drink. It was good, clear water, the best she had drunk in moons.

"I can't see very well," she said softly. The sun blazed overhead, and shadows fell only when nephilim scudded across it. The world seemed fuzzy and far too bright; it was like looking through sunlit glass.

Treale took a pomegranate from her pack and cracked it open against her knee. She handed half to Mori.

"Your eyesight will improve," she said firmly. "Eat, Mori. Eat and you'll grow strong again."

Her voice didn't waver, but Mori saw tears in the young woman's eyes. She looked down at her pomegranate. Looking at the bright red color helped her focus her eyes, and she blinked a few times. She scooped seeds out and ate them, then closed her eyes and sighed. They were the sweetest, most wonderful, magical things she had ever eaten; they exploded in her mouth and shot healing energy through her. Her body shook with it.

A shadow fell over them. A nephil screeched above and swooped so low, its wings raised sand around them. The creature overshot them and soared over the city ahead, crying to the sun. More followed, a flock of rot and screams, their wings spreading their stench.

"We shall feed on dragon bones!" they screeched. "We shall drink dragon blood! Hail Solina. Hail the Golden Queen!" They beat their wings and swirled across the desert sky. "We are free! We will eat dragon flesh!"

Treale huddled closer to the old falcon statue that rose above them; the sand below and the limestone beak above formed a hollow. Mori pushed herself back and huddled by her friend. She began to shiver.

"How did Solina free the nephilim, Treale?" she whispered. "My books said the Ancients imprisoned them years ago."

The squire placed her arms around her, pulled her close, and held her. She too was shaking. Sand stung the welts on Mori's back, mingling with the pain in her belly and head. She watched as the beasts dived and cried overhead.

"Don't worry about those creatures, Mori," Treale said, holding her. "I'll get you out of this desert. I promise. We're going to fly north to a beautiful forest, and we'll find lots of food there, and we'll live there together." Her tears fell. "I promise. Do you believe me?"

Though Mori shook and her own eyes dampened, she nodded.

"Will Elethor be there?" she whispered. "Is Bayrin waiting in that forest too? And Lyana? They're waiting in that forest for us, right?"

Treale hung her head low and said nothing. A tear streamed down her cheek.

Mori bit her lip. "I thought not," she whispered.

With a sniff, Treale raised her head, looked into her eyes, and pulled her into a soft embrace.

"I pray that they live, Mori," she whispered. "But if they're gone... if you and I are the only ones left... then we must survive. We must escape and we must live alone. You understand, right?"

Mori nodded, a lump in her throat. "We will live, Treale. We will get out of this awful place." Her lip trembled, and the statue shook behind them with the shrieks of the beasts above. "We'll find that forest, and we'll find lots of food and water, and we'll survive."

Treale sniffed again and knuckled her eyes. "Can you fly, Mori?"

"I don't know. Let me eat a little more. Let me catch my breath. And then we'll try to fly. If I can't, will you let me ride you—you a dragon and me a human?"

Treale laughed through her tears. "You'd fall straight off! But if you can't fly, I will hold you in my claws, and I promise to be gentle."

They finished their pomegranate, then some bread and cheese Treale had pilfered from the dungeon, and Mori felt some of her strength return. The world still seemed too bright, and her limbs too shaky and weak, but she managed to push herself up to her feet.

"We'll walk a little farther," Treale said. She pointed ahead. "See the mountains there in the west?"

Mori squinted, able to see only a tan smudge. She nodded. "I see them."

"None of these creatures fly there. But we will. We will rest there among the stones for the night, then keep going. The swamps of Gilnor lie a few days northwest. We'll find more food there—fish and frogs to eat—and we'll find shelter under trees." Treale's voice trembled as she spoke, but she clenched her fists and plowed on. "We'll fly north from the swamps. A few days' flight will take us to the forests of Salvandos. That's where the true dragons live, and they can protect us. We can be there this moon, if we fly fast enough."

"The salvanae!" Mori breathed.

She had read many books about them. True dragons of old, they had no wings, no limbs, and no human forms; they flew as great chinking serpents, wild in the forests and mountains, forging no metal and plowing no fields, yet studying the stars and singing many old songs. Mori had seen a salvana once—the priest Nehushtan, a wise old dragon who had visited Requiem a year ago.

She lowered her head. Memories of Requiem flowed over her, as powerful as whips: Lacrimosa Hill where she had stood with her brother, the library with the leather books, and her canopy bed where she would laugh with Bayrin. Her trembling returned, and tears filled her eyes, but she knuckled them dry. She could not panic now. She could not weep now. They were still in danger; there would be time for tears later.

"Let's go," she said. "We'll walk to the mountains as humans so the nephilim don't see us. We'll fly from there. I'm strong enough."

They began the journey. Mori walked with her arms slung across Treale's shoulders, and the young squire held her waist and helped her every step. The nephilim kept swarming above, screaming of the dragons they'd eat. If they saw Mori and Treale, two haggard women, they did not see them as prey. When one landed in the desert before them, and hissed at them, Mori nearly fainted with fright. The nephil, however, only tossed its head, spraying drool, and took flight again.

"Dragons!" it screeched. "Solina will feed us. We will feast upon them!"

Mori tightened her lips and kept walking toward the mountains. "Come on, Treale. Let's hurry. I reckon Solina told these creatures they can only eat prisoners and dragons, not her people. They must think we're Tirans. But once they get hungry enough to forget orders... I want to be far away."

They seemed to walk forever. The sand burned Mori's bare feet, and the sun pummeled her. When evening fell, she looked behind her. The city of Irys was distant now, a patch of stone under the red sky. Nephilim still bustled above it, cawing and swirling, landing and soaring. None now flew over Mori and Treale; they were safe from them here.

When Mori looked west toward the mountains, she let out a sigh. They still seemed so distant, leagues and leagues away, no closer than they had ever been.

"Once we get to those mountains, we can fly," Treale said. "We'll be far enough from the nephilim. They're staying at the city, and they won't see two dragons from there."

Mori nodded. Yet how far was enough? She felt weak, and her eyes rolled back. When she blinked, she found herself sitting in the sand, legs splayed out.

"Oh, Mori," Treale said softly, knelt, and touched Mori's forehead. "I'm sorry; I pushed you too hard. We'll rest for a bit here, okay? We'll keep walking toward the mountains later, and then I can fly and carry you."

Mori nodded, head spinning. Treale let her drink some more; there were only a few sips left, and Mori left the last one for Treale, yet the squire insisted that she was not thirsty. They nibbled on more bread and cheese as night fell. The sun dipped behind the horizon so fast here in Tiranor, not a slow melting sunset like the northern ones of Requiem, but a plunge into darkness. The stars emerged overhead, piercing bright, millions of them. The Draco constellation shone in the north—the stars of their home.

"Can we sleep a little, Treale?" Mori whispered. "I'm so tired. So tired. Can we sleep just for a little?"

Treale nodded. Nothing but leagues of sand surrounded them, but thankfully the wind lay low, and the dunes did not swirl. Treale laid out her cloak, lay down upon it, and Mori lay beside her.

With the sun gone, it grew very cold very fast. The day had been so hot, and sweat had drenched the two women, and the sun had burned their skin. Now it felt like winter, and Mori shivered. She clung to Treale, sharing her warmth. Weariness tugged on her as tightly as chains.

"Mori?" Treale whispered. "Do you remember my canopy bed in Oldnale Manor, the one we'd sleep in as children? Remember how we'd hide under the blankets, pretend it's a palace, and read books? Let's pretend we're sleeping there now."

Mori smiled, remembering that great bed with its oak posts, soft mattress of feathers, and woolen quilts. She imagined that she lay there again, and slowly the beating of her heart eased.

"Thank you, Treale," she whispered. "Thank you for coming for me."

They slept embraced, their breath mingling.

They woke to a dawn of shrieks and rot.

Mori opened her eyes and shivered. She had not expected to sleep this long, yet the morning rose around her, and she still lay by Treale. The desert shook around them. Nephilim swarmed above, their wings tossing the sand into clouds. Mori coughed; the sand entered her nostrils and mouth. Treale woke at her side and coughed too, and they could barely see through the sandstorm. The shadows of the nephilim shot overhead, wings beat, stench flared, and shrieks cracked the air.

"We seek dragon blood!" they howled. "We will find the dragons, and we will feast! We fly to blood and organs and sweet marrow. We rise, we rise!"

Mori and Treale lay huddled together. The sand rose and stormed around them. The horde seemed to swarm forever, blasting their faces and fluttering their hair and cloaks with beating wings. Finally the last nephil disappeared overhead, leaving the sand and stench to settle. Globs of nephil drool and pus littered the desert like boils upon patchy skin.

Mori rose to her feet and stared north. Her heart thrashed against her ribs, and her legs shook. She shielded her eyes with her palm and stared after the dwindling nephil army.

Stars, she thought and her breath quickened.

"Treale!" she said. "Treale, they... they seek dragons!"

The young squire pushed herself to her feet. Sand filled her long black hair, painting it yellow. She shook that hair and patted sand off her tunic.

"I heard!" she said. "Bloody stars, trust me, I heard; they've been screaming about that for two days now. That's why we're walking in human forms, isn't it?"

Mori wheeled toward her, and a smile spread across her face. She grabbed her friend's shoulders. "But Treale! Don't you understand? How did I not see this earlier? If they seek dragons, that means others still live! More Vir Requis survived, not just you and me!"

She trembled and panted, still grinning. *Bayrin! Bayrin might be alive! And my brother Elethor, and my friend Lyana, and maybe more—many more.*

Of course, if they did live, they were in grave danger. Solina had summoned these new beasts to hunt them—just like she had summoned the wyverns and phoenixes. But still, they could be *alive*. That filled Mori with such joy that she lifted her chin and began walking again, not even waiting for Treale.

"Mori!" Treale said behind her. "Wait *up*. Mori!"

But Mori would not wait. She kept walking, head high, biting her trembling lip.

They're alive. I know it. They have to be. Otherwise Solina would never have sent these beasts to find them.

Treale rushed up beside her, buckling her cloak and tossing her pack across her shoulders. They walked through the sand, stepping around the globs of nephil drool.

"Mori, please," Treale said. "I... I hope they're alive too, but... I don't want us to get our hopes up. Okay, Mori? You understand, right?" She looked down at her feet. "Mori, we both saw the wyverns destroy Nova Vita. It was a slaughter. I don't know if anyone else escaped. It could be Solina lied to these nephilim, or maybe only a very, very small handful survived in the mountains where the miners work."

Mori stopped walking and turned to face her friend. She sniffed and tightened her fists.

"Bayrin is alive," she said. "I feel it. I know it. Elethor and Lyana are alive too. They are great warriors and... stars, Treale. Solina wouldn't wake this horde of demons for a few miners. She sent them to catch Elethor! He's always been the one she wanted. This whole war started because of this... this unholy obsession she has with him.

Elethor is alive, and if he's alive, I bet he kept Lyana and Bayrin close to him. We'll find them, Treale." A tear rolled down to her lips. "I won't stop looking. I believe."

She looked behind her; the city was distant and the nephilim had left it. She looked ahead; the horde had disappeared over the mountains.

Now we fly.

Mori summoned her magic and shifted.

Her wings wobbled. She tried to take off, flew a few feet, and dipped. Her claws hit the sand, and she kicked off again, flapped her wings with all her strength, and rose into a tottering flight. It took several heavy strokes to fill her wings with enough air and rise higher. She dipped again, snarled, and finally managed to rise and glide.

I will find you, Bayrin. I will find you, Elethor and Lyana. I swear.

Yet as she flew, she wondered: If truly she found Bayrin, would he even recognize her now? Whom would he find when he held her in his arms? Not the old Princess Mori, the timid girl whose lips he would kiss, who would laugh at his jokes. No; she could barely remember that Mori anymore. She did not know who she was now. A princess of Requiem? A famished prisoner, her back scarred and her mind forever haunted? In the dungeons of Tiranor, had something broken deep inside her, something that could never heal? She did not know.

"You are Mori," she whispered as she flew. "You are Mori, Mori, *Mori.*"

She might not know what that name meant anymore, whether it was the name of a princess, a prisoner, or a survivor, but she would not forget it. She would cling to herself. She would hang onto that name like a rope, for below her spread an endless pit and the reaching claws of monsters.

She flew over the mountains, their peaks carved from tan, bare rock. Treale flew at her side, black scales shimmering under the sun. The Tiran Sea shone blue and white to the northeast; distant beyond that horizon lay the ruins of Requiem, too far to see from here. When Mori looked northwest, she could just make out a green haze: the swamps of Gilnor. Beyond them lay a wilderness of forests where lived the salvanae, the true dragons... and safety, and hope, and a dream.

They flew toward that distant green patch, two dragons in an endless sky.

ELETHOR

The southern swarm grew, a stain upon the sky, and the distant shrieks rose.

Elethor stood upon the mountain, clad in plate armor. His leather glove creaked as he gripped his sword's hilt. He stared south. Fall was fading into winter, and the forest trees were nearly bare now; the branches and trunks of birch, maple, and beech grew dark from carpets of orange and red. Cold wind ruffled Elethor's hair and stung his face. Clouds veiled the sky and a drizzle fell.

"With rain and wind," Elethor whispered, "with bare trees and bare hearts; thus did winter find us."

It was an old poem. He could no longer remember the poet, but he remembered Mori quoting those words every winter by the fireplace. She would shudder, and he would laugh, muss her hair, and tease her for fearing the wind and rain and coming cold. She would smile hesitantly, and they would drink mulled wine and stoke the fire.

Yet now the storm does rise, and we are bare before it.

The dark cloud was spreading, still leagues away but moving fast. Thousands of beasts seemed to fly there, black and red and crying into the wind. Even from here, Elethor could detect their stench; they smelled like rotten corpses. They were mere specks from here, but when he squinted, Elethor could see beating wings, glints of sun on armor, and lanky limbs.

Nephilim. The spawn of demons and mortal mothers. He gripped his sword tight. *Stars, Solina, what have you done?*

He looked below the mountainside to their camp. A thousand souls lived there—people who depended on him, people he had protected for moons now, people who might die this evening. They could hear the distant shrieks; as they moved between the trees, the survivors cocked their heads, listened to the southern cries, and began to whisper. A few men drew swords.

Elethor snarled, fear gripping his heart like claws. He stared at the spreading shadow. It was buzzing and shimmering, a foul tapestry. How long before it reached them?

He missed Lyana and Bayrin so fiercely his chest tightened. He did not relish the thought of fighting without them, yet they had flown west and east, seeking aid.

Will you fetch aid for a pile of corpses?

An old man walked up the mountainside, clanking in armor. A scar rifted his creased face, and braids filled his white beard. A patch covered his left eye, and his gnarled hands clutched a sword and shield.

"Garvon," Elethor said and nodded his head. The old man had fought in the City Guard for forty years; he was one of the only guards to survive Nova Vita's fall.

"My king." The old man's breath rattled. He spat, then turned to stare south. His eyes darkened and he grumbled. "Bloody bollocks, what are those?" He covered his eyes and squinted. "Wyverns? Stars, there's an army of them."

Elethor shook his head and spoke softly. "Not wyverns. Nephilim."

Garvon grunted and stared at him with his one narrow, shrewd eye. "Nephilim? My king, they're only a legend. Don't tell me you believe—"

"I believe what I see, Garvon, and those are no wyverns." Elethor inhaled deeply. "They're flying our way. They know we're here."

Garvon flexed his fingers around his sword hilt. "They're just scanning the forest. We've seen Solina patrol here before. We're hidden under the trees; they won't find us."

Elethor looked down at the camp. A moon ago, leaves had covered these trees, and not even wyvern eyes could see through their cover. Today the branches were bare. From here upon the mountainside, Elethor could see huts and tents. They had covered their dwellings with woven curtains of leaf and vine, but that would not fool seeking eyes.

"These are no scouts, Garvon. This is an army, as you said." He grunted. "Solina would not invade Salvandos with an entire army; she would not risk angering the salvanae. Not unless she knew we were here." He began walking downhill. "We evacuate. At once."

"My lord," Garvon began, chin raised, "I say we stay. We fight. We slay them upon the—"

"The days of fighting are over," Elethor said, still walking downhill. "At least until Lyana and Bayrin return with aid. We flee to the temple."

Garvon muttered as he walked downhill, breath snorting and armor clanking. "That temple might make us miss the nephilim. I prefer fighting beasts I can see, rather than ghosts. Beasts you can cut and burn."

They had discovered the temple three moons ago, a network of ruins a few leagues north in the forest. Elethor had wanted to set camp there, to hide among its fallen statues, crumbling archways, and dungeons. The others—everyone from Garvon to Bayrin and Lyana—had adamantly refused, quoting old tales of the ghosts who dwelled in those ruins.

The Ancients built those temples, Lyana had warned, *and some say their ghosts still haunt the place. Let us hide among trees, not old stones that still whisper.*

Yet now these trees were naked, and stones could protect them, even if they had to share those stones with spirits.

He reached the foothills and entered the camp. The distant shrieks rose louder now. The survivors stood still, staring south. Children raised wooden swords as if, with enough courage, they could slay any enemy. Wounded men lay legless in carts, faces pale. Mothers clutched babes to their breasts.

One thousand and fifty-four souls. The last lights of Requiem.

Elethor climbed onto a fallen log. He gripped Ferus's hilt so tightly his fingers ached. The people came to stand around him, forming a ring in the forest. Elethor looked from face to face. They were pale. They were afraid. These were not fighters; nearly all their fighters had died in Requiem. These were elders, children, mothers, wounded.

"People of Requiem!" Elethor said, looking from face to face. They stared back silently. "Queen Lyana and Lord Bayrin have flown to fetch aid; they will return with it, I promise this to you. But now we must move. Now we must flee danger. I will lead you north through the forest, and we will hide among the ruins of Bar Luan. We will find safety there until help arrives."

The people exchanged dark glances. They whispered prayers and curses. One old man drew his sword and a child whimpered. They had all heard stories of Bar Luan, the fallen temple of the Ancients. In a thousand bedtime stories, they had heard of the ghosts who wandered there, the spirits that sucked the blood of the living, and the old pain in the rocks.

Yet what choice do I have? Elethor thought. *We can face old stories. Or we can face beasts that fly upon the sky.*

The distant shrieks rose higher—cruel, inhuman shrieks, high-pitched like shattering glass. A stench wafted on the wind, scented of corpses. A child began to cry, and a few of the wounded whimpered. A young woman cursed and drew a chipped sword.

"Be calm!" Elethor said. "Danger approaches; the enemy flies from the south. We will hide in the temple, and we will find safety there. I promise this to you. I swear it on the name of my fathers. Now move! Walk in human form. Stay under the trees and wear your cloaks of leaf and vine. Move silently, move fast, and stay under the cover of the branches. The temple is three leagues away. Follow me now!"

He stepped off the log. The ring of people parted, and Elethor began walking north. His heart pounded so madly he thought that, were he not wearing a breastplate, it could leap from his chest. He walked silently, lips tight, hand still gripping his sword. Around him, the people glanced at one another uneasily.

"Follow, now!" Garvon hissed, moving from survivor to survivor. "Do not pack. Leave your things! Move—no, leave your supplies. Move!"

Behind them in the south, the nephilim shrieked. Elethor marched among the trees, leaves and twigs snapping under his boots. Behind him the people walked, faces pale, clutching spears and swords or simple staffs they had carved from fallen branches.

Please, stars, don't let them see us, Elethor prayed silently. *Let us live until Bayrin and Lyana return.*

They moved through the forest in single file, silent. These people had fled the phoenixes into the tunnels under Nova Vita, then the wyverns; they knew how to move silently and swiftly. Strings of leaves covered their heads and cloaks, red like the forest around them. Eyes darted. Voices whispered. Fingers twisted around weapons.

"Legion, Legion!" rose a distant shriek behind them, curdling Elethor's blood. "You promised flesh! You promised dragon bones. We hunger! We thirst!"

Elethor gritted his teeth. Around him, the survivors whispered and a few mewled. The shrieks still sounded distant—leagues away—but louder than the crash of columns.

"We must feast! We must drink dragon blood." The cries rolled across the sky, loud and shrill as snapping bones. "Where do dragons hide?"

Requiem's survivors watched the skies, clung to one another, and raised their weapons.

"Keep moving!" Elethor hissed. "Garvon, keep them moving."

A hundred men and women served in their new army, a force Elethor had dubbed the Camp Guard; old Garvon led them. These soldiers, clad in dented armor and bearing longswords, moved along the line of survivors, rallying them forward. They kept moving through the forest. Elethor quickened his walk to a run; the others ran behind him.

"I am Legion!" rose a cry from behind. The stench of rot blazed. "I am Prophet. I lead you to dragons! A camp, a camp! Dragons were here. Dragons are near! I smell them, brothers and sisters. I smell sweet dragon blood to drink, and bones to crack, and marrow to suck, and meat to lick, and souls to break. Dragons flee! Dragons will die."

A shadow shot above the branches overhead. The survivors bent, wailed, and pointed. The shadow circled, then soared again, and Elethor snarled.

Stars save us.

He had seen illustrations of nephilim, those spawn of demons and their mortal brides, great lanky beasts with bat wings. In real life, they were more hideous than anything an artist could draw. The nephil above looked, Elethor thought, like a strip of dried meat, its fingers clawed, its mouth full of teeth like swords. A halo of flame encircled its head. The creature howled, and trees shattered, and the survivors covered their ears. The sound was so loud Elethor shouted through his clenched jaw. The scream pounded through his chest; it felt like it could snap his ribs.

"Shapeshifters, shapeshifters!" cried the creature. More shadows shot overhead. "Humans walk, humans smell like dragons. Feast upon them! I am Legion. I am Prophet. I bring you blood and bones!"

Three nephilim swooped, crashed between branches, and landed on the forest floor before them.

Elethor snarled, shifted into a dragon, and blew a stream of fire. Around him, men of the Camp Guard shifted too and blew their flames. The nephilim screeched and burned, and a fourth one swooped from above. Its claws reached out, grabbed a child, and ripped her apart. Blood spattered. People wailed.

"Shift and fly!" Elethor shouted. "Fly, Vir Requis! Into the sky."

They screamed. They wept. They shifted into dragons—elders, mothers, youths. A few Vir Requis were mere babes or toddlers, too young to shift; their mothers carried them in their claws.

Elethor crashed between the branches into the sky. Thousands of nephilim swarmed and howled. At his left, one swooped and grabbed a young red dragon. The nephil ripped off her head and swallowed it; the dragon's body returned to human form and crashed down. At Elethor's left, a nephil crashed into a silver dragon, slashed its claws, and gutted the dragon as easily as a fisherman gutting his catch.

"Fly, Vir Requis!" Elethor shouted. "Fly north. Fly to the temple!"

He could see Bar Luan perhaps a league away, rising from the forest. A few staircases, a crumbling archway, and craggy walls remained from what was once a sprawling complex; these remnants would have to serve them now. Dragons began flying toward it, blowing fire over their shoulders at pursuing nephilim. Elethor rose, blew a flaming jet at a beast, and ducked to dodge its tumbling body. Thousands of the creatures covered the southern sky, swarming forward.

"Fly, Vir Requis!" he howled. "Hide in the temple." He roasted another nephil, a scaly beast clad in rusted armor, and rose higher. "Camp Guard, rally here! Hold them back. Battle formations, here!"

A clanking white dragon rose ahead, horns long and eyes red—Garvon, chief of the Camp Guard. A gash ran down his side, seeping blood, but still he fought, blowing fire at nephilim above. A dozen other dragons, wearing the great dragonhelms of the Camp Guard, rose around them and blew their fire.

"Hold them back!" Elethor shouted. "Let the others flee. Flame the beasts!"

Behind him, the women, elders, and children were fleeing north. Before him and his fellow soldiers—less than a hundred dragons—the nephil host spread. Thousands of beasts, maybe tens of thousands, covered the horizon. They screeched to the heavens, and the trees below cracked and fell, and boulders rolled. The earth itself seemed to shake.

Hovering in midair before the swarm, Elethor bared his fangs and growled. Around him, his fellow dragons beat their wings and smoke rose from their nostrils. Elethor's heart pounded, and fear and rage throbbed through him, tingling from his tail to his horns.

"Soldiers of Requiem!" he said to the dragons around him, a mere handful of warriors before the swarm. "You will hold your ground. You will hold the beasts back. You will buy our people time to flee to safety."

Behind him, Elethor heard the survivors of Requiem fly farther; they would soon reach the temple. Before him, the countless nephilim screeched and soared and circled in the air. They flew in no battle formations like wyverns or phoenixes; this was a mob of devilry.

"Legion!" they howled. "Legion! Prophet of the Fallen!"

The great nephil, their champion, rose from flame. His halo of fire screamed. His body was lanky; his ribs pushed against skin like dried parchment. He howled to the sky, teeth long and thin and white, and his wings sprayed fire as he rose. His cry was so shrill it raised boils across the nephilim around him.

"I am Legion, I am Prophet!" he screeched. "I have led you to freedom. I lead you to dragons. Feast upon them!"

The thousands of beasts howled, beat their wings, and shot forward.

The dragons roared their flames.

LYANA

She crouched between the roots of fallen trees, stared downhill, and cursed.

The Tiran camp sprawled a mile away, covering the scorched earth. Sooty palisades, carved from uprooted trees, encircled a mass of tents and huts and campfires. Thousands of men swarmed there. Many were soldiers, clad in breastplates of pale steel, suns upon their shields. Others were masons; they bustled across scaffolding, raising walls of stone.

They are building a fortress here, Lyana thought. *A great barracks in the heart of Requiem.*

She growled and clutched her sword Levitas. Once fields had swayed here. Once House Oldnale had plowed this land, growing barley and wheat and sweet peas. Today the farms were gone, the earth scorched. The old bricks of Oldnale Manor, where her squire Treale had lived, lay in wheelbarrows within the Tiran camp; those old stones of Requiem were now growing into the Tirans' fort.

"I swear to you, Treale," Lyana whispered, crouched behind the roots of the fallen tree. "I will avenge you. I will return to this place someday, and I will burn those who defile your home."

A screech rose from the camp, and Lyana winced. Even here, a league away, the sound throbbed through her chest. She pulled her cloak tighter around her, narrowed her eyes, and snarled.

A dozen nephilim guarded the camp below, patrolling the palisades of sharpened spikes. Each stood as tall as a dragon, dwarfing the Tiran men. Their bodies were emaciated, dried flesh clinging to bones, yet their claws and teeth were long and white; Lyana could see their glint even from here. Bat wings beat against their backs, stirring ash beneath them. Lyana had been traveling across the ruins of Requiem for ten days now, and she had seen their destruction everywhere: their drool upon forest floors, corpses of animals torn apart, and trails of the rot they leaked.

Lyana longed to fly down there. She long to test these beasts in battle—to see how fast they flew, to blow her fire upon them, to kill them upon the land they infested. Yet she could not—not here, not alone.

We need more than dragons now. We need the men of Osanna, and the griffins of the east, and the salvanae of the west. We need aid or the world will fall.

With a grunt, she turned away from the roots and began moving downhill, away from the camp. Her cloak fluttered in the wind, revealing the armor she wore underneath: the ancient, silvery armor of a bellator, a knight of Requiem. Her scabbard and helm bore engravings of the Draco constellation, the sigil of her order.

The bellators have fallen. I am the last of their number. She walked down into the wind. Dry leaves fluttered around her boots and her cloak billowed behind her. *Yet I still serve my stars. Now. Forever. Until my last breath.*

She walked upon the scorched earth, moving between fallen trees and dead cattle until those stars glowed in the sunset. Smoke still blew above Requiem, hiding all but the dragon's tail above, yet still Lyana gazed upon those lights, and she prayed to them.

"I still fight for you, stars of my fathers." She drew Levitas, ancient sword of her order. "I still fly under your light."

As the sun dipped below the horizon, she shifted into the blue dragon and took flight. Nephilim patrolled this land; she had seen countless of the beasts while walking across Requiem, peering at them from between trees and boulders. In the darkness she could fly silently, fire in her maw, sky beneath her wings. She dived through the cold, long night.

The land soon changed below, the scorched fields giving way to lush dark forests. Forts rose from the trees, their battlements alight with torches. After days of ash and soot and mud, Lyana was leaving the ruins of Requiem; she flew now over the eastern lands of Osanna, ancient realm of men. It was a vast land; Lyana had visited here before as an envoy of Requiem, but she had seen only small parts of the kingdom. Osanna stretched from northern Fidelium, mountains where the undead rose from tombs, to the southern port of Altus Mare, whose ships navigated the Tiran Sea and sailed east to Leonis, land of griffins.

She flew for hours, crossing forests, mountains, and fields, before finally spiraling down to a silver lake under the moon. There she lay upon grass, drank from the water, and slept until the dawn.

She awoke to see two cloaked archers pointing arrows at her.

With a snarl, Lyana leaped up and began to draw her sword.

"Freeze!" shouted one of the archers, voice ringing deeply from the shadows of his hood. "Release your sword or you'll die before you draw the blade."

Lyana bared her teeth at the men. Both wore green cloaks, and beneath their hoods, brown scarves covered their faces. Leaves and vines covered them, and swords hung from their belts. One man was short and squat, his wide shoulders tugging at his cloak; the other was tall and lean. Something about them seemed familiar, though Lyana could not place them.

She growled. "I am Lyana Eleison, Queen of Requiem, and—"

"We know who you are," said the taller, leaner man, the one with the deep voice. "Release your sword."

Both men drew their arrows back farther; the bowstrings creaked. With a grunt and hiss, Lyana released her sword's hilt, letting the blade fall back into its scabbard. The two men stepped forward and grabbed Lyana's arms.

Lyana growled, tugged herself free, and shifted.

She took flight, a blue dragon with fire in her maw.

Below her, the two men shifted too and soared, bronze dragons with long white horns.

"Stars!" Lyana shouted, beating her wings. The grass below swayed, and waves raced along the lake. "You're Vir Requis. How dare you threaten your queen?"

Seeing them as dragons, she finally recognized these two. She had seen them in Requiem's northern mountains; they were brothers and miners of iron ore. The older, taller one was named Grom Miner, she remembered. The younger, squat brother was named Gar.

"We are no longer in Requiem, Lyana Eleison," said Grom; his scales were a slightly deeper shade of copper. "And you are no longer our queen, if indeed you wed the Boy King Elethor in your exile. All titles are forsaken in the ruin of the world, and every dragon is master of himself now. We will take you to our camp, and you will answer to our new lord."

Lyana snarled, and fire flicked between her teeth. These two dragons were burly and long, far larger than her own short, slim form, yet she knew that she could kill them. She was fast. Her fire was hot. Her claws were sharp. She had trained to fight in Castra Draco, garrison of Requiem's fabled Royal Army. These two had perhaps grown strong from digging mines and hauling ore, yet Lyana had slain phoenixes and wyverns, and she could slay these two.

And yet... and yet they were still her kin. They were new survivors when she had thought none existed. She spat her flames into the lake.

"You call yourselves your own masters, fellow dragons of Requiem," she said. "Yet now you speak of serving a new lord. Are you free dragons or servants?"

Gar Miner—the younger brother—spoke for the first time. He was a shorter dragon than his brother, but burlier. He spoke in the high voice of a man just leaving his youth.

"We are free dragons," he said. "Yet we choose to fight for the Legless Lord. You will follow us. You will answer to him, and you will have a choice to serve him too, or you may leave these lands and find your own fortune."

Lyana growled deep in her throat. She had not come here to Osanna for this; she had flown seeking aid from the king of men, and then from the eastern griffins. And yet here hid more survivors of Requiem, perhaps many more. She could not forsake this chance to meet them, to bring them back to Elethor's camp.

"Show me to your lord," she said.

Grom Miner nodded and growled. "We walk. In human forms. We live in Osanna, and the cruel Queen Solina still dares not invade this land, yet we've seen her beasts fly overhead as scouts. We walk hidden. We walk quietly. We will not fly as dragons again."

The bronze brothers descended and shifted back into human forms upon the lakeside. Lyana landed beside them and shifted too.

"Follow," said Grom. He turned and began walking into the forest.

Lyana snarled at him. She was Queen of Requiem; she followed no one. And yet Grom was walking among the trees already, and his younger brother Gar was caressing his bow. Growling, Lyana followed, and the three moved through the forest.

They walked for a long time, and the forest thickened. The oaks grew twisted and tall here. Moss covered the boles and mist floated between them. Back in Salvandos in the west, where Elethor ruled his camp of survivors, the autumn leaves had fallen and covered the forest floor. Here they still grew bronze and dulled gold, metallic and hard and barely rustling. Lichen hung from gnarled branches, brushing against Lyana's cheeks, and the air smelled of loam and stagnant water. She could not see the sky or sun—the canopy was thick as a roof—yet the brothers seemed to know their way. They walked assuredly, boots crunching branches and twigs.

Lyana guessed it was near noon when a stench rose on the wind, twisting her gut. Flies buzzed. With a snarl, she drew her sword, but the brothers only snickered.

"No need for blades here, my *queen*," Grom said, speaking the last word as an insult. He led them around a boulder and pointed at a thick oak. Upon its trunk, tied with ropes and chains, hung the corpse of a nephil.

"Stars," Lyana whispered.

Nausea rose in her. She had never seen one of the beasts so close before. Patches of dank scales covered its flesh like lesions, and its claws curved, long as sabres. Its bloated head bustled with insects; the eyes were already gone. Worms crawled upon its cleaved skull, and dried entrails hung from its slashed belly. Half the body was burnt with dragonfire, the other half lacerated with claws.

Squat young Gar smirked. "Figured we'd leave the bastard here—a warning to his comrades. I killed this one myself." He thrust out his broad chest. "Burned him dead."

Lyana spat in disgust. "Bury it," she said. "It stinks."

"We want it to stink, *your highness*," Gar said. "Let its brothers smell it. Let them smell their death on the wind and know that more death awaits them here."

Lyana whipped her head toward the brothers and glared. "You are a boastful couple." She growled. "You hide here in disguise, and you dare not shift and fly, yet you brag of slaying nephilim. Do you know how many of these creatures fly in Requiem, seeking us? Thousands. *Tens* of thousands. Armies of them muster, and more keep flowing north from the desert. You burned one? Swarms of them will fly here; they will cover the world. Do you think the stench of one will deter the rest?" She marched toward Gar, grabbed his collar, and bared her teeth at him. "You are a foolish boy, and when this corpse's comrades arrive, you will die squealing." She twisted his collar tight, constricting his breath. "I've seen many boys like you die squealing."

The young miner paled, and for an instant his lips shook. Then he raised his chin, shoved her off, and smoothed his tunic.

"Be silent," he grumbled, though his voice shook slightly. "Follow. We're almost there."

They walked past the corpse—Lyana nearly gagged as the flies buzzed near her—and moved down a leafy slope toward a stream. The water rose past their ankles, and beyond it stood a hill with trees so thick, they had to push branches aside and climb over roots and boulders. Finally, below the hill, Lyana saw the camp.

Her heart leaped and tears dampened her eyes.

"So many," she whispered.

Only a thousand Vir Requis lived with Elethor in the west; Lyana had thought them the only survivors of Requiem. Yet here lived many more—this camp was twice the size of the one Elethor led, maybe larger. Children ran playing around boulders, holding dolls woven of leaf and grass. Young women whispered around campfires. An old man stood upon a boulder, leading a congregation in prayer. A palisade of spikes surrounded the camp, and men stood guarding it, armed with spears.

A tear streamed down Lyana's cheek, and her legs trembled. "So many still live."

The brothers tried to grab her arms and lead her. Lyana wrenched herself free and began marching toward the camp, holding her head high. She let the wind billow her cloak open, revealing her knightly armor. At times like these, Lyana missed her old mane of fiery red curls; it used to draw people's attention like a beacon of fire. Solina had sheared that hair last year, and now only a finger's length grew upon her head. Today these embers, a memory of a great flame, would have to do.

"My lady!" Gar cried behind her. "I mean, Lyana! I mean—newcomer. Halt! We will escort you into our camp."

Lyana ignored him and kept marching. She made toward a gateway in the palisade where two guards stood, bearing cracked shields and makeshift spears. They wore old, dented breastplates; one from the armories of Requiem, another stolen from a dead Tiran and still bearing the Golden Sun of Tiranor. When Lyana tried to march between them and into the camp, they moved closer together, making to block her way.

"Move!" Lyana barked and shoved them back. When they tried to grab her, she glared and bared her teeth at them. "I am Lyana Eleison, Queen of Requiem, your mistress. If you touch me, I will cut off your hands."

She gripped her sword's hilt and drew a foot of steel; it gleamed and the guards hesitated. Not wasting another moment, Lyana strode into the camp.

"Who leads this place?" she called out. "Bring him before me."

All around her, people abandoned gardens, wheelbarrows, toys, harps, and weapons. They began to gather around her, staring and whispering to one another. She heard her name spoken in awe. She knew these faces; she had seen them labor in Requiem's fields, dig in her mines, and forge steel in her smithies. She saw no nobles; the last lords and ladies of Requiem had fallen. Here were the commoners of Aeternum's Kingdom.

"Who leads you?" she repeated. She stepped onto a tree stump and wheeled her head around, seeking a ruler. "Bring him to speak with me."

Grom approached her, tall and grim, his ill-fitting armor clanking beneath his cloak. He cleared his throat and smirked.

"It will be... difficult to bring the Legless Lord here. I think you will find it easier if we took you to him."

Lyana gripped her sword tight and frowned. She was queen to these people; would she approach this Legless Lord, a son of Requiem, as an ambassador? She grinded her teeth.

"Very well," she said. "If truly this *lord* of yours— and I use the term lightly—has no legs and cannot approach me, take me to him."

She did not like this. These people had missed her coronation in the wilderness of Salvandos, yet they still knew her as the Lady Lyana, a knight betrothed to their king. And yet they did not bow before her.

I will find no loyalty here, she thought. *Titles still mean something in the west, where King Elethor protects his people; here they are forgotten.*

The brothers led her down a dirt path between gardens, tree stumps, and rows of game hanging from poles. A hall rose ahead, built of boles still rough with bark and the stumps of felled branches. Those branches, still leafy, formed a rough roof. The structure looked long enough to house a dragon.

They stepped through its makeshift doors, which were carved of branches and rope, and into a shadowy chamber. The air outside was cold and wet; inside the hall was hot and stuffy and scented of pine. A campfire burned upon the earthen floor, its smoke rising through a hole in the roof.

"My lord!" called Grom, standing at Lyana's side. "We have found another survivor. She is Lyana Eleison, once a lady of Requiem's courts; we found her by the eastern lake."

A cough sounded behind the campfire; a man sat there, hidden behind the flames. The coughing went on for a long moment, then ended with a wheeze. Finally the man behind the fire spoke, voice raspy.

"Bring her closer, Grom. Let me see her."

Grom and Gar grabbed Lyana's arms yet again. She tried to shake herself free, but the brothers gripped her firmly, and they pulled her forward. She grunted but walked with them; she was more curious to see this man than to fight his minions. They walked down the hall and around the fire, and there she saw the Legless Lord.

He was an older man; she guessed him sixty years old, maybe older. His cheeks were stubbly, his long hair grizzled. He wore a brown leather tunic and sat in a chair of twisting oak roots—a mockery of Requiem's old throne which had stood in its palace. Upon his knees, the man held a sword with a dragonclaw pommel; forged in dragonfire in Requiem's Castra Draco, Lyana thought. His legs ended below those knees, and cloth wrapped the stumps.

"Lyana," he rasped. Coughs seized him again, and he brought a handkerchief to his mouth. It was a moment before he could speak again. "Lyana Eleison, once a lady of Requiem; I am glad to see you survived the carnage. Welcome to our camp."

"Dorin Blacksmith," Lyana said, eyes narrowed. She recognized this one. He had forged steel in Nova Vita smithies, and he had served in the City Guard during the war, though last time she had seen him, he had walked on two legs. "I too am glad to see you live; I fought with you against the wyverns. I saw you slay two. You fought well, my friend."

The blacksmith hacked a laugh, then coughed again. "Yes, I slew more than two. The last one did this." He swept his hand across his stumps. "You have emerged unscathed, I see, though perhaps with less hair."

She took a step closer to him, shaking off the brothers' hands.

"Dorin," she said, "King Elethor lives. He reigns in exile, leading a camp of a thousand Vir Requis. We still fight. We will assault Tiranor and we will slay her queen. Fly west with me now, join King Elethor, and we will rain fire upon the enemy."

Coughs interrupted Dorin's sigh. He dabbed his lips with his handkerchief. "Damn smoke and damn ash." He cleared his throat; a rough, rusty noise. "Since the fires in Nova Vita, my lungs are ruined." He hacked again, then *tsk*ed his tongue. "Do you see the ruin of war? My lungs. My legs. These ragged, haunted people I lead. That is what your King Elethor brought us; that is what he will bring those who still follow him." He shook his head. "Fly west to join the boy on another adventure? I think not. We've had enough of war; now is our time to grow gardens, to build halls, to find a new life here in the east. Requiem is fallen, my child. Her columns lie smashed, and her halls shattered; her cry is silenced. Let us find new spring here—in Second Haven—a new kingdom for the children of Draco."

Lyana raised her eyebrows. "*Second Haven?* A new kingdom?" She grabbed the man's shoulders. "Damn it, Dorin, Requiem still lives. Requiem is not a piece of earth; she is starlight, and she is the magic inside us. King's Column still stands; Requiem still roars. You are one of her children, and Elethor Aeternum is still your king."

Grom and Gar grabbed her and tugged her back. Lyana snarled, spun, and kicked at them. She hit the elder on his shin, and he raised his fist. Lyana leaped back, drew her sword, and nodded to him.

"Go on," she said softly. "Go on, Grom Miner. Make your move. You can soon become a Legless Servant to your Legless Lord."

The lanky miner rubbed his shin and spat. He looked at Dorin, hesitating. The Legless Lord grumbled and raised his hands.

"Brothers!" he said. "Leave her be. Lyana! Sheath your sword; we draw no steel in this hall."

She raised that sword higher. "You look upon Levitas, sword of Lord Terra Eleison, a Light of Requiem. I draw and raise my steel where I please, Dorin. You were a blacksmith once; you should show more respect to a blade of legend."

He sighed again, breath rattling like dice in his lungs. "I was a blacksmith; that is true. And these two brothers were miners; they are guards now. You were a knight; now you are a guest. Requiem has fallen. Her legends are nothing but burnt scrolls. Lower your sword; its history means nothing in Second Haven."

Lyana growled. "Nova Vita has not lain fallen for a year, and you forsake all memory of her halls and heroes?" She spat at his feet. "You fought nobly for Requiem over her capital; now you defile her. You may stay here, Dorin Blacksmith, upon this mockery of a throne you have carved. I lead these people west—with or without you."

She turned and marched back toward the door. She trudged out into the camp, stepped onto a boulder, and raised her voice.

"Children of Requiem!" she called.

Women planting seeds, men carving spears, and children weaving baskets looked up, pausing from their work. Lyana raised her sword so the light caught it.

"I am Lyana Eleison!" she shouted. "I am wed to King Elethor Aeternum, son of Olasar, descended from Queen Gloriae. I am Queen of Requiem. King Elethor still lives! Requiem still fights. Join me west, and—"

Pain shattered against her nape.

Lyana fell from the boulder and hit the ground.

She flipped over and tried to raise her sword, but a boot pressed down on her wrist. The brothers stood above her, and behind them sat the Legless Lord in a wheelbarrow.

"Tie her up!" the grizzled old man shouted. "Guards, tie her to the tree."

Lyana kicked and nearly freed herself, but more men rushed forward. She leaped and tried to shift; they grabbed her legs, and one man swung a club. Pain exploded across her, her magic fizzled, and blood dripped into her eye.

She hit the fallen leaves.

Men leaped onto her, and dirt filled her mouth, and she couldn't even scream.

ELETHOR

Behind him, the dragons fled toward the temple ruins—mothers, children, elders. At his sides, a hundred dragon warriors flapped wings and blew fire. Before them, the army of nephilim spread, covering the sky and horizon, a buzzing horde of countless demons.

As their wives, children, and elders escaped, Elethor and his dragons shot forward, roaring fire.

The nephilim crashed against them.

Elethor howled and blew his flame. The fire crashed against one nephil, and the beast screeched and fell. Two more nephilim flew at him, one from each side. Elethor spun and clubbed one with his tail, driving his spikes into its rotted flesh. The second nephil crashed into him and grabbed hold like a great spider clutching its prey. Teeth bit into Elethor's back, and he roared. Claws ripped at his flank.

He dipped in the air, twisted his neck, and bit into the nephil. It felt like biting mummified flesh. The beast opened its mouth and screeched; the sound was so loud and shrill that when it faded, Elethor heard nothing but ringing. He flamed the beast, and when it screeched again, the call washed over Elethor like white light.

It fell. More swooped from above. There must have been ten thousand.

Stars, give me strength. Let me hold them back just long enough—long enough to let the others flee into the temple, to hide among its stones and shadows.

"There, my Lord Legion!" rose a voice from the mass of nephilim—the rumble of a dragon's voice. "The brass dragon! That one is their king. Feast upon him, my lord!"

Elethor flamed one nephil, clawed another, and looked up toward the voice. He growled and rage flared within him, spilling between his teeth in rivers of fire.

A gray dragon flew ahead between the nephilim, his eyes red, his mouth open in a gloating, snaggletoothed grin. Elethor knew this one.

"Nemes," he growled.

So that is how they found us.

Roaring, Elethor beat his wings and rose higher. He blew flame and flew through the fire, shooting toward the traitor.

Nephilim crashed into him. Teeth bit and claws swung; he felt them tearing off scales. He roared and blew fire in a ring. They surrounded him, a cell of putrid flesh and rotting eyes. Their wings blocked the sky. Their sores oozed pus. A claw lashed his wing, tearing a rent through it.

"Nemes!" Elethor shouted. He barreled forward through the beasts, seeking the gray dragon. He had never felt such bloodlust, such a craving to kill and destroy his enemies; today he hated Nemes more than Solina herself.

"Elethor!"

Garvon's gravelly voice rang out. The burly white dragon rose and tugged at him, pulling him back into a ring of other dragons. They blew fire, holding back the beasts.

"Garvon, he betrayed us!" Elethor said. "Nemes—the gray dragon. Help me find him."

He whipped his head from side to side, seeking the traitor, but saw only nephilim. The trees below cracked and fell under their shrieks. The half demons chewed severed limbs of Vir Requis, tossed their heads back, and swallowed greedily. When he glanced behind him, Elethor saw his people vanish into the distant temple, scurrying into its crumbled halls and secret tunnels. He looked back south, seeking Nemes again, and growled.

I will find you yet, Nemes, and I will burn you with my fire.

He spun and began flying north to the temple.

"Fly, warriors of Requiem!" he shouted. "Fall back to the temple. Fall back!"

They flew around him, bloodied and slashed and panting. They blew fire over their shoulders, burning nephilim, yet the swarm spread for miles; they seemed endless. Elethor beat his wings madly. A nephil swooped from above, and claws thrashed, and Elethor banked. He soared, flamed the beast, and clawed another dead. More rose below them, and Garvon rained fire upon them.

A hundred dragons had remained to hold back the swarm; perhaps twenty still lived. They raced over the collapsing forest toward the temple. Every moment, another one fell. Nineteen remained. Then eighteen. Soon only a dozen. In death, their magic left them, and they crashed into the trees—torn apart and splattering blood upon the fallen leaves of autumn.

Finally Elethor and his surviving warriors reached the temple. The ruins spread below them like the scattered bones of a stone giant.

Nobody knew the age of Bar Luan; books from a thousand years ago called these ruins ancient. Walls carved with reliefs of men and beasts rose from the forest, crumbling and mossy, chunks of them missing as if giants had chewed upon them. Some walls cradled dark archways with stairs that plunged into darkness. Others lay fallen. Great stone faces, carved larger than dragons, stared stoically from some walls that still stood; other faces lay fallen and overgrown with moss and vine.

The roots of great trees clutched these ruins, twisting over them like woody tentacles or the wax of melted candles. Years ago, paved roads and courtyards had spread here; today trees and roots broke through the cobblestones, casting them aside like discarded dice. Years ago, pyramids had risen here from the trees; today only one remained standing, its stairs so chipped they would send climbers tumbling.

Bar Luan, Elethor thought. *House of ghosts.*

They called it a temple; it looked more like a city. Ten thousand people could have lived here, maybe twice that many. Elethor thought the place nearly as large as Nova Vita.

"Go, into the doorways, into the halls!" he shouted. Dozens of doorways filled the walls, leading to chambers and dungeons. They were small passageways built for the Ancients, a people short and slim; the nephilim would not fit through.

Elethor dived toward one doorway, a narrow opening with a lintel shaped as a stone lion. Before he could land, two nephilim swooped and crashed into him, shoving him against cracked cobblestones.

Elethor writhed beneath them. He whipped his tail, hitting one beast. It screeched, deafening him. Again ringing rolled over him; he could barely hear anything else. The second beast bit, driving teeth into Elethor's left shoulder, the one already scarred from wyvern acid. He bellowed, kicked, and rolled. They slammed into a wall, sending it crumbling. The nephil roared, and Elethor beat his wings. He rose ten feet and rained his fire, catching the nephilim before they could rise. They blazed, screeching and kicking, knocking into walls and statues. Stones cascaded and fallen leaves burned.

Elethor looked around him; he could see one last dragon land, shift into human form, and run into a doorway between hanging roots. The rest had either hidden in the ruins or lay dead.

Above the ruins, thousands of nephilim blocked the sky.

Elethor growled, resisting the temptation to fly at them; he still craved to roast Nemes. Instead he shifted into human form and ran toward the doorway.

Nephilim swooped behind him.

Their claws scraped against the cobblestones.

Elethor leaped into the doorway and rolled.

Behind him in the courtyard, the nephilim shrieked. They bit at the doorway. Their claws reached into the darkness, each as long as Elethor's sword. He drew that sword and slashed at them. He cut one finger off—it was longer than his arm—and black blood sprayed him. Their teeth snapped at the doorway, their eyes blazed, and rocks tumbled.

Elethor retreated deeper into darkness. The walls were built of rugged bricks overgrown with moss. The ceiling was low, only a finger's length above his head, and the doorway only five feet tall; the Ancients must have stood hardly taller than children. Elethor walked around a bend, moving out of the doorway's line of sight. When he stepped a few more paces into darkness, he bumped against something soft.

He turned to see two children kneeling in the shadows, a boy and a girl with muddy blond hair. Elethor recognized them as twin children from his camp.

"Aw da monstews outside?" asked the girl; she looked to be about five years old.

Her brother raised a wooden sword. "I'll protect you."

Elethor knelt by the children and examined them for wounds; they were bruised and muddy and scratched, but otherwise unhurt. When he looked behind him, he could no longer see the doorway, but he could still hear the nephilim shrieking. The twins clung to him, one clutching him from each side. They shivered.

Nemes, Elethor thought. His old servant. A Vir Requis. *How could a son of Requiem do this?*

As the children embraced him, Elethor's head spun with rage. Solina had betrayed him, but she had always been a daughter of Tiranor; this was a stab in the back, and Elethor swore that someday, somehow, he would reach Nemes and slay him.

The nephilim shrieked outside. The temple shook and dust fell from the ceiling. The rage and darkness of an ancient horde howled outside, and Elethor held the twins close, shut his eyes, and struggled to breathe.

BAYRIN

He woke up with a stiff neck, Piri still cuddling against him.

Merciful stars, he thought and sighed. His every part ached, and he had barely slept with the girl clinging to him.

It's an amazing discovery, he thought. *A creature for one of Mori's bestiaries—half woman, half leech.*

"Up, up!" he said. "It's morning."

He struggled to rise, but Piri only mumbled, scrunched her lips, and wrapped her arms more closely around him. She kept sleeping. For such a slim young thing, she was surprisingly strong, pinning him down.

"Piri Healer!" he said with a groan. "Stars, get *off.*"

The girl was intolerable. Throughout the night, whenever he would crawl away from her, she would snuggle closer, trapping him in her embrace. Whenever he did fall asleep, moments later she would mumble or kick her legs, waking him. And now dawn had risen, and still he could not extricate himself.

Bayrin groaned and let his head fall back onto his pack. He looked up at the sky. Clouds rolled there beyond the branches of maples. It would be a long day of flight, and Bayrin knew his wings would ache, but anything was better than lying here.

"Merciful stars, Piri, will you wake up?" he said. He grabbed her arm and tried to pry it off, but she clung tight.

A distant cry sounded.

Bayrin frowned.

He raised his head and stared. In the distance between trees, he could just make out dark forms in the sky. Shrieks rose, closer this time.

Oh stars.

"Piri!" he said. "Wake up!"

The screeches rolled across the sky. Long figures were flying there like dolls made from sticks, distant but moving fast. A stench of rot wafted through the forest.

Nephilim.

"Piri, Piri, wake up!" He shook her. "I really think you need to wake up now, Piri!"

She scrunched her lips, squeezed her eyes tightly shut, and mumbled. "What, Bay? I'm sleepy."

He managed to pry her arms off, leaped up, and stared east. *Damn it.* A hundred of the creatures flew there, moving straight toward them, and their cries rolled across the land.

"Bay?" Piri sat up and rubbed her eyes. "What's that sound?"

He grabbed her and pulled her to her feet. "Look!"

"Hey!" The young healer wrenched herself free. "Watch who you tug, Bayrin Eleison! I—"

Her eyes fell upon the approaching nephilim and she paled. She grabbed him and pulled him down. They ran at a crouch, grabbed their packs and blankets and pots, and scurried behind a fallen log.

"Bloody stars, Piri," he whispered, "I think you could have slept through the Griffin War."

She elbowed him. "Shush! And stay down." She tugged his cloak over them; leaves and twigs were still woven into it. "Be quiet for once, Bayrin."

"Me?" He bristled. "I—"

She dug her elbow sharply into his stomach. "Shh!"

They crouched under the fallen tree and stared between its branches. The stench of the nephilim flared. Two years ago, after the phoenixes had crushed a building in Nova Vita, Bayrin had helped dig up the ruins. Beneath a fallen wall, they had revealed a rotted corpse, and the stench had nearly knocked him down. These nephilim smelled the same way, but the stench was older somehow: rotten flesh mixed with old leather, dust, and mold on cold stones. Their wings beat, sending leaves flying across the forest floor. Their mothers had been human, and their bodies bore humanoid shapes, though their ribs thrust out like those of birds, and their limbs were stretched like men pulled off the rack. Patches of scales clung to their skin, not bright like the scales of dragons, but rotten like lesions of leprosy. Their faces were bloated like waterlogged corpses about to burst. They screamed to the sky and their claws caught the sun and blazed. Their flesh was perhaps rotten, but those claws still looked sharp and hard as freshly forged blades.

Bayrin grabbed his sword and growled. A hundred or more of the beasts flew above. If they saw him and Piri, could the two flee fast enough? These creatures swarmed as fast as swooping dragons. Bayrin pushed himself deeper under the branches.

He waited for the nephilim to overshoot him and disappear westward. But they circled above like a murder of crows, and their nostrils flared, sniffing as loudly as steam rising from smelters.

"Dragon flesh!" they cried, and their drool rained. "We smell dragon flesh, comrades! Crunchable bones, and blood to sip, and sweet organs to suck on, yes comrades. Dragon flesh hides here! Sweet bone and vein!"

Piri cursed and whispered at his side. "Bayrin, they smell you!"

He peeked between the branches and his stomach sank. The nephilim began to dive down. It happened so quickly, Bayrin barely had time to gasp. A few landed ahead, scattering leaves with bony, clawed feet like those of vultures. One landed behind him, mere feet away, and its swollen head thrust down. Its nostrils flared, and its milky white eyes widened. It opened a mouth full of razor teeth and howled, blowing back fallen leaves.

With a roar, Bayrin leaped forward, drew his sword, and sliced the creature's eyes.

It shrieked.

Blood splattered the leaves.

"Fly, Piri!" Bayrin shouted, leaped, and shifted. His wings beat and he crashed between three nephilim who still flew above. One dived screeching behind him, and he spun and flamed it.

"Piri!" he cried, rising higher and blowing fire.

"Bayrin, here!" she shouted. She flew ahead, her lavender scales flashing between the rotten beasts. She blew fire, flaming two.

He shot toward her. They soared higher. They flew back to back, blowing fire in every direction. The nephilim screeched and surrounded them. One rose from below, and Bayrin knocked it aside with his tail. Another slammed against them from above, and claws tore at Bayrin's back. He roared and gored the beast with his horns.

"Piri, follow me!" he shouted. "I'm breaking through."

With a great roar, he shot forward, claws slashing and fire blazing. A nephil clawed his flank, and he howled. He barreled through them, revealing the western horizon, and shot forward. Teeth bit him. More claws cut him. He kept flying, screaming and blowing his fire.

He glanced over his shoulder and saw Piri flying beside him. Behind them, a hundred nephilim screamed and followed.

Clear cries bugled ahead.

Bayrin looked back to the west, and his breath left him.

Beautiful, he thought. Tears came to his eyes. *Stars, it's beautiful.*

Over the forest flew a horde of salvanae, true dragons of the west. They had no human forms like Vir Requis; they lived feral in the woods and mountains, wise and ancient beings. They had no limbs or wings; they coiled upon the air like serpents upon water, a hundred feet long. Scales shimmered and chinked across them. Their horns were long and bright, and their beards and mustaches fluttered as they flew. Their eyes were like crystal balls, spinning and glowing and topped with long white lashes. A thousand or more flew there, a tapestry woven of silver and gold. As they charged eastward upon the wind, they bugled their cries again, sounding like trumpets of silver from castle towers.

"Bloody stars, the cavalry's arrived!" Bayrin shouted.

He shot toward them, Piri at his side.

Behind them, the nephilim screeched to the sky. The earth shook below. Trees shattered. A boulder cracked. Bayrin screamed with the pain; the sound thudded against him and left his ears ringing.

The salvanae ahead trumpeted again, and this time, their voices pealed with rage. They stormed forward, serpentine bodies undulating upon the wind, beards fluttering. The nephilim screamed, beat their tattered wings, and reached out their claws. The two armies drove toward each other over the toppled forest.

"Up, Piri!" Bayrin shouted.

He soared in a straight line, teeth grinding. Air beat his face. His head spun. Darkness spread across his eyes. Piri flew at his side, growling.

Screams exploded below them as the armies clashed.

Bayrin spun in the air and swooped. Below him, the salvanae were trumpeting their cries. Lighting shot from their maws to slam into nephilim. The beasts burned and screamed. Their claws tore into the salvanae. Scales showered like spilling jewels, and the blood of true dragons rained.

Bayrin blew his fire, drenching a nephil below him. Piri swooped at his side, and her own fire took out another beast.

The sky blazed with battle. Lightning bolts flew everywhere. Fire blazed. The bodies of salvanae and nephilim fell around them, and the forests below caught flame. One nephil shot forward, and its maw opened so wide Bayrin thought its head would split in two. It drove teeth into Piri's shoulder, and she cried out; suddenly she sounded so young to Bayrin, a mere girl.

He roared and drove forward. He leaped onto the nephil, bit down, and tore into its neck. Its scales cut his mouth. Its rotten flesh oozed. He spat out a chunk and bit down again, and the nephil shrieked, releasing Piri. She dipped in the sky, blood streaming down her shoulder.

The nephil turned toward Bayrin, half its neck missing. Black blood spurted from it, and it laughed, a bubbling laughter full of dragon blood. Its eyes were mad, burning with sickly white light.

"Mortal child," it hissed through its laughter. "You do not know what you face. Legion rises! The Fallen rise! Your souls will scream in our darkness. We—"

Bayrin bathed the creature with flame.

It shrieked and fell. When its body hit the forest, it cracked open like a rotten fruit.

Bayrin dived and flew toward Piri. She was wobbling, still aflight but barely higher than the trees. Blood coated her shoulder. He nudged her with his wing, and she gave him a weary smile.

"You saved me, Bayrin."

He looked above him, waiting for nephilim to swoop. He found only salvanae above, and when he looked over the forest, he saw bodies everywhere, two hundred or more; about half of them were the nephilim, their corpses leaking pus and blood. The rest were golden and silver salvanae, the light dimmed from their eyes, their bodies hanging from the trees like the discarded skins of great snakes.

Piri landed in a clearing, shifted into human form, and clutched her wounded shoulder. Bayrin rushed toward her, and she gave him a wan smile.

"My hero," she said and kissed his cheek. "I'm never letting you go now."

Despite the horror, fire, and blood around them, Bayrin rolled his eyes.

The salvanae spiraled down above them like streamers. Soon they hovered a few feet above the clearing, scales chinking like coins. They blinked their crystal eyes, and their long white lashes fanned the grass. Their beards hung low enough to brush the ground. One of them, a dragon of white scales, lowered his head and blinked at Bayrin and Piri. He exhaled through his nostrils, fluttering his mustache and blasting the two Vir Requis with air.

"Children of Draco!" the salvana said. His tufty eyebrows pushed down over his crystal eyes. "A great evil followed you into our realm—an ancient curse. You have brought the Fallen here! We have heard their tales. Our forefathers whose souls fly among the Draco stars have fought these beasts before; they are the spawn of demons. Why have you brought this curse into our land?" The salvana tossed his head back and cried in mourning. "My brothers are slain! Salvanae have fallen! Curse this day."

Bayrin reached into his pack and began rummaging for bandages.

"Save your curses for later," he said. "My friend is wounded, and I have a feeling more of these nephilim are on their way." He looked up at the salvanae. "Queen Solina of Tiranor freed them. She cursed this land, not us. I am Bayrin Eleison of Requiem. Take me to your halls, and I will speak with your leader, the priest Nehushtan." He looked at a dead nephil which leaked blood upon a tree. "Our trouble with these bastards is just beginning."

LYANA

She sat tied to a tree when the nephilim lumbered into the camp.

The tree was an ancient oak, twisting skyward as tall as a palace, and its roots rose around Lyana, coiling and smoothed like the Oak Throne of Requiem's fallen hall. The tree grew in the southern corner of the camp behind piles of firewood; she could see nobody from here other than a distant guard in a tree.

It was seven days since she'd entered Second Haven, and she had spent these days sitting upon these fallen leaves, her wrists bound behind her back and tied to the trunk. The rope was ten feet long, just enough to let her sneak into the bushes when nature called, but too short to reach the huts, gardens, and people of the camp. Twice a day, the bronze brothers would bring her game and wild berries and oats. She ate at her tree. She slept at her tree. She wondered sometimes if she would grow old and die at her tree.

The seventh morning dawned clear and cold; winter was almost here, and the sun seemed small in the pale, cloudless sky, unable to warm her. Lyana shivered in her cloak and gave the ropes a good morning tug, but once again could not break them.

"Here," said Grom, the elder of the bronze brothers, who came trudging through the fallen leaves toward her. "Eat, dog."

He tossed a bowl of stewed greens and venison her way, spilling half onto the ground before her. Lyana glared, wrists bound behind her back. With a growl, she leaned down to grab the food in her mouth. Grom stood above her, smirking.

Before Lyana could take a bite, she heard the shrieks.

The sound tore across the camp, and Lyana winced and yelped. Grom covered his ears. It sounded like steel scratching along stone, like mountains shattering, like ancient souls torn in two. The camp shook with it. The shriek died for an instant, leaving Lyana's ears ringing, and then ten more cries answered it, and Lyana screamed.

Grom fell to his knees and clutched his ears.

"Grom!" Lyana shouted. "Free me. Nephilim. Free me!"

He looked up at her, gasped, and turned to flee. He kicked the bowl of food as he went.

"Grom, damn you!" Lyana shouted. "I will rip your guts out and feed them to the beasts!"

Shouts and screams sounded through the camp. Lyana leaped to her feet, ran ten steps, and the rope yanked her back. From here at her tree—stuck between a palisade on one side, a copse of oaks on the other—she could see nothing. She tried to shift—she had tried it a thousand times these past few days—and failed again, the ropes tugging her back into human form.

"Grom!" she screamed. "Damn you! You will hang for this in the court of my king!"

Fire blazed and heat washed Lyana. Ahead above the trees, she saw dragons take flight. A few were tough, hardened warriors roaring fire. Others were elders missing teeth. A few were youngsters, barely larger than horses. She could catch only glimpses of them between the branches. She saw a nephil shoot above, baring its fangs. She heard a dragon scream.

"Grom!" she shouted.

Screeches rose. Claws grabbed the trees before her and yanked them out. The roots pulled from the soil like hair pulled from a scalp, showering dirt. A nephil stood before her, holding an oak in each hand. The beast tossed back its rotted head, howled at the sky, and threw the trees aside.

Then it saw Lyana, its white eyes widened, and it snarled. Drool splattered. It came lolloping toward her on clawed feet.

Lyana stood with legs parted, rocking on her heels. Her wrists were still bound behind her; the rope which tethered her to the tree stood taut, a good ten feet long. She narrowed her eyes, staring at the approaching beast, and bared her teeth.

The nephil reached her and slammed down its claws.

Lyana leaped aside.

The claws slammed into the earth, digging ruts. The beast thrust its maw forward, teeth jutting out like rusted blades.

Shouting wordlessly, Lyana leaped back, allowing the rope to spin her around the tree like a tether-ball. She placed the trunk between herself and the nephil.

"God damn you, Grom," she muttered. If only she could fly! Stars, if only she had unbound wrists and sword in hand!

The nephil screeched, shaking the earth, and raced around the oak. It thrust down its jaw, and Lyana leaped back again. Its teeth dug into the earth. It raised its head and howled, a shattering sound that splattered drool and earth and dry leaves.

Lyana pressed herself close to the tree trunk, narrowed her eyes, and nodded at the rotted giant. The rope which ran between her wrists and the trunk lay loose at her feet.

With a howl, the nephil lashed its claws.

Lyana leaped forward, tightening the rope between herself and the trunk. The nephil's claws severed it.

Shouting hoarsely, Lyana ran through the camp. The nephil raced behind her. Its jaws lashed down, and she rolled. Its teeth missed her by inches. She leaped up and tried to shift, but could not; she was free from the tree, but the rope still bound her wrists behind her back.

Dragons and nephilim howled above her. Children ran through the camp. Lyana scurried forward. She looked over her shoulder and saw her nephil leap skyward like a giant, rotten grasshopper. The beast came plunging down toward her, and Lyana screamed and turned her head aside.

Fire blazed.

Through squinting eyes, Lyana saw a legless red dragon—Dorin Blacksmith!—crash into the nephil an instant before the beast could hit her. Dragon and nephil tumbled, rolled through the leaves, and crashed into a tree.

Lyana leaped up, whipping her head from side to side. The battle raged around her, nephilim and dragons slashing and biting and burning.

A blade. I need a blade!

Her eyes fell upon Grom.

"The poor fool," she muttered.

The miner lay in human form, his legs bitten off, his eyes staring lifelessly. He still clutched a sword in his hand—*her* sword, the ancient blade Levitas. The leaves around him soaked up his blood.

She ran toward him, turned backward, and crouched. She ran her wrists against Levitas, cutting the rope.

Three nephilim flew above, howled, and came swooping toward her.

The rope fell off her wrists.

Lyana grabbed her sword, shifted with it, and soared.

A blue dragon, she roared her fire, bathing the creatures. She shot through her own flame, lashed her claws, and crashed between the blazing nephilim. They fell around her, burnt and lacerated.

Lyana soared higher, rising from flame. Dragons and nephilim fought around her. She slew one beast with a blast of fire, then spun and swooped, the sun at her back. She crashed between the treetops into the camp, swung her claws, and ripped the head off a charging nephil.

Wails rose behind her. Lyana landed and spun around. A nephil was chasing a group of toddlers too young to shift. The children leaped under a fallen bole, which the nephil began to slash at. Still in dragon form, Lyana charged and leaped onto the nephil's back. It bucked, and she dug her teeth into its shoulder.

Gooey blood filled her mouth. The nephil screeched and she pulled it backward, allowing the toddlers to flee. She crashed onto her back, the nephil writhing above her. Lyana pushed her tail down, thrust herself up, and tossed the nephil forward. When it spun toward her, she flamed it and it fell.

She looked around the camp, panting. The battle was over.

The nephilim all lay dead, their corpses oozing pus and black blood thick with worms. Some lay burnt, others slashed with claws, their entrails dangling and their innards bustling with cockroaches. Many Vir Requis lay dead too, a hundred or more; they were torn apart, limbs strewn, heads severed. Some were half-eaten, and their blood stained the teeth of the fallen nephilim. Huts and trees burned, and living dragons flew between them, patting down the flames with tails and wings.

Lyana's head spun. She shifted back into human form and clutched her sword. Her hand trembled and her breath shook in her lungs.

War. War and blood and death again. She gritted her teeth, forcing down the horror. *You are Lyana Eleison, Queen of Requiem, ruler to these people. You will not panic. You will not faint. You will stay strong.*

A hoarse cry rose through the camp. Lyana drew her sword, for an instant sure a nephil still lived. She looked up to see Gar Miner walk through the camp, the younger of the bronze brothers. He howled and wept, carrying the body of his fallen brother.

"Dead!" he cried. "My brother is dead!" The short, burly miner looked at Lyana and his eyes blazed. "She led them here. Lyana Eleison arrived in our camp, and these beasts followed her." Tears ran down his cheeks. "She murdered my brother!"

He lowered his dead brother to the ground, knelt over him, and wept.

Around the camp, people muttered and stared at Lyana. One man, his arm lacerated, spat and glared. Two young men grabbed spears, and Gar rose to his feet and grabbed a club. They began to advance toward Lyana, stepping over corpses, and blood coated their boots. Lyana snarled and raised her sword.

"You accuse your queen of treason," she said softly. "Come lay this charge before my sword; Levitas will cut your lying tongues from your mouths." She spat toward them. "I've slain more of Solina's beasts in this war than you have thoughts in your skulls. If you accuse me of treason, I will slay you too."

They kept advancing toward her, raising their weapons. Ash and blood covered their faces.

"You are no queen in Second Haven," said Gar. He limped; a gash ran down his leg. "You are a stranger here, and you've brought only blood to this camp. Your blood will be the last shed here."

The men charged toward her.

Lyana growled and raised her sword.

"Cease this madness!" rose a shout over the camp.

A legless red dragon dived down from above, wings raising a cloud of fallen leaves and dirt. Snorting smoke, Dorin landed by the combatants. He shoved his head between them, nudging Lyana away from Gar and his comrades. He blasted more smoke from his nostrils and grumbled. When Gar tried to step around him, Dorin slapped him back with his wing, and the miner's club thumped to the ground.

Dorin shifted back into human form. He lay legless upon the leaves, his grizzled hair and beard matted with dirt and soot. He grumbled and pushed himself up onto his elbows.

"Gar," he said and coughed. Soon his entire body shook as he hacked. "Gar, fetch me my seat. Go, son."

The young miner still shed tears. He looked at Lyana. He looked back at his dead brother, and a sob racked his body. Finally Gar stormed into the wooden hall—half its roof had collapsed—and emerged carrying the mock Oak Throne carved from roots. He placed it upon the forest floor, grabbed Dorin under his arms, and lifted him into the seat.

The Legless Lord sat in the forest, and slowly the Vir Requis of his camp gathered around. Many clutched wounds.

Dorin shouted, voice hoarse. "People of Second Haven! Hear me. Hear your Lord Dorin. This camp is lost; Queen Solina knows we are here, and she will send more of these beasts our way. We must leave this place."

All around, men and women wailed, whispered, and looked from side to side. Gardens lay trampled. Huts lay fallen. The palisades were smashed.

Lyana lowered her head. She knew what these people were thinking.

They spent moons building this place, she thought. *They believed their life could spring anew here—a new city for the children of Requiem, a new haven. Now they relive the destruction of Nova Vita. Now again they are refugees.*

She stepped toward Dorin and bowed her head.

"Lord Dorin," she said softly; for the first time, she gave him the honor of a title. "You fought nobly. You saved my life." She held her sword before her, blade pointing down. "Fight by my side. Fly with me to Confutatis, capital of this kingdom you hide in, and speak with me to the king of men. Let us Vir Requis form an alliance with Osanna." She raised her sword. "We will not just flee. We will not hide. We will *fight*."

Dorin stared up at her from his seat, eyes narrowed and shrewd. His lips tightened and he clutched the armrests.

"How can we fight such evil?" he said, voice low.

She grabbed his shoulder. "We fly south. We fly to Tiranor. Solina is sending her wrath north, emptying her lands. We will fly to those lands and rain fire upon her." She tightened her fingers around him and stared into his eyes. "Fly with me, Dorin. The days of hiding are over. Fly with me, sound your roar, and blow your fire with mine. A dragon needs no legs, only fire and wings."

He glared up at her, lips tightened and trembling. Finally he coughed, spat sideways, and stared back at her.

"I will not serve you as some man-at-arms." His fists shook around his seat's armrests. "My sons served your husband, the Boy King Elethor. They fell upon his towers. I flew for Elethor. I lost my legs in his service. No, girl. My days of serving Elethor are over. Requiem is fallen, and he has no titles in these lands, nor do you."

Her lip curled. "Requiem did not fall. She lives in the west, in Salvandos, among tree and stone, a light in our hearts."

Dorin snorted. "Then let Requiem remain in the west." He swept his arm around him and spoke louder. "This is Second Haven! This is a free realm. Look at our banners upon the trees; they fly still." He looked back at her with narrowed eyes and spoke softly. "But yes, Lyana. I will fly with you. And I will rain fire upon those who destroyed our camp. I will not bend the knee before King Elethor even if I still had knees to bend. Let Requiem and Second Haven fly together, two free nations aligned, and together we will crush this desert queen."

Lyana stared at him silently. The man still spoke treason. To secede from Requiem meant to hang from her walls.

She lowered her head. *Yet those walls are fallen. And I cannot fight this entire camp, nor will I kill my own people.* She heaved a sigh. *Bloody stars, but Elethor will kill me when he hears.*

She nodded. "We fly together, Dorin. Requiem and Second Haven. Let us seek what allies we can in these eastern realms—men and griffins who will fight at our side." She gripped her sword and snarled. "And then we will set the desert aflame."

ELETHOR

She lay nude beside him, golden in the dawn. The light cascaded
through the window, dappling her with pale mottles. She smiled at
him—the smile that showed her teeth—a smile so rich and full and
singing of purity, and a smile so rare these days, so precious to him.
Her platinum hair cascaded like a moonlit river, hiding her breasts, so
pale it was almost white, and Elethor ran his fingers through it. He
touched her nose, marveling at the golden freckles he loved, and ran
his hand over her body, tracing her curves from shoulder, down her
ribs, into the deep valley of her waist, and finally up the hill of her hip.
He had caressed her landscape countless times, and every time he lost
his breath at its beauty.

"Solina," he whispered her name. Daughter of sunlight, the
name meant in her tongue. Sun of his life.

They lay in his bed upon blankets of green and silver wool—the
colors of Requiem. Around them stood the statues that filled his small
house upon the hill: marble elks with antlers of gold; a wooden turtle
with jeweled eyes he had carved for Solina; and statues of Solina
herself, nude or clad in flowing robes of marble.

"They are all away," she whispered, leaned forward on her
elbow, and kissed his lips. "Today is ours."

He looked outside the window above and breathed in the clear
air. *A free day. A day for us.* His father, his brother, the Lady Lyana,
even his little sister—they had all flown to distant Oldnale Farms for a
feast. The courts of Requiem had emptied; only he, Prince Elethor,
remained to rule.

*But I intend to spend the entire time here in bed with this very beautiful,
very naked woman.*

He ran his hand again over her curves, from waist to hip and
back. She reached under the blankets, sneaked her hand into his
pants, and closed her fingers around him. She smiled softly and kissed
him. They had made love last night for what seemed like hours; in the
dawn, he loved her again until she screamed and scratched his back so
violently, he bled.

A day for us. A free day. A perfect day.

They held each other close in bed. They closed their eyes under the soft light, and they slept again, and they did not wake until noon.

Finally Solina rose from the bed, walked to the window, and stretched before the trees that rustled outside, nude and golden and drenched in light. She was a work of art to him, greater than any statue he could sculpt. She looked over her shoulder at him.

"Wake up, sleepy," she said. "I'm hungry."

She stepped toward the bed, pulled the blanket off him, and wrapped it around herself. He rose with a grunt, embraced her, and kissed her head. They held each other closely for long moments before breaking apart, stepping into his pantry, and rummaging for food.

They filled a basket with bread rolls, a jar of preserves, smoked sausages, a slab of butter, a wheel of tangy cheese, and hard yellow apples. They took their meal outside and sat upon the grass beneath the cypresses. She wore nothing but the blanket wrapped around her shoulders; he wore only his woolen trousers. Below the hill where Elethor had built his home rolled the city of Nova Vita: the palace of marble columns, the domed temple, and the cobbled streets that snaked between birches.

That palace is empty now, he thought. *The day is ours: a day of sunlight, a day of peace, a day of Solina.*

"What will we do today?" he asked as they ate. "Walk through the forest? Go swim in the lake? Maybe visit the library and read old books?"

She yawned magnificently. "Too hard." She lay back on the grass, and her hair spread out around her like molten white gold. The sunlight danced upon her face. "I'm just going to lie here all day." She reached out, grabbed him, and pulled him back. "And you will lie here with me."

He lay on his back watching the clouds, and she nestled against him, and soon she slept again. He kissed her forehead and held her in his arms, and her breath danced against his neck. He closed his eyes, Solina warm against him.

This is the best day of my life, he thought. *Here and now, this is perfect. This is all I ever want. Never let this end.*

A shriek tore the day.

Elethor opened his eyes and found himself in darkness. Solina slipped into shadow, and he tried to grab her, and his heart ached at her loss, and then the shriek sounded again and he covered his ears.

He rose from the cold stone floor and looked upon a shadowy, dusty tunnel. His body ached, and dried blood covered his left arm. At his side, children cowered and held one another. The shriek sounded again, coming from far above through walls of stone—the nephilim circling above the temple ruins.

Elethor clenched his jaw. His dream faded, the last warmth of sunlight and Solina's embrace falling into a deep, throbbing cold.

He grimaced. He had slept in his armor, and every muscle and joint in him groaned. The mossy brick walls pressed close around him. The root of a great tree thrust down through the ceiling, splitting the room. Behind the root, a dozen more Vir Requis huddled—the young twins and ten others who had scurried inside. They had been hiding here for six days now, drinking what rainwater dripped through the ceiling and eating only what supplies they had carried in their packs and pockets.

The screech sounded again from outside, a cry torn in agony. The tunnel where they hid shook and moss rained from the ceiling's bricks.

"Something is going on out there," grumbled Garvon. The leathery, one-eyed man huddled against a wall, his white beard caked with mud. "I don't like this."

Elethor frowned and found himself agreeing. The past three days had been eerily silent. They had heard nephilim pacing and grunting outside, sometimes shrieking in rage. They had heard other Vir Requis shout from their own hideouts in abandoned cellars and halls. But this—this cry of agony—was new.

"Something is hurting them," Elethor muttered. "That is no scream of rage or hunger. It's a scream of pain."

Were the other Vir Requis emerging to fight? No; he heard no dragon roars. Did Bayrin return with the salvanae or Lyana with griffins? Elethor could not hear them either; salvanae bugled and sang in battle, and griffins let out eagle cries.

Garvon rose to his feet. His hoary head nearly hit the ceiling. He drew his sword with a grunt.

"Get ready," he said and spat. "They're planning something."

The nephilim screeched again, and a new stench flared from outside, one of blood and sour milk and worms. Elethor could not see outside from here—the tunnel curved, sealing them in shadow. He began walking toward the bend. He had to look outside, to see what new devilry festered there.

Garvon grabbed his shoulder. "I go first."

The old man shoved Elethor back, trudged around him, and walked down the tunnel toward the exit. Elethor drew Ferus, his old longsword, and walked close behind. The stench invaded his nostrils as violently as demons thrusting into mortal women.

The crumbly doorway stood before them, lichen hanging from the lintel. Elethor frowned and Garvon muttered. For the past three days, nephilim had stood here, reaching claws and teeth through the doorway like cats pawing at mouse holes. Today Elethor saw sunlight through the doorway, no claws or teeth blocking the exit. The screeches rose outside, and the stench of blood and rot swirled so powerfully Elethor nearly gagged.

Garvon kept advancing toward the doorway, sword raised. Elethor walked close behind. Soon they stood in range of thrusting claws; Elethor saw their grooves cut into the walls and floor.

"Careful, Garvon," he said.

The old soldier froze, spat, and cursed. Elethor looked over Garvon's shoulder into the forest. He felt the blood leave his face.

"Stars," he whispered.

The nephilim stood in a ring outside between fallen statues, crumbling walls, and trees that grew from cracked flagstones. Between them lay a howling nephil. She was a female, Elethor saw; her rotted breasts hung loose like bags of sour milk, and her shrieks sounded almost human.

They are half human, he remembered with a chill, *the spawn of demons and human mothers.*

The female nephil dug her claws into the earth, tearing stone and root. Her screams rose. Her legs lay open, and blood sprayed from between them. She gave a great howl, and a warty head began to emerge from her womb. The mother screeched. Her spawn's head burst out, coated in blood and mucus, and screeched.

"Stars damn it, oh stars damn it," Elethor hissed through clenched teeth.

The nephil spawn thrust its claws out, tearing the opening wider. Its mother wept and screeched, and the nephilim around her roared and reached for the heavens. The spawn fell into the dirt, coated with blood, and bit off its umbilical cord. It stood the size of a man, its wings limp and dripping, its flesh already rotten and covered in boils. It wailed and leaped onto its mother. It grabbed onto her breast and began to feed, not drinking milk but tearing into the flesh, feasting like a wolf upon prey.

Garvon growled low in his throat. "Bastards."

More blood gushed from the mother.

Another spawn began to emerge, wailing and clawing and biting its way out. Soon the second beast began to feast, ripping into its mother's flesh. Across the forest ruins, more shrieks sounded, followed by the shrill wails of spawn.

"They're small enough to enter the tunnels," Elethor said softly.

Garvon stared at him, teeth bared. "They're too young; they're babes."

"Babes who are tearing apart grown nephilim and eating their flesh." He grabbed his shield from over his back and slung it onto his arm. "Garvon, I—"

A squeal rose outside, cutting off his words. One of the spawn leaped off its mother, face smeared with blood, and stared right at them. Its eyes burned with white fire. Its lips pulled back, revealing long teeth like daggers. It came racing toward them, squealing and snapping its jaws.

Garvon cursed and raised his sword.

The spawn reached the doorway, leaped into the tunnel, and crashed onto the old man.

Elethor yowled and thrust his sword, but could not reach the spawn without cutting Garvon too. The old soldier screamed and hacked at the creature; it was nearly as large as him. Garvon fell. The spawn opened its jaws wide, bit down, and tore into Garvon's head. With thick claws, it cracked the skull open and began to feast.

Elethor screamed, heart thrashing, and thrust his sword.

The blade slammed into the spawn's chest, and blood sprayed.

The beast writhed upon the sword. It lashed out its claws, mewling. Elethor raised his shield, and the claws slammed into it, scattering chips of wood. Screaming hoarsely, his boots sticky with blood, Elethor pulled his blade back and swung it down. He cleaved the demon open from collarbone to navel, and centipedes fled from its body to scurry across the floor.

Elethor gagged. His head spun. The spawn fell dead, and Elethor stepped toward the doorway and chanced a look outside. He cursed. More demon spawn were racing across the forest and leaping into burrows, doorways, and tunnels. Among the ruins, other pockets of surviving Vir Requis fought. They swung swords from under fallen statues and collapsing roofs. Beyond an expanse of trees rose a crumbling hall; great stone faces stared stoically from its walls, mossy and green with vines. Nephil spawn were climbing the walls and trying to crawl into holes and windows. Fire blasted from within, roasting the beasts; dragons hid inside.

Shrieks sounded ahead. Elethor snarled. Two demon spawn came racing toward his tunnel, eyes blazing and teeth stained with blood.

Elethor raised his sword. The two nephil infants crashed into him, jaws snapping; they were nearly his size.

He roared and shoved one back with his shield. The other lashed claws, scratching across his breastplate and raising sparks. Elethor drove his sword's crossguard into the beast, and its skull cracked, and it howled. The demon behind his shield began biting at the wood, and Elethor drove forward, crushing the beast between his shield and the wall. Another spawn came racing from the forest and leaped onto him, and Elethor crashed down. Within an instant, three of the beasts were atop him, biting and slashing, and one's claw broke through his breastplate to scratch his chest. Elethor screamed and saw nothing but their rotting faces.

A blade whistled overhead. Steel crashed into a spawn's head, crumpling it like a tin mug, and the creature fell. Elethor leaped to his feet, swung down his sword, and slew another. At his side, he glimpsed one of the survivors, a boy of fourteen named Yar. The boy was trembling but managed to swing his sword again, stabbing another spawn. They swung their blades together, and soon the last of the creatures lay dead.

Yar shook, bent over, and gagged. Elethor placed a hand on the boy's shoulder. The corpses lay stinking; cockroaches and worms fled from them.

Elethor stepped over the corpses and looked outside. Across the forest, more female nephilim were falling over, howling and tearing down trees, and spawning their vermin. Hundreds of the infants shrieked.

At least, Elethor thought wryly, *we didn't meet any ghosts.*

"We can't fight them," Yar whispered, trembling. "So many. Hundreds."

Elethor grunted. "We're trapped in here." He stared at the youth. "Yar, carry the toddlers with you; they are too young to shift. Fly behind me. We're breaking out."

The youth trembled and clutched his sword before him. "There are thousands of nephilim out there. Where will we go?"

Elethor stared outside into the forest; he could see the vermin emerging from rotten wombs, crawling to the breast, and feasting upon the meat. In moments, they would be racing here to feast upon Vir Requis too.

He clenched his fist. *Damn you, Solina. Damn you, Nemes.* With Garvon dead, Yar was the only survivor in this huddle old enough to fight; the others were mere children. *There is no more safety here.*

"Yar," he said, "listen carefully. There is a wide hall among the ruins—about five hundred yards from here. There are stone faces on the walls, and the roots of trees clutch the place, sending trunks up through the ceiling. Don't look outside now! Some Vir Requis hide there, and they hide as dragons; I saw their fire blasting out the windows. Our burrow is too small; we cannot hold back these spawn with our swords. The great hall is wider. We can crouch there as dragons and join our fire to those who already hide there."

Yar's hands shook around his hilt. "My lord, five hundred yards... stars, we'll never make it. They'll tear us apart."

Ahead in the forest, the fresh spawn raised their faces from the bloodied torsos of their mothers, stared toward the tunnel, and hissed. With screeches, they came racing toward them.

"They'll tear us apart here," Elethor said. "Yar, get the others! Follow me to the hall!"

Snarling, Elethor raced outside into the forest, shifted into a dragon, and blew his fire. The nephilim howled and swarmed toward him.

BAYRIN

Bayrin had heard tales of Har Zahav, the mythical golden mountain of the salvanae. In old books, he had read how Kyrie Eleison and Agnus Dei, the great hero and heroine of Requiem, had visited this place to summon the salvanae to aid them. Those books described a volcano of pure gold rising from the forest, above it a sky full of the true dragons. In countless illustrations, tapestries, and paintings Bayrin had admired the scene: the two Vir Requis, among the last of their kind, flying to the golden hall under a sky of coiling, glittering salvanae with flowing beards and crystal eyes.

During the journey here, Bayrin had imagined himself like Kyrie Eleison, the old prince of Requiem, and imagined Piri as Agnus Dei, the fiery warrior-princess. He had imagined them too flying among wise salvanae toward a mountain of wonder and magic.

Now Har Zahav rose before him, the golden mountain of legend, and Bayrin's eyes dampened at its glory lost. Nephilim had flown here. Whatever beauty had once shone here had fallen to their rot.

"Stars," Piri whispered, flying beside him. Her eyes dampened. "Stars, Bayrin, we're too late."

A battle had raged here not long ago. The pines lay smashed and burnt below. The mountain did rise ahead—triangular and golden like in the paintings—but blood and ash now coated it, and the corpses of both salvanae and nephilim lay upon its slopes. More bodies littered the forest below: salvanae torn into segments, the glow of their eyes dimmed, and nephilim charred with lighting, their corpses bustling with maggots.

"When the wyverns attacked last year, we found no allies," Bayrin said softly. "The world did not believe that Solina could threaten it too. Stars, Piri. Look at this world now."

Those salvanae who had first found Bayrin and Piri in the forests now flew around them. At the sight of their bloodied mountain and the corpses of their brothers, the salvanae tossed back their heads and cried with grief. Their calls rang out like mournful bells, like forests weeping, and their tears fell as rain into smoldering fires.

"Salvandos!" they cried. "Salvandos, land of the true dragons! We will avenge you, land of Draco. Your beauty rivaled the light of stars, Salvandos! You were brighter than sunlight, sweeter than wine."

Gliding beside him, her lavender scales glimmering under the veiled sun, Piri looked at Bayrin with soft eyes.

"Are the other salvanae all dead?" she whispered.

Bayrin looked ahead across the smoldering forests to the mountain. He squinted and then breathed in relief.

"Look, Piri," he said and pointed a claw. "Some still live."

A group of salvanae rose from the mountain, their scales splashed with blood. They coiled skyward, wailing in grief, then dived down the mountainside toward their slain kin. Flying serpents, they had no limbs or wings, and Bayrin caught his breath, wondering how they would lift the bodies and carry them to burial. The salvanae opened their mouths wide, tears in their eyes.

Piri gasped and looked aside. "Stars, Bayrin! They... stars! They're eating them!"

As he glided toward the mountain, Bayrin stared with disbelief. Piri was right. The living salvanae took the tails of their fallen into their mouths. They began to swallow the fallen like snakes swallowing their prey. As they ate the dead, more salvanae coiled above, singing songs of mourning. The clouds parted, and rays of light fell upon the golden mountain, and the song rose like the keen of harps. Bayrin knew he should be horrified. *Stars, they're cannibals!* And yet, as he glided upon the wind, this act—the consumption of the fallen—seemed not obscene but deeply sad, deeply respectful.

"It's a last honor," he whispered. "The fallen will become part of the living. Their blood will live on."

When the bodies were gone, the salvanae rose—heavier and rounder—into the air. They coiled toward the top of their golden volcano and vanished inward into darkness.

Above the mountain floated a great, golden salvana with a flowing white beard. He came flying across the charred forest toward Bayrin and Piri; they met above golden, bloodied foothills.

"Children of Draco," said the salvana, and his eyes shone with tears.

Bayrin recognized him; here was Nehushtan, High Priest of Salvandos. Bayrin had seen the wise old dragon in Requiem; Nehushtan had visited Nova Vita a year ago to meet with Elethor.

Sudden rage filled Bayrin, erupting from his nostrils with puffs of smoke. He wanted to slash his claws at the old salvana, to slam him against the mountain, to burn him dead.

When the wyverns attacked, you abandoned us! he wanted to shout. *Elethor begged you for aid, and you refused. Look at you now! Look at your dead.*

He fumed, unable to speak. Nehushtan only looked at him, tears in his eyes. When Bayrin looked into those great, glittering orbs like crystal balls, his rage faded. Such sadness lived in those eyes, such regret.

I am sorry, those eyes seemed to say to him, and starlight swirled inside them. *I am sorry and I will forever mourn.*

Hovering in midair, Bayrin snorted smoke and looked aside.

"Nehushtan," he said. "I am Bayrin Eleison, a son of Requiem, and this is Piri Healer, a daughter of our stars. We come on behalf of King Elethor and Queen Lyana. Let us fly into your hall. Let us speak." He looked over the bodies of nephilim that still littered the mountain and forests. "We have much to discuss."

Smoke rose from scattered fires. Ash painted the sky. The stench of rot filled the air. Salvandos burned, and the salvanae above wept, their tears falling as rain to wash the blood and soot. Bayrin thought back to that day eight years ago when Solina had fled Requiem, scarred and screaming of vengeance. Now that vengeance burned the world.

Nehushtan turned and began flying around the mountainsides, and Bayrin and Piri followed. Upon the western slope, they found more bodies, blood, and rot. Hundreds of nephilim lay dead upon the foothills like great insects swept down a river. A great hole loomed open in the mountainside, its rim showing the marks of claws and teeth. The mountain was not solid, Bayrin saw, but hollow; through the hole, he saw salvanae coiling among orbs of floating light. They seemed to fill the mountain like ants filling a hive.

Beard flowing like a banner, Nehushtan coiled through the air, flew into the hole, and vanished into the mountain. Bayrin glanced at Piri, and she looked back, eyes sad. They flew side by side, heading over the bodies and through the gaping hole. They entered the hall of Salvandos.

The mountain's innards loomed around them, a cavern the size of a city. Glowing orbs floated through the hall, casting their light upon golden walls and burrows. The place indeed seemed like a great hive; salvanae coiled through the air, flowing from and into round passageways. Far below upon a polished floor, a pile of nephilim lay dead and burnt between fallen boulders. Several dead salvanae lay around them, torn apart.

Nehushtan flew upward and crashed between a cluster of floating orbs, sending the balls of light flying. Bayrin and Piri flapped their wings, rising after him. He led them to a wall of pods like a honeycomb. Thousands of the alcoves covered the wall; the heads of salvanae peeked from some, their eyes blinking and their beards hanging.

Nehushtan hovered before one pod. He turned to look at Bayrin and Piri and nodded.

"You will spend the night here," the old priest said. "Inside you will find sweet fruit and sweet water, and you will rest." His lips pulled back, revealing sharp teeth, and his brows pushed low; suddenly his face was terrible, a mask of rage. "And tomorrow, children of Draco... tomorrow you will fly with the hosts of Salvandos. Tomorrow we will fly to blood and death and song. Tomorrow we fly to war."

With that, the true dragon flew away into shadow.

The entrance to the pod was round and narrow; it could perhaps fit a slim and long salvana, but not a bulky dragon of Requiem. Bayrin clung to the opening with his claws, shifted into human form, and climbed in. He looked over his shoulder to see Piri do the same.

The pod was long, round, and narrow—a cozy little nook. Standing here in human form, Bayrin felt like a small forest critter nesting in a hollow log. Fresh leaves carpeted the floor, and the walls were carved of smooth stone. In the back lay clear, round vessels holding fruits, wine, nuts, and leafy greens. At first Bayrin thought these made of glass, but when he lifted a sphere, it burst and spilled berries into his hands.

Bubbles, he thought and began to eat. The berries too burst when he ate them, spilling juice down his throat. He began tearing into the other bubbles and feasting.

"Come on, Piri!" he said through a mouthful of almonds. "It's good."

He looked over his shoulder at her... and the rest of the almonds fell from his gaping mouth. She stood naked before him, holding her cloak in one hand. Her body was tall, lithe, and tanned. She let the cloak drop and took a few steps toward him.

"Bayrin," she said softly. "Forget about your belly for now. Take me instead."

He sighed and rose to his feet. She took his hands and smiled at him, a smile that began seductively but ended trembling, and her eyes dampened.

"Piri!" he said and touched a tear on her cheek.

She placed her hands in his hair and kissed him deeply. Her lips were soft and full, and her tongue sought his, and her naked body pressed against him. For a moment Bayrin closed his eyes, overwhelmed with the warmth and softness of her.

Then he broke their kiss and looked aside.

"Piri, I can't," he whispered. "I'm sworn to another."

She touched his cheek, tears in her eyes. "I know, Bay. I miss Mori too. She was my princess and my friend. But... it's been moons now. We lost so many in Nova Vita. I loved Mori, but we have to move on; we have to realize she is gone. I am so sorry for your loss, Bay, but..." Her tears flowed. "But *I* love you. *I* need you now. I've loved you for years, Bayrin—since our first kiss four winters ago under the stars. You remember that night, don't you? Will you not return my love now, here, as the world burns?"

She tried to kiss his lips again, but he turned his head, and her kiss landed on his cheek.

"Bay," she whispered, held his head, and turned it toward her.

He stepped back and held her waist, keeping space between them. He stared into her eyes.

"Mori is still alive," he said, unable to keep anger away from his voice. "I know it. I can't betray her." His voice softened and he held her hands. "Stars, Piri, you are beautiful. You are kind and brave and you are..." He couldn't help but look down at her naked body, then up again, and a sigh fled his lips. "Stars, but you *are* perfect. But I can't. Not while there's still a chance Mori will return."

She nodded, tears on her cheeks, and closed her eyes.

"Then hold me one last time," she whispered. "Please, Bay. Hold me just once and hold me tight, because I'm so scared."

He held her close, his arms around her, and she laid her head upon his shoulder.

Behind her, a figure stepped into the pod. A voice rose, high and hesitant.

"Bayrin?"

He looked over Piri's shoulder.

His breath died.

At the doorway, clad in a white cloak, stood Mori.

ELETHOR

He flew across the temple ruins, roaring fire.

"Vir Requis!" he shouted. "Fall back to the main hall! Fall back! We gather in the Hall of Faces."

That hall, once the central temple of Bar Luan, rose at the back of the ruins. Over thousands of years, the rest of the complex had fallen to the encroaching forest; roots, trunks, and branches had gradually broken down Bar Luan's outer walls, smaller homes, and statues. The great Hall of Faces, however, still stood. Its walls were pockmarked and green with moss. The great stone faces upon those walls, each as large as a dragon, were smoothed with countless winters of rain and snow. Holes gaped open in the walls, punched by tree roots or the slow pummeling of the years.

Today fire blasted from those holes, burning the spawn of nephilim. Some dragons hid inside that great hall; there was safety there, Elethor thought. But many Vir Requis—hundreds of them, perhaps—still hid across the rest of the complex. These ones crouched in human forms. They hid under fallen statues, inside the small stone homes of ancient monks, or in tunnels that had once led to cellars. These hideouts had protected them from the fully grown nephilim; those beasts were too large to enter burrows where humans could fit. Now, as Elethor flew above the ruins, the spawn of nephilim scuttled across the ruins like cockroaches, entering every hollow and hole and feasting upon what flesh they found. Hundreds swarmed.

Three nephilim took flight from a craggy wall and flapped toward him. Their claws reached out, and their teeth snapped. Elethor doused them with fire. More nephilim soared from the ruins below and crashed into him. Elethor swiped his tail and crushed one's head. Another clawed his legs, and Elethor howled and flamed it.

"Vir Requis!" he shouted. "Fly with me! To the hall!"

A few Vir Requis burst out from their hiding places. Three children—just old enough to shift—emerged from a cellar, shifted, and took flight. Nephilim screeched and swooped toward them. From under a statue rose a silver dragon; she clutched her babe in her claws, a boy too young to shift. Three youths ran from inside a crumbled old home, took flight, and roared fire.

"To the Hall of Faces!" Elethor howled. "Enter through the windows at the back."

He flamed another nephil. To his left, three dragons soared. Nephilim crashed into them, claws swinging. One of the dragons screamed, then fell as a bloodied human girl. Beneath Elethor, three graybeards ran from a cellar, swinging clubs at nephil spawn. One old man fell, and the spawn leaped onto him, and blood sprayed.

The nephilim covered the sky. More kept rising from the trees. Elethor cursed and began flying toward the temple, spraying his fire.

"Fly!" he shouted. "Vir Requis, to the hall! Follow!"

Dozens of dragons soared around him, blowing their flames. Walls of fire rose around them. Nephilim tried to break through. They blazed and screeched and fell. The trees below kindled, and smoke filled the sky. Elethor coughed, barely able to see. More dragons kept rising from below. More nephilim crashed into them, biting and clawing. One crashed onto Elethor's back, and its teeth scraped his shoulder, and he roared and bucked. He slammed his tail like a scorpion, driving its spikes into the nephil; as the beast fell, he flamed it.

"To the Hall of Faces!" he cried. "Enter the windows."

He began circling the great, crumbling temple. Through holes in the walls and ceiling, he saw hundreds of Vir Requis inside. Most huddled in the center of the temple in human forms. The rest stood as dragons at the walls, blasting fire from windows, archways, and holes.

"We're sending people in!" Elethor shouted at them through a hole in the roof. "Make room!"

The dragons inside nodded, pulled back from one window, and opened a path for survivors. At once, the nephil spawn began clattering up the wall outside toward the window. Elethor swooped and whipped his tail, shoving them off. He blasted flames against the wall, burning the others.

Teeth bit into his wings, and he dipped several feet. Spawn covered him, biting and clawing. Elethor growled and shook, but they clung to him. He crashed onto the forest floor, and the brood crawled over him like ants over a discarded piece of fruit. Elethor roared and rolled and blew flames, but the spawn seemed endless.

Roars sounded above. A yellow dragon dived, shifted into human form, and leaped onto Elethor's back. It was Yar, the youth who had shared Elethor's tunnel for six days. He began swinging his sword, knocking the spawn off.

"Yar, shift and blow fire!" Elethor shouted. "Help me hold them back."

The boy nodded, leaped, and shifted back into dragon form. He and Elethor stood flanking the window, blowing flames at the encroaching spawn. Two walls of fire spread from the temple across the complex, creating a corridor.

Dragons dived into the corridor of fire, shifted into humans, and began leaping through the window into the temple. Soon a dozen had entered, and more kept landing between the streams of flame. Elethor dug his claws into the earth; he had maybe a few more breaths of fire in him before he would need rest.

Three young dragons landed in the corridor, shifted, and began running toward the window. An adult nephil swooped from above and tore into them. Its claws ripped them apart and the beast howled, tossing limbs aside like a child tossing toys.

Elethor growled and turned his fire toward the beast, crossing his flames with Yar's. The nephil shrieked and burned. More came flying from Elethor's other side, and more spawn began crawling atop him. He roared and fell back against the temple, cracking the wall, and tore the beasts off. He looked up to see thousands fly toward him; they covered the ruins.

"Yar, get inside!" he shouted. "Into the temple."

The yellow dragon growled at his side, clawing at demon spawn. "Not without you, my king."

"Go now, Yar! I'll hold them back. Go!"

He trundled toward the boy, shaking spawn off his back, and whipped his tail, knocking more beasts off the yellow dragon's back.

"Go!"

Yar blasted fire at the sky, catching a diving nephil, and shifted. He leaped through the window into the temple.

Elethor stood outside the walls, alone with the nephilim. The covered the ruins before him: the forest floor, the trees, the crumbled walls, and the sky. He could see nothing but them, a tapestry of the Abyss. Their eyes blazed, burning white. Their tongues lolled, raining drool. Some had swollen, distorted heads that leaked pus. Others had gaunt, long faces lined with spikes. Some had nothing but great mouths full of teeth, their entire heads made only of jaws.

"Elethorrr...," one hissed, a great nephil that hovered among them. Its wings spread wide, and it sat upon a throne of flame. A halo of fire wreathed its brow, shrieking like a storm, and blood coated its maw. It was the largest among them, a leader of darkness.

"You will leave this place," Elethor called to it, standing before the temple window. "You will return to the Abyss."

The nephilim tossed their heads back and howled. They laughed and snapped their teeth and beat their wings. Severed heads and limbs cracked inside their jaws. Their leader rose higher upon a throne of fire. Its halo blazed white-hot.

"I am Legion!" it screeched, its voice so loud and shrill, Elethor roared in pain and trees cracked across the ruins. "I am Prophet! I serve the great Queen Solina. I have feasted upon the sons of dragons. I will feast upon their king! Your doom is near, King Elethor of Requiem. Your blood will be my wine, and your spine will feed my children." It howled, pus and blood spraying from its maw. "The time of the dragon ends, King Elethor. Your kingdom is fallen. The world burns and we, the Fallen, feast. The nephilim rise!"

All around Legion, the thousands of nephilim repeated the cry. "We rise! We rise! We feast!"

How can we fight such evil? Elethor thought in a daze. His head spun. He felt weak. He could barely cling to his magic. *How can we fight countless of these demons, creatures risen from ancient evil? How can Requiem survive such malice, such might?*

He thought of Lyana, his wife, the love and light of his life. He thought of Mori, his sister whom he had vowed to find. He thought of all those people who had died under his banner, and those who still lived behind him.

I am still their king. Even now. Even as our light fades. If we die here, let us die with a roar that will sound across the world.

He sounded his roar. He blew his fire at the Prophet of the Fallen. The blaze crashed into Legion, and the nephil screeched to the sky.

Elethor shifted into human form and leaped through the window. He rolled into the temple and the arms of fellow survivors. At once two dragons thrust their heads to the window and shot fire outside, holding the swarm back.

Elethor lay in human form, bruised and cut and bleeding. He struggled to his feet and looked around him. His breath left his lungs and the weight of mountains seemed to lie upon his shoulder.

So few still live.

Several hundred Vir Requis huddled here, bloodied and bruised, clinging to one another. This was all that remained of his father's nation. Dragons stood along the walls and clung to the ceiling, blowing fire outside, holding the nephilim back.

But they will break in, Elethor thought. *They will break these walls and they will tear us apart—elders, mothers, children. They will feed the horde and King's Column will fall.*

"Come back to us, Lyana," he whispered, voice hoarse. "Come back to us, Bayrin. Bring what aid you can. We cannot wait."

He didn't even know if his friends could find them now. If Bayrin and Lyana returned to their abandoned camp, would they know to head to Bar Luan? Were they alone here, and no aid could reach them?

The sun set outside. Darkness covered the world. The nephilim howled and slammed against the walls. Dust and moss fell and babes wept. Fire blew. Elethor shifted back into dragon form and replaced a young dragon at a window. He blew his fire, not knowing if they'd last the night.

LYANA

They flew north across the plains, heading toward the ancient capital of Osanna, and found it burning.

Lyana had been to this place, the legendary city of Confutatis, many times. She had flown here with her father to visit the king of men, a wise old grandfather with a flowing white beard but pitch-black eyebrows. The people of Osanna had no magic; they could not become dragons like the children of Requiem, but rode horses and shot arrows, forged steel and wove silk, wrote ancient books and studied the stars. They were an ancient race—their history stretched back as far as Requiem's—and wise.

As a youth, Lyana had read many stories of Confutatis, the White City: how the twins Osira and Osari had founded the city, carving its first bricks three thousand years ago; how Confutatis grew from a simple village of farmers to a great metropolis of towers, amphitheaters, castles, and a million souls; and of course, how the tyrant Dies Irae conquered Confutatis, forged his center of power here, and led the griffins from this place to destroy Requiem, leaving only the Living Seven among the ruins. Confutatis was a city of ancient secrets, of old blood, of steel and light and stone. For three hundred years now, the priest-kings of the Earth God had ruled here, honoring a strong alliance with Requiem—an alliance Lyana was depending on.

And today... today when she needed this city's strength most, she found its walls crumbling.

She still flew several miles away, and shadows still cloaked the world; dawn had just begun to rise. But dragon eyes were sharp, and Lyana snarled. A hundred nephilim encircled the city, tearing down walls and towers with claw and tooth. Arrows rained upon them from the battlements. More nephilim flew above, dipping to claw at soldiers who manned towers or ran along snaking streets. Three nephilim barreled into one of those towers, a great spire of marble and gold; it crashed onto the streets below, burying men beneath it.

Stars, Lyana thought, *is no place upon this earth safe anymore?* Solina's arm had grown long enough to cross desert, sea, forest, and plains, even to this distant northern city.

She turned to look at the dragons who flew around her. Dorin flew to her right, an old red dragon with no back legs, his wings whistling with holes. At her left flew Gar, the young miner, a burly bronze dragon with fire in his jaws. Behind them flew the survivors of Second Haven: three thousand men, women, and children. Their eyes widened with fear, and they blasted fire.

Lyana raised her voice and cried to them.

"Soldiers ahead!" she shouted, smoke fuming from her nostrils and mouth. "Women and children behind. Battle formations—like we drilled. Go!"

Wings creaking, Dorin snarled at her. His eyes blazed.

"You will lead our last survivors to die upon the walls of a foreign city?" He turned to the dragons behind them. "Dragons of Second Haven! This is not our war. We have come for aid; we find death. Fly back! Back to the forests! To—"

Lyana slammed into him, shoving him into a tumble. He glared and snapped at her, and she pulled back and hissed. Flames sparked between her teeth. She and Dorin circled each other in the sky, glaring and snorting smoke and flames.

"You have played your little games of dominion, *Legless Lord*," she said, spitting out the last words mockingly. "Yet Confutatis still stands; she is besieged but still fights. We will fly to her aid."

She looked back at the battle. Trebuchets swung upon the city walls, tossing boulders onto the Fallen Horde. One boulder crashed into a nephil, crushing the beast upon the plains like a great insect. Other nephilim still swooped above the city, lifting men from towers and feasting upon them. Arrows thrust out from the creatures, but seemed barely to faze them; their hunger was too great. Some soldiers of Osanna upon the walls, tall men clad in steel, saw the dragons and raised a cry.

"Requiem!" they cried. "Requiem flies to our aid!"

The nephilim screeched, turned, and saw the dragons too. They raised their arms and howled, and a city wall cracked, and the land itself shook. Dozens of the creatures began flying south toward Lyana, Dorin, and the thousands behind them.

"We flee now!" Dorin said, glaring at Lyana. "That is my order; these are my people."

Lyana looked back at the dragons; they hovered in midair, torn between their queen and their new lord. She looked at the nephilim; they flew across the plains, bat wings beating, teeth bared and glinting in the small morning sun.

"Dorin," she said softly. "Dorin, I led your son in battle."

His eyes narrowed. He sucked in his breath. Smoke plumed from his clenched jaw.

"He was brave," Lyana said softly as the nephil horde approached. "He was among the bravest dragons I knew. He charged into the host of phoenixes, and... I could not save him. But he saved me. He saved many."

Dorin hissed and flames shot from his mouth. "You will not mention my son! You—"

"Dorin, do not flee from this battle. If truly you lead these people, you must fight for them." She looked back at the nephilim; they flew only a mile away now. Her jaw twisted into a crooked smile. "We can take them."

Dorin stared at her. He stared at the dragons behind him. He stared at the enemy and grunted. Finally he bucked and roared.

"Dragons of Second Haven! Leave none alive!" He blew his fire, clawed the sky, and charged toward the horde. "Slay them!"

A hundred dragons, warriors of Second Haven, sounded their cry and charged.

The nephilim crashed into them.

Lyana blew fire. She slammed her tail's spikes into one nephil's head, punching through its skull. Her claws slashed another. Three nephilim crashed onto her, clinging like spiders onto their prey, and teeth punched through her scales. She roared and clawed at them, dipping in the sky. Another soared from below and slammed into her belly. The beasts enveloped her, crushing her and biting, and she howled.

Stars damn it.

With a deep breath, she shifted into human form.

She slipped between their claws and tumbled toward the ground.

Wind roared. The nephilim shrieked above and swooped. Before she could hit the ground, Lyana shifted back into a dragon and soared, shooting fire. Her blaze caught the swooping nephilim and she knocked between them, clawing their burning forms. They fell around her, blood and worms spilling from their wounds.

She soared to fight among her comrades. The dragons flew back and forth, blazing their fire. These ones had survived the phoenixes, the wyverns, and the attacks on Second Haven; they were scarred and battle-hardened, and they killed with grim intent. Nephilim fell before them, blazing.

A few of the beasts dipped, flew beneath the warrior dragons, and crashed into the women, children, and elders. Screams rose. Claws dug into dragon flesh. Dragons returned to human form and tumbled, and nephilim caught them in their jaws and feasted.

Lyana howled.

"Circle the group!" she shouted to her fellow warriors. "Above and below!"

She swooped, slashed a nephil's swollen head, and flew under the mothers and children. Nephilim swarmed her way; she blazed them with flames, and above her, the young dragons screamed. At her sides flew the other warriors, circling the weaker dragons, forming a shield of scale and flame around them. The nephilim kept charging at them. The dragons kept blowing their flames.

Finally only three nephilim remained. They howled, spraying fountains of saliva. One reached out and grabbed the leg of an old, female dragon. He pulled her from the protective ring and bit deep, and the old dragon returned to human form. The nephilim tore her apart and fed upon her.

Lyana roared and charged at them. Fire blazed at her side; Dorin flew there, howling. The two dragons—blue and red—crashed into the feasting nephilim, clawing and biting and thrusting their horns. The beasts fell dead, and Lyana roared to the sky.

She looked back at her people. Some had fallen; their bodies lay upon the fields below. Most still flew, scales splashed with blood and soot. Heart hammering, Lyana whipped her head back toward the city. Dozens of nephilim still flew above the walls, insects above a prized morsel.

"To Confutatis!" Lyana cried and roared a pillar of flame. "Slay the beasts upon the walls and towers!"

Three thousand dragons streamed toward the city, raising a roar to shake the earth. Lyana flew at their lead, blowing fire and howling, a hoarse cry of rage, of pain, of loss—a cry for the death of her parents, for the fall of her palace, for the fading light of her people. She flew to aid others. She flew to slay her enemies. She flew as queen, as a woman haunted, as a blue dragon with so much fear and pain inside her that she could never heal. She shot over the city walls. Above the towers and streets of Confutatis, she crashed into nephilim and slew them with fire and claw.

When all the creatures lay dead, diseased corpses strewn across streets and roofs, Lyana landed upon a steeple that rose among cobbled streets, dwarfing the houses and shops beneath it. Her fellow dragons landed upon roofs, towers, and walls around her, panting and tossing their heads to scatter their smoke. Around them across the city, soldiers ran in armor, cheering and crying for Requiem.

We slew them, Lyana thought, snarling and baring her teeth. *We slew the bastards, and we will slay Solina next.*

She kicked off the steeple and rose into the sky.

"Dragons of Requiem!" she shouted. "We've secured the city. We've shown our strength! We—"

Shrieks rose in the south.

Lyana's heart froze.

Hovering in midair, she turned to see a bustling swarm cover the southern horizon.

They had slain a hundred nephilim. Ten thousand more now cried for blood and stormed toward the city.

Merciful stars.

Below Lyana, Osannan soldiers ran along the streets, drawing swords and arrows; they heard the distant shrieks. Around her upon the towers, walls, and roofs of the White City, her fellow dragons snarled and stared. They were weary. Blood coated their scales. So much of the city lay fallen around them, towers smashed and walls fallen and houses crushed—the work of but a hundred nephlim. Now thousands flew from the south, and Lyana trembled and spat flames.

"Stars bless us, Requiem," she whispered. She landed back on the steeple. She could not win this fight, she knew. Not with only three thousand dragons, most of them elders and children. Not with only men living in this city, soldiers so small and frail by the cruelty and might of the Fallen Horde.

So here my life ends, she thought, *far from Requiem and far from my king—here, upon the white walls of Osanna's Jewel, will I die with fire.*

The screams rose from the south. The eyes of the nephilim blazed. Their wings rose and fell like a cloud of locusts. All around Lyana, dragons snarled upon roofs and men drew arrows upon walls.

Dorin perched upon a temple's dome beside her. He looked at her, and his eyes were weary; so much pain and whispers of blood filled them.

"Lyana," he said softly. She had never heard him speak softly before. "Lyana, you are brave, and you are strong, and you fought well. But now we must flee. We have shown our honor here, but this is not our war."

She glared at him, and her claws dug grooves into the steeple.

"This is Solina's horde!" she said. "These are the beasts that ravaged our camp. Here is our war—it flies toward us."

Dorin sighed and gestured at the city that sprawled around them. "In Confutatis? City of men? We are Vir Requis, Lyana. These are not our walls to die upon. This is not our city to protect."

"Our walls fell!" She snapped her teeth. "Our city, which we protected, burned. I will make my last stand here if I must. If here is my end, I will make it an end for poets, and I will rise to the stars knowing that I died fighting my enemy, not fleeing into the wilderness to die alone and old many years from now, still haunted by my cowardice."

Dorin shook his head, and smoke streamed between his teeth. "Cowardice, Lyana? Is it cowardice to seek life when death looms with certainty? Is it cowardice to survive, yes—to flee—when there is no chance of victory? No; I call that prudence. Your valor will have you die upon walls not yours. What honor is there in that? How will your death protect those of our people who still live? I would rather live as a man than die as a dragon. In the forests we survived."

"Until the horde found us," she said. "How much longer do you think we can hide? The nephilim cover the world; stand and fight them here, Dorin. With me."

And yet... and yet her words tasted stale to her. She wanted to roar them with conviction, to rally his heart and hers. But was this valor truly foolishness? Was his wish to flee not wisdom? And had she—Lyana herself—not fled from Nova Vita as its walls fell and the dead burned upon its streets?

The nephil army was close now, so close that Lyana could count the teeth in their jaws. She flapped her wings and rose higher, and flames filled her maw. She growled and her wings sent dust flying across the city below.

Maybe I am foolish, she thought. *Maybe he is wise, and I am but a headstrong soldier dreaming of glory. Let him flee then; let him survive. But I am Queen of Requiem, and the scourge of my people flies before me, and I will roar my fire. If I must stand alone, I will die with my fire and the song of my stars—foolish perhaps, but I am a warrior, and I will die as one.*

The Fallen Horde stormed across the fields, a tapestry of claw and fang, a night of rot and malice. Dorin grunted, gave Lyana a last glare, then took flight and began to flee north. A few dragons began to follow him.

Be strong, Lyana, she told herself, staring south as the horde approached. *Be strong and you will soon fly to your parents, to Orin, to all those who fell.*

Darkness covered the city.

From the east, like a sun rising, sounded the cries of new dawn.

Lyana turned her head, looked eastward, and tears filled her eyes.

"Hope," she whispered. She raised her voice and roared to the city. "Griffins! Griffins are coming! Dragons of Requiem, rally here! Griffins fly to aid."

Flocks flew from the dawn, half eagles and half lions, great beasts the size of dragons. Sunrays rose around them. Lyana had never been to their home, the mythical Leonis Isles across the sea. She had seen only one griffin before, Prince Velathar who had visited Requiem a year ago. Now thousands flew from the rising sun, a golden dawn aflight.

Seeing the host, the nephilim wailed and covered their eyes with their claws, blinded and hissing. A few turned to flee. Others howled and faced the sun.

The two hosts crashed above the ancient walls and towers of Confutatis.

Lyana soared and blew her fire.

BAYRIN

"Mori?" he whispered.

Inside the golden mountain of the true dragons, he stood in his pod, embracing a very naked Piri. Before him at the doorway, Mori stood with wide eyes and trembling lips.

Bayrin gasped and froze, barely able to breathe. How could this be? How could Mori be here? She looked almost like a ghost, so frail and pallid Bayrin thought he might be seeing a spirit. She was thinner than he'd ever seen her, her cheekbones prominent, her eyes large and gray, her arms sticklike and neck too thin. Her skin was milky white and dark circles surrounded her eyes. And yet it was her, and she was alive, and she was beautiful and fragile and *real*.

Still embracing him, Piri looked over her shoulder and saw the princess. She gasped, pulled away from Bayrin, and grabbed her cloak from the floor. She covered her nakedness and retreated to the back of the room, eyes wide and mouth hanging open.

"Mori," Bayrin said, and his eyes stung, and his heart thrashed. He took a step toward her. "Stars, Mori, are... is it really you?"

She looked at him, frozen. She looked toward the back of the room where Piri stood, cloak wrapped around her. Mori's eyes dampened. She turned, shifted into a golden dragon, and flew away from the pod.

Bayrin leaped out into the darkness. The cavern of the golden mountain loomed around him, its walls lined with countless more pods like a beehive, its empty spaces lit by flowing orbs of light and the shimmer of salvanae scales. He shifted and flew, seeking Mori, but salvanae flew everywhere—thousands of them. He could not see her.

"Mori!" he shouted, flying inside the mountain. He knocked through a cluster of floating orbs; they scattered, tossing light and shadows. "Mori!"

He glimpsed a slim golden tail behind a group of salvanae. He flew in pursuit. Salvanae streamed everywhere around him, flying serpents moving so quickly they appeared as streams of light. As he flew, Bayrin kept having to dip, rise, and skirt the coiling creatures.

"Mori!" he cried out. "Stars, Mori, come talk to me."

He barreled through a group of salvanae; they bugled in surprise and scattered. He dived between floating orbs and saw her there. She flew away from him, descending deeper down the mountain into shadow.

"Mori!"

He dived after her, calling her name. She flew beneath a cluster of salvanae elders who crowded around glowing runes, their eyelashes beating and their beards dipping as they prayed. Stars, she was still so fast! Bayrin flew after her, incurring clucking tongues and grunts from the salvanae elders. He saw Mori soar toward a wall of more pods. She approached one pod, shifted into a human, and ran inside.

Heart pounding, Bayrin followed. His claws grabbed the pod's rim. He shifted into human form and crawled inside like a bee entering its hive. This pod looked much like the one he shared with Piri: long, round, and simple. Fresh leaves covered its floor in a rug, and bubbles of food and wine lay upon them. Mori sat by the far wall, her back to him.

Bayrin approached her, walking gingerly upon the carpet of leaves. When he reached her, he knelt and hesitantly touched her shoulder. She cowered at his touch and huddled deeper into the corner.

"Mori," he whispered. "Stars, Mori, I... I can't believe you're here! I missed you. Mori?"

She looked over her shoulder at him. Tears filled those huge gray eyes Bayrin had dreamed to see joyous.

"Bayrin," she whispered. A tear rolled down her cheek.

He embraced her, but she felt wooden and stiff, and she did not return the embrace. She was so thin, so pale. Bayrin closed his eyes. This was not how he'd dreamed of meeting Mori again. For moons, he had wanted nothing else, and his fingers still shook with the shock of it. In endless dreams, she would run toward him and crash into his embrace, and they would kiss and laugh and tell stories of daring escapes. Not... not this, just silence and Mori so still in his arms, a porcelain figurine.

"Mori," he whispered again. "I'm so glad you're here. Stars, I missed you, Mors." His voice cracked and his eyes dampened. "You don't have to tell me what happened. Not now or ever, if you don't want to. I'm just so glad you're here. I'm not going to let you go again—ever, not ever, Mori. I'll never let you out of my arms. If we have to, we'll just stay like this forever."

She looked up at him, blinking tears from her eyes. "Is... I saw Piri. Is she...?"

Bayrin found himself weeping. He hated showing such emotion; hated it! He had not cried since he was nine and Lyana had kicked him too hard. Today he could not help it. And yet he laughed—he laughed through his tears until his chest shook.

"Piri! Stars, Mori, the girl in crazy. You remember how she used to follow me around, right?" He kissed her cheek. "I love you, Mori. Only you. Now and always. Nothing happened between Piri and me. She tried to seduce me; I refused her. You've always had a talent for showing up at just the wrong moment! Remember how you once walked into the armory just as I was, uhm... testing Lyana's dress?"

"You were going to put it on!" she said, and now a soft smile trembled on her lips.

"I was not! I was only holding it against me to see if... I accidentally stabbed it with my sword."

She laid her head against his chest.

"I know," she whispered. "I know, Bay. I believe you."

He did not have to ask if she meant the dress or Piri. He leaned back against the wall, and Mori wriggled until she nestled in his arms. He held her very close for a very long time, and they said nothing more.

A hole upon the mountainside, a remnant of the nephil attack, gaped open not far outside their pod. Through it, Bayrin could see into the wilderness. The sun began to set, casting rays of orange light upon the forest. In the evening, the priest Nehushtan flew to their pod, coiling and chinking, and summoned them to a council.

"We will meet under the stars and discuss the evil that stains the world," he said, his tufted eyebrows curved in sorrow.

Bayrin and Mori followed him in dragon forms, and they flew out the mountain and above the forests. Sunset gilded the land, and Bayrin looked at Mori as she flew. She looked back and gave him a soft smile, and despite the ruin of the world, and the evil that still lurked in the desert, Bayrin was happy.

Mori is here. There is still light in the world.

Nehushtan led them to a grassy hill that rose from a forest clearing. Ten great stones rose here, each larger than a man, arranged like the Draco constellation. Night fell, and blue runes glowed upon the stones, and the true stars shone above. Fireflies swirled around the henge, adding their glow. All around the hill, the forest rolled into shadow, the trees mere black hints like charcoal etched onto obsidian.

Above several stones hovered elder salvanae. Their eyes glowed silver and gold in the starlight. Their bodies coiled behind them like banners in a breeze. Their beards were long and their brows furrowed, and their breath steamed in the night.

Upon a pair of stones perched two dragons of Requiem—unlike the salvanae, they had stockier bodies, four legs, and wings. Even in the dim starlight, Bayrin recognized Piri's lavender scales; it was a rare color in Requiem. The other was a slim black dragon, and Bayrin gasped when he recognized her.

"Treale Oldnale!" he blurted out, hovering above the henge. "Bloody stars, I haven't seen you in ages. Where the Abyss have you been?"

She raised her chin at him. "Probably having a rougher time than you, Bayrin Eleison. Now sit down and don't be rude. We have a council to attend."

Blinking in amazement, Bayrin landed upon one of the boulders. His tail flicked against the grass below, and a silvery rune glowed upon his perch, warming him. Mori landed upon another stone, and the high priest Nehushtan flew to hover above another. All the stones were now occupied, the stars shone, and the council began.

"An ancient evil has fallen upon our land," said Nehushtan. He blinked, and his great white lashes fanned the grass below. "Thousands of winters have passed since blood spilled in our land, and we were young. We saw the demons of the Abyss rise to crawl upon the earth, and we saw them choose mortal brides. We watched, weeping, as their spawn grew into rotted giants, as the Fallen Ones—the nephilim—roamed the world, neither men nor demons, half-breeds torn in anguish. We watched them burn trees, smash rocks, and feast upon living flesh. We fought them. We slew them. Now they rise again, and we weep, for our sons and daughters have fallen and now fly among the stars."

The salvanae all looked up toward the Draco constellation and sang prayers, for the true dragons—like the Vir Requis—worshipped the stars of Draco.

They too are Draco's children, Bayrin thought. *They too are dragons. They are cousins to us Vir Requis—different from us, but sharing our light.* He sang their prayers with them.

As they sang to the stars, he looked at Mori. She sat beside him upon a boulder engraved with a crescent rune. She was looking skyward, and the starlight glimmered in her eyes and upon her scales. Warmth filled Bayrin in the cold night. He reached out his tail and coiled it around hers. She looked at him softly and nodded, and their tails braided together in a warm grip.

Other dragons spoke next. Treale spoke of seeing Solina raise these beasts in Irys, capital of her desert realm, and send them to feed upon dragon flesh. Piri spoke too, talking of King Elethor and his camp in the eastern forests where a thousand Vir Requis lived. Finally Bayrin himself spoke, describing Elethor's wrath and plans to invade Tiranor and slay its queen. Only Mori did not speak, but every time the word *nephilim* was uttered, she gave his tail a squeeze.

The salvanae elders talked too. They talked as the stars wheeled above: of Solina's evil, of the souls of the fallen, of the sadness in their hearts. They bugled to the sky their rage and mourning.

Bayrin listened to them pray, talk, and sing, and slowly fire grew inside him. He mourned too—for his slain parents, for his fallen friends, for his kingdom that lay in ruins. Yet perched here upon this stone, he found mostly rage inside him—a rage against Solina's cruelty and the murder of so many. Finally he could bear it no longer. He released Mori's tail. With three great flaps of his wings, he rose to hover above the henge, and he blasted fire skyward.

"Hear me!" he said. "We have mourned here for hours, and the stars have turned; soon dawn will rise. I'm done weeping! Solina brought death here. She bought blood and misery. I say we repay her in kind." He blasted more flames; they danced against the dragons' scales. "I am a warrior of Draco. You can fight too. Fly east with me to King Elethor and his camp. We'll join our forces there, and we'll fly south as one... and we'll slay this mad queen upon her desert." He sounded his roar. "What say you?"

At his right side, Piri and Treale both snarled, flapped their own wings, and tossed their heads back. Lavender and black dragons, they blew pillars of fire skyward. Heat blasted Bayrin to his left, and he turned to see Mori roaring her own fire. Bayrin joined his fire to theirs. Four flaming pillars crackled and spun and blasted heat, and the dragons of Requiem sounded their roars.

The salvanae looked at one another, and their bushy eyebrows furrowed. They were peaceful beings, wise and ancient and sad, and yet now their lips peeled back, and their fangs shone, and they became terrible to behold. A fire burned in their eyes, and lightning crackled in their maws, and for the first time, Bayrin saw them not as old wise priests, but as warriors.

They tossed back their heads and roared their wrath, and they shot lighting to the stars.

"We will fly!" they cried. "We will fly! We will avenge our brothers. We will fly!"

Their roars seemed to shake the forest, and Bayrin grinned as his flames flowed.

Yes, he thought. *Yes. To fire. To blood. To ruin. To the desert and to Queen Solina.*

"We will fly!"

SOLINA

In the bowels of the Palace of Whispers, she sat in a hall of stone and shadow. Nephilim swarmed around her. They scuttled across the dusty mosaic floors, clung to the ceiling like bats, and climbed the limestone columns. Three knelt beneath her, heads downcast and wings splayed out; they formed her new throne, a seat of living rot and scale and bone. The spine ridges of two beasts formed her armrests, and their claws formed the legs of her chair; a third nephil rose behind her, a backrest of scales and boils, and its head drooled and hissed above her own.

"Children!" Solina cried, her voice ringing across the hall. "Feast! Feast upon the bones."

They howled and fed upon the bones of prisoners she had tossed them, cracking them open to suck the marrow. This chamber, here in this desert palace, loomed thrice the size of her throne room in Irys; ten thousand nephilim fit inside it. They roared all around, drooling and screeching and clawing the floor and walls. Solina imagined that their cries carried to every hall, tunnel, and chamber throughout this great palace—an edifice the size of a city. Their cry would ring across the desert too—across the world.

"Do you hear it too, Elethor?" she whispered. "Do they scream for you?"

The nephilim that formed her throne cawed and writhed, and she stroked them. They drooled and their white eyes narrowed. She had sent Legion himself, king of these beasts, to fetch her beloved. She had sent more to every corner of the world: to the wilderness of Salvandos where true dragons flew, to the plains and cities of Osanna where men rode upon horses and knew no magic, and even to the distant isles where griffins flew.

"You will find no place to hide, Elethor," she said, stroking the nephilim she sat upon. "In every corner of this world, my children will hunt you. Any allies you enlist, my children will kill them. You cannot stop them. You cannot hide from me." She clenched her fists and grinned. "I will *bring you here*."

She stood upon her throne of living flesh and raised her arms. All around her, the Fallen Horde flew in a storm, wings beating and teeth snapping.

"The flesh of the world is ours!" she called. "The bones of your enemies will be your prize! We will never fall!"

They howled around her, a myriad of demons, bodies lanky and rotted like corpses, wings full of holes, mouths full of blood. They roared and praised her name, and the chamber shook.

"Hail Solina! Hail the Golden Goddess! We are free!"

She walked down a nephil's spine as if descending stairs, crossed the hall between the beasts, and left the chamber. When she closed the doors behind her, she could still hear them sing her name and growl and feast.

Solina walked down a corridor of shadows. She gripped her twin sabers at her sides, and her lips tightened. She had her power. She had her glory. But one thing she still missed; one prize she would still claim.

She walked through the palace for a long time.

She walked down hallways where dust and cobwebs covered old murals of beasts and men. She climbed chipped staircases lined with statues of slender, solemn Ancients, their heads oval and their eyes staring. Finally, after what seemed like miles, she stepped through a doorway into the Hall of Memories.

She stood before the great, dark cavern and a shiver ran through her.

The chamber was vast, larger even than her throne room; she could have fit a palace in here. Columns surrounded the chamber in a ring, supporting a shadowy, domed ceiling. Below the doorway spread a black pit; the bases of the columns faded there into shadow. Solina had tossed stones into that pit before and could not hear them hit the bottom; perhaps there was no bottom and the darkness led to the Abyss itself.

In the center of the chamber, a great stone well rose from the darkness like a tower rising from a moat. A bridge crossed the pit, leading from the doorway where Solina stood to the towering well. She began to walk. The stone bridge was narrow, barely wide enough for her to cross. On both sides loomed the pit; cold air rose from those shadows to sting her cheeks. The columns that surrounded the chasm frowned upon her, ancient sentinels of stone. The hall was so silent Solina could hear her own heartbeat.

Finally the dusty, chipped bridge led her to the towering well.

The well was wide—wide enough for a dragon to swim in—and pale bricks formed its rim. It seemed less like a well from here, and more like a pool upon a tower top. Water rose to the brim, silver and opaque and perfectly still. A staircase led from the edge down into the water.

Solina stood above the pool. She lowered her head, and the cold wind played with her hair. She breathed deeply, in and out, again and again. All around her lurked the shadowy pit.

The place of my heart. The innermost whispers of my soul.

She stepped onto the staircase that led into the pool. When her sandals touched the first step, the water rose over her ankles, cold and warm at once, both soothing and stinging like a memory of lost love. She kept descending, taking each step slowly. The water rose to her knees, stung the jewel at her navel, and finally rose to her neck. She raised her head, closed her eyes, and took a deep breath. She descended the last step, and the water covered her.

When she opened her eyes, she saw feathery white light. A warm breeze caressed her skin and hair. Slowly the light parted like silk curtains and she saw it.

A tremulous smile touched her lips and tears stung her eyes.

"Home," she whispered.

Marble statues filled the small room, carved in her likeness. Tapestries hung from the walls, and plush rugs covered the floor. Upon shelves stood the wooden statuettes he would whittle: deer, leaping fish, and her favorite—a turtle with emerald eyes he had carved especially for her. Upon a table stood a plate of bread rolls, a bowl of apples, and a jug of wine. His bed stood under a window, topped with quilts and pillows, the place where they would kiss, love, sleep, and whisper all the whispers of their hearts.

Outside the windows the day was clear and warm. Birches and cypresses rustled upon the hill, and the scent of jasmines wafted. Only scattered white clouds filled the blue sky. Birds chirruped and bees bustled around the honeysuckle. It was spring in Requiem, a day of peace, of warmth, of him and her.

A day for us. A free day. A perfect day.

The cruel King Olasar, his pitiful daughter Mori, the haughty Lady Lyana and Prince Orin—they were all gone to Oldnale Farms far in the east. Nova Vita was theirs, just hers and Elethor's—a spring for their love, a spring to lie in bed and hold each other, to sit upon the hill and watch the trees, to be free, a day of no fear, no hurt.

She looked around his chamber. Marble statues. Shelves with books and geodes and his carvings. The table with the bread and wine. His bed of quilts. And silence. Waiting. A loneliness like a house after death.

"I created this for us, Elethor," she whispered. She tasted her tears. "You remember. It was the best day of our lives. A day for us. A perfect day."

She had found this old place in this old palace: the Memory Pool, a place where she could weave her dreams. The Ancients, it was said, would enter this pool to return to their childhoods in old age, to revisit old ghosts before the great journey to the world beyond. Solina had only bad memories from her childhood, memories of the dragons slaying her parents, of captivity in the hall of the Weredragon King. But this memory... this memory from only a decade ago... this was pure. This had been—*was!*—her one perfect day, the one perfect piece of her soul.

"You remember, Elethor." She lay upon his bed and looked up at the ceiling. Cracks spread there like cobwebs, but they were beautiful to her; she knew each one. "You remember how we lay here. We made love three times that night, and you were *so lazy* in the morning. You didn't want to wake up. Do you remember?"

She was weeping. Her tears flowed down her cheeks and dampened the quilt.

Why did such pain have to fill this world? Why had so much fire burned her? She was but a mortal, but a frail woman, and she had walked through fire, blood, and death. She had fought the dragons and slain them, and she had raised beasts from the desert, and she had done great things upon this earth.

"But this is all I ever wanted, Elethor. This day again and again and again. A day for us. A perfect day. I will bring you here to this Palace of Whispers, to this Memory Pool, and you will be here with me." She clutched the blankets. "We will be here forever."

She turned her head aside, blinked the tears from her eyes, and pulled a blanket over her. She felt so cold and she longed for his embrace. She looked outside the window at the clouds that glided, and she missed him so badly that her insides ached and she could barely breathe.

LYANA

Corpses littered the city. Thousands lay dead here, Lyana thought—tens of thousands. She flew over Confutatis, her heart a block of ice.

The ancient capital of Osanna was home to a million souls, a great labyrinth of white stone and cedar. Its walls had stood for thousands of years, and its towers kissed the sky. Today holes peppered those walls; in some parts they had fallen completely. Towers lay smashed, crushing houses and streets beneath them. Everywhere she looked—in gardens, squares, and streets—dead nephilim lay rotting, cut with griffin talons, pierced with arrows, or burnt with dragonfire. Many griffins lay dead too, their wings torn off and their bellies slashed. Vir Requis lay dead in human forms, indistinguishable in death from the corpses of Osannans; many of this city's people had fallen too, bitten apart by the feasting horde.

The stench of rot and blood filled the sky. Outside in the fields, living dragons and griffins stood side by side, digging mass graves and shoving piles of bodies into them. Flies buzzed and crows feasted.

Again you bring death, Solina, Lyana thought as she circled above the city like one of the crows. *Again you bring blood. But now not only Requiem knows your evil, Solina. Now the world will fight you with one great cry. You have kindled a fire you cannot tame.*

The sun set upon a city of blood and tears.

Bells of mourning rang in the night.

Lyana found a cobbled square beneath an archway, curled up in dragon form, and slept dreaming of white demon eyes.

Dawn rose, and three monarchs met in the Palace of Osanna. Upon his throne of giltwood sat King Shae, elderly ruler of Osanna, his beard flowing and white, his eyes sad and wise beneath black brows. Before him stood Vale, the Griffin King, his breast mottled white and his yellow eyes solemn. Lyana stood there too, Queen of Requiem, clad in her silvery armor, her sword upon her waist and her helm upon her head. Three rulers of three great kingdoms; they stood silently as funeral bells rang across the city and echoed in the palace hall. They stood here alone.

It was Lyana who spoke first.

"King Shae," she said. "We must attack Tiranor. Join your forces to mine and let us strike the desert." She pounded fist into palm, then turned to the Griffin King. "King Vale, most noble of beasts! The nephilim attacked your homeland too. Now fly with us. Let griffins fight with dragons; let talons and claws join in war. Together we will topple the halls of the desert queen."

She had expected a long day of arguments, of pounding fists, even of pleading.

Instead she got two nods, one from each king.

In the hall of Osanna, she closed her eyes, clutched trembling fingers behind her back, and whispered.

"Thank you."

She left the palace with more fear in her belly than during the battle.

Fire and blood will cover the world, she thought. She stood outside the palace doors, shifted, and took flight. *No place is safe now; no land will be spared death.*

Lyana had never been particularly pious. Her mother had been a priestess. Her friend Mori had spent hours in the temple, singing old songs and praying to the stars. Lyana had always preferred drilling with her sword, or roaring her fire, or polishing her armor; her weapons and strength had been her gods. Yet today she flew outside the city, walked through forests in human form, and prayed.

"Please, stars of Requiem," she whispered among the naked trees. The first snows of winter glided and clung to her cloak and hair. "Please, stars, do not let the light of the world go out. I am afraid. I am afraid for my husband. I am afraid for Mori and for Requiem." She closed her eyes and clenched her jaw, and pain dug through her. "I am afraid for myself. I miss my parents and I'm so scared."

Tears filled her eyes. She could not remember when she had last cried. She spent all day here in this forest, and when night fell she looked up at the stars, and sang to them softly, and clutched her sword's hilt so tightly that her fingers ached.

"I am Lyana," she whispered to those distant lights, the constellation Draco, stars of her fathers. "I am Queen of Requiem. I am your daughter. I will walk in your light, stars; this I swear. Light this long, dark night."

She slept among the trees in dragon form, curled up as snow coated her blue scales. Dawn rose pale around her, and icicles filled the forest, and Lyana took flight. Osanna rolled cold and glimmering around her, but when she looked south, Lyana could imagine the desert, and there the sand was hot and the sun burned her.

LEGION

Legion licked his chops and snapped his teeth and slashed his claws. He grinned and howled and tasted the blood of dragons.

"We are strong!" he said, his cry rising and tearing the air and cracking trees and boulders. He flapped his wings and rose upon fire. "We feed! We feed!"

Across the ruins, the Fallen Horde roared, swirled across the sky, and covered the ground, an endless swarm. His children screamed and laughed and flew around him, thousands of his spawn torn from the wombs of his wives. Already more nephilim rutted in the dirt, and rotted wombs swelled, and more beasts burst through flesh to feast upon their mothers.

"The world imprisoned us!" Legion cried. They answered his call with thousands of screams. "Now we kill. Now we eat. Now we drink blood. We are the nephilim! We were the Fallen. Now we rise! We rise!"

Countless screams shook the world, boulders rolled, trees fell, and the ruins crumbled below.

"We rise!" the nephilim howled. "We rise!"

Legion flew around them, blood roaring, halo flaming, tongue licking, wings beating. He rose. He rose! He fed. He ate! He killed. Solina freed him! He was a god. He was Prophet. He was Legion.

"The dragons cower!" he shouted. "The world trembles. We are strong! We are Nephil. We are Enemy. We are Nemesis. Our jaws will crush their spines!"

As he flew drooling, he caressed his belly. His own womb swelled, and he felt the vermin kicking and biting inside, drinking his blood and eating his innards.

Soon, precious spawn, he thought. *Soon you will burst from me too, and you will eat my flesh, and you will grow to lead this swarm.*

He landed upon the roof of the crumbling temple. Blasts of fire burst from within. The flames sprayed from every window and hole. One flame blasted not two feet from Legion, clawing at the sky, and heat baked him. The vermin bustled inside his womb, and Legion heard their muffled screams.

Yes, Legion thought, *yes, the fire burns us, my vermin. But not for long.*

They are weak. They are afraid. We will eat them, and their blood will nourish us.

He spread his wings wide, curtains of black leather, and raised his claws. His halo blazed and screamed. He howled to the sky of nephilim, and they swirled above and around him, a storm of rot.

"Tear down these walls!" he shouted. "Drag the beasts out and rip them apart! Feast, nephilim. We rise! We rise!"

They howled around him and the ruins shook.

"We rise!"

ELETHOR

"Break down the walls!" the beasts screeched outside. "Break them down!"

They huddled in the darkness—a few hundred Vir Requis, perhaps the last of their kind. They were ashy, bloody, and famished. They crowded together, mothers embracing weeping children, youths clutching swords, elders whispering. Around them rose the walls of the ancient temple—mossy bricks, roots and branches pushing between them, as old and brittle as the scrolls of ancient scribes.

Outside the horde cried for blood. White eyes like smelters blazed at every window and hole. Claws tore at every brick. The ceiling was crumbling, and through it the Vir Requis saw no sky, only more fangs and blazing eyes and claws that thirsted for blood. Countless of the creatures swarmed there; they covered the sky, the forest, and the ruins, breeding and multiplying until it seemed the world itself would crash beneath them.

Elethor shifted into dragon form, moved toward a gaping hole in the wall, and replaced a weary silver dragon who blew fire there. The silver stepped back and shifted back into human form—a weary, gaunt woman. Elethor placed his maw into the hole and blew his flames, driving back the nephilim who clawed and bit there. His flames roared and crackled, flowing over his vision, but in his brief pauses for breath, Elethor saw the horde and fear clutched him.

Thousands. A hundred thousand. More. They covered the sky and land, a mass of scale and rot; he saw no end to them.

Elethor howled as he sprayed his fire. He could not hold them back much longer. They had moments before they grew too weary for fire, before these walls fell and the demons drowned them.

Finally his fire was drained. He pulled back, panting, and another dragon replaced him. Elethor shifted back into human form and stumbled into the center of the room. His people crowded around him, wailing and staring from wall to ceiling.

At every window, doorway, and hole, dragons stood blowing fire. No more than a dozen dragons could fill this crumbling hall; if more Vir Requis shifted, they would crush one another.

Bricks shifted.

Claws drove past stone.

A hole crashed open in the southern wall, showering dust. A nephil's arms reached inside and slashed, lacerating a Vir Requis child. The boy fell, his belly sliced open. Elethor screamed and swung his sword, cutting the nephil's arm. Black blood showered, and the arm withdrew. At once Yar, the young yellow dragon, leaped toward the new opening and roared fire. The nephilim outside shrieked.

"The ceiling!" somebody shouted.

Elethor looked up to see bricks shift. Fangs burst between the stones, and a hole gaped open, raining rock and dust and moss. A nephil's jaw thrust in, snapping, and Vir Requis screamed.

"Burn it!" Elethor shouted, and one Vir Requis—an old graybeard—shifted and roared fire at the ceiling.

Claws thrashed at the northern wall, tearing a window wider. A nephil reached into the hall, claws lashing, and a woman fell, her arm severed.

Elethor shifted back into dragon form, raced toward the new opening, and blew more fire. The nephil screeched. Elethor's flames were weak now, mere sparks. He was too weary. When another dragon replaced him, Elethor could barely stand. He shifted into human form and looked around him.

"Mama," whimpered a child and clutched her mother.

"Stars of Requiem," whispered an old woman, holding her husband.

And so it ends, Elethor thought. His armor felt so heavy; such a weight to bear. *So does Requiem fade away, a small lingering light crushed under darkness.*

He looked up. Claws and teeth lashed at the ceiling, tearing stone from stone. All the terrors and evils of the world were digging in.

"Requiem," he whispered. "May our wings forever find your sky."

These were the ancient words of his people. Now the survivors repeated them as the claws tore the walls. A hole cracked open in the ceiling, and bricks rained, and a sickly red light fell. The nephilim shrieked and cackled.

No, Elethor thought. He snarled and drew his sword. *No, we will not fade like a guttering candle. We will die in a great pillar of flame.*

Yar stumbled toward him, panting and coated in sweat; another replaced him at the window. He stood by Elethor and bowed his head.

"My king," the boy said.

No, not a boy, Elethor thought. *He is a man today.*

He clutched Yar's shoulder.

"Yar, you fight nobly for Requiem." He looked up at the ceiling where claws tore brick from brick. He lowered his voice. "Yar—fly with me."

Yar followed his gaze. The ceiling was trembling. Bricks and dust and moss fell, and the nephilim howled there, eyes blazing.

"To the sky," Yar whispered.

"To death," Elethor said. "To glory. To our starlit halls."

Yar bared his teeth, nodded, and clutched Elethor's shoulder. "We will fly, my king. We will fly there together."

The temple shook and the shrieks nearly deafened them. King Elethor gave the orders, and the dragons pulled back from the walls, and the survivors crowded in the center of the hall. All around them the walls shook, the claws reached in, and the shrieks echoed. Elethor held his sword high.

"Vir Requis!" he shouted, voice nearly drowning under the screams of the horde. "We fly now. We find our sky. Shift, dragons of Requiem, and sound your roar! Let the sky shake with the song of dragons!"

In the darkness of night and demon siege, after seven days of hiding in shadow, the dragons of Requiem emerged from their temple and crashed into the sky.

Elethor led the charge, a brass dragon with rippling scales and bright horns. His fire rose before him, a pillar of flame to lead their way. At his sides flew his soldiers, battle-hardened dragons with dented scales and broken claws, and their fire rose like the columns of afterlife. They shot through the collapsing roof and soared into a sky of demons. The nephilim spread endlessly into the night; thousands upon thousands covered the sky, a sea of rot and scale and blazing eyes.

The dragons soared upward, flames and claws carving their way. Behind Elethor and his warriors flew his people, the elders and mothers and children, and they too roared and blew their flames. The dragons of Requiem rose, a few hundred souls in an endless ocean, and all around them the darkness closed in.

Requiem! We will find your sky.

To the stars that hid above beyond the cruelty of Solina. To that sky. To the white halls of afterlight. They flew to glory and death.

"To death!" his warriors shouted at his side. "To fire!"

From the east, dawn broke and distant cries answered their call.

Elethor turned and saw light blaze over the battle, overflowing him with white. The eastern cries rose, and the nephilim howled in fear, blinded with the light, their dark scales bleached. They hissed and clawed at one another and wailed to the sky. Elethor looked into the light, and his eyes watered.

"Lyana."

She flew from the dawn, a blue dragon with sunrays bursting around her. She sounded her roar, the song of Requiem, and blew her fire. She charged toward the nephil horde. Behind her from the light emerged more dragons—thousands of them in every color, all blowing their flames, a great host of Requiem roaring its song.

Tears filled Elethor's eyes.

More Vir Requis live. Lyana found them. We are not alone.

The nephilim howled, heads whipping from side to side. Some turned to flee. Others screeched and cowered. Some bared fangs and raised claws. Lyana and her dragons crashed into them, and the world exploded, and beams of dawn blazed through the Fallen Horde like spears of light.

Eagle cries rose in the north, and Elethor turned to see a griffin host—ten thousand beasts or more—their fur and feathers golden in the morning, their beaks wide and their talons outstretched. Riders sat upon them, clad in the armor of Osanna, bearing bows and spears. This host too charged toward the nephilim, ablaze in light and crying for battle. The nephilim wailed and fluttered before them, pierced with arrows.

From the west rose a keening song, clear and cold as winter dawn.

Elethor turned and lost his breath.

"Salvanae," he whispered.

The true dragons flowed from the west, wingless and long, coiling and uncoiling in the sky like serpents upon water. Their beards fluttered like banners. Their crystal eyes shone. Their scales rippled and they trumpeted their song. Among them flew several Vir Requis, flapping wide wings, and Elethor wept in the sky.

A golden dragon flew among them.

Mori. Mori.

From the west, the salvanae crashed into the nephilim, and lightning flowed from their mouths, and their teeth bit the demon host. The nephilim howled in fear. They scattered. They fled. They died and fell upon the scorched earth.

The battle raged through the dawn and day, a tapestry of light and darkness, a song of blood and fire. The armies of the world crashed over the ruins of Bar Luan, and nephilim rained dead, and finally the survivors of the horde turned to flee. Screeching and licking their wounds, those nephilim who still lived flew southward, and the griffins and salvanae chased them and slew them over the forest, so that only a handful escaped bloodied and wailing to their desert queen.

When the sun began to set, Elethor landed upon the ruins of the world, his scales dented and chipped. Nephil corpses piled around him, hiding the forest; countless rotted and bustled with flies, and even the crows would not touch them.

He looked toward a crumbling wall that rose from the carnage. A golden dragon perched atop it, gazing upon the battle with soft eyes. Elethor flew and landed upon the wall too, and the golden dragon looked at him. Elethor's limbs shook and his eyes stung.

"Mori?" he whispered.

She shifted into human form and stood before him, as pale and wispy as a ghost, and her hair fluttered in the wind. Her gray eyes stared up at him, huge pools like oceans under clouds. Elethor shifted too. They stood upon the wall, and he touched her cheek, not sure if she was real or a spirit.

"El," she whispered. "El, we saw the ghosts! The ghosts of Bar Luan! We arrived at your forest camp, and they were fleeing the nephilim, and they summoned us here. Ghosts are real!"

Right then, Elethor did not care about the dead, only the living. He blinked tears from his eyes. He pulled his sister into his embrace and almost crushed her, and he rocked her in his arms, and he whispered her name again and again.

A cackle rose beneath the wall.

His sister still in his arms, Elethor turned and looked down. Upon a pile of nephil corpses lay a bloodied, laughing man. His left arm and both his legs were severed. Blood oozed from his stumps, caked his long white hair, and covered his face, and yet still he laughed hoarsely and coughed.

Elethor growled.

"Nemes," he said through clenched teeth.

The traitor looked up at him, spat blood, and laughed some more.

"You have failed, Elethor," he said, blood in his mouth. "My Lord Legion has left this place; you could not kill him. He returns now to his palace in his southern empire, and he will return, mightier than ever before." Nemes had only one hand left, but he clenched that fist as if clutching onto life itself. "You will bow before him!"

Gently, Elethor removed his arms from his sister, climbed off the wall, and stood before the hacking man. He drew his sword and held it above Nemes.

"You did this, Nemes," he said, chest tight. "You caused this death. You were a son of Requiem! You lived under my roof."

The wretched, dying man spat blood and hissed. His eyes blazed. "I *served* under your roof—like a worm crawling through the dirt. My father served you, as did his father; our backs nearly broke from bending to you and yours." He spat more blood, spraying Elethor's boots. "But now I bow before Legion, a great lord of darkness. Soon you will bow too, and your back will break, but that will not save you, *boy king*. You will beg and plead for mercy, but my Lord Legion will lock his jaws around your spine. He will snap you in two before devouring you." Nemes snorted and swept his one arm across the battlefield. "Who do you bring for aid? Griffins? Dragons of the west? Pathetic creatures. Do you think they can hold back the darkness that rises in the south? You have tasted but a bite from Lord Legion's feast. His greatest power still lurks in the desert, and he is coming for you, boy king. You cannot hide from him, only die. Only die."

Elethor growled and placed his sword against Nemes's neck.

"Soon you will be silent," he said. "You have betrayed your people, Nemes; for this *you* will die."

Silence fell over the battlefield. Elethor was vaguely aware of more Vir Requis coming to stand behind him: Bayrin, Lyana, Treale, and others. They stood silently, watching.

Nemes hacked more blood and laughed again. "I'm already dead, boy king," he said. "So are you. You don't know it yet. But you will. When the jaws of my lord close around you, you will." He coughed blood. "Go on, boy. Go on. Kill me. You were always a coward. You cannot even do this. But I am strong, Elethor, more than you can imagine. I—"

Elethor drove his sword down, piercing the traitor's neck.

He pulled his blade back, stumbled away, and Mori crashed back into his embrace. Bayrin wrapped his arms around them, and Lyana followed, then the others. They stood together, wounded and burnt and bloody survivors upon a mountain of corpses.

Holding his sister, wife, and friends, Elethor looked south. The ruins and bodies stretched for miles, but beyond them hung a cloud and dark mist.

Solina waits there, he thought. *That is where we fly. Into darkness. Into the very lair of madness.*

He held his friends and family close and shut his eyes, and the pain grabbed him like demon claws.

BAYRIN

He walked through the ruins of Bar Luan, calling her name. Ash covered his face and he shouted himself hoarse, but could not find her. He shifted, flew as a dragon over the carnage, then landed and turned human again. He walked among the dead—so many men and beasts rotting and bloody.

"Piri!" he shouted. "Stars damn it, Piri! Where are you?"

A few others had joined him. Treale walked among bodies across the ruins, armor sooty, also calling the healer's name. Many others searched for survivors: mothers cried the names of their children, wives called for husbands, and even griffins cawed and searched for their fallen comrades. Bayrin moved among the crowds in a haze. His heart would not slow down nor his fingers stop trembling.

"Damn it, Piri!" He shouted himself hoarse. "Piri, where are you?"

Clouds roiled overhead, and rain began to patter. Blood ran in rivulets between the corpses. Rainwater streamed off fallen trees and walls. Bayrin walked around a great, smashed carving of a stoic face—it was large as a dragon—and over the roots of a fallen tree. Dead nephilim lay around him.

"Piri!" he shouted, seeking her in the mud and ruin.

"Bayrin?"

Her voice was so soft, so timid and afraid, that tears leaped into his eyes.

He ran toward her voice. He found her beneath a fallen wall. The stones buried her up to her chest. She looked up at him, only one arm free, and smiled softly. Her head lay in the mud, rainwater flowing around it. Blood soaked her healer's robes.

"Stars, Piri. Hang on."

Bayrin trembled and grabbed the fallen wall. He shouted and grimaced, but it would not move. Piri lay there, watching him, the sad smile never leaving her face. Blood matted her dark braids.

With a growl, Bayrin shifted into a dragon, grabbed the wall with his claws, and pulled at the bricks. The wall crumbled in his claws; it was like grabbing sand. He roared, eyes stinging, and tossed the bricks aside until he revealed her body.

Oh stars.

He shifted back into human form and knelt above her, tears in his eyes. Her body was broken. Every bone in her must have snapped. Bayrin blinked, barely able to see. He touched her cheek.

"Piri, you're going to be fine. I'm going to take you home."

She raised her good arm. It trembled. She touched his cheek and smiled and whispered. He had to lean down to hear her words.

"Bayrin," she whispered. "Bayrin, do you remember Requiem?"

He smoothed her hair. "Of course, Piri."

"I'm flying there now, Bayrin. I can see them." Tears flowed from her eyes. "I can see the columns again, all in silver and moonlight, and I can see my parents there and all those I could not heal." She trembled in the mud and rain. "Bayrin, do you remember how I sneaked into your room once? Remember how surprised you were? And how we kissed, and you said that I was so beautiful?"

He laughed through his tears. "I'll never forget."

She laughed too, a weak, broken sound. "It's a good memory. I never forgot it." She sniffed, eyes red. "It was my best day. I love you, Bayrin. I love you. No! Don't say anything back. I know, Bay. I know." She caressed his cheek. "Be with her, Bayrin. Take care of Mori and be happy with her. Protect her. Promise me."

He nodded and whispered, throat tight. "I will."

"Will you hold me, Bay? One last time?"

He held her in the mud, her head against his chest. She held him with one arm and smiled softly, and her breath died. She stared over his shoulder, and he held her against him, and he wept for her. He placed her down, kissed her forehead, and closed her eyes.

"Goodbye, Piri. May the song of harps lead you to our starlit halls. You will find Requiem's sky. You will fly home."

He shifted into dragon form. He lifted her body gently in his claws. He flew with her. He flew for hours until he found a hill far from the battle, a sanctuary where he could not see or smell the death. Pines rose twisting here, their needles rustling in the wind and coating the ground, and pinecones lay strewn and glistening in the rain. Between the pines he could look west to distant, lush forests, a river, and a lake where deer herded. A quiet place. A peaceful place. A place of pine, water, and memory.

He buried her there and placed his sword upon her breast, a sigil of honor for a soldier of Requiem. He rolled a boulder onto her grave, and with his dagger, he engraved it with her name, a birch leaf, and the Draco stars. He whispered.

"Goodbye, Piri Healer, a daughter of Requiem, a healer of starlight."

He flew back to their camp, found Mori, and held her, and they stood silently together for a long time.

ELETHOR

He stood upon the mountain, the wind ruffling his hair, and gazed upon a host like a frozen sea. Snow swirled through the air, coating the mountainsides, pines, and wrath of wounded nations.

Below him in the valley stood the survivors of Requiem, all in dragon forms—over three thousand of them, joined from his camp and Second Haven. Every Vir Requis old enough to fly and breathe fire stood here in the snow, smoke pluming from their nostrils, frost upon their scales.

East of them stood a host of griffins, over twenty thousand strong, snow in their fur and rage in their eyes. King Vale stood at their lead upon a boulder, the greatest among them, his head raised and his talons like great swords.

Beyond the griffins, an army of salvanae coiled above a frozen lake, as large and mighty as the host of griffins. The true dragons hovered, their long bodies undulating like waves, scales chinking like purses of jingling coins. Their beards were long, their eyes blazing, their breath fuming.

Finally, in a field of grass and stone, stood the soldiers of Osanna. Fifty thousand rallied here, each warrior bearing a sword, spear, and bow. Their breastplates and shields sported engraved bull horns, the sigil of Osanna's Earth God, a deity of all things growing and good and a nemesis of Tiranor's flaming lord. These warriors would ride to battle upon the beasts that flew. From the backs of griffins and dragons, they would shoot their arrows and toss their spears, and when they landed in the cities of Tiranor, they would draw swords and fight the enemy in streets and halls.

"A hundred thousand men and beasts," Elethor said softly as snow swirled around him, coated his beard, and frosted his armor. "Will it be enough?"

He turned to look at Lyana who stood at his side. She reached out, took his hand, and squeezed it. Their leather gloves creaked.

"All free nations fight against the evil in the south," she said. "It will be enough, or we will perish. But fly south we must. I would rather die charging into evil than waiting for it to come."

Her hair, shaved off in her captivity last year, now grew several inches long. It fell across her brow and ears, little cascades of orange curls kissed with snow. Her eyes, green as a spring forest, stared deeply into his. Fields of freckles spread across her pale face; Elethor knew and loved every one.

He looked south over forest and mist, imagining the desert. *Tiranor*, he thought. So many times, Solina had lain in his arms, or walked with him through the forests, or stood with him upon the hill, and spoke of her desert realm. She would describe dunes kissed golden with dawn, oases lush with palms and birds, and towers of limestone that rose capped with platinum. She spoke of the dragons burning those trees and toppling those towers, and how one day she would restore her land to glory. She spoke of a magical realm of secrets, a desert paradise of pomegranate wine, figs sweet as honey, smooth myrrh and chinking gold—a land of beauty, of wonders, of ancient wisdom.

"We will live there together someday, Elethor," she had whispered so many times in the halls of Requiem, her eyes rimmed red and her fingers clutching him desperately. "It will be our place, our secret land of magic. We will rule there together, queen and king of the desert, so far from the dragons who hurt us."

Elethor had never been to Tiranor, the land that Solina's heart had always beaten for. Now he would see those towers, those oases, and those statues and steel and treasures.

And we will burn them. Stars, Solina, we will burn your land and burn you. He clutched his sword so tightly his fist trembled. *You drove me to this, Solina; now Tiranor will rise in flame.*

"The north has mustered!" he cried to his army, palm coned around his mouth. "We have gathered our hosts, and we will crush the desert. We fly at dawn tomorrow. Rest tonight, northern warriors. Tomorrow we fly to victory!"

They cheered, a hundred thousand warriors roaring for victory and vengeance and flame. But Elethor only stood, jaw squared, chest tight. He could not roar with them. He could not find joy in this; the fires of war had never lit his heart, and even now, with so many dead behind them, he could not summon the flame that drove Solina, that drove these warriors below the mountain. He held Lyana's hand tight and looked at her. She looked back up at him, lips tight, and nodded.

"I fly by you, my king," she said. "Tomorrow and always. Our wings beat together, and our fires will light the long, cold night."

He spent that night in a tent the men of Osanna had brought upon griffinback. The tent was wide, its walls woven of thick green cloth, and they had set a bed, a table topped with candles, and a tall bronze mirror within it.

Elethor stood before that mirror and gazed upon himself. It had been moons since he had looked at his reflection. Tonight he barely recognized himself. Two years ago, when Solina had invaded Requiem with her army of phoenixes, he would look into his mirror and see a thin, pale young man with soft cheeks—a boy who pined for his lost love, who shunned the court, who hid within his walls, sculpting his desire over and over. Today, Elethor did not find that boy staring back from the mirror. He was not yet thirty, but looked older; his beard had thickened, his body had grown gaunt and hard, and lines marred his brow. Instead of the soft woolen tunics of a prince, he wore the steel plates of a soldier. Mostly his eyes had changed; they were sunken, hard, and dead as the ruins of a fallen kingdom.

I look ten years older than I should, he thought. *And I have the eyes of an old man.*

Lyana came to stand by him and placed her hand on his shoulder. She was barely taller than that shoulder, and so thin, but her eyes stared into the mirror with all the strength and grief of an aging, hardened warrior. If he was a battered longsword forged in dragonfire, she was the blade of a knight, scarred with a thousand nicks but strong as the steel of ancient heroes.

She helped him unclasp his armor, piece by piece. She placed his pauldrons on the table, then his greaves and vambraces, and finally his breastplate. When he stood before her in his damp woolen tunic, she placed her hands on his shoulders. She stood on her toes, her eyes still haunted, and kissed his lips.

He began unclasping her armor, buckle by buckle. He moved slowly at first, placing every piece of steel aside. But soon his fingers grew rough, and she gasped as he pulled at the straps, tore her breastplate off, and tossed it aside with a clang. His chest was too tight. His heart pounded with too much pain. He clenched his jaw and swallowed, forcing the terror down, and tugged the lacings of her tunic. Fabric ripped in his fingers, and he let out a hiss that felt almost like a snarl, and tore at her clothes.

She winced and sucked in her breath. "El..."

He put one hand on the small of her back and pulled her against him. He tugged at her clothes almost violently until she stood naked, and his eyes stung, and his heart thrashed against his ribs, and his fingers trembled, and he kept seeing them—kept seeing the demons tear at the walls, pull brick from brick, slash his people apart until their blood gushed and their limbs fell.

"El, please," she whispered.

He realized that he was grabbing her so tightly his fingernails had cut her. He released her and took a shuddering breath. She stood before him, naked in the candlelight, her hair a pyre of flame. The scars of war covered her flesh, but she was beautiful to him. He sat on the bed, and she stood before him, and he reached up and touched her cheek with trembling fingers.

"Lyana," he whispered. "I..."

I'm afraid, he wanted to say. *I can't stop seeing the blood. I want to roar in rage and fly to battle as a hero, but I can't stop my chest from hurting, or my stomach from feeling so cold and tight.*

But he could say none of those things, and he knew she understood. He saw it in the softness that filled her eyes, and he felt it in her fingers as they touched his hair.

He pulled her onto the bed, and placed her on her back, and when he climbed atop her and loved her, he closed his eyes, and he could barely breathe. But he made love to her—no, not love, but something rougher this night, something that felt more like a battle, like a war against demons, and sweat drenched him, and he *hurt* her. Stars, he hurt her until she gasped and bit into the blanket and cried.

When it was over, and he lay beside her, he found that tears filled his own eyes, and he pulled her against him and held her so tight he nearly crushed her.

So many died. So many gone. So many will still die as we fly into the southern horde.

She kissed his lips.

"I am yours," she whispered. "In bed. In battle. In the glory of our halls when we rebuild them—or in the starlit halls of our fathers. You are my king. You are my husband. You are my love." She held him tight and closed her eyes. "We fly together, Elethor; always."

They slept holding each other through the long, cold night.

TREALE

She stood upon the cliff, the wind in her hair, and looked at her king. Treale had dreamed of this for so long—to finally stand beside him again. He was so close now she could reach out and grab him, yet he had never seemed farther to her, not in all the forests and deserts she had hid in.

Once more they stood upon Ralora Beach. Last year she had stood here with Elethor and three thousand dragons, a green army awaiting the southern fire. Today a hundred thousand warriors covered the cliffs, hills, and beach: griffins, salvanae, soldiers of Osanna, and dragons of Requiem. Last year Solina had lured them here, allowing her forces to crush Nova Vita. Today Elethor had decided the queen's fall would begin in this same place.

You are thinking of her now, Treale thought, looking at the young king. He was staring south, the wind ruffling his dark hair. *You are thinking of Solina, the one you loved, the one you vow to kill. But I am thinking of you, Elethor. I am thinking of the night I kissed your cheek, and I am standing here beside you, and you cannot even see me.*

Treale lowered her head, and the wind played with her long black hair, scented of the sea. She closed her eyes. So many nights she had dreamed of him! When she had lain curled up in charred forests, fleeing the wyverns, she had pretended to still lie by his side like that night upon the hill. When she had huddled in alleys in cruel Irys, or crawled over dunes that burned her, or trekked through the swamps of Gilnor to seek sanctuary in the north, she had thought of him. She would remember talking to him about her puppets, and kissing his cheek, and sleeping all night by his side under the stars, feeling safe by her king. And then... and then after all those long moons, she had met him again! She had returned to him. She had flown with true dragons and fought by his side, driving the nephilim from the ruins of Bar Luan.

And he had gone into his tent.

And he had taken Lyana into his bed.

And her heart had been broken; it still felt like shattered clay in her breast.

Oh, he had given her a compulsory embrace, and squeezed her shoulder, and thanked her for saving his sister. He had kissed her forehead, then pulled Mori into his arms again and nearly crushed her, and not a moment later he was walking with his soldiers and talking of battles, and Treale had remained standing in the ruins, cold and alone.

You have Mori now, she thought, looking at him. *You have your sister whom I saved. And you have your wife, whom I serve. And you have me, Elethor. You have me always; you had me since that night upon the hill. And still I wait for you. Still I stand by your side, but do you see me here?*

She walked across the cliff, moving closer to him, until she stood a foot away. Lyana stood at his other side, clutching her sword and also staring south. Mori stood beyond her, clad in armor—Treale had never seen the princess in armor before—and hugging herself. None seemed to notice her.

"My king?" Treale said softly. He seemed not to hear her, and she touched his arm. "Elethor?"

He seemed to wake from a dream. With a quick draw of his breath, he turned toward her, and his face softened.

"Lady Treale," he said.

Not his love, she thought. *Not his wife or sister or even a friend. A lady. A cold title for a court.* Her eyes stung and she blinked. She wanted to grab and shake him, to yell at him: *Don't you remember that night? Don't you remember how you told me your story, and I told you mine—about the puppets, and Oldnale Farms, and... I kissed your cheek, Elethor, and we slept side by side. And now I am only a lady, this... this cold warrior like the thousands of them?*

But she could say none of that. Not with his wife by his side or even with Mori there. So Treale only swallowed and spoke soft words.

"I will fight by your side, Elethor," she said. "I will not leave you. I promise. You have my fire—always."

She lowered her eyes, the shame burning through her. *Of course,* she thought. Of course he was so cold to her. She had abandoned him in battle last year. When the wyverns had flown toward Nova Vita, she had defected. She had left his army despite his orders, had flown to Oldnale Farms and found her parents dead. She had deserted him; of course he would not show her the warmth he showed Lyana and Mori.

I'm a traitor to him, she thought, and her throat constricted. She looked away lest he saw the tears in her eyes. *I saved his sister, but he still remembers my sin.*

The wind blew, and she lowered her head.

The invasion of Tiranor began with rain, wind, and beating waves. The dragons of Requiem took flight first, three thousand in all—all Vir Requis old enough to shift into dragons and fight. Today they were all soldiers. They roared and their scales clanked and their wings thudded, rippling the sea. Upon every dragon's back rode a soldier of Osanna, clad in steel and armed with bow, spear, and sword. Their bull horn banners streamed, and their shields caught the sun. They shouted for their land, and the dragons roared, and they raced across the sea into a horizon of rain and cloud.

Behind them, the salvanae and griffins took flight too, a great host nearly fifty thousand strong. Upon their backs too rode soldiers of Osanna, clinging to their saddles. The army soon covered the sea like a great cloud, shimmering and snorting and rippling the water beneath them.

Never had the world seen so many beasts fly together, Treale thought. Poets would sing of this day until the world fell.

She flew, a slim black dragon with fire in her nostrils. Upon her back rode an Osannan soldier, a young man with a stubbly face, an impish grin, and a shock of brown hair.

"Stop dipping so much!" he shouted down to her. "By the Earth God, you do wobble when you fly."

She growled over her shoulder and found him grinning.

"Be quiet, Jadin," she said and gave him her best glare. "Stars, you farm boys do whine a lot."

He snorted. "I haven't seen my farm in a year now. I'm a soldier; don't you forget it. If we meet any nephilim, it'll be my bow shooting at them."

It was her turn to snort. "And my fire. I think they will barely notice your puny little arro—OW!"

He had dug his heels deep into her flanks. Treale grumbled and cursed. She was a dragon of Requiem! It was ridiculous that she should wear a saddle like a horse. And yet the Osannans had insisted, saying something about how otherwise, they would fall and drown in the sea. Flying with Jadin upon her back, Treale did not think that would have been so tragic.

"If you do that again," she said, "I'll bite your legs off."

He flashed a grin. "I'll stop if you stop wobbling."

She grumbled, looked back forward, and beat her wings with grim intent. She tried to forget he rode her. It would be a long flight. The sea stretched for many leagues between southern Requiem to the northern shores of Tiranor. Even flying at top speed, it would take hours to reach Tiranor, perhaps all day.

Jadin began to sing old, rude limericks—something about the beasts he'd slay, the women he'd bed, and the gold he'd plunder. Treale grumbled and snorted fire and kept flying.

She looked to her left. Elethor flew there, Lyana and Mori at his sides.

The royal family of Requiem, she thought. *The man I love. The man so close and so far from me.*

Behind them, the army spread like a great tapestry, a league long. Treale looked over her shoulder at them, so many dragons and griffins and men. She imagined this army sweeping across Tiranor, claiming city and fort; the world had never known such might. And yet...

Fear pounded through her. She had seen the nephilim. She had seen them slay so many. She had seen the Lord Legion rise, a great beast all of scales and horns and rot, his halo flaming like a sun. Could they truly kill this dark god? Even with all their might, could this northern alliance truly defeat Solina, or would they crash against the shores of Tiranor?

A growl rose in her throat.

Perhaps we fly to death, she thought. *But I will fight by my king. I will never more abandon him. I will show him that I've grown brave.*

She narrowed her eyes, snarled, and flew.

They flew for a long time.

Dawn turned to noon, and the sun burned above; already it felt hotter than the sun of Requiem. They kept flying. Treale's wings ached and she snorted smoke. Her lungs blazed. She wanted to slow down—her body screamed for it—but when she looked around her, the other dragons still beat their wings mightily. Treale growled and kept flying.

"Stop wobbling!" Jadin said on her back. "Treale, darling, are you getting tired?"

"Tired of hearing your voice, boy," she said. "Save it for your battle cries."

The noon sun trailed down in the sky. When Treale looked behind her, she saw that the army's formations had loosened. Griffins, salvanae, and Vir Requis now trailed behind her, the slower flyers dragging like a wake. King Elethor, however, flew far ahead of her now; Treale could see his brass scales glinting hundreds of yards ahead. By his side, she saw Lyana's blue scales, Bayrin's green ones, and Mori's gold.

I will fight by their side.

Treale snarled and flew faster.

"That's more like it," Jadin said. "Go, little dragon, go!"

Treale's breath ached. Her eyes stung. Her wings screamed with pain. The sun hung low in the sky when finally she saw rocky beaches ahead leading to a dead, golden desert.

"Tiranor," she whispered.

She drew flame into her throat, bared her fangs, and shot forward. Soon she flew by her king. Elethor was staring ahead with narrowed eyes, and smoke streamed from between his teeth. She gave him a nod and a grim smile; he returned the same.

"I fly by you, Elethor," she said, fire flickering in her mouth.

He growled and stared forward, and his claws flexed. "Be strong, Lady Treale. Be brave. We fly together." He looked at her and his eyes softened, and Treale could weep, because she saw that he *did* remember, that he too had never forgotten that night. "Stay safe, Treale. You are among the bravest, strongest dragons in Requiem, and you will make me proud this night."

I love you, Elethor, she wanted to say. *I love you always; from that night upon the hill until today and every day after this one. Always. Always.*

Yet she did not have to utter those words; in his eyes, she saw that he knew, and that though he was wed to another—though he loved Lyana with all his heart—he loved her too. That soothed her. That would give her strength this night.

Lyana came to fly at their side, flames snorting from her nostrils. Bayrin and Mori joined them, flying so close their wings almost touched. Behind them spread thousands of other dragons, the last of their kind, and as the sun fell, their flames lit the darkness.

They streamed toward the Tiran shore.

The sun dipped into the sea.

From the dunes of Tiranor, a dark host rose, and countless nephilim soared, screeched, and flew toward them.

LYANA

The sky burst with the demon horde.

The beasts swarmed from the sands, myriads like clouds of locusts. Lyana roared, beat her wings, and drove forward. Her fellow dragons roared at her sides, and behind them cried the griffins and salvanae. The beasts ahead shrieked, their voices so high-pitched and deafening, the dragons' riders screamed.

Stars save us, Lyana thought, fear chilling her. *They knew we were coming. They knew where we'd land. These are no mere sentinels patrolling the border; this is an army bred to crush our invasion.*

"Hang on tight, Wila!" Lyana shouted to the woman who rode her, a young captain of Osanna. "This is going to get rough."

She stormed forward. The nephilim shot toward her, eyes blazing and jaws snapping and bat wings wafting their stench.

The two armies crashed above the beach.

Dragons slammed into nephilim. Fire exploded and rained and shot in pillars everywhere. Claws lashed and fangs bit, and from the backs of dragons, a rain of arrows whistled, red shards in the firelight.

"Lyana, your left!" Wila cried from her back.

Lyana banked and saw a nephil swoop her way, claws outstretched. Wila shot her bow, and an arrow slammed into the beast; it bucked and shrieked and kept swooping. Lyana roared her fire, and the nephil blazed.

Lyana banked again, narrowing dodging the flaming beast as it fell. Wila screamed and held out her shield, and the nephil's claw scraped against it before the beast crashed against the beach below. Lyana soared and blew more flames. More nephilim fell before her. Claws and teeth shone everywhere.

Stars damn it! Lyana thought. With Wila on her back, she could barely fly properly. She could not soar straight up, or spin, or whisk like a bee between the swarming enemies; Wila would fall. Lyana gritted her teeth and flew onward, lashing her claws and blowing her flames as Wila shot arrows.

"Crash through them!" Elethor roared somewhere above her. "Past those cliffs—land above them!"

Lyana looked up, seeking her husband. The sky was burning. Dragons, salvanae, and griffins flew everywhere, crisscrossing and scattering and regrouping and all roaring their cries. Nephilim crashed against them—some of the beasts swung curved, rusted blades—and blood splattered. Bursts of dragonfire exploded. When howls sounded in the south, Lyana looked to see new combatants arriving: hordes of burly wyverns blowing acid and phoenixes crackling with fire. They too crashed into the battle. The sands below turned red with blood. Bodies rained and piled up and drifted into the sea. Lyana couldn't even see the sky, only beasts and men screaming and killing.

This should not have happened, Lyana thought in a daze. Her eyes blurred. *They knew. They were waiting for us. They are too many.*

For an instant Lyana froze, barely able to fly, barely able to breathe. She had fought many battles. She had slain Tirans in the Phoenix War when they first invaded her land. She had walked through the Abyss and fought its creatures. She had defended Nova Vita even as it crumbled under wyvern acid. She had fought hordes of nephilim above cities and temples. And yet this... Lyana had never seen a battle like this. Hundreds of thousands of creatures flew and died here, spreading for a league around. To call this a battle, she thought, diminished its magnitude; here was a great song of blood and flame and carnage.

I never knew, she thought, eyes stinging. *I never imagined. We should have run. We should have hidden. We will burn the world from this place.*

"Lyana!" Elethor shouted. He dived toward her, blew fire over her shoulder, and a nephil shrieked behind her.

She snarled. She soared. She fought.

The battle raged through the night—a night of dragon wings and fire and rot. The dead covered the beaches and cliffs. They bobbed upon the water like thousands of fallen leaves. When dawn rose, it rose upon a world drenched in blood. When the battle finally ended, there were no songs of victory: there was only weeping, screaming, and everywhere the dead and wounded.

Lyana landed upon the cliffs of Tiranor. She shook so badly Wila nearly fell off her back. When the woman dismounted, Lyana shifted into human form and stood trembling.

Stars save us, she thought, looking over the beaches below.

"We won," Wila whispered. Blood splattered the soldier's pale face, and she clutched an arm that still sizzled with acid.

"Nobody won this slaughter," Lyana replied and leaned against her, so weary she could barely stand.

The hosts of the enemy lay dead, but so many of their own lay among them. Tens of thousands of corpses covered the beaches: piles of nephilim bustling with gulls and crabs, men and women slashed with claws and burnt with fire, and salvanae and griffins torn apart.

Among the dead, thousands of wounded screamed and wept and begged. Men clutched at stumps or spilling entrails, calling for their mothers. Young women—torn from their homes into a war their brothers could no longer fight alone—lay burnt and swollen and screaming. Healers in white robes rushed among them, trudging through puddles of blood, but there were so many hurt, so many dying; every moment, another screaming warrior fell silent, voice forever lost.

Elethor landed beside Lyana, brass scales charred and chipped. He shifted into human form. Blood splattered his armor and sweat dampened his hair. He took Lyana's hand and they stood together, gazing down upon the landscape of death.

ELETHOR

He walked along the beach, blood sluicing around his boots. The dead rose in hills around him, stinking under the pounding sun. Crows and gulls flew everywhere, picking at the flesh. Nephilim lay broken and burnt, their foul innards leaking from their mouths. Griffins and salvanae lay in heaps. Men and women too lay dead, torn apart into mere hints of humanity.

"Elethor," Lyana said softly at his side. "Are you sure?"

He nodded. "We'll find one here."

They kept walking—him, Lyana, and a dozen of their men. The tide was rising, grabbing bodies and pulling them to sea, then tossing them back ashore covered with seaweed and salt. Crabs and flies bustled across severed limbs and heads and burnt corpses.

Wounded Tirans, their armor and bodies broken, writhed in the sand among the dead. Half were wyvern riders, their mounts dead beneath them, slashed with griffin talons or burnt with dragonfire. The rest had flown in phoenix forms; bolts of salvana lightning had crushed their magic and charred their bodies. Most were dying, barely able to whimper, common soldiers with no ranks upon their shattered armor.

They will know nothing, Elethor thought.

"El," Lyana said softly. "Should we heal them? We can't just... just leave the wounded here to die. We—"

"First we will find what we seek," he said. "Then we will heal whoever we can."

They kept moving through the bloody sand, at times climbing over the corpses of beasts. Finally Elethor found what he sought and stopped walking.

The Tiran officer lay on the beach, clutching her slashed stomach. Blood seeped between her fingers. Her breastplate was shattered—it showed the form of dragon claws—but upon her pauldrons Elethor could still see golden suns. This one was of high enough rank to serve him. He knelt by the woman.

"You are a captain," he said to her.

Blood covered her lips. The sides of her head were shaven, revealing sun tattoos, and several rings pierced her lips and brows.

The hair that grew from her scalp spread out around her, platinum stained red, and more blood splashed her golden skin.

"I..." She licked her lips and coughed. "I will not talk."

Elethor tightened his lips. Rage flared in him. She would not talk? He would make her talk. He would stab at her wound. He would stab her eyes. He would hurt her until her bones cracked, and she screamed, and—

No. He clenched his jaw and looked away. *No, I will not torture a prisoner. I am not Solina. I will not let that rage overcome me.*

He looked back at the wounded officer. She lay clutching her belly, and her blood kept trickling; so much of it already soaked the sand.

"We can heal you," he said. "You need not die here, bleeding in the sand among the corpses of your comrades. We can give you silverweed to ease the pain, bandages, and water to drink. But you must tell me what I need to know."

She gave a weak cackle, spitting blood. "My queen was right." She laughed hoarsely, a hideous sound, and blood stained the rings piercing her lips. "She told us this King Elethor was a weakling, a soft boy. I never imagined how soft you were." She managed a snarl. "But we are strong, boy king. We will never fall. The Tiran empire rises, and Queen Solina leads her to glory. You will *die*, weredragon, you and all your kind."

He leaned down; their faces were but inches apart. He stared into her mocking blue eyes.

"We will die, Tiran? We crushed you at this beach. We claimed your shores. We drove you out of our lands, and now we drive into yours. Who is weak, Tiran? I, a king who conquered, or you, a wounded soldier in the sand?"

She laughed, and more blood trickled down her chin, and her armor clanked as her chest shook.

"Drive into our lands? Weredragon, you have seen nothing of our strength. You fought but a drop from our ocean, and this drop ravaged half your forces. Do you think you can move beyond these shores?" She coughed a laugh. "The might of Tiranor still awaits you, weredragon. I wish only that you live to see it all, but you will be crushed too soon. Even as you linger here, my queen breeds new hosts. Even as I lie dying, she gives life to a million more nephilim."

He bared his teeth and glared. "My father burned Irys to the ground and killed its monarchs; I will do the same."

The Tiran spat blood at him. "You are not fighting Irys now, boy. You fight the Palace of Whispers, a god of stone, a city in the mountains. You will crash against its walls. From within its chambers, Solina will send forth her wrath, and you will die, weredragon. You will die screaming and begging to worship her."

He rose to his feet and wiped her blood off his cheek. He turned to Lyana and his men.

"I've heard enough," he said. "Fetch healers; treat her as well as you can. If she dies, bury her with the rest."

He shifted into a dragon, took flight, and soared above the cliffs. Before him, plains of rock and dry scrub rolled for leagues, finally giving way to dunes and distant southern mountains. Heat rose in waves. Even in winter, the sun pounded the Tiran landscape; it baked Elethor's scales and blinded him.

When he looked east, he could just discern a distant green line leading to a delta—the Riven Pallan and the city of Irys, capital of this land. They still lay a day's flight away. When he looked west, Elethor saw the desert roll to distant tan mountains against a white sky, mere hints of color from here. Somewhere in those mountains rose the Palace of Whispers, he knew, the ruins where Solina lurked and bred her beasts.

He looked down at the desert below him. His camp spread here, a league from the sea. Whoever had survived the slaughter upon the beach bivouacked upon the plain. Griffins stood to one side, frozen like sentinels of stone. Salvanae hovered around the camp, coiling and chinking, their beards dipping into the sand. Soldiers of Osanna were erecting tents and campfires, and the scents of sausages, breads, and wine filled the air.

Finally, the Vir Requis camped to one side, the smallest of the hosts. They stood in human forms, gazing south upon the desert, solemn and silent. Most of them were not soldiers; they were mothers, fathers, brothers, sisters. They were the few who'd survived the attacks on Nova Vita and the slaughter in Bar Luan. They were the last light of Requiem, and they stood here wounded and gaunt and grim, and they comforted Elethor even more than the might of griffins or the wisdom of salvanae. They were his people, and their fire burned deep and hot within them.

As the sun set, spreading orange and red fingers across the desert, Elethor met with his generals upon a rocky hill.

At his right stood Lyana, clad as always in her silvery armor, her helmet upon her head, her sword and dagger hanging from her belt. Beside Lyana stood her squire, the young Lady Treale; she wore armor engraved with a sheaf of wheat, the sigil of her house, and the wind played with her long black hair. To Elethor's left stood Princess

Mori, clad in the armor they had forged her, its steel engraved with a two-headed dragon, sigil of House Aeternum. Bayrin stood there too, the wind in his red hair.

Elethor looked upon them—a wife, a sister, his dearest friends. His heart gave a twist. Suddenly he loved them so much that it hurt. These were the dearest people in his life, the people who had flown through fire and blood for him. There were none braver in the world, he thought.

I wish you were here with us, Orin. I miss you, brother.

He thought of those who had died in this war: his brother, his father, Deramon and Adia, Piri Healer, and so many others. So many extinguished lights.

But we still fight for you. Your light still guides us—always.

Before him upon the hill stood his allies: the Griffin King Vale, his fur kindled with sunset; wise old Nehushtan, High Priest of Salvandos; and King Shae, his beard white and flowing, ruler of Osanna. Between the allies stood a table topped with candles, wooden carvings of griffins and dragons, and a parchment map of the desert. Standing over the map, Elethor looked at his companions one by one. They stared back in the sunset. He took a deep breath and began to speak.

"We invaded Tiranor with a hundred thousand warriors. Twenty thousand of them died upon the beaches." He lowered his head. "Their memory will light our path. We will forever sing of their sacrifice and courage in our halls."

The others bowed their heads and whispered prayers. A few had tears in their eyes. When the moment of prayer ended, Elethor spoke in a deep, firm voice.

"We cannot rest here long," he said. "We won a battle, but Solina is not idle. Already she musters new forces; we must continue our assault with all the might and speed we can muster. We believe that Solina lurks here." He tapped a western mountain upon the map. "The Palace of Whispers—a great fortress built into a mountain, once the domain of the Ancients, now a lair of her devilry. She is... creating, summoning, or breeding nephilim there. It won't be long before she hears of our invasion and strikes our camp."

Bayrin snarled and pounded his fist against the map. "Then let us fly to her! We'll attack that mountain with everything we've got. Soon it'll be called the Palace of Solina's Blood... and Guts." He tapped his chin. "Yes, Guts too; I like that."

Elethor was about to reply, but to his surprise, it was Mori—shy, timid Mori who never spoke in their councils—who replied first. Her voice was soft, and her lips trembled, but she clutched her luck finger tight and spoke for all to hear.

"We must attack Irys too." She looked at the map and spoke as if to herself. "Maybe Solina now lives in the mountains. But Irys is where her palace is, where the capital is, where she..." Mori swallowed and reached out to clutch Bayrin's hand. "We have to attack it. We have to burn it down."

Bayrin held her hand tight and pulled her closer to him. Mori bit her lip and said no more.

"Princess Mori is right," Elethor said and nodded. "We will attack Irys too. The city still holds the garrisons of her men, phoenixes, and wyverns. It still holds her palace, her greatest symbol of power. We must topple that palace, crush her forces there, and cut off the capital from the rest of this desert."

Lyana spoke up, chin raised.

"Irys gets its supplies from the river," she said. She ran her finger along the map, tracing the Pallan down from Irys in the north. "It snakes many leagues down to here, its sister Iysa." She tapped the map at the southern city. "Here in Iysa is where Solina forges her steel, grows her grains, and mints her coins. The supplies flow up the river on a thousand ships." Lyana snarled. "We will boil the river. We will burn all ships along it and crush southern Iysa. Without the river and her southern sister, the capital will dry up and die like an old fruit."

Elethor nodded. "We'll have to guard the northern sea too. Solina still commands many forces in the ruins of Requiem—wyverns and riders, men-at-arms, warships, phoenixes, and hordes of nephilim. These forces will not sit idle in Requiem's ruins when Tiranor itself is under attack. They will fly to Solina's aid. We must prevent them from returning into the desert."

For a long time the council talked. The sun disappeared and the stars emerged, brilliantly bright above the desert. No moon shone. The camp slept below. And still the council talked.

Finally at midnight, Elethor rolled up the map and nodded.

"We all know our tasks." He looked at the wise salvana who coiled before him, crystal eyes glimmering. "Nehushtan, you will guard the northern seas, preventing Tiran aid from the north. Take with you five thousand salvanae; you will need them to patrol the coasts."

The High Priest nodded. "The dragons of Salvanados shall keep the coasts secure. This I vow to the stars of Draco that shine above. They bless us this night. We will succeed, King Elethor."

Next Elethor turned to look at Lyana, and he felt some of his fear melt. His wife looked up at him with her green eyes—eyes that for years had taunted him, that for years he hated to see, yet which now spoke of her love, which now lit his heart.

"Lyana," he said. "You I will send south. Fly along the Pallan; burn any ships that sail north. Fly until you reach southern Iysa and burn her smelters, her mines, and her shipyards. Take with you a thousand dragons and ten thousand griffins; bear on your backs soldiers of Osanna to fight among the streets. Nehushtan will cut off Irys from the north; you will crush the south."

Lyana nodded and held his hands. "I will not let you down, my king. We will take Iysa and the river."

Mori spoke up again, chin raised. Her lips trembled but her voice was strong. "And I will attack the capital of Irys." She clutched the sword that hung at her side. "I will fly there. Bayrin can fly with me. We will burn them." A strange fire lit her eyes; Elethor had never seen such fire in her. "We will burn their palace, and burn their soldiers, and burn them all." She nodded, face pale. "We will burn them all."

Elethor placed a hand on her shoulder. "Are you sure, Mori?" he said softly. "You can fly south with Lyana if you want; she will keep you safe."

Mori shook her head. "No, El. I'll do this. I... I have to. I want to fight in Irys; that is where my battle lies." She held his arm. "I promise you, El, I will fight well. We will take the city."

"And I'm going with you!" Bayrin said. He placed an arm around Mori's waist and pulled her close. "Just don't fly so fast you leave me behind."

Elethor smiled softly; seeing his friend hold his sister close comforted him. If anyone could keep Mori safe, after all, it was her personal guardian.

"Yes, Bay, you will fly with Mori to Irys," he said. "And you will take with you twenty thousand griffins, dragons, and men." His voice hardened. "The Palace of Phoebus must fall."

Mori nodded. "It will fall."

Elethor turned to look west. In the darkness of night, he could not see the distant mountains where Solina lurked, but still the shadows chilled him. He thought of that day long ago—*their* day, a perfect day in his home upon the hill—and he thought of Solina slaying children in Requiem, kidnapping Mori, and screaming that she would slaughter them all.

You wait for me there, Solina, in darkness. You vowed to light the world; now you lurk in shadow. We will meet again in the mountains. No more words. No more memories. Now we meet with flame and steel and blood.

He spoke softly. "And I will fly to the mountains. I will lead a host against the Palace of Whispers. And I will kill Solina."

For the first time in the council, young Lady Treale spoke. "And I'm going with you."

Her eyes shone in the moonlight. Her lips tightened. Elethor remembered that night upon the hill when those lips had kissed him, when those eyes had seemed so warm and comforting in the night. Her kiss had given him strength then, though he had never dared tell her that, and even now, looking upon those lips, those dark eyes, and her flowing black hair soothed him.

"But Treale," he said, "you squire for Lyana. Will you not fly south with her? Will you not fight at her side?"

The squire looked over her shoulder at Lyana, then back at Elethor. She raised her chin higher and shook her head.

"Lyana is no longer a knight, but a queen," Treale said. "And I'm a warrior. My lord, I..." She lowered her head. "When the wyverns attacked, I... I let you down. I am so sorry, my lord. I fled from battle then." She raised her eyes; they shone with tears. "But I will not let you down again. You are my lord, my king, my guiding star. Let me reclaim my honor. I will fly by your side, King Elethor, and I will sound my roar, and I will slay our enemies. For you, my king." She drew her sword and knelt before him. "My sword and flame are yours."

The council dispersed in the night, each member retiring to a quiet place to rest until dawn. Around the sleeping camp, salvanae circled in vigil, their bright eyes piercing the night.

Elethor stepped downhill toward a tent of lush, crimson fabric. He stepped inside to find beds soft with quilts, tables topped with untouched meals, and candles casting their flickering light.

His family shared the tent with him. Mori and Bayrin nibbled a cold dinner, then lay down in a plush bed; the princess slept with her head upon her guardian's chest. Treale, like family to them, curled up in her own bed and slept clutching her sword to her breast.

Elethor could not eat nor drink. He removed his armor, lay upon his bed, and stared at the tent walls. The pain still clutched his heart; it had not left since Solina had returned to Requiem two winters past. Perhaps this pain had not left him since Solina had fled into her exile nearly a decade ago.

Lyana slipped into bed with him. She huddled close, wrapped her arms around him, and her lips touched his ear.

"Will you sleep?" she whispered.

He looked aside and saw the others sleeping. He looked back at Lyana.

"I will sleep," he whispered. "Lyana, this... this might be our last night together. I don't know what tomorrow will bring."

She touched his cheek. "It might be our last night," she agreed. "But I don't think it will be. We've survived this long, and now we are strong. Now we fly with aid. We will win this, El."

He held her close and shut his eyes. They stung; he dared not open them lest they shed tears.

"I love you, Lyana," he whispered, holding her like a drowning man. "I am so sorry, Lyana, for the man that I was. For the man who pined for Solina. For the man—no, the boy—you tried to reach, but who pushed you back. I remember myself in Nova Vita before this all began—a dour youth who shunned you, who shunned the court. And I'm ashamed." His throat tightened. "Will you forgive me for those years, Lyana? For those years I yearned for Solina and forgot about you, about my family?"

She kissed him. "Only if you forgive the woman I was then—the woman who would pester and lecture you. Stars, I drove you crazy!"

He laughed, opened his eyes, and saw her smiling mischievously. He mussed her hair.

"Oh, I'll never forgive you for that," he said. "What was it I called you once? Intolerable and overbearing?"

"And supercilious," she said with a grin. "I think you called me that too. Big word for you, El. I was impressed."

He gave her a mock shove, then felt the coldness between them and pulled her back into his embrace. She laid her head upon his chest, and he stroked her hair.

"Goodnight, Lyana," he said softly.

She raised her head, kissed his lips, and cuddled against him.

"I love you too, Elethor," she whispered. "Always."

The candles guttered into darkness, and they slept.

SOLINA

She lay in his bed under the quilts. She paced his room and caressed the marble statues he had sculpted. She lifted the wooden turtle he had carved for her, kissed its head, and placed it back upon the shelf. She stepped outside and gazed upon the trees. She dreamed. She missed him. Loneliness clawed at her and stung her eyes.

I am so sad without you, she thought, pacing his chamber again and again like a prisoner in a cell. *I am so alone. I want you with me.*

But it was time to leave this place. It was time to rule. To conquer. To slaughter his people and bring him here—to warmth, to memory, to light.

To me.

She stepped toward the door of his chamber, placed her hand on the knob, and closed her eyes.

I wish I could stay here forever. She was young here, only twenty-three and still bright with youth, and her face was unscarred, and no pain or hatred or death filled her heart. *A perfect day.*

She tightened her lips, twisted the knob, and opened the door.

She stepped out of memory and into the chamber.

She walked up the stairs, emerging to the rim of the well. All around her spread the Hall of Memories, its columns rising from darkness to the shadowy domed ceiling. The pit surrounded the well, spreading all around her like a moat around a tower. Once only shadows and wind had filled this pit. Today her glory festered here.

"My children," she whispered.

The spawn of nephilim filled the pit, biting and mewling and clawing at one another, their bat wings beating and their eyes leaking pus. Each was the size of a man already, and they were growing larger every day, the strong feeding upon the weak. They writhed in the pit like a pile of maggots. A million or more rotted here. The strongest rose to the top, teeth bloodied and bellies bloated with the flesh of their brothers. For a mile deep they festered, stinking of decomposing flesh and blood and nightsoil.

"You will rule the world someday," Solina said softly. She stood upon the bridge, looking down at them. They reached out to her, claws shaking and glimmering with blood. They hissed her name.

"Sssolina... Sssolina..."

Mature female nephilim clung to the columns around the pit. Fifteen of them screamed here, bellies bulging and contracting and birthing more spawn into the pit. Blood poured down their legs, and nothing but wounds now spread between their thighs, and still their spawn burst out screaming and hungry to fall onto the million others.

Lord Legion himself clung to the sixteenth column, father of his brood. He licked his lips, gazed upon his wives and children, and gave a toothy smile. His drool rained.

"My queen," he said to her, bowing his horned head.

"Your brood is strong, Legion," Solina said to him from the bridge. "They will consume the world."

The great nephil hissed. Twenty feet tall, his body like a blackened cadaver, he spread out his bat wings, lovingly embracing the stench of his spawn. He inhaled and licked his chops.

"*He* will lead them when I'm gone," Legion said. "*He* will be the greatest among them, a devourer of the weak, a conqueror of dragons."

Solina smiled and placed her hands upon her belly. She could almost feel her son wriggle inside. She could almost hear him screech.

The weredragons killed my child with Elethor, she thought and closed her eyes. *But Lord Legion has given me a new heir, and he will be greater. He will rule this world.*

She still ached from the night she had allowed Legion to know her. Her belly gave a twist, and Solina gasped. That was his son. That was the demon child within her. His claws tugged at her womb, still too weak to break through.

But soon, my child, she thought. *Soon you will emerge into this world and be my heir, a great king the world will cower from.*

She opened her eyes and looked back at Legion.

"Keep mounting the females," she told him. "Again and again. We need more. I want them pressed against the ceiling until they crack it. Very soon, Legion, we will have enough to cover the sky of the world."

He nodded, fangs bright with drool.

"For you, my queen, I will create a mountain of spawn."

She nodded and crossed the bridge. As she left the Hall of Memory and marched toward her throne room, she caressed her belly and smiled.

LYANA

She flew across the desert, fire in her belly. Behind her flew ten thousand warriors, a swarm of dragons and griffins bearing archers on their backs. They flew low. The desert raced below them, boulders blurring into streaks. The sun pounded above. The air whipped them and screamed in Lyana's ears.

"Here we are, boys," Lyana called over her shoulder. "Stay low and burn those sails!"

The River Pallan stretched across the desert ahead, a scar of blue and green rifting the land. It flowed several leagues away; they would be there in moments. Reeds, palm trees, and fields of barley grew alongside it. Upon the water rose hundreds of white sails, each emblazoned with the Golden Sun of Tiranor.

These waters will boil, Lyana thought, *and the trees and sails will blaze.*

She looked to her left. Far in the north, she could just make out a sprawling patch of brown and green. Distant white towers rose from it, mere twigs from here. There lay Irys, capital of Tiranor, a hive of a million souls. A second army flew toward it, a cloud in the northern horizon; Mori and Bayrin flew there with thousands of warriors.

But that is their battle, Lyana thought and looked back east. *Here is mine.*

The Pallan flowed so close now, Lyana could count the sailors' shields. She growled and filled her maw with flame.

"Burn every last ship!" she shouted to the dragons, griffins, and soldiers who flew behind her. "Sink them all."

She streamed forward, leaving the desert to dive over fields and trees. Irrigation canals stretched below her like blue cobwebs, and farmers dashed to hide in their homes. Behind Lyana, her dragons roared, her griffins shrieked, and their riders—men and women of Osanna—sounded their war cries.

Lyana reached the water. She banked and dived to skim southward along the river. Rushes and palms billowed at her sides, bending under the flap of her wings. Ships rowed and sailed beneath her, and she bathed them with flames.

As her fire rained, arrows soared. Lyana roared. Arrows clattered against her scales. One shot through her wing, and another slammed into her back leg. Upon her back, Wila of Osanna fired down her own arrows, screaming the battle cries of her people. One of her arrows pierced a Tiran sailor upon a ship, sending him plunging into the water.

Around Lyana, dragons and griffins swooped to tear and burn the ships. Arrows flew in both directions, fired by both northern riders and Tiran sailors. Several griffins crashed dead into the river, their necks pierced with arrows. The ships rocked madly and sails blazed. One dragon screamed, arrows in her neck, and shifted back into human form; she crashed into the water.

Lyana rose higher, arrows whistling all around. The river stretched before her, a great stream that flowed into the southern horizon; it ran for so many leagues it could take days to clear. She snarled and dived again, raining fire on more ships. More arrows flew. One scraped Lyana's cheek, and Wila shouted upon her back.

"Five damn arrows in my shield!" she cried to Lyana. "Bastards."

Lyana could not spare the woman a glance, but she heard the whoosh of Wila's arrows flying by her ears. Two arrows pierced sailors upon ships below. The sails and masts blazed.

Lyana growled, flew along the water, and dived again. More ships burned, and more griffins and dragons fell pierced with arrows and spears.

Screeches sounded in the south.

Black shadows took flight.

"Here they come!" Lyana shouted over her shoulder to her warriors. "Griffins—into battle formations, go! We'll hold them back. Dragons, you keep burning those damn ships!"

She growled, beat her wings madly, and shot forward. A hundred nephilim rose from the trees alongside the riverbanks like giant diseased crows. They shrieked and drove toward her. Lyana roared and blew her flames. Griffins shrieked around her and reached out their claws. The nephilim crashed against them with thuds and exploding fire.

Blood splattered the trees and turned the rivers red. Dragons shot below, spraying fire. Ships burned and sank. Arrows filled the sky. Nephilim rose everywhere, and claws thrashed at Lyana, and she roared and bit into diseased flesh, then spat out maggots. Griffins shrieked and fell and clawed all around her.

Lyana shot between nephilim, soared higher, and gazed south. The river stretched into the horizon, thick with hundreds of ships. All along the riverbanks, more nephilim were taking flight. Southern Iysa still lay too far to see.

But we will reach the city, Lyana swore. *We will pave a path of fire toward it, and we will burn it down.*

"Dragons, keep burning the ships!" she shouted. "Griffins, battle flights of four—hold those nephilim back!"

The griffins and nephilim crashed and bit and clawed, and blood sprayed in mists. Below, dragons flew against the ships, and smoke rose in plumes.

Lyana cursed as she killed. It would be a long, bloody flight south.

ELETHOR

They streamed across the desert, thirty thousand strong, a swarm of dragons and griffins all bearing archers of Osanna upon their backs. The dunes raced beneath them and the mountains loomed ahead.

Elethor bared his fangs.

Thirty thousand. It was the number of souls who had lived in Requiem before the wyverns attacked. Thirty thousand. They would crush the Palace of Whispers and they would catch Solina and they would burn her.

"We will show you no mercy today, Solina," he hissed as he flew, flames in his mouth. "We will take no prisoners. You will stand no trial in our fallen halls. Today you die."

Scales clanked and fire blasted. Treale darted up to his side. The black dragon stared with narrowed eyes, teeth bared. A snarl left her maw, and a dragonhelm rose upon her head, crowned with blades.

"My king," she said and gave him a deep stare. "I fly by your side. I will kill for you. I will burn the enemy for you."

"Not for me, Treale," he said. "For Requiem. For the souls of our fallen. For the souls who still live."

All around them flew their warriors: dragons of Requiem with flames in their nostrils, true dragons of the east with fluttering beards, griffins with beating wings and yellow eyes, and upon every beast's back a warrior of Osanna bearing arrows and spears. They flew grimly, staring ahead in silence, rising and falling like waves upon the wind. Thirty thousand—a great northern host of light and fury.

The dunes rolled below, soon giving way to rocky fields, boulders, and hills. The noon sun pounded when the host flew over the mountains, and their shadows raced across rocky slopes. Nothing lived here; Elethor saw no plant or beast. There were only these rocky peaks, this white sky, and this glaring sun. The silence unnerved him and he growled.

Where are you, Solina?

They kept flying, a cloud of scale and steel. The mountaintops jutted beneath them like the fallen bones of ancient stone gods. Finally they saw it ahead, and Elethor hissed and his heart twisted.

The Palace of Whispers.

It still lay leagues away, but even from here, Elethor could barely believe its size; it looked larger than a city. He could not decide whether the Palace of Whispers was a mountain covered with towers, archways, bridges, and walls, or whether he flew toward a fortress so massive it had grown to mountain size. Hundreds of towers rose here, and hundreds of windows and archways led into shadows. All were built of the same tan, hard limestone of the mountains around them; Elethor could see no other color. The Ancients had built this place thousands of years ago, and time had done its work. The towers rose, craggy and twisting like stalagmites. The walls lay crumbling and bent like castles of sand after a wave. And yet, despite its age and dilapidation, this place still held power; Elethor felt it emanating like heat.

He kept flying toward the mountain. His host flew behind him. Elethor growled deep in his throat.

It's too silent, he thought. *Damn too silent.*

He could see no movement upon the towers or walls of the great fortress. No nephilim shrieked or flew. No banners fluttered. The ruins seemed dead, and that unnerved Elethor more than a cloud of demons.

"I fly with you, my king," Treale said, voice strained. Upon her back, her rider—a young man named Jadin—nocked an arrow.

They flew closer. The mountain grew ahead. Soon it loomed before them, a monolith large enough that nations could live within it. Still silence covered the land; Elethor heard nothing but the beating wings and snarls of his host. No Tiran soldiers. No nephilim or wyverns or phoenixes. Nothing but desert wind and those old stone battlements.

Only a league separated them from the palace now. The towers and walls dwarfed them. Thousands of windows and archways peppered the mountain like maggot-holes. And still—silence. Stillness. Nothing but rock and wind.

A creak sounded.

A twang followed.

Something moved upon a tower ahead.

Elethor growled.

A lone trebuchet had fired. The missile flew their way—a round ball of clay. It arced in the sky, dived down toward them, and slammed against a griffin.

An explosion tore the sky.

A boom rang out so loudly Elethor screamed. Light blasted. The impact tore the griffin apart; the beast scattered into gobbets of flesh. Flames burst out in rings. Ten more griffins—those who surrounded the one hit—tumbled down, lacerated and bloodied, wings and limbs torn off.

"Tiran fire!" Elethor shouted. "Keep flying—topple those towers!"

He had barely finished his sentence when a hundred twangs sounded ahead. A hundred clay balls flew toward his host.

"Dodge them!" Elethor howled. "Fly higher!"

He soared. Upon his back, his rider—a gruff, mute knight of Osanna—fired an arrow and hit a clay ball two hundred yards away. It burst with light that blinded Elethor, and the blast of air sent him spinning backward. He crashed into a griffin, beat his wings, and rose higher. His warriors were scattering. Explosions rocked the sky, one after another. One clay ball slammed into a dragon, light blazed, and blood and flesh flew. A single, severed arm tumbled down toward the mountains.

"Keep flying!" Elethor roared. His ears rang. He did not know if anyone could hear him. "To the towers! Burn those catapults. Treale—with me!"

The black dragon flew above, scales splashed with blood. She nodded, dived, and flew at his side. They drove toward the fort's towers. Hundreds rose ahead, and more catapults fired. More balls of clay arced through the sky.

Elethor darted left and right, dodging the missiles. Treale flew at his side, whisking around like a bee set to sting. The clay missiles missed them, and explosions blazed at their backs, blasting them with heat. The two dragons flew toward twin towers that rose ahead upon a peak; each held a catapult and Tiran soldiers in tan cloaks.

"Treale, burn the left one. I've got the right!"

He swooped toward the tower. The Tirans fired arrows. Elethor roared. One arrow snapped against his shoulder. Another thrust into his leg. He spewed a jet of fire.

The tower top blazed. Men fell burning and rolled. The catapult rose in flame. To his left, Treale blew fire against the other tower, and its men burned and fell like comets to thump against the mountainsides.

Elethor looked back at his army. Most were still flying toward the fortress. From a hundred other towers, more missiles flew. Every second, a blast blazed across the sky, and more dragons and griffins fell dead.

"Attack the catapults!" Elethor shouted. "Tear them down!"

A flight of griffins—four swooping birds—flew down toward one tower. A clay missile flew and slammed into one beast. The griffin burst into blood and gore. One other griffin shrieked and tumbled, burning. The remaining two swooped and their talons tore down the catapult. Arrows pierced them, they crashed upon the tower, and the Tirans leapt onto them with swords.

"Treale, there, the walls!" Elethor said. "Dive with me."

She snarled and flew toward him. They swooped together. Below upon a snaking wall Tirans were firing three more catapults. Behind them in a ditch, baskets lay stacked with balls of Tiran fire—a hundred or more.

The two dragons blew their fire, drenching the wall.

"Treale, soar!" Elethor shouted. "With me!"

They began to rise, flying straight up.

White light flooded them.

The sky burned.

Flames licked their feet and Elethor could hear nothing but the ringing, see nothing but white light. He thought that he had died, that he flew in the afterlife of starlight.

He could see the faces of his family—Orin, his father, and his mother. They awaited him, clad all in white, and smiled. They reached out to him.

"Elethor!" they cried. "Elethor!"

I'm flying to you... I can almost reach you... I...

"Elethor!"

A tail slapped against him. He looked and saw Treale flying by him. Ugly welts spread across her tail and back legs.

"Elethor!" she said. "The fortress—look."

He turned his head and looked down. He flew so high, he could cover the fortress with his feet. Dust rose in clouds. Elethor spun and began to dive, Treale at his side. When they grew closer, he saw it.

A great hole stretched across the fortress where the Tiran fire had burst. The opening loomed fifty feet wide, large enough for dragons to fly through. Inside, Elethor saw burrows and halls where men raced.

"We're going in, Treale," he said. "Can you fight? Is it bad?"

She snarled and howled in rage. "I can fight! I fight for you, my king."

For the first time, Elethor saw that the rider on her back was gone. Her saddle was singed black. When Elethor looked over his shoulder, his stomach plummeted and he wanted to gag. His own rider still sat upon his saddle—a charred corpse with a gaping skull.

Elethor cursed, tore off the saddle, and let the man fall; they would have to bury their dead later. He dived. Treale dived at his side. They pulled their wings close and curved their flight, racing toward the opening in the mountainside.

"Griffins and dragons!" Elethor roared as he flew. "Into the mountain! Into their halls. Rally here—we enter the darkness."

Thousands of dragons and griffins heard his cry and flew around him. Clay balls shot toward them. Blasts flared. Fire blazed. Griffins and dragons tore apart. Elethor roared, shot a stream of fire into the hole, and men inside burned.

He was first to enter. He dived into the opening and blasted fire in every direction. Upon staircases, bridges, and crumbling floors, men screamed and burned and fell. Arrows clattered against his scales. One slammed into his chest, and Elethor howled and snapped it off. He blew more fire.

He landed upon a rocky floor. Around him loomed a cave carved by the blast. Along the walls, halved hallways and chambers crumbled. It looked like a great ant hive that a giant had punched. Men scurried everywhere, firing arrows, and Elethor blew more flames. Treale and other dragons flew into the cave behind him, and their fire turned the place into an oven.

When the flames died, they revealed a chamber full of charred Tiran corpses. Elethor flapped his wings, grabbed onto the opening of a corridor, and shifted into human form. He ran into the shadows to find more Tirans firing arrows. He raised his shield, and the arrows peppered it. Men shouted and raced toward him, swinging swords.

Treale leaped at his side, her own sword blazing. Elethor raised his blade and snarled. Behind them, more of their warriors—soldiers from both Requiem and Osanna—raised their swords.

They had entered the mountain. The search for Solina began.

MORI

The skies above Irys, ancient capital of Tiranor, swirled with blood, fire, and endless beasts of scale, feather, and rot.

Everywhere Mori looked she saw them. Salvanae streamed around her like banners in a storm, shooting lighting from their mouths. Griffins shrieked and swooped, talons outstretched, to tear down buildings. Dragons blew fire across streets and forts. Upon their backs, the soldiers of Osanna shot a rain of arrows that clattered against streets, rooftops, and the armor of Tiran soldiers.

The warriors of the enemy were not idle. Nephilim filled the sky like murders of undead crows. Phoenixes blazed and shrieked and crashed into dragons, burning them down. Wyverns beat their leathern wings and spewed their acid; the foul liquid tore into bodies and rained blood upon the city below.

Mori had seen the fall of Nova Vita, but she had never seen such slaughter, tens of thousands falling together, and a city of a million souls—twenty times the size of Nova Vita at its largest—burning and crumbling. As she flew between the beasts, her heart pounded, her eyes stung, and she could barely breathe.

"Bayrin!" she shouted. "Come with me. We're going to the palace. I know the way."

She winced, snarled, and pulled her wings close to her body. She dived, skirted around a soaring wyvern, and arced over a nephil. She dared not breathe fire—not yet. She needed to save her flames.

"Mori!" Bayrin shouted behind her. "Bloody stars, Mori, you know, we are part of a phalanx, and—damn it!

The green dragon cursed, swerved around a phoenix, and barely dodged two swooping nephilim. Mori spared him only a glance. She kept flying, dodging the creatures, seeking the palace between the flames.

"Princess Mori!" cried the rider on her back, a young man of Osanna. "Mori, wyvern on your tail!"

"Shoot the rider!" Mori replied. "Keep your arrows flying!"

Crossbow bolts whizzed around her. Upon her back, she heard her rider respond with arrows. Mori kept flying, rising and falling between the combatants. Behind her, she heard Bayrin cry for their phalanx—a group of one hundred dragons and salvanae—to follow.

Mori could not even spare them a glance. She had to find the place. She—

There! Among flames and smoke ahead spread a cobbled square, an expanse large enough for armies to muster upon. Mori knew this place. Here was the Square of the Sun, a sprawling disk of stone in the south of the city.

This is where she whipped me. Mori clenched her jaw and swallowed. Her eyes burned and she could barely breathe. *This is where she chained me for the crowds to see. This is where I screamed and bled.*

Pain pounded through Mori. She could feel those whips upon her back again, tearing her skin, tearing her mind; she had never imagined pain could blaze so powerfully, shake and claim and twist her insides until she could not bear it. She could feel the chains around her wrists again. She could see the cruel jailor and feel his rough fingers forcing her jaw open. Mori screamed. She dived down, blasted fire at two nephilim who rose toward her, and skimmed along a street. She roared her flames, and men and women fell dead before her. Mori screamed and flew through the stone canyon.

Queen's Archway rose ahead. Roaring, Mori flew under it, her claws grabbing soldiers like an eagle grabbing prey. Past the archway, she soared high above the Square of the Sun, soldiers still screaming in her claws. She tossed the men down, knocking them against their comrades below, and bathed the square with fire.

The Palace of Phoebus rose before her from flame. A great staircase led from the square below to the palace gates. The Faceless Guardians flanked the ivory doors, statues that rose taller than dragons.

That is the place. That is where she hurt me.

Mori roared and wept. She flew toward the palace. Arrows fired all around her. Two shot through her wings. Another pierced her shoulder. On her back, her rider screamed and fell silent. Mori kept flying, howling, rage and pain tearing through her.

She flew up the stairs, clawing men apart, and soared up the palace walls. She bathed those walls and towers with fire.

Roars sounded behind her. The dragons of her phalanx descended upon the palace, howling and blowing flames. Their tails lashed at towers. Their claws tore at walls. Nephilim flew to face them. Mori roared and shot flames at the beasts. One nephil grabbed her leg, and she clubbed it with her tail, tearing the beast off.

She flew higher, shooting up in a straight line. Before her rose the Tower of Akartum, the tallest spire in Tiranor, perhaps in the world; it scratched the sky, looming above the city like a great needle of stone and platinum. Archers lined its top, and arrows flew, and Mori roared her fire until the archers burned and fell. She circled the tower, tears in her eyes. The city spread burning below her.

I screamed. I hurt. I cried. I will always scream, Solina. Always. Every night I will scream in my dreams, and every night I will feel those whips again, and I will destroy this place. I will crush these stones that held me.

She slammed her tail against the tower, again and again. She screamed. Stones cracked. Mori howled and barreled into the tower, claws lashing, teeth biting, eyes weeping. Bricks rolled.

Always. Always, Solina. Always you will hurt me. But know this—know that I'm the one who crushed your glory.

The Tower of Akartum cracked. With one more swipe of her tail, Mori sent it crashing down.

The great pillar of stone slammed into the palace. The roofs below collapsed. Walls fell. The lesser towers crumbled. Dust rose in clouds, and the dragons howled and soared.

The Palace of Phoebus, Solina's ancestral home, fell below them into a ruin of flame and dust and blood.

Mori rose higher, tears in her eyes, until she flew so high the cold air spun her head and she could barely see the streets below. When she looked over her shoulder, she saw her rider dead, pierced with a dozen arrows. Below across the city, fires burned and thousands of warriors flew and killed and died.

ELETHOR

They charged down the hall, a thousand warriors swinging blades, trampling corpses beneath them. The soldiers of Requiem charged with longswords, clad in breastplates bearing the Draco stars. The soldiers of Osanna fought at their side, bull horns engraved upon their armor, their one-handed swords lighter but fast as striking asps.

"Get to the staircase!" Elethor cried, sword drenched in blood. He swung that blade with both hands, cleaving the armor of a Tiran warrior. "Take those stairs!"

This place had once been a banquet hall, Elethor thought; faded murals of feasts covered the walls, featuring the Ancients dining on roasted ducks, bowls of pomegranates, and peacocks still bright with feathers. This had been a place of life; today death filled the hall.

Dozens of Tiran soldiers stood between Elethor and the staircase leading deeper into the fortress. They wore armor so pale it was nearly white, the breastplates sporting the Golden Sun of Tiranor. Their sabres swung, spraying blood in arcs, the pommels shaped as sunbursts. Their visors swooped like beaks.

Columns rose every few feet, supporting a low ceiling. Torches crackled. Along the walls, archways led into deeper shadows; more soldiers fought there. There was no room here for dragons or nephilim; here was a war of blade and armor, of hacking forward every foot through blood and entrails and corpses.

"Elethor!" Treale shouted at his side, her sword clanging against Tiran sabres. "What's up those stairs?"

Elethor took a sword's blow to the breastplate and cursed. He swung Ferus down, severing the Tiran arm that had attacked him. With another swing, he slew the man.

"I don't know!" he shouted back. "But we've got to move deeper. Let us fill every corridor, chamber, and staircase in this place."

He had no map of the palace. He did not know where Solina hid. *We will fill this mountain like water spilled into an ant hive,* he thought. *Wherever you lurk, we will find you.*

Finally, with a sword swing that clove a man's helmet, Elethor reached the stairway across the banquet hall. He shouted orders, and his forces split into five phalanxes. Each phalanx—a hundred soldiers strong—dashed into another hallway or chamber, leaving the banquet hall littered with corpses. Elethor ran up the staircase, leading his own phalanx, a hundred warriors of both Requiem and Osanna.

You cannot hide, Solina, he thought as he raced upstairs. *We will bang down every door and overturn every brick until we find you.*

Tirans raced down toward him. Blades swung and men fell dead, and Elethor kept climbing. Treale fought at his side, eyes narrowed and lips tightened; the staircase was only wide enough for two to fight abreast. Their hundred warriors ran behind them, awaiting their turn to fight.

"Solina!" Elethor shouted. He slew a man and climbed another step. "Solina, come and face me! Emerge from hiding, or are you a coward?"

A Tiran ran down toward him, thrusting a spear. Elethor cursed and dodged the weapon; it thrust between him and Treale.

Their swords both swung, tearing into the man. They kept climbing. Through the walls, Elethor heard the battle ring across the palace; thousands of his troops were racing through the darkness, filling the mountain.

They fought for every step. They slew a dozen men before they burst into a second chamber—a columned hall lined with archways and torches. Murals covered the ceiling, depicting birds with the heads of men, and a dusty mosaic sprawled across the floor, its stones forming dolphins in a green sea. Fifty Tirans filled this chamber, and with battle cries, they charged forward.

"For Requiem!" Treale screamed and ran toward them.

Elethor ran at her side, and blades swung, and behind them their comrades burst into the chamber. Steel rang and blood washed the floors. Sabres slammed into Elethor's armor, denting it; he could feel his flesh bruising beneath. One sabre cleaved his pauldron, cracking the steel but only nicking his flesh. He kept swinging Ferus, painting the room red.

"Solina!" Elethor shouted. "Damn it, Solina, come face me!"

He snarled as he fought. Sweat drenched him. His wounds blazed. Solina could be anywhere in this fortress; how could he find one woman in this labyrinth? Perhaps she wasn't even in the mountain; perhaps she had fled to fight at another front. He swung Ferus at her men, craving to swing the blade into the queen.

"Solina!"

He charged through the chamber, his warriors at his sides. They barged through a doorway, fought up another staircase, and ran down a corridor, cutting men down. All across the fortress, Elethor heard steel ringing and men shouting; his other phalanxes were spreading across the place, filling every hallway, staircase, and chamber like poison seeping through veins. When he passed by an arched window, Elethor saw griffins and salvanae still fighting outside; the onslaught of Tiran fire had ended, and now nephilim—too large to fight in these halls—were charging at the beasts.

They raced through an ancient library, its shelves rotted away, its scrolls disintegrating under their boots. By a stone door, Treale slew a man, letting the crumbling papyrus drink his blood. For a moment no Tirans charged at them, and Treale leaned against a wall, lowered her head, and breathed raggedly. Blood covered her armor, helmet, and sword. Elethor stumbled toward her, leaned against the same wall, and for a moment they panted together.

"El—" Treale said, coughed a few times, and tried again. "Elethor, I... I can smell them. Rot. Worms. Nephilim are here."

Elethor nodded and wiped blood and sweat off his brow. Northern men, both of Requiem and Osanna, trudged through the dust toward them, blades raised and armor dented.

"The bastards are fighting our griffins outside," Elethor said.

Treale shook her head. "No, Elethor, there are nephilim in here. Inside this mountain. The rot is rising from somewhere deep inside." She shuddered. "There's something festering in the heart of this mountain. It's the stench of nephilim, but somehow worse, more powerful."

Elethor sniffed. He could smell the blood, the crumbling scrolls, and their sweat—and overpowering it all, the stench of nephil rot. Treale was right. This stench wasn't coming from outside—at least, not all of it. A hive of these creatures lurked deeper. He raised his blade.

"Follow your nose, Treale. Wherever this smell is coming from, I wager that's where we'll find Solina."

They broke down a door, charged into a corridor, and slew three more men. Their warriors ran behind them.

They combed the palace for hours. They kicked down doors of corroded bronze. They swung their blades. Blood washed the palace and corpses piled up. A hundred warriors followed Elethor down a columned hallway; a dozen died when Tirans charged from one chamber. A dozen more replaced them, rushing down a staircase from a room they had claimed. This palace was a great, dusty hive of ancient stones and smashed statues. They fought hallway by hallway, room by room, bridge by bridge. Elethor thought the labyrinth would never end, and yet the smell grew stronger, and he moved deeper into the mountain. He left all windows far behind. The only light here came from the torches men carried. These halls were old, older even than the ruins of Bar Luan. Dust rose to their ankles, and wind moaned like ghosts.

"Down here, Elethor!" Treale shouted at his side. Her eyes were wide, and her chest rose and fell as she panted. "I can smell them. Here!"

She ran down a spiraling staircase. Elethor ran at her side, and dozens of their men followed. The stairs corkscrewed around a towering statue of an Ancient, his face stoic and his sandstone robes cascading like silk. At the foot of the statue, the stench of rot flared so powerfully Elethor nearly gagged.

A rough hallway plunged downward, its walls lined with torches. At the tunnel's end rose doors of bronze, large as the gates of palaces. Firelight limned the doors; flames burned behind them. Grunts, snorts, and gurgles rose from the chamber beyond.

Nephilim.

Elethor paused and looked at Treale. She raised her blade and stared back with tightened lips. Their men crowded behind them, armor dented and bloody, eyes grim.

"Once we enter, Treale, shift into a dragon," he said. "If nephilim are back there, the place is large enough to shift."

She nodded. "We'll break down the doors and burn them all."

She took a step back, raised her shield, and made to charge down the corridor. Elethor placed a hand on her shoulder, holding her back.

"Wait, Treale," he said softly. "Before we go in there..."

She looked up at him with huge, dark eyes like pools of endless night, and Elethor swallowed, suddenly not sure how to proceed. They had survived this far, but now a fear gripped him like icy fingers around his spine. Treale's eyes seemed so large to him, so young, so loyal. Despite all the men she had slain, she seemed a mere youth to him now, an innocent young woman blinded by love for her king.

And he was afraid for her. He was afraid for all those who followed him, who obeyed his orders without question, who plunged into darkness to fight at his side. If too many nephilim lurked beyond these doors, there would be no sky to flee to.

It is victory now, Elethor thought, *or death—death for me, my men, and this young woman who only a few years ago placed a frog on my dinner plate, then fled squealing and laughing, a child with no care in the world.*

"El?" she whispered. "Are you all right?"

He held her shoulder. "Treale, if we don't make it out of here, I want you to know something."

Her lips parted, and Elethor knew she was remembering that night—that night upon the hill where she had kissed his cheek, where they had talked about their lives, where for one night Elethor had forgotten about Solina, forgotten about Lyana, and had almost loved her, almost left the world for her. He had thought about that night often, and today in her eyes, he saw that she had never forgotten—that she had relived her lips upon his cheek countless times.

"What is it, El?" she whispered.

"Treale, you fought bravely. You proved your honor. Whatever happens beyond those doors, you are Requiem's finest; never doubt that. Will you kneel before me?"

She gasped, swallowed, and nodded. She knelt, caked with blood and ash, and held out her sword in open palms.

"I, King Elethor Aeternum," he said, "knight you a bellator of Requiem, a warrior of starlight. Rise, Lady Treale Oldnale."

She rose, tears in her eyes.

"But I ran from battle," she whispered. "When the wyverns attacked, I—"

"You flew to find your family," Elethor said. "I will not fault you for that. And damn it, Treale. You saved my bloody sister, for stars' sake. That's got to count for something, no?"

She laughed, eyes damp. "A knight, Elethor! Bloody stars. Two years ago I thought I'd be a puppeteer." She wiped her eyes, clutched her sword, and nodded down the hall. "Now that I'm a knight and about a hundred times braver, are you ready to go kill the queen?"

He nodded. She clasped his shoulder and bared her teeth. He gripped her shoulder too. They shared one long, final stare, then turned and ran shouting down the hallway. Their men screamed and charged behind them. They smashed against the bronze doors.

These doors were ancient, forged thousands of years ago, and they crashed open, and Elethor and Treale burst into a great chamber.

Countless nephilim screeched, white eyes blazing like molten fire.

Elethor shifted into a dragon and spewed his flames. Treale shifted too and her fire screamed across the chamber. Nephilim shrieked. Fellow Vir Requis burst into the room behind them, and more dragons blew fire, and nephilim crashed against the ceiling and walls, and a column cracked.

The hall blazed, an inferno of flame and flesh and scale and tooth. A nephil burst through fire and thrust claws, and Elethor roared, blood upon his chest. Another nephil leaped onto Treale and knocked her down, and she rolled and wrestled it, her tail flailing. The beasts flew everywhere, a great living mass, and Elethor lashed his claws, bit maggoty flesh, and whipped his tail.

A flaming halo crackled, and a towering nephil rose ahead, wings spread out like the sails of a demon ship. Lord Legion shrieked, and the sound cracked the walls, and rubble fell from the ceiling. Men died in his jaws, and the Nephil King laughed, and all around him his minions spread, an endless sea of the fallen.

We cannot win this, Elethor realized, and fear clutched him, and for a moment he froze. *They are too many. I led my people to death.*

Legion chewed and swallowed men, licked his lips, and charged toward Elethor. Legion's great arms swung, and Elethor blew his fire, but the arms slammed into him. He flew and crashed against a wall, cracking it. More nephilim mobbed him. Three beasts dragged Treale down and bit into her back, and she screamed.

"Enough!"

The voice rang across the chamber, clear even over the shrieks and roars.

The nephilim froze.

Elethor fell, wheezing, and his wings draped at his sides. He looked up to see Solina sitting upon a throne of living flesh and scales. One of the nephilim formed her backrest, its head above her own, drooling upon her. Two more nephilim formed her armrests; she laid her hands upon their ridged spines. A crown like claws of gold rose upon her head. Nephil drool and pus covered her white gown, and the creatures of her throne licked her with long, white tongues.

"Elethor," she said with a crooked smile. "You cannot win this war. Look around you! A thousand nephilim fill this hall. You have brought...." She squinted. "Oh my, Elethor, but you have only one dragon left, a scrawny female one too."

Elethor growled and looked around him. A hundred men of Osanna and Requiem had charged into this chamber with him. They lay dead upon the floor, torn apart, limbs scattered and bodies crushed. Already nephilim feasted upon them, sucking up bodies like owls sucking up mice.

Only Treale still lived. The young black dragon lay on her belly, and Legion stood above her, his claws pressed down against her neck. Treale growled and tried to rise, but could not. Legion smiled above her, tongue darting, and his halo flamed blue.

Elethor looked back at Solina.

He roared and blew a jet of fire toward her.

She leaped back, and several nephilim slammed against Elethor. Claws swung. Fangs dug into him. He screamed. He burned them. His fire exploded and showered back upon him. Blows thudded against him, and a nephil clawed his cheek, and pain blazed, and more claws slashed his belly, and he roared. Claws drove into his back, and Elethor howled, and his magic left him.

He crashed to the floor in human form.

Legion lolloped toward him, grinning. The Nephil King reached down, wrapped his claws around Elethor, and lifted him like a demonic child lifting a discarded toy.

Elethor hung in the air, dazed, the claws nearly crushing him. Legion shook him wildly, and Elethor's head spun, and he could not see or breathe. All around him the nephilim leered and howled.

"Enough!" Solina shouted again.

The nephilim froze. Legion stood holding Elethor in one fist, pinning his arms down. Blood dripped into Elethor's eyes, and he could barely breathe. It felt like Legion's grip would snap his ribs.

He looked aside and saw that Legion was clutching Treale in his other hand. She too had resumed human form, and she hung in Legion's grip only feet away from Elethor. Blood dripped from her, and her face was pale. She whispered to him, but her voice was so weak Elethor could not hear.

"Treale!" he cried hoarsely.

She gave him a pleading look, eyes full of pain. Her lips uttered his name silently.

"Legion, hold them before me," Solina said. "Hold them still."

She rose upon her throne. The nephilim that formed her seat shifted, creating a ramp of spines and ribs. Solina descended and walked across the bloody floor, hands on the hilts of her sabres.

When she reached Legion, the nephil lowered Elethor and Treale in his claws, holding them a mere foot above the floor. Elethor struggled and kicked and screamed, but could not free himself.

Solina touched his cheek, and her eyes softened.

"Still you fight," she whispered. "Even when all your hope is lost. Still, here in my hall, you struggle."

He spat out a tooth. Blood filled his mouth.

"Fight me," he said. "You and me. No dragons. No nephilim. Just the two of us—sword to sword."

She raised her eyebrows. "Are you..." She laughed. "Are you challenging me to a duel? This is no epic poem of olden days, Elethor. This is no romantic farce." She caressed his hair. "I don't wish to fight you, El. I never did. All I ever wanted was peace."

He laughed mirthlessly, hanging in the claws. "Peace? You wanted peace when you slew my family? When your beasts crushed my city? When you slaughtered children in our tunnels?"

She placed her hands in his hair. She kissed his ear—her lips were soft and full—and whispered.

"I slew them, Elethor, so that we could have peace. So that all those who taunted us, who tried to stop us, who whispered against us—so all of them went away. I killed them, and I will kill everyone else, until all the world is just you... and me." She nodded up toward

Legion, whose head drooled above them. "Show him, Legion. Kill the girl."

Elethor shouted.

Clutching Elethor in one hand, Legion tossed Treale down from his other hand. She slammed hard against the floor, and her blood splattered.

"Treale, shift!" Elethor cried.

She looked up at him. Legion's claws thrust. Treale rose to her feet and began to shift.

A claw crashed through her breastplate.

Treale gasped. Her magic vanished. She hung upon the claw, head and limbs tossed back, gasping. Her legs kicked in midair. Blood filled her mouth.

Legion shook his claw and flung her back down.

"Treale!" Elethor shouted. He howled. With strength he had not imagined in him, he tore at the claws that clutched him.

"Let him go, Legion!" Solina said and laughed. "Let him see her!"

Elethor crashed to the floor, banging his knees. He rose, rushed to Treale, and knelt over her.

His eyes stung. His breath caught. She lay on her back, a hole in her chest. She trembled and gasped, and her hands reached toward him. Blood poured from her chest.

"El," she whispered.

With shaking fingers, he tore off her armor. He rifled through his pack, pulled out a bandage, and placed it against her wound, knowing that it was too late; the blow had pierced through her. He held her, one hand under her head, the other against her cheek.

"I'm here, Treale," he whispered. "I'm here."

She convulsed, legs twitching, chest rising and falling. She could barely speak.

"El," she whispered. "El, do you... do you remember that night?" Her body shook like a fish on a boat's deck. "Do you... do you remember? Under the stars, how... how I kissed your cheek?"

He held her and caressed her hair. "I remember, Treale. I never forgot. Ever."

Her blood flowed, and her trembling eased, and she smiled with blue lips. "El, do you remember how we talked about puppets?"

He blinked tears from his eyes. "I remember," he whispered.

"I... I liked that night," she said. Her breath shook. "El, can I... Please, can I kiss your cheek one more time? Please. I want to... I want to pretend I'm there." Tears flowed down her cheeks. "I want to be back on that hill under the stars."

He lowered his head, and she kissed his cheek with trembling lips, smearing him with blood. He kissed her forehead and caressed her hair.

"Don't leave me," she whispered.

"Never," he said. "Never, Treale. I'm here. I'm right here. Tell me about your puppets. Tell me about all the shelves and piles of them, and all the puppet shows you performed."

She placed her arms around him. A soft light touched her eyes. She trembled against him.

"I had...." Her tears fell. "I sewed them, Elethor, so many... so many. Hundreds of puppets. Green ones. Yellow puppets. And..."

Elethor lowered his head and a silent sob shook his chest. He laid Treale down upon her back. She stared up, mouth open and eyes glassy. His tears wet her face, and with a bloodied hand, he closed her eyes.

Goodbye, Treale. Fly to your puppets. Fly to our starlit halls and wait for me there, and one day you will tell me all about them again.

He rose slowly to his feet.

He turned toward Solina.

He raised his sword, howled, and lunged at her.

She only stood, sighing, as nephilim swooped toward him, and claws grabbed him, and he screamed as wings and scales and rot covered his world.

LYANA

Ships burned along the Pallan, a line of fire blazing across the desert. Once this river had teemed with life. Merchants, soldiers, and fisherman had sailed upon their barges and cogs. Reeds, palm and fig trees, and rustling fields had lined the riverbanks. Ibises, falcons, jackals, and hundreds of other animals had drunk from these waters. Today under the cruel sun the river crossed the desert like a scar, her sails, trees, and farms burning, her animals fallen or scattered.

This place was the vein of Tiranor, Lyana thought, *pumping blood to her capital. Today we burned this vein and left Irys to choke and rot.*

The capital perhaps was choking now, but her sister city—Iysa, great southern jewel of the desert—still pulsed. Lyana kept flying south, her host around her: thousands of dragons and griffins all bearing riders. Before them in the desert, the Pallan widened into a sprawling oasis, and here rose the white walls and towers of Iysa.

Lyana had heard stories of this city. Here did Tiranor build her ships, forge her steel, and mine her jewels. She had imagined a place bustling with enemy forces: battalions of archers upon the walls, phalanxes of wyverns and phoenixes circling overhead, and swarms of nephilim festering and screeching for blood.

Instead, as she flew toward the white walls, she found a ghost city.

The walls of Iysa stood barren, their battlements like sun-dried jaws upon sand. The towers stood silent; no war horns blew upon them, and only a single, tattered banner flapped from one, hiding and showing the Golden Sun. Lyana frowned, flying closer. Behind her flew her warriors.

"It's too quiet," said Wila, her rider. "Nephilim guarded every cog along the river. Won't they guard a city?"

Lyana sniffed. She could smell the rot of nephilim, but could not decide if they lurked here in hiding, or had left their stench and fled. She flew higher and over the walls. Below her, the streets of Iysa spread like a barren labyrinth. Shops, temples, forts, homes—all lay silent and still. Lyana saw no movement but for a few flapping tunics upon lines and a dog that fled into an alley. Docks stretched into the river, naked of ships.

When Lyana looked south of the city, she saw many footprints in the sand heading toward distant hills. She squinted and gazed into the horizon; she could just make out fleeing beasts aflight, perhaps wyverns or nephilim.

"They fled the city," Lyana said. "They heard of our approach. They ran rather than fight."

Lyana heard the creak of Wila tugging her bowstring.

"I don't like this," the rider said. "Nephilim—the spawn of demons—fleeing from battle? Something is wrong here. This is a trap."

"Let's be careful," Lyana agreed. "As far as we know, Solina loaded up the city with Tiran fire, and some poor bastard down there is just waiting for us to land so he can blow the place up."

They circled above the city—dragons, griffins, riders. Their wings scattered dust and leaves and bent the trees below. By a domed temple, movement caught Lyana's eyes. She stared down, squinting, to see several men cowering in a courtyard. They wore rags, iron collars encircled their necks, and dust filled their white hair. Welts and blood covered them. Chains ran from their ankles to heavy iron balls the size of watermelons, too heavy to even drag.

"The city folk left their slaves," Lyana said. "Those too old, weak, or wounded to flee with them."

She circled above the temple. Rough bricks formed its dome, and several palm trees swayed alongside it. When her shadow fell upon the slaves, they wailed and covered their heads. They were thin, ribs showing between the tatters of their rags, and whip lashes covered their backs. Blood stained their lips.

They're dying of thirst and heat, Lyana thought. She looked around the city, cursing. *Damn it.* She could still smell rot here somewhere—did nephilim hide in these houses, or did their stench merely linger? Was this a trap and the slaves the bait?

She looked over her shoulder at her rider. Wila sat with an arrow nocked, her face stern and her golden hair billowing. Her breastplate bore the bull horns of Osanna in silver, and a golden pin—shaped like the walls of Confutatis, the White City—clasped her gray cloak.

"Wila," Lyana said, "keep that arrow nocked. We're going to help these men."

Wila frowned. "My lady, I don't like this. Nephilim waited for us on the beaches. They hid along every league of the river. This place is too quiet. I say we burn the damn city from the air."

A sigh clanked Lyana's scales. "I would, but... Wila, too many innocents have died. We have slain too many women and children. How many cowered in the hulls of the ships we burned—the wives, sons, and daughters of merchants shipping supplies to Irys? How many women and children now hide in that northern capital as dragons rain fire upon it?" She shook her head. "We do not crave the death of our enemy's innocents. We are not Solina; she slew our children with relish. I have killed my enemies, Wila, and perhaps while doing so, I have killed innocents too, bystanders whose only sin was standing too close to those who seek my own death. This will haunt me. This blood I cannot wash from my hands. This blood I had to shed. But here in this city, seeing abandoned slaves cowering below me, I cannot blow my fire. If I did, would I not be as Solina is? Fighting a monster, would we not become monsters ourselves? I will save them if I can. If I can save the innocents of the enemy, perhaps after all this blood and fire, I can save my own soul."

She dived toward the courtyard. Her claws clattered against the cobblestones, and the chained slaves whimpered.

Lyana whipped her head from side to side, sniffing the air. The drool and pus of nephilim seeped between the cobblestones and puddled in a corner; the stuff reeked. The creatures had been here not hours ago.

"Please," whispered a slave, an old man with a white beard. "Please don't hurt us, don't burn us, please..."

Still in dragon form, Lyana approached the chained men. In the sky, griffins and dragons circled over the city; some were descending to land upon roofs and streets. The chained slaves flinched whenever a shadow crossed them.

"I'm not going to hurt you," Lyana said. "Where are the nephilim? Where—"

Stars.

Lyana growled and took flight.

Stars damn it.

These slaves were not chained to balls of iron. They were chained to clay balls of Tiran fire.

She had not soared fifty feet when the temple ceiling crashed open, the doors shattered, and nephilim burst screeching outside.

The air cracked. The Tiran fire exploded below. Fire raged and white light flooded Lyana, and the slaves' blood splattered her. Her ears rang, and claws grabbed her leg, pulling her down. She roared.

As she plummeted, she glimpsed the rest of the city. From every temple, fort, and hall, nephilim burst into the sky. Tiran fire exploded. Flames and blood showered across Iysa.

Lyana crashed back onto the temple courtyard. One nephil grabbed her leg, and three others leaped onto her. The slaves were gone; nothing remained of them but blood and gobbets of flesh. The temple walls had shattered opened; archers stood there, and arrows flew at Lyana.

She roared and blew her fire. Upon her back, Wila screamed and fired her own arrows. Lyana's flames crashed into a nephil, slamming it against a wall. Another leaped onto her shoulder, and claws dug, and Lyana screamed and bit. Her teeth sank into the beast's flesh, and she tasted its rot and maggots.

"Take her alive!" shouted a Tiran soldier in the temple. "Her horns are gilded—this one is a noble. Take her alive!"

Lyana screamed and flapped her wings, struggling to rise. She kicked wildly, freed herself, and flew ten feet.

Three more nephilm swooped from above, crashed down onto her, and she slammed into the cobblestones again. They cracked beneath her. She roared and blew fire.

"Wila, run!" she screamed. She did not know if her rider even lived. Arrows peppered her, clattering against her scales. One pierced her chest, and Lyana roared in pain, and claws tore at her, and teeth bit, and pain flooded her.

Light and song and ringing flowed across her.

Her magic tore free like a bandage from a wound.

She lay in human form, the nephilim dwarfing her. She gripped her sword. She drew a foot of steel. She screamed and claws grabbed her, tightened around her like a girdle of bone, and lifted her.

She screamed and kicked and spat, tried to shift again, and shouted every curse she knew. She was still screaming when they shoved a sack over her head, and wings flapped, and her legs kicked in midair. Wind whipped her, her head spun, and terror pulsed in her chest.

ELETHOR

Legion's claws wrapped around Elethor's chest, pinning his arms down and nearly cracking his ribs. Elethor could barely breathe, barely make a sound. His wounds burned; so many cuts and bruises and welts covered him, he felt like a slab of beaten meat. He tried to shift but could hardly muster the power to stay conscious.

"Yesss," Legion hissed. The nephil was carrying him down a dark hall, his clawed feet clattering. "Yessss, struggle, weredragon. I like it when you struggle."

The demon's tongue dipped to lick Elethor's cheek. Elethor grunted and closed his eyes. The beast's head rose above his own—the creature stood thrice his height—and his jaws leaked drool and pus that stank of corpses.

"Soli—" Elethor began, but Legion squeezed his claws tighter, suffocating his voice.

The queen walked ahead, not turning back to regard him. She held a torch, lighting walls covered in faded murals depicting the Ancients battling serpents and raising fire in their palms. As they moved down the hall, Elethor shut his eyes and thought of Treale.

Fly to our starlit halls, daughter of Requiem, he thought. *Await me there among the souls or our fallen. You sing now among them.*

Solina led them through many halls, stairways, and doors, until finally she brought them to a towering archway whose keystone sported engravings of lions. Solina walked through the archway, and Legion—carrying Elethor in his grip—followed.

They entered a hall the size of a palace, easily the largest chamber Elethor had seen in this mountain. He thought that the fallen courts of Requiem could fit into this chamber with room to fly around them. Limestone columns rose from shadow to support a wide, domed ceiling like a stone sky. In the center of the chamber, a tower rose from a pit; a bridge led from the doorway to the tower top.

Solina took several steps onto the bridge, turned around, and smiled at Elethor.

"Welcome," she said, "to the Hall of Memory. Legion! Carry him onto the bridge. Let him see what lurks below."

She smiled crookedly, turned her back toward them, and continued walking across the bridge.

Elethor snarled and struggled against Legion's claws, but they squeezed further, and he was so tired, so hurt, his skull too tight, his chest aching. He wanted to scream, to break free, to lunge at Solina and kill her. And yet he could barely keep her in focus. He had lost too much blood, had fought too much, hurt too much.

Legion began to walk along the bridge, his claws clattering and scraping again the stone. Clanking, squealing, and screeches rose from the pit below, and a stench wafted so powerfully Elethor choked and gagged. Legion laughed—a sound like snapping bones—and held Elethor over the pit.

His breath left him.

Elethor closed his eyes.

He knew then: There was no hope. Not for him and not for his people fighting across the desert.

This flight south was folly. This was all in vain.

The spawn of nephilim filled the pit below the bridge, spreading all around the tower. Their eyes burned red. Their claws and teeth dug at one another's flesh, feeding and licking and sucking blood. They screeched to see Elethor hanging above them. They leaped and tried to claw at him, nearly reaching his feet. Countless filled this place, a writhing mass like a nest of maggots.

"Do you like them, Elethor?" Solina cried ahead, voice echoing. "My servant Legion spawned them himself. A million writhe below you, growing larger. The strong, you see—they feed upon the weak. They climb the mass. They will soon be large enough to fly and cover the world." She looked over her shoulder, and her eyes softened in mock concern. "I am quite afraid, my dear Elethor, that they will soon feed upon the rest of your weredragons."

Then she laughed, turned back toward the tower, and kept walking across the bridge.

Legion hissed and his drool sprayed. He followed, carrying Elethor farther along. As they walked, the nephil spawn leaped at the bridge, clawed at its edges, then fell back into the pit. Their veined wings beat uselessly, still too brittle for flight. They screeched and licked their maws.

"Weredragon blood!" they cried, voices shrill like possessed children. "Let us eat his organs!"

They walked for what seemed the length of cities before the bridge reached the tower. Upon the tower top lay the still, silvery surface of a pool.

It's some kind of well, Elethor realized. *A towering one rising from the demon pit.*

Solina stepped onto the pool's rim, placed one foot into the water, and looked over her shoulder. Her eyes again softened, but this time Elethor saw no mockery in them, only old sadness like a lone doll upon a shelf in an abandoned home.

"It's time, Elethor," she said. "It's time to go home."

She stepped into the well, moving deeper and deeper down hidden stairs until her head disappeared underwater.

Legion hissed and chuckled. With a screech and spray of rot, he tossed Elethor forward.

Elethor tumbled and crashed into the water.

Silver streams flowed across him. His blood seeped and rose through the water like red ghosts. He sank. He closed his eyes. He thought of Lyana's green eyes and hands in his, clung to her memory, and waited to die.

Warmth fell upon him.

Sunlight played against his closed eyelids.

His body felt...

Whole, he thought. *Healed. Young.*

His pains vanished like a nightmare fleeing the dawn. He could not remember feeling so nourished, healthy, and strong in years. Softness caressed him; he lay in a plush, warm bed.

He opened his eyes and inhaled softly.

My bed, he thought. His eyes watered. *My bed at home. In Requiem.*

Not the cold, hard bed in Requiem's palace, a great thing of dark oak the kings of Requiem slept in. No—this was *his* bed, the one he had built himself for his small home upon the hill.

He was in that home now. A tear streamed down his cheek. He had not seen this place in two years—not since the phoenixes had burned it. He sat up and looked around, eyes stinging and breath shaking.

Shelves lined the walls, brimming with leather-bound books, geodes, rolled-up maps, and wooden figurines he had whittled. Larger sculptures of marble stood upon the floor: Solina in her youth, nude and beautiful as sunlight over the forest. Outside the windows—stars, how could this be?—he saw Requiem. Not Requiem as he knew her now, burnt and fallen and crawling with beasts. This was the Requiem of his youth. It was spring, and the sky was blue, and dragons glided outside—not haggard survivors, but gleaming dragons of blue, gold, and green.

"I'm home," he whispered.

He left the bed and found that he wore a green tunic with a silver collar—stars, he remembered this tunic!—and that his body was younger, slimmer, not scarred from war. He looked at his shoulder where, a year ago, wyvern acid had burned him; the flesh was unblemished. He touched his cheeks and found them smooth, his beard gone.

Are these the halls of afterlife? he wondered. He had always imagined them like glittering columns and starlit halls. This felt more like a memory come alive—a memory of youth when everything was bright, fresh, and pure in the world.

He moved through his room, laughing softly, disbelieving. He ran his fingers over his cherrywood table. He lifted the statuette of a turtle, the one he had carved for Solina. He looked out the windows to see Nova Vita roll across the hills, bright in the spring sun, her birches rustling.

This is Nova Vita years ago, he realized. The potter shop below the hill was only being built now. The cypresses outside his window were still young.

It's ten years ago, he thought. *Maybe nine. And I'm only eighteen here, a mere youth and prince, not a haunted, scarred king.*

Under scrolls and books, he found his handheld mirror and looked upon his reflection. His cheeks were softer. His brown eyes had seen less pain. No scar rifted his face; that face was young, thoughtful, and pale.

"Solina always did say I was too pale," he mumbled.

"You always were," came her voice from behind him.

He turned to see her at the doorway, and his breath left him.

She stood barefoot, leaning against the doorframe, and gave him a crooked smile. She wore one of his old tunics. It was loose around her, and she was naked beneath it; he could see the golden smoothness of her legs and the tops of her breasts. Her hair cascaded over her shoulders, rivers of platinum like water under moonlight. She was young here in this memory, closer to twenty than thirty, and her face glowed with youth, and her blue eyes stared at him with all the temptation and coyness of forbidden young love.

She's beautiful, he thought. This was not Queen Solina, the cruel tyrant of Tiranor, the mad woman she had become. No. This was *his* Solina, the young Solina he had loved, the Solina he had pined for, the Solina she had been. This was the woman who had filled his bed for years, then his dreams for years after that. This was Solina of sunlight, of stolen kisses, of maddening love and sex and flame.

"Solina?" he whispered.

"I am here, Elethor," she said. She walked toward him, took his hands, and smiled. "It's me, El. It's me. Do you remember?"

Her hands were soft and warm. He held them and looked at her, and looked around, and his eyes dampened again.

"I remember. Solina, how—"

She placed a finger against his lips.

"Does it matter?" she whispered. Her smile left her, and her lips trembled, and she embraced him. She clung to him desperately, and her fingers pressed against his shoulders. "Hold me, Elethor. Hold me tight."

He held her. They stood like this for long moments, and her tears wet his shoulder. He caressed her hair, and suddenly he was no longer King Elethor of Requiem, a jaded warrior. That man faded away, and he was Prince Elethor again, eighteen years old and caught in her light, and this was *real*. This was him again. This was home, this was youth, and the world was bright and no darkness could fill it.

"How can this be, Solina?"

She looked at him. A tremulous smile found her lips, and she touched his cheek.

"I made this place for us," she said. "Do you remember this day? It's the day your father, brother, Lyana, and all the others flew east for some fair. You and I remained here in Nova Vita—no duties, no dinners, no obligations, just... us. Just a perfect day of sunlight and being lazy and..." She lowered her eyes shyly. "And making love." She looked back up at him, her eyes damp. "It was our day. A perfect day. It was the best day of my life, El—the best one ever. It *is* the best day. We can relive this day now! Again and again forever, and... and the others will never come back. There will never be war here, or pain, or exile, or any of those bad things. Just you and me, young forever, in love forever. Our perfect day."

He pulled away from her, walked to the window, and looked outside upon the hills of birches and cypresses. Above in the sky, the dragons glided. Solina came to stand beside him and placed a hand on his shoulder.

"Where are we?" he asked.

"In Requie—"

He turned toward her. "Solina, where are we?"

She looked aside, eyes pained. "Does it matter, El? Does it matter where this place is? It's real to me. It's real to you." She looked back at him, tears trembling in her eyes. "Don't you remember?"

He placed his hands upon the windowsill, lowered his head, and understood. He spoke softly.

"We're still in Tiranor. We're in the bowels of the mountain, and around us the nephilim spawn, and... this is some... some illusion of the water. Of the pool we entered." He grabbed her arm. "Isn't it, Solina?"

"So what if it is!" Her face flushed. "So what, Elethor? Who cares what lies out there?" She swept her arm around. "*This* is what matters. This place, not anything else. These books, and statues, and... and, Elethor, the turtle you carved me. You remember the turtle." She pressed herself against him and tried to kiss him. "I love you, Elethor, and that is what matters. That is all that matters. And you love me too. Here you do. Here you've always loved me."

He sighed and lowered his head. "It's not real, Solina."

"My memory is real. This day existed, El. It was real years ago; it's real again, real enough. It was my best day. Have you forgotten it?"

He looked around him, seeing his books, his sculptures, his bed. He looked at Solina—his love.

"I remember," he said softly. "It was my best day too."

Tears streamed down her cheeks and she embraced him. They stood together by the window, holding each other close.

"Then let us stay here," she said. "Your city that you loved still stands here. The people whom you loved still live. I will leave the Memory Pool sometimes—to govern my empire, to deal with the dirt, blood, and cruelty of the world. You can wait for me here, and read your books, and sculpt your statues. I will return to you every day. We will make love every night. Like this forever—young and happy. Out there, in the world, we are killers, Elethor. I killed so many; you did too. Our bodies are scarred there, our souls cold and drenched with blood. But not here. Here we are young, and good, and pure of heart." She touched his cheek. "It's finally over, El. All the pain. My exile. Our war. It's over now. The pain is gone, and nothing but joy and light remain."

He looked at her young, earnest face, unblemished by the scars of war. Her skin was smooth and supple, a soft golden hue, and freckles covered her nose. Her eyes were deep blue, her lips full and pink, her hair so soft in his hands.

Is this not all I ever wanted? he thought. *Is this not what I spent years yearning for? Is this not perfection, eternal bliss?*

He breathed deeply, and his chest ached. He had it here—all he had desired! He could spend the rest of his life in his home with the woman he loved, the woman who had claimed his soul and still clutched it, the woman who—

The woman who slaughtered children in our tunnels, a voice whispered inside him. *The woman who slew my father and brother. The woman who destroyed my kingdom and butchered my people.*

He thought of Lyana, his wife. Here, a decade ago, he hated Lyana—an imperious youth who would lecture him about this or that until he wanted to strangle her. And he thought of Lyana the woman, his wife, a warrior who had fought at his side, loved him, and flown through fire and death with him—a woman braver than any he had known, a woman of a heart pure and strong like steel forged in dragonfire, of soft light and goodness and eternal sadness, a woman who would always fly by his side.

I loved Solina in my foolish youth, he thought. *But I walked through the Abyss with Lyana, and I loved her as a man, and I fought with her for all that we believe in, for all that our people hoped and killed and died for.* Solina was a flame, a fire that had lit his youth, flickered bright, and spread into a wildfire that burned him. But Lyana was no flame—she was starlight, blinding in the darkness, guiding him home.

"And what of those who still live?" he said, voice suddenly hoarse. "What of Lyana, my sister, and the others?"

Something dark crossed Solina's eyes. Her jaw tightened. She looked aside and spoke tautly.

"They will live," she said. "I will not kill them. I will not hunt them. You have my word, Elethor. I vow to you." She looked back at him and again took his hands. "If you remain here with me—with your Solina, with your love—I won't harm any more of your people. Those who still live can leave this land, fly into exile, and find whatever life they still can."

He tore himself away from her. He walked to the back of the room where his statues stood. He faced them: likenesses of Solina carved in marble. A sigh ran through him, and he closed his eyes.

"No," he said softly. "No, Solina. You say we are young here and pure. Are we pure, Solina? What defines our evil—our actions or our hearts? You slew my family. You butchered my people. You—"

"Not me, Elethor! Not this me. Not this Solina here." She walked toward him and grabbed his arm. "Not this Solina who stands unscarred before you."

She breathed heavily, chest rising and falling, and she was beautiful, and young, and temptation itself barefoot in dawn's light.

"That evil is inside you," he said. "It always was; I was blind to it. I saw your beauty. I felt your kisses. I ignored the cruelty of your heart. Your hands slew my family years from now. Your heart drove those hands; it has always beaten inside you. I will not stay with you here. I will not be part of this mockery, this fake dream, this—"

She slapped him—a slap so hard he sucked in breath and saw stars.

"You will!" she hissed between clenched teeth. Her eyes blazed. "You will stay with me here, or she will die, Elethor. She will die in pain. I will kill her." She spun toward the doorway and screamed. "Legion! Bring the whore!"

The door to Elethor's chamber creaked open.

The nephil's head thrust inside, nearly as tall as a man.

Elethor growled and instinctively reached for his sword, only to find it missing. The sight of this rotted, bloody creature here, in perfect old Requiem, spun his head. Legion grinned, and his fangs shone, and his drool pooled on the floor. Dried blood encrusted the spikes and horns across his head, his halo crackled, and worms crawled inside his left eye.

Like a scuttling insect, Legion crawled into the chamber—even crouched, he barely fit through the door. Rot dripped from him to seep across the floor, and his stench swirled, thick as moldy stew in the air.

Then Elethor saw what Legion clutched to his belly, and he let out a hoarse cry.

Holding her close against him, Legion carried a bloodied, bruised Lyana.

"Lyana!" Elethor shouted and made to grab her, but Solina held him back.

"Don't move, El!" she warned, her breath against his ear. "If you move, he will crush her. See how frail she is! See how sharp his claws are around her little ribs."

Elethor froze, head spinning and breath panting. Lyana moaned, her eyelids fluttered, and she looked up at him. Her one eye was swollen and bruised. Her lips bled. When she saw him, she gave a soft gasp and whispered his name. This was not the Lyana of ten years ago, the imperious girl with the upturned nose and bouncing red curls. This was the Lyana he had married, her hair shorter, her eyes deeper and wiser.

"Lyana," he whispered.

He looked into her eyes and saw fear, anger, and pain, but above all love for him and Requiem, a brittle strength like an old sword drawn for one last battle.

"Look at her," Solina whispered. She stood behind Elethor, her hand on his shoulder, her lips against his ear. "Look at her there, bloodied and nearly crushed in the claws of my servant. Look at her, the great knight, the proud queen, the loving wife—look at her. Broken. Weak. Almost dead."

Elethor would not remove his eyes from Lyana, but he spoke to Solina.

"She is stronger than you will ever know, Solina," he said. "She is stronger than you will ever be."

Solina took a step forward, touched his cheek, and whispered.

"We will see, Elethor. We will see." She turned toward the nephil and his prey. "Legion! Kill the girl. Kill her like you did the last one."

Legion grinned and raised Lyana toward the ceiling, and his jaws opened, and Lyana cried out.

"Wait!" Elethor shouted.

Legion froze, holding Lyana a mere foot above his jaws.

"Wait!" Elethor repeated. "Solina, wait."

The Queen of Tiranor smiled softly. She nodded at Legion, and the nephil lowered Lyana to his breast and held her close, a spider clutching a fly.

Elethor lowered his head, pain pulsing through his chest like demons inside him, scratching at his heart and ribs. Again he saw all the dead: his father, his brother, Treale, and countless others, all dead for this war between him and Solina. He could bear no more—not Lyana. Not her. He clenched his fists at his sides, turned toward Solina, and stared at her.

"Let Lyana go," he said, "and I will stay with you here." He exhaled slowly and lowered his eyes. "You win, Solina."

"El," Lyana whispered. "El, I—"

The claws tightened around her, constricting her breath and voice. Blood trickled from her lips.

Elethor stepped toward his wife, heart wrenching. He wanted to touch her, comfort her, hold her and whisper to her, but Legion's foot thrust out and kicked him back, and Elethor fell several paces. Solina caught him, wrapped her arms around him, and stared into his eyes.

"You made the right choice, Elethor," she said. "You grieve for her now; I know. You will forget her in time. You will forget her and you will love me again." She turned to her demon. "Legion! Take the girl back to the bridge. Let her go! She is free."

The nephil bowed his dripping, spiked head, and his tongue lapped up drool from the floor. Clutching Lyana to his belly, the creature retreated back out the door, leaving a trail of slime.

Elethor gave a wordless cry, wrenched himself free from Solina, and ran after them. He passed through the doorway, and stench hit his face, and shrieks filled his ears, and he found himself standing outside the pool again. Around him rose the columns of the Hall of Memory. Below in the pit, the million nephil spawn rotted and shrieked and fed upon one another. Legion was already retreating along the stone bridge, moving from the Memory Pool toward the archway that exited the chamber.

"Elethor!" Solina cried behind him.

He ignored her and raced along the bridge.

"Wait!" he shouted. "Solina, let me speak to her! Let me say goodbye. Then you may have me."

"Put her down, Legion!" Solina shouted. "Let him speak to his whore!" She laughed. "Let them cry together one last time; it will amuse me."

The vermin in the pit screamed and leaped and clawed at the rims of the bridge. Their father, the towering Lord Legion, cackled and tossed Lyana down. She thudded against the bridge, and the vermin all around clattered and screeched and clawed, grabbing at the bridge and trying to reach her, then falling back into the pit.

Elethor ran. He reached Lyana, knelt above her, and held her, and for a moment he could not speak from pain. She was hurt. They had removed her armor and torn her clothes, leaving her ragged and bloodied. Dirt and ash matted her hair and caked her face.

"Lyana," he whispered. "I'm here. I'm here."

She struggled to her feet and stood on trembling legs. Elethor held her waist, and she placed her hands on his shoulders. They stood in the center of the bridge. Solina stood behind at the pool; Legion retreated to stand at the archway. All around in the pit, the wretchedness and darkness of the world screamed and bled and fed, their cries echoing in the chamber.

"Elethor," Lyana whispered and tears filled her eyes. "Elethor, no."

He touched her hair. "It's the only way, Lyana. Leave this place. Fly to the others. Find Mori and Bayrin and whoever still lives and flee this desert. Promise me, Lyana."

She stared at him, and her eyes hardened, but then she trembled and pulled him into a crushing embrace. They held each other as the creatures screamed all around.

"I love you, Elethor," she whispered, her head against his shoulder. "I love you always, my husband, my king. They will sing your name in the halls of Requiem. Always."

He touched her cheek and looked into her eyes—those eyes that would once taunt him, madden him, infuriate him... and which now spoke of Requiem's halls, of warm embraces on cold nights, of her steel and fire and love that had taken him through this war, that would remain inside him even in the very pit of darkness.

"I love you too, Lyana," he said. "More than the fallen halls of our fathers, and more than memories of spring. You must lead Requiem now. Our people will follow your fire, and it will lead them home. Two winters ago, I told you this in the Abyss: Whatever strength I have is yours. I will keep you safe, then and now, even in the heart of darkness. Leave this underground. Find our sky. Lead our people to light." He took her hand and placed it against his chest. "I cannot fly with you now. But I will think of you upon the wind, and I will smile, and I will wait... I will wait until we fly together in starlight."

She tightened her arms around him, and they kissed—a deep kiss that tasted of blood, tears, and memories of home, a kiss of fire such as they had never shared, a last flame of stars.

Claws grabbed Lyana's shoulders.

Legion pulled her back, wrenching her from Elethor's arms, tearing their kiss apart.

"Elethor!" she cried, eyes wide.

Legion began dragging her back along the bridge. She reached out to him. Their fingertips touched, shooting warmth through him. Then the beast pulled her into shadow, and she cried his name and disappeared under the archway into darkness.

Elethor stood alone upon the bridge, cold and empty, and stared at the archway.

Goodbye, Lyana. May your wings find our sky.

He turned back to face the Memory Pool. Solina stood there upon the bridge, her eyes soft. She stepped toward him and held his hands.

"You did the right thing, El," she said softly. "I know how much I hurt you. I see the pain in your eyes. But I only hurt you for us, Elethor. For our life. For our memories. Lyana was never yours, El; you know that. She tempted you. She stole you from me, and she hurt you too, and you weep for her now. But you've chosen me. I always knew that you would." She kissed his lips. "You've returned to me at last—to your Solina." She wept and held him. "It's over,

Elethor. It's finally over, and we are together again. Come, Elethor. Come with me into the pool. It's time to go home."

Her kiss stung against his lips. Her hands touched his cheeks. Her eyes were huge, drowning in her pain and madness. He touched her hair, and she smiled at him tremulously.

"Goodbye, Solina," he whispered. "I loved you once. I loved you for years. You held me for so long. But that boy in the pool, a boy caught in your light... he is only a memory too." He kissed her cheek. "Goodbye, Solina—fire of my youth, flame and curse of my life."

Standing before her, he shifted into a dragon.

Solina gasped and fell back.

Elethor beat his wings. The vermin below screeched. He soared in the chamber and blew his fire, and roared, and his cries echoed. As Solina lay upon her back and the spawn howled, Elethor shot forward and slammed into a column.

"Elethor!" Solina screamed. She rose to her feet. The firelight painted her face red. "Elethor!"

He slammed into the column, again and again, howling his rage and blowing his fire.

"Legion!" Solina screamed. "Legion, kill the weredragon!"

The nephil screeched outside. Claws clattered. Elethor blew a stream of flame at the archway, and Legion screeched. He kept slamming against the column. Cracks raced along it.

Fly from this place, Lyana. Fly far. Lead our people home.

He slammed into the column once more, and it cracked.

Elethor pulled back, wings beating, and watched the column fall.

It crashed into the pit, crushing spawn beneath it. Legion leaped into the chamber, and Elethor blew his fire again, and the nephil screeched and blazed. Solina screamed upon the bridge. Cracks raced along the ceiling, and chunks of rock fell.

Elethor flew and slammed into another column.

Rocks rained from the ceiling. The second column collapsed, and the spawn below wailed, and Elethor slammed into a third column until it too cracked. The pillar crashed down onto the bridge, crushing it. Solina screamed and leaped back. The bridge crumbled, and the ceiling rained stones, and Solina fell back into the pool. She vanished underwater as all around, columns fell, boulders rained, and vermin screamed and died.

Bricks buffeted Elethor. A chunk of the ceiling crashed down against Legion, and the blazing nephil tumbled into the pit. At once his spawn covered him and began to feast, ripping at their father's flesh, tearing gobbets loose from bones. The prophet howled, voice rising into a storm, so loud and shrill the sound cracked another column. Then the vermin grabbed Legion's jaw, ripped it free, and burrowed into his head. Soon they were feasting upon his eyes and maggoty brain. Legion's flaming halo gave a last crackle and guttered away.

Fly, Lyana, Elethor thought. *Fly far and never return.*

Rocks slammed against him. A column crashed and hit his tail. The walls crumbled, falling and burying the vermin beneath them. A blast shook the chamber and fire blazed outside. Another blast shook the palace, and Elethor realized: The hoards of Tiran fire were bursting.

A final crack raced along the ceiling, and the chamber collapsed.

Rocks slammed into Elethor and he fell. Bricks pummeled him. Dust blinded him. Only the Memory Pool remained standing now; the palace crumbled around it. Blinded and roaring with pain, Elethor crashed into the pool.

He slammed against the floor of his old home in Requiem.

Silence rang in his ears.

The fire, the screeches, the crumbling of columns—all was gone.

Here, he heard nothing but a breeze in the birches outside, the song of birds, and the flap of distant dragon wings.

A moan sounded behind him.

Elethor pushed himself onto his elbows and turned to see Solina on the floor. A great chunk of column pinned her down. Her blood seeped from beneath it.

"El," she whispered. Blood stained her lips. "El... will you hold my hand? For the end?"

She reached out a trembling, bloodied hand.

A boulder crashed through the ceiling and landed beside Elethor. It cracked the floor, shattered his bed, and knocked him down.

He lay beside Solina, and bricks rained onto him, falling through the ceiling of his home. Fire blazed above.

"El," she whispered. "Hold my hand. Please."

She reached out, grasped his hand, and held it tight.

"I love you, Elethor," she said. "I'm sorry. I'm sorry for how much I hurt you. All I wanted was to be with you here. I'm sorry."

Rocks rained. His home trembled. A column tore through a wall, and his shelf of books and statuettes crashed down. His marble statues fell and cracked. The wooden turtle shattered.

He tore his hand free from Solina's.

He crawled toward the fallen wall. A brick slammed onto his back. He dragged himself over the debris and outside onto the hill.

He crawled a few more feet until he lay in spring grass. Birches rustled at his sides, and the city of Nova Vita rolled below him, towers and roofs emerging from a verdant forest. White clouds glided above, and the dragons flew, shimmering bright under the blue sky.

It is a beautiful place, Elethor thought and smiled softly. *It is home. It is the best memory of my life. It is a good place to die.*

Chunks of column, wall, and ceiling fell from the sky and crashed into the forest. Elethor lay back in the sunlight, took slow breaths, and let his hands play with the grass. Above him in the spring morning, the sky fell.

LYANA

She hovered outside above the desert, watching the Palace of Whispers crumble.

Blasts of Tiran fire sounded across it. Lights flared. The towers upon the mountaintop crumbled first, raining dust and bricks upon the walls below, and then those walls too fell, and soon all the bridges, archways, and pathways of this ancient edifice collapsed. Dust rose in a cloud and rolled across the desert. Some nephilim tried to escape. They burst from the ruins, only to have boulders, fire, and crumbling towers crash against them and bury them upon the mountainsides. Griffins fled shrieking.

Nothing will escape, Lyana thought. *All that lives there dies.*

She watched, eyes damp, wings flapping as she hovered before the ruin.

"Elethor," she whispered.

Love of my heart. Light of my life. My husband. My king. Goodbye, Elethor. You fly now to your brother and parents. You will dine at their side among the glittering columns.

She let out a sob.

"And watch over me, El. Watch over me from the stars, for I'm afraid and alone."

Wings thudded behind her. Snorts rang through the air. Lyana turned to see Bayrin and Mori flying over the mountains from the east. They were ragged, scales stained with ash and blood, and they panted as they flew. When they reached Lyana, they hovered at her sides. They gaped at the crumbling palace, tongues lolling.

"Bloody stars!" Bayrin said and spat flame. "We heard you were captured and chased you for three days, Lyana. What the Abyss is that?" He gave her a sidelong glance. "Did you blow up that mountain?"

Lyana lowered her head. Below her, dust and debris rolled across the desert.

"It was the Palace of Whispers," she said softly. "The lair of Solina and all her devilry. Elethor destroyed it."

Mori gasped. "Elethor!" the princess said. "Lyana, is... And Treale..."

Bayrin snorted smoke. "Stars, Lyana, where are they?" He looked around from side to side, as if seeking them. He sucked in his breath and looked back at the clouds of dust. "Lyana, are..."

Lyana looked at her brother. He appeared blurred to her, and she blinked, and her throat burned.

"We have to leave, Bayrin," she whispered. "We have to fly north. Back to Requiem. Please, Bayrin. Take me home."

She could speak no more. Her eyes stung too much. She turned and flew over the desert, fleeing this place, fleeing the pain inside her. Bayrin and Mori flew at her side, wailing and roaring flame, and their tears fell upon the desert. They understood, and they sounded their cry, a great song of mourning and pain for their fallen, for their king, for their guiding star. Lyana roared with them, a keen of starlight.

For Treale. For Elethor.

They flew for a long time.

They flew over dunes. They flew over the ruins of southern cities, their palm trees charred, their rivers littered with burnt ships, their towers fallen. They flew north over the sea, ragged survivors behind them, a thousand Vir Requis haunted and wounded and crying for their fallen. They flew over the ruins of Requiem: her blackened forests, her hills littered with dead, and finally her fallen courts among the ash of King's Forest.

His words echoed in her mind. *You must lead Requiem now. Our people will follow your fire, and it will lead them home.*

Once Nova Vita had stood here, a city of new life, a revival for Requiem among the holy birches. Once towers had risen here, white and pure against the sky. Once harpists had played music here in white halls, and dragons had flown overhead, singing the songs of their people. This had been a city, a hope, a living dream, the heartbeat of a nation.

This is where my parents raised me, Lyana thought. *This is where I loved Orin, and where I loved Elethor, where I was knighted and where I fought, where I watched columns fall and dead rain.*

She landed in the ruins of the palace. A single pillar rose from the debris, three hundred feet tall, its capital shaped as dragons: King's Column, raised by the first King Aeternum millennia ago. Even the cruelty of Queen Solina could not topple it, and all the claws of her beasts could not scratch its marble. Lyana shifted into human form, held her sword before her, and knelt before this column. It led from ruin into starlight, from death into hope, from memory into dream.

"This is where I fought, this is where I killed, this is where so many died," Lyana whispered. "And this is where I will lead. I swear to you, stars of Requiem. I swear to you, Father and Mother. I swear to you, my Elethor. I will lead Requiem in your path, and I will rebuild her halls, and starlight will forever shine upon us."

She turned from the column and looked over the ruins.

Her people stood there, a thousand Vir Requis dressed in white, Requiem's color of mourning. Many here were wounded. Many were scarred, limbless, broken—but strong.

Yes, they are still strong, Lyana thought, looking from face to face. Their eyes were grim and haunted, but determined. *We will rekindle our fire.*

She climbed onto a fallen column and stood before the crowd. Bayrin and Mori stood before her, hand in hand. The others sprawled around them over the strewn bricks, toppled columns, and smashed statues. All looked upon her. They had flown south in winter, and snow had covered these lands. Today spring warmed Requiem, and among the ruins, Lyana saw birch saplings sprouting.

This forest will live again.

Upon the column, Queen Lyana Aeternum spoke to her people, voice ringing clear above the ruins.

"We gather in desolation," she said. "We gather in grief. We stand here in spring to mourn our long winter." She looked from person to person—elders with white hair, children with solemn eyes, and warriors with scarred faces and scarred souls. "Today we all mourn a loss. Everyone who stands here grieves for family, for friends, for loved ones. We grieve for those who died. We grieve for our fallen kings. Let us look to our sky, and let us pray for them."

They raised their heads and stared into the sky of Requiem. It was a clear spring sky, cold and bright and empty of clouds, yet Lyana thought that even in the light of day, she could see the Draco constellation, the stars of her fathers.

You are there now, Father and Mother, she thought, and a soft smile touched her lips. *You are there, Orin and Elethor. You watch over me. You are with me now. I can feel your light upon me, and I am afraid, but I know that I am never alone.*

She returned her eyes to the crowd.

"We are the survivors of Requiem," she said. "And we are her hope. We are Vir Requis, and we have known pain, and we have known tears, and we have known too much blood, too much death. But we are strong, and we are eternal; forever our starlight will glow. It has glowed here for three thousand years since King Aeternum raised this column and carved our stars into its stone. Queen Gloriae found this column standing in ruin after the great wars three hundred years ago; she rebuilt these halls and let starlight fall upon them. King Elethor led us to victory and to hope, and now this torch of starlight passes to me. And I vow to you, children of Requiem, I will rebuild these halls, and we will watch this forest bloom again." She raised her voice and cried to the stars, knowing that Elethor could hear her. "Requiem! May our wings forever find your sky."

All across the ruins, the survivors of Requiem repeated her prayer.

Standing upon a smashed mosaic, Mori smiled at Lyana, her eyes soft and warm. She knelt upon the broken stones before her queen.

"Queen Lyana," she said softly. She held her sword before her upon open palms. "I serve you, my queen."

Bayrin knelt too, blade held before him. Behind them, more people knelt, and soon a wave flowed across the survivors. They all knelt before Lyana upon the ruins, eyes gleaming, lips whispering.

Lyana stood before them, and her eyes stung, and she tasted a tear on her lips.

"I will lead them well, Elethor," she whispered and looked to the sky. "I will lead Requiem down a path of starlight, and I will not stray from it to the left or right, and I will honor your memory. I swear this to you, my husband. I swear this to you, stars of my fathers."

Those stars now did shine in the sky; Lyana could see them, and she laughed through her tears.

The birch saplings rustled.

Spring turned to autumn. The leaves turned red and scuttled across the ruins of Requiem.

All around the city, masons and carpenters toiled, and smithies rang, and people bustled. The first homes stood upon hills, and new columns rose in the ruins of the palace. The farms gave their crops, and baking breads, foamy ale, and hot apple pies filled Nova Vita with their scents, and for the first time in years, Lyana heard laughter ring through the city. Life and light shone.

On a cool autumn morning, Lyana lay upon her fur rug in the small, hillside temple they had built. She dug her hands into the fur and closed her eyes, but she did not scream. Mori clutched her one hand, and Bayrin held the other, and with a gasp and joyous pain, they had another in their family.

Lyana held her son to her breast, smoothed his hair, and smiled.

"Our son, Elethor," she whispered and looked to the ceiling. "He looks like you."

Mori laughed and gasped at the babe.

"Look at his hair!" the princess said. "It's brown like mine. And his eyes, Lyana—they're green like yours." She gingerly touched the babe's head. "What will you name him?"

Bayrin cleared his throat. "She's going to name him Bayrin, of course. After me. What do you think?"

The babe mewled and fell asleep against her, and Lyana stroked his hair, feeling warm and safe.

"I will name him Elarath," she said softly. "And I will raise him to know of his father, and his grandfather, and the great kings who came before him. He will be a great king too someday."

Bayrin patted the child and smiled down upon him.

"Your father was a good king, little one," he said. "You better follow in his footsteps, or Uncle Bayrin will make you regret this day."

Mori punched him, and Bayrin gasped and feigned indignation, and Lyana smiled and held her son close.

"Sweet El," she whispered to the child. "The birches whisper, dawn gilds our mountains, and light shines upon the forest. You are home, El. You are home."

MORI

Mori stood upon the fortress walls, watching winter's first snow fall.

The flakes swirled, glided, and coated the forest below. The trees spread into the distance: young pines, birches, and maples rising from memories of war. Icicles hung from their branches, and the snow soon covered the forest floor, a glittering carpet like fields of stars in a white sky. All around Castellum Luna, this small southern outpost, the snow and light of winter rolled into the horizons.

Mori took a deep breath of the cold air. The wind kissed her cheeks, billowed her hair, and sneaked into her cloak. She looked down at her hands and caressed her luck finger, the sixth finger on her left hand.

You've always brought me luck, she thought. *You've always helped me.*

She placed her hands upon the battlements and looked back into the southern horizon, watching the snow glide down and coat the trees. It was four years to the day since she had stood here, a frightened young girl, and watched the first phoenix rise from the south.

I was so afraid then, Mori remembered. *Everything scared me: the creak of armor, the rustle of leaves, and the wilderness that rolls on forever like a sea.*

And now... who was she now? No longer a youth. No longer so afraid, perhaps. Four years ago, she had come to Castellum Luna as a frightened girl, and here her world had burned around her. Now she stood here as a woman, older, stronger, a lady of this fort. She ruled Castellum Luna now.

"And I will not let these walls fall again," she whispered. "I will be the eyes of Requiem and her long arm in the wilderness."

She held her luck finger and thought of Orin. He had stood here upon these walls four years ago and fallen.

I will stand here every winter, Mori thought, *and I will remember you.*

Footfalls sounded behind her, and Mori turned to see Bayrin climbing the stairs from the courtyard. She smiled down at him, and he joined her upon the walls. In his arms he carried their little bundle wrapped in furs. Mori felt her heart melt like butter over hot bread. She took her daughter from her husband's arms, held the child close, and kissed her forehead.

"Good morning, Treale," she whispered.

The babe reached out and touched her cheek and smiled. She was a child of pale skin, red hair, and large gray eyes. Mori thought her the most beautiful child in the world.

"I swear," Bayrin said, "I've never seen a babe go through so many swaddling clothes. We're going to need a whole castle's worth of them delivered down here. Does Lyana's baby soil himself this much too?"

Mori cooed at the child. "Don't listen to him, Treale." She kissed the babe. "If he complains some more, bite him."

Silently, she added words she would not speak aloud.

May you never know loss, my child, she thought, holding Treale close. *May you never know war. May you grow in a world of peace, knowledge, and light. May your soul never be broken like mine.*

She looked toward the southern horizon. Four years ago the flame of Tiranor had risen here. They had tortured and killed her brother within these walls. They had raped her by his corpse as she screamed. They had flown north from this fortress until they reached her city, and they toppled it.

Mori closed her burning eyes.

How do I go on? she thought. *How can I be a mother to Treale when still the nightmares fill my every night, when still the pain clutches me and does not let go, when still the loss pounds through me?*

She blinked and looked south through her tears. She knew the answer. She knew that this pain would never leave her: the pain of those she had lost, of her shattered innocence, of her captivity in Tiranor. Those memories would always haunt her. Those scars would forever clutch her soul, and many years from now, she would still wake up in darkness, afraid and trembling and back underground in chains.

Some scars do not heal, Mori knew. *Some memories do not leave us. Some hurts are too great; they will forever be within me.*

She looked at her child, an innocent babe. Treale reached out toward her, fingers grasping, lips smiling. And Mori smiled back.

But I have Treale, she thought. *And I have my husband, Bayrin.* Her tears fell. *And I have some light in my life. Stars of Requiem—let whatever light still shines upon me, and whatever joy still fills me, be a beacon for my daughter. I will raise her in your light, and may she never know the pain I feel.*

Bayrin placed an arm around her and held her close. Mori hugged her daughter to her breast, and they stood together on the wall, watching the snow fall.

THE END

NOVELS BY DANIEL ARENSON

Standalones:

Firefly Island (2007)
The Gods of Dream (2010)
Flaming Dove (2010)

Misfit Heroes:

Eye of the Wizard (2011)
Wand of the Witch (2012)

Song of Dragons:

Blood of Requiem (2011)
Tears of Requiem (2011)
Light of Requiem (2011)

Dragonlore:

A Dawn of Dragonfire (2012)
A Day of Dragon Blood (2012)
A Night of Dragon Wings (2013)

KEEP IN TOUCH

www.DanielArenson.com
Daniel@DanielArenson.com
Facebook.com/DanielArenson
Twitter.com/DanielArenson